THE
DREAM LORDS

First printing: 2024

ISBN:
Trade: 978-1-960381-31-6
Hardcover: 978-1-960381-32-3
eBook: 978-1-960381-33-0

Cover: Anton Oxenuk

Originally published by ZEBRA BOOKS, New York as THE DREAM LORDS, Volume 1, *A Plague of Nightmares* (First printing: February 1975, Second Printing: July 1977), THE DREAM LORDS, Volume 2, *Lord of Nightmares* (First printing: November 1975, Second Printing: August 1977), and THE DREAM LORDS, Volume 3, *Bane of Nightmares* (December 1976).

INTRODUCTION TO THE SECOND EDITION

The Young Devil Rides Out

In the summer of 1968 I first began writing the books that were eventually to be published under the general title of THE DREAM LORDS at the tender age of nineteen. I was working in a branch library in Birmingham (England, not Alabama) and had avowed since I could first wield a pencil that I would one day write story books. (As I grew older and, arguably, wiser, I changed that to novels.) Each day, as I shuffled and re-shuffled the stock of that branch library, it struck me that there was actually no rule that said I had to wait until I had either retired or reached some advanced age before I should convert this promise into deed. That realisation, coupled with a series of high-octane surges of inspiration in the form of certain authors (to whom I will refer to in more detail shortly), led me to get down to the nitty-gritty, to use the appropriate jargon of the time.

I started with a ruled notepad and a variety of coloured Biros. I scribbled down ideas, plots, characters, histories and anything that would have a bearing on the epic adventure that I had in mind. I drew up maps and sketches of citadels, even drawings of some of the mutated creatures who would roam the pages of my odyssey. In those days, computers were something you read about, mainly in science fiction stories, and the expression "word processing" was, to me at least, unheard of. In fact, in my naivety as an enthusiastic young novelist, I was not even in possession of a typewriter. Regardless of such a minor detail, I gathered together a pile of loose papers and began work on the actual novel itself. The book had a working title of *The Barbarians*.

I dug out from my hitherto forgotten pile of things not to throw away in case they came in handy eight or so school exercise books that I had not used at school. Into these I copied up my scruffy first draft, in my best *joined up* handwriting. It was pretty large, but it was legible. It took me about a year, but eventually I did finish the book and it ran to all eight of those exercise books. During its writing I had tremendous encouragement from my colleagues in the library where I worked, and their help in getting me to beat the thing into better shape was absolutely invaluable.

By the time it was completed, it had become apparent to me that if I were to submit the work for publication, I would need to get it typed up. Nothing daunted, I bought a second-hand typewriter—a dinky little portable beast. The result was a blotchy, mega-scruffy manuscript and an even blobbier carbon copy.

But one better quality typewriter and another re-write later, I was ready to send out *The Barbarians*. In order to ensure that this introduction is not longer than the actual novel that follows it, I'll move forward a bit—the book was accepted for publication by Zebra Books in New York. I was a happy bunny. It was now 1974 and at twenty-five years old, I was going to rock the world of fantasy. Now, I should have added a bit earlier that I had good advice from several people who knew a whole lot more about getting published than I did (which at the time was zilch). In summary they said things like, "start with short stories, not a novel" and "keep your first novel fairly short, say 60,000 words" and "never write your first novel in the first person." So what did I do? Yes, you are absolutely right – my first work was this novel, it was over 120,000 words long and it was in the first person.

However, here we were in 1974 with an offer to publish. It was suggested that I revise the book into 2 or even 3 volumes. What did I think? Hell, this was a chance to do it in 3—fair enough, I would split the existing manuscript into the first 2 volumes and write new material for the third. Done deal. So my third book was commissioned and contracted *before I had even written it*. Hey, this was really cooking with gas!

In February 1975, the first volume was published by Zebra. I had, in my youthful zest for garish titles, called it *A Plague of Nightmares*, which seemed to me to be suitably emotive, evocative and—well, appropriate. (Volume 2 was to be *Lord of Nightmares* and the final volume would be *Bane of Nightmares*.) Someone at Zebra, who may (wisely, I suspect) have thought my garish titles a bit too—well, garish—hit upon the idea of giving the series the overall title THE DREAM LORDS. Each volume came out under that heading, but with my own titles as the individual volume titles. I thought at the time that it was a Good Idea and I still do.

So, patient, probably dozing-off-to-sleep reader, the current reprints are all coming out under the heading THE DREAM LORDS. We have not added the garish sub-titles to each volume, but please feel free to think of each volume under those original headings. Or, if you like, think of the entire epic as *The Barbarians*.

Okay, so what else have I changed?

It did occur to me that as I needed to transcribe my original manuscripts into word processing documents (yes, I am up to speed now, but I daresay the version of Word that I am using is a score or more versions older than the latest one) I would have an ideal opportunity to do a real re-write of each volume. After all, I was now writing with the experience of having had twenty-five books published (oh yes, and some short stories, too). Thirty-seven years after I finished the manuscript for Zebra—I could do wonders with that manuscript. Michael Moorcock does it annually to all his 900 books, doesn't he? He must be a very patient guy. I still enjoy reading his books, so it must work.

However, as I started work preparing this first volume for its new printing, I decided that I would limit my revisions. I wanted to keep the spirit of the originals, warts and all. Well, not *all* the warts, to be honest. I have removed some of the real howlers (including the spelling errors I found—come on, the original proofs were set before IT spell-checking conveniently arrived) and here and there I have changed a word or clumsy sentence to convey more precisely what I was trying to say. Otherwise what you are about to read is pretty much the original yarn, as it was, bludgeoning its way on through to the last page. The enthusiasm, inspiration and exuberance that literally flooded me when I wrote the book(s) may not have created the finest fantasy work since Homer, but it is the drive that all writers must have if they are to create. I well remember writing the books and all those emotions, as if I were still sitting in my attic room in Birmingham (England not Alabama).

Not all my subsequent works infused me with such a rush of blood! But today, as I am in the process of writing what will be my thirty sixth published novel, I am, mercifully, excited by it—that must-have ingredient, that drive, is there. I am no longer sitting in my attic room in Birmingham, having long since exchanged it for my current abode in remote, rural Devonshire, a couple of miles from the sea.

What were the books that inspired me in that heady summer of 1968? The ones that gave me the last push I needed to get those notebooks and papers out and start work on *The Barbarians*? Most of them will become obvious to anyone reading my epic. The John Carter novels of Edgar Rice Burroughs were still clutched in my hands as I wrote. The later ones had only just come out in the UK in paperback, and I had been a devout fan for several years. A year or so before I started to write, I had been completely knocked out by Frank Herbert's *Dune*, a book which I must have read half a dozen times since. And, on a slightly different tack—the Black Magic books of Dennis Wheatley, such as *The Devil Rides Out, The Satanist, To the Devil a Daughter* and…well all of them.

Plus, naturally, the grand-daddy of them all, *The Lord of the Rings*. If, like me, you read it when you were nineteen and at a time when you hadn't read a million other fantasy epics, it will have been something that has stayed with you for life (unless you hated it, of course). You think you'll never find another book that will come close. (In my case, not many have, but that's my problem.) Preparing THE DREAM LORDS for reprinting, I can see exactly how and where those wonderful books influenced me. I never intended to pastiche them or pinch their ideas or emulate their styles, but they are all in here somewhere! Oh and yes, I had read quite a lot of H.P. Lovecraft and I'm sure some of that is here, too. (Just to digress for a moment—my favourite HPL yarn is **The Shadow Over Innsmouth**, and it still influences me today. My novel, NIGHT OF THE HEROES, has its climax firmly fixed in a setting that is pure HPL.)

You may be interested to know that authors who I had not read at the time I wrote *The Barbarians*, were Robert E Howard, Jack Vance, Fritz Leiber, Leigh Brackett…pretty well all the sword and sorcery and top fantasy authors. So when the first volume of THE DREAM LORDS originally appeared, with the legend "in the tradition of HP Lovecraft and Robert E Howard" I was a bit bemused. And the cover! Given the wonderful covers usually available on the sword and planet or sword and sorcery paperbacks, this one was, well, a disappointment. It must have dawned on Zebra that it had done them no favors either, because not too long afterwards, they reprinted the book, with a brand new cover, the first by a new artist (his first, in fact) Tom Barber. It's a stunning picture of the Four Horsemen, and you'd be forgiven for seeing a likeness to LOTR's Nazgul. Beautiful piece of work, Tom.

The second volume of the trilogy came out with a Jack Gaughan cover, which would normally have been a real plus, as he was a regular for many of the top US paperback publishers, notably Ace Books. But I was even more disappointed with it than the first volume's cover. Zebra again reprinted the book, with another Tom Barber cover, a big improvement. With one glaring error. They put "volume 3" on it. I don't know how that affected sales, but it sure as hell didn't help! When the third volume came out, Tom Barber had again produced his excellent work for it, and at least it also had "volume 3" on it.

The 3 books were now in splendid company, with the Robert E Howard revival in full swing: THE DREAM LORDS sat alongside new pastiches of Bran Mak Morn (Karl Edward Wagner), Black Vulmea and Red Sonja (David C Smith and Richard Tierney), although it always seemed odd to me that my books were advertised as "in the tradition of Conan" when they'd been written prior to my discovering the Hyborian barbarian.

Pulp fiction was enjoying a grand revival in those days, and I suppose it was inevitable that it spilled out into the movies. In 1977, 2 years after the first DREAM LORDS book was published, the colossal blockbuster *Star Wars* hit the big screen. I watched the movie for the first time and it came as a bit of a shock—after all, here we had Imperial troops, light sabres, Darth Vader, the Force, etc., etc...uh, not that different to the contents of the DREAM LORDS books. Coincidence? Synchronicity? Probably. Wouldn't have been the first time. And I'm not bitter about the fact that *Star Wars* has conquered the known universe and grossed half the riches in it.

I'm content to tell myself that if Zebra had published the books with those Tom Barber covers at the outset, with the correct numbering sequence, well...who knows? This might be the 50th edition you're holding and I might be word processing this intro on a very large yacht somewhere off the Bahamas, or the Seychelles, or…

Nevertheless, as I write this, some 48 years after it began a life in print, here is THE DREAM LORDS, my first foray into the world of writing, still dear to my heart, and ready, I hope, to quicken the pulses of a whole new generation. Star Lances at the ready—

Adrian Cole,
Devon, England,
2023

THE
DREAM LORDS

Adrian Cole

Cirsova Publishing © 2024

Table of Contents

Book I: Rebellion

Much has been written by historians about the Dream Lord Empire, from its beginnings in the remotest deeps of time to the even darker days of its fall. It is a history steeped in obfuscation, mystery and deceit, for there are many who might profit or suffer from the numerous truths, or indeed mendacity, twisted into the threads of the telling.

Galad Sarian, son and heir of a Dream Lord, provides us with a record of his own experiences at a crucial time in the great changes that shook the Empire to its roots. Impetuous, impulsive and at times dangerously arrogant, the young Sarian undoubtedly endured tribulations that would have unseated the reason of many less determined men.

In translating Galad Sarian's personal records, the historian Nandorkanthas has declared that he has used very little licence and has remained faithful to the youth's narrative and style, colorful though it may seem. Other sources may be consulted on the events of Galad Sarian's life, and it is agreed that in the main they do correlate with his personal records, while it should be acknowledged that such historical material remains sensitive to this very day.

The revelations in the Nandorkanthas version are unquestionably dark and disturbing, but may be closer to the truth than the more literate, sanitized versions.

*- from **The Annals of Enlightenment**, official archives of the Empire.*

CHAPTER I
What Dark Dreams May Come

Since my earliest days, I have feared darkness, for it is the stuff of evil, the fabric from which nightmare is woven. Although it brings rest to the body, it does not always soothe the mind in the way that the Dream Lords would deem it. Even as a child, during the long hours of darkness that cover my native planet, my mind was seldom at peace when I slept the true sleep, seeing strange and unbidden visions not sent by the makers of illusions who rule. Even the cloak of dreams that the Dream Lords draped over me could not stave off the searching tendrils of the nightmare realm, so that a hint of other powers fretted at the edge of my awareness. Sometimes I awoke with a soundless scream and sometimes my fear was such that I sought comfort with my father—he was never too exhausted by his trying position of Dream Lord to put me at ease. Yet as I grew older, my dreams became wilder, until I began to dread some terrible climax to them, as though a renegade Dream Lord was abroad in search of a tool to oust his masters. My fears became realities as the darkness took substance, sucking me into its living depths.

How well I remember that night! Sleep did not come easily to me then, as it had not of late. I had dreamt strangely of Zurjah, my homeworld, seeing it not through the vivid eyes of the image makers, but as from an alien viewpoint, cold and inhospitable. It was colder than usual and winds drove thick mists about the stark mountains and cities, sending people hurrying indoors to shelter and warmth, ripping aside the garments of the world to expose raw bones of rock and crag. Thick swathes of fog and gaseous mist billowed around the huge planet, only faintly penetrated by the sun, itself so dim and distant as to be almost invisible.

Tonight the soothing power of the Dream Lords could not touch my mind, and now it seemed to drift free of their ministrations. Dreams and realities blended, bearing me onwards to some unseen destination. The night and the cold darkness seemed to bear heavily down on me as I wrestled in my bed. The sumptuous luxury of the room had dissolved, and I felt thick skins and robes around me like the pelts of some shepherd from the world's rim. A dim shaft of grey light cut the gloom of my chamber, filtering through the narrow slit in the solid stone of the wall. Solid stone? Another dream then—the fabulous castle of the Dream Lords was never so primitive. As I stared from eyes that seemed drugged, I looked at the window and a slight illumination passed quickly across it—one of the moons hurtling madly around on her interminable voyage.

Shortly after that, the thought blanket of the Dream Lords must have lulled me—together with the sleep serum I had taken—and I appeared to succumb. But my sleep held all its worst terrors.

The dream always began the same of late, which in itself was wrong. If the Dream Lords had sent it as a diversion or a morsel on which to think and learn, they would not have done so more than once. But it had become repetitive, like some nocturnal obsession.

In it, I could make out a vast plain, stretching away for eternal distances, covered with cities and forests, sleeping peacefully under a bright moon. Then there would come a series of violent flashes in the sky, whereupon showers of fire descended on the tranquil plain. Beneath the now black skies, I would see tall cities—as large, and some larger, than Zurjah itself—engulfed in black clouds and in flames of colossal height. There would be people streaming from one place to another, helplessly, but none seemed to escape the destruction.

I would see rivers boiling, spilling over their bubbling torrents and devouring whole forests; others rushed headlong for miles only to be swallowed up by gigantic cracks. Mountains heaved and twisted, while great sparks and embers cascaded continually down from the heavens. The climax of the dream was always the most fearful part.

There would come a gradual silence as the effects of the turbulence died down. Here and there, people stirred from the ashes. Then, faintly at first, but growing louder, would come the unmistakable drumming of hooves. And then I would see them, these haunters of my very soul—four titanic masked riders, mounted upon huge stallions, riding forward and thrusting crackling lances of fire at all who survived. I would see all this as a survivor myself, lying defenceless on that bare plain. Nearer they would come and louder thundered the hooves, until at length, seconds before I, too, must be ridden down, I would awake, shuddering in terror.

That cold night, years ago, I had that same dream, no less pregnant with terror than before. I awoke shaking, bathed in perspiration. All around me, the pitch night pressed down and the very air seemed alive with unseen phantoms, as though I had brought them with me from the black gulfs of my mind. Try as I would, I could no longer sleep. I saw in my mind's eye those remorseless riders galloping on, driving everything before them, leaving behind them chaos and total destruction.

Zurjah is very silent at night. The Dream Lords give total peace and tranquillity to all the citizens with the strength of their thought blankets. Would that I had received the same blessing. From the vast city outside I heard not a sound, nor from the cloudy sky. I closed my eyes, certain that sleep would not return that night. Something was wrong. I sensed it instinctively. I was awake—returned for a short time to my real body, my physical self, which we Zurjahns do so much without, evolving as we are towards an expression of thought rather than matter. Awake—and aware of some new challenge to my reason.

The thick furs and pelts that I had sensed earlier were still around me. Yet this was no dream. I sat up in the freezing air. Again I was perplexed, for I *knew* that I was not dreaming. Wrapping myself up in the strange furs, I crossed to the slender window and peered out into the murk. I almost drew back in awe. This must be some new test of the Dream Lords, I thought—some new physical dimension of their powers—to try my character because I was heir to my father's place as Dream Lord amongst them. Beneath me the city lay grim and misty, stretching away for miles into the shadows. It was no longer the glorious, inspired metropolis of gods, but a grimy, chilling sprawl of stone. The castle of the Dream Lords from which I gazed out was not as I knew it. Clouds were forming thickly around the turrets and battlements, while thin, wispy fingers of mist crept up the rocky walls from below. The building reeked of age and decay. True, it had been here for untold centuries, but not as a crumbling ruin from out of my people's darkest ages. Why were the Dream Lords showing it to me in this horrifying guise?

A test, I told myself. I was the heir of Dotas Sarian, Dream Lord of Zurjah, controller of millions of minds, and on his passing I would be invested with all his knowledge and power. For the good of the Nine Worlds. Long had I contemplated these powers, for now having only a minute portion of them, and I longed for the day when the full knowledge would be mine. But I knew I had to be patient. I wished my father a long life, though I feared for his health even in my youth. No doubt he was now dreaming, just as the city below dreamt, content and peaceful.

I eyed the unfamiliar swirling vapours, streaming across the lurid sky that should not have been there. Above me loomed the turrets and parapets of the castle, shrouded in darkness of a very real nature. The fortress looked hostile and foreboding, a symbol of dominance and power of an evil nature. For a brief second, I thought that some other power—some power opposed to the Dream Lords—was showing me all this. I shrugged the thought away.

Now, as I gazed up at this alien castle, I saw a glimmering window, high on one of the towers. I frowned. Why should there be a light at this time? There was no reason for anyone to be awake, for days on Zurjah are full and tiring for the people. Then I smiled to myself; perhaps someone else had broken dreamsleep.

Eventually, beginning to feel a little colder, I turned away, settling once more on the warm but inhospitable bed. I sprawled across it but could find no comfort. Sleep persisted in evading me. My mind wandered from thought to thought, then bobbed back to the light above. That light—I kept visualising it. It taunted me with its twinkling. Again I rose and went across to the window. The light was in a turret over to my left, high above the buildings around it and completely isolated. I recognised that tower now! People called it the Finger of Dusk and hinted at it as a source of nightmare and menace, though the Dream Lords drew a mental drape over it so that no one knew of its real purpose.

My mind whirled with the dusty thoughts that the tower had stirred—sorcery of the ancients, magic and all manner of peculiar doings, things from the recesses of man's mind, impossible imaginings. It was said to hold forbidden secrets, knowledge that the Dream Lords had stumbled on and found best left alone. Perhaps that lonely turret was the source of my own warped thoughts. I smiled. I would find out.

I wrapped my furs even more tightly about me. Beside the bed were thick boots which I laced on. I would play this strange game of illusion with whoever it was that taunted me. My door was no snugly fitting steel panel of warmth, but a great carved wooden one. I opened it and stepped into the empty passage. There were no Imperial Guards slouched against walls or standing stiffly at corners, for there are no enemies of the Empire on Zurjah. It is the Center of peace, and should anyone wish to break into the castle, well, he would get no further than wishing.

Yet the anachronisms surrounding the castle persisted, for I found a guttering firebrand in a wall socket. As I lifted it to light my way, the shadows danced and receded noiselessly into the corners. The Dream Lords could send their minds back into time, but not their bodies. I felt as though I had gone back aeons—but how?

I moved on down the circular passageway, my light picking out the paintings and etchings on the rock walls. These at least were familiar, though the walls seemed to have aged greatly. The paintings had been done centuries before, as long ago as Man's first steps on the Nine Worlds, which some of them depicted. They made

19

a lurid background to my progress, flickering and contorting in the glow of the sputtering torch. I traversed several crossways and stairs, the way being familiar although the masonry was not, until at length, having met no one, I came to the stairs that led up to the fabled Finger of Dusk.

Once there had been a constant watch kept here, but it was no longer deemed necessary. Fear was deterrent enough to keep out the curious. There were strange inscriptions on the walls, together with drawings of fierce warriors and wild beasts doing battle. I found myself unable to unravel the paradox of time implied here—had I been projected into the future or back into some dismal prehistoric chapter of the castle?

My light showed an old, seldom-used stairway that wound up into the heart of the tower. The darkness seemed to palpably struggle with the light, and for a moment I hesitated to go on. But the smoking torch lit the way and I began the climb. It grew colder as I ascended, as though I were being exposed to an external atmosphere. The sense of the alien became ever more oppressive.

I heard little scratchings in the thick dust, and whenever I held the light near a turn of the stair, I would just miss seeing some tiny body scuttle away. There were spider webs, too, hanging like mouldering curtains across the spiral ceiling. Fronds of thick web hissed as the flames of my torch singed them asunder.

After a long climb, I found myself in a circular room, in the middle of which rested a ladder that led upwards. The room seemed to contain little of interest—just dusty shapes of all sizes, draped with old cloth and cobwebs—like something from out of a time dream. My attention was drawn to the scarred ladder, a primitive wooden device. I lifted high my firebrand to see what was above. There was a trap door, though closed. As I put my foot on the bottom rung of the ladder, I heard unusual sounds in the room, muffled by the dusty objects. I stood rigid, holding my breath and listening intently. From inside one of the dark shapes near a wall came the unmistakable sound of birds.

I could not fathom their use, unless it was in connection with something I had heard only smatterings of in old tales. It was said that small creatures had once been used in rituals connected with devilry and witchcraft. I shuddered, but told myself to forget the fables and the legends of lost aeons, though it was not easy to push them aside.

I wedged my torch between some boxes before ascending, then climbed, determined to investigate further. Thin shafts of light could now be seen to knife from under the trap door. I paused, hearing the rising wind buffeting the time-worn walls outside. Cautiously I moved upwards until I reached the door. It was wooden and bore a strange emblem on its surface, that of a winged horse. I tried to peer through the cracks, but it was impossible.

I gave a gentle tap. There was no response, so I tapped again. Yet again, no response. Pushing upwards with my shoulders, I found that the trap opened easily. Letting it down gently, I climbed into the room. It was an uncanny place—stranger than any that I had ever seen, in either reality or dream travel.

Peculiar, ethereal light flickered about the circular walls, throwing great shelves, hangings and carvings into grotesque relief. This light came from one huge candle resting on a very ancient table—a table carved of some substance hitherto unknown to me. All around the wall those shelves stretched, littered with books, scrolls, phials, implements and assortments of nameless oddments. The books were of all shapes and sizes: pamphlets, notebooks, huge tomes and grimoires. Some were beautifully bound, with letters of gold, all in languages with which I was not at all familiar. There were even bones there—human or not I could not say—and a multitude of jars with weird contents. All manner of colours flickered back at me from the incongruous selection of bric-a-brac. The roof disappeared into a conical mass of dust-laden beams and cobwebs. Great bizarre tapestries hung along one part of the wall, with intricate patterns of gold, silver and bronze intertwined across them. Thick carpets of crimson and maroon stretched across the floor in a subdued blaze of colour. On the tables before me were yet more books, great thick volumes, some open with quills and ink beside them.

I moved silently across to where one of them was lying and gazed at its yellowing pages. I could not decipher the words, written beautifully in some strange, archaic language. As I stood there, mesmerized by the incredible surroundings of this forgotten sanctuary, I felt like an intruder in another dimension, centuries and light years from Zurjah.

"So you have come at last," said a gentle voice behind me. The effect was startling, but I managed to remain calm. I turned slowly, and my eyes beheld yet another incredible sight. A man who had once been very tall but who was now bent with age stood before me, dressed in clean, white robes, thin straggles of wispy hair about his head like pollen. His wrinkled eyes were crystal clear and sparkled like sunlight on water; his arms were hidden in the folds of his creased garments. His face was a maze of lines, bespeaking great age and my gaze was drawn to the golden chain about his neck, upon which hung a medallion, stamped with a great winged horse.

"Welcome, Galad, and peace to you," he smiled. His voice was oddly hypnotic, so that at first I was suspicious. How did he know my name?

"I am sorry to disturb you, old man, but I saw your light from my chambers below and was puzzled," I said.

"Yes, yes," he nodded, showing for the first time his long, tapered hands, which he rubbed together for warmth. "Have a seat, my boy." So saying, he motioned me to a splendid chair, carved from something stronger and darker than any wood, with coiled serpents appearing to wriggle up its legs. When I had seated myself somewhat uneasily, my host sat down in a huge chair draped in purple velvet and I wondered at the display of material wealth. It would not be unusual for a normal Zurjahn to collect things from different ages, but it would be a peculiarity for anyone of power. The old man's eyes twinkled as if he were picking through my thoughts. He seemed to have been expecting me, and I wondered if he could be the worker of the illusions I had seen below in the castle, for illusions they must have been.

"And what brings you to the lair of the terrible sorcerer, eh?" he chuckled, though there was no hint of evil in the sound. My brows contracted at the ancient word. He scrutinized me from head to toe and I shifted uncomfortably, feeling irritated by his inspection.

"As I said, I saw the light. All Zurjah sleeps at this late hour, and it is unusual to see a light, especially high up in the isolation of a turret." It was a subtle challenge, but under his steady gaze I felt it was I who would be interrogated.

"Ah, so you were also awake. That, too, is strange," he mused, gently stroking his gnarled chin.

"Yes, I could not sleep, despite the Dream Lords' controls," I said, locking straight into the eyes that held a hint of mockery. He smiled back at me, biding his time, as is the way of the aged. Silence had descended like a calm, blanketing even the raging elements outside. Then I recalled his use of my name.

"You appear to know my name."

"I know many things. I know that you are Galad Sarian, son of Dotas Sarian and heir to his position as one of the Dream Lords of Zurjah. You are, let me see, twenty, yes, twenty years of age and are as yet unwed—"

"Your knowledge whets my curiosity. How is it that you know this? We have never met before tonight."

"As I have said, I know much. I have seen you in the castle and in the city many times, and I have sensed your movements in dream travel. My little friends downstairs, who gave you such a start just now—"

"The...birds?"

"Yes," he laughed. It was a warm, melodious sound. "They travel all over Zurjah and bring me much news of the real world." He smiled and leaned forward. "And they have brothers and sisters elsewhere who are not averse to doing errands for an old man." So saying, he sat back and let me contemplate, though I was yet perplexed.

"I am too old to travel in my physical body," he went on presently, "but I like to know what is transpiring about me. You enjoy physical pleasures, being a youth, is that not so? Riding, for example?"

I nodded cautiously. I spent much of my time with horses; they were my great passion. But anyone who knew me, and he knew of me at least, knew this.

"Horses will play a major part in your life, Galad," he mused, turning his eyes up to a spot in the rafters. "You are a man of action rather than words and mind travel. This dreaming life governed by the laws of the Dream Lords is not for you, is it? You crave the outdoors—the physical, even though they say evolution is discarding such principles." He looked across at me and I involuntarily shuddered. The Dream Lords knew my weaknesses.

"What you say is true. But it is true also that I am a misfit within my own species."

"Perhaps, perhaps," he agreed, turning his eyes away from me again. "You have your place, though. And what of your skill at arms?

How does it progress?" This time his words startled me and a tension slipped back into the atmosphere. If the Dream Lords got to know my skill with weapons, I would be punished. It was strictly forbidden by law for any but the Imperial Guards—the peace keepers—to bear arms of any kind. Was this man, then, some inquisitor, set here by the Dream Lords to test me?

"I didn't mean to alarm you, my boy," he said with some degree of warmth. "No. No. You need not fear me. I am not the Dream Lords' creature, I promise you. Your secrets are safe here, but all the same, I am curious."

Doubts for my own safety persisted, but I needed to find out more about this lonely character.

"Since you ask, I will tell you something of it, though you appreciate my surprise. I am proficient in a number of weapons, mostly of a primitive type. I could match the skill of any Imperial Guard, sword or light rod."

He smiled at my boast and stood up, moving gracefully to another book-strewn table. He began aimlessly browsing through a large open book.

"What else will you tell me of yourself? Tell me, Galad, what of this—feeling of apartness you have? You do not succumb to Dream Lord thinking. Your own dreams must be disturbed. Tell me of them; they reveal so much." He said this casually, though his attention was not on the book. I felt uncertainty welling within me again, tinged with anger.

"Explain yourself," I snapped.

He frowned.

"Softly. Do not be so belligerent. There is nothing for you to fear in this place. The Dream Lords cannot hear us or tap your mind. I have sealed the room. Now, I mentioned dreams."

"You are indeed a sorcerer if you know the nature of my dreams," I replied, my face flushed. It came to me then that it could have been this very man who had sent the dreams to me, seeking some way to control me. He set a firm hand on my shoulder and shook his head benignly.

"You must learn to control your temper, Galad. It is one of few dark traits in your character. Good. You will learn to trust me in time. I am not one of the evil powers you have realised exist. Oh yes, they are abroad. But you will see. Now, relax and tell me about these dreams that so haunt you."

The softness of his voice and his commanding nature were as a salve. I felt the truth drawn from me like a lifted weight as I began describing in detail my worst dreams, or rather the nightmare. He nodded occasionally, sighing as he laid back comfortably, his eyes remaining closed. I felt much relief in telling him all this, for I had found no one previously whom I could trust. Father had long since tired of my problem and these days it served only to anger him. The old man stiffened slightly when I mentioned the four riders, but remained silent until I had finished, hands clasped together under his chin.

"What does it all mean?" I asked. "Can your wisdom fathom all this? Perhaps, as has been whispered, my mind is defective. Much more of it and I shall be locked away like yourself," I declared.

He opened his eyes and sat up, regarding me again. "Shreds of understanding cling to what you have told me. Your dream is not of Dream Lord making, be assured. Other powers have touched you."

For a moment I could say nothing. Then I broke the cold silence. "There is evil in this?"

"Of sorts. A cosmic circle nears its fullness. You are an important part of the final movement. But I will explain your part later. First, you must know of other things."

I felt colder. Who was this man that he had power that must be equal to that of the Dream Lords?

"You realise that from the moment that you saw the light in my turret to this that you have been awake, alive, dwelling not in a dream but in reality?"

"The castle…its unfamiliar guise…the city below…so, so impoverished…you have powers of illusion to match those of the Dream Lords?"

"I have. But all that you have seen tonight is no illusion! Tonight I have cast aside the black velvet of the Dream Lord illusion and have shown you your homeworld as it really is—your castle as it really is. Oh, you do not credit the truth of my words. You will."

"But why? Why have they done this? Is Zurjah really such an accursed world—old, decaying, primitive?"

"You will understand. Somewhere deep within your mind is a hereditary memory of what life was once like for Man, and it is that memory that causes your inner conflict with the Dream Lord illusions. Your subconscious rejects their lies. But let me go back in time.

"Many, many years ago," he began, "when Zurjah was a vast, empty waste, void of any life, there were other worlds spread over the heavens. On one dwelt Man. His world was full of life and very powerful, teeming with jungles, swamps, mountains, lakes, animals of all kinds and consisting of many nations. These nations grew and grew to such a degree that it seemed that the planet must wither and die under their billions. So some of the people built the huge solar ships and sailed across the black gulf of space to land on sister planets. Gargan was the first and later Zurjah. But there were many left behind and still they multiplied, until one day there was a great and terrible war (that of which you dreamt, or part thereof) and the planet was almost destroyed. So while Zurjah and Gargan grew strong, Ur, for so is the planet named, perished and her few inhabitants struggled among the ashes—her just reward.

"As you know, Zurjah became a great power, ruling in time the entire system of planets local to her sun and she enforced a rigorous code of peace upon them—a not unsatisfactory way of life. But not happy for Ur. Ur had to be made an example of so that Man's future would avoid such a retrogressive step as the war that had so nearly destroyed him. Here on Zurjah, the channelling of evolution to the development of the mind and the new powers its understanding had unleashed progressed—the Dream Lords came to power, controlling the entire Empire, their word absolute law. They strove towards a mental existence, trying eventually to slough off their physical trappings. And they decreed that the primitive world of Ur become a prison world, so that its terrible, war-like barbarians could be enslaved, never to grow strong and destroy again." Here the old man paused, allowing his words to fasten in my mind.

"But you are speaking heresy! Man came from *Ur* to Zurjah?"

"Yes. You have seen the murals on the castle walls, heard of the legend of the far homeworld?"

Indeed I had, as had all men, though it was only fable. It told how, an unknown age ago, men had come from the stars and settled on Zurjah, adopting it as their home, growing stronger and peopling other worlds.

"Are you telling me the fable is true?" I asked.

"Yes, it is all historical fact. Man has evolved from Zurjah for centuries, classing all other races as sub-species."

"But you are saying that we are all one race. We—" I began, realising the fantastic implications involved.

"Yes, except for one or two races indigenous to the worlds we usurped, such as the Garganians and the Aquanx, whose histories extend back beyond even Man's in time."

Both of us sat silently and thought deeply for a few moments.

"This has become dangerous knowledge, as you know, Galad. A terrible secret. A curse lies on Ur. She is now a shackled nation, and her people—our people—are slaves," he sighed, and somehow I knew that he was telling the truth. It was an incredible story, for Ur was treated with utter contempt by all of Zurjah and the most rigorous restrictions were placed on her natives. Yet to think that they were our ancestors—it would be unthinkable for any Zurjahn to accept it.

"How do you know all this?" I asked suddenly. His smile was gone now and his brow was furrowed with genuine worry.

"My father, Saul Morley, or Solmor as he became known, founded the doctrine of the Dream Lords. I was alive at the time, thousands of years ago though it was. I myself have lived on Ur, and I took part in the voyage across space. You may have heard my name."

Here he paused and there was no hint of madness in his eyes, only sorrow. I nodded for him to go on.

"I am Chalremor," he whispered, and with that one word, all the fear, the superstitions, the shadowed dread, came flooding back to me. *Chalremor*. A name more spat upon than any other I had heard. He had bowed his head as if in silent prayer. I was utterly amazed, for the name Chalremor was as much held in contempt as that of Ur, for it was the name of the legendary prophet of the Barbarians of that desecrated planet.

"You are Chalremor?" I could not hide my surprise.

"Yes, Galad, I am he." He stood up and again absently walked over to the big tome.

"So, if I am to believe you, the old legend did not lie. And the ways of the Dream Lords are *not* the natural ways of Man. But…the Dream Lords have long had it proclaimed that you are dead. Why have they imprisoned you, instead of killing you? Your name always causes anxiety, and ever do I hear such words as 'traitor' and 'warmonger' coupled with it. On all Zurjah no name is more reviled."

The old man allowed himself a smile. Something of his calmness was returning.

"So I can believe, my boy. But I seek only to bring peace—true peace—to my forsaken people. Now, take your father, Dotas. He knows of my political leanings and of the secret—"

"My father *knows* all you have told me?" I gasped, appalled.

"Indeed. The Dream Lords know all. In time it would have been revealed to you, but in a different guise, shrouded in the illusion that these hypocritical seekers after the sublime traffic in so misguidedly. They deem it their duty to preserve the evolution and eternity of Man, so the truth is a closely guarded secret. You see, were it known, this secret, there would be the most unethical political upheaval of all time, in which the structure of society would be brought crashing down. All of the Nine Worlds would be involved. Man would return to a state of barbarism—so they believe. But the cosmic circle will knit once more."

"Yes, but the price for the present peace, surely it is too great—an entire planet enslaved?"

"Ah, but the Dream Lords see through different eyes. The point that they make is that the so-called Barbarians are bellicose and warlike and would almost certainly misuse any power given them. Man hates to admit his failures, Galad. He would rather hide them under a thick carpet of deceit. Zurjah thus prefers to divorce herself from the violent rabble of Ur and likes to think of herself as the mother planet from whence all came. That is why the voyage across space is only a legend and, even so, the source is said to be beyond the stars. So you see, were it known throughout the Nine Worlds that we are all Barbarians…" Chalremor threw up his hands in a gesture of resignation.

"I understand. And you are the one person who could reveal the truth, outside of the Dream Lords," I said.

He came and stood before me, touching my shoulder in an almost fatherly way. I felt surprisingly at one with him. Some force within me responded to what he had told me.

"Yes and no," he answered me. "You asked me why I have not been, ah, eliminated. Well, the Dream Lords are wise, chosen for their integrity and political skills as well as for their mind powers.

They have a more subtle way of dealing with me."

"Imprisonment?"

"Well, yes. But that is not all. For example, you have just told me that you constantly hear such words as 'traitor' and 'warmonger' bandied about with my name. This is where I am wronged. My own story is a long one, but suffice it to say that years ago I slighted the Dream Lords—my own father, in fact—because of their determination to enslave Ur. So I cut myself off from society. I turned for a pastime to the study of the mind, including all its blackest aspects. I learned many of the sciences that have been lost to so-called Barbarian man and touched on evil powers that are as real as you and I. There are no gods, Galad, but a capacity for evil exists and there are those who would tap it. Because of my secretive work up here in the Finger of Dusk, people think evil of me. They see me as a wicked Barbarian demigod, hurling spells and curses at them from the lofty ramparts of my den. A relic from an age of sorcery."

He straightened himself and I could not suppress a grin at his visage.

"But I have come to learn much. For example, how old do you think I am?"

"Earlier you hinted at an age that I could only guess at. I had thought it a jest."

"No, no. I am almost three thousand Ur years. The secret of longevity is one of many that I command." He chuckled impishly, reminding me for a moment of a mischievous child. Again I found myself believing his words, nevertheless. Age has become meaningless amongst the Dream Lords.

"And now the masters of Zurjah point and say 'behold the gatherer of devils and demons', and all Zurjah shudders and replies, 'here is evil indeed.' Yet it saddens me, Galad, for all that we joke and make light of it, as men will with all heavy burdens. And mine has been heavy. Heavy indeed." At this his head dropped a little and his eyes held a faraway look.

"So you will spend the rest of your days in solitude, old man," I said softly and he looked up as if suddenly remembering I was there.

"I am old, Galad, older than a score of lifetimes. No matter," and he waved aside my sympathetic look. "Now it is beyond my power to go back to my people and lead them out of their misery. I am beaten on all sides, hemmed in to an old castle, hidden away with spiders and rats." His face seemed to light up and he gave me a penetrating look.

"They need a powerful leader, a strong man who can stand against the Dream Lords and their beliefs. I said there are no gods…maybe I am wrong. I have read the signs. I spoke of the cosmic circle—the wheel of change that turns and returns to its beginning. Man's cycle goes ever thus. Achievement, progress, change and finally a titanic struggle ending in cataclysm. Now the circle will knit again. The struggle will be with us soon. There is a darkness that even the Dream Lords must face. Your nightmare is an intimation of it. You will be involved. Your destiny has reached out to claim you."

He was talking beyond me again and had risen to what seemed a fuller height. He remained silent and motionless, so that the death-like stillness fell over us both, more tranquil than before. From the dim void a thousand faceless voices and more awaited an answer. I swallowed hard, sensing, as I did in my nightmare, a coming crescendo. Beads of perspiration began to trickle down my forehead. Steel tentacles were grasping my spine, and more than ever I felt that in all this cog of history and intrigue, there was a place I must fill.

"You are…trying to enter my mind," I whispered hoarsely, thinking that Chalremor was thrusting a dream of his own making upon me. He spoke down to me as I clutched at the sculptured serpents.

"I have seen the Pale Horse, Galad. I have looked upon the awful Rider. I have seen the very face of the Rider…I have looked into his eyes. And I saw therein visions of things that shall come to pass. For the Rider came to me in a dream together with three other Riders, even as he came unto you. These things have I told you, Galad Sarian, for you were the Rider of my dream, and behind you came the hosts of Hell itself." His voice rose powerfully and the elements came to life.

Chalremor was standing high before me as I cowered back. His arms were outstretched, and rods of light seemed to crackle from them. The air became taut and vibrant, and a terrific din arose like a million voices raised against each other. He was filling my mind with yet another awful vision.

A great shaft of light scythed across the outside world, sending glittering needles of yellow heat across the room, whilst powerful winds tore at the walls around us. All the colours known to the mind fizzed and sparkled about the place as purple dust tinkled amidst the beams like glass, yellows and golds hopped around the shelves, chased by winking stars of blue and twinkling greens. This chaos of noise dulled a little as cascades of fire-rain poured in torrents down upon the ancient roof. I buried myself in the chair, my contorted mind swimming before such terrible power. The worst experiments of the drug searchers could never have found such a kaleidoscope of madness.

"You must fulfil the destiny given to you, Galad," came a rumble like thunder. "Go and seek the darkness that festers like a sore upon the blackened face of your home. Destroy it for all time and bring the people into light and joy. For unto you is given the power to kill with sword and with hunger, with plague, death and with the beasts of the earth."

More sparks showered across the confines of my mind. The room began to spin violently as the noise grew. Thunder, lightning and all manner of hubbub burst asunder. I tried to rise, staggered and fell, and as I crawled, the zigzag of the carpet pattern began to change and blur. I covered my head but could not shut out the noise. It came from within, I knew. Then, rising to a terrible climax, the noises died abruptly and the blinding light faded. Once more I was alone in the dusty tower with the candle. Chalremor had vanished.

I lay there panting. As I was about to rise again, I thought I heard a faint sound in the distance. No, it was imagination. Had all this been a dream? I refused to believe that, despite the dramatic culmination. That sound…there! It came again. Far away, but coming closer. The sound of hooves. I began to perspire again, trying to fathom from which direction they came. As they drew inexorably nearer, I screwed my eyes up and fell back. The hooves began to pound closer. Terror clutched me.

Suddenly everything had gone silent. Slowly I opened my eyes. The room had a pale glow to it, giving an impression of some presence. Chalremor returned? I turned over. I nearly bit off my tongue in fright, for there above me stood a huge, pale horse, snorting and shaking its massive head. On its broad back sat a tall, armoured figure, its head encased in a mask cast from a human skull.

As I watched, wide-eyed in terror, the rider threw back the mask. I stifled another scream—for the face of the rider was *my own*. The horse reared and I rolled to one side, rolling, rolling, until I pitched into oblivion.

CHAPTER II
The Cold Light of Day

I opened my eyes and blinked in the morning light. How I came to be back in my bed—the narrow, foamy bed of every day that I was used to—I could not say. Pictures of conflicting light still befuddled my awakening mind as I sluggishly sat up and gazed around my room. Nothing appeared to be amiss and I saw it as I saw it normally. Then for a moment, the contours blurred and I made out the stark reality of the night. I tried to force my mind to reject what Chalremor had shown me. Surely I had dreamt the events of the night! I shook my head and slipped from the bed, glad of the warm air.

Puzzled by what had happened in the night, I reached for and swallowed two white pills which had the effect of making me light-headed and seemingly weightless. I drifted languorously to the window, and leaning out I looked up into the clear sky at the Finger of Dusk. It jutted defiantly into wispy clouds, and as I looked, I thought that I could make out one or two tiny shapes fluttering around its hazy silhouette. I looked down at the city below, my lids heavy from the effects of the pills. Zurjah spread gloriously before me, but as I lingered, I saw the grim scenes of the night superimposed upon it.

"Galad, are you awake?" came a deep voice from outside my chamber. I recognised it at once as that of Gundar Sabian, personal Master at Arms of my father and lifelong friend of both of us.

"Surely. Come in, Gundar," I called, turning away from the window and the conflicting images below. Although Gundar was my elder by many years, he treated me as a very close friend and it was he who secretly instructed me in swordplay and weaponry, himself being an expert. He had been brought up amidst the wars of mastery on Ur and other worlds, having led an active, warrior's life with little recourse to the ways of his masters, the Dream Lords. But they had good use for men like him; otherwise their own way of life would have been impossible. Gundar had little time for dream time or mind travel, and although he sympathised with my dislike of my Dream Lord training, he nevertheless worried about my recalcitrance. The metal door slid shut behind his vast bulk.

"You slept long and deep, my lord," he grinned, his huge face split with pleasure. He was as perfect a physical specimen as our race had evolved; his body boasted rippling muscles which tugged and strained against his splendid leather and bronze harness. He wore as usual his green tunic, the colour signifying his rank, and carried his heavy helmet with its green plume under his arm. His hair was jet black, thin and cut very short to his bullet head, his jaw firm and dark with the first suggestion of wiry bristle, his eyes blue and without the wide stare of the Zurjahn dreamer. At his side rested his star lance, a rod that could liquefy bare rock when operative.

"Greetings," I smiled. "Yes, I have been asleep, but hardly passed a peaceful night. But then, when were my dreams not troubled?" I added, though still smiling.

"You must sustain your physical self, sire. I know how anxious you are to keep fit. As it is long past the early meal, I might suggest one or two inconspicuous corners of the castle where you could take refreshment," he winked.

"Yes, and I can readily guess the nature of the refreshment to which you refer, aside from the food, you old villain," I said. His humour often infected me, and this particular allusion to one or two of the serving wenches with whom he had shared more than a casual relationship brought a further smile from me. Gundar, like the other Imperial Guards and commoners on Zurjah thought nothing of indulging in physical love, whereas the Dream Lords frowned on it for its own sake, seeing not only as the prime means for propagation. As a future Dream Lord, I was expected to indulge in the mating of minds only, though I had long since committed the supposed sin of physical love, as Gundar well knew.

"Do not worry about food," I said, tapping his rounded stomach. "You dwell too much on it." For answer, he swelled his chest and laughed.

"True enough, sire. But see, I have roused you. There are eavesdroppers enough within the castle walls ready to whisper to Dream Lord ears news of your late slumber should you not make at least a token appearance. Your reputation for turbulent dream sleep—"

"Enough of such talk, Gundar. I have sober mood enough."

"As you will, sire. But come and join me for a time at least. I have to inspect the Guard at the main gates, as Bortan has injured himself—singed by his own heat ray. The Dream Lords would do well to slow such a clumsy buffoon down with their drugs. He's far too exuberant for one of his position, although I suppose it's well to be keen." He led me to the door. I smiled again, for Bortan I knew well. He was another of big stature, though not so big as Gundar, and all the castle spoke with both awe and amusement of the rivalry between the two veterans.

"Very well, Gundar. Let us to the gates," I nodded.

After I had floated briefly in a current of warm air-bath, I rejoined him and we stepped on to the awaiting hoverdiscs outside my chambers. We skimmed down the metal corridors which had been so grim and silent by night and which now hummed with the flashing by of other hoverdiscs—those of officials, Imperial Guards, nobles, merchants, bankers and clerks—all gazing like sleepwalkers into their own private thoughtscreen. An image flashed on my inner eye of the bare stone walls in which guttering torches coated the ceiling with smoke. Was this castle really an illusion, or had Chalremor tricked me?

We curled to a halt and hovered inches above the steel floor of a large balcony overlooking the Inner Courtyard of the castle, a great semi-circular space where all those entering the castle were inspected or recognised. I stepped down from the hoverdisc and leaned on the balustrade. Opposite Gundar and I were the main gates, through which all visitors and businessmen must pass. Sensitive detector robots and sensors screened the gates and all coming in or out, making it impossible for unauthorised persons to pass. Imperial Guards marched to and fro amongst the people working below, while three small shuttle craft were being unloaded to the left of the court, by the warehouses.

"Large grain consignment from the Garganian fields," commented Gundar, nodding at the busy overseers as they tallied the servo-robots' haul. The main gate was open and through it now came a small, rather solemn procession. This was led by two colourful beings astride hoverbubbles, the larger, outdoor versions of the hoverdiscs. The pennants which these two held aloft bore mottos with which I was only vaguely familiar. They kept very rigid and statuesque and Gundar was showing more than a passing interest in their military demeanour. Behind them came an aircar, its slim sides emblazoned with various unusual designs. A huge flag fluttered from the top of the vehicle, and at its rear came another hoverbubble, followed by a large contingent of infantrymen, all dressed in yellow coats. Presently the company was called upon to identify itself under scrutiny of the detectors.

"Sarban Handor, shipping merchant and fleet owner of the Sarban Merchant Navy of Aquarn and his retainers, all being loyal to the Zurjahn code and servants of the Dream Lords," replied one of the leading riders to the formal challenge at the gate. His eyes stared fixedly ahead, his body proudly held to attention. An impressive sight, I thought. No doubt the riders at the fore had high positions in the Sarban consortium.

"Zurjah greets Sarban Handor, who is expected. Allow my men to escort my lords to their quarters within," said the Imperial Guard after the sensors approved the newcomers. The procession moved into the castle. The parent ship would be safely berthed at the spaceport down in Zurjah.

"A fleet owner from the ocean planet, Aquarn, eh?" I mused.

"Yes. Come to discuss trading rights and shipping problems with some of the native Aquanx delegates. The Dream Lords will be presiding over the case for the next few days. And no doubt Sarban Handor, who was probably drowsing in that sleek aircar just now, will have his wings trimmed a trifle," my companion snorted.

"Oh?" I detected petulance in his tone.

"They looked very noble in their yellow uniforms, don't you agree, Galad? The Dream Lords are not impressed by these private armies, though. They imply aggression. There is only one army—the Imperial Guard—and it exists solely to maintain peace. This colonial would do well to remember that. There is no cause for him to behave like some Barbarian warlord!"

Normally I would have been amused by Gundar's offended pride, typical of his warrior breed, but at mention of the Barbarians I was alert.

"I don't understand you," I said.

"Well, the Barbarians are the only people with hostile armies.

And if one lives on a peaceful planet like Aquarn, one should have no need of an army, or navy. The native Aquanx are friendly. So why should Sarban Handor keep such retainers?" He scowled deeply at the idea.

"I agree with you. But the Barbarians would seem to need their armies, is this not so?"

"Huh! Rabble, that's all they are. Vermin obsessed by war. I spent long hard years on Ur and have taken many a cut from their cruel steel. All they can do is kill, kill, kill, almost destroying their entire planet, piling it high with dead. What is the purpose in that, eh?" The heated words were spoken like a challenge.

"How much of it is our doing? Perhaps war tires them as it does us. Perhaps they seek peace. Oppressed as they are by our forces, they could never find it." I had to be careful in this matter, for to arouse suspicion would be to alarm my old friend. What I had said would normally have been unheard of—a slight to the master race. Gundar eyed me oddly.

"You speak of the Barbarians, Galad. If you ever meet one, you will understand. However, I had better get on with the business of the morning. I must see to the inspection."

He grinned and the tension between us dissipated. I was relieved as he stepped on to his hoverdisc and spiralled down to the courtyard. Thoughts of Chalremor were still fresh in my mind, and for a while I closed my eyes and clung to the balustrade. Voices crowded in my head, seemingly at odds with each other. I felt lethargic, as though about to plunge into a deep dream, my mind severed from my body and free to float in a vast inner space. Contorted images confronted me as the wrinkled face of Chalremor insinuated itself into the pattern.

"Drink from my power, Galad," said his voice. "The Dream Lords are as yet unwary of me. Let me rend their fog of illusion and show you reality."

I lifted my heavy lids with effort and stood like any Zurjahn dreamer who has inhaled his herbal vapours. Gundar descended a flight of cracked stone steps and stood before the Guards had stood up for him. I saw as through a frosted pane. The Guards were as stiff as rods, etched against a background of bleak walls that looked like a primitive temple to long-forgotten gods. Gundar strode up and down the ranks, dwarfing even these mighty warriors, here and there adjusting a harness strap or tightening a shield grip. The shields were almost as high as the men, painted deep blue, engraved with a big, golden "Z" and running into a point at the base. But the paint was rusted and chipped as though time had eaten at it laboriously. Beyond the ranks I saw horses—never usually allowed in the castle—snorting and prancing, bedecked for war. I shook myself and drifted back to a moment of emptiness.

Then Gundar was dismissing the parade and presently his hoverdisc swirled up from the courtyard to join me again on the balcony. Below me I saw everything as I was used to seeing it. There were no horses here now, only hoverdiscs and airwheelers.

"And what are your duties for today, Galad?" said Gundar, unaware of my bemused gaze. "More study, I'll warrant. Your mind will burst with knowledge before the Dream Lords have done with you. I shall be a little busy myself, for I have to supervise arrangements with the entire Navy of Aquarn, or its officials at least. Sarban Handor is in my charge, too. He's a particular old demon—obsessed with precision." But Gundar was grinning: few things in life ever got the better of him. His words drew me back from that abyss of uncertainty. The Dream Lords had cast a thick web of illusion over this place, it was true. I could not hide from it, but I could see glimpses of reality through it, now that Chalremor had opened my mind. I had to challenge my father and the Dream Lords on this.

"You meditate deeply," said Gundar quietly.

"There is a cold air stream in the castle," I replied.

"Only in your head, surely. Are you troubled?"

"I have been wondering—"

"Ah. You cannot deceive one who knows you as well as I. You have been unsettled in mind since first I disturbed you. Now then—out with it. You know you have my utmost confidence, Galad," he said, clapping an arm about my shoulders. We guided our hoverdiscs into the castle.

"You are right, of course. I am troubled in mind," I sighed, searching for words to express my dilemma without indiscretion.

"Oh-ho!" he laughed. "Can it be a girl, then? Your sins have found you out? You are to be a father, perhaps? Fry me, but that would rattle the Dream Lords! But who? Taria, or dark-eyed Meline, with whom I saw you only yestereve?" He was enjoying himself enormously, and I could not help but laugh at his banter.

"I wish it were that simple. But you are unkind to those two ladies. No, the nature of my problem is such that between us we could not solve it, Gundar. It is no light matter."

His face altered at once, showing a concern I knew to be genuine. "A secret, then?" he said, lowering his voice.

"Gundar, you know me well enough to know that if I could, I would explain it all to you, for do I not always? We have no secrets from each other."

"Of course," he affirmed without hesitation, nodding. "I forget sometimes that you are the heir of a Dream Lord and owe your prime allegiance to them. I would have it no other way. But I can see that something has greatly disturbed you. This morning when I first saw you, I sensed some cloud, some oppression over you; and just now, the constriction of your speech when we spoke of armies and war. Are you sure I cannot help?" His features had hardened, though with concern, not anger. He let his hoverdisc glide to a halt and I stopped.

Before us was a brightly painted mural. I gazed at it, and Gundar, too, looked up, probably seeing as little as I.

"I'm not sure how best to express my desires in this. What I really need is—"

"Go on," he said, patiently.

"—a meeting with my father. An audience."

At this his jaw dropped and he had difficulty masking his astonishment. "An *audience*! But—"

"I assure you I would not ask for such an outrageous thing if I thought the matter slight," I returned, cutting him short. I fixed his eyes with mine. For a moment he was perplexed, but presently he nodded gravely.

"No, no. I know that you would not, Galad. But this deeply perturbs me. Am I to learn nothing?"

I shook my head despondently. I felt closer to him and his physical way of life than I ever would to the vague image-wrought worlds of the Dream Lords, but I dared say nothing to him of what I had learned. "I will not compromise you, my friend."

"Well," he shrugged, doing his best to remain unruffled, though I could see that he was hurt by my silence. "I can try and arrange such a meeting—but when, that is the question? This Aquarn shipping problem is going to take up some time, and it goes into its first stage today." He frowned down at the hoverdisc, thinking very hard. "It must be soon?"

"I must speak to Dotas as soon as possible. I cannot let the matter drift to the back of my mind by waiting. Is it not possible for me to see my father before the merchants of Aquarn assemble?"

Gundar stroked his chin and thought for a moment.

"Very well, I will see what I can do, my lord, but you must know that you ask much. Go to the Hall of Light and await me there," he said at last. I sensed something, almost an alienation, that I did not want, but there was nothing I could do.

"You are a good friend, Gundar. I would not ask this of you, but…"

"Aye," he nodded. "Well, then, the Hall of Light. And now speed is of the essence. I shall return at once." He gave a cheerful if uncertain smile as he twisted his hoverdisc away and skidded towards a private corridor that would take him up into the heart of the castle to the Dream Lord chambers and my father. I sent my own hoverdisc in a swirl to the nearby Hall of Light, musing again on Chalremor.

What did he really expect of me? I knew little of Ur, my scant knowledge as limited as that of any of the Zurjahn commoners. It was a prison planet, mostly consisting of blasted desert, on which the scum of the Nine Worlds accumulated in the gigantic prison city of Karkesh. Many tales were whispered of the Barbarians who roamed the wastes, a fearful horde, whilst I had also heard stories of ferocious and hideous beasts. However, men are prone to exaggeration and superstition; the planet was reputed to be a terrible one nonetheless.

I reached the Hall of Light, stepped off my hoverdisc and let it glide to a halt near the doors. I walked across the marbled mosaic floor and sat down at the far end in one of the comfortable chairs, which at once began to purr as it gently saw to my comfort. This was a beautiful sanctuary, for it captured light in many forms from the five globes of encased fire that hovered in the air below the shimmering ceiling, sixty feet above. Tall sheets of glass of varying colours lined the Hall, twinkling and glittering like a million stars. Beams and rays of light sparkled in all directions and reflected to and fro like sun on a rippling lake. The Hall of Light was like a shrine, where the weary came to relax and have their minds purged of doubt and worry by the hypnotic effects. I closed my eyes and wondered if this place, too, was an illusion of the Dream Lords, but my image of it did not change.

I sat there for a long time, a feeling of well-being gradually seeping into my veins, until at last my reverie was broken by the sound of footsteps. Gundar was coming across the Hall. He had a troubled look about him and appeared tense. He came and stood before me, no trace of a smile on those dour features.

"I have spoken with Dotas Sarian, your father," he almost intoned and I nodded. The gems on the grip of his star lance scattered darts of light across the Hall. I waited.

"He is angry," Gundar went on, his eyes half-closed as if he had just come out of a deep slumber. Had the Dream Lords read sympathy for me in his mind and wiped it away?

"I hope he directed his anger at me and not you," I replied, rising as I spoke. Gundar waved me back, but nevertheless I stood.

"Aye, but have no fears for me. I can handle Dotas. He listened." Something of the old twinkle came back into his eye. I felt the atmosphere tauten like a bowstring, and for a moment I regretted having used my friendship with him and his with my father.

"And will he see me?"

"Yes. Though it surprises me. He will send for you soon. But, Galad, be careful. I don't know what it is that troubles you, but it distresses your father more. The Dream Lords are very busy of late. Dotas at first waved me aside, but eventually consented to your plea, although he is even now greatly surprised and much disturbed that you should choose such a trying time for an audience. Being his only heir, you have been given special consideration by the Dream Lords, which no other would have. They would speak with you on other matters, it seems." Gundar looked grave.

"I will use my time well," I assured him.

"So be it. Now I must be about my duties. I trust I will find you in a lighter mood next time we meet." He turned to go, and I noted with some relief that the shadow of a smile had crept back to his features.

"I am grateful," I told him.

"Thank Dotas, not me! I am merely a messenger between you rulers! Well, I wish you good fortune. Choose your words well." This time he grinned then waved himself away to his duty with the

Guards.

So Dotas would see me! Could he have foreseen the importance of my talking to him? Had he in any way sensed the forces at play in the castle last night? And what were these 'other matters' that the Dream Lords wanted to discuss with me? My future, perhaps, though that was now no longer clear to me. I sighed, relaxing again in the comfortable chair.

As I sat there, once more lost in thought, I heard gentle footfalls crossing the floor somewhere behind me. Silently I raised myself a little and peeped over the back of the chair. It was Taria, the beautiful daughter of Bordin Sulian, one of the nobles. It was plain that the blonde girl had not seen me, for she was walking in the direction of the main exit. I was in two minds whether to call, when just then she looked around and with a little gasp, saw me.

"Galad!" she cried and, lifting her pretty skirts, came tripping over to me. As always, she looked stunning to my eyes, with her silken hair cascading over her pale shoulders. She had on a modest purple gown, laced with gold trimmings, revealing her neckline and shoulders, falling away in many folds to her feet. It was the fashion for women to cover themselves, no matter how beautiful of form, and I felt my pulse quicken at the memory of Taria's true form. We were closer than the Dream Lords would dare guess—or permit. She came before me now and smiled beguilingly, displaying perfect teeth.

"Taria, sweetest daughter of all Zurjah! And where are you hurrying to?" I grinned, badly feigning pomp. She wrinkled up her nose in mock scorn. Her eyes were wary, though, for she lived in constant fear of the Dream Lords. I, however, always felt immediately comfortable and relaxed in her company. So many other girls of the castle set my teeth on edge, especially in the presence of nobles. Taria and I had grown up together, and she was but a year younger than I. I had watched her grow up from a tomboy into a maturing woman of no small beauty, and I loved her above all others. Many were the occasions where I had indulged with other girls in the mating of minds—that helter-skelter rush into a kind of mental ecstasy—and I had even broken my Dream Lord directive and taken a few physically. But that was the heat of curiosity. My feelings for Taria went so much deeper.

She gave a pout and curtsied like a naughty child caught playing in forbidden territory.

"To the gardens, sire. Will you not accompany me?" I felt a pang of regret about not being able to go, for Taria more than anyone could salve my nerves now. But it was not the time. The Dream Lords would send for me and seek me out until they had found me. If they found us together in our secret place, I would be kept from her forever. I sighed dramatically.

"Alas, I cannot at this time, Taria. Business presses me. But I will join you later, if it pleases you." I gave her a crooked smile, for I enjoyed teasing her. Her eyes widened and she flushed.

"Oh, I see," she said with more than a hint of irritation. "And whom does this 'business' concern? Perhaps my lord Galad has taken to thought projection and prefers lessons with Meline to airing himself in the gardens? The sublime unification of mental energy presents an alluring pleasure, no doubt?" Her mood was typically playful, but I felt the barb beneath it.

"Upon my honour—" I began.

"Upon your *what*!" she laughed, darting a glance at the doors.

"I am sure my good lady is being over-imaginative! There is nothing between Meline and I. Why, we merely speak courteously to each other on the relatively few occasions that we—"

"Oh, come, come my lord. Why, only the other day on the Upper Terrace…"

"Taria!" I exclaimed. I remembered the incident to which she referred only too well, but felt amused and flattered by her evident concern. I chuckled and motioned her to a seat. She scowled, unmoving.

"I do believe your are jealous," I taunted her. At that, Taria gasped indignantly. Her eyes blazed with a new passion, and my smile widened. Forgotten were my troubles of earlier. The world seemed very remote when we engaged thus in lovers' banter.

"How *dare* you! Jealous indeed! Why, I—" But here she was cut short by the sigh of hoverdiscs and the marching of feet. Three Imperial Guards, complete with star lances and shields, stood behind her. As she wheeled around, one of them stepped forward, saluted me, bowed to her and spoke.

"The Dream Lords command the presence of Galad Sarian, heir of the Dream Lord, Dotas Sarian, immediately. I and my two accompanying men are to escort the Heir to their chambers, as is their will."

He bowed again and I nodded to him. I could sense the colour draining from my cheeks. Taria was gazing at the man in abject disbelief, her hand over her mouth. I tried to smile at her, but she stiffened with unease.

"Well, business calls," I muttered limply. As I passed her, I whispered so that she alone could hear. "And shall I come to the gardens after my lessons in thought projection?"

Normally her eyes would have dropped and she would have no doubt given me a delightful blush, but she had sensed at once the gravity of the situation, though she could have had no idea of what was wrong.

"Yes, yes of course," she said softly and it buoyed me. With that I joined the three Guards, who had been standing rigidly to attention, their own thoughts as masked as mine. We left the Hall of Light, allowing a somewhat bewildered Taria to go to the gardens alone.

CHAPTER III
Through the Veil of Illusion

As my three escorts and I hovered up the central cone of the castle that leads to the chambers of the Dream Lords, I went over in my mind the events of the night that had led me to my present course. Was I justified in seeking an audience too soon? I had been criticised more than once for being of an impetuous disposition. Yet somewhere within me was embedded a compunction to see this through, as though Chalremor had laid upon me an aegis of sorts. I told myself that if what he had shown me was the truth, it would only have been a matter of time before the Dream Lords divulged it to me anyway. So I went to them, compelled by instincts that were even older than I was.

The Guards halted outside a sealed chamber and after an uncomfortable glance at the blank door, departed. I waited in silence. Presently the door slid aside and I stepped off the hoverdisc and entered.

Inside it was dark. The door slid shut. I walked forward, my eyes seeing nothing in the blackness.

"I am here, my Lords," I said, for I knew that somewhere in the space-dark void before me the Dream Lords were watching. I felt my stomach knotting, for I knew well enough that they could draw me into a dream and search the innermost corners of my mind. However, I wanted to converse on a physical plane, so that my faculties were not dulled by their hypnotic processes. Presently a light shone dimly around me as though through a mist.

"You are recognised, Galad Sarian," came a sibilant voice. I walked forward. I could have been standing on a vast empty plain out in the wilds of Zurjah for all that I could see by the faint luminosity. The Dream Lords rarely showed themselves. From here, in the heart of the castle, they made the laws and kept the peace for all the Nine Worlds, their power supreme and never questioned. A feeling of hopelessness and insignificance seemed to permeate the misty atmosphere around me, but I drew on Chalremor's words and power for encouragement.

"While we respect Galad Sarian as an Heir to the Dream Lord triumvirate, we expect him to respect us, for we have a full agenda ahead of us this day. We have to wrench ourselves from the sublime privilege of thoughts to clad ourselves in physical form in order to appear before our subjects from Aquarn. Therefore we hope Galad Sarian has strong motives for summoning us at such an unseemly time." The voice drifted out of the ether, though I made no attempt to pinpoint the direction. The air was suffused with emotions and thoughts, the current of which the Dream Lords could direct at will. But for the moment they did not wish to bend my will to theirs— they would hear me out.

"I believe my reasons to be of the utmost importance," I answered firmly, surprised at the mettle in my own voice. I sensed within the air now some new force, something which drew about it its own cloak of shadow, as though it moved independently of the Dream Lord will. But there was nothing evil about it, nothing daunting. Rather, it gave me strength and I realised that it must be Chalremor's thoughts intruding here, showing me that the Dream Lords were not omnipotent and giving me the courage to face them.

"Certain contradictory realities have come to my notice. There are things within the castle that are not as they would seem to be, things which would be alarming and considered preposterous to the people of Zurjah. I have learned also of a forbidden secret, long repressed, of such a terrible nature and seemingly so blasphemous to our race that I hesitate to bring it before you. Especially as it is no secret to the Dream Lords, who keep it from the Nine Worlds," I said to the void. I had said more than I had meant to, but my tongue ran its own course. The suggestion of Chalremor's presence and intervention was strong. Was he somehow manipulating my words?

"You are setting foot on dangerous ground, boy, if you think to interfere with Dream Lord affairs," came my father's voice, terse and brittle with warning.

"Perhaps. But I need you to put my mind at ease. I will speak to you of this secret and its source."

The void was silent, uncommitted. I went on, like a child finding his footsteps through an unstable terrain.

"I have learnt that the castle and the city are not as the people believe them to be. Zurjah is not as perfect a world as they think. It is inhospitable and alien to our species, tamed by our science and forged into a home for us, but draped in the false perfection of your illusions. Why? Because Zurjah is not our homeworld. Our homeworld, according to the old legends, is beyond the stars. Our race came from there aeons ago and tamed the Nine Worlds. So tell me, where did the migration of old set out *from*?"

For a while my words met with only that pulsing silence, but I had the fear that some colossal beast was awakening from the slumber of centuries, a dragon of retribution. The voice of Laomidian, said to be the most advanced of the Dream Lords, came sternly to me.

"We are accustomed to your—youthful—ways, Galad, and have come to expect a *strangeness* about your mind and its divergent workings. But we fail to see the nature of your present—dilemma. As for the migration of old, why, we all know the legends, how our ancestors are said to have come from afar, settling on Zurjah and spreading throughout the Nine Worlds. There is no proof, no written history to show that such a migration took place, but as it is only a legend, we do not trouble ourselves with it. Our purpose here—and yours—is to govern our race and the lesser races. As to the legend, well, all legends are enigmas of sorts. Do you question it or find fault with it? Perhaps you have some—other—theory." The voice was calm, reassuring, but served only to put me on my guard. I was in no mood for easy mollification.

"On the contrary, my Lords, I am not here to criticise the legend.

Rather, I believe it to be truth. Man did come from elsewhere. But I fault the source pointed to by the legend. I believe the source is much nearer than your servants have been given to understand."

This brought a deeper silence, the implications of which were obvious. The Dream Lord aura dimmed; they were annoyed at my persistence.

"Explain yourself," came Laomidian's now icy tones.

"Very well, my Lords. Let me present a hypothetical case, the better to clarify my point. Imagine if you will, a solar system not unlike ours, with some nine or so planets, only two or three of which are inhabited by various species. Suppose that one of these planets has an intelligent, powerful race on it and that this race grows so rapidly that the planet can no longer contain it. What can the people do? Only one thing seems logical. A migration to a neighbouring planet is undertaken. But while this is being effected, let us say that a war breaks out on the homeworld, a war so terrible that it is crippled. Subsequently the migrating people become the stronger— they have taken with them an advanced technology and their finest scientists, now lost to their planet of origin. These emigrants treat their homeworld with contempt because of what has happened and in time they even return to enslave its decimated populace, using it rebuild the stricken planet."

My words met with the silence of stone.

"I submit that all these things could have transpired in this very solar system. I could even name those of the Nine Worlds—"

"Enough of this fantasy!" My father's voice cut the air like a blade. "As you say, this is pure hypothesis. On what do you base such unfounded and illogical conclusions? This is speculation of the wildest kind. It is both unwarranted and inflammatory." It was only too evident that I had stabbed at a Dream Lord nerve.

"I fail to see why this is so improbable. Take, for example, Ur, the prison world. She is crippled, is she not, by a terrible war and has lost countless millions. Is it so unlikely that Man travelled to Zurjah to escape such a war?" I bit back, the other presence around me a subtle shield against the threat of harsh recriminations.

Vidor Karset, last and youngest of the Dream Lords, spoke then, his voice sharp and scathing. "One moment, Galad," he said from the darkness. "The implications of what you suggest are laughable to as advanced a race as ours. Are you to have us believe that Ur, a prison planet, peopled by a primitive species of savages, whose only occupation is war and destruction, is the real home of our kind?" He said this with such loathing that I recoiled from his belligerence as though from a fist.

"I cannot state it as a positive fact, no. But it is not for me to do so. It is for the Dream Lords to answer my question. I have a right to know the truth."

"Don't be a fool, Galad!" rasped my father, and at that moment I knew that Chalremor had not lied.

"We are all of Ur, are we not?" I said to Dotas's weary plea. Deadly silence hung like a pall around me. Eventually it was Laomidian who answered.

"That is a question that you have no right to ask, in spite of the importance of your potential status, Galad Sarian. The Dream Lords, who make the unquestionable laws for the whole of the Nine Worlds, have passed a judgement on Ur and her people for their terrible crimes. That sentence remains in place. To suggest, even to hint, that we Zurjahns are one and the same race is not only blasphemous, it is sinful—evil! *Who put such foul heresy into your mind?*"

For a moment I was completely nonplussed. I dared not mention Chalremor, for they might not only deride him, but they might also wrench him from his tower and destroy him. I was forced to answer quickly.

"I...I have had a series of visions, showing me what must have happened," I blurted, immediately realising that my defence of my statements would be weak. I felt the shadow of Chalremor draw back, as though sensing its own sudden vulnerability. Presently it was gone. "My dream sleep is often interrupted by visions not of the Dream Lords' sending."

The voice of Vidor, confident, assured of victory, came coldly at me, and I felt like some insect, about to be crushed.

"I have heard something of your disturbed dreams, Galad," he said and I cursed to myself. "Perhaps Dotas, your father, knows considerably more than I do on the subject and could illuminate us further. I always think first hand knowledge serves understanding so much more than say, a psychometer reading."

"Indeed," sighed my father, and I knew it for a sigh of relief rather than exasperation. "It is true that from early youth, Galad's mind has fought against the principles of thought guidance and mind control.

He has been cursed with resultant dreams and nightmares. It has been like a disease almost, but I have never given up hope that he will one day outgrow it. I still believe that with the right treatment, he will oust the evil in his mind and become a respected and reliable Dream Lord."

"It seems to me," interrupted Laomidian, "that for the time being, you are still plagued with these perverse dreams, Galad. You are at an age where it is easy to—*romanticise*—places like Ur far too much. Now you have connected it with the old legends and concocted a remarkable fairy tale. But it is high time you learned to distinguish dreams from reality. Outside you will find Zurjah as you have always known it—and this castle. Your visions of Zurjah as an alien world are an illusion of your own making, a fantasy for your physical being to dwell in. Once your mind has—matured—you will no longer need to worry about a physical environment."

"You have yet to answer my question," I persisted. I sensed their awe at my temerity.

"I will give you an answer, Galad," said Vidor tartly. "I tire of this juvenile insubordination. My answer is this: go back to your studies and put the problems of governing the Empire from your mind. Apply yourself to your duties more forcefully. Get the wisdom of experience inside you; open your mind to the powers we can lend. Discard this wretched craving for physical pleasures and take a mind-wife until it is time for you to produce an heir. We know something of your self-indulgence—let there be no more such ill-advised conduct.

"One day you may be fit to inherit your father's position, but put aside your fascination for mythology. And now, leave us. We have important affairs to see to. Do you not realise that we have to scotch the rumblings of a possible naval upheaval on Aquarn as a matter of urgency? We are faced with a complicated situation, and to discuss it with the ambassadors and merchant delegates who have travelled here requires us to be in full readiness. We cannot afford to jeopardise the solution of such a vital problem by listening to any more of the unfounded ramblings of a youth troubled by visions! I speak for the three of us when I say this. We refuse to be further troubled by you."

The others said nothing.

"Then it is agreed that the matter is closed," Vidor concluded.

"I thank my Lords for their indulgence," I managed to say, through my suppressed anger.

"We shall retire," announced Laomidian. "You are dismissed, Galad Sarian."

I knew that it was pointless addressing them further, so I turned. The door of the dark chamber slid open, and I blinked as I stepped out into the light. Bortan awaited me, his face a blank mask. Unless I missed my guess, he had been inhaling drug fumes. I got on my hoverdisc and frowned at him.

"You are to come with me," said Bortan listlessly. I did as he bade me, skimming through a juncture of corridors to a narrow door. This was the private apartment of my father, and I knew that anyone trying to go within would be scorched alive by the eye of the door sensors without clearance.

"Dotas awaits you within," said Bortan, and I noticed that his right arm was wrapped in sticky folds. Gundar had told me of his accident.

"I hope your arm will soon be healed," I told him, but he spun his hoverdisc and skimmed away. The door slid open. It was safe to enter.

The room was warm, with a few furnishings placed about it for convenience more than for decoration. At its far end, a window of curved glass overlooked the city far below. Storm clouds were streaking together outside, gathering in black strata across the mottled heavens. The speed of the piling clouds was remarkable, the colours vivid, forces at work that suggested furious clashes of the elements, a lurid and almost terrifying scenario. I stood by the window and watched in amazement. This was Zurjah as I had never seen her before, as she really was.

There was a movement beside me, and I turned to see Dotas, my father, clad only in a simple, grey gown.

"There is a storm brewing," he murmured, without so much as a glance at me. Dazzling lightning outside lit up his face, making of it a mask of pain. It was evident that he was making no attempt to shield me from the true nature of Zurjah. No Dream Lord imagery softened its ferocity, its *alienness*.

"Yes, father," I said. He turned around slowly, his white brows contracted in a frown. The lines of strain on his face were clear, and I realised that he was a sick man, for all our sciences. I had suspected as much the last time I had seen him, but he seemed paler than before. My mother's death a year ago had put premature years on him, for she had been his one great comfort, whereas I seemed only an extra burden. There were rings under his hollowed eyes, and his skin was criss-crossed with wrinkles.

"So you have stumbled across the secret of our inheritance, my son. There you see it, that pandemonium, a living hell that requires all our super science to quell. I will no longer shield your eyes from it. But your actions were indiscreet, thoughtless! I would have given you a private audience here after Gundar spoke to me, but the others knew something was amiss. So they told the Guards to bring you to the Mind Chamber." He was not incensed as I expected, but controlled his irritation well. I felt my cheeks flushing.

"I expected to be laughed at," I admitted.

He raised his brows. "I see," he sighed. "And what did you expect to achieve?"

"I don't know—some compromise, I suppose. I wanted the truth and now I have it. But I was horrified by what I learned—the thousands upon thousands on Ur, no more alien than ourselves. It is an unpleasant thought," I said softly.

He clenched his fists and scowled, and I noticed a thin bead of perspiration trickling down his cheek. He was controlling himself with an effort. "They are barbaric savages, nevertheless, more detrimental than useful to Man's evolution. How can we forgive them their sins? Their kind caused us to migrate to new, often hostile planets—such as you see out there in that madness—and while we struggled, they almost destroyed our homeworld. It was a beautiful world once, Galad, with wonderful cities, forests, sun-kissed oceans and fertile valleys. But now it is a scorched, charred desert, filled with twisted, gnarled caricatures of life. And the Barbarians? You will never educate them. *They are a different race now*. Forget any grandiose thoughts of reuniting us. As long as they are our slaves, we shall have the peace we need to survive and evolve." He had turned to look out of the window into the raging murk. Drops of rain had started to splash down on the sill.

"Zurjah is no home for us, father. See how hostile, how repellent it is! Would that we had a beautiful home such as you have described. Perhaps a place like that could cure you of whatever it is that is eating away at you," I said.

"What do you mean?" He whirled on me, angry now, shaking not with rage but with some other emotion, perhaps linked to the disease from which he suffered.

"You may be a Dream Lord, father, but you cannot escape physical reality. You are ill, do not deny it. And I am saddened." I had spoken very quietly, and his eyes dropped.

"I am strong yet, have no fear. Now you see why I am concerned about your affairs. You will wear my robes of office one day. Sooner than either of us would want. This accursed planet wears away at our withered bodies, but I will end my days here. Ur, and the poisons that the Barbarians unleashed in their mad wars, seethed there and did their work well. Many of us, your *mother* included, inherited that curse."

I realised in that moment how deep my father's bitterness ran. I saw also just how alien an environment Zurjah was to us, and the irony of that served only to inflate my hatred of it.

"You need not remain here, father. Listen to me. What I have told you and more I have heard from one who believes that Ur can be saved, even restored."

But at these words, the cold crept back into his voice and his anger flared anew. "So! *That* is where you have got all this from! Long has the Finger of Dusk been quiet. I should have realised, fool that I am. Can you deny it? That you have been corrupted by that evil mind-warper, the conniving reptile in our midst! He has enchanted you with his tricks—is it not so?" he snarled, and his bitterness took me by surprise.

I could only nod, so taken aback was I by his outburst.

"How? How did that accursed charlatan penetrate our shields and corrupt you?" he asked, eyes ablaze.

"You do him an injustice to label him a charlatan—"

"Listen to me, boy," he went on, slowly trying to calm himself. "I know the old man in that place from years ago. A medical genius, they said. Hah! Little good it did us in our efforts to scotch the snake of Ur's poisons! He could not save—those who were afflicted. He appears to be the essence of goodness, but don't be fooled. He is the serpent in our garden. Throughout the history of Zurjah he has sought to disrupt the Dream Lords at every turn, but we have always thwarted him. He is an unstable man—if man he is—who wields great power among the Barbarians. They call him their prophet.

Should he make his own power manifest, he would almost certainly bring the Empire to ruination. That is why he is kept safe here in the castle. He is not put in the cellars because the people think him no more than a harmless, doddering mystic. But he has black powers, so it is well to be wary of his cunning. He would twist your very reasoning."

"He is as old as time, is he not?" I asked.

"So it is believed, and some say he was here as long ago as the first colonisation. But how could that be so, unless by some pact with the darker powers that dwell in the depths of the mind. No, Galad, there is something forbidding about him. Has he poisoned your mind?"

Dotas was showing genuine concern now, becoming worried as he usually did that I was straying from the path that the Dream Lords were carefully preparing for me. The rebel in me was aroused, though, and his words did not deter me. I still sensed the deep injustices of Man's history. And the Dream Lords had lied. Ur was homeworld.

"Perhaps he has. But I believed that he told me the truth. You paint a night-black picture of him. And you do hide the face of Zurjah from its people. Are you hiding the face of Chalremor? I feel for his cause and the slaves of Ur. The stories that reach our ears from Karkesh are not pleasant, stories that freeze the marrow in one's bones more readily than that hell-world outside. Can you not at least destroy Karkesh and let the people on Ur dwell in peace? Let them rebuild their world, even if you want no part of it?"

"Karkesh is not pleasant, Galad, that is true. But it was not built for luxury, nor for a model species. We fill it from the Nine Worlds with criminals, misfits and lunatics—"

"Exactly! How can you remedy a sickness if you encourage it? Surely there must be some humanitarian way of treating the people of Ur! Are we not like savages ourselves if we treat our fellows as we do?"

"*Fellows*! That is a dire misconception." Dotas grew angry again. A vein pulsed near his temple, and he glowered at me, framed in the window behind which the elements raged with full force. Lightning was flickering incessantly over the city, throwing the tallest buildings into garish luminosity. I knew that Dotas was possessed of surprising physical energy, yet I feared for his health.

"I have heard enough!" he said with finality. His hatred of what our ancestors had done to Ur was a blinding obsession with him, that and Ur's part in my mother's illness. I sensed that there was more in the latter than I yet understood.

"You must learn to accept the situation, is that clear?" he went on. "I speak to you now more as a Dream Lord than as a father. We have made our law regarding Ur and it will not be changed. To overturn it now would mean a backward step in our evolution and lead inevitably to our extinction. The Nine Worlds would all become dead. Such behaviour as yours is usually punished as heresy and you would be executed. However, the Dream Lords have recognised that you have been the subject of evil intervention and have passed the matter off considerately. You are fortunate that the others are understanding. There are other indiscretions of which they could have rightly accused you, but it shames me too much to speak of them here. It now remains for you to forget about Chalremor, Ur and all that concerns them."

"It will not be so easy to dismiss them from my mind."

"I forbid you to press further in this matter!" he stormed. His eyes closed and a short spasm of pain shook him. I reached to help him but he shrugged me off.

"The more adamant you become, the more I am intrigued," I persisted, a little petulantly, but I was annoyed by his rebuttal.

Infuriated now, Dotas smacked his fist into his open palm. Somewhere above, a cavernous boom rolled across the heavens, a perfect counterpoint to his fury.

"How dare you argue with me! If you were to have spurned the Dream Lords thus, they would have severely reprimanded you— perhaps more than that. But I am your father and I am telling you for your own sake not to meddle in affairs the implications of which you cannot begin to understand. "Well?" he paused. "Do you yet persist?"

"I want to know more about Ur," I said simply, myself exasperated by his stubborn refusal to admit to the facts that glared so intensely at us.

He exhaled a deep sigh and ran his skeletal fingers over his face. "Very well," he said, after some thought. "I can see that Vidor Karset is right. I would not have punished you, but you must learn. I want you to understand why we treat Ur as we do and why we are determined to continue to do so. You know almost nothing of her history. Here on Zurjah we have reasons enough for keeping it in shadow. Unfortunately Chalremor has stirred up inside you a primitive longing, which I myself have felt, I confess. But it is little better than a death wish and must be repressed.

"When you have acquainted yourself with Ur's history, as you will in time, you will be in a better position to take on the responsibility of Dream Lord. The knowledge you have now has come too soon. I am old, my son and there is no point arguing about that. It is before my time, yes, but I am weak and have fewer years left to live than I would wish," he said, lifting a hand to still me.

"All the more reason why I must learn, father. From my knowledge I can perhaps better the ways of the Nine Worlds."

"Perhaps, Galad, but you are yet young and young ideas are hard for such old heads as mine to accept. But know this—you have disturbed the Dream Lords, particularly Vidor. They want this idea of yours eliminated from your head. They hate to think you may become a champion of the Barbarian cause, as Chalremor is. He would have become a Dream Lord once, but he contradicted the laws and you see how far it has got him: eking out a solitary existence in his crumbling tower. But enough of him. Your future is of paramount importance now. As to that, my colleagues have made a suggestion to me and left me to decide whether or not to put it into effect. In fact, I shall," he nodded, crossing to a seat and dropping into it.

"What suggestion?" I asked, at once suspicious.

Dotas ran his hands through his greying hair. "My remedy, or should I say, our remedy, is temporary dismissal from Zurjah," he replied, watching my reactions closely. The thunder and lightning wreaking havoc outside had become very remote to my ears. I felt bewildered.

"Dismissal!" I echoed in disbelief.

"It amounts to that, but perhaps the word is ill-chosen. However, to your friends and fellows in the castle, that is how it will appear. We cannot afford to have you starting inappropriate chains of thought among them. If they know you are being sent offworld, they will know that it is part of your treatment," he explained.

It was my turn to display anger.

"Offworld! But to where am I being sent?" Nothing could have prepared me for this, though I remembered Chalremor's warning that my destiny was reaching for me.

"Gargan," replied Dotas coolly. My mind was racing. Dotas watched me, but I kept calm. Gargan was a prosperous planet with its own indigenous race, and its ties with Zurjah were strong. But I would be totally cut off from all I knew.

"Gargan," I repeated. "But to what end?"

"Yes. You seem surprised, but need not be. You say that a physical existence appeals to you. We shall test that attitude on Gargan. Life is hard there. You will go to Melkor, its principal city and there learn all you need to about preparing for Dream Lordship. By the time you return to us, you will be ready to exist on a new level of consciousness. Ur will no longer trouble you."

"For how long is this to be?" I asked anxiously.

"For three years," he said calmly.

I felt numbed. "You cannot mean this. It is too sudden. I refuse to go! Surely you cannot have decided upon such a course of action so quickly!" I protested. My training was supposed to have been completed on Zurjah among friends—and what of Gundar and youths of my own age with whom I consorted often, Handin, Bolt and Sunian. What of Taria! How could I pass three years without her? But somehow I shielded my thoughts.

"It is an idea which I have toyed with for this last year and more. Zurjah will depress you even more than it has, now that you know its true nature. Gargan is healthier, but you will love it no better. The culture there will do you good, reconcile you to your Dream Lord duties. As for my final decision, that was now. You force me to take action. If you remained on Zurjah, Chalremor would find a way to corrupt you further."

"You are adamant, then?" I said, and he nodded.

"We are," he replied, and I felt renewed bitterness at that. He had said 'we,' though he seemed to be hiding behind the word.

"And when am I to go?"

"Soon," he replied quietly and rose slowly, again focusing his attention on the clamorous storm beyond the window. I still felt confused. Events were rushing about me, running ahead of me, leaving me behind, baffling and bewildering, spinning me in a vortex of chaos. Dotas spoke into my thoughts.

"We will talk of this again soon, Galad. In the meantime, prepare yourself."

He was far away now, thinking no doubt of the planets and stars hidden by the masses of heaving cloud around us. I spun on my heel and left, thinking also of distant places.

CHAPTER IV
Secret Meetings

As I left the apartments of my father, my mind raced with a crossfire of conflicting thoughts. A curious mixture of regret and excitement bubbled inside me over my banishment to Gargan. In some respects it was unfortunate; to all intents and purposes, I had been cast out, like blighted corn. My going to Gargan meant my complete divorce from all my friends and indeed my whole way of life. On the other hand, it presented me with a challenge, opening up the chance of an adventure which appealed to my physical nature. Shrugging with uncertainty, I decided to go to the gardens and seek Taria.

The corridors and shafts of the castle were no longer busy, as most people were concluding their morning's work and preparing for the second meal. My meeting with the Dream Lords had left me without an appetite, so I took my hoverdisc down to the Middle Terrace, where the gardens of the castle were situated. At the modest wire gate to these gardens there were never any Guards, which was well, for it would have been considered unusual for someone like me to enter. When I knew that I had not been observed, I docked my hoverdisc and passed into the fascinating world of greenery and tranquillity and felt immediately refreshed.

These gardens were almost as old as the ancient castle itself and had been cultivated as a sanctuary where the common people of the castle could find repose. The Dream Lords and the senior orders had no need to come here, concentrating as they did on a non-physical existence. So, although I would never be forbidden entry, it would concern the Dream Lords that I should spend time seeking physical pleasure.

The gardens were housed in a giant dome of crystal, stretching over a considerable distance, and the temperature inside was kept at a constant level. Here were conditions far more suitable to Man. But then I paused. Was all this illusion! The thought appalled me. I concentrated hard on my surroundings, certain that I could penetrate any false guise. But nothing changed, and I felt relief that the Dream Lords had maintained this reality.

Walking through the meandering paths and smelling the scented flowers of all shapes, colours and sizes, I felt a weight lifting from my mind. The paths were of sand, gravel, shingle, earth and grass, and some were of rock, criss-crossing the vastness of the gardens both openly and secretly. I knew my way around them well, yet there were others I had not discovered. As for the plants and vegetation that walled in the paths, they came not only from some parts of Zurjah (though rare and exceedingly strange) but also from others of the Nine Worlds. There were shrubs, bushes, hedges and trees, all varying in height, expanse and colour; light greens, yellows, mottled greens tinged with brown, reds and deep sea greens, all motionless in the still air, trembling now and then when a small winged creature or insect alighted on their colourful verdure. A thin, wispy heat haze filtered its way like mist through the silent branches and droplets of silvery condensation hung poised on countless boughs, reflecting needle-thin rays of light from the glittering artificial suns high above.

All around me stretched a carpet of floral magnificence on gently undulating ground. A light green sward of grass formed a surface for all manner of blooms—every conceivable colour studded the resplendent mantle. There were funnel-shaped flowers of white with purple leaves and thick stems and minute golden flowers that clustered thickly in tiny groups. Insects of all sizes hopped and crawled amongst the growths with complacent abandon. It was their sanctuary, too. Here and there a radiantly coloured bird swooped down and was then gone again into the great banks of foliage.

I strolled peacefully on, pausing under the shadowy bough of a tall needle-tree, sniffing with pleasure the scent of resin that was somewhere oozing gently from the bark of the dormant giant. I could smell also the refreshing fragrance of the needles. How much more natural was this heady perfume than the drugs of the Dream Lords!

So far I had heard only the distant whisper of rain high up on the crystal dome above, but passing through the needle-trees into the open once more I heard from somewhere ahead the babbling of a tiny stream.

Presently I came to a little bridge in a willow-encased clearing. Over this, tiny fingers of some creeping plant were slowly finding a tentative hold and across the rails on one side trailed the pure white flowers of some luscious plant, whose thing green tendrils were searching for further grip on the splintery wooden surface. Beneath this bridge a miniature stream of pure sky blue trickled idly between scattered yellow-brown pebbles and stones and along each earthy bank occasional moss-strewn rocks rested immobile against the foam. The stream issued from a waterfall a few yards into the trees and it twinkled as it cascaded playfully down the slippery rocks behind, blurring them.

I watched the water with the deep fascination that all such miracles of true nature hold for me, knowing that it would be a short while before I lost sight of them, maybe forever. I leaned on the creaking rail for some time, then felt the slightest of movements behind me. Gently turning, I met the innocent gaze of Taria, who was standing silently on the edge of the bridge. She had changed into a long, white shift and her beautiful hair hung down on to her shoulders, like the water that splashed down the fall. Her eyes regarded me expectantly.

"You are even lovelier than the gardens," I observed truthfully, offering my hand.

"I am sure you do not mean it. Words come easily to a scholar," she smiled, her blue eyes dropping under my gaze. She took my hand and came to me. I put one arm around her slender waist and bending down, kissed her gently. She responded warmly, putting her arms about my neck, drawing me closer. It was not safe for us to be like this here in the open, but we had become so close to each other of late that our desire was not easily curbed. I smiled inwardly when I thought of the first time I had missed her and touched her tongue with mine, so that she trembled and drew back in fear of me, thinking me a beast intent on stealing her virtue. Now she had learned to respond to my affection. After a while, I disengaged myself and smiled into those sparkling eyes.

"The daughter of a nobleman should be wary of these gardens and the denizens that lurk within," I laughed.

"I have been to our place," she said. "But I grew restless and walked, so happening by here. I have not been seen." It was not likely that we would be recognised, but the Dream Lord sensors ranged wide and could have come upon us by chance.

"I was on my way there, thinking to find you. I stopped by the waterfall, for such things always fascinate me." She smiled at my words and turned to it.

"You have taught me to love its beauty. I was blind to this and more when the Dream Lords chained my eyes," she said.

"It reminds me of your hair," I told her, running my fingers through those silky tresses. She shook her head and laughed.

"Words, words. Now, tell me, for I have been beside myself with anxiety, how did your affairs with the Dream Lords go?"

I felt myself jarred back to the matter in hand. I sighed deeply, slightly annoyed that she should have brought it up. I turned to the waterfall, my arm still about her waist. "Not well, I fear," I said.

Taria said nothing but leaned her head against my chest, waiting patiently for me to speak, if speak I would.

"Let us go to our sanctuary," I said at last, having decided to confide to her all that had occurred and the impending consequences. I could only be honest with her. She nodded and we walked hand in hand through the balmy gardens and along hidden paths until we came to a secluded spot, overhung with mossy boughs and surrounded by tall grasses and shimmering ferns. This was our own special sanctuary where we often came to hide from the world and as far as we knew, no one else had discovered it. A tiny stream gurgled swiftly through the bottom corner of the leafy glade, while white and yellow flowers dotted the mossy floor.

"You are melancholy today, Galad," said Taria as we sat on the lush, dry grass. I lay back, resting my arms under my head, staring through the tangled branches above at the distant sky. She came and knelt by me, concerned by my mood. I smiled at her.

"Oh, look!" she cried, like an excited child, pointing across the clearing. "What is it?" she asked.

I grinned, watching the furry body of a four-legged vole scuttle into some bushes and vanish. "Only a torpe," I said, gripping her wrists and pulling her across me. "He could be no softer to touch than your fair skin," I added playfully.

"You are a—"

I kissed her before she could speak further. We embraced for long, warm moments before breaking apart again.

Taria eyed the bushes. "It was such a sweet little thing. Will you not catch me one?" She looked down at me, eyes alight with mischief.

"You shall have a thousand." I closed my eyes for a while, but could sense her eyes still on me.

"What is it, Galad? Please tell me. I know that something is wrong," she said soothingly, trailing her fingers across my shoulder.

"Nothing. It's just that…well…I've had another of those fearful dreams."

"Oh," she sighed. "Will you never be rid of them?" It was something we had discussed often.

"One day I will," I assured her. There was another pause.

"Is that why you went to the Dream Lords?"

"Yes, that was partly it. For the rest, I met an old man last night and he solved some of my riddles for me. He told me the meaning of the dream," I went on and her eyes widened with interest.

"Old man? Where? Who?" she asked with mounting excitement.

I ran my fingertips down her cheek. "Well, you remember the stories that we heard as children about the sorcerer?" I said, lowering my voice and widening my eyes in mock dread.

She wore an expression of genuine awe. She was always a wonderful audience. "Of course—the one locked away in the Finger of Dusk. Who has not heard such tales?"

"Yes, though he is not chained up. Last night I went into the Finger of Dusk—"

"Galad!" she interrupted, amazed, as if I had told her I had entered a cage of wild beasts.

"Listen!" I scolded. "This is true. I went there and I learned something of great interest from the old man who dwells within. A secret that disturbs me and that caused distinct unrest amongst the Dream Lords when I confronted them with it." I paused, reflecting on their anger.

"Go on, go on," she prompted, filled now with curiosity.

But I shook my head slowly. "I dare not disclose too much of what I know yet. Not until I have learned the truth behind the matter. Already it has put me deeply in trouble and cost me the favour of the Dream Lords. Even my father is angry."

At this Taria frowned. "I am hurt to hear this, Galad. But I do not understand what you have done. This old man…I have heard strange tales about him. Has he…has he…"

"What?"

"Has he somehow intoxicated you?" she asked with a hint of dread in her voice. Her expression was amusing, but the subject sobered me.

"No, no. But his secret has upset the Dream Lords. It concerns the true heritage of our species, which they are keeping from the Nine Worlds."

"And is this old man mad, as people say?"

"Far from it. It would seem that, in this affair, the Dream Lords are mad."

"Galad!" she gasped. "What are you saying?"

I shook my head at her. "The old man is a visionary, a prophet. One day the knowledge he possesses will be shared by every man on the Nine Worlds."

"Oh," said Taria, dropping her eyes. "And you cannot tell me."

"I dare not. Not yet. Besides, it will only trouble you. I would not have that. And if the Dream Lords somehow knew that you had found out, they would be cruel. So do not press me more," I told her, but I knew she would not rest until she knew more.

"But the Dream Lords. What did they say? And your father?" she insisted, gripping my arm. I winced inwardly, fearful of telling her the truth. She sensed some withdrawal within me though.

"Well, what is it?" she repeated. I flinched. I must tell her now, I thought, no matter how it will hurt her—and me. It had to be told.

"They are sending me away," I said, avoiding her eyes.

"Away!" she cried. "But where?" Her grip on my arm tightened. As I looked up into her face, I felt a pang of remorse. I was the one who had led her from the path of her own duties and taught her my own ways. Now I would have to leave her. I said nothing for a moment, but eventually answered her.

"To Gargan." It was almost a whisper. She gaped with disbelief and shook her head.

"Oh, no, no, Galad. They would not send you so far away. They can't do such a thing. I will not let them!" Her head shook violently from side to side, swirling and twisting her silken hair. "I shall tell my father. He is not without influence. He can see the Dream Lords and plead—"

"I would that he could. But it is too late. I must face this tribulation alone. My own father has decided on this himself. It is the will of the Dream Lords, and no one can alter their decisions." I turned to her again. She was upset but cloaked her feelings well.

"For how long must you be gone?" she asked, flushing. Each question sent me sinking deeper into a well of despair. I had never known its like before, for only now was the true depth of my love for Taria brought home to me. We existed not as separate entities, but as one.

"Tell me, Galad. I must know," she implored.

"Three years," I whispered and she sat back, aghast, raising her hand to her mouth. She bowed her head and covered her eyes. Slowly I sat up and put my arm around her shoulders. It grieved me deeply to see her reaction.

"You must not worry," I said, trying to soothe her, but with little success. I inwardly cursed the Dream Lords for their stupidity in curbing natural human nature. Taria meant more to me than any duties they would want me to follow. When she lifted her eyes, there were tears coursing down her cheeks.

"Three years. What am I to do?" she cried, searching my face for an answer. I drew her close, and she buried her face in my robe, shaking now with silent sobs. I felt renewed anger rising above my sorrow. If I had not acted so rashly, Taria and I might never have faced this situation. Instead we could have been preparing for marriage—a marriage that would have had the blessing of the Dream Lords, her father and everyone that knew us.

"It is done, Taria," I said solemnly and she looked up at me with red eyes.

"Must it be soon?" she asked, gradually winning back her control. I nodded gravely.

"But know this. I will come back. I have been a fool, I see that now that I am with you, but I shall return once I have paid my slight to the Dream Lords. For three years I must work hard and prepare myself to become one of them. I must dedicate myself to work in these lonely years, Taria, and I shall come back to you, I swear." Such must have been the substance of many avowals from young men throughout history, and rash though it may have been, it was said honestly enough.

"I am sorry to appear foolish," she stammered.

I shook my head.

"I cannot help my feelings for you, Galad. No matter what you have done, or who you have offended, be it all the Nine Worlds, they will remain the same. I have always loved you and always will. The Dream Lords can never erase that from my thoughts," she said simply, and I felt another stab of pain at her words.

"I have often wronged you," I told her. "Teased you by flirting with others. But what we have shared is sacred to each other. No one else could ever command your place in my life."

She began to cry again.

"I love you," I told her.

We sat together in silence for a long time after that, comforting each other as best we could. Throughout the rest of the day we made love—physical love that the Dream Lords in their ignorance frowned upon amongst the higher orders, unless for the express purpose of propagation—lingering on every precious moment, holding it close, afraid to lose it now that we knew we must. This was part of our lives that could never be reversed, and I knew that Taria was as averse to Dream Lords ways as was I. However, she could not risk her safety and would have to wait until I had the power and position to alter the laws. My sojourn on Gargan would at last grant me that power.

Eventually, as evening was drawing about us, for even the gardens are given night, we left our haven and came again to the little bridge. The stream still sparkled with life as it always would, unconcerned with the troubles of men. I embraced Taria tenderly, the memory of her warm, soft body a drug to me.

"We shall come here every day until the time of my going," I told her reluctantly.

"Yes. Every day. I will look for you tomorrow at this same place," she assented.

We kissed one last time, and then she was out of my arms and down the bridge. I watched her slowly run along one of the paths that led away into the bush. She turned for a brief moment, and then the gardens swallowed her up. My heart was heavy as I turned up the gentle rise directly ahead and started back to the castle interior. Darkness already seemed to be drawing in around me.

I had gone but a short distance when my attention was drawn to a cluster of tall ferns on my right. Several birds flew out from them as though frightened. Looking closer, I perceived that the ferns were waving wildly about as though buffeted by a strong wind. Yet the gathering gloom about me was still and silent. Slowly I crept over the grass, covering the twenty or so yards that separated me from the shaking ferns. Their trembling stopped quite abruptly.

"Who's there?" I challenged. I parted the ferns and drew back in surprise. There stood a grim, shadowy figure, wrapped up in an ethereal space-black gown, hunched in silence before me. Its face was completely obscured by a thick hood. A shiver of apprehension went up my spine.

"I am a friend, Galad Sarian," said a sepulchral, vaguely familiar voice from inside that hood. The atmosphere around us had died to an utter silence, as if all life in the gardens had suddenly petrified. In all the universe there seemed to be only the two of us.

"Why do you go about thus?" I demanded.

"If I were to be seen, I would be destroyed," the voice replied. I recognised it now. It was the old man from the tower, Chalremor. His presence filled me with mixed feelings—sympathy, anger, uncertainty.

"Why are you here?" I snapped.

"I cannot project this image for long. Great forces for evil are at work, even here. They seek me. Listen! You are leaving Zurjah soon?" The question surprised me.

"How did you know that?" I failed to see how he could have eavesdropped on Dotas without being detected.

"No matter how. I know and see much, as I have said before. But we waste vital time. I have something for you," he went on hastily.

I took a step back, still in awe of him.

"Do not fear me, Galad. There are others who would harm you, but not me. Now, take this." So saying, he held out something that shone in the fading light. It was the same golden medallion that I had seen round his neck in the Finger of Dusk. Unable to resist, I reached out and took it, frowning at the winged horse engraved thereon.

"Keep it safely about you at all times. That is imperative. When you reach Ur, your life will depend on it. You *must* trust me."

"Why does my father not? Why does he hate you so?" I blurted, recalling the words of Dotas, the accusation in his voice.

"There is no time—"

"I will have an answer. That, or take back the medallion."

"Dotas blames me for the death of your mother. I tried to save her—and many others—but the havoc unleashed on Ur had done its terrible work. The power was not given to me to turn back the damage. When you reach Ur, you will know why."

"Ur, you say," I replied with some surprise. "But I am to journey to Gargan." The figure remained completely still.

"I know where you are bound for, Galad Sarian. You will make many journeys. But at all times remember to protect the medallion, for it will protect you. You will be known by it. Now, I dare not tarry longer."

"Wait!" I cried, trying to move forward, but found myself rooted.

"Seek the lion, but beware of the goat," was the last thing he said, talking once more in riddles. I started to speak, but the figure's image dissolved like mist and was gone. I shook my head as though to clear it of a dream. The medallion was still clutched in my hand, as real as I was. The powers of the old man were no small thing, it seemed. I lifted the medallion and pressed my fingers to the embossed markings. They were strangely warm.

My future was to be decided on Gargan, and from there I hoped to come home to a better understanding of life and to Taria, but Chalremor had hinted at further events elsewhere. Could he see into the future? And what powers for evil did he fear? Now I was faced with a choice. Either I must dispense with the cause which he had called upon me to resolve, or I must forswear my duty as a future Dream Lord and take it up. Whichever it would be, that choice did not seem to be mine to make.

CHAPTER V
On to the Red Planet

My stay on Zurjah was to be short, for only eight days passed before my father summoned me and told me all was ready for my journey to Gargan. I parted from Taria with a heavy heart, and she herself braved our separation well, entreating me to return as soon as I might, while I solemnly avowed to do so as soon as time would allow. I loved her and was loath to leave her, I confess, but something lurked at the back of my mind, put there by my two meetings with Chalremor. I knew he would be with me for a long time still. Visions of Ur still flashed across my dreams, but none so violent and disturbing as I had known before.

It was Gundar Sabian who escorted me to the Zurjahn spaceport, and our parting was an unhappy one. Gundar knew that when I returned, I would be a changed man, a man who would very likely have no more time for such physical pleasures as riding and combat such as he had taught me. One gift he gave me—a star lance encased in a sheath of silver. It was forbidden to all but Imperial Guards to wear arms, but as an Heir I was made exempt.

So Gundar departed silently, and I was left to await my Garganian escort in private. I had been furnished with very little information by the Dream Lords, so I did not know what to expect. Presently an official-looking uniformed man entered the room and bowed.

"My Lord, Galad Sarian?" he asked in a soft voice. He was Zurjahn, after all, and had the droop-lidded eyes of a dreamer.

"Yes. I am Galad," I nodded. He bowed, came forward and shook hands briefly. His uniform was smart and he was unarmed and bareheaded, so that I could see his sparse, thinning hair. I estimated his age to be in the fifties, while his manner and bearing suggested a man of learning and culture. There was much dignity about him; he would be high in the order of the Dream Lords.

"I am Ardat Vellor, from the principal Garganian city of Melkor. I was sent to meet you here, acting on your father's instructions. It is a trifle stuffy here, I admit, but at least it is private. Once we are on board, we shall be more comfortable," he said in his soft, relaxed tones.

"You know my father?" I asked, and his solemn features melted into a smile.

"Indeed, sire. He and I studied together when he was on Gargan many years ago. We still have occasion to correspond frequently. I am Lord High Tutor." His words struck a chord in my memory.

"Of course. Ardat Vellor: now I recall you. Forgive my rudeness, sir, but my mind has been befuddled by this journey. Yes, you are a teacher on Gargan. My father has spoken of you," I nodded.

He appeared pleased that I had remembered him, and I saw him to be a man who counted honour highly. "Just so. And now it seems I am to be your tutor, sire. The prospect is most pleasing. I am profoundly honoured," he said with obvious pride, his eyes sparkling. Then he stopped with ill-disguised shock. I followed his gaze down to my star lance, which I had strapped to my thigh.

"But what is this, my lord? Armament?" He asked softly, with some concern.

"There is nothing to fear. I travel new ground, peaceful though it may be. I am the son of a Dream Lord and I feel secure with this," I told him, trying to make light of it, but he remained uncomfortable in its presence.

"But there are guards at home—"

"It is nothing. I am a cautious man." I allowed my tone an edge that implied finality.

"As you wish it," he assented, though plainly not at ease. I wondered how close a friend of my father's he really was and just how closely my activities on Gargan would be watched.

Our voyage was uneventful and during its passage I was able to learn much of the world which I was to visit for three years. Ardat was happy to tell me as much as he knew and we grew friendlier to one another.

"Of course, civilisation on Gargan is far older than our own, my boy," he said. He had discarded the formality of calling me "sire," much to my approval. "Yes, Garganian legends and histories date back through the bygone centuries. In many cases fact and fiction are not easily discernible. There is much superstition and myth, and as one may expect of so ancient a world, its beginnings are completely obscured. The indigenous Garganians remain a matter for our constant fascination and are consequently a mystifying race."

"And the planet itself?"

"Oh, Gargan is an equally fascinating planet, totally unlike Zurjah. It hasn't always been as it is now, for when Zurjahn colonists first arrived it was cold and arid—dying. Now it is more hospitable, though far from the warmth and comfort of the mother world from whence you come. Gargan has a thin atmosphere and most of its surface area is unproductive. The Empire has but a few colonies on the planet—well, we are alien to it—and these have to be housed under colossal domes. As you know, our scientists perfected the wheat hybrid that flourishes out in the fields beyond the crater zones, but neither we nor the Garganians can spend too much time out on the surface. Harvesting is done mostly by robotic means. It is generally agreed by archaeologists that many, many years ago the surface was thick with vegetation and that Gargan teemed with life.

"Melkor, my city home and largest of the Zurjahn settlements, lies quite centrally (both geographically and in the settlement complex) and is built inside one of the planet's smaller craters, which has been domed over. The planet is riddled with craters as you probably know."

"I envisaged a virtual desert planet, Ardat. What of trees and forests? Do they grow anywhere?" I asked.

"Oh, yes. There are a few forests and woodlands in the equatorial regions, such as that in which Melkor lies. They were dwindling before Zurjahn colonists had arrived, but we have effected a revival of some species. The more we can cultivate these areas, the better our chances of strengthening the already thin atmosphere. But there is little water to sustain them. Our rainfall is very limited. However, Melkor has its own artificial reservoir—a nearby crater which has been flooded—and on its shores several large forests do flourish. To the west of Melkor lies such a forest, called simply the Ancient Forest, as it was here before Man came and dates back into Garganian history—one of the few we saved."

"And will I have the chance to see it?" I asked, never having seen a living forest. There are none on Zurjah, real or imagined.

"I very much doubt it, my boy," he grinned and then leaned forward with an amusing air of mystery, as if he expected the walls to be listening. His whole attitude was not unlike that which Gundar assumed when telling me scurrilous tales of his past.

"You see, we rarely travel into it. The Garganians fear the place and call it haunted, yet this is probably only superstition," he smiled.

"You don't seem sure," I replied, amused by the suggestive pause.

"Well," he went on, raising his brows, "they do say—"

"Go on," I urged, for the element of superstition never failed to intrigue me.

"Mysterious occurrences have been reported," he said with a frown.

"Such as?"

"Mm," he mused, and I sensed a change of mood in him, for something unpalatable had evidently come to mind. "Probably just Garganian folk tales," he went on, obviously having decided to dismiss the matter. I did not press him, and there was a brief silence before he resumed his talk.

68

"Melkor itself is a wonderful city, a tribute to Zurjahn technology. It is built to suit even the high standards of the homeworld and was constructed deliberately away from Garganian labyrinths, so that we interfere as little as possible with their way of life. We are gradually achieving harmony with them, and the actual Garganian population is growing all the time. In fact we have a number of first rate lecturers in the Culture Center who are Garganian. After all, who better to discuss Garganian life with than the people themselves? It is intriguing to trace the evolution of an alien species."

"What are they like, Ardat? How do they differ from us?" I asked, knowing next to nothing about them.

"They are much the same. Structurally—I should say, physically—they are identical, apart from having a smaller build with a large chest to accommodate the lungs and they have larger eyes. Both of these are adaptations to suit a changing environment and have not always been thus. In fact, since we Zurjahns have been here, certain other biological changes have evolved. You see, as you probably know, the gravity of Gargan was not strong enough for the first colonisers and so they had to create an artificial gravity in the dome cities and surrounding lands. At first the Garganians kept away from these 'heavy areas' as they called them, although men did venture into the local labyrinths to contact the Garganians."

"What are these labyrinths?" I interrupted.

"Forgive me for not elucidating. Due to Gargan's dying surface, the Garganian race, which once dwelt on it as we dwell on Zurjah's surface and as the Barbarians dwell on Ur's surface, had to retreat underground in order to ward off extinction. They built labyrinth colonies. Over the centuries they have filtered into Melkor and other of our own cities and slowly these have evolved a stronger type, such as now dwells in harmony with Man. Their future is brighter than that of the vast majority of Garganians, who have little to do with us, scattered as they are under the planet's surface, well away from the 'heavy areas.'

"Today's Garganians are probably far more docile than their ancestors, but have never been truly peace-loving. In years gone by, they were a race of many tribes, waging constant war with one another, almost to the point of extinction. This is thought to be the main reason for their gradual decline, so that now there are few great, ah, shall we say, tribes and many little isolated communities.

Of these latter, we know little, for they keep strictly to themselves. It seems that all the lesser species of the Nine Worlds are doomed to extinction at their own hands. Witness the Barbarians. Without Dream Lord rule, both Ur and Gargan would be devoid of native races."

I made no comment. It would not be wise to arouse Ardat's suspicions about my loyalties.

"However, any changes we have made on Gargan have been as much to Garganian advantage as to our own."

"Despite all the wonderful things we appear to have achieved, I would have thought the Garganians must have been highly disparaging when we first colonised the planet, particularly when we imposed the Empire's peace laws. Especially when, as you say, they are naturally so bellicose." Clearly Ardat had no doubts that Man had come from Zurjah, and I wanted to see what he knew of early Garganian colonisation.

"No, there was no violence. In fact, they welcomed the Zurjahns and are now honoured to be members of the Empire. I suppose it is because they are, for all their aggressive traits, a sentimental race and respect empires and armies to the point of worship, particularly one like ours which has almost achieved a unified Gargan, something her entire history could never do. However, there are rebel factions, of course. This is a natural thing for these people, but they cause minimal trouble," he added thoughtfully.

"Is it likely that they will?"

"Oh, no. I shouldn't think so, Galad. I do believe there is a—how can one put it – ah, a 'secret sect' I suppose. They have a strange name, too. What was it again?" He scratched his wispy locks.

"I am intrigued," I told him with a chuckle.

"Ah, yes; the Brotherhood of the Ram…no, no, Goat. Yes, that was what Pthorthe called it; the Brotherhood of the Goat. Though the name is an enigma, as the goat is of Zurjahn origin," he laughed.

I forced a smile, though I must have paled. My mind cast back to the gardens on Zurjah and the spectral shadow that had warned me to be wary of 'the goat.' Could this be mere coincidence? My reverie was dispelled by the chuckling Ardat, who fortunately had not seen my surprised reaction to the name.

"Yes. The society plans to 'overthrow the unmitigated dictatorship of the alien invader' or words to that effect. It happens from time to time in Garganian history. They are not taken seriously, if they really do exist, and in any case they have yet to prove violent. We have a very large army of Imperial Guards stationed here, just in case we do have difficulties, though we don't brandish it like a fist, you understand." He smiled as if to reassure me.

"Yes, I believe there is a training area on Gargan, now that you mention it. I have friends in the Imperial Guards on Zurjah," I said, deciding not to arouse Ardat's curiosity by dwelling too long on the secret society he had mentioned.

In this way, Ardat and I talked away many hours and I learned much about Garganian life. The Imperial Guard Center was far from Melkor in the Red Mountains, where the conditions—as Gundar had once remarked—were frightful. Improper gravity, thin air and freezing cold were the curse of all who toiled there. So I was to have little chance of keeping up with my personal physical regime. My life of the past would change.

My thoughts strayed often to Taria, so it was with difficulty that I concentrated on what Ardat had to say. He was only too willing to furnish me with all of his vast knowledge, but on the subject of the actual Zurjahn colonisation of the planet, he was always elusive and managed to enshroud the facts in enigma. My growing belief in what must really have happened was sustained, though to confront him with my misgivings at this time would have been both tactless and unproductive.

Our ship docked south of Melkor in a subterranean spaceport and we took a fast surface glider into the domed city. The landscape that I saw flashing past was red and dusty, pocked with small craters and crossed by cracks and chasms. I had little time to study it as we were soon within the dome and Melkor itself. The city was bright but so geometrical as to be devoid of any artistic beauty. Built for economy as it was, I suppose the planners had little time to devote to its decoration. I learned later that its actual Zurjahn population was small and that servo-robots and computer systems did most of the maintenance and labour here. Although Ardat was proud of the city, I knew that it was not a place where any Zurjahn would come to of free choice. There were scientists here and archaeologists and all manner of men devoted to improving Garganian ecology and environment, but that was all, save for the occupants of the austere edifice that was to become my home.

This was the Culture Center—a block of rock that thrust up from the floor of the crater like a barren interloper amongst the rectangular buildings, its craggy walls split and honeycombed with grim passages and rooms, like some ancient, monastic retreat. Here the students of Dream Lord lore lived frugally. In such surroundings, their physical life was not encouraged and they spent most of their time developing their minds, taking drug courses and studying, a way of life which I was expected to follow. Indeed, which such minimal scope for extra-mural interests, how could I think of abandoning the path set for me by the Dream Lords? I entered the frowning portico of the Culture Center like a condemned man.

Gargan was to be my prison for three years.

The hall which I entered was vast, being lined with bare stone seats, tables and shelves full of books, pamphlets and papers. It was decorated with splendid tapestries and occasional bronze statues of odd mathematical forms. It was here, too, that I had my first glimpse of a native Garganian.

He was sitting peacefully in a chair across the hall, deeply immersed in some thick volume, now and then turning a page with the faintest of rustles. He was quite small and had a ruddy complexion, his features being sharp and bony, his eyes larger than a man's. His black hair was very short, not even covering part of his ears, as does the Zurjahn style. He was dressed in a short, dark tunic and wore laced shoes, his skin having a marked red tincture to it. (This latter characteristic tended to develop in men who spent much time on Gargan, being attributed, as I learned, to the sun's radiation.)

I did not stare too closely at the Garganian, for fear of being offensive, but turned my attention back to Ardat. He had been indulging in light conversation with an official at the reception counter and the Imperial Guard who had come to join them. The latter watched me with interest and was evidently puzzled by my star lance, which still rested at my side in its sheath. Ardat touched my arm and introduced the Guard.

"This is Dworl, Galad, who supervises the Guards here in the Culture Center, though there are but a few. His job is purely one of appearances, you understand, there being no trouble here. If at any time you wish to go out and see something of the city, Dworl will see that you get an escort fitting for an Heir of the Dream Lords."

"Your servant, sire," Dworl acknowledged, with a bow. I nodded, though the prospect of a chaperone annoyed me. So I was not to be trusted alone in Melkor?

"I am grateful," I replied, hiding my feelings. I rarely formed an opinion of a man until I knew him, but this Dworl I took an instant dislike to. He was a tall, lean soldier, with noticeable eyes that darted to and fro like those of a snake, and he had a thin, vicious-looking mouth. His dark hair was cut short, though not so short as the Garganian's. His whole bearing was one of arrogance. I hid my resentment and distrust in silence.

"Perhaps my lord would like me to take his weapon and see that it is carefully stored until such time as he will need it," suggested the lean Guard. Ardat looked askance.

"Thank you, but it will not be necessary. I will set the star lance aside when it seems fitting to me," I replied rather curtly, my hand on the weapon's hilt.

"Star lance?" repeated Dworl. "An advanced weapon for such a place as Melkor, sire."

"I am the Heir to the Dream Lord, Dotas Sarian. It is as much a ceremonial badge of office as much as anything. I am sure you would not question my right to display it?"

He straightened and bowed once more. "By no means, my lord."

"Galad," Ardat began, "perhaps, under the circumstances—"

But my glare silenced him. "I think that I should honour my rank by carrying the star lance. You need have no fears of my using it. It is purely a symbol."

"Of course," nodded Ardat with a painful smile at Dworl, who turned and left us. Ardat then led me to my rooms.

They were grim and austere, and I thought back to the night that Chalremor had ripped aside the Dream Lord illusions and shown me their castle as it really was. This barren rock was not unlike it, cold and cheerless, an incentive to leave for the comforts of a more salubrious homeworld. Ardat left me in the dim chambers, promising to return after I had 'settled,' to conduct me around the Center.

I uttered more than a few curses to myself. To have come to this was a bitter blow. Taria would be beyond my reach for three years. Nothing could soften the sadness and anger I felt at our passing. There would not even be anyone like Gundar to unburden my heart to. Even other students here would be wary of conversing with the heir of Dotas Sarian—for all they knew, I might be a spy. Loneliness closed in on me like a grey fog and a deepening resentment of everything Zurjahn began to settle on me.

CHAPTER VI
A Prisoner without Chains

For the next year I had little choice but to study hard in the Culture Center under the patient tuition of Ardat Vellor and his monk-like fellows. I had decided quickly to apply myself to the task of preparing for my future role as a Dream Lord, and with such little room for distraction and diversion as the dreary environment offered, I began to settle into the work. To have done otherwise, I soon realised, would simply have led me down a path of frustration and desperation—even madness.

I spent much of my time in the libraries, which had an incredible stock of archives, records and texts. These I pondered and read constantly, sometimes deep into the dusk, and my whole time became devoted to my task. In time I almost forgot the events that earned me my dismissal from Zurjah and I became engrossed in my work. The speeding passage of time and the thought that Taria awaited me were now my cheering incentives.

I studied law, geography and politics, all being vital subjects to the workings of a Dream Lord. Sometimes my work was done without artificial aid, but often it was done under the control of the psychometers and the insinuator machines. With the knowledge that I was accruing, I could turn my thoughts to problems such as Ur when I became a Dream Lord. My father wrote often, expressing his pleasure in knowing that I worked so hard. It was good to know that I had brought him some comfort, although I felt saddened by his refusal to allow my correspondence with any other on Zurjah, especially Taria.

During the year, I saw much of Melkor and something of the surrounding terrain—the foothills of the stark Red Mountains and the sweeping plains of dust and the huge craters. The "heavy area" stretched for many miles and I was never allowed beyond it. My sorties by surface glider were always accompanied by three of Dworl's Imperial Guards, sombre men who had little to say for themselves. In fact I had meagre companionship. Apart from the families of the scientists and some of the high ranking officials, there were only the Guards and the other students at the Culture Center, and most of them were wary of me. Perhaps they had been instructed not to get involved with me.

However, my loneliness was not to be prolonged. By now my knowledge of Garganian life was advanced and Ardat informed me that I was to be introduced to a Garganian elder who was an expert in all the fields I was studying in Garganian law, politics and geography. He was named Pthorthe and was a likeable old fellow with greying hair and white whiskers (unusual for Garganians) and although not nearly as tall as my own six feet, reminded me more of a man than one of his own race. Ardat placed me in his keeping, for he was to teach me the Garganian language of which I still knew only basic words. And so began a close friendship. I was treated as a social and mental equal, which warmed me at once to my new colleague. The marvellous old man and I got on extremely well and shared a good many daily hours discussing and arguing policy and other matters.

Some months after we met, he invited me to his house, which is a great honour for a man. It was in the residential area of the city, two miles from the Center. The house was lavishly decorated and had an atmosphere of Garganian antiquity about it that fascinated me. We sat by a sprinkling fountain on his lawn and watched it play. Water is a particularly precious commodity on Gargan and fountains are to be found in all homes, reminding the people, so Pthorthe told me, of the times when it was hard to find underground. That was before Man came and melted parts of the polar ice. Now the water from all Garganian fountains goes through a cycle so that none of it is allowed to flow back into the dust plains and seep away forever.

We sat in the still air of the quiet suburb, the dome barely visible so high above us. Outside it the sky was dark blue with wispy clouds drifting occasionally across.

"This is a very tranquil planet, Pthorthe," I said, turning to the old fellow.

"Ah, but yes. We are a docile race, are we not, Galad?" He smiled. His face broke into a maze of wrinkles, and I wondered how old he was in Zurjahn terms.

"Your people seem very content with life, from what I have

seen," I agreed.

"And why not? We are tired; we are a people living in the memory of our past, basking in the light of bygone events. Our existence is dwindling like the waters of our planet," he said sadly. Like most Garganians, he had a penchant for melancholy reflection.

"There is life left yet on Gargan, old friend," I said. "Why—there are many of you scattered beneath this vast world. Why should you perish?"

"Oh, in time Gargan will die. It is like a great organism that has reached its maturity and gone beyond. It is a very, very old planet, older by centuries than Man. Even he, with his miracles of science, will not save it when the time comes. One can delay death, but not prevent it. Someday soon, I feel Gargan will sigh peacefully, like the old man he is, and give up his last gasp of thinning air, so that all remaining of his tired body will be the dust." He spoke in a doleful voice, hands under his chin, eyes far away.

"You are too pessimistic, Pthorthe," I chided, though his words moved me. "But tell me," I went on, seeking to turn his thoughts to the past and away from the sadness of contemplating the future, "what of Man? What do you know of our history?" My interest was casual, having been aroused by his comment on Gargan's age.

"Man is young," he smiled warmly. "I know something of his history. Such a devious history…mmm, it is an interesting tale."

"Tell me about it," I said, leaning towards him. He nodded, sat back, completely relaxed and looked up into the hazy heavens.

"Man came to Gargan many years ago. At first our people were frightened, for they knew that a race that could master the void of space must surely be powerful. But we were to become allies, not slaves, for the men were not hostile." He had closed his eyes and was sitting in a trance-like state. There was a pause, and for an amusing moment, I thought he had dozed.

"Were there many men?" I prompted.

"Not at first. Then they came in great numbers. But they did not interfere with us. They built their splendid homes above ground and lived in peace. They made improvements, giving the ageing world a new life, so that some of our people thought of them as gods, for had they not made it possible to live on the surface again? We have such an abundance of gods and deities that there was ample room for a new pantheon." I grinned at this remark, having found Garganian religion as frustratingly labyrinthine as their underground homes.

"Where did they build? Here?"

"Yes, some came here and over the years built this city from out of the crater dust in which it stands. A wonderful achievement. Other cities were built elsewhere, but that was all long, long ago," he nodded to himself, sighing deeply.

"And where did they come from?" I went on. At once I realised the implications of what had seemingly been an innocent question. I had asked it without thinking, falling subconsciously into the trap of my old ways. Pthorthe did not notice my momentary discomfort.

"From Zurjah, I suppose. And before then from the stars. Man has ever been a race for reaching out and moving onwards. From whence exactly amongst the stars…well, there is a legend, is there not?" he asked, opening his watery eyes and looking meaningfully across at me.

I frowned at his deep blue stare. "A legend…yes," I murmured.

"Oh, you have another theory, then?" he asked, a faint trace of amusement on his lips. Unease was stealing upon me, and I hesitated to speak my mind. Pthorthe should by rights be Ardat's man. Yet…

"One must be careful what theories one forms about history," I answered, deciding to be wary.

Pthorthe could see that I was tense, but he still smiled. "But you do have a theory," he persisted, interlacing his fingers.

"I have a few ideas of my own, yes. But speculation is of no importance and carries no weight in the face of fact," I said negatively, deciding to avoid the issue. I averted Pthorthe's gaze. If Ardat discovered that I still persisted in clinging to the things that Chalremor had told me, my father would be notified. I would be punished. So I held my tongue. Pthorthe, however, was not prepared to let it pass.

"I, too, have—shall we say, certain theories," he chuckled. "But, of course, I am a discrete person, as you will have discerned. Theorizing about the source of Man is a delicate matter, is it not? The ears of the Dream Lords are sharp, and they are quick to correct recalcitrant beliefs."

I twisted uncomfortably under his mischievous stare.

"I imagine a man of your learning must know much of the truth," I said at length.

"I do. I do indeed. And do not be alarmed when I tell you that I know why *you* are here, my Lord," he asserted quietly. His words startled me. He had not called me 'My Lord' since our earliest meetings.

"I see."

"Oh, I am not your father's spy. As I said, I am a discrete man. Your theories and heresies—if such they are—will not pass beyond my walls."

There was another pause while we studied each other, I searching his face for reassurance. Although I tried to relax, I could feel, almost hear, my racing pulse. What did he know?

"Well. So you know of my 'unacceptable behaviour on Zurjah and of the Dream Lords' disapproval?"

"Yes. But you need not be disturbed. The Dream Lords were frightened, were they not? But wait. Before I speak of these things to you, I want you to feel sure you can trust me," he added genuinely. His eyes held a sincere look, though I felt insecure.

"Beneath your tunic, concealed from prying eyes, you wear a medallion, stamped with a winged horse."

I caught my breath at the words, for they were so unexpected. But it was true. I still wore the medallion. For some reason I had never taken it off, keeping it, I suppose, as a symbol of my independence.

"You see," went on Pthorthe, "I am a friend to the old man in the Finger of Dusk." At his words, I recalled my meeting with Chalremor, and all the enchantment came crowding back into my mind.

"You knew him?"

"He has been here. Not for many a dusty year, it is true, but he has been to this very house, sat in that very same seat..." He nodded passionately at the one in which I sat, and I resisted the desire to leap from it.

"Here?" I echoed in puzzlement.

"Aye, but it was long ago. But I remember it well. And although he has gone on to a cobwebbed existence, his agents are active all the time—everywhere. His eyes can see what you and I cannot," Pthorthe continued, a little excited. Presently he sat back again, smiling.

"So you see, I know about you, Galad. More than you would like, I think, but you must not fear or mistrust me, for the old one I hold in mighty esteem. Mighty esteem."

"It was a shock to me that you had met him. Tell me more of this, for every tale I hear of him is as unlike its predecessor as water is unlike rock."

"I will. Years ago he was schooled in that very same Culture Center in which you are now taught by Ardat. Yes, and he went on to become Governor of Melkor, a high Zurjahn honor." As Pthorthe revealed more, all my inner conflicts surged up anew, for there had to be a story behind this so-called sorcerer. I remembered Dotas telling me that Chalremor had once been heir to the Dream Lords.

"Then the old man did not lie?"

"No, Galad. Did you doubt him?" asked Pthorthe softly. I shook my head slowly.

"Since I have met him, no. The actions of others have taught me that he spoke the truth. Chalremor..."

"Hush, my boy. Do not speak his name. Our lives would be in jeopardy should it reach the wrong ears in this city. Ah, how he has been reviled by his own kind. Man has aimed his self-hatred not at himself but at the one who justly accuses him of his crimes. Man will not admit his folly."

The words thrilled me. The name "Chalremor" echoed and re-echoed in my mind and seemed to be taken up by the giggling waters of the little fountain. His power could still reach out over unguessable distances and touch me.

"You must tell me the full story of this man, old friend, for I have only the threads," I said with hushed enthusiasm.

"Very well," Pthorthe assented gladly, then launched into another fascinating and enthralling tale, another chapter in Ur's forbidden history. "To begin with, as you have been told, Man came not from the stars, but was spawned on Ur. Ur had a turbulent history, Man being as warlike a creature as we Garganians, and despite the frequency of its wars, the planet became overpopulated. Man was forced to find a new home; he did—Gargan, the nearest of his neighbors. One of the first men to arrive here was the father of the Wise One, as the Barbarians call the old man in the tower. His name was Saul Morley—Solmor to the Garganians and, more simply, Sol.

"Sol brought his family here—Elenore, his beautiful wife, Beatrice and Deirdre, his two fair daughters, and his proud son, the Wise One. Shortly after, as Sol had foreseen, a terrible and bitter war broke out on Ur, the like of which the planet had never known before, almost destroying it, and what last of the survivors could, came here and settled on Gargan with the earliest colonizers to begin a new life. They were full of sorrow and sadness, but were determined and resilient, winning our respect, promising that never again would men be allowed to unleash powers the likes of which had blasted their homeworld.

"Eventually, as I told you, the Wise One became Governor of Melkor, while his two sisters lived normal and contented lives in Tsune and, alas, died years since. Then came trouble. By now Sol had gone on to Zurjah, a titanic planet, which none believed could ever be tamed. However, Sol had brought the wonders of a highly advanced science from Ur, and with this he settled on the inhospitable Zurjah, and beyond belief were the marvels he wrought there. The surface was altered in part, the atmosphere was changed..."

He went on, almost as totally wrapped up in his tale as I was. He characteristically added a detail here, then digressed elsewhere, until I thought he would never reach his goal. But such is the way of old men when relating past events, and I let him meander in peace.

"By the by, Garganian science owed everything to Man's. We squandered our chances of advancement in war, intent only on subjugating each other in petty, tribal struggles for millennia; such a waste, such a criminal waste," he sighed.

"You spoke of brewing trouble."

"I did indeed. Sol mastered tempestuous, uninhabited Zurjah, and there set up a new culture, a new way of existence, and almost a new species. The Dream Lords were set up in power—men who had developed their mental faculties to such a level as to be able to use new powers. Dream control, mass hypnosis, illusion, shape changing, and many more. Over the next thousand years, Zurjah grew strong, her Empire having dominion over all the inner worlds. All men answered to the Zurjahn seat of power. It was then decided by the Dream Lords that Gargan must officially join the Empire, coming under Dream Lord legislation for its own benefit and security. However, the Wise One disagreed strongly with any notion that the Garganians should be made subjects of an alien Empire, and he argued bitterly with his father and his fellow Dream Lords.

"But as always, the wishes of the Dream Lords were realized and the Wise One resigned in anger, saying that he had betrayed his allies and his friends, the Garganians, whom he had come to love dearly. As to the Empire, there was no trouble there. Garganian officials welcomed these gods of peace, for they respected the power of the Empire and the salvation it offered. Some of us had realized the folly of war in light of what we had seen of man's scientific achievements, the likes of which our own race had never known. Even so, the Wise One had a growing dislike for the Empire's power. It would abuse it, he said, and it would shackle freedom the way Man had done on his native Ur. Sol, his father, felt sure that it would preserve peace.

"Sol tried to persuade his son to remain on Gargan as Governor of the whole planet's colonial system, but it was no use. His son refused the post and was given instead the leadership of the first scout force sent to explore Ur. Three years later, Sol died, having lived to an impossible age, for Man had learned not only to stave off the death of planets such as Gargan, but also to prolong his own life. With Sol's passing, a law was made on longevity, giving the Dream Lords the power to bestow it on those whom they chose.

"The Wise One was not elected to become a Dream Lord when Sol died; his disagreement over the Gargan affair had left his ideals in serious question. Instead he devoted his time to Ur, trying to rebuild it from the ashes left by the war. A colony at last sprang up on the site which is now Karkesh. The Wise One travelled far and wide, discovering a great diversity of life, and meeting the people who were to give him his name. He was like a god to these Barbarians (as they were named) and became known as their prophet. He promised these survivors of the war that one day he would give them a new world and universal peace, restoring them to their old status. For they had become primitive and backward, lacking sophistication and even the rudiments of technology.

"However, his wishes were thwarted once again by the Dream Lords. What he found when he returned to Zurjah sickened him to the depths of his soul. The Dream Lords had a master plan for Ur, and this it was that so horrified the Wise One. Ur was not to be welcomed back into the Empire, but was to be spurned and turned into a prison planet, while her people were to be enslaved, so that they could never rise and destroy again. Ur's history was to be rewritten, as was Man's, and the place became accursed. Thus did the Dream Lords, masters of terrible weapons themselves, say that Ur's people—simple, grovelling savages—were not to be trusted.

81

So Man denied that he was Man and became another race, whose source was 'beyond the stars.' Ironic, is it not? How foolish. But such is pride.

"Reluctantly and with a heavy heart, the Wise One informed his loyal Barbarians of what had been decreed, and he swore to have his revenge. 'If they choose not to be men, then they are alien usurpers,' he told them. Heartbroken, he returned to Zurjah, determined to thwart the Dream Lords whenever he could. He confined himself to study and mastery of new powers. He kept himself informed of everything that went on around him. He knew what passed on Ur, Gargan and all the other worlds. And he waited until the time to strike back came.

"He had confined himself, but he was not to be left alone, for shortly a new side to the Ur problem showed itself. It had to happen, just as he had forseen. Someone stumbled onto the darker powers of the psyche and wanted to use them for his own betterment. A rival power for the Dream Lord supremacy stretched itself and prepared to challenge them."

"Rival power?" I said, surprised, for the Dream Lords had no enemies that I knew of.

"Oh, yes. The Wise One spoke of the nature of Man and said, accurately, that throughout his history a wheel had been turning. Each successive age of development and refinement of civilization was always followed by a struggle and then a period of barbarism. It began with the old cycle of the Gods. The Gods would fall out, argue, fight, then destroy everything in a cataclysm, leaving the whole cycle to begin again, with new Gods to rule. And so, said the Wise One, would the cosmic wheel of Dream Lord power turn. They would clash with evil powers of their own strength and meet their Armageddon. This time the scale would be greater than ever before and the nine worlds would perish."

"He told me a cosmic wheel was coming to a close...'a ring will knit' I think he said," I interrupted.

"Just so," nodded the Garganian.

"What leads him to believe this? Another war on Ur?"

"Daras Vorta became Warden of Ur and that was the sign the Wise One had awaited. What do you know of this man?"

"Vorta? Not a great deal. A military figure, full of ambition, as I recall."

Pthorthe frowned. "Then there is much more I must teach you if that is all you know of Vorta. The Wise One knew him to be an intensely evil man—he had had brief encounters with him here on Gargan—and through his spies the Wise One learned that almost as soon as Vorta and his foul ways were established in Karkesh, the city had become the haunt of terror. The Wise One once more appealed to the Dream Lords, who summoned both him and Vorta. But Vorta has the tongue of a demon. He accused the Wise One of conspiring with the Barbarians in an attempt to reunite them against Zurjahn authority. He produced Barbarian prisoners who swore this was true. They had been tortured and promised freedom by Vorta's thugs if they would denounce the Wise One. So the Dream Lords found for Vorta and against the Wise One.

"They were angry, for there were many tribes of Barbarians roaming free and unshackled on Ur. The Dream Lords determined to uphold their policy on Ur's enslavement. Peace at any price, they insisted. Thus the false prophet, as they called the Wise One, was imprisoned. In the Finger of Dusk has he languished since, while a darkness gathers about the Dream Lords. The rest of the sorry history you know, Galad," Pthorthe concluded. He sat back, breathing deeply, giving me a moment to digest all that I had heard.

"For the first time the picture is clear," I said.

"It is well. You see the greatness of this man. I myself am not a man, I am a Garganian, and proud of it. But I see in him a greatness, glory and dedication to his people that surpasses all other. To stand beside him is to stand beside a god. I became a sworn ally to his cause, not only because he is a friend, but because of his love for his people, and that he believes no matter how dark the night, a new day will dawn. He fights the senseless barbarism that has all but wiped my race away and that will wipe his own race away if it is not stopped.

"So do you see your place, Galad?" he ended.

"My place?"

"You are his last hope. In you he sees his last weapon, his sword, his staff. He has shown you the fallacy behind Dream Lord ideology. You must use your scant power carefully," he went on passionately. The weight of my responsibilities had suddenly magnified. Yet I felt helpless.

"I shall do what I can, and can do no more. When I am a Dream

Lord, my will shall be known," I said, but I was seized by many doubts.

"The circle knits, my boy. Do not let events carry you; you must be the master of your own destiny. But for now, I am tired. I will rest and we will speak of these things another day." He waved his hand casually, showing me that for the time the matter was at an end. He closed his eyes and drifted into sleep, leaving me to contemplate his revelations in the serenity of the cool air. I sighed. For over a year I had let Ur slip to the back of my mind. Now it was resurrected, this true motherworld. Pthorthe, I knew, had been assigned to teach me more than Ardat Vellor would ever realize.

CHAPTER VII
A Clash of Steel

Now that I knew the full facts surrounding Chalremor, I found it difficult to study. Only now did I realize the true importance of his schemes to unshackle the Barbarians, and how much of a key I was in these schemes. At least I knew that I was with him. Yet what could I do here on Gargan? What, indeed, could I have done on Ur? The situation seemed completely hopeless and I began to despair. However, that I was to tread became clear, for soon after I had visited Pthorthe, a series of rapid and unforeseen events occurred.

The star lance that Gundar had given me hung in its silver sheath on the gloomy wall of my apartment. Usually I wore it whenever I left the Culture Center and left it where it hung if I remained in the building. Today I took it down and admired it before belting it on and strapping it to my leg. I had it in mind to visit one of the balconies where certain hydroponic experiments were being conducted.

On the balcony that overlooked the plain buildings of the city, I thought over the events of the past beneath a clear sky. There was no one outside to disturb my thoughts, and no one to fuss over the plants that lined the rock wall of the Center. Below me was a thirty foot drop to the streets of Melkor, which were usually silent in this area.

I had been leaning on the parapet, lost in thought for some time, when a movement below caught my attention. A large square was directly beneath me, and creeping stealthily across it, peering this way and that, moved a furtive, grimy figure in dusty, ragged clothing, with a mop of tousled black hair. It was mid-afternoon; the square beneath and the immediate surroundings were devoid of activity in the oppressive heat. Besides this, the very nature of the man's skulking attitude made me at once suspicious.

Suddenly three Imperial Guards burst into the square from the passageway from which the man had just emerged, and seeing him, shouted out a challenge. I was too high above the scene for the words to be audible, but the man was evidently terrified. Nevertheless he broke into a run, and for the first time I noticed, with mild surprise, that his wrists were shackled. A fourth figure joined the trio, and I recognized Dworl, the Sergeant of the Guard of the Center, a man whom I intensely disliked and had never trusted. I had made a point of avoiding him.

Dworl barked something at the fleeing fugitive, who immediately stopped, turning helplessly. Then the three Guards strolled over to him lazily and roughly gripped him. They awaited Dworl's command. He spoke, and two of them forced the unprotesting man to his knees, holding him there while the other ripped the shirt from his bronzed back. Dworl unfurled from beneath his cloak a vicious looking whip of black leather, and in its many tails something gleamed in the bright sunlight—copper, perhaps, or lead shot.

Standing menacingly above the helpless man, Dworl said something, and in reply the prisoner appeared to spit. Horrified, I watched as Dworl brought up a booted foot, violently kicking the man in the face, while the two men held him down, laughing grotesquely. Never before had I seen such a cowardly act, and it filled me with rage and loathing. My blood began to boil as I discarded caution and climbed over the parapet, dropping noiselessly several feet to a nearby sloping roof which adjoined the Center.

My movements had gone unobserved, so I quietly slid to the edge of the roof and dropped onto yet a lower roof. From the cool of the shadows I saw the Guards mercilessly twist the prisoner around, and Dworl lashed out with the whip, leaving thin lines of spreading scarlet across the helpless man's back. As he struck, Dworl laughed, but the brave victim uttered no sound at all. I reached the ground silently, remaining unseen. Dworl struck again, and I could hear the cruel chuckles of the others. Their words were now audible in the humid air.

"Beg, you Barbarian dung! Come, let us hear you crave mercy. I'll have you crawl on your belly, weeping every inch of the way back," snarled Dworl, lashing out again. The man's back had become a hideously dissected mass of crimson, staining redder the rusty dirt around the tableau. I felt sickened, and could restrain my anger no longer. With as little sound as possible I stepped out into the light.

"Stop that at once!" I commanded vehemently. The four guards looked around in horror, sweat glistening on their startled faces. Dworl lowered his whip slowly and glowered at me from beneath his plumed helm. The glare of the sun was behind me and he squinted.

"Who *dares* to interrupt—oh, it is you, sire," he said, contempt his tone rich in contempt. The others were puzzled, looking to Dworl for a lead. He remained unperturbed, blowing a drop of sweat from those cruel, thin lips. I had drawn my star lance in the shadows and had it now out of sight, both my hands clasped behind me in a seemingly casual fashion.

"What, may I ask, is the meaning of this unprecedented little episode?" I asked, my voice level. I walked slowly forward. My eyes never left Dworl's, for my anger had yet to cool. Dworl finally looked away and pointed his ugly whip at the lacerated man.

"A runaway, sire. Trying insolently to avoid his share of the work in the sewage clearance," he said coldly, his wicked mouth twisted with contempt. He rubbed sweat from his jaw.

"Sewage clearance," I mused. "Surely there is a fully automated system for such work. What crime has this man committed that he should be appointed to do the job of a machine?"

"He is from a Barbarian slave party, sire."

"Explain yourself," I said, my frown deepening. What was a Barbarian doing on Gargan? The three Guards were fidgeting restlessly, but Dworl remained outwardly calm.

"The Governor sometimes finds it necessary to import slave parties for some of the more unpleasant work, sire. We keep a small pen of such dung. There is at present a fault in F sector of the drainage channels below the city and this excrement was one of the assigned party to clear the blockage," said Dworl.

I looked at the man. His gaze was on the leaded thongs of the whip, which were aimlessly tracing trails in the bloodied dirt. So this was a Barbarian?

My stomach knotted at the thought of slave labor. Surely the Dream Lords had not condoned this?

"Is this true?" I asked the prisoner. The Guards stood him roughly to his feet, turning him to face me. His face was brown and stained with dirt, blood and sweat, while a bluish bruise had formed under one eye. His damp hair flopped into those piercing eyes, eyes which now looked hard into mine. I felt an overwhelming pity for him as he stood, almost on the point of collapse, defiant before me.

"Well?" I asked again.

"I have done nothing, Zurk," he said simply and lowered his head. Pthorthe had told me that the word "Zurk" was the contemptuous nickname the Barbarians gave to all Zurjahns. As the man bent, his body gave a slight tremor, and his eyes darted back to mine, then down to my chest. I realized at once what had startled him. I had on only a loose, open tunic, due to the heat, and had foolishly forgotten fully to conceal the medallion of Chalremor. The man had instantly recognized it.

"You are a liar!" snapped Dworl, drawing back the whip for another blow. I sensed the move instantaneously and moved faster. I took one step back, swung up the star lance in a glittering arc from its concealment, and swept it swiftly down, scorching the haft of the whip inches from the hand that held it. It fell smouldering to the ground, sending up a tiny dust cloud. Dworl whirled away from the star lance, teeth barred, furious with rage.

"My lord, you should not meddle in matters which do not concern you! This man is a criminal—"

"Then return him to his duties," I retorted. The Guards gazed nervously about.

"Yes, of course, sire," Dworl said hurriedly. "But he needs a lesson for attempting to escape. He is dangerous. These Barbarian dogs must be taught that we are the masters," he argued, throwing down the remainder of the useless whip haft. His flaunting of my authority rankled with me.

"That may be so, but only a coward kicks a defenceless man in the face. An animal would not sink as low," I said, putting as much contempt into my voice as I could. I could ill hide my seething hatred for this man Dworl. He epitomized everything evil in Zurjahn ways. The prisoner eyed me with some reverence. The others sensed the electricity that was at play in the angered air around us. There was a long pause.

"It is easy to insult when one carries a star lance, my Lord," Dworl replied slowly, measuring his words and lowering his voice. His men sensed trouble and shifted uneasily. They knew my rank, my high position. Dworl was taking an immense gamble by questioning me. But I had shamed him unspeakably by comparing him to an animal. I sensed that his pride could not bear such an insult.

"Then give me a sword," I said, unstrapping my silver sheath. I slipped home the star lance and dropped it at my feet. Dworl motioned for one of the Guards to toss me a sword. I caught it as Dworl haughtily unsheathed his own blade.

"Now we are even," I breathed, moving away from the star lance, crouching for battle. I was being rash, perhaps, but Gundar's teaching was still fresh within my mind. I held out my sword, crosswise at chest height.

"I shall not kill you, upstart, but you will learn better manners in front of your master, for none has outfought me yet," he sneered.

"Will you slay me with words, animal?" I taunted, and at that he swore crudely, his face reddening, and he made a move forward.

"You have asked for this. My three men are witnesses for me, and they shall speak in my favor when the time comes to explain why you lie bleeding abed. And they will all relate, with much disgust, how the ignoble Galad Sarian attacked an Imperial Guard during his line of duty, not with a sword, but with a star lance," he gloated, and his words cheered his men, who saw in them a possible way out of the dilemma into which he had led them.

"Let us see you fight, then!" he suddenly challenged, darting forward, thinking to take me unawares. I had expected such an elementary move and was not fooled. Despite the unnerving strategy, I eluded the lunge with ease, and shielding my body, aimed a swift kick at his right knee, on which he was temporarily balanced. Unprepared for such a crude trick, he stumbled over heavily with an oath, completely taken by the rapid speed of the move. Had I wished to finish him then, it would have been an easy matter to rip him open where he lay, but such was not my desire. Gundar had taught me that to enrage an opponent to madness weakens him more swiftly than long combat.

I allowed Dworl to get up. He cursed foully, coming at me again, but this time wary of any dirty tactics. Our swords clashed in the sun, and crackling sparks danced and flew in the air around us. Suddenly it was Dworl's turn to use underhand play. He feinted a drop to one knee, and as he rose, scooped a handful of dust accurately into my eyes. I staggered back, fighting to see, and faintly I made out the whistling sword of my opponent, splitting the air above me. Instinctively I parried his terrific, double-handed blow, my weapon ringing along the length of his, and with a splintering crash, his sword snapped at the hilt and clanged heavily in the dirt. My arms shook from the impact, and I knew that the blow would have killed me. But I was his match, and my own pride revelled in my new-found skill.

I rubbed my irritated eyes and held Dworl, now less anxious to continue, at bay. He stood quite still, then with no warning, drew back his arm and flung his shattered hilt at me in desperation. I stepped aside, and holding my sword as one would a club, lashed out at the hurtling remnant, sending it tumbling end over end across the square. A gasp escaped the watching men, and Dworl stood aghast.

For the second time he knew that I could run him through.

"Another sword, there," I called, much to the horror of the Guards. After a moment, one of them threw his blade to the smirking Dworl. He caught it and came on at me again. We engaged further, and it soon became apparent that he was not a skilful swordsman but a man who depended on foul tactics and brute strength as one usually finds with bullies. Nor had he been well trained. My own superiority in that field now allowed me to toy with him. This made him furious, for the Guards could see his blundering ineptness, and he had to put more into his sweaty task, determined not to back off or lose more face. I became more confident and, I confess, a trifle careless, for he drew blood on my left arm. He grunted with satisfaction, and now it was my turn to be angered.

Stepping forward, I cut away the cloak from his shoulders with one contemptuous sweep, and it hung limply from his right arm. Taken aback, he stumbled in its folds, and I followed up by scything through the plumes of his helmet. Behind me I heard chuckles of mirth from the Guards. Deeply disgraced, Dworl recovered himself and aimed a wild, despairing blow at my throat, but I evaded it with ease. Lifting my weapon, I sank its singing steel into the white fingers that held his sword. Blood was quick to spurt onto the scuffed ground, and with a scream of agony, Dworl dropped his blade. He grasped his fist to his stomach, pouring forth a torrent of invective. The fight was at an end.

Dworl dropped to his knees, head bent low towards his stomach, the man doubled up, fighting the waves of agony that must have coursed through him. I brought my blade very slowly up until it rested beneath his clean-shaven chin. Beads of sweat, mingled with tears of pain, ran down my blade. I forced his head up. He drew in great lungfuls of air.

"You deserve to die, Dworl. You are a filthy insult to the name of Zurjah. However, we are supposed to be a civilized species. I cannot spit you as I would an animal. Get away from this place and lick your wounds. And in future, control your manners in my presence, or *you* will be the one working in the sewers." I had almost expended my hate. He closed his eyes, moaning and trying in vain to stem the rapid flow of blood from his ruined hand. I saw his blade in the dust beside him, and next to it, one of his severed fingers. Disgusted with the whole episode, and more by my own bestial rage, I turned to the proud prisoner and the horrified Guards.

"You!" I shouted, pointing to the nearest. I plunged the sword into the ground. "See to him," I said, indicating Dworl. The Guard nodded submissively, blanching at the crimson sheen on the blade. He ran to Dworl and helped him to his feet. I picked up my star lance and unsheathed it. I walked to the prisoner.

"All of you," I said. There was a hush, apart from Dworl's groans as he was led away by his fellow. Even he turned to face me now.

"You have seen a Guard beaten with a sword. The sword is the only weapon allowed you Guards on Gargan, apart from the spear. This is a star lance," I went on. I gripped the handle and twisted it, sending a leaping tongue of white heat curving upwards in an arc to sputter harmlessly down on the ground sixty yards away. The Guards all gasped, for as I had surmised, they had never seen a weapon like this before. I switched off the fire stream.

"Weapons like this are not to be trusted to anyone. There would be no one left on this planet if the likes of you were let loose. You call yourselves a superior species, but you are no better than Barbarians."

I ignored their glares and waved Dworl and his escorting Guard away. The barbarian watched them go.

"May all who kiss the backside of the Goat reap such a harvest," he muttered, and I wondered at his words.

"What is your name?" I asked softly, my calmness returned.

"Tegara Sahdi, master," he replied.

"I shall remember you. Do not despair," I said, and his eyes fell again to my medallion.

"Are you indeed from the One?" he whispered, so that the others could hear nothing.

I nodded abruptly. "Tell them on your return to Ur that they are not forgotten," I breathed.

I turned to the two remaining Guards. "I am shocked by what I have seen here. I expect you to execute your duty like human beings. For this episode, you deserve to be cast out of the Imperial Guard, never to wear sword for the Empire again. However, military and political matters are not yet my major concerns, so I will let this pass. This man is to be treated properly. If he is not, I will have you before the Governor himself. Understand that, and mark it well!"

They nodded, muttering. Tegara Sahdi said nothing, but I read thanks and something else in his eyes before I walked back to the Center. He knew I was powerless to free him.

Above me, a bird of some description fluttered up into the rocks of the Culture Center, and I may have imagined it, but I thought that in its beak it carried one of Dworl's severed blue plumes.

CHAPTER VIII
The Shadow of the Goat

"Your life is in grave danger," said Pthorthe. We were in a private room of his house, deep underground, where there was no possibility of our being overheard. Pthorthe's apparent anxiety that morning when we met in one of the libraries at the Culture Center had set my nerves on edge. Since I had disgraced Dworl a few days before, I had expected some kind of reprisal. I did not press Pthorthe for details at once, knowing that he would furnish me with them all in good time.

"From what?" I now asked, startled by his disclosure. His brows contracted in a deep scowl.

"From that very source of evil which you have been sent to destroy," he said softly, as though afraid to say it even in this sheltered place. I shared his fears, for it was not usual for him to seem so insecure.

"From Ur?"

"Yes, from Ur itself. I have told you something of Daras Vorta, have I not?"

"Yes."

"Well, I will tell you more, for circumstances force me to hasten. Vorta was born here on Gargan, that you know already. While he was here he made many friends, most of them unpleasant, ambitious men, I might add, and after some years he founded a cult that began practising evil and delving into forbidden realms of Dream Lord powers."

"Evil? I don't understand," I said, frowning almost as deeply as he.

"All in good time, Galad; be patient. Yes, Vorta is a terribly evil man, for he has certain powers now that are above those of a normal man. Moreover, he is a psychopath—when one has learned some of the things that he has one's mind can hardly remain stable—so he is doubly dangerous. I told you of the cult he started here; the details of this are too heinous to relate," he went on grimly, and his expression was one of loathing.

"The Brotherhood of the Goat?" I guessed, and at once he whirled, eyes aflame.

"Exactly! Do you know of it, Galad?"

"A little. Ardat mentioned it once, although not in connection with Vorta. The Wise One told me to be wary of the Goat," I added.

Pthorthe nodded. "Yes, yes. The Goat. Vorta's self-appointed title. Ardat has heard of the cult from myself and from others, but little suspects its true function. People think it is a Garganian secret society for the overthrow of Zurjahn rule, but it is in fact the tool in the hands of a madman. Now that Vorta has the huge fortress of Karkesh on far off Ur to hide in, he has developed his foul Brotherhood to a greater extent.

"The Dream Lords do not realize this, for Vorta is as cunning as a demon, but Karkesh has become more than a prison city—it is a living hell, made for the sadistic pleasures of the vile Warden who rules it like an Emperor. Vorta used countless numbers of his helpless prisoners as victims in his ungodly rituals to appease the hungry appetites of the disgusting gods that he serves." Pthorthe paused, face clouded with revulsion. I had never heard him speak with belief about any kinds of deities before this. Perhaps it was more Garganian superstition.

"How am I implicated in this?" I asked, more than a little uncomfortable.

"Recently I have feared developments in the Garganian underworld, and now my worst fears have been confirmed. I have not had all the facts—and still I lack details—but I see something of Vorta's plans. My spies, as faithful to the Wise One as to myself, keep me well informed, and from these sources I keep as well informed as possible. They tell me that events are coming to a head. And you are the keystone."

"How so?"

"Vorta has it in mind to test his powers to the full. He plans to overthrow the Dream Lords," Pthorthe replied. It seemed preposterous.

"If this can be proved, then they must be informed."

"Not yet. The time is not ripe. The Dream Lords laughed at the Wise One before, and you they banished. We must wait for the exact moment. Listen to me. Vorta is subtle. I have sought vainly for a way of thwarting his plans from here, but to no avail. He has mastery of Ur and the Imperial Guard there. Now he covets mastery of Gargan. He will cleverly play off the Garganians against the Imperial Army here, himself an apparently ignorant spectator. When the Garganians rebel, as he is planning they shall do, he will emerge as the head of a new religious order."

"How? How could your people accept him?"

"The Brotherhood of the Goat serves two purposes. One is to pave the way for all manner of foul acts and rituals to further delve into the darker powers Vorta has tapped, and the other is more practical. Vorta's identity is not known to the Garganians as head of the cult. They believe the Goat to be the spirit of some deity that has returned to cajole them into rising against the Zurjahns. I have preached to underground centers against this, but Garganian blood is Garganian blood. The Goat promises victory."

"So there will be a rebellion? A war? Yet—your people will be massacred," I cried.

"No. Vorta works from within. He controls the Imperial Guards on Gargan...many of the high ranks are members of his cult."

"This is evil news, I confess. Then after the revolt?"

"There will be little violence at first, and nothing to implicate Vorta. Then his next step will be to put your cousin, Ravas Tarak, on the Dream Lord triumvirate in your place—"

"Ravas! Why, that's insane! That fawning idiot—"

"Think, Galad, my boy," Pthorthe cut me short. "You are here on Gargan, completely at the mercy of Vorta's agents. Ravas Tarak, fool that he is, is next in line to you to succeed your father. If you were to die...well, you can see what will transpire," he said simply. I nodded, realizing he was right.

"Just what does Vorta intend? Where is Ravas?"

"Ravas skulks in Karkesh, a puppet in the hands of Vorta, who promises him a share of controlling the Nine Worlds," replied Pthorthe, spreading his hands in frustration. I could not help but groan.

"That is worse news, Pthorthe. Ravas is so gullible, a fop— and he detests me; he's never concealed the fact. In the hands of such a man as Vorta, he would be putty, I know."

"I fear that I have worse news yet, Galad. The reason I brought you here is that Vorta now knows your every move. He had not known until recently that you were here in Melkor, and now that he does, he sees it as the opportunity he has dreamed of."

"Surely he would not kill me here? That would be madness," I said, shaking my head in disbelief.

"Not kill you at first, no. But if he were to kidnap you..." He left the sentence hanging. He was right.

"You think he will?" I asked, wondering myself what plans must be forming even now in the mind of the evil Warden.

"Certainly. He has everything to play for. He will kidnap you and have the Dream Lords informed that it was the work of the Garganian rebels. It will be called a gesture against the Empire. The Governor of Melkor, Wortan Heynar, would be empowered to take reprisals. He would recall his crack troops from the Red Mountains."

"How could Vorta benefit from this? The rebels would never

triumph—"

"Heynar is Vorta's right hand man in all of this."

"Heynar, too?"

"Just so. He is loyal only to Vorta, as corrupt as only the Warden of Ur could have made him. And he has orders to take you."

"And Vorta will kill me."

"Your body would be found, after the rising, and a number of Garganians would be arrested and executed. All Zurjahns not loyal to Heynar would be killed by the Garganian rebels, and Heynar would be master. The Garganians would be told by the Goat to serve him, and Heynar would have little trouble convincing the Dream Lords that he had subdued the uprising. Vorta would then be master of this world. Shortly thereafter, Ravas Tarak becomes Dream Lord without a slight and the cancer spreads."

"How is it that Vorta found out about my whereabouts?"

"You skirmish with the Imperial Guard, Dworl. You did well, striking a blow, unknown to you, against one of Wortan Heynar's leading cut-throats," he said, allowing himself a chuckle.

"And you are certain that Heynar will have me taken?"

"Vorta is not the only man with spies in this city. His own deceit has cost him the secrecy of his plan. He has Garganian allies, but there are those who know how ruthlessly he would murder any of us whose existence became inconvenient. I have eyes and ears everywhere. Vorta rules by terror. The common Garganian fears the Gods, and the power of the Goat is manifest now. A Garganian would sell his brother rather than face the wrath of the Goat."

"Then what am I to do?" I asked, baffled. I was to be the focal point of affairs. I dared not return to Zurjah, where I would surely be scoffed at and returned.

"I must use the *phorud*," I half heard Pthorthe mutter to himself. It was a Garganian word for which I knew no equivalent.

"Yes," he said. "The *phorud* is your only chance, though there will be those who will question my sanity in protecting a Zurjahn. I will explain. You know that here on Gargan there have always been groups of my people agitating for reform— and some for radical reform. Vorta has used such enmity against Zurjahn rule. But it is the Garganian way to agitate. We are a dying race, so we enjoy our minor intrigues and plots against authority. It reminds us of the old glorious days of Empires we knew. There are foolish diehards amongst us, and although they do no real harm with their so-called daring exploits, they often need help in extricating themselves from the clutches of the Imperial Guards.

"That is where the *phorud* comes in. When one of my people comes to me and he needs to get out of Melkor quickly, I smuggle him out through the *phorud*. Sometimes I have to employ, ah, more energetic means than are generally required, to get someone out of prison, perhaps, but things are well organized. I have a long line of contacts, like a channel, all of whom are loyal and dependable. They come from all over the city and beyond it. There are certain members who would sell any Zurjahn to the Guards, but I will pick my accomplices in your escape carefully."

"You will smuggle me out of the city?"

"It is the only thing to do under the circumstances. As long as Vorta keeps a constant watch on your whereabouts, you are in danger, for he will certainly strike. His power reaches into all but the remotest corners, so you will not be safe in Melkor. It is imperative that you leave the city."

Pthorthe was deep in thought, and I realized this solution of his must be the only viable one.

"It will be hazardous, for there are those amongst my people who would slit your throat with no remorse."

"Where am I to go?" I asked, for my knowledge of the terrain was minimal.

"Difficult...difficult. I have friends in other places—distant Garganian labyrinths where even the Gods could not reach you. But the plans of the Wise One are jeopardized. Events are going too quickly for my old head. We had planned to get you to Ur," he said, shaking his head dubiously and wringing his hands.

"Ur? How could—?"

"It could be done. But now...it is too soon, and too dangerous. You must go into hiding and Vorta must be tricked into believing you dead or lost. Only then will he cease to search you out."

"And when am I to leave the city?"

"It cannot be too soon. I will begin arrangements at once. You must leave tonight," he said after brief hesitation.

"Tonight! But what of Ardat?"

"It is best this way. I will find a way of letting your father know you are safe." Pthorthe sighed and I nodded wearily. We fell silent, both lost in thought. Then Pthorthe rose and began pacing the room.

"It must be tonight, then. I will make the necessary arrangements and secure the first contact. Be prepared. I shall await you in the main library after the last meal."

"How am I to leave you when I am sure to be escorted?" I protested. Even now there were three Imperial Guards outside his house, ready to return with me to the Center.

"Meet me after the last meal. I will see to everything."

*

That evening I met Pthorthe as arranged in the main library. He appeared calm, but there were additional lines of strain across his face.

"Tell the officials that we are attending a Garganian function to do with harvesting," he said as we approached the doors. I had always to produce my identity discs when I left the Center so that a number of Guards could be assigned to accompany me. The official on duty examined my discs briefly and nodded. He was familiar with my regular passage to and fro.

"If you'll wait one moment, sire, I will call for an escort."

He spoke into his communication unit. Pthorthe and I exchanged brief glances, but said nothing. I had taken my usual precaution of strapping on my star lance, though the Guards were used to my wearing it. Presently three of them emerged from a corridor and bowed.

"Your escort, sire," said the official. "May I know where you will be going, so that it can be registered?"

"Of course. I attend a Garganian debate on new harvesting techniques. My Garganian tutor, Pthorthe, will be with me throughout its duration."

"Thank you, sire," said the official, noting it down. I signed some papers for him, then nodded to Pthorthe and his Guards. Pthorthe and I walked to the doors, the three Guards behind us, faces devoid of emotion.

"Excuse me, sire," came the voice of the official.

"Yes?" I said, turning.

"Has Ardat Vellor been informed?"

There was a moment of uncomfortable silence.

"Naturally the visit is under his auspices," I said a trifle coldly. Another silent pause followed, and I sensed Pthorthe tensing beside me. The official had only to check and we would not be allowed out.

"Very good, sire," he said after a moment, and without another glance I turned and left the building.

"You have a plan to be rid of these mummies?" I said softly to Pthorthe as we reached the broad avenue. The Guards refrained from breathing down our necks, but were never far behind.

"Have no fears," murmured Pthorthe.

"Excuse me, sire," said a gruff voice from behind.

"What is it?" I retorted irritably.

"Would my lord prefer to travel in a transporter car? One can be readily summoned," began one of the Guards.

"It will not be necessary," put in Pthorthe. "We go but a short distance."

The Guard's questioning eyes remained on me.

"We will walk," I told him firmly and turned my back.

Pthorthe led us along one of the many broad pavements. The sky had turned to twilight orange, a few streaks of light across the horizon, the buildings like gaunt blocks of stone, draped in darkening shadows. We walked down a number of side streets, the bots of the Guards always echoing back at us from the walls. At length Pthorthe stopped at the end of a narrow alleyway.

"This is the place, sire," he said, raising his voice so that the Guards could hear.

Their spokesman came forward and peered into the gloom of the alley. He drew his sword.

"I will lead, sire," he said in such a tone as to imply that it was not to be questioned. I drew aside. He stepped into alley, which was wide enough to accommodate only one man's passage at a time. Pthorthe followed him, then I, then the remaining Guards. The darkness closed in and a chill crept into the air. My hand went to the grip of my star lance.

We came out into an ill-lit square, which appeared to be deserted. The leading Guard turned to Pthorthe.

"Where to now, old man? I like not this dingy place."

Pthorthe glanced nervously about and for a moment I sensed that something was amiss. The square was small and bare, with a number of black alleys opening onto it.

"I am debating which exit to take," mumbled Pthorthe. "My memory is not so good these days."

The Guard grunted but I shot him an angry gaze. His fellows shifted in the pale light of the solitary glowbulb. The next moment there came the sound of movement from one of the adjoining alleyways across the square. Suddenly a small transporter car, not much bigger than a Zurjahn hoverbubble, turned into the square and came straight at us. Pthorthe jerked me to one side as the car zoomed down upon the leading Guard.

He made a dash for safety, but as the car drew abreast, a shrouded figure straightened up from its tiny cockpit and an arm drew back. The Guard's head snapped back, and with a torn off gurgle he sank to his knees. Blood spurted from where a blade had lodged in his throat, and he fell onto his face.

The other Guards had their swords out as the car spun in a tight circle. Pthorthe and I watched, amazed and horrified. The car tried to smash the Guards down, but they moved quickly to one side, slashing with their blades at the occupant. Swords clanked down on metal as the car veered away and turned for another attack. I slid my star lance from its sheath, my immobility gone as I realized this could be one of Vorta's kidnap attempts. The car missed the Guards again and this time the driver misjudged his turn, and with a screech of metal on stone, the vehicle went into a spin, showering the square with sparks as it ploughed up the paving stones. Its nose smashed into a jutting buttress, buckling up and catapulting the driver against the wall like a sack of wheat. He rolled over, half stunned.

The Guards leered at one another and slowly moved over to where he was sprawled, swords ready to finish him.

"We are lost," muttered Pthorthe in horror.

"What?" I asked bemusedly, watching the two Guards standing over the recovering driver.

"Flee while you have the chance and the Guards are not looking," hissed Pthorthe.

"But the danger is past! Vorta's attempt here has failed."

"Not Vorta...that man is ours! He was to lead you to the *phorud*."

My mouth fell open and I stared at the helpless figure. Two swords rose cruelly, ready to shear his head from his shoulders. I needed no further thought. My star lance came up, I aimed, twisted the grip, and a thin flame shot outwards, throwing the square into lurid illumination. I directed the arc of fire and scythed down the two Guards. Their swords clanked to the floor as they let ut brief shrieks, their backs scorched and charred.

Pthorthe drew back in momentary horror. He had never seen such a weapon in operation before. The fire beam retracted into the star lance as I switched it off. I ran forward, ignoring the two smouldering corpses, and helped the driver of the transporter car to unsteady feet.

"What manner of blade is that, that it can send fire at the enemies?" grunted a voice from inside the man's dark cowl. He had spoken in Garganian, and I replied in the same language.

"Are you hurt?"

Pthorthe came shuffling over and asked the same question, but the man was only shaken.

"Then we must be on our way before a patrol stumbles on this chaos. The whole square was aglow when you fired that accursed thing," grumbled Pthorthe.

I slid the weapon back into its sheath.

"There are clothes in the car with which to disguise yourselves," said the cowled one. I found them without difficulty.

"Where will you go?" the Garganian asked of Pthorthe.

"I cannot return to the Center after this. When these bodies are found it will be obvious that it was Galad who killed them. I will be implicated at once as I am registered at the Culture Center as having left with Galad. I will be thrust into Heynar's hands and no doubt he will use psychometers to drag from me everything I know."

"But," I interrupted, "you would have been implicated anyway, surely."

"No. I was to have been trussed and left in the street. I would not have seemed party to your abduction. Heynar would probably have believed you had been abducted by men under Vorta's command, and so not pressed me for details. But now I must leave Melkor at once. I dare not return."

"Then let us begone quickly!" snapped the Garganian. He wheeled and led us into another dark alley. As we wormed our way down it, I called a halt.

"What is it?" breathed Pthorthe.

"Wait," I commanded. Something in the air had brought me up short. My blood ran cold. There was something intangible about the atmosphere, but I could feel the darkness being probed. Some power was searching for us...not just patrols, but something deeper, like a beam of mental energy. It came from within, and I realized it must be some telepathic resource from the Center. The Dream Lords had the power of mind-search, as they called it...could this be Ardat? I could close my mind off to it and shield all three of us, but instead I opened my mind. If I could get Pthorthe to safety…

But the force that sought us tried to sweep in like a black tide of nausea, and I knew at once that it was pure evil. It could only be Vorta or his allies. I shut it out and yelled at my companions.

"Hasten! Vorta's dark forces are on our track."

We threaded our way through endless passages and back streets while Pthorthe gasped that we must get outside the dome and into the labyrinths if we were to get away.

At last we came to a main street, not far from which rose the glint of the dome. Our guide peered out from the cover of the shadows.

"We have little hope of making a rendezvous with the *phorud*. Too much time wasted in flight," he said. "But there is a drainage system not far from here. The dome's wall is a mile off. If we can get through the sewers, we can get out into the labyrinths. I know a way."

"Then lead on," said Pthorthe. Our guide nodded. He looked around him again, then sprinted across the road. Pthorthe and I followed. We made it safely and began moving down side streets. Presently we pulled up as our guide pointed.

"There," he said. I looked and saw a huge tunnel appearing in one of the walls on a level below our own. There were narrow steps leading down to it, and as we descended, I saw that the tunnel was fed by a swirling river of filth—the sewage from this section of Melkor. We were halfway down the steps when a cry went up from above.

I turned to see a Guard leaning over the wall and challenging us. Without hesitation I aimed and burned him to a cinder, his corpse toppling over the wall and splashing into the grim waters below.

Pthorthe nodded as we went down. The guide turned to us as the tunnel mouth loomed above us.

"Our problem will be the darkness," he said simply.

I pressed the haft button on the star lance, and it glowed with a dim blue radiance.

"We have light for as long as we need it," I told him with a smile, which he returned.

"Then we should succeed. Let us be gone."

He slipped into the beckoning shadows, and I helped Pthorthe up on to the ledge that ran alongside the river of filth into the earth.

CHAPTER IX
Death Beneath the City

As we moved silently down the gentle gradient of the path, our outlines faintly limned in the dull glow of the star lance, the only sound that came to our ears was the gentle swirling of the waters beside us. A numbing cold crept into our bones and our breath puffed out in front of us in white clouds. I repressed a shudder with difficulty, for the darkness thickened as we descended, darkness that would be the ally of Vorta's sinister agents as much as it would be our own. After we had gone a considerable distance under the city, our guide halted, head up, as though sniffing the pungent air like some human tracker hound.

"I hear something above the noise of the waters," he said softly. Pthorthe and I listened but heard nothing. We moved on apace, then our guide halted again.

"Switch off the light for a moment," he said. It was the last thing I wanted to do, being fearful of that abysmal darkness, but I complied. Instantly we were plunged into total darkness, as though a sheet of blackest night had been flung over us. I gripped the star lance the more tightly.

"There," came the whispered voice of our guide. "Up ahead. Can you see it?"

"I see nothing," muttered Pthorthe, but my eyes were growing accustomed to the pitch darkness.

"Lights," I said, for I could faintly make out a number of tiny dots way ahead of us.

"We will have to advance with care. And keep our light extinguished," said the guide.

"What is it?" I asked as we moved forward again.

"There is a minor junction somewhere ahead, where two subsidiary channels feed into this one. Shortly after we pass them, we plunge down and out of the dome. The lights ahead are one of two things. Either Wortan Heynar has learned of our flight already and set up a line of Guards, or it is the automatic sewage system at work."

"The drainage automatons," I nodded. "Let us hope it is them."

There was a large number of various robots programmed for duties in Melkor and out on the Garganian terrain, and provided they were not interfered with or balked of their duties in any way, they worked in total oblivion, mindless of their human masters. Their movements and functions were constantly transmitted and charted in a number of special Centers in the city, so that the work of any one robot could be followed. If these were robots ahead of us, our chances of slipping by unobserved would be excellent.

A droning sound came to us as we neared the glowing lights. I saw the two tributary sewers feeding into the main one, and it was here that the work was in progress. We were lucky, for a party of robots was busily engaged in clearing a minor cave-in. Some of the curved slabs that formed the side of the drain had cracked and fallen, allowing several tons of earth to half close the mouth of one of the adjoining sewers. The robots moved around jerkily, scooping up the fallen earth and heaping it into hover-trucks. From time to time, as the trucks filled up, they turned and disappeared up the other tributary sewer.

"I see no Guards," said our guide. Sometimes it was necessary to have a human overseer on a difficult job. We moved under cover of darkness to within fifty yards of the work party.

"We cannot cross without being seen," said Pthorthe, almost in despair. I gripped his arm reassuringly.

"Yes, but they won't stop us. They won't even consider us or register our presence. We are as unimportant to them as vermin would be," I told him. Our guide seemed satisfied that there were no other obstacles to our progress, so he beckoned us on. We had moved but a few yards when a sound nearby drew my attention. I turned to see one of the robots on the other side of the drain. It had stepped out of the shadows and it seemed to me that it was *watching* us.

"Get down!" yelled our guide, falling flat. I dragged Pthorthe to the floor, just as a beam of heat smacked into the wall behind us.

"A Guard," gasped Pthorthe.

"No," said the guide. "An armed robot. Heynar must have one posted at every sewer exit to Melkor. He's taking no risks."

I had never properly seen an autoguard in action, and had no taste for it now. These robots were very sensitive to movement, equipped with highly developed visual abilities, and had heat ray propellants in each arm. These locked on to the targets automatically and only missed rarely. The next burst from the autoguard would roast us all. I swung my star lance round as the robot aimed, and I fired. The machine blew up in a cloud of smoke and a sheet of orange flame. A section of sewer wall cracked.

"We must run," I said, struggling to my feet. "As soon as that explosion registers on some central monitor, there'll be an army of Guards down here."

Without pausing to discuss the matter, we headed for the junction. But robot activity had stopped. The robots began to arrange themselves in formation, across the path we had to take. We pulled up short in our tracks. Pthorthe turned to me.

"What is happening?"

"Heynar is no fool," I breathed. "These robots must have a secondary programme. If anything goes wrong down here, this is what happens. Heynar must have foreseen something like this. If we got past his autoguard, it would forewarn these. Our presence here is already registered."

There was about a score of robots facing us. The guide turned to me.

"What about your weapon? You can cut an army down with that," he said, apparently eager to see me use it.

"Heynar could not have foreseen that I had one of these," I agreed, but again I was mistaken. There came a commotion from the open tributary sewer on our right. I had levelled the star lance, ready to scythe down the ranks of stationary robots, when a number of figures burst into view.

"What is happening?" cried the perplexed Pthorthe again.

A group of ragged men had been herded out into the main channel. They were pushed and kicked by a dozen Imperial Guards, and they fell to their knees or staggered into the line of robots. At once the robots snatched at them and held them in front of them, like shields. The Guards stood behind the robots, swords drawn.

"Get behind me," I told Pthorthe and the guide. "They may have heat guns."

I still held the star lance ready, but did not fire. I realized now what game Heynar was playing. The struggling ragamuffins that the robots held were a Barbarian slave party, or so I had surmised. I could not fire without killing them. A Guard stepped forward, peering into the darkness that still half cloaked us.

"Galad Sarian!" he shouted, his voice a sneer. I recognized him at once. It was Dworl, his right arm covered and in his left a new sword.

"Sarian!" he repeated venomously. "I know you are skulking in the filth out there! Show yourself before I have your miserable friends gutted before your eyes."

Pthorthe tried to draw me back, but I pushed him and the guide against the confines of the curved wall. I went slowly forward.

"We meet again, Dworl," I said.

"So you are there. It had to be you! Surrender yourself to me at once." His eyes were blazing fanatically, full of renewed hate. I lifted the star lance and aimed it at his chest.

"A twist of the haft and you become ashes," I said, but the bluff was impotent. He pointed with his blade to the prisoners. "If you use that thing, they all die!" he snarled. The Imperial Guards lifted their swords and touched their points to the backs of the slave party.

"Cut them down!" cried one of the prisoners to us, and others joined in.

"Aye! We have nothing to live for on this hell world! Fry the stinking Zurk!"

"Silence!" roared Dworl, whirling his sword. I would gladly have cut him down, but I would not cause the deaths of these men.

"You must kill the Guards if we are to flee," said a voice beside me. It was the Garganian guide.

"But the slaves will die," I grunted.

"We have no choice."

I was about to argue, when a sound behind me drew my attention. I looked back up the worm-like tunnel down which we had come. An airboat was sweeping down upon us, the beam of its nose-light blazing like a small sun in the distance.

"There is no way out," called Dworl.

I clenched a fist in exasperation. I would not give in. The airboat came gliding closer, a score of Guards dotting its rails.

"Pthorthe!" I called to the darkness. "There is no need for you and our friend here to be taken. Go back and find another way out."

"But you'll be killed—"

"Go!" I shouted. The guide slipped from beside me and went to Pthorthe. I heard them talking. The airboat drew ever nearer. Dworl paced toward me, his confidence growing.

"Throw down your arms, Sarian!" he snarled.

"Go while there is still time," I called to the two Garganians.

"The Gods be with you," said Pthorthe, and they began making their way back up the huge drain. Beyond them the airboat came gliding, its beam bathing myself and the robots in lurid light. For a moment the light swept from side to side and I saw the two fleeing Garganians. Just when it seemed they had not been noticed, the light locked on to them and they stood paralysed with fear. I took a step forward, but the damage was done. A spear flashed down from the narrow deck of the airboat, and with horror I saw Pthorthe's body jerk backwards and tumble over the walkway into the sewer. It had happened so quickly I hardly knew it was real. The other Garganian turned and fled, but the airboat swept down and a flight of wicked spears tore into him and sent him spinning and tumbling to his death.

I ran forward, my mind seething with anger, my own safety no longer important, and cursed the airboat's crew in the vilest terms. The craft bore down upon me, my figure silhouetted in its glaring nose-light. I saw the faces of the Guards on board, as the men gesticulated and pointed gleefully. Bracing my feet, I lifted the star lance and took careful aim. An arc of white hot flame soared upwards and took the airboat in the underbelly. For seconds the ship was aglow, but nothing happened. Then an explosion rocked her underside and the craft turned in mid air, spilling Guards and accelerating madly.

I watched it spin like a top, discharging its crew members who smashed like broken dolls on the slabs and sewers below. The airboat whined wildly, flames gushing out behind it as it plummeted onwards. It screamed past and I turned to watch its path. The Guards by the robots fled in terror as the ship bore down on them. Dworl dropped his sword and backed against the wall, eyes wide and jaw slack.

I realized then what I had unwittingly done, for the helpless prisoners were still gripped by the robots, which stood unmoving and stone-like, totally unaware of the death that shrieked towards them. I watched in horror as the slaves screamed as they tried to free themselves, but to no avail. The burning airboat tore into the sewer waters and ploughed on remorselessly, bursting through the robot ranks and destroying everything in its path. There came a series of explosions and a wall of flame leapt up at the curved roof.

Through the flames and fallen earth I could see that not one of the robots had survived. Their shattered husks littered the sewer sides, and in all that wreckage could be seen no trace of a human body. I had killed them just as the Guards would have, had I killed Dworl. My blood ran cold when I saw what I had caused. I swore by my father that the Governor would pay for this.

I walked to the edge of the wreckage. Nothing moved as the smoke cleared.

"So you killed them after all," came a voice almost beside me. I whirled, star lance at the ready. It was Dworl, his features twisted in a grimace of hate and glee. He held a sword in his one good arm, but it dangled beside him.

"Wortan Heynar will send other airboats. You cannot evade him. And if you do, where will you hide? The Garganians would kill you, those that don't work for Daras Vorta and the Brotherhood."

His lips curled in a sneer. I wiped sweat from my face, controling my breathing with an effort. On an impulse I levelled my star lance at his chest and fired. His eyes widened in terror.

But nothing happened. I switched it off and on, with no response. I had been in darkness too long, and the last colossal burst at the airboat had expended the star lance's stored solar energy. I would have to expose it to sunlight before it could be used as a heat thrower again.

"Hah! So you have only a bar of metal to protect you," he laughed contemptuously. He lifted his sword and stepped forward. "Then I will take you to Heynar in pieces. He cares nothing for your life, as long as he has your corpse!"

So saying he made a lunge. I leapt back. It was true the star lance was no longer an effective heat thrower, but its secondary energy source had not been drained. It could still be used as a heat rod. If I pressed the haft button and the rod glowed blue, Dworl would know at once and retreat. So I allowed him to think I was fighting with just a long bar of metal.

"I owe you this cut," he said as he lifted his blade for the kill. His sword came down and I held my rod before me. As soon as the weapons touched, I pressed the haft button. The rod glowed blue and a current shot through Dworl's sword and into his body. He screamed as the heat charred him, his body convulsing and twisting with the agony. I switched off and his smouldering remains fell to the cold floor.

"Stay exactly where you are!"

The imperious voice split the smoking air. I looked up from where I stood, ankle-deep in filth, to see the sides of the sewer lined with Imperial Guards, These were the men who had leapt aside as the airboat had come crashing in on the robots and slaves. Their spokesman must have seen my fight with Dworl, so he knew the star lance was not as potent as it had been.

"You cannot take all of us. Throw me your weapon and we will spare you your life."

"To have the Governor murder me?" I laughed, but there was no amusement in my voice. I still felt more angry than at any other point in my brief life. Pthorthe's death had wrought a change in me.

"You must take that chance, Galad Sarian."

"Then you must kill me now," I challenged. I pressed the haft button, and the star lance glowed deadly blue. The Guards murmured among themselves. Fortune smiled on me in one respect—none of them had spears. I began moving through the debris, working towards the junction and the big drain that would lead me to freedom.

"Take him!" shouted the leading Guard, but the men were reluctant to move.

"Cowards! There are a dozen of us. He cannot take us all." So saying, he led the attack, knowing that if he did not, his men would let me go. I swung my weapon, and they kept out of range.

"Surround him."

I tried to reach the relative safety of a wall, but the Guards were ringing me. Suddenly I leapt forward, slashing from side to side, my rod crackling against the swords of two Guards, who shrieked and fell back unconscious. I spun and almost lost my footing, and another Guard ran in. His blade cut the air, but my rod rammed up into his stomach, burning a hole in his flesh, and he stumbled away in mortal agony. Sparks flew in the air as I parried three more thrusts, and the Guards began to realize that they must disarm me or I would kill them all.

I sidled along the wall, keeping my weapon in full view of the remaining Guards. They were wary of it, drawing back and watching their leader. He scowled angrily. An idea had come to me, but it would need speed and deception. Two hovertrucks rested by the mound of fallen earth where the robots had been working. If I could get into one, I could yet escape the city walls.

"I stood now at the junction of the sewers. The Guards were in a half circle around me, their swords ready to dart in at any sign of weakness in my defence. I had no doubt that they would kill me now. Their blood was roused by the havoc I had wrought. But if Gundar could have seen me now! He would have been proud of his pupil. And although I faced the prospect of a cold death, I thrilled to the activity and sheer physical enjoyment of the contest.

"You cannot win in the end, my Lord," said the wily spokesman again. "In a while the air will be full of craft. You will be finished. Surrender now, or Wortan Heynar's revenge for all this will be terrible."

I watched the man. He was playing for time, and it rested in his favor, not mine.

"Very well," I said, still with the mind to take a hovertruck. I walked towards him, my weapon held innocently at my side. He frowned, slowly raising his arm to take it. The Guards watched, momentarily relaxing.

"A wise decis—" began the leader, but as his hand came up, I leapt forward, the star lance brushing his arm. He screamed as the heat burned him and I tumbled him into the waters, thrusting past and splashing knee-deep in filth to get at the hovertrucks. The Guards were momentarily stunned, but with a cry they gave chase.

Within moments I had leapt astride the control bubble of the first hovertruck. I rammed the lever into elevate and hovered a few feet above the ground. The Guards were only a few feet away as I spun the truck, which tilted dangerously under the uneven load. Swords clanged on the rounded nose of the vehicle, narrowly missing my legs. I swung my rod to keep them at bay, then moved off.

Once I was above the waters of the main drain, I headed downwards, ever nearer the city boundary. Behind me there were angry shouts as the Guards pursued me along the drain banks. Two others had started the remaining hovertruck and were also giving chase, but the machines were very slow and cumbersome, their purpose being to transport as heavy a load as possible, rather than to carry things quickly. So my progress was slow, and the Guards along the banks were not hard pressed to keep apace, though they had to sprint.

It seemed that I had only to outwit this last threat to my safety, when a new one arose. Somewhere in the distance, a high wailing began, and I recognized the sirens of at least two airboats. Heynar had wasted no time in replacing the one I had destroyed. How far was the sewer exit? Much further, and I would never make it.

I looked back over my shoulder and cursed. The other hovertruck was gaining. In my haste I had unknowingly picked the truck with the heaviest load. The pursuers had a near-empty vehicle, and it would be a short time before they overhauled me. The drain was steepening in its descent, and I knew that after all I could not be far from the city boundary. Down I went, the Guards still running not far behind on the bank, the hovertruck nearing, and the sirens wailing louder in the middle distance.

Suddenly I brought my craft around. The others were nonplussed and kept straight on, unable to turn at the speed they were making. With another wrench on the controls I sent my vehicle directly for theirs. It was too late for them to avoid the collision. My truck was due to meet head on as I leapt over the side and tumbled into the foul waters. My shoulder hit something hard, and needles of pain shot through me as I fought to regain the surface. As my head came above water I saw the two hovertrucks crashing into the wall, their riders helpless to avoid the impact.

I was rushed headlong away from the crash as the waters spilled downwards. Total darkness swallowed me up like the maw of some subterranean colossus.

CHAPTER X
Conspiracy

I was rolled and swirled about in the evil-smelling waters, my body buffeted along, my breath driven from me for what seemed an ageless period. Over and over I fought to keep my head above the stinking waters which tried to drag me under to oblivion, and it was only with the grimmest determination that I kept a firm grip on my star lance. Eventually I felt the solid chute of the drain slide away and I was tumbling in mid air, tons of water falling with me into some dismal unseen gulf. My battered body splashed into a new surface of water and I felt myself sinking deeper and deeper, the life draining away from me. But I clawed my way upwards. There was no light to guide me and I might have been immersed in tar for all I could see, but some primitive instinct forced me to cling to life with every last ounce of energy I possessed.

Just when it seemed I was beaten, my head broke the surface of that hellish pool and I sucked in great lungfuls of fetid air, gagging as I fought to folat upon the surface which was thickly covered with scum. Behind me I heard the cascading of the fall, but still I could see nothing. With my last resources, I swam slowly and painfully away from the sound of the falls. I had no way of knowing how far this subterranean pool extended, or if there were any means of egress. I could only go on the words of the Garganian guide, who had said this way led to the outer world. Perhaps I was already beyond Melkor. If I could get to dry land, the star lance would provide me with illumination.

I gagged again and barely kept from sinking, when my feet touched something solid. I kicked out and worked my way forward. At last I was in shallow water and I struggled to rise through thick suds of foam. The stench was unbearable, my whole body coated in muck, my hair plastered to my head. Coughing and vomiting water, I splashed through the scum to the edge of the pool.

Once on firm ground, I fell to my knees and wiped some of the foul muck from me. I tried to switch on the star lance, but the last of its energy must have been nullified in the water and I hoped that it had not been permanently damaged. Lying on the slippery rocks, trying to get back my rasping breath, I wondered what Taria would have thought of me, could she have seen me. I smiled in spite of my position. Whatever happened to me now, it could hardly be a worse experience than the one I had just been through.

Still I could see nothing, not even my hand in front of my face. And had there been any sounds from any direction, they would have been covered by the tumbling cataract. With aching limbs, I got to my feet. I could not stay and rest for long, for the water was icy and I had grown bitterly cold. I pushed on across the rocks, the surface of which was treacherously broken and uneven.

After some time I found a wall; it was etched and rugged like some natural surface. I had no choice but to follow it, so I moved along. The ground flattened out into a sand-like basin and progress became easier. I tried my star lance. It flickered briefly and went out. I knew that the water in the pool must have an outlet, but I could only hope it was not below the surface, for nothing could induce me to dive into it again.

Further along the wall I stumbled. My star lance seemed useless, so I sheathed it.

Presntly I came to a turn in the wall. It had been abrupt and I tried to reach across to see if it was an opening. Fumbling in the dark, putting my feet cautiously in front of me, I decided that it was an exit to this huge cavern, but how big and to where, I could not say. I entered. The sandy floor underfoot continued, sloping downward.

Abruptly something clanged behind me. I whirled, all my terrors of darkness screaming inside my head, for I could see nothing. I whipped out my star lance and readied to strike. For long moments I stood as still as death, hardly daring to breathe, but there was only the sound of the falling water, now some way distant.

Then another clang, similar to the first, came from the direction I had been going, and I turned, uncertain how to protect myself. Could there be robots even down here, working in the dark?

Before I could deliberate further, I was suddenly bathed in blinding light. My eyes ached against such an abrupt, intolerable glare, and I screwed them shut, almost dropping my weapon. I tried opening them and found adjusting to it painful, but in a few minutes I could see. I was in a narrow passage and the way I had come was closed off to me now by an iron grill. I had been trapped, whether by accident or design.

Furiously I pushed the grills in turn and tried to weaken them, but they were immovable. A harsh laughter rang in the passageway. I looked in every direction, but could see nothing. The ceiling was ablaze with the strange light and from this direction came a voice.

"Resistance is useless, my Lord."

"Who speaks?" I demanded angrily, but for answer I heard more mocking laughter.

"You are late for your audience with the Governor. His patience wears thin."

Abruptly the lights went out and silence fell again. The air grew colder and somehow denser, and after some time I realized that some kind of gas was being fed into the passageway. It was impossible to escape it, and a short while later I must have become unconscious.

*

My next recollections were blurred and misty, like some tortured dream, half-truths and hideous unbidden thoughts all spinning and twisting away madly into a bizarre fabric of nightmare from which no pattern could emerge. People I had known, mixed with people I had never met, flashed throughout the blended visions, uttering muffled, unintelligible sounds, while the distant booming of my heart throbbed as an intermittent background to the colorful blaze of the phantasms that whirled about me.

Time had lost its meaning, so that when I at last opened my eyes, I felt completely disjointed. It was with difficulty that I was able to go back over some of the past. I remembered the passage...the gas. Now I looked about me. I was strapped to a bare slab in a white room, all manner of technical equipment around me. I could not sit up, but behind me I made out the unsettling contours of a psychometer, the machine that could be used to either fill a human brain with information, or drain it. I had trained my own mind in many Dream Lord ways, but if they had used the thing on me while I had been drugged, I would have put up very little resistance to its questioning.

However, neither Wortan Heynar nor Daras Vorta stood to benefit from probing my mind; it was enough that they had me at their mercy.

I fought my bonds for some time, to no avail, and then the laboratory door opened. A wizened man stepped in, garbed in a grey robe. Behind him were four burly Imperial Guards, their spears almost scraping the low roof of the room.

"Awake?" said the scientist rhetorically.

I merely scowled.

He turned to the Guards. "We've scraped the filth off him and had his weapons sent on ahead. You may take him now." The scientist pressed a button somewhere beneath my slab and my bonds slipped aside. I sat up at once.

"You are to come with me," said one of the Guards, stepping forward and bowing slightly. He was clean shaven and his narrow features were marked with a number of small scars. His spear tip wavered close to my eyes.

"I gather you had an active time down in the drains," he went on, his eyes narrowing to two slits. The scientist was busying himself somewhere else in the laboratory, apparently no longer interested in me.

"Give me a sword and I'll teach you manners in front of a Dream Lord heir," I retorted. The spear tip drew back and the flat of a sword blade smacked against my face. I felt a trickle of blood.

"You are a dead man," said the Guard brutally, his spear tip now beneath my throat. "Now get to your feet."

I obeyed. Resisting was pointless, for these Guards would happily spit me and carry my corpse to Heynar with no fear of reprisal if I offered challenge.

They led me through a maze of bare passages and corridors and halted outside a metal door on which an emblem was stamped: a thin diagonal yellow streak on a background of dark green, which was the emblem of the Governor of Melkor, Wortan Heynar. The door slid aside and a spear point dug into my spine.

"Enter," came an indistinct voice from within. The Guards helped me on my way with a further push. Although the room beyond was poorly lit, it was exquisitely decorated. Thick carpets stretched the length of the floor and rich curtains and drapes of velvet hung the walls. A small rock garden was the centerpiece, with a miniature waterfall beside it. The air was thick with perfume.

My eyes fell upon an intricately carved desk on the top of some broad steps. It was covered in charts and what looked like maps of Gargan. Behind this desk sat the man I took to be Wortan Heynar. He was surprisingly young for a Governor, in his thirties, I thought, though his eyes, ringed with darkness, and his gaunt features had aged him prematurely. His thin brown hair was flat to his anaemic face, and his narrow, grey eyes darted to and fro like a nervous bird's. Some disease had pockmarked him, and his stringy body was emaciated by the unknown depravities in which he must have wallowed.

"Ahh...Galad Sarian, I take it," he said with a faint smile. "You have found your way to us at last." Behind me the guards were very much alert to any movements I made.

"You will pay for this with your head, Heynar," I said arrogantly, and the spears touched me menacingly.

"Oh, I think not, sire. You have had your vengeances already, I believe. Slaying some of my best men—Dworl, too, whom I loved dearly. All that vile killing down in the sewers. In exchange we have only the corpses of two miserable Garganians—a poor swap! Or were they special, eh? Perhaps you have certain tastes of which I have not been told..."

"Hold your foul tongue, or by the Dream Lords—" I surged forward, choked with anger at his unpleasant words. He was up and had leapt back in a flash, moving sinuously and quickly like a snake. Yet he need have had no fear, for the Guards rammed their spear butts into my sides and smashed me to my knees before I had taken two paces.

"Peace, young Galad, I was merely teasing you," Heynar said sibilantly, his eyes watching me the way a predator might study an intended victim. It infuriated me further, and had I been free I would have strangled him on the spot.

"A poor swap it was," I snapped. "I should have exterminated the rest of your vermin."

"Enough of that! Forget about killing, dear boy. And forget any childish plans you may have of escape. It pains me to say it, but you are as good as dead." He paced nervously about, then began idly inspecting a chart on one of the tapestried walls.

"If you would kill me, why not do it now?" I snapped.

"Oh, no. I could not do such a thing. Violence upsets me, dear boy. I couldn't bear to see such a fine young man as yourself put to the sword." There was something deeply unsettling about his words, and the tone in which he uttered them that made me shudder.

"However," he went on, "Daras Vorta will kill you, make no mistake about that. He has been contemplating doing so for a long time. And afterwards, your heir-ship to Dream Lord rank will be conferred on your sweet cousin, Ravas, whom I get along with so well." His many rings glittered in the subdued lighting as he watched my reaction with interest.

"The Dream Lords would never accept him," I said, though with less confidence than I felt.

Heynar's pencil-thin brows twisted themselves in a frown. "You disapprove of my friendship with Ravas? You are young, and possibly a little naive."

"Nothing of your world, or of Vorta's shocks me. More importantly it does not shock others. These things are well known,"

I said, bluffing him. I could see that my words had to some extent alarmed him. He paced about, a little restlessly.

"I doubt that," he said, but his tone implied the lie.

"Vorta's days are numbered."

His lip curled in a contemptuous sneer. "Your opinion is of no consequence. You are missing. No one knows where you are. The Garganian underground has already been blamed for your murder. You will never be seen by your allies again, and no one will ever be able to prove that Daras Vorta had anything to do with your disappearance. Your two Garganian friends will have their corpses left in such a place as to convince their fellows that it was you who killed them, and your name will be a vile word amongst the natives of this planet."

He straightened himself as if his words had given him confidence.

"So you believe."

"It is true!"

"The Garganian underground will spit upon your cheap lies. They are not so easily fooled."

"Then let them believe what they will!" he said indignantly, but I knew my words had cut into him. "When Daras Vorta has you in his hands, nothing and no one on the Nine Worlds will save you."

"Where is Vorta?"

Heynar chuckled. Again he paced about, brushing dust from one of the exotic wall hangings.

"You will meet him soon enough. Your Garganian friends have a special rendezvous with him." He left the raised part of the room and came towards me. The Guards rested their spear points on my chest. One movement and they would push them home.

"In Melkor?" I breathed.

Heynar stood before me. I saw that his eyes were painted, and there was a faint aroma of perfume about him that made me shudder anew.

"Perhaps. But now that we have you, our plans for the overthrow of the Dream Lords can begin in earnest. To begin with—"

"The Garganians will rebel in the name of their new religious master, the Goat," I said calmly.

Heynar flinched and drew back as if I had struck him. "You knew this..." he muttered, his eyes darting to the blank faces of the Guards.

I laughed.

"Where are the results of the psychometer test?" he shrieked. The Guards looked uncertainly at each other.

"Well?" persisted Heynar.

"I assumed they were brought to you earlier, sire," replied one uncertainly.

Heynar scowled, then wheeled and went to his desk. He thrashed about amongst his papers, then came back to me with a triumphant grin, waving a sheaf of them in one hand.

"Whatever you know is in here," he said, grimacing as he began to read. The smell of his sweat mingled with the pungent aroma of perfume.

"I told you, Vorta's plans are known."

He remained motionless for long moments, until he had digested the contents of the report. He smiled at me.

"Ah, so there. You do know a good deal. But any allies you may have will be powerless. And your test supplied us with some interesting facts. Your weaknesses are...interesting."

He began walking about again and I felt uncomfortable. The psychometer can read everything in one's mind if one is open to it. Under the drugs, I must have been very vulnerable.

Abruptly Heynar thrust his hideous features close to mine. "Is she beautiful, this woman?" he sneered.

I resisted the urge to reach out for his throat.

"A soft spot?" he said, grinning and straightening up. "You cannot afford the luxury of a nerve point, Galad. The young lady...Taria, was it? Yes, well...you have strayed a long way from the straight and narrow of Dream Lord law, have you not? And you have the temerity to accuse *us* of doing so!" He laughed drily and flung down the papers.

"So," he went on, as my blood began to congeal in my veins, "you know that Vorta will incite a rebellion—a war—and that Zurjahn power on Gargan will change hands. *I* will rule, and the Garganians will obey me, the servant of the Goat."

His eyes gleamed with the lust of a fanatic.

"How will Vorta achieve it? The Garganians are not fools."

"No? They are an old race, full of superstition and belief in old gods and strange deities. Vorta is like a demi-god to them. He has as much power in his single brain as the entire Dream Lord triumvirate!

You will see when he tests them. And it will begin here. He will release all the wildest nightmares of Garganian myth and drive the whole nation into frenzied rebellion against Zurjah. He can give the people illusions to match the illusions of the Dream Lords—nightmares to match your wildest imaginings. He has been to the innermost recesses of Garganian intellect, faced the whole gamut of their ancient beliefs, and he can bring it all to life."

"Then he is here," I said apprehensively.

"He will come when he is ready."

"Do you really believe he can face the Dream Lords?"

"You will see. With Ravas amongst them, they cannot hope to stand in his way."

A door had opened somewhere beyond the hangings, and a figure moved from behind them and into the room's shadows.

"Who speaks my name?" said a piping voice. I felt a renewed wave of revulsion. Ravas Tarak stepped into the light and approached.

"Ravas, my dear," said Heynar nervously. "You shouldn't have burst in like this—"

"Nonsense. I heard my delightful cousin was here. Oh, Galad, and here you are. My, but what a wretched spectacle. Have you displeased the noble Governor?" He came closer to me, but not too close. He was tall and thin and his hollow eyes were even more darkly rimmed than those of Heynar. His fingers were like wire, twisted about each other in constant agitation and worry.

"Your life of folly will undo you this time, Ravas," I said coldly, but he sniffed indifferently and turned to Heynar.

"You look distraught, Wortan," he smiled.

Heynar turned away and again looked through his papers. "I will be more myself when this wretched rebellion is over with."

"You worry too much," said Ravas. He turned to me. "Your father will be distressed to hear of your demise." He walked to a Guard and gently took his spear from him.

"They will never accept you as an heir," I said bitterly.

"Oh, but they will," he said, tracing patterns on the carpet with the point. "You see, I have been hard at my studies away on Zurjah. The Dream Lords are impressed by my efforts. They whisper amongst themselves that perhaps I have reformed after all. I no longer appear to indulge in all the little temptations of the wilder life. So—another few months and I will be strongly considered. There will be much sadness when your unfortunate carcass is returned to your homeworld, and I shall be foremost among the mourners, of course. After your funeral, I shall present myself to the Dream Lords and declare that I am repentant of all my sins. Your death will have brought me to my senses. Oh, yes, Galad, they will accept me, I assure you."

"They will read your lies in your mind."

"No," he said, again shaking his head. "Daras Vorta will protect me from that. He is strong enough."

He played with the point of the spear, pricking his thumb and drawing a bead of blood. Heynar winced.

"I wonder whether Vorta would be annoyed if I were to run you through now."

"Ravas, there is no need for such behaviour. If you must spill blood, do it elsewhere," said Heynar nervously.

"If you are a man," I said coldly to Tarak, "then give me a sword and face me in equal combat."

He laughed. "And be spitted where I stood? You are a fool."

"Take him away," said Heynar, gesturing to the Guards. They prodded me to my feet. Ravas Tarak returned the Guard's spear. I left without another word, my spirits very low.

CHAPTER XI
The Voice in the Shadows

I was imprisoned in a small cell. It was no filthy hovel, with begrimed walls and straw bedding, but a clean, heated apartment with several furnishings, including a soft bed, lighting, and a regulated heating system. The room had been divided in two by a force screen, so that I could not reach the door. For some reason the clothes I had been wearing when I had been taken, together with my star lance in its silver sheath, were resting on a small table by the door. However, there was no way I could reach them, and if the weapon had been put there to frustrate me, it served its purpose admirably. There appeared to be no way out of the dilemma, and I resigned myself to a confrontation with Vorta.

How long I was left in the room, I cannot judge. From time to time a small wall panel slid aside to reveal food and drink, and I drank and ate with no fear of being poisoned or drugged. Heynar's methods would be more straightforward when my time to die came.

Eventually the door to the room opened, and I heard an altercation outside. In a moment a tall Imperial Guard thrust himself into the room, in full regalia. Behind him two others argued with him about something, apparently his entrance.

"But, sir, we have strict orders from the Governor himself," protested one of them uncomfortably.

"And I said you have no need to be perturbed!" snapped the intruder. He stood at the other side of the force field facing me, his face the hard, scarred face of a veteran, his frame strong and solid with muscle. The two other Guards stood by the door, their swords drawn. They exchanged nervous glances, and one of them depressed the tab that slid shut the door behind them.

"So," said the man who faced me, thumbs dug into his wide leather belt. "This is the rebel who wrought so much confusion in the drains."

I had been sitting on the bed when he entered. I made no move to get up and said nothing, watching him placidly.

"Vorta can have him!" he scoffed. "But I wanted to meet the man who had cut down so many of us. The man who went up against a handful of Guards, armed only with their swords, and cut them down with a star lance."

"Have no fear, sir, he will be made to suffer for that," said the other. The officer bent down and scowled at me.

"My brother was among the men you butchered," he said venomously, his eyes like slits, hot as coals.

I stood up slowly. "Did they tell you of the slave party that died down there, too?" I said, matching his stare.

"Barbarian offal! You speak to me of slaves! You murdered my brother and his fellows in cold blood."

"I think you had better return to—" began one of the Guards, his arm gently resting on the officer's.

"I'll return when I'm ready!" he fumed, swinging his arm into the face of the man behind, who staggered back. The officer drew his sword.

"If you want to argue with me, I'll cut your heats out!" he snarled, turning on them. His temper was at boiling point and the Guards drew back.

"Heynar will punish all of us if the prisoner is harmed," said one lamely.

"I will be responsible," retorted the officer. His eyes turned from the two men to the table by the door, and he stared at it for a moment. He walked over to it, sheathing his sword.

"What is this? Hell's teeth! Is this the weapon?" he murmured. He looked at me in triumph. "This is the star lance, is it not?"

I stared at him but made no reply. He picked up the gleaming sheath and carefully drew out its rod. The two Guards were now very tense, their fingers whitening where they gripped their blades.

"Yes, this must be the weapon." He turned to the Guards. "Raise the force shield."

The Guards' jaws fell. They made no move, eyeing each other uncertainly.

The officer pointed the star lance at them. "Raise the force shield, or I will fry you where you stand!"

"Yes, sir," muttered one, and depressed another tab. There was a humming in the air before me, and the invisible field had been removed. The officer turned once more to me.

"I am not going to kill this man. As you told me, that pleasure belongs to Daras Vorta himself. But he has a lesson to learn."

He came forward slowly, watching my every move, though I kept very still. With a flick of his thumb, he switched the rod on, and it glowed a dull blue. I realized he knew how to use it. As the weapon came closer, I stepped back until my back touched the far wall of the cell. The two Guards looked on unhappily, beads of sweat coating their faces.

"I should burn out your eyes and your tongue for what you did," said the officer, the glowing end of the rod only inches from my face. Terror clawed at me, my mouth had dried up and my bowels felt as though they would melt, but I tried to mask my fear. The rod's heat made my face sweat as the sadistic officer lowered the weapon and touched it to the ends of my hair. They singed and he drew the rod away with a short barking laugh.

"Shall I scorch all your hair? It's far too long for a man. Vorta would be offended by it." He singed more of it, my neck burning at the proximity of the dreadful weapon. The Guards were not so apprehensive now that they thought the officer only wanted to indulge in a little torture.

"And is this the badge of your office?" said the man, his eyes dropping to my chest, where my medallion hung. For some reason it had not been removed by my captors; no doubt they attached no significance to it. The officer lowered the star lance so that its tip came within an inch of the medallion. I controlled my breathing with difficulty.

"A winged horse," he said indifferently. "A Dream Lord symbol, I suppose. It will not help you here."

His cruel eyes bored into mine. I could not move, though. One touch of that rod to my skin and I was dead. I could not look down. A smile twisted his lips, and he touched the rod to the medallion. Instantly his face screwed up into a mask of agony and he flew backwards, showers of sparks and light bursting between us. My chest burned for an instant and I felt buffeted as if by a huge fist. I sprawled sideways, shaking my head to clear it. The officer was contorting himself horribly, shrieking with pain. The air stank of ozone, and the star lance lay buzzing beside the man's smoking body.

The Guards let out cried of alarm and rushed forward, swords ready to cut me to pieces if I moved, but I was almost unconscious. They saw me slump over and attended the officer.

"By the darkness, he dies!" cried one. They loosened his tunic, but the twitching body was still.

I had no time to waste as I fought to keep conscious. Had I made a play for the star lance, the Guards would have been quicker. It was near my feet, so I tried a desperate ploy. I drew my heel back and aimed a kick at the haft of the weapon. It shot across the floor, still glowing the deadly blue, and skidded into the boots of one kneeling Guard. As soon as the rod touched him, he shrieked as the current shook him, falling dead beside his officer. The other Guard yelped and stumbled aside, practically dropping his sword in an attempt to get clear.

In that moment I was up and racing for him. He lifted his blade as I came at him, but I kicked out at his hand and heard the snapping of its bones. The sword spun away and my fist smashed into the bemused Guard's face. He went down and rolled over. I reached for the star lance and came for him again. It was cold-blooded, but my life was at stake if the Guards took me. I touched his chest, and he died as his companions had.

Without further ado, I raced to the door. I had no idea which part of the building I was in, or at which level, but I would find a way out or kill anyone who tried to stop me. Before I ran down the corridor, an idea struck me. I stepped back into the cell and slid shut its door. It had occurred to me that I would only have to be seen to be instantly recognised as an interloper, so I would need a disguise, albeit a temporary one. So I began stripping the officer. His harness and some of the material of his tunic was charred, but I could not afford to be critical. His helm was intact, and in a few moments I was regaled like a Zurjahn officer. I strapped on my star lance sheath, slid the weapon home and walked out of the cell and down the corridor.

I had decided to make my way downwards. Somewhere below me would be the drains, and if I could get access to a hovertruck and pretend to be supervising some of the robot workers, I could slip back into Melkor and perhaps get into the Culture Center. I would have to rely on Ardat Vellor for help. Something of the events in the sewers could have found a way to his ears. And if he knew of Pthorthe's death, he would surely be even more in sympathy with me.

My thoughts were interrupted by the appearance of four Guards from a sub-corridor. Their cheerful manner and casual banter led me at once to believe they were off duty. Once they saw me, they saluted and I nodded calmly as they passed me. I found some stairs and descended. Some way down a side door opened and a man in officer's uniform stepped out. I smiled briefly and went on down, but I could feel his eyes boring into my back.

"You have business below?" he said.

I turned to look up. "I have indeed. And you'll pardon me if I say that I don't think my orders are any concern of yours."

He scowled and came down the stairs slowly.

"I do not recall your face."

There was no use in further pretence, so I pulled out the star lance and went up at him. His eyes widened, but he had half expected some trouble so was quick to leap away. He reached the doorway from which he had emerged, and his palm smacked up against the wall and an alarm button. I cursed as he pulled his sword out, but one sweep of the star lance and he was electrocuted.

The damage was done, though, for I heard another door opening and before long there were footsteps coming up from below and raised voices from above me. I was trapped in between two advancing groups of Guards. I could lay them all low if they only had swords, but there were certain to be some with heat guns. Pausing only for a second, I pushed open the door the officer had emerged from and went in, closing it behind me.

I was in darkness for a moment, then the star lance lit up my surroundings. It was a narrow corridor. I wasted no time in fleeing. The walls were made of stone and were cold and dripping. I ran on as quickly as I could in the enclosed space. Behind me I heard distant sounds—possible pursuit—so I hurried on. I came to some narrow, cracked stairs and stumbled down. At the bottom was a maze of tiny passages, and I darted into one of them, trusting that my pursuers would be lucky to take the same one.

This passageway went downwards so that the musty smell of the stale air and the evidence of earth walls made me think I was below the actual level of the building's foundations. My progress was restricted by the lowness of the sagging ceiling, and I stopped to listen. It seemed that I had lost the pursuit, for I heard nothing from back the way I had come. However, I decided to see where this passage led; perhaps it would provide me with an unexpected escape route.

For some distance, the passage sloped lower, then it levelled out. There were scarred wooden doors on either side, all of which were bolted. I had gone deep down into the darkness when from somewhere ahead I thought I heard muffled voices. I flicked off the star lance glow and stood in darkness, keeping very still. A faint alternative glow came from ahead, and I could finally discern the outline of one of the doors. I advanced cautiously. The door to one of the adjoining chambers was open, and from within came the voices.

I looked around the door. Light came from a grille in the low ceiling of the dusty chamber, which itself was empty. It was from the room above that the voices came. I flicked on the lance to see if there was any means in the room by which I could reach the grille. In one corner an old table rested on its side. I dragged it under the grille and climbed up.

Peering through the iron railings of the small grille, I saw the high roof of the chamber above me. The voices came from up there, but were indistinct. I dared not risk moving the grille in case it was in view of the speakers. It was no use, so I left the room and continued down the passage. I had not gone far when a small stairway led off to my left. It could lead me into the chambers above, so I climbed it. After a while I came to another grille, this time set in the wall, so I was able to see within.

The chamber was rounded and broad, with weirdly exquisite paintings on its far wall. Thick velvet drapes hung from above and the air was choked with incense. As I watched, a figure moved into view not far from where I crouched. I gave an involuntary start—it was Wortan Heynar. His eyes were lowered and his expression crestfallen. He paced about like an agitated midwife, tugging at his hair and playing with the sleeves of his coat.

"I assure you there is no cause for undue alarm," he said to someone I could not see. "There is no possible way in which he can escape this building. I have sensors at every door, every portal, every window, every drain. Sarian will be found, I swear it!" His voice quivered with excitement, and I grinned. But the voice that answered him filled me with loathing, and a new horror crawled up my spine like a current of cold air. It was extremely deep—unnaturally so— apparently booming out from its mouth as though from a cavern. There was a cloying air of evil about the resonant tones, a current of reptilian coldness, as though the very words could poison the air, and I realized with a new shudder of revulsion that it could be none other than that of Daras Vorta, the Warden of Ur.

"It would be most unfortunate for you, Wortan, should this young man evade you after all. While I appreciate the crass stupidity and criminal ignorance of your private army of morons, I do not tolerate your own lack of initiative. You had the man in a cell under close scrutiny, yet he escaped you."

"Only for a short spell, my lord, I assure you. At any moment my guards will bring me his corpse. It is not conceivable that he could..."

"Don't repeat yourself, Wortan. My patience is hardly inexhaustible. Besides, even if the wretched individual does break free of your supposed infallible defences, he will not make for Zurjah and the Dream Lords. Not yet, anyway." There was an oily undercurrent of conceit about the words. I craned my neck, but could see nothing beyond where Heynar stood.

"I don't quite follow, sire," said Heynar.

"No. Well you must think. You presented me with a psychometer reading on the Sarian youth. Yes? And what was the one particular weakness we noticed?"

Heynar thought for a moment, and a fresh wave of terror threatened to engulf me when he answered.

"The girl! Sarian lusts after some Dream Lords wench."

"Exactly. Taria, daughter of Bordin Sulian. When Sarian realizes what plans I have for his beloved chattel, he will not leave Gargan."

"Plans, sire?" repeated Heynar, his eyes glinting with renewed confidence. I tried the grille, but it could not be broken. Even the star lance could not warp such strong bars quickly.

"Let it be known amongst the underground channels, your own men, those faithful to you in the *phorud*, those in your pay in the Culture Center, and the Brotherhood, that the hour of the uprising is near at hand. There will be a gathering in the forest and on the altar of the Goat will be seen such sacrifices as have never been seen before. And have it known that this Taria will be used as the central sacrifice. Wherever Sarian is, whoever is protecting him, the word will reach him."

"It shall be done at once, sire."

"Sarian will not be able to resist coming to her aid. When he sees her stretched on the bloody stones of the forest altar, he will betray himself to us."

"You have her, sire? Already you have procured—"

"There is no man or woman on the Nine Worlds outside of my power, Wortan. You would do well to remember that."

I had gone as one dead, my hands almost crushing the bars at what I had heard. Taria in the clutches of this monster! But he had been right. I would not rest until I had freed her. I would not be able to sleep knowing he had her in his foul clutches. But at least I had been forewarned. Somehow I must find a way of thwarting him.

"I shall have Galad Sarian for you before the day is out, though," persisted Heynar.

"If you say so. Then both of them can be sacrificed. The Garganians are already anxious to lay hold of the Zurk responsible for the deaths of two of their closest allies. It will only take a few more days of preparation and the revolt can begin. Be sure to have your most loyal troops hidden when the time comes. Once the Garganian hordes pour into Melkor, they will be so maddened as to kill any man that stands before them. And the nightmares I shall conjure up will not be pleasant for you to look upon."

"I will await your final command with all eagerness," said Heynar with a low bow. After he had risen, the conversation appeared to be at an end. Heynar strode out of my line of vision and silence descended. Then the lights went out and I was alone with my thoughts. What manner of horrors would this rebellious Warden unleash? I had heard from more than a single source that he had powers to equal those of the Dream Lords. And even they were too far away to be of help when Vorta struck. But he was here on Gargan at least. If I could somehow reach him, I would end his life at a stroke and the reign of terror would end as abruptly.

Now I had to get out of the building, whether Taria was in it or not. I would have to rely on a surprise attack. There could be no way I could baffle the whole alert defence system of this place, so I would have to attack from without. Vorta had mentioned the forest. It could only have been the Ancient Forest, of which Ardat Vellor had warned me. A center of Garganian mythology and superstition. It would be there that Vorta would enact the final part of his evil drama.

I scrambled back down the stairway to the earth passage below and went on down as far as I could. My star lance showed the way. A long way on, my nostrils picked up a familiar and unpleasant odour. The sewers! Inspired by the knowledge, I ran on, the glimmer of lights not far distant. Yet I was cautious. Heynar had told Vorta that his sensors guarded every exit. I would have to fight my way out.

At length I came to the end of the passage. It gave way into a huge tunnel, like some deep subterranean cavern of mine workings, and peering over the lip of the precipice, I saw the outpourings of one of the sewers some way below me. At the bottom of the cavern, some fifty feet away, a pool filled with slime was emptying out from another tunnel opposite. I had no intention of jumping into the filthy water, remembering the last time it had happened. There was a rough ledge working its way down the rock face, and after sheathing my star lance, I tried it.

Once at the bottom, I stood beside the pool and looked around me. There appeared to be no robots or Guards, so I darted down the tunnel opposite. I had gone but a few yards when a brawny arm shot out and hands closed over my mouth and throat, and I felt my star lance whipped away from my side.

"Here's another of the Zurk bastards!" said a gruff voice in the poor light, and a knife touched my ribs under my harness.

"Slit his throat and feed him to the sewers with all the others."

"He struggles like an eel, lads. Come, who'll strike the first blow?"

The hands around me tightened, and I saw knives glint in the cold air. With whoops of enthusiasm, my captors made ready to butcher me.

CHAPTER XII
Flight in the Underworld

A knife gleamed before my throat, ready to slash me open and spill my life blood out in the musty passageway deeps below Melkor. I was powerless as it rose for the death blow, gripped by the arms of the sweating bodies around me.

"Hold, Zarrak!" cried a voice in the gloom, and the knife hovered for a moment. "More light here!"

A sputtering torch was thrust near me, thick black smoke coiling up towards the damp roof. I coughed and struggled but could not break the hold.

"By the Sacred City!" cursed a gruff voice, the man drawing back the torch. "Release him at once."

"Release him!" protested a chorus of angry voices.

"Aye. This is no Zurk, despite the trappings he wears. It is the youth from the Wise One. Chalremor's prophet. See the medallion..."

"Argh, the bastard has filched it, Tegara—"

"Tegara!" I said.

"Aye, master. It is I, whom you saved from a beating at the hands of the Zurks. I know this man, lads! His name is Galad Sarian, and he has been sent to us from Chalremor."

The men drew back from me as if I were some fabled demigod. I grasped Tegara's arm and clapped him on the back.

"Allow me to humbly apologize, master," he said with a reverent bow. The other men also bowed and I felt a trace of embarrassment.

"If you employ yourselves in slitting the throats of Heynar's men, your work is worthy. But tell me, how came you to this place, and where are your overseers?" I asked.

Someone handed me back my star lance and I nodded to him as I strapped it on. Tegara explained what had befallen the Barbarian slave party.

"There was a cave-in in one of the sewage exits and a blockage that caused a reservoir of filth to build up. The robots are no use under water, so we were given the foul job of clearing the obstruction. I escaped from my escort once, and it was you who saved me when I was retaken. Not long since, there was another cave-in the waters having undermined a considerable part of the drain walls, and in the resultant chaos a party of robots used for earth clearing and their trucks were buried, along with a handful of the Imperial Guards. We turned on the few remaining of our tormentors and plunged them into the sewers after taking their weapons. Now we hide ourselves until we can find a way out into the city and freedom. We expect to be killed, for there must be thousands of Guards up there, but we will strike a blow for Ur before we go down." There was a suppressed cheer of enthusiasm at this last remark and I smiled grimly. A handful of men, all armed with knives, swords and chains—they would have lasted only minutes up there in the city.

"I have a better idea," I said.

"My lord?" replied Tegara, and there was a hushed silence. The men were not sure of me—the uniform disturbed them.

"I have just escaped from the clutches of the Governor. The buildings above us are alive with Guards searching for me. They will be armed with their most dangerous weapons. If we go back now, it will be to a swift demise. Now, I was told by the Garganians—the natives—that it is possible to get outside Melkor, outside its dome, and take refuge there."

"But, master," said one burly slave, "we will be hunted down like vermin. Let us go into the city and wreak as much havoc as we can before we die, for we know we can never get off this planet."

"Listen to me," I told him firmly. "We might yet get away."

I told them then of all that had befallen me since Pthorthe had led me away from the Culture Center for the last time. I explained what evil schemes Vorta was brewing, and how he would incite the Garganians to rebel. The slaves were impatient and then horrified as I told them about Vorta's intentions of sacrificing not only Taria, but others as well. They knew only too well the horrors that were perpetrated in Karkesh, from whence they had been brought. After I had talked to them and reassured them of my confidence in at least upsetting the evil warden, they were with me. We would not rush blindly into the city, but try and get out into open country.

"Can men survive out there?" asked one.

"As long as we stay within a radius of about fifty miles of Melkor, the gravity and atmosphere will support life."

"Then," said Tegara, "let us leave this festering hole and seek some clean air."

"Aye!"

"Lead on to the sunlight!"

"Have your swords ready," I told them. "There will be Zurjahn blood to spill yet."

They whooped at that, and I followed Tegara down the passage to the place where the sewer had caved in. It struck me then how completely I was with the Barbarian cause now, for I had my weapon to use brutally against any Guard, or indeed, man, who stood against us. All the remnants of Dream Lord culture and sophistication had dropped away from me and I had become a physical, ruthless predator. And although my heart was heavy with fear for Taria's life, I felt a strange elation at being so free of my old ways.

"This is the place," whispered Tegara. He drew me to the shadows, and the men kept out of sight behind us, the last of their torches doused. My star lance came out of its sheath, but I kept it off, for some of the ceiling lights were still on down there. I looked at the scene before me. Tons of earth had blocked the drain and a lake of excrescence had dammed up behind it. Several hovertrucks were overturned and half-buried, but there were no signs of Guards.

"How thick is the wall of earth blocking the drain?" I asked Tegara, but I realized he would only be able to guess. The earth touched the drain roof.

"Can't tell, for we fled once we had disposed of the Guards. We never thought to try and get out of the city."

"Then we must try and find a way through."

"It could be yards thick, master," he said softly.

"Set up guards further up the drain. If anyone comes it will be from the main drain. You and I will climb the wall of earth and try to burrow through. It is our only hope, Tegara."

He thought for a moment, then nodded. He turned and gave a handful of the men orders to go a little way up the drain and watch for signs of Zurjahn approach. Then he and I ran across the walkway beside the drain and struggled up the sloping embankment of earth. Anxious moments passed as we reached the top. It had the look of the impassable about it, but I managed a grim smile. I dug frantically at the top of the earth, scooping great handfuls to one side, but there was always more. Tegara helped me. Below us the men watched the drains carefully, and suddenly a shout rang back at us from up the drain.

"Zurks!"

"By the City!" swore Tegara through his teeth. "We are trapped! This accursed mound may go on for miles."

"How many?" I yelled. The men were scuttling down the drain and they all stood at the bottom of the mound, looking up helplessly.

"The drain goes far into the distance and there are two flickering lights."

"Airboats!" I said. "We'll have to flee into the passages. We can't hope to—"

My words were cut short by a whirring. Instinctively I ducked as something thumped into the earth beside me. I jerked aside, for it was a roughly cut arrow. My eyes swiftly scanned all sides to discover the source, and Tegara cursed, sword ready to cut into any assailants.

"It seems the scum have surrounded us," he breathed.

"I'm not sure. The Zurjahns don't use arrows."

"Then who?"

"Ah—there's your answer."

I pointed to a spot near the opposite side of the drain, where the earthfall rested up against its side. In a recess in the wall stood a young boy of about fourteen, or so he seemed, a fresh arrow nocked to his tiny bow.

"The Zurks come at great speed!" yelled someone below. I acted quickly, running towards the young archer.

"All of you! Get up here and prepare to sell your lives dearly!"

called Tegara, and the men at once began scrambling up the bank side. I approached the youth uncertainly, but a broad grin split his features. He was a native Garganian!

"Why do you attack us?" I called softly. He shook his head, and I realized I had spoken in Zurjahn.

"We are friends. Put down your bow."

He grinned self-consciously and was about to reply when something back up the drains must have caught his eye. He stooped down and craned his neck to see, then a look of fear clouded his face. He turned to me and waved me to him.

"This way, this way!" he cried. "There is a way out." My heart leapt at his words. I turned to the others and shouted for them to follow. The Garganian youth was standing in what I now saw to be a passageway which had been revealed by the earthfall. In moments I had jumped alongside him, giving his shoulders a pat.

"The Zurks are almost upon us," said one of the men, and I could see the sweeping beam of an airboat nearing us in the drain.

"But—but—you are Zurks, too!" gasped the boy as the ragged Barbarians leapt for the safety of the passage.

"The Zurks are our enemies," I told him. We are friends of the *phorud*."

I was hoping the word meant something to him and I was lucky, for his eyes lit up.

"The *phorud*! Then you must escape."

"Where does this passage lead to?"

The last of the men had scrambled up beside us, darting fearful looks at the oncoming airboats. They could not understand what the boy and I were saying and stirred restlessly.

"Out of the city to the labyrinths."

"Then lead us there," I said, motioning the men to move away and out of sight.

"I cannot take you to the *phorud*..." said the boy, with an apologetic shrug. I pushed him gently down the passage with a last look at the drains behind us. The first airboat came hovering into view.

"What is your name, boy?" I said as we broke into a run, now out of sight of the Zurjahns as we scurried away into the earth like rats.

"Zartol, sir," he said.

"Well, Zartol, we owe you much for saving us. The Zurks would kill us if they found us."

Tegara was beside me. I flicked on the star lance and threw the narrow tunnel into eerie radiance.

"We will guard your back," said Tegara. "If the Zurks give chase, we will keep you occupied while you flee."

"I think I can foil their pursuit," I said. I had noticed a series of cracks in the earth walls of the tunnel, probably caused by the earthfall nearby, and by inserting the star lance I was able to loosen the wall. Motioning the others aside, I prodded at the walls and soon had another minor fall started. I leapt back just as part of the roof thumped down and I nodded with satisfaction at my handiwork, for the passage was suitably blocked. Should the Guards come this way, they would assume the passage unusable.

"Now, Zartol," I called to the boy. "Take us to the labyrinths."

We trooped down the dark passageway, the men in high spirits now, some even whistling or humming. To be free of the Zurk yoke was like an impossible dream to them. I was not so cheerful. How could our small band hope to defy the massed forces of Wortan Heynar and the unknown powers of Daras Vorta? We could warn the Garganians about the evil inherent in the Brotherhood of the Goat, but would they listen?

A thought had stirred in my mind. Something Pthorthe had said. He had preached against the Brotherhood, but to little avail. For some reason the awful cult appealed to the Garganians, and with a flush of understanding, I saw why. If Vorta had the same powers of illusion that the Dream Lords possessed, he could bend the Garganian will to his desires. And now this youth was leading us to the Garganians, who would in all probability bind us and take us to their new-found god, the Goat. Zartol may have meant well—any enemy of the Zurjahn Guards would be a friend to him and his people, surely—but I decided we could not take the risk.

"How far to the labyrinths?" I asked him, for we had journeyed far down the claustrophobic tunnel.

"We are outside the city, sir. Another half mile or more to go."

"Then it would be best if we went our ways in secret," I told him. The men were listening, although they could not understand. They sensed by my worried features that all was not as well as it might be.

"But you will be protected," protested the youth. "I will find men who can take you to the *phorud*."

"No," I demurred gently. "You must know, Zartol, that not everyone agrees with the ways of the *phorud*. There are those of your people who see the *phorud* as a threat to peace on Gargan. If these people know that we—and we are men, not Garganians, is that not so?—if they know we flee other Zurjahns and seek the *phorud,* they may fear the wrath of the Zurjahns and give us up to them."

"Then I will hide you until I can seek out someone from the *phorud*," the boy said anxiously.

"We cannot take that risk, Zartol. If you would truly help us, take us somewhere where no one will find us. We must make plans quickly for a strike against the Governor soon."

The boy was nonplussed, but the worried faces of my companions and the urgency in my tone must have won him over.

"Very well, sir. I know of a nearby warren which will take us away from my people's labyrinths, but you will be going into dangerous country."

"Lead us there," I encouraged him. He nodded and proudly motioned us to follow him down the earth tunnel. Soon we reached a junction, and it was indeed like a warren, for scores of tunnels branched off into the darkness. Zartol had no hesitation, however, in choosing a passage and leading us down it, and I explained to the men why I thought it best if we avoided the Garganians. I told them also that Heynar had had my name blackened amongst them after Pthorthe's death and that my safety would be in jeopardy. As we filed down the winding tunnels of the underground maze, which Zartol seemed to know in infinite detail, I asked him something of himself.

"What brought you to the drains?"

"Oh, that, sir. Well, I discovered the old passage some time ago and often use it to spy on the Guards. It leads far into the city and has many spy-holes. I have never been discovered, and if my father knew of my secret visits he would be greatly angered. I have always wanted to join the *phorud* and fight the invaders, but always have I been laughed at and told to get on with my chores. Other boys my age are not as keen as I on joining the *phorud* and often they laugh at me and avoid me. So I go my own way."

"It is well that you do."

"Yes. If you had remained where you were, the Zurks would have killed you all. I have seen them kill before."

"And now you have the chance to really help strike a blow against them."

"I am honored. My weapons are yours to command."

His enthusiasm had surprised me earlier, for we were a ragged, unkempt band, our appearance that of savages or criminals, yet Zartol had sided with us almost at once. Now I saw something of his reasoning.

Further along the tunnels we went, and now I saw roots and weird growths lining the sides. I questioned him about these, and he said that he was leading us to the one place where few people ever dared venture.

"I have been there many times," he said boastfully. "I have spent nights on the surface, with a small fire to keep me warm. I do not fear the place as others do."

"And where is this place?"

"The Ancient Forest. It stretches for a great distance and hides many secrets of Garganian history. I have often stumbled upon crumbling ruins or seen strange shapes from my treetop hideaways."

My heart jumped at his words. The Ancient Forest—this was where Vorta would hold his final diabolic rituals and set the Garganians at the throats of the Zurjahn forces.

"How well do you know the Forest?" I asked.

"I have travelled far and wide within its confines since I was a child—another fact that I have hidden from my father. Other boys keep away, frightened of the spirits and evil ones who dwell there."

"And what do you know of these...evil ones?"

Zartol was obviously uncomfortable. He shrugged.

"I keep away."

"You have seen things, then?"

"Sometimes at night there are lights deep in the Forest, near the old ruins of a certain temple. But I do not go too close. I have heard things. I was frightened. If it is the Goat people, I have no wish to confront them."

"The Goat people?" I said with some amazement.

"I know little about them. My father used to frighten my mother and sisters with tales of the half beings who dwell in the forest and eat wayfarers so that people would be too scared to go into the Forest. I did not believe him until I glimpsed the temple glade. But

I will hide you far from this place, for the Forest is deep and wide and could hide a thousand like you."

I gripped his arm.

"That is well, Zartol, but would you lead us to the forbidden glade if I asked it? You need not tarry once you have shown us the way."

His eyes widened in fear, but he tried to mask it.

"I...would be leading you to your deaths, sir."

"Our most hated enemy is at the heart of the black practices you speak of. The one who rules the Zurjahns whom you hate so. If we can surprise him at his work, the rule of tyranny will be over."

Zartol was both excited and appalled by the news. "It is an evil place," he said again. "And I have heard the awful chanting of many voices. Can such a small band as we are destroy all of the Goat people?"

I shook my head at him.

"You have only to show us the place, then flee back to your people. I would not ask you to risk your life with us."

Zartol looked indignant. His chin jutted out and he clasped his bow firmly. "I have made my choice, sir. I will take you to this place, and I will stand with you. I will not flee."

"Yet you know more than I the dangers of this place."

"Yes, so you will need my guidance," he persisted.

"Zartol," I said evenly, resting my hand on his arm so that we stopped walking. "I must tell you that none of us expects to come away from this alive. We are few and there are many enemies. All we wish is to destroy the man who controls them. We will gladly forfeit our lives to that end. But you can escape and warn your people about what has happened."

"No," he said stubbornly. "There should be a Garganian amongst those who would rid their world of its worst oppressor."

There he had me, and I nodded with a wry grin.

"You are a brave boy. Your father may not approve of your decision, but he would be proud of you."

His face lit up at that and we moved on. I called Tegara to my side and told him where we were going.

He nodded grimly. "Fate has sided with us for awhile," he said, going back to tell the others.

Zartol led us deeper into the tangled maze, the way often being choked with pale growths and hanging lichens, but we got through.

The tunnel widened and became like a vast low-roofed cavern, peppered with pillars. I examined these and saw them to be thick tree roots, gnarled and twisted like the supports of some monstrous crypt.

"The Forest is above us," said Zartol.

"Let us rest here, then," I said. The men dropped down silently, their nerves now wound up for our last move against Vorta.

CHAPTER XIII
The Ancient Forest

We emerged from the seclusion of the underground burrow in the tranquillity of the Garganian twilight, and found ourselves surrounded by the age-old growths of the Forest. We gazed speculatively at the motionless and vast expanse of uncanny forest around us. These incredible trees were twisted and gnarled into every conceivable shape; some looked like caricatures of bent old men, others were tall and straight, with curling branches and thick, leathery leaves. A powerful scent of wood and dried undergrowth came strongly to us, intermingled with something intangible. It was not unpleasant, but had a strong alien quality to it.

I felt uneasy in the darkness, but doubly so for this peculiar forest was utterly motionless: not a leaf wavered. It was as if the whole forest had been petrified, or cursed by some mythological wizard from its aeon-old past. We moved deeper into the foreboding entanglements and the trees became taller, their branches more thickly intertwined, so that very soon we were in almost total darkness. We dared not strike a light, though. The rushing moons of silver above threaded no fingers of light into this tightly webbed forest. Useful progress would be impossible, so I called a halt to our movements.

"We had better save our energies and find a place to sleep. The trees should offer us the cover we need."

Shortly thereafter we had all found lofty perches for the night. Zartol assured me that this part of the Ancient Forest was well away from the old ruins and that he doubted if anyone would come nearby. I settled myself as comfortably as I could in the crotch of an old tree, the silence around me like a thick blanket. It struck me then that

Vorta might seek me out as he had when Pthorthe, the Garganian guide, and I had first fled to the sewers, so I did my best to weave a mental barrier around the men as protection against such a probing. Then I drifted into a fitful sleep.

It had been a long while since I had been disturbed by dreams and nightmares, but now I suffered a new attack of them. At first I seemed to be floating in a blended sea and sky of deep blue light, which seemed to have no horizon or boundary, like a limitless eternity of space. Sometimes a vague shadow would pass quickly by, as though veiled in mist, and strive as I did to see clearly, I caught only hints of the flashing visions. There were different sounds, like muffled voices, throbbing nearer, but pulsing away before I could catch the words. Then I saw globes of darkness as black as deep space floating in spinning orbits at the limits of my vision. They swam nearer, hovering to and fro, exuding a nameless terror, an aura of palpable evil. My body curved and twisted as it drifted, but the black orbs drew closer.

Nearby flashed a ray of gold, and presently it bathed me in its glow, so that I was near blinded. I did see the black orbs, though, darting at me and shying away as the light struck them. A thick whisper seemed to emanate from the golden light, and somehow I thought of Chalremor. Then a huge shape looked before me, a nightmarish horror of night, with blazing eyes and horns. The light receded, then pulsed brighter, and the flapping of wings drew near to blot out the awful vision. A winged horse of white light flew by. A leering skull peered at me, and I saw my own eyes reflected in the sockets.

"Use your powers..." murmured a soft voice like a cooling stream. "The Dream Lords have taught you how to use your mind...soon the Pale Rider must mount..."

I tried to fix on the source, but wisps of thick cloud swirled from the sea and spiralled around me like fronds of web. Other voices susurrated in the air, and there was shrill laughter. Black globes whirled close again, but were again urged away by fingers of golden light. Vorta's voice babbled from some inner recess of my mind: "...when Sarian realizes what plans I have for his beloved mistress, he will not leave Gargan..." And the leering face of Wortan Heynar formed out of the swirling mist before dissolving. A sense of impending storm and brewing elements permeated the air of the dream, and I knew that Vorta was preparing for his murderous coup. Once more his black-globed probes sought me, but the golden light yet protected me and they whirled away. My dreams became more peaceful, interwoven with an undercurrent of calmness and encouragement from a source that could only be Chalremor. It was as though he had sent his mind out over the millions of miles that separated us to comfort me.

When I awoke in the early hours of the morning, I knew that Vorta was aware of my presence. He had known that I would respond to the bait of Taria. But I knew also how I must fight him. I must exercise my own powers of illusion and use my own mind. But it would be a desperate struggle.

My chest burned and I looked down. The medallion glowed very faintly in the first rays of day. Chalremor's talisman. Perhaps it was the medium by which he could reach me. Well, I would certainly need to draw something from his strength if I were to triumph. My thoughts were disturbed by a movement beside me. Zartol, who had been sleeping nearby, had awakened, too, and had stretched himself.

I called to him cheerfully. I had pulled out my star lance and let it rest in the sunlight. It would draw in solar energy and before long be the potent weapon I was familiar with. Zartol watched it in awe.

"How long will you hide here?" he asked me.

"We cannot waste time now, for we are discovered. You need not fear the trees and undergrowth—there is no one hidden there. But the Goat knows we seek him. You had best lead us to the ruins. Only there can we confront each other. But, listen. Is there a secret way? Can we get to the ruins underground, or must we walk in boldly?"

I had no intention of doing so, for it would be impossible to take Vorta by surprise.

"The ruins are built on solid rock," said Zartol with a shake of his head. "Only by passing the portals can you go within to the place of the altars."

I frowned. Had I come this far in my cause against Vorta only to be thwarted? I looked at the stirring men around me. Scarcely a score of us and all but myself armed only with simple weapons. I examined my own weapon. There was one faint possibility. Now that the star lance was fully charged, it could be made to melt even bare rock. I could burn my way under Vorta's temple, although even this thought filled me with apprehension. How could I hope to shield myself and the men from the one place where Vorta's concentrated power would be at its strongest?

"Do the tunnels under the earth run near to the ruins?" I asked Zartol.

"I think so, but I have never ventured close."

"I must get beyond the portal, or our cause is lost before we begin. Will you lead me as close as you can?"

"Very well," he said, but he was white with fear.

"Good lad. With your help we shall overcome the Goat yet. Tegara!"

"Master?"

"I have had time to fathom a way of pitting ourselves against Vorta and his forces. Let us to earth and I'll unravel it to you."

We slipped to the ground once more and took to the burrows beneath. I explained what I thought would be our best strategy of offence and we spent the day arguing around it, assessing each move as best we could. Now all that remained was for us to station ourselves near the ruins so that we could await the fated night when Vorta would arrive and begin his dealings with the forces of darkness. At first it had struck me that we might after all, be able to secrete ourselves among the ruins, but Zartol told me they were overrun with Garganians loyal to the black Brotherhood. The altars were always tended.

And so we took shelter as close to the crumbling portals as we dared. We fed off the mushroom-like plants that Zartol brought us and waited anxiously for signs of movement. For the next two days there was an endless procession of garbed acolytes passing from the Forest byways into the huge grove beyond the portals. My men frowned at the large numbers, thinking, no doubt, that our cause would be hopeless.

After three days there were no more grim shapes forthcoming from the silent verdure. I sensed within me that it would be tonight. Vorta would inject his followers with the fervor of religious mania and send them out from the Forest and into the city. What he had a mind to do, I was yet to learn. I watched sullenly as the moons of Gargan rose. The minutes dragged by, and we listened for the first grim hints of activity from the grove of the altars that seemed to draw tighter its veils of darkness.

Tegara looked at me and his mouth twitched nervously. He had heard something. I listened attentively, then nodded. A distant chanting had started up, deep and doleful.

"It is beginning," murmured the Barbarian.

"Then I must begin our strategy. Zartol, are you sure you want to see this through? If you wish it, you can return to your people now. I will find my way from here."

But the brave Garganian lad shook his head. He was trembling, but adamant. He would lead me as close to the ruins as the tunnels permitted. With a frightened glance at those distant stones he stood over the burrow in the earth and drew back the concealing branches. I clapped Tegara on the shoulder.

"We part for the last time," I said sadly.

"The power of light be with you, Galad," he nodded.

"You know what to do."

"As soon as the Garganians prepare to leave the ruins, we will block the portals and sell our lives as dearly as we can. We may not stem the flood, but we will give them cause to reconsider their assault on the city. And you—"

"I will try for Vorta's life. Whether I succeed or not, I cannot expect to survive long. If there are gods watching over the Nine Worlds, they will claim us all tonight."

I gripped his arm in farewell and followed Zartol into the burrow. He led me through a low maze of earthworks. Somewhere ahead were the ruins. I flicked on the star lance to show us the way, and as I followed Zartol I began concentrating with all my mental faculties on shielding both of us from the natural mind defences that Vorta would have constructed against me.

Through the narrow confines of the earthen tunnels we groped our way, Zartol knowingly by-passing the offshoots of other workings. Eventually he stopped and turned to me, his voice low, his eyes darting around us for fear of catching sight of some eavesdropping enemy.

"The tunnel curves away from the rocks here. Beyond this wall lies the rock on which the place of the altars is built."

"Then I will make my own tunnel. It is not too late for you to go back," I added, but again he shook his head.

I ushered him behind me and pointed the star lance at the rock wall, twisting the haft. A needle of white heat shot outwards, searing the rock, which quickly began to melt away like butter. The light seared our eyes, but the work went fast. How long the energy of the lance would last, I could but guess, although my progress was quicker than I had hoped. Soon I had seared a molten tunnel well into the rock wall, and Zartol and I drew ever nearer the place of the altars that lay beyond the portals above us.

We had gone a considerable distance into the rock when I stopped. The melting stone glistened wetly in the glow of the firelight. My mental shield appeared intact—there was a good chance that Vorta would not expect an attack from below. The only danger was that he would sense the released energy of the star lance. Now I used my acute mental powers to try and detect sounds from the surface. There was something very audible on the very edge of my range, somewhere ahead, above and to my left.

Apart from this vague guide, my work with the star lance was random. When I finally reached the point where I thought we were somewhere below the place of altars, I diverted the tunnel to one side and at another sufficient distance began working my way upward. The lance was losing its power, so I would have to break surface soon. I turned to Zartol, who was warily watching our rear.

"We will be out in the open at any moment," I told him. "Just pray that it will be in some spot away from the gathered servants of the Goat. As far as I can tell, they are some way over to our left."

The next moment a rush of cool air fanned my face, and I knew that the star lance had burned its way to the surface. At once I switched it off and kept as still as I could. There was only a ring of darkness before me, a starless sky. Faintly in the distance I heard the weird ululations of the worshippers. I raised my head a fraction above the lip of the opening.

It had been a lucky strike—that, or the Gods had favoured me. We had come up inside a walled chamber of some description—a dark tomb with only the merest slit of an opening to allow in the torch-lit ray of yellow from the outside world. I helped Zartol up, and we stood by the aperture and looked out.

Below us was the place of the altars. A huge crowd had gathered to praise the new Goat god, and all were kneeling, their hands waving in supplication to the three flat blocks of carved stone that made up the altars at the head of the clearing. Huge monolithic blocks surrounded the glade, their blackened sides marked with fantastic cabalistic signs. Braziers of hot coal lined the walls of these blocks, sending thick black clouds of smoke up into the Garganian night.

Zartol sucked in his breath, and I patted him gently to try and calm him. The sight must have been doubly disturbing for him, for it was like something out of the oldest of Garganian legends. Not for centuries had such a primitive spectacle presented itself to Garganian eyes. For here were all the trappings of a savage, primordial religion: the bloodied altars, the reeking incense and choking smoke plumes, the half-naked bodies swaying restlessly and sinuously to the monotonous wailing of the chant, the aura of evil. Behind the altars stood the priests of the cult—or so I took them to be—dressed in skins and animal hides, their heads covered by hideous masks complete with curling horns. And behind them was the opening of a cave-like tomb, a great gaping mouth of darkness from which emanated a miasma of evil, a sentient power of maliciousness and corruption. There would I find Daras Vorta.

As I took in the gently undulating multitude below me, I felt something searching the air of the clearing and knew it for Vorta's mind. Like a living tentacle it was seeking my place of refuge. He knew I would be here somewhere. But the grim mausoleum in which Zartol and I were hidden stood at the very edge of the ring of monoliths, and if Vorta had penetrated my mind shield, I had no way of knowing.

"I can hardly believe what I see," whispered Zartol.

"These are the so-called Goat people," I told him softly. "Not spirits or demons, but men, both Zurjahn and Garganian."

"Yes. Garganian. Yet I am amazed because there are members of many tribes, some from afar. How is it that they come together peacefully to worship a common God? It is not heard of..."

"The Goat is all-powerful," I said, wondering at his words.

What next transpired filled me with revulsion and loathing, for a handful of captives were dragged screaming before the altars, and with clinical precision they were sacrificed in the name of some unspeakable deities and their collective blood put in a huge bowl. Servants of the priests then went among the worshippers, flicking upon them the blood of the slain. Zartol had turned away, but I watched in disgust. Such a barbaric practice had not been known for millennia. How could these people indulge in such foul rituals?

Then a familiar voice came across to me from the heart of that

143

cavern behind the altars on which the dead sacrifices lay naked and white. Daras Vorta's sepulchral tones echoed from the darkness and dead silence fell upon the hundreds of watchers.

"Children of the Goat! The spirits of your gods are pleased to see you assembled here. Though you have waged incessant war on each other for all recorded time, yet have you answered the plea of the Goat, greatest of all the Lords of Darkness, and come together against your deadliest foe. Your deadliest foe, Children of the Goat, that is daily thrusting deeper into your labyrinths and bringing alien ways to your world of Gargan. Your deadliest foe, that daily mocks the old ways, the old Gods, and daily reduces to ruin the temples and sacred laws of your pantheons. Your deadliest foe that sows it wheat and reaps its harvest to feed its own numbers so that more can come to aid in the usurping of your world. Who else but the accursed Zurk invaders? With words and weapons of forbidden power have they wrested your world from you.

"But the spirits of the Gods are no longer sleeping. I, the Goat, have the power to wake them and allow them to walk once more among you—to lead you to victory over the hated Zurks. The Brotherhood of the Goat is strong—too strong for the godless men who rule in the domed cities. And not only do I see Garganians from every part of this world, but there are the humble converts from the very heart of the enemy's camp. Oh yes, Children of the Goat, there are Zurks among your numbers. But they are as you, and live only to serve the Gods that are your masters.

"Together will you throw down the invaders in the name of the Goat. Under me you shall regain your former greatness, for I shall restore Grgan to its former days of wonder. There will be seas here again, and tropical jungles and all the things you hear of in distant myths. And once more shall the Gods of old return to rule and bless you."

The silence was absolute. Not a soul moved. Every eye was fixed on the cave mouth, though Vorta did not show himself.

"Tonight shall your resurrected Gods lead you against your foe! They will be conjured from their ancient resting places. You will see them! Touch them! Now—as the blood of your sacrifices bathes you, I turn the key that sets you free."

From beside the altars I saw the one sight that I had dreaded seeing most. For there, struggling helplessly, her hands chained, her clothes torn almost from her pale limbs, was Taria. My whole being trembled as I remembered how it had been to touch that fair skin. I frantically aimed my star lance through the aperture, fixing on the nearest goat-helmed man that held her. I fired, but the weapon was useless, its energy expended in the making of the tunnel.

Helplessly I watched as my beloved Taria was flung across one of the altar slabs. She was brutally spread-eagled, her head thrust well back so that her soft throat gleamed in the baleful glare of the smoking braziers. A libation cup was held beneath her neck, ready to catch her sacrificial blood once the dreadful cut was made.

"Here is the lover of one of your most hated enemies!" came Vorta's booming voice. "The wanton slut who allowed herself to be caressed by the murderer who fled the corpses of his Garganian victims—Galad Sarian, the Zurk who cut down the men who trusted him. This is his mistress. Her blood will be a potent charm against Zurk power. Blood for the Goat, blood for the Gods, it will revive them, it will strengthen them!"

I clawed at the stones before me, trying to get through. The tomb had a door, but swinging it on is massive, hidden rollers was agonizingly slow. Below me I saw the priests ready their knives to slit Taria's throat. Zartol had fled behind me, too terrified to watch. Somehow I pushed the huge portal back and stood outside on the top of a broad stairway. The priests stopped and looked up at me, their faces masked by their grim hoods.

"So you have come, Galad Sarian!" laughed the voice of Vorta. "See him, Children. This is no God from the past. It is the Zurk murderer! You are too late, Sarian! Already I have summoned the spirits."

I could only stand there with my star lance glowing dully, my eyes fixed rigidly on Taria's uselessly thrashing form. Another peal of mocking laughter came from the cave. I made to rush through the throngs of leering Garganians, but I could not move. Somehow Vorta's power held me rigid. I could only watch as the priests lowered their knives and allowed Taria's blood to flow into the libation cup.

CHAPTER XIV
Warden of Hell

Standing on top of the broad stairway, at the foot of which milled the howling throngs of Goat-worshippers, I cried out my anguish at the sight of the dreadful sacrifice being made on the central altar at the other end of the clearing. My own mental agony plus the strength of Vorta's hold on me forced me to my knees. My weapon all but fell to the ground beside me. Beyond the yelling hordes, a group of shrieking acolytes leapt up beside the altar, dipping their hands in Taria's blood, so that I lost sight of her pathetic, still body.

"And now let the spirits walk among you again!" came the sneering tones from the cavern. The air around the clearing was thickening as though a fog had descended. The Garganians had fallen to their knees, ignoring me as new events transpired about them. Dim shapes had begun to form in the mist. From out of the ground they filtered like wisps of white silk, these shadows of men and creatures from an age of fable. I could sense what Vorta was doing, but the gathered acolytes were completely under his influence.

Vorta was exerting his Dream Lord-like powers and creating a wave of illusion, based upon the imagination of the Garganians. From the darkest corners of their minds he was creating a nightmare army of fantastic beings: Gods, demigods, gibbering demons and crawling things. Palsied, rotting corpses emanated from the monoliths and from the bloodied earth came reptilian creatures with glistening skins, bloated and toad-like. There were screams and shrieks of fear amongst the Garganians, but Vorta's voice spoke calmly to them, exhorting them to remain where they were, for these horrors were their allies.

Because of the tremendous strain Vorta had to exert to control so many minds, the mind-grip he had put on me was lessened. I refused to accept the reality of the monstrosities that flapped about the monoliths like huge carrion-eaters, or the be-slimed serpents that slithered through the grass, or any of the horrendous, fanged liches that walked unsteadily amongst the Garganians. For brief moments I was able to see the scene below as it really was (the way Chalremor had shown me the true Dream Lord castle) and there were only the uncertain Garganians and their Zurjahn allies.

146

I wrestled with Vorta's hold on me and felt it weakening. Somehow I got to my feet, a sheen of sweat coating my face, my hair damp and straggling over my ears. I gripped the star lance. It could not spit fire, but it was still usable as a heat rod. If I could get to Vorta, I would unleash my fury.

I knew I had to fool the Garganians first, for unless I fought my way through their masses, I would be overwhelmed by their sheer numbers, despite my weapon. Painfully I went down the steps, concentrating all my mental energy on battling Vorta's mind grip, so that all the conjurations and nightmares he had released came right back into focus around me. The air was dense and cloying, permeated with a charnel stench, and the acolytes of the Brotherhood rose and bowed before the array of demonic entities that sprung out of the ether among them.

Thick tendrils of fog swathed everything so that my features were obscured as I came within the clearing and forced my way through the throngs ever closer to the cave where Vorta sat. Baleful eyes glowered at me as the demons and visions of hell watched, but I alone knew they were blind eyes.

"See your Gods!" came Vorta's gleeful voice. "Touch them! They will lead you down into the city. No one can stand against them. The gates will be open. Go forth and tear out the hearts of the Zurks! Scatter the alien usurpers to the wind. Make them as dust!"

An evil chanting and cheering broke out as the host of nightmare shapes began floating like wraiths towards the end of the clearing where stood the portals. I prayed that my faithful Barbarian friends would stand firm and shut these loathsome things from their minds. I had warned them what Vorta would send against Melkor, and that if they could find the effort of will, they would not be harmed by them. As long as they stood their ground and fought off the Garganian hordes, there would be a chance for Vorta's defeat.

I pushed on through the Garganians, who moved themselves like soporific automatons, following the lead of the nightmare demigods. If Vorta sensed my approach, he made no attempt to stop me. His whole mind must have been concentrating on holding this fantastic feat of illusion. By a supreme effort of will, I shrugged off the last of his binding mental chains and thrust my way to the very foot of the altars. The priests barred my way, their eyes betraying their recognition of me, and I lunged at the nearest with my star lance. A ring of fire burst around him as he tumbled down the steps.

Swinging that deadly blue bar of light, I leapt up the remaining steps, smashing the weapon into the face of another priest and booting him angrily aside. The cave mouth loomed. Behind me the Garganian forces were moving ever nearer the portals of the place of the altars, and soon the Barbarians would have to engage them or flee.

Three more priests came at me with cruel, spiked spears, but I contemptuously drove my weapon into their faces, sending showers of sparks flickering in a deadly aura about me. I was getting closer to the place where Vorta was hiding. At last I had cut down the final few defenders. Now I would put Vorta's physical powers to the test. I sprang into the cave mouth with a howl of triumph, holding high the star lance.

I almost dropped it in horror at what confronted me. The cave was *empty*. Solid walls of rock surrounded me on three sides, and all that the cave contained was an earthen floor on which peculiar markings had been scratched. A roll of thunder-like laughter split the air around me.

"Welcome, Sarian!" boomed Vorta's evil voice.

"Come and face me, you scum," I shouted, but another peal of laughter greeted my challenge.

"You cannot win! Young fool, Sarian, you cannot hope to stand alone against my powers. Even now your pitiful Barbarians will be massacred and soon Melkor will fall to my gloriously repulsive army."

"You cannot fool everyone with this illusion. There are many who know your plans. Come and face me, or have you no ounce of honor in your stinking carcass, you murderer of women!"

"Alas, poor Taria. Yet she served her purpose well."

"Come and face me, you bastard!" I snarled, spinning to search every wall for signs of a crack or a hidden door. Vorta was there somewhere and I would tear down the whole tomb to find him.

"I fear that it is not possible for me to be with you in the flesh, much as I would like to be."

"I will find you, Vorta, by the stars, I swear it..."

"Yes, but not on Gargan."

"You speak in riddles..."

"If you seek me here, you will be disappointed. I am not here in a physical sense. Foolish youth! My powers are immense! Why should I travel across the void to do my will? This place on which you stand is a catalyst for mental energy. What you hear is a mental projection. If you would face me in the flesh, you must travel far—"

"I will tear Melkor stone from stone!"

"Hah! Your search would be fruitless. For I am on *Ur*. You must seek me in Karkesh if you would confront me." Again, he laughed.

"You lie!" I cursed him.

"Then sunder all Gargan to find me. You will fail. And now, if you must fight me, use your own mind. I will thrust you into a madness of your own making!"

A blinding bolt of light struck me and I knew that he meant it. He would be deadly. I staggered out of and away from the cave, my head ringing. Only the glowing radiance of Chalremor's medallion brought me to my senses. I dashed down the steps by the altars into the now empty clearing. Behind me the laughter of Vorta roared out at me from the cave.

"All is lost, little Galad Sarian! Soon I will be master of the Nine Worlds!"

Deep within me some other force stirred, as though it had been slumbering until it was needed. Animated by my hatred of Vorta and my extreme horror at what he had done to the one thing more precious to me than a universe of worlds, I drew on my deepest forces of mental strength. It seemed to me then, staggering as I did through the smoke-wreathed clearing, that Chalremor whispered in the air.

"I am with you. Fight his illusion with your own illusions. Break the grip of the Warden on the Garganians. Cloak yourself in illusion and cast down the nightmares he has brought into the world. They only exist because the Garganians believe in them. Shake their faith in their invulnerability."

I shook my aching head. From somewhere I heard the drumming of hooves. The fog became a wall of darkness, and I clawed my way forward. A neighing behind me made me turn. In the gulf of night that surrounded me I saw the huge pale horse of my vision in the Finger of Dusk. This was part of the illusion I must cloak myself in to face the Garganians. With all speed I bent my mind to conceiving my illusion, and with the faint power exuded by Chalremor's influence, I surpassed my expectations.

In a moment I had become a giant figure—a warrior of steel astride a pale horse, my star lance glowing with heat, ready to oppose Vorta's illusions. This was to be a battle of minds—of wills—but to the Garganians it would be an earthly struggle of demigods. I spurred the charger forward and came in sight of the rear ranks of the Garganians. They turned and screamed in terror as they saw the skull-faced rider bearing down upon them, their ranks parting like corn in a high wind.

I galloped through, bending from side to side and smashing down as many as I could. I could see my faithful Barbarian swordsmen standing in a line across the portals, faced by the crawling ranks of Vorta's nightmares. With a spurting of dust, I burst through the last of the Garganians and wheeled before the hellish army. As one they turned and their eyes blazed hatefully at me. And every pair of eyes was identical—the eyes, I realized, of Daras Vorta.

The only hope I had of thwarting Vorta was to catch him unawares. With a confidant shriek of derision, I goaded my steed forward and leapt over the first rank of corpse-like images. The Barbarians saw me drawing near the portal and were in two minds whether to flee. For a brief moment I stood before them in my true guise.

"It is I, Galad!" I shouted. "Ignore these horrors. I told you Vorta would try and trick your minds! Slay the Garganians—they are real enough!"

"The Pale Rider!" cried Tegara, eyes wider in horror than before as I again became the skull-faced rider. I whirled to renew my battle with Vorta. The Garganians were stupefied that such a figure as I should have emerged to do battle *against* their Gods. But doubtless they saw it as a typical quarrel, for the pantheons of Garganian deities are so complex as to allow for perpetual struggle.

A cascade of sparks lit the darkness of the Ancient Forest as I clashed with the flying things that swooped at me. I whirled my star lance this way and that, scything wings from one beast and scorching another so that it flapped to earth in a shower of flames. The Garganians paused to watch only for a short while, then seeing the Barbarians, hurled themselves forward with all the fanaticism of religious mania.

As I warded off the host of obscene opponents that Vorta's will pitted against me, I caught an occasional glimpse of the slaughter between the portals. Tegara and his men were the staunchest of heroes, spitting or slashing down enemy after enemy. Their desperate efforts seemed tireless as they hewed and parried with all the pent up fury of their imprisonment and abuse. Blood drenched the floor of the Forest, and a pile of Garganian dead mounted so that each new adversary had to climb over the slain to get at the Barbarians.

However, holding this human dam was impossible. Although each Barbarian hacked to pieces a score of opponents, one by one they were ripped down and trampled upon. Tegara swung about him with a berserk ferocity that was the scourge of all who came within range of his slashing, bloody sword. How many Garganian dead choked the portals was impossible to say, but at last even Tegara fell to their knives. Not one of the valiant Barbarians survived. It had been a desperate, pitiful struggle, but the Barbarians had gone to their deaths gloriously, after the fashion they loved best and knowing that even one blow against Vorta would bring their people a step closer to freedom.

It was my own turn to come under the murderous harassment of the enemy. While scores upon scores of jubilant Garganians clambered over their own heaped dead through the portals, a trio of grinning antagonists closed with me. As I swung at these creations of Vorta's, I saw to my consternation that the majority of his nightmare legion had swept ahead of the Garganian forces, and unless I could dispose of these three quickly, they would fall upon Melkor. Heynar would have left them the means of ingress and then sealed himself and his faithful troops up in his building.

Three winged fiends clawed at my head from above, while the snapping fangs of a slavering beast-god went for my steed's hooves. I thought of the flying horse of the medallion and concentrated my mental powers the harder. As I smashed to a bloody pulp the brains of the first advancing beast, I took to the air as my charger spread its huge wings. It bit into the neck of one of the flapping reptile birds and the thing fell to the ground with a last feeble screech.

Serpents hissed from the ground below, lifting high their scaly necks in an attempt to bring me down. The other winged demons closed but my star lance was a blur in the air, scattering them. I swooped down and decapitated a roaring demon, then plunged the end of the rod full in the mouth of another. I could not tell if Vorta's strength was waning. My own seemed to grow with every blow that I smote. I felt as if my will was asserting itself slowly over his.

I wanted to end this fight and pursue the Garganian force, but Vorta kept me at bay with his winged creatures. Five more materialized and I was forced down to earth. If they overpowered me, I would be helplessly struck down and held until Vorta could send out human agents to bind me. On and on the savage fight raged. I slew beast after beast, fiend after fiend. Eventually I heard a voice from near the portals.

"Galad!" it called over and over. I whirled my steed, just in time to see a small figure come into view.

The youth gawked at me in amazement. I was pressed by three towering skeleton warriors, and underfoot a clutch of serpents were trying to bring the stallion down.

"But...but...who are you fighting?" said the astounded boy.

I smashed aside another antagonist and slipped away from the others to stand before Zartol. "Can you see nothing?" I asked him.

"No, sir. Only the silent trees."

"No demons or spirits of the old Gods?"

"I don't believe in such things," he said, but his eyes swept the trees for the slightest sign of movements.

"Here is one boy you cannot fool, Vorta!" I yelled to the sky. There was an impatient groan, as though a wind had passed through the Forest, and one by one I saw the nightmare phantoms of my assailants fading back into Vorta's mind. I stood on firm ground again, the Garganian youth beside me.

"Who were you fighting?" he asked again. I smiled and clapped an arm on his shoulder.

"It was like a bad dream," I told him. "I saw terrible ghosts and sights to frighten the bravest of men. But my mind is cleared of them now."

"And the Goat people?"

I scowled at the trees. Vorta's will had waned under my determination and Zartol's innocent mind, so he must now be concentrating on the illusions he wrought over the Garganians.

"They march on Melkor. There will be a gate open for them. There has been treachery."

"Then how will you stop them?"

"I do not now," I said, shaking my head in bafflement. I walked to the portal, where the bloody bodies of the gallant Barbarians were surrounded by a hundred dead foes. I felt a wave of sadness rushing upon me like a tide, as I thought of Taria. Her cold, lifeless body must even now be lying somewhere amidst the altars in the clearing. Yet I could not bring myself to go and seek her, for the sight of that once-warm flesh I had known so intimately would have so sapped my strength that Vorta would have been able simply to smash me down so that everything I had fought for would be lost. Instead I used my seething hate as the foundation for a new offensive.

I lifted my medallion and pressed my fingers to the embossed horse.

"If you can hear me, Chalremor, and if your mind can fathom the vast gulf of space, lend me what you can of its power."

Zartol stood back, no doubt thinking I must be mad.

"You must help me now," I told him.

"How?" he said uncertainly.

"I want to set Vorta's forces against Heynar. I must try and divert them. My will against Vorta's. Concentrate on the Governor's buildings. Will the Garganians to go there. Use every ounce of your mind to think only of that. The Garganians to attack Heynar's buildings."

Zartol nodded, mystified, but closed his eyes and was silent. I thought I had detected something, like a voice from far away."

"...I will lend you all the power I can...fight him to the end...the wheel turns..."

Chalremor had somehow answered, but I knew his power would be small. I threw all my own powers into trying to counteract Vorta's will once more.

It was as though my spirit had swept up into the night to stand on some empty plain that shifted as restlessly as an ocean of fire. And not far from me a cloud of chilling evil pulsed and throbbed, its will contesting mine. Everything I had ever loathed, every shred of revulsion I had ever felt, I recalled now and built up my determination to foil it. I brought light on to this astral wilderness, but black clouds spewed from the shape before me and obscured it. Other golden lights flared on the horizon, and I knew Chalremor was pitting his weakened resources against the madness of Vorta's will.

I threw sheets of living flame at the darkness as it gathered and tried to blot me out and rivers of heat flowed into it. Light and dark, battling furiously as they had since the universe began. Time became a mere word. The war of our wills went on. Vorta tried to throw me by showing me illusions of Taria as she had been on that foul altar, but I countered with images of his own death and of a great goat drowning in a pool of molten fire.

From the horizons, the light grew in intensity. Where there is light, darkness cannot linger for long. A sunburst overhead was followed by another. Vorta's whirling clouds of night were fading! Now the cloud dwindled rapidly as star showers filled the horizons.

I opened my eyes and stared down at Zartol. He was still thinking hard. I joined my mind with his, directing my will out from this cold Forest...out over the crater rim...out to the gates and dome of Melkor, where the Garganian hordes gathered.

Whether Vorta had fled temporarily I could not tell, but I felt exultant now, having realized for the first time what it was like to have full Dream Lord powers. My confidence grew. I would turn Heynar's treachery upon him. I would will the Garganians to rid Melkor of all Vorta's foul allies.

"Keep thinking of the Governor's buildings," I said softly to Zartol. He opened his eyes and nodded, his face very serious in the starlight.

"Good. We shall triumph after all. Come, let us get to Melkor. Do you know a quick way?"

"Yes, sir."

"Then we must hasten before Vorta tries to reorganize his forces. Once he controls the Garganians in Melkor, we are lost."

CHAPTER XV
The Fall of Melkor

Zartol and I stood on the lip of the crater in which the dome of Melkor had been raised. We had left the gloomy Forest and followed close on the tracks of the Garganian rebels, but we had arrived too late to stop them from entering the city. I had sent out a mental bolt of determined energy in an effort to warp Vorta's illusions and turn the rebels upon Heynar's fortress, but I could not say whether I had been successful.

We made our way down the escarpment to the bridge that led to the huge air valves of the city. Although the atmosphere and gravity outside Melkor had been adjusted to suit human habitation, the inside of the dome was more carefully controlled. Temperature and rainfall were artificially controlled within the dome so that hydroponic and botanical work could go on the more successfully.

Once Zartol and I had reached the bridge, I pulled out my star lance. I could see that the first part of the air duct was open. No one appeared to be guarding it or shutting it against infiltration. We ran across the curving bridge and into the duct. There were no Guards or signs of life. Heynar's treachery was evident, then, for the Garganians had passed unmolested into Melkor. I found the huge wheels that closed the valve walls, and soon Zartol and I were in an enclosed chamber as the outer wall of the dome slid shut. I opened the inner valve and we went out into the streets of Melkor.

"They have been here," murmured Zartol, for there were signs of vandalism. Several corpses littered the now deserted streets. We rushed into the city, following the trail of debris—wrecked transporter cars, overturned hovertrucks, and worse. Within moments we were faced by a trio of burly Guards. They saw the worn and battered Zurjahn uniform that I was wearing and lowered their weapons.

"Are there more Garganians to come?" said one, and I knew him at once for Heynar's man.

"We are the last. The valves are closed," I replied.

"Then soon the city will be truly ours," said another of them, laughing coldly.

"Where is the bulk of the rebel forces?" I said.

The Guards all pointed in vague directions.

"Wherever their whim takes them, I suppose."

There was a sudden blast from beyond, and a wall of black smoke coiled upwards towards the dome roof. Minor explosions rent the still air and black clouds billowed from the near horizon of rooftops.

"They have begun," laughed another of the Guards, jerking a finger in the direction of the havoc. Then his jaw fell slack.

"Horns of the Goat!" swore one of his companions. "Heynar's fortress! The fools are assaulting the Governor!"

I winked at Zartol, who seemed bewildered by all that was happening. The Guards rushed down the street towards the distant explosions.

"We've done it!" yelled Zartol jubilantly. "We've turned the rebels on their masters."

"Aye, lad. But there's work to be done yet. Are you ready with your sword arm?"

For answer he nodded vigorously and wielded his tiny blade. I urged him along with me. I was not senselessly risking his life, for I had automatically put up a shield around him that no enemy would penetrate while I stood by. We rushed down the streets to find an abundance of corpses, both Garganian and Zurjahn. There had been terrible fighting here. But the main Garganian spearhead had responded to my mental commands as I bested Vorta in our mental struggle and had made for the Governor's bolthole.

We turned a corner and came face to face with a party of fleeing Zurjahns.

"Run, brothers!" they yelled as they scuttled past. "The rebels are inside the Governor's walls, sacking and killing. All the devils in hell are loose!"

Zartol and I ignored the fleeing soldiers and made straight for the blazing fortress doors. I saw down an alleyway a small passenger transporter and pulled Zartol into the cockpit. Minutes later we swooped away from the entry hall into the buildings, where thick palls of smoke were blackening the walls and swirling indifferently over the charred corpses of the fallen combatants. We still had not found the rebels. They must have split up and poured down as many passageways as they could find, putting everyone they found to the sword.

I sped the car to the main spiral, and took us up. It was Wortan Heynar that I sought now. If I could get to him and cut him down, Vorta's coup would be smashed completely. I could call in the Dream Lords or have a fleet of Empire starships land to maintain order.

Zartol used his bow with stunning accuracy wherever he came across Heynar's Zurjahns trying to escape. I had told him not to kill any of his own people unless it was in self-defence, for they were like puppets in the hands of the Gods, and not themselves. Yet the Zurjahns within these walls were all corrupt—the elite of Heynar's traitors. Now we had come to the levels where the fighting was at its grimmest. Swords clanged and clashed, warriors screamed and flung themselves upon their foemen, heat guns stabbed living tongues of flame at helpless aggressors.

The corridors were lined with the dead and moaning wounded. Still we passed upwards, knocking aside handfuls of terrified defenders. I burned my way through doors of steel and turned the transporter ever up the spiral towards Heynar's last refuge. The bloody carnage around us was terrible. The Garganians were hurling themselves like madmen at the Zurjahn troops, who were whittled down with deadly speed. The loss of life was terrible on both sides of the affray. Hundreds of Garganians had died under the heat guns, but still they came on. No longer had they the nightmare army of their spirits to lead them, for Vorta had long since given up and withdrawn his mental presence. Yet the fervor of fanaticism was upon the rebels and they fought on doggedly.

At length Zartol and I broke through the last ranks of Zurjahns of the upper levels and I smashed the car into the doors that protected Heynar's private apartments. I yelled savagely as we broke through, my star lance raised to slash aside any that opposed us, but the chambers were empty. I skidded the car to a halt on the rich carpets, springing off and ripping down curtains and drapes in a last desperate bid to find Heynar.

Outside us we heard the cries of combat where the ragged remnants of the Zurjahns and the final assault of the maddened rebels had crashed together on the spiral.

"Search every corner!" I called to Zartol. He nodded and prowled about manfully, ready to kill for me if need be.

"No need! No need!" came a high pitched voice. I whirled from an alcove and stared at the far end of the chamber in fury. Heynar had appeared from behind a pillar, his eyes wide with hatred and madness, his gaudy clothes creased and ripped.

"You seek me—you have found me, Sarian! But your victory is not to be! You cannot destroy the powers of the Goat..." he babbled, and I could see that he had taken a heavy dose of some drug. Even so, he was dangerous, for the muzzle of a heat gun pointed at me. He would not have to be accurate with the small hand gun, for one blast would send a sheet of flame at me.

"Surrender, Heynar!" I called. "Your men are dead around you. Vorta has withdrawn his power to Ur. Here on Gargan, it is smashed."

"No! Lies! You think to trick me with filthy Dream Lord illusions. My fortress is filled with loyal Guards! Out in the city the rebels are putting the last of your Zurjahn people to the sword."

His weapon wavered but I dared not move.

"This time, I will kill you myself!" he said hysterically and the gun levelled in my direction. But Zartol was quick to see my plight. With a coolness and deliberation that made mockery of his youth, he aimed his bow and sent a frail arrow speeding across the chamber. It lodged in Heynar's forearm, and the heat gun fell to the carpet. Heynar yelped and stumbled backwards, and I sprinted forward, leaping up the stair to where he knelt. His bloodied fingers stretched for the heat gun, but I kicked it away and followed up by driving my foot under his chin. His head snapped back and he sprawled, unconscious.

"That was a fine shot," I said to Zartol, who had another arrow nocked and ready to send into Heynar's heart.

"Shall I kill him now?"

I shook my head.

"Not yet. Go and see what is left of the battle outside."

Reluctantly he lowered his bow and went to do my bidding. I slapped Heynar's face until he came around. As he opened his eyes, I stood over him, the blue glow of the star lance illuminating his haggard features, turning them almost demonic.

"Spare me! Spare me!" he screamed, covering his face with his elongated fingers. I felt no compassion for him.

"Heynar, you snivelling scum! Listen. I have seen men whipped in your name. I have seen men thrust into stinking sewers and made to work with the filth that clogs them. I have seen men goaded to madness and thrust into bloody turmoil. And I have seen men sacrificed on foul altars to serve your master. And worst of all, I saw a girl, a slip of a girl, a creature as helpless as any you could find on any of the Nine Worlds, thrust upon a slab and foully murdered! Now you ask for mercy. The only mercy I will show you is a speedy death," I ended angrily, tears in my eyes. I lifted the lance to finish him. He writhed in agony before I had touched him.

"Wait! Wait! You are wrong. She lives! She lives! Your heart's desire was not murdered."

My hands gripped his throat in a vice-like grip and I thrust my face inches from his.

"What lies are these? I saw the sacrifice with my own eyes!"

"A trick, a trick. I swear by all the powers! It was an illusion. Vorta used your fear for her life to fool you."

"You *lie*!" I cried, but my heart thumped against my rib cage in renewed hope. Heynar struggled and screamed for mercy.

"No, no, no! I swear it. You believed what you saw in the Ancient Forest. Vorta knew you would. The girl he used was like her. You believed it was Sulian's daughter, so the illusion was a success."

"Then where is she?" I snarled. My hands grew tighter around his throat. His eyes screwed up tightly, tears running down his cheeks.

"She is on...you're strangling me..."

"*Where is she?*" I shouted again, twisting him even more violently.

"...on...Zurjah"

I flung him down and picked up my weapon.

"It is true, Galad! She has never been touched. All Vorta used was the superimposed mental image you had of her that we took from the psychometer reading."

But I was not listening any more. I understood what Vorta had done. Taria was alive...at home, untouched by these vermin. I laughed, throwing my head back. Then, with a contemptuous twist, I ended the life of Wortan Heynar with as little remorse as I would have had he been a rat.

"A noble killing," purred a voice behind me. Quick as light I spun, my star lance ready to strike any enemy that dared attack. My eyes filled with a new loathing. It was Ravas Tarak, my sickly cousin. Behind him stood a troop of Zurjahn spear men, their weapons ready to pin me to a wall at a word of command. I would still have leapt for the throat of Ravas, but I could not.

For his wiry arms were around the neck of Zartol. There were tears of frustration in the youth's eyes as the knife touched his skin.

"Let him go," I said quietly to Ravas.

"I'm afraid not, Sarian. He is my guarantee of your surrender. Throw my men your weapon and give yourself to them. Your life will be forfeit otherwise. But first, you will see this child murdered before your eyes. I promise it!"

I knew he meant it, but I made a last plea.

"If I surrender, will you release him?"

Ravas sniggered. "Your concern for him moves me. But, yes. Turn yourself over without further bloodshed and I will set him free."

I read the protest in Zartol's eyes: he was too terrified to speak. I nodded to Ravas and threw my star lance to the Guards. Ravas thrust Zartol aside as his men moved in on me.

"There, boy," he told him. "Run away back to your tunnels. I have my prize."

"You can do no more for me, Zartol," I told the sad youth. "But remember this—we have triumphed today. The power of the Goat on Gargan is no more."

He wiped at his tears and then turned quickly and ran away. Ravas's chilling laughter followed him.

"Yes, Sarian, a noble fight! You have indeed upset the Warden's schemes. But you were lucky."

"Perhaps," I said as the Guards bound my wrists. It was pointless resisting now. All I cared was that Taria lived.

"Oh, you were. Vorta had to fight from afar. You were here. But I am alive. I shall still take your place among the Dream Lords. In a while we shall leave Gargan, so that when Ardat Vellor and the appropriate authorities have had time enough to tidy up the last of the mess around us, they will think that Heynar and his men died trying to save the city from an uprising. Vorta's power on Gargan has only been temporarily—"

"No," I said, with a contemptuous smile.

"What do you mean?"

"Vorta's power here is smashed for all time. A new reign of Dream Lord control will follow this. Vorta will have to be content to sulk in his prison city on Ur."

Ravas made to argue heatedly, but his eyes dropped, and I knew that I spoke the truth. In time the Dream Lords would realize the truth about Vorta, and Ur would be purged.

"You have earned yourself death for your part in this!" snarled Ravas suddenly. He slapped me hard across the face.

I laughed at him. "Then kill me. I am satisfied. The knowledge that Vorta is beaten is enough for my peace of mind. And before Heynar died, he told me that Taria lives and is unharmed."

Ravas swore crudely.

"So do your worst," I said.

"Very well. To the victor the spoils."

There was a commotion from outside and presently a runner joined us.

"Sir!" he addressed Ravas with a curt salute. "The ship is ready. We have to leave with all haste. The Zurjahns are aware of what has gone wrong. They move against us. An Empire vessel is even now on its way from the motherworld."

"We are not lost yet. When we have left, no one will know that Ravas Tarak was here," said my cousin with a sly grin of satisfaction.

"And you will still be a mystery," he said to me. "All Zurjah will think you dead, though you will be far, far away."

"You cannot hide me unless you kill me."

"Vorta will decide. We leave at once for Ur and Karkesh."

So this was to be my reward. To be delivered into the hands of the madman I had defeated. It was a cruel blow, but my own success had softened it. Taria lived! Gods, but that was a blessed relief beyond dreaming. And she would be spared the knowledge of my own passing. I was satisfied. In my short life I had known what it had been like to fight, to ride, to live, and to live as a man should. Even death could not take that from me.

Book II:
Revolution

CHAPTER I
City of a Million Sighs

I opened my eyes in evil smelling darkness. Cramped around me in the humid air were the sweating, naked bodies of a slave party, chained ruthlessly and without compassion by their Zurjahn masters to the steel cell walls. My own wrists chafed where the cold chains rubbed at them. I had long since ceased to pull at the rings that held me. Voices muttered in the darkness and men coughed, weakened bodies racked.

"How much longer aboard this hell-ship?" I asked of the shadows, nudging the elbow of the reeking man next to me.

"Who knows? What makes you so anxious to return to Ur? Surely anything

is better than the pits of Karkesh."

I fell silent again. Time had lost its meaning on this grim voyage, and most of the chained slaves were taciturn, for they had been brought with me from the planet Gargan, where they had enjoyed a temporary respite from the rigors of the prison planet, Ur, to which they were now being returned. As I huddled in the oppressive air, my limbs cramped and soiled, I reflected on the cruel twist of fate that had thrust me into this pool of hopelessness, snatching me away from the world of the Dream Lords, who ruled the nine worlds.

The Dream Lord Triumvirate ruled the solar system, the nine worlds out from the sun being Los, Varga, Ur, Gargan, Zurjah (said to be the motherworld of men) Solcis, Urse, Aquarn, and furthest away, Dor. Of the varying anthropomorphic species indigenous to the nine worlds, the Dream Lords of Zurjah were the most advanced n the evolutionary scale. Their mental faculties and powers of telepathy, illusion, telekinesis, and the like had made them prime rulers, enabling them to direct their own destiny and their peoples' toward the ultimate ends that they had chosen for each, gracing themselves with the ability to perform technological miracles together with a close understanding of longevity. Their law was absolute law to the lesser races of men, and to enforce the Primary Law of peace, their Imperial Guards were present everywhere in the Empire. Only the simplest of weapons were allowed outside the hallowed halls of Dream Lord authority—even the Imperial Guards were permitted star lances and light rods in time of emergency only.

The other subspecies of the Empire included the Aquanx of the planet Aquarn, a peculiar amphibian race who dealt only rarely with men of the Empire, the Garganians, the majority of whom spent their lives under the ground in a vast network of labyrinths, and the enigmatic Barbarians of Ur. It was with the latter that my own fate had become inextricably wound up. They were considered to be the most primitive and savage race of the nine worlds, having in centuries gone by almost destroyed their planet completely in a war of devastating proportions. For this reason they had been subjugated and oppressed more than any other race in the Empire, Ur having been declared by the Dream Lords to be a prison world. Principal city of this desecrated world was Karkesh, city of chains, and called by its persecuted slaves the city of a million sighs. It was for here that our craft was bound.

Sitting in the rank air and silence of the cell, I saw in my mind the images of the all-powerful Dream Lords, who had set me on a tempestuous course in life when they had rejected me from their halls. Of their Triumvirate there was Laomidian, Vidor Karset, and Dotas Sarian, my own father. He was aging rapidly, his body eaten slowly away by some wasting disease that not even Zurjahn science could eradicate. I, his only son and heir, had been scant comfort to him, for I seemed to him to persist in contravening all known codes and ethics paramount to Dream Lord doctrine. I loathed the Dream Lord ways, preferring to test my physical abilities rather than concentrate on developing my mental powers, upon which Dream Lord evolution placed such a high value. Befriended and secretly encouraged by Gundar Sabian, a high ranking Guard and a veteran of many old campaigns, I had indulged in activities far below my appointed station—riding, fighting, physical exercise, and love-making. This last was a strong Dream Lord taboo, only being permitted in a mental form known as the "mating of minds" and then later within the bounds of sanctioned wedlock for the specific purpose of procreation. But I was incensed with love for Taria, daughter of a Zurjahn nobleman, and we had refused to give up our secret trysts.

My father's despair at my waywardness reached a climax when I succumbed to the teachings of a true renegade to Dream Lord beliefs, who had been imprisoned in a private tower. This ancient man, named Chalremor, taught me that our race was spawned not on Zurjah but on Ur, the chastised prison world, and that the hallowed Zurjah was a false motherworld. He had imparted to me a dreadful series of truths that showed vividly the fallacy of Dream Lord illusion, and I realized that my heart was with the old man— he did not lie. After that, I had demanded of the Dream Lords a fair reason for the suppression of the Barbarians, but I was told they were a sub-species who must pay for their crime of nearly destroying Ur.

For my heresies, I was banished by the Dream Lords for three years to Gargan, a harsh world, where it was hoped that I would learn to despise an uncomfortable physical existence and return to Zurjah more prepared to adjust to my true role in life. But it was not to be, for events on Gargan had thrust me closer to the truth of Chalremor's teachings. From a Garganian teacher named Pthorthe, who had been an ally of Chalremor's in years gone by, I had learned that the burden of Ur had increased. The Warden there was Daras Vorta, a vile and ambitious man, bent on overthrowing the Dream Lords themselves and wresting from them the control of the nine worlds. Part of the evil Warden's plan had been to kill me and ultimately to place my cousin, Ravas Tarak, on the Dream Lord Triumvirate, in my place.

Vorta had power on Gargan as well as Ur. He had established the Brotherhood of the Goat, a hellish cult aimed at recruiting Garganian dissemblers and promising to revive old and forbidden gods so that Zurjahn power might be broken. The cult even had its turncoats from the Empire, for the very Governor of Gargan's principal city, a man named Wortan Heynar, had been a depraved underling of Vorta. I had barely escaped the clutches of this Governor and, together with a band of escaped Barbarian slaves (who had been imported by Heynar for labor of the vilest kind), had slipped away into the sewers and labyrinths of the Garganian underworld.

I realized that Vorta had mental powers akin to those of the Dream Lords and that he intended to use them in spreading an illusion of nightmares among his Garganian acolytes. His plan had been to conjure up the spirits of the old Gods, and they were to lead the rebellion against Zurjahn rule. I had been forced to call upon mental resources of my own that had been slumbering, and in a titanic battle of minds had broken Vorta's hold on the Garganians and had turned them against their evil masters. Vorta had, however, foiled my attempt to kill him, for his mind had been powerful enough to operate not from Gargan, but from Ur. Furious, I had broken into the last of Wortan Heynar's defenses and throttled the treacherous Governor. Vorta's power on Gargan had been smashed, for already a Zurjahn fleet had been on its way to investigate. But my own triumph had been short lived, for my detestable cousin, Ravas Tarak, had snatched me at my moment of victory and now promised me a grim death on Ur at the hands of the man I had defeated, his evil master, Daras Vorta.

It had been a cruel twist of fate's knife that had cast me here, unless it was the hands of the soulless Gods that Chalremor had spoken of, for he had promised me that I would go to Ur, where my true role in life was to be enacted. I foresaw little hope. Ravas Tarak had laughingly thrust me aboard the slave vessel, down in the hold with the Barbarian slaves that had been forced to work at repairing the huge sewers of Melkor, Heynar's city. Nothing would allay my cousin from delivering me into the hands of the Warden of Ur, who still set himself up against the power of the Dream Lords, rulers of the nine worlds. Vorta had two reasons for wanting me dead. First, I was yet Heir to the Dream Lord Triumvirate, where Vorta had plans to set Ravas Tarak upon my seat. And secondly, I had thwarted his plans to grasp power on Gargan, from which Ravas had found it prudent to fly in all haste. Now the prison world drew nearer, and I could not escape it and the prediction that Chalremor had made. I must go to Ur, the last refuge of the madman who dreamed of unparalleled power.

I languished for what must have been weeks in that stinking hold and had little to say to my fellow captives. I rarely saw them, even when the crude meals were served and passed resignedly around. And they wanted little to do with me, or indeed with any of themselves. On Gargan I had met another such party of Barbarians, and they had died helping me to oppose Vorta. The sorrow of their passing weighed heavily upon me now.

This sadness was as nothing to the void left in my heart by the knowledge that I would probably never see Taria again. Ah, but still her divine image floated before me—the beautiful creature with whom I had spent so many hours and with whom I had learned the true depth of mortal emotion. She it was who taught me the fallacy of the cold Dream Lord doctrines, did she but know it, and yet now

I would go to my doom, and she would never know the way of my going. Daras Vorta had played me foul on Gargan when he had tricked me into believing he had sacrificed her, but now I knew she lived and I longed for her touch just a final time. But it would be denied me, and no one would know my true fate. For I had already accepted that but one fate awaited me—a swift demise at the hands of Daras Vorta. Talk of escape was not only madness but also a depressant, for these men were without hope, as were all the people on Ur. The prison world toiled under the Zurjahn yoke, and the primitive people could never hope to break it. I could not insult these sorrowful men by kindling their hopes. It had been my ideal to champion the Barbarian cause for freedom, but chained in the black hole of this vessel, I knew only the uttermost depths of despair.

At last the voyage came to an end. We had landed on Ur, and a restlessness

stirred the slaves. Some broke down and cried shamelessly, while others bore things with amazing stoicism. Lights blazed in the hatches of the cell as hard-faced Imperial Guards thrust in their heads. They unchained us all, swords ready to slit the throat of any recalcitrants, but no one opposed their rough handling, not even I, who once would have fought to the death.

The Barbarians were bundled out, until only I stood ringed by the cruel Guards, their weapons wavering at my breast in the glowglobe light. I was naked save for a filthy rag about my loins, my hair was matted and unkempt, and my body was covered with grime and sweat. The Guards looked at me scathingly as though I were some lower form of life, but I hid my humiliation under a bland gaze.

Presently there were footfalls in the corridor without, and a familiar figure stooped in the hatchway and entered. Ravas Tarak stood before me, a haughty look on features drawn by the excesses of his life style, a gleam of scorn in his eyes.

"Alive, I see," with a flick of his oiled black hair. A strong scent of perfume pervaded the cell, despite the accrued filth here. Ravas was like a younger version of Wortan Heynar, the treacherous Governor I had throttled with my bare hands on Gargan. I had wondered about the true nature of their relationship, and the death of Heynar was, I felt sure, the real reason for Ravas Tarak's deep hatred of me.

I looked stonily at him, but said nothing. It would do me no good to scream oaths that could only be impotent.

"Good. Then it is time for you to meet the Warden of Ur. But before you do, Galad Sarian, let me say that I pray nightly to the Dark Powers that he will grace me with the privilege of destroying you." His feral eyes gleamed with deep hate, but I was not to be provoked. He snorted with disgust and turned on his heel.

"Where is Drusea Mordan?" I heard him snap.

"At your disposal, sire," came a voice.

"I go straight to the Warden. Bring the prisoner."

"At once, my Lord."

A man came into the cell and eyed me warily. He was a rugged, middle-aged fellow in a smart red tunic, with a little harness, bearing the insignia of vessel Captain on his sleeve. He held a polished steel helm beneath his arm and stood stiffly before me. After a brief inspection, he led me through the walkways of the ship. Behind us a score of Imperial Guards had materialized, their spears clasped to their shoulders, their short swords clanking against their thighs. My legs were not shackled, but my wrists were to remain chained. When we had reached a tall door of concave steel, Drusea Mordan halted.

"I gather you have not been to Ur before," he said softly. I shook my head, scowling at him.

"The Warden has expressed a desire to have you placed before him, complete with all your faculties. I doubt if he would appreciate it if I were to deliver you to him blind. Shield your eyes."

I must have looked uncomprehendingly at him.

"Ur is millions of miles closer to the sun than is the homeworld, or indeed Gargan from whence we have come. You will grow accustomed to the sunlight by degrees. Shield your eyes."

This time I did so. Seconds later, the door slid to one side. Despite having my hands over my face, I sensed brilliant sunshine flooding the ship. My eyes began to smart. Mordan took up the loose end of my chains and led me on to a ramp. I was pulled forward, unable to look about me in the intolerable glare. It was as if I had entered a furnace, the air around me baking, and the searing heat of the ramp burned my feet so that gasps of pain escaped my lips. Drusea Mordan tugged at the chain, and I had to stumble along behind him beneath this scorching sun.

Painfully I made my way down the metal ramp until the Captain pulled me up. I jerked to my knees, rubbing at my eyes. A few ill-concealed chuckles came to me from the Guards behind, and the first stirrings of my old anger moved within me. It seemed I was to be subjected to the most humiliating form of degradation at the hands of Vorta's minions.

"Try to adjust your eyes gradually to the sun," suggested Drusea Mordan.

On my knees now like some beaten beast, I allowed a little light to filter through my fingers. It was a painfully slow process, but at last I was able to peer with streaming eyes. I was standing on a huge platform, high up above what must be the city of Karkesh—the only point on Ur where Zurjahn spacecraft could land. This must have been the Space Receiver Station, for at its corners I made out the observation towers of starship control. At periodic intervals around the edge of the huge platform were dotted Imperial Guards, standing stiffly at attention, their nine-foot javelins pointing at the cloudless, azure sky. Either Vorta delighted in showing his military strength, or he was being ridiculously cautious with me.

Behind the rigid Guards, I saw buildings and spires sprawling away in all directions for miles. Beyond the ugly city was a flat, indefinable plain—not unlike the barren Garganian terrain, though far lighter in color—stretching away to meet low-lying hills beyond. From all over the vast city, smoke curled up in wisps or billowed in black clouds, up into the clear vault above, while a gentle breeze wafted the unclear air across the landing platform. The city of a million sighs seemed an apt description of this place.

"On your feet," said Drusea Mordan, yanking on the chain. I did as bidden angrily. In front of me, a huge glass-like dome loomed up at the end of the glistening air-deck. I was now led into this. Ranks of Imperial Guards lined the walls of this building. I was taken up in lifts, along carpeted corridors, up stairways, and always the way was lined with the grim Guards. There were no hoverdiscs or signs of Zurjahn technology at its more advanced, but the décor of the lavish palace, for such it was, came close to the artistic beauty of the places I had known on the planet of my birth.

Drusea Mordan led me at length to some engraved doors. We entered and an involuntary gasp escaped me. We were in the highest part of the palace dome, the entire top of it forming one bright hall. Sunlight streamed in between the thick steel girders of its framework. Skies of that incredible blue were all around, easier for

171

me to look at now, seen clearly through the huge glass windows of the superstructure. Below me the dazzling floor stretched away for yard after yard, and with a start I realized that it was of pure gold, inlaid with fantastic silver patterns and weird hieroglyphics. Fifty yards ahead, in the center of the hall, a tall dais of bizarrely etched steps reached up a height of some twenty feet. High above it, in the apex of the dome, was suspended a pair of immense ivory horns, and I frowned at their significance.

Hundreds of Guards lined the perimeter of this monstrous hall, and two long columns of three rows each stretched on either side of the thick purple carpet which reached luxuriously to the foot of the empty dais. Mordan stood behind me and pushed me forward. I walked slowly to the column of glittering marble. Rare gems of all colors were embedded in its stonework. The chamber was Vorta's holy of holies and bespoke his power. I had brushed with him once, and though I had defeated him then, seeing this sea of military might, I began to think it may have been only a temporary victory. The last vestiges of hope were drifting away from me.

We reached the foot of the dais and stopped. Drusea Mordan bowed to the horns, though I could see no one else here other than the array of Guards. Then I became conscious of a faint whirring which seemed to be coming from inside the dais. An air of hushed expectancy hung over the assembled multitude. As I looked up, a strange throne rose into view on top of the dais. It was made of solid, shining gold in the shape of a goat's head, with two curling horns in its crest, and its entire surface sparkled incredibly with myriad twinkling diamonds, rubies, onyx, pearls, and other precious gemstones. Two huge opal eyes gazed sightlessly out across the hall, and below them was a gaping mouth. In this, on a carved seat of gold, sat the man who could only be Daras Vorta, Warden of Ur.

I was aghast. Never before had I seen such a hideous monstrosity of a man. His enormous, bloated body was dressed in colorful robes of shimmering silk, hung with bracelets, necklaces, and amulets. The thick, pudgy fingers were heavily ringed, and Vorta wore a scabbardless star-lance which gleamed like the sun itself, the haft studded with gems. Atop his completely bald head sat a scintillating diadem, encrusted with yet more valuable jewels. Amidst all the finery was his face, distorted in its ugliness, transformed by obesity. His bloodshot eyes goggled hugely like a madman's out of red-

172

rimmed sockets, and beneath those disturbing eyes, heavy bags hung, products I was sure of bestial practices and debauchery. All his features were lined, and his flat, squashed nose had two gaping nostrils, themselves creating an impression of skeletal eyes. Vorta's mouth was generously thick-lipped, the upper of which hung pendulous and bright red over the lower. Not only was he bald, but his face was hairless, and lines of weariness and grossness scoured the shining forehead. The whole unhealthy visage was a ghastly corpse-pale.

It was the first time I had seen Daras Vorta, and I looked upon this atrocious entity in disbelief. It could almost have been the malign entity of some foul conjuration from the blackest depths of man's mind, but it was no illusion. Vorta dipped those thick, tentacle-like fingers into a bowl of meat, sucking with greasy lips at the morsel he withdrew. His two saucer-like eyes mooned down at me hungrily. They were larger than the eyes of a Garganian.

Drusea Mordan fell to his knees and bent down to touch his head to the bottom step. The undignified act disgusted me as much as Vorta repulsed me. "Almighty Vorta, Lord of Ur. Your humblest and most unworthy servant, Drusea Mordan..." began the Captain.

"Yes, yes! No need for this superfluous introduction," came Vorta's voice. "I have eyes. Galad Sarian stands before me. You may quit my sight, Captain." The voice I had heard before, and still it filled me with deep loathing. It was a deep, sepulchral sound, giving me the uncanny feeling that some evil force was using Vorta as a medium. Mordan went deathly pale at the petulance in that booming tone and scuttled away quickly. Vorta paid his fleeing form no heed, his vile eyes fixing on me with relish.

"My dear, dear Galad Sarian," he said after a long pause. My name echoed back at me from the glass walls as though to emphasize my subjugation. I held myself straight, determined not to be the butt for his contempt. I closed my mind tightly to any mental probes he might send out, and assumed an affronted air of disdain. Vorta went on speaking, pausing only to wipe away a trickle of saliva from his chin.

"I have awaited this moment with such eager anticipation. Since you confounded my schemes on Gargan, I have wriggled like a spit worm, twisting and turning with the burden of waiting, day after day. I was foolish enough to underestimate your by no means trivial powers. However, it may now be safely assumed that your powers are of no consequence. You are most welcome here to my own little Empire." He spoke each word slowly, pronouncing every syllable clearly and with precise deliberation.

"You have much to answer for, Warden, both to the Dream Lords and the wretches of this world," I replied. The echoes had hardly died when a heavy blow fell behind my ears and stars of pain exploded inside my skull. I staggered forward, sprawling clumsily across the steps. I shook my head and heard Vorta's rumbling laughter above me. Despite my efforts, I was too dazed to rise.

"It is blasphemy to address the Warden unless told to do so!" shouted a voice behind me. I looked back to see the Guard who had struck me with his sword hilt. Now it was the point that menaced me.

"Enough! Let him up," ordered Vorta. "There will be time enough to teach him respect. Forgive my impetuous servants, Galad."

I glowered as the Guard backed off, and I managed to get shakily to my feet. "When the Dream Lords realize I am here, your ambitions will be concluded," I said bitterly.

Vorta laughed. "The Dream Lords want as little to do with Ur as is necessary. Their life on Zurjah and the evolution of the Zurjahn race is all they really think of. They are content to allow their trusted Warden to deal with the problems of Ur. I have a free rein here. Oh, true, they send ambassadors for occasional reports, but I am always ready for them. So you need not look to your father and his fellow Dream Lords for help. Here, you are my toy."

I said nothing. He was right. Ur had been as good as abandoned to him, an obvious embarrassment to the Zurjahn elitists.

"I will not play with you for long, though. As to your future, I shall put your mind at rest. You have only a few days to live."

I greeted this news with no show of outward emotion. I had not expected to outlive the hour.

"I shall commend your soul to the Great Horned Master. Shaitan, ruler of the dark worlds, will suck your soul to his breast for eternity. And soon it will be time for him to return to this plane of existence."

Vorta's expression was enraptured, though I did not pretend to understand his evil words. I knew the powers of his mind and his ability to blanket others with dreadful illusions, but I could see through them. He had tricked me only once—that terrifying moment

174

when I thought his black-souled priests had sacrificed Taria on a cold alter on Gargan. For that alone I would find a way of destroying him if it was at all possible.

"There is little more to be said," he went on, still gloating at me. "Ravas is safely with me once more. And now that I have seen you, I am content."

"Make no mistakes with me, Daras Vorta, for by the deeps of space, I will destroy you!"

Vorta hissed with mirth like some sibilant reptile. "Your threats are empty. You will go to the amusements and no doubt acquit yourself well, but you will die. Ravas Tarak will be watching. He will kill you even if you somehow defy the amusements."

"What amusements?"

"You will see. Brusiphylon?"

The man who had felled me stepped forward. Now that my head had cleared, I could see that he was a full General.

"Conduct Sarian to the prepared chamber."

"At once, Lord," said the General with a low bow. He gripped the chains that bound me and prepared to lead me away. Vorta pulled him up with a sharp cry.

"Stay! Before you leave, Sarian, I am curious. That bauble about your neck. Is this some token from your lady love on distant Zurjah?"

I glowered at Vorta. The golden medallion, stamped with a winged horse, had been given to me by Chalremor, the man whom the Barbarians called their prophet, and he that had told me the truth about Ur. I had worn the medallion since the day it had been given me.

"Ah, no. Wait," grinned Vorta. "My memory must be palling. On Gargan you were given a mind check by a psychometer. Wortan Heynar furnished me with some interesting results. You have, if I recall it rightly, a special sympathy with the Barbarians of Ur. And your medallion is a symbol of your beliefs. Very commendable." He sucked at one of his thick fingers. "Well, if the bauble is to recommend you to the rabble of this world, then you must wear it. Where you are bound, it will show them how powerless and doomed you are. Take him away!"

And so I was removed from the palace. Brusiphylon and his Guards took me deep down into the bowels of Karkesh. We passed

175

through two levels of the palace block and then through two levels of underground cells and cages, where thousands upon thousands of prisoners were entombed in the dim, stinking atmosphere. Surely the Dream Lord envoys must be unaware of the horrors here. Zurjah had drained the wastes of Ur as well as the other worlds of their criminals to stock this atrocious prison city, and the miserable wretches would be entombed here until merciful death claimed them. Some would be fortunate enough to go to the surface or to other worlds for slave labor.

As the lift sank lower, so did my spirits. Once past the lower levels we came to the pits which had been hewn out of solid rock. They housed the worst criminals that the Empire could provide, and the ventilation was terrible. No light penetrated the abysmal gloom, save for that of a few sputtering torches. I could hardly believe that men could subject their own kind to such misery.

I was marched through foul-smelling tunnels, and everywhere I looked I saw hopeless despair in the haggard faces of the poor devils behind bars who watched me pass. From near and far I heard hideous screams rending the choked air, and despite the acrid heat, I shuddered. Eventually we passed through a long, low tunnel and stopped at a small cavern at its dingy end. Here some thirty men were penned up in a low cell set in the rock wall. Outside the cage sat a gnarled, bronzed dwarf, almost asleep. A huge ring with dozens of keys hung from his thick leather belt, which was all the repugnant little beast wore. He bounded to his feet as we entered, squinting from watery eyes, and something about him sent a wave of nausea over me. He was deformed in an indefinable way—human but not quite so—and I later learned that he was a mutant, or a throwback from the time of the toxic war of so long ago.

"Another one for you, Yarkeron!" snapped the General, giving the peering form a kick.

The dwarf scowled and came over to me, and I saw that one eye was completely closed. "Uh. Fine lookin' specimen. Soon sweat the meat off him. What's he done? Don't look like no Barbarian to me," he cackled.

"This one is very special, so take good care of him, you festering rogue. He is to be saved for the personal attention of the Warden himself," said the General. The rugged men in the cage were looking at me with undisguised pity.

176

"Is he, indeed! Well, well. Special, eh? He may grace the Sacred Alter of the Ram, then! Ha! Ha! I will treat him most carefully, noble master. Nothing but the best for this pretty boy! Heh!" Yarkeron cawed, jumping up and down like one demented. A murmur came from behind the bars.

"Quiet, you devils!" screeched the dwarf, leaping at them with evident bravado for Brusiphylon's benefit. Several of the prisoners spat and Yarkeron leapt back. He turned to me.

"Manacle him to that wall, where I can keep my one eye on him," said the gargoyle-like creature, pointing to the rock face opposite from which two rusty chains hung. He shuffled over, taking out his rattling keys, and having decided on one, undid the dangling manacles. Brusiphylon motioned me to them. I slowly walked over, and the General snapped them on my wrists. My back was to the damp wall, and my raised arms hung from head height.

"Remember what I have said," Brusiphylon told the dwarf. "Vorta has a special purpose for this man."

The evil keeper cackled, showing toothless, blackened gums. "Fear not, master. None shall feed him but I."

Brusiphlon nodded, apparently satisfied, then turned and marched briskly up the passage, vanishing in the cloying gloom. Yarkeron hobbled closer and peered up into my face. As I looked into his own twisted visage and smelled his rancid breath, I wondered if he could see aught at all.

"And who are you, my fine fellow?" he asked haughtily.

I said nothing, and he became angered. The silent prisoners were pressed up against their bars, watching expectantly in the poor light.

"Have you no tongue, eh? Vorta cut it out? Or are you too fine a gentleman to talk to the likes of me? Well? Shaitan's Horns, but I'll make you talk!" he yelled, trying to force open my mouth with his grubby fingers. In disgust, I kicked out furiously, hitting him fully in the stomach, and with a piercing yelp he catapulted backward and crashed into a jutting rock outcrop. I fully expected him to renew his attack, but he limped off painfully down the passage, muttering curses and spitting. After that he treated me with more respect.

"Well struck, stranger," said a firm voice from opposite in the crowded cage. A tall well-built man of about forty was looking at me from brown, piercing eyes. He had a bushy black beard and thinning, wispy hair. His body, dressed in the filthy skin of some unidentifiable animal, had with stood the ravages of the cell exceedingly well, and the man looked like some proud warlord or warrior. The other men were all as filthy as the big man, still chuckling at Yarkeron's discomfort. There could be no mistaking them—they were true Barbarians.

"Old Yarkeron has been in need of such a kick for many a long day," the tall man said with a smile, and I nodded.

There was little light, but I could see that he was huge, with thick arms and rippling muscles. How he kept fit down here was a mystery.

"Such an unsightly little beast I have rarely seen," I said.

"Aye. But his heritage is not his fault. Since the war there have been many strange things seen on the surface. One is sickened by them but can feel pity for them also. My name is Thuran, stranger. May I ask yours, and from what part of the world are you? You have the face of a southerner, from what I can make out."

The giant exuded warmth and seemed to inspire confidence in his fellows by merely being with them. I was certain that I could trust him, but I would have to be tactful.

"I am called Galad Sarian, and I was born not on your world, but on Zurjah."

"Zurjah!" Thuran's face clouded and there were murmurs at his shoulder. "You are a Zurk," he said coldly, and in that one word was more hatred and distaste than in any other I had heard spoken.

"I am the sworn enemy of those who have imprisoned you and those who chastise you," I told him, but his frown deepened, and he did not seem satisfied with my answer.

"All Zurks are cursed among us!" he replied bitterly.

"Wait!" a voice called from among the men. One of them was desperately pushing himself through the others in a rough attempt to get to the bars. Grudgingly the men parted. The man was badly scarred and absolutely filthy; his hair and beard were caked with filth. His eyes widened in the flickering torch glow as he saw me.

"I have heard rumors on the surface," he began. "Words have been whispered among the slaves. You all know I have come down here of late," sent the bent figure. The others assented. "Up there I heard from a man who had been on Gargan half a year gone, maybe less—time means nothing to a slave. The man spoke of other slaves on Gargan who had talked to one of us called Tegara Sahdi. Sahdi worked the sewers on Gargan, but by luck he broke free once. His Zurk masters would have killed him, but a youth saved him. Sahdi swore to his friends that the youth was the One who would be sent by the Wise One. He would be Chalremor's staff."

"What are you saying?" growled Thuran.

"All I am saying is that it was believed on Gargan that the Chosen One was there. His words to Tegara Sahdi were encouraging. And he wore the medallion with the winged horse."

"I have heard this tale," commented a voice.

"And look," said the first, with an air of reverence and humility. "The man before us wears a medallion."

"Who are you?" Thuran demanded of me, his tone still hostile.

"I told you I have come from Zurjah. And your friend on Gargan did not lie. I was there. I am from Chalremor," I said as calmly as I could, and my words had a devastating effect on the prisoners. An excited cry broke from all of them save Thuran. He alone was skeptical.

"He shall be cast out from the very camp of thine enemies," someone muttered in the shadows. The responsibilities that Chalremor had once put upon my shoulders had been suddenly thrust upon me and at a time when I was most helpless. What did these men expect of me? Did they think me some god, some worker of miracles?

"Can you prove that you are from the Wise One?" said Thuran. The medallion was in shadow.

"You," I said to the man who had spoken of Tegara. "You said my words to Tegara Sahdi were encouraging. Did you learn what I said to him?"

"Why, yes, you..."

"I told him that those on Ur were not forgotten."

The man looked to Thuran, his mouth slack.

"Well?" said the huge warrior.

"That is the very thing Tegara passed on."

Another murmur broke out, and much to my surprise, the men began to drop to their knees.

"He is young, as the prophet foresaw," said one.

"If this be true," said Thuran, lowering his voice, "and you are the Chosen of Chalremor, then the world will rejoice. Are you our savior?"

I felt myself on the horns of a dilemma, for how could I claim to be a savior, when I had but a few days to live? Yet if I denied it, the last dreams, the last hopes of these desperate people would shatter. I thought of the cunning of Vorta—he must have foreseen this confrontation. My hate welled up anew and I gripped the chains that held me.

"Yes, Thuran! I come from Zurjah, the heart of this cankered Empire. And though the blackest Gods of the nine worlds face us, we will tear them down. But for now, you must pretend not to know my identity. Should it be known among the Zurks and to that fiend, Vorta, all our hopes would be as the dust."

"The Lion will roar loudly when this news reaches him," said Thuran. He seemed to have accepted me, though not as completely as his fellows.

"I was told by Chalremor, my guide in all things, to seek the Lion. What can you tell me of this?" Well did I remember Chalremor's enigmatic parting comment.

"You do not know who the Lion is?" said Thuran, and I could see the surprise on his face. I could not blame him for being wary.

"Chalremor was careful what he told me and what he left as mystery, for the Zurks have powers to drain a man's mind. I was told to look for the Lion, no more. You know of it?" There was an uncomfortable pause, as though I had said something amiss.

"All men have heard of the Lion. The Warlord of the Barbarians. I know him personally, for I serve as General in his army. Or did, until I was taken," said Thuran coldly. "That is by and by. There are those among our enemies who know the name Lion, too—those that are alive."

A whoop of pleasure went up at this and I peered anxiously up the passage to see that Yarkeron did not come scuttling back to investigate. But he did not come. Now I must do what I could to reassure the men that I was not a Zurk spy. Already I had discarded the word Zurjahn for its more scathing form, Zurk. And though I had been condemned by Vorta, it had become vital that I convince these men of my belief in their cause. Thuran was the most doubtful, but as I began to speak more of Chalremor and of Zurjah where he was imprisoned, the big man warmed to me.

"Then you will take me to the Lion, should we break free of this cesspool?" I asked him at last.

"With all haste," he nodded. "But to escape? There is nowhere more dismal and more guarded than Karkesh."

"We will escape," I promised him and the Barbarians held themselves up, nodding and almost believing that impossible promise. I cursed inwardly. To be here on Ur, so close to the people that I knew so much about, yet to be chained at the mercy of Daras Vorta. I allowed my mind to drift to Taria and the painful thought that she would not even know that I had died, if Vorta had me erased. Although it would have been blasphemous to say it, even now I would have gladly given up my Dream Lord heritage to Ravas Tarak for one last meeting with her. Yet I was in no position to make such a demand.

CHAPTER II
Carnage in the Arena

In the bowels of Karkesh there is only the half-light from torch-glow and the acrid stench of smoke and incinerated humanity. Penned like animals, it was small wonder that the Barbarian prisoners had come to the bitter end of their hopes. My own hopes were minimal. I slowly won the respect of Thuran, but he knew our situation was impossible. From the men in the cage I learned that we were all to die in a series of episodes called the amusements. Apparently Daras Vorta held these amusements at certain times in his necromantic calendar to sate the appetites of his Brotherhood and to cut down the number of prisoners that swelled the cells. I had heard of some of Vorta's bestial atrocities when I had been on Gargan, so I expected the worst kind of treatment.

The day came when we were to face the amusements. A detachment of Guards arrived and roughly bundled the men into the corridor, chaining them all together and prodding them forward with sharp javelins. I was released and escorted with them. We wound our way through the pits and out into a labyrinthine sequence of corridors until our escort halted us. We were then pushed into a small, bare chamber, and the door slid shut behind us, cutting us off from the Guards. Then a panel in one of the walls opened to reveal an assortment of swords, shields, clubs, knives and spears.

"What manner of game are they playing?" muttered one of the

Barbarians, eyeing the weapons warily.

"This is the way of the amusements," said Thuran. "We are to select our weapons. Then we must face whatever they have prepared for us."

We had little choice. If we were to die, then let it be with a sword or a weapon in our hands. Silently we chose. Soon afterward another door slid open, revealing a dark corridor. There came a faint sound, like a roaring or rushing of wind.

"Well," said Thuran, "there is but one way out of here now. Through yon passage. The gods know what lies beyond, but we'll receive no mercy by standing here."

"Aye," returned another. "Let us show these Zurks what it is to die like men."

Then we crept stealthily along the corridor. Behind us the door slid shut and for a moment we were in complete darkness. My fingers tightened around the haft of the rusty sword I had chosen. Ahead of us a tall door hummed wide, and for a moment the light dazzled us. But we moved through into its glare. I was astonished at what I saw. For here was a gigantic chamber, another huge dome with glass superstructure, encircled by a high wall of smooth, metal plates. Above this wall in a circle were tier upon tier of milling people, and it was the sound of their cheering and yelling that we had heard from within.

We moved dazedly out into the dust of the arena, and I could see scattered carcasses of horses, men, and strange beasts. The crows caught sight of us and gave a roaring hurrah of encouragement. So these were the amusements of Daras Vorta—a primitive arena where the rites of ancient history were brought to terrifying reality. The Barbarians bore the sight of it imperturbably, and I marveled at their coolness.

I looked up at the howling multitudes. There were bright colors and gaudy flags up there; banners and pennants fluttered limply in the breeze of the ventilators, and trumpets blared discordantly from all areas. The arena was perhaps two hundred yards across, and at one end a huge gate opened into it, while opposite us loomed a dark, black tunnel, about twenty feet high. From its depths came a hideous roar, which was echoed and drowned by the seething crowds above us. My eyes went from the trappings of a regal balcony, thronged with what looked like nobles and generals, to the tunnel.

My mind must have been vulnerable in that moment, for a presence flashed inside me. I had put up a mind shield from the moment Vorta had taken me, but in this instant I had relaxed it, and Vorta was quick to mind speak. His serpentine tones hissed inside my head and my companions sensed me stiffen, though they could not hear the evil one.

"Look your last on life, Galad Sarian," Vorta mocked. "Look around you and see the servants of the Goat. My people now. No longer submissive to the soft ways of your Dream Lord lieges. No longer fawning to the weak ways of the Empire. Look around you and see a new breed of men—men who lust for power, physical, sensual, *actual*. Men who gladly drink from the fountain of the Goat and Shaitan, its glorious master. His time has come. Your feeble friend Chalremor was right when he told you of the cosmic circle that knits. Shaitan has come again, and soon the last of his enemies will be flung down. So go to your doom knowing who is master now!"

The voice was gone as quickly as it had come, and I put up the mind shield again. I looked at the minions of the Goat. Chalremor had told me that the Dream Lords would face their greatest test, and he had been right. My thoughts were shattered by Gastar, a muscular Barbarian beside me. He gripped my arm and pointed to the tunnel.

"An ibathene!" he cried despondently.

I saw the dark of the tunnel moving, and from its murky depths, a weird creature came into view. I had never dreamed such a monstrosity could have existed. It came into the light and gave vent to a hideous screech. If this was another of Vorta's illusions, I would soon know. But it was real enough. It was some species of giant lizard, scaly with four huge paws armed with six claws each, and changing in hue as I watched from a dull green to yellow, orange, then dark maroon. The most amazing part of this gruesome beast was its armored head, which consisted mainly of a cavernous mouth filled with row upon row of pointed yellow teeth. At first I thought the beast had a ruff, but saw after a moment that it was made of solid bone. The creature had only one eye and this dangled obscenely from a stalk in the center of its forehead. As the beast slithered forward on its great white belly, it swung its twenty-foot tail and slammed it with a resounding clang into the side of the tunnel. The crowd howled in delight.

"What in creation is this monster?" I breathed.

Gastar wielded his sword and never took his eyes from the lumbering colossus before us.

"Ibathene. A giant lizard from the swamps beyond the Poison River. How they have captured it I cannot imagine. Since the war, many such horrors have reared up from the worst regions."

"We are doomed," said Thuran grimly. "But we will show the Zurk scum that we are not afraid."

The ibathene bellowed as we rallied to Thuran. The grotesque eye of the beast swung in our direction and stared fixedly at us. All down its back the webbed spines quivered, then with another ear-shattering shriek it lumbered ponderously but with deliberation toward us. We backed off fearfully, though the beast drew inescapably closer.

"Beware its tongue, sire!" warned Thuran, but almost as he spoke, the unusually long, red tongue came shooting out of that gaping mouth, uncurling as it split the air, and wrapped itself wetly around an unfortunate Barbarian. He screamed once, dragged toward the awful mouth. I was jarred from inactivity by the horror of the situation and at once sent a bolt of mental energy at the beast's nerve center. Vorta must have anticipated that I would try my Dream Lord powers, for he put up a mental shield so that my energy was deflected and was of no avail. The struggling warrior was whipped off his feet, pulled to the mouth of the beast, pulped by the constricting tongue and ground mercilessly by those infinite teeth. The crowd howled with delight, but we stood rooted, sickened by it.

"We must act swiftly!" I cried, snatching the initiative from the bemused Thuran. "Gastar! Take half the men and cover the right flank of the beast. Thuran and I will take the left. We must outmaneuver it and keep away from its mouth."

"Beware its tail, then!" Gastar shouted back.

And so we attempted to encircle the beast while it roared, and shook its many spines. Tongel, one of the youngest of us, ran recklessly forward and cast a spear at its eye, but with uncanny speed the stalk swung aside, and the missile bounced harmlessly off the armored collar. Then with one lightning movement, the curious reptile snatched up the lad in one of its terrible foreclaws and fed him whole into its enormous mouth. Its fetid breath came over us in nauseating waves as we tried desperately to run to its rear.

Gastar and his followers had rushed to its right flank, but the huge creature had seen them, and it lurched around, darting out its whip-like tongue. Two more of our luckless number were reduced, and Gastar was forced back under the shadow of the arena walls. The roar of the lusting crowd swelled while the beast finished devouring the helpless, thrashing men. It might have been sated by its grisly meal, but I sensed Vorta's mind stinging the beast to a blind rage. It advanced again, sweeping up six more men in its cruel claws, lowering its head hungrily to rend them. As it did so, brave Gastar and his remaining men charged forward hopefully, throwing spears, clubs, even swords in a vain attempt to damage that single eye. How could we hope to stop such a creature?

"Attack it!" I shouted above the deafening din, and before Thuran and the others knew what I intended, I had sprinted at the ibathene, avoiding its flicking tail, and launched myself recklessly at its back. I had formed an insane plan, but no matter how hopeless it was, it had to be tried. In the meantime, Gastar's men were all either dead or had been badly mauled, while somehow that gallant warrior had reached the lowered head and leapt on to the beast's nose. I stood shakily on the spiny back, but for a moment the beast had not noticed me. I could hardly keep my balance as it shook its head from side to side. Gastar was still hanging on miraculously to its flaring nose, and somehow he managed to swing his weapon, intending to slice into that extraordinarily agile eye-stalk. As the beast roared and twisted, Gastar struck, but before the blade could hit home, he was tossed high up into the air.

I fell across one horny shoulder as it happened, watching helplessly as the tumbling Gastar fell in a twisted jumble into the very jaws of the beast. With a sickening crunch those jaws closed, and the bleeding corpse was flung impassively aside. By chance Gastar's sword bounced down the scales of the ibathene's back to where I lay, and in a flash I reached out and snatched it up. Below me, Thuran and the remainder of the men gazed hopelessly on as I began the precarious ascent of the ibathene's pulsing neck. Sensing me at last, the beast began to try and shake me loose, but I took a firmer grip on its tough, plated scales.

"Hold on, by all the Powers!" yelled Thuran from the ground. The men were dodging about in the flying sand as the creature's claws churned up the arena floor. The crowd was ecstatic, eager for more blood. Vaguely I saw one of the Barbarians make a wild run at the beast with a javelin. He got right under those sharp foreclaws, for so intent was the beast on dislodging me that it had not seen him. The man drove the javelin between its legs, deep into the soft underbelly, then drew a curved sword from his belt. With an ear-splitting shriek the beast bent its head, lifted one bloody paw, and brought it smashing down on the daring but foolhardy man.

While the beast tore at the javelin with its mouth, I climbed up to its forehead between the ears, hanging tightly to the bucking armor neck plates. The crazed ibathene then temporarily forgot about the embedded javelin and me and turned to the returning handful of men, who were again trying to outflank it. In turning, the beast had brought its long tail up against the arena wall and used it like a battering ram, hammering the wall repeatedly. Metal sheets were buckling and twisting away from the wall, and beneath them stone slabs and walls of earth were splintering and collapsing with a sound like thunder, showering the squealing crowd with chunks of flying debris.

Swaying dangerously, I firmly gripped a scaled joint between two plates and lifted the sword high. Then I dug it down as hard as I could, to a depth of three feet between the beast's plates. The creature screamed louder than before and began thrashing about convulsively, contorting itself into the most fantastic shapes. Still I hung on, though my tired arms felt as though they were slowly being wrenched from their protesting sockets.

That thick, swirling tail was creating havoc with the wall. It lashed madly at the tortured metal as though it were the source of the beast's pain, and the wall was collapsing into fragments under the ruthless onslaught. Pandemonium had broken out among the adjacent spectators as a whole section of the crowd fell screaming into the bedlam of the arena. Almost at once the former spectators were trampled to death by the rampaging, pain-wracked ibathene. I wrapped my left arm around the protruding sword haft, gripping the handle tightly. I wanted to deal one last blow before I too was killed. Steadying myself as best I could, I wrenched out the blade and swung it. With an almighty lunge I brought it down upon the dodging eye, and the beast began shrieking hideously as I rained down blows that tore into the living flesh and organ.

The mighty head lowered as I struck repeatedly for all I was worth, drawing as I did on unknown resources of energy. Behind me the swinging tail still smashed the disintegrating wall of the arena to rubble, sending scores of Karkeshians tumbling to their bloody deaths. A terrified melee of people were fighting each other in an attempt to escape, while hundreds lay maimed and dead below. Thick clouds of dust were billowing out and blanketing almost the entire inner dome. Wearily I managed to bring down one last blow at the gore-soaked, sticky eye-stalk before my receding strength was finally drained. As the beast roared and shook in agony, I slipped from my perch and fell backward, narrowly missing those sharp spines. I rolled down the arching back and came to rest on the huge tail that had so pulverized the walls. One rapid jerk of it sent me sailing across the scattered debris that now filled this side of the arena. I landed with a jarring crunch amidst a pile of broken stonework.

Bruised, cut and ripped, I gasped for breath, completely exhausted. Looking up through misty, sweat-filled eyes, I saw Thuran lying dead, not twenty feet away. The whole incident had been so pointless. One last look showed me that they were all dead. I had known them but a short time, but already I thought of them as brothers—as close to me as any men I had known. I would have gladly made a home among them. Now only blood-soaked bodies lay around me, far and near. Some writhed in the last spasms of agony, some half protruded from fallen rock, others lay mangled and tramped. Vorta had had his way. But the ibathene was dying, that much at least we had accomplished. My head sagged in the dirt. I coughed through dusty layers of pain and sank into unconsciousness.

*

I awoke in a pool of agony. My whole body ached and throbbed as I lay in the choking dust. It was pitch black around me. Night? My mind whirled. I still lay in the arena, and the shadows of the dead were all around me. But why had I not been taken to Vorta so that he could laugh over my corpse before disposing of it? I thought of the bedlam in the arena as the ibathene, itself now a huge, cold bulk nearby, had died. Vorta must have thought me dead. I had been unconscious for hours. My mind would have been blank all that time. Perhaps the arena was being avoided for a time, until the beast's death had been confirmed. I got to unsteady feet and made for the shelter of its carcass. My movements would have to be quick. I had no idea how I could slip away from the carnage, and it struck me that Vorta could pick up my corpse at his leisure. Here in the heart of his citadel I was as much a prisoner as I had ever been.

Hardly had I stationed myself behind the outstretched claw of the ibathene when strong arms locked around my throat. I cursed for being so careless, fighting for breath.

"Galad!" gasped my attacker, releasing me at once.

I gasped myself, for it was Thuran, whom I thought dead. I gripped his arm.

"Thuran, and alive, by the stars!"

"The Gods indeed protected you," he whispered. "But we are not safe yet. I have watched the arena for two hours. The Zurks are taking away the dead. See! They come."

He pointed to the far end of the arena, where glowbulbs danced in the air. Beneath them a party of Guards was walking into the dark arena. There were less than a dozen.

"We must arm ourselves," I whispered.

"We cannot fight them without rousing others. Somehow we must take their tunics. You see this huge monster behind us? Aye, well it will be taken out into the desert and left for the vultures. A party of slaves will heave it into a cart and drag it forth."

"How do you know this?" I asked him.

"I heard two of the Zurks. They walked amidst the dead, searching for your body. Vorta has told them to bring it before him. But the Gods are with us, for the Zurks are in no hurry. They will not look again until daybreak. By then we will be gone."

I grinned in the faint glow. Voices sounded close at hand. Then two officers came into view around the shoulder of the dead ibathene. Thuran and I drew back into the darkness.

"Ho, Valkin, there was a slaying for you! Were you in the stands today? By the Horns, it was a slaying!" said one of the shadowed forms.

"Aye, and a hundred or more of our numbers buried withal. The Warden sat as one bloated with pleasure."

Thuran and I watched as the two Guards moved closer, listening to them discussing ways and means of moving the bulk behind us. Then, swift as light, Thuran leapt out on the first, his fists ramming into his face. I was upon the other, my knee in his back, arms about his neck. With a jerk I snapped his spine and let his corpse sink to the ground. I whipped out his sword and plunged it between the shoulder-blades of Thuran's struggling opponent.

"Quickly, Galad. Change clothes before we are discovered."

Thuran dragged his victim deeper into the shadows, and in moments we had dressed ourselves of the regalia of two Imperial Guards. We waited in silence for sounds of the other Guards. Presently a droning sound announced the arrival of a cart at the gates. It was a simple, wheeled contrivance, and I wondered why Vorta did not employ an aerolift or a number of hovertrucks. I soon saw why, for the cart was to be drawn by a party of slaves. I scowled when I saw how they were treated. The Warden missed no opportunity to punish or torment them.

For the next hour my heart beat heavily against my ribcage as Thuran and I, posing as Guards in the burial detail, helped load the massive carcass of the ibathene up on to the cart. Our officer's uniforms impressed the other Guards, and in the dim light of the glowglobes our faces were not scrutinized. The Zurjahns were as anxious to get away from the arena and back into bed as Thuran and I were to escape. Eventually the cart rolled forward, with Thuran and I applying whips to the belabored slaves. Our faces were grim, but it had to be done convincingly. The procession struggled painfully through the empty streets of the dirty city. It was incredibly large. Soot and grime stained its foreboding walls and towers, which clustered together tightly, showing filthy, garbage-strewn alleys and back streets. An air of filth and intense evil hung over the whole place like a black miasma.

We came at last to the gates, and again I felt a pang of fear. There was an inspection. Up on the ramparts a score of javelins stood out against the night sky. Smoldering braziers poured thicker fumes of darkness into the heavens as swords clanked in the gateway. Thuran cracked his whip and yelled out at the men below us.

"Ho! Open yon gates, by Shaitan! Must I sleep in the streets to please you? Come, I have a wife abed in the city. Let this rabble through."

There were grumbling answers in the dark, and at last the inspection appeared to be over. The gates creaked open and the desert lay before us.

"Mind you bring them all back!" called a voice in the battlements and a chorus of laughter rang around the begrimed walls.

"Aye, I'll be back," Thuran muttered under his breath. "And next time I'll not be short of friends."

CHAPTER III
Death in the Cursed Forest

The struggling prisoners labored sadly under the cracking whips of the Imperial Guards of Karkesh, and the huge cart bearing the dead ibathene rumbled out into the gloomy desert. Once the burden was well clear of the city, Thuran and I dropped silently from our perch, rolling into a gully.

"The Guards will have the carcass taken well out into the desert. Come, let us vanish before they know we are gone," urged Thuran, and we made our way down the crumbling gully, which I gathered was a dried up stream bed. We picked our way in and out of the jutting rocks, and the sounds of the rolling wheels grew softer and softer. Thuran knew the terrain intimately, even in the dark. He had told me there were many miles to go.

We were to make for the lair of the Lion, the Warlord whom I had heard so little about. Thuran had been reluctant to say too much to me while we had been incarcerated, but now that we had fought in the arena together, he became more trusting and more talkative. I learned more about this persecuted world as we sped into the night. Thuran was a General in the collective armies of the Lion, and it had been whilst raiding a northern satellite of Karkesh, Pyron, that he and Gastar had been taken. Thuran had lost all his men in the raid and felt very bitter about it—doubly so now that Gastar, his closest friend, was dead. But my appearance, together with our miraculous escape, had done much for his spirits. On more than one occasion he made reference to the Horsemen, and my mind went back to my first confrontation with Chalremor and the dreams of my youth when the four grim horsemen rode.

As the night wore on, we fell silent, conserving our energy beneath the bright eye of the moon as we threaded our way through gullies and rills. The landscape was bare and dry, and I learned that most of Ur was charred and blackened—an inhospitable desolation where life had been horribly changed and mutated by the war of so long ago. There were vast areas where no living things could venture and bizarre forests where parodies of life vied for control, ghastly vegetables and animals alike waging perpetual battle. The rivers were mostly poison, the lakes full of black mire, and swamps abounded. All life forms were tainted with the curse of the war. Even so, Thuran and the Barbarians regarded the Zurks as the worst of their enemies.

We fled into the desert, skirting the fringe of one of the dreadful wastes. Thuran drove me on remorselessly. By day the sun was scorching, and my skin dried and my throat seized up with dust. Waterholes were scarce and not always usable. Karkesh we left far behind, but I began to doubt my own ability to go on much further. Yet Thuran had said we must make for the north and for the Forlorn Mountains where we would find the citadel of the Lion—the one place where a Barbarian would be safe. The fabled City of Light it was called, for the Barbarians worshiped light. I could understand that in view of the dark powers that Vorta courted.

Many times on that dreadful journey across the dry landscape, Thuran was forced to carry me and revive me when all seemed lost. Somehow I clung to life as hour after hour passed murderously by, agonizingly slowly, and still the relentless sun burned down from the pure blue and cloudless heavens. Vultures wheeled ever above us, making no sound, hoping for our deaths. We rested at intervals amongst the stones, coughing and gasping. The air was the first free air I had taken and thus the fullest and sweetest I had ever breathed.

At last, after days of weary travel, we topped a ridge, and far below, swathed in a white envelope of mist, was the incredible sight that Thuran named the Cursed Forest of Amazar. It stretched as far as the eye could see to the east and north east, being lost in the steaming vapors that clung cloak-like above it. Thuran pointed to it with a satisfied nod, but the prospects of entering such an eerie place daunted me. I had come to Ur, the homeworld, only to find a planet more alien to man's ways than I could have foreseen.

As we descended the barren slope and made for the forest, the air became thankfully cooler, though my apprehensions grew. The trees were incredible to behold as they rustled in the rising steam. Some were tall and thin, others were sixty feet thick, while more were willowy and covered in multi-colored fungi. Huge green leaves and dusty toadstools sprouted upward into the treetops, and bright, spiky flowers of every conceivable color swayed slowly in the silent wind, like moody ghosts. It was getting ominously dark as we entered the fascinating entanglements of thorns, ferns, vines, creepers, and bright, dripping blooms. I heard distant roars, but Thuran did not seem to take any notice. The place was pervaded with hidden evil.

On our journey over the desert we had several times seen dust clouds as Zurk riders must have sought us, but now Thuran assured me we would not be followed. Only those who knew the forest intimately would dare set foot in it.

"Keep close to me, Galad. Some of these plants are carnivorous. You may find a vine entwining itself around you, so draw your sword and be ready to hack. A barbed leaf might snap its sharp jaws at you, and other plants may close around your feet like hungry rats. See? Those yellow monstrosities are covered with a pasty substance. Once stuck on that, you will never tear free," Thuran warned, pointing to a bushy plants with several stems, on top of which grew gaudy yellow flowers.

We chopped our way through the weird underbrush, our bodies soaked in condensing steam. Underfoot there were soggy mosses and stagnant, weed-grown pools, and with horror I saw that some of the plants actually retreated away from our swords. Thuran drove his blade into a huge funnel-shaped purple flower, whose tentacles had sought to enmesh him and it *screamed* as sickly green sap oozed from the gaping wound. As the tentacles waved and became limp, Thuran wiped his blade in a handful of blue grass.

I had never before seen vegetation of such hues, but here it grew in frenzied profusion. In fact, everything grew so rankly that some of the carnivorous plants fought each other in gruesome, misty tableaux. High up above, in the entangled vines and mildewed branches, vague forms shrieked noisily in the misty light, but Thuran payed them no heed. The vegetable life appeared to be a far greater hazard than the animal. We passed through two gigantic cabbage-like growths, which guarded the way like monolithic titans, and Thuran cut some round, red-skinned fruits from a swaying bough beyond.

"These will have to do for our night's meal, though it will be a change from desert rodents. And there is our bed for the night—a *fanphal* tree," he said, pointing.

I looked up at the tall moss-grown trunk. It had no branches, but hundreds of spiky projections, some of which were broken off. On its top a collection of thick, maroon leaves stretched for yards into the soaking twilight. The spikes made a natural ladder and soon we were among the cushion-like leaves, in the midst of which grew an orange bloom. My bones ached and my head rang with the effort of our journey, but I felt able to relax for a short while. I ate of the fruits Thuran had given me and shortly after, with night closing in rapidly, fell asleep.

*

The following day, after a night without incident in which I restored some of my waning energy, we pressed on into the forest, bound for a tree village called Vendl in which Thuran was known. We stopped in a clearing, and Thuran procured more fruit. He sliced the top off one colorful specimen and bade me drink. I was surprised by the sweetness of the liquid. We had started on our way again when Thuran stopped abruptly, listening intently.

"What is it?" I asked him.

"It has gone strangely silent. Normally the forest is a perpetual hive of sound. Something is amiss."

Leaves stirred softly in the waking sunlight. We peered all around the grassy glade but saw nothing. Then without warning, a piercing shriek rent the silence asunder and I looked with alarm on the unsightly figure that swung toward us on a long vine. In its teeth was gripped one of the four-foot *fanphal* spikes, and I could not help but gape at the abnormally uncouth man, if man it was, that bore down upon us.

"Mutant!" cried Thuran, lifting his sword. The creature landed only feet away, snarling as it snatched at its crude weapon. Its eyes blazed maniacally, and I saw that they swiveled about independently of themselves in their wrinkled sockets. Before I could retreat, the beast attacked. It stood on all fours to a height of four feet. It had thick, stocky legs and bloated, muscular arms, but all four limbs were much shorter than a normal man's. It had seven fingers on each hand, and six toes to each foot. The beast was entirely hairless, but had a strange red comb running along the top of its head.

Thuran dodged its flaying stroke and made a quick thrust. His sword sliced into the warty skin, drawing thick, oily blood, while the creature gave vent to an awful scream. It swung wildly at me, and I brought my sword down heavily onto its hunched shoulder, digging deep into that stinking hide. Thuran had recovered his balance, and now he used both hands to chop down hard into the back of its skull with his sword, cleaving it apart to the shoulder blades. The thing collapsed, dying at once, as a foul smelling substance gushed from its fatal wound.

"There will be more of these abominations," said Thuran, leaving that malformed body behind as we crossed the glade. Sure enough, we had not gone far when we heard sounds of pursuit crashing through the undergrowth behind us. A pack of mutant men had got our scent and were howling like ravenous wolves. We ran carelessly through the forest, dashing across another small clearing. With no warning, Thuran fell headlong into the swampy reeds, tripped by a twisted creeper. I hacked at the accursed plant as it began entwining itself slowly around my dazed companion's leg, and it recoiled at once.

However, it was too late to get away, for the mutants were upon us. They stood at the edge of the glade, not thirty yards behind, screaming and howling madly. Such a formidable band of ghouls is hard to picture. They were entirely hairless and naked, and their scrawny bodies were covered in boils and sores, scarred horribly. They swung their assorted weapons meaningfully—clubs, gnarled branches, thick roots and *fanphal* spikes—drooling and slavering like demons from hell itself. Standing there on twisted, repulsive legs, dancing wildly, they worked themselves into a frenzy, preparing to charge, while I stood over Thuran, my sword ready. I would kill many before they overcame us, I avowed. Then with more horrible screams they came at us.

I dealt the ugly, grotesque leader a sweeping blow which almost took off his head, drenching myself in sticky gore, and booted one dwarf hard in the groin. He rolled backward, knocking over some of his deformed fellows and balking others. Those that fell into the reeds at the side of the clearing found themselves under attack from the tentacles and jaws of the jungle as they snapped and swung in the damp air. Thuran had staggered to his feet, mud soaking his tunic, his temple gashed, but he prepared for the onslaught.

As the ferocious mutants came on in force, we fought back to back, hacking and slicing, dealing out death on all sides to the horrific brutes. Thuran was a mighty fighter, and he severed arms and legs and split skulls with all the deadly verve of a natural warrior. Body after body piled up around us as the mutants came on, their blood-lust aroused by the flowing gore of their fellows. Then behind me I heard Thuran grunt, and he fell sideways into the heaped dead and lay still. Swinging my blade in great, circular arcs, I whirled around, laying three triumphant faces bare to the bone. One bent beast tried to bring his club down on Thuran's bleeding head, but I took its arm off at the elbow, and the creature rolled into the swamp screaming. All around me the mutants were fighting the incredible carnivorous plants, which were now thrusting into the sweltering grove in alarming numbers, as though summoned by the blood. The whole jungle seemed to have gone mad.

I was fighting now out of sheer desperation, turning this way and that like a cornered rat, standing unsteadily over the unconscious Thuran, and all seemed lost, for there were far too many assailants for me. I buried my blade into another mutant heart, and before I could withdraw it, another one of them lifted a twisted branch and prepared for a blow which would inevitably brain me. I faced death with the knowledge that this time there would be no reprisal, Then, to my surprise, an arrow appeared in the breast of my assailant, and with a soundless glare, he toppled into the mire. All around me, mutant after mutant began to fall prone, until only a few remained, snarling and growling at the hail of arrows preparing to meet any new attackers. Utterly spent, I dug my blade into the hill of carnage, resting my arms on its haft. The glade was choked with arrow-filled corpses and presently I heard cries from the trees beyond.

I gazed through stinging eyes as sweat bathed my whole body, knowing that I had fought my last that day. The mutants had turned to meet the new source of attack, and it amazed me that they did not flee. Their brains must have been as stunted as they. Bursting out from the trees with whoops and yells came a swarthy, mounted band of men, their skins painted in greens and browns to blend with the forest. They fired their arrows with deadly accuracy into the ranks of the charging mutants. At their head rode an immense warrior, swinging a huge, double edged ax above his long, black mane. It was a wonder that his horse could support such a vast bulk. With a great shout, the man bore down on the leading half-man, scattering heads like flowers as he passed.

Up in the trees there were winged shapes, little leathery creatures that would swoop down to suck at the blood of the fallen. These *vampas,* as Thuran had called them, were shrieking down, maddened by the noise and the blood, and the archers laughed grimly as they shot them down, again with uncanny accuracy. Within moments the band of riders had completed the slaughter, emptying the air of *vampas*, killing the last mutant, and cutting now at the seething plants. Hardly able to stand, I bent down and examined Thuran's head. He was badly bruised, but still lived. I looked up to see the eagle-eyed warrior glaring angrily down, and I forced myself to my feet amidst the carnage, leaning on my sword haft.

"We owe you our lives," I panted. The gaudy hues daubed on the chest of the warrior swelled as he laughed, a deep, booming sound like thunder.

"Indeed you do, Zurk. But when we have done with you, you will wish the mutants had finished you!" he bellowed, and his men laughed with him. "I know not what two Zurk bastards do in my forest, but I thank the Powers for delivering you into my hands."

With sagging shoulders I pulled my sword free of the corpse-strewn mud. It came away with a dull sucking sound.

"Let us hang them up for the *vampas*, Ool," suggested one of the archers. The big man swung his ax across his shoulder and chuckled.

"There will be time enough for sport when we return to Vendl. First we will hear what they are doing in this place. No Zurk dares Amazar's hell unless for good reason."

"You are from Vendl?" I interrupted.

The giant's smile faded, and he frowned. He leaned forward. "I am."

"Then it is you we seek."

"Indeed?"

"Yes. Do you know this man?" I said, pointing to the senseless Thuran.

Very slowly the giant dismounted, eyeing me warily, and his men fitted arrows to their strings, fearing an attack. I stood well away as Ool turned Thuran's face toward him with the beautifully engraved ax handle. He stared down contemptuously at the Zurjahn uniform for a moment, then gasped.

"By the Sacred City! My eyes lie to me! It is Thuran! Why, the Zurks took him months since!" he said in disbelief.

"We garbed ourselves in Zurk blue to escape, and have crossed

196

the desert to find you," I explained.

Ool knelt by Thuran's side and turned to his men. "There'll be no more killing here. This is Thuran, first warrior to the Warlord. The Gods are smiling upon us once more!" At this a great roar came from their throats, and they leapt from their mounts and splashed forward, clustering around us to confirm the news.

"And who, friend, might you be?" Ool asked.

"My name is Galad," I said. I would let Thuran speak for me when he came to.

"Where are you from?"

"From the south." I had no intention of raising their hopes or suspicions of me by saying I was from their prophet. There would be a correct time for that later.

"The south? Beyond the wastes? Some have said there would be lands there. Well, Galad, if you are truly a friend to Thuran, you are welcome here. You must forgive our attitude, but times are hard. Your Zurk uniform belies your fealty. However, anyone who comes with Thuran is our friend. Now, tell me, is he badly hurt?"

"I think he is only stunned. He will soon mend once he is properly tended."

"That is good. Hi! Stand back, you gawks! Help me get Thuran on to my horse. We must away to Vendl with all haste."

Our party was mounted in moments, and I clung to the back of one of Ool's men. We spurred through the sucking swamps and into the uncanny forest. For hours we rode, hearing all manner of weird calls and roars from the steam around us, but we reached the village in safety. Most of its houses were built high in the trees and were well camouflaged. Rope ladders and vines hung down from them into a large, stockaded compound below. In an adjacent compound the horses were kept, and I could see that Vendl was a strong garrison, for there were many horses. Row upon row of spears lined the compound walls, ready for use. Further along beyond the horse compound I heard occasional roars, which I recognized at once as those of ibathenes.

As we rode into the clearing, men came running to tend the horses, and I jumped lightly down. Ool joined me. A ring of painted warriors scowled at me and my hated Zurk uniform. Hands went to bows and daggers, but Ool moved the men away. They were fierce-looking savages, their hair braided, their faces daubed with green and yellow, and their manner was that of the fighting breed. So these were the true Barbarians of Ur, I mused, the men whom the Dream Lords saw fit to treat as primitives. Perhaps they were, but after what I had been through in Karkesh, my heart was with them. I considered myself a Barbarian, and a Zurjahn no longer.

I looked about me, seeing the fires glowing, and in their heat the smiths tempered soft steel, bending it into swords and long curved bows. Vendl hummed with activity, and the atmosphere was ever one of preparation for battle. War, it would seem, was not far away. Women carried tall pots on their heads, flashing me inquisitive glances as they passed through the compound to the forest's edge. Ool clapped a huge hand on my shoulder.

"I shall take Thuran to the old witch woman, Afagal. She knows some of the lost ways and will do what is needed to revive the General. Meanwhile, I have had pigeons sent to the Sacred City, telling the Warlord of his return. I take it you and Thuran are bound for the Sacred City?"

"Aye, to the Warlord."

"It is well. I will not press you for your reasons. But tell me, is the south readying for war? Have you your armies there?"

"You will soon know," I promised him.

"Aye, I understand, lad. Say no more. The very sky has ears. Come, let us to my house. You can eat and rest, and tell me of your escape from the Black City. We get few visitors here in Vendl, especially now that we are readying. I hear that Annulian moves against Pyron in the north soon. There lies a sign that the war is beginning. I know not your own feelings, Galad, but something in my bones tells me that the Four Horsemen are even now preparing to ride. I am a warrior, anxious for battle! I search for signs with every sunrise! But, come. Food and drink in exchange for your tales."

CHAPTER IV
Came a Pale Horse

I allowed Ool to believe I was from the south, and he did not press me for details of my mission in his part of the world, for one of the major traits of the Barbarian personality is secrecy. The big man accepted me; the fact that I had been befriended by Thuran spoke volumes in my favor.

We had plenty to eat and drink, and I bathed in a tub of icy water. Afterward I was left to sleep. Some time before evening I arose and went down into the village. Ool had told his warriors that I was no Zurk spy but a man to be trusted, so I was allowed freedom to see the village. I had discarded the dusty uniform of the Zurk officer and wore now a simple smock. Chalremor's medallion I kept hidden in its folds. I had been careful to hide it from Ool's eyes.

Descending to the palisade, I went first to see the horse compound. It had been a long time since I had ridden or even seen a horse. The gates were open and men were passing in and out. Walking over, I looked in, and when I was sure my presence alarmed no one, I went boldly in. There must have been over a hundred fully fit horses in that long enclosure, and I watched avidly as they frisked about. This was the prime strength of the Barbarian armies—their horse power. Every Barbarian warrior worth his honor had at least one horse. By contrast the Zurks of Karkesh had only minimal cavalry forces. The Imperial Guards were dependent on vehicles within the city and sky rafts without. The sky rafts ran on fuel and thankfully could only manage short journeys from Karkesh and the satellite towns. Vendl and, indeed, all the Barbarian settlements were either camouflaged from the air or were too far from the Zurk outposts to be known.

I watched the horses with a silent nod of approval. Then one of the men came over from where several of the stallions were being rubbed down, leaning next to where I held the rail.

"Good day," he said cheerfully.

I returned his greeting and friendly smile.

"You are the man who came here with Thuran, the Warlord's General."

"Yes. I am called Galad."

"My name is Erl. I am one of the tenders of the horses here in Vendl. I noticed your interest. Are you an admirer of horses?"

"That I am, Erl. I love horses. I have done so since first I stood up. There are few where I came from, though," I told him, and it was no lie.

"I see," he replied, but refrained from asking me more about it. "Still, we have plenty here in Vendl and there are ample stabled in the Forlorn Mountains. When the Warlord leads us against the Zurks, everyone shall be provided for."

"Yes." I nodded.

"If you are a lover of horses, there is something of interest you might like to see beyond the paddock."

"Is that so?"

"Aye. There are some expectant mares in the stables." He seemed pleased to note my deep interest.

"Really? Where is this?"

"Would you like to see them? Ool told me you are to have the run of the village."

"Certainly. Lead me to them."

"Come with me," he said in a conspiratorial voice. He conveyed an attitude of secrecy with his hushed voice, though it was merely his way. I followed him around the long paddock, and we went through an exit in the palisade and into a small clearing. Several stables lined its sides.

"See? Some of the mares have foaled already," he cried, delighted.

And it was so, for in some of the straw-filled stables we saw mothers licking the newcomers to the herd. Up ahead a small crowd of men gathered expectantly around the last stable. It seemed that one of the mares was just about to give birth.

"We are in luck," said Erl, chuckling. He strained to see over the backs, but I could not force a view, so waited behind the sweating ranks of the men. The sun was low in the heavens, peering through the weird forest beyond the stable. A sudden joyful murmur went up, then unaccountably turned to one of dismay.

"What is it?" I asked Erl, who was frowning.

"Nothing. It is—" He stopped in mid-sentence.

I pulled him gently aside and at last got a glimpse of the inner stable. The mare lay in the shadows, and before her in the straw lay a tiny, pale-colored foal. Its skin was wet and the color peculiar, unique. The men were shaking their heads sadly.

"What is wrong?" I asked softly, and instantly those near me looked at me with renewed suspicion.

"See how pale the foal is! It is mutated!" cried someone at the front.

"It must be killed," said another.

Then an odd thing happened. One of the midwives was handed a short sword, and he prepared to destroy the newborn foal. I cried out in dismay at this rough justice.

"*Stop*! The foal lives. Why must you kill it?"

A gasp of disbelief came from the crowd at my words, and the men parted to let me through.

"What do you mean by this?" demanded the midwife angrily, though withholding the death-blow.

"There is nothing wrong with the foal. See, it stands already! It seems a healthy beast despite its pallor. Why kill it?" I persisted, standing beside the unsteady foal.

"Are you insane? All mutations are killed at birth. Nothing born with the taint of Shaitan is tolerated. The very color of its skin points out that it is a blasphemy. Only the Fourth Horseman will ride a steed with this hue. Are you unaware of the legend, outlander?" he shouted. The word of my coming from outside had spread quickly.

"I care not for your legends! Leave the foal alone!" I stormed, for cruelty to horses, and indeed all animals, I had always detested. My temper had flared quickly, particularly as the warrior had insulted me. The men around us were beginning to mutter unpleasantly. Chalremor had warned me to curb my temper under stress, but I bowed now to pride, not discretion.

"Stand back, interferer!" snarled the midwife, lifting his weapon for the fatal wound.

I acted with greater speed than he, for before he could destroy the tottering foal, I kicked him full in the face, and he tumbled back into the straw. That face contorted with rage, he fumbled with the blade, but I had my own out in a second. Something kept the crowd at bay. They could have dragged me off easily, but something intangible— their superstitious natures, perhaps—held them back.

"Dare you protect this blasphemy?" hissed the midwife through clenched teeth, and the crowd murmured.

"The foal is helpless against your cruel blade, despite its unnatural strength. I do not understand why you would kill it, but you will have to kill me first," I snapped angrily, ready to sell my life dearly. The others moved back.

"Very well! That I shall enjoy," sneered my opponent, coming cautiously forward. His short sword was half the length of mine, but he did not seem to care. I could see by the way he held it and poised himself that he was no novice.

"Open him up, Holjeen!" someone called, and the crowd began to urge him on.

He jabbed, and I parried to the right, using my sword to hold his blade down. Then I used one of Gundar Sabian's ungallant but effective shock tactics: I punched him swiftly and hard under the nose with my free arm. He fell back with a grunt, spurting blood over the straw, and before he could recover I trod on his weapon.

"I trust you expect more mercy from me than you would show the foal," I said quietly, laying the point of my sword at his throat. He saw death in my eyes and knew that I would kill him if he did not give up his intentions of killing the foal. I felt the anger within me subsiding. From behind me came a disturbance.

"Galad!" some one shouted. I turned abruptly. It was Thuran, a deep frown etched on his rugged face.

"Thuran! Are you recovered?"

"That is no matter. What do you mean by this? Have you lost your senses?" He came forward.

I was in no mood for reprisals. "It seems to me that these people have lost theirs," I replied coldly. "They would destroy a newborn foal."

"You should not have interfered. Our business is not here, but with the Warlord. You could have been killed," he said in annoyance, uncomfortably conscious of the awestruck men around him. They must be wondering why he had not ordered my immediate execution.

"Do not think to chastise me, Thuran," I said, and something in my voice made him pull up sharply. It was only my anger bubbling up anew, but he may have thought it something deeper.

"Be still, Thuran," said a croaking voice from behind him. I noticed its owner for the first time. She was an aged crone, dressed in black satin robes, leaning heavily on a twisted stick. At sight of her the company drew well back.

"The witch has come," I heard someone say fearfully.

"It is Afagal," murmured another.

"Quiet, you fools," warned a third.

"Who are you, stranger, that questions the laws of the Priests of the Inner Sanctum of Annulian?" She addressed me in an almost inaudible croak, like a voice from the spirit realm. I could see none of her face, for it was heavily hooded. She leaned forward on her stick, almost bent double and little more than three feet high. Her words meant little to me.

"I am Galad Sarian," I said haughtily. No one moved in the tense atmosphere. Thuran was frowning at the old hag, although he evidently respected her. Beyond him now I could see Ool coming from the horse palisade.

"An unusual name. Where do you come from?" asked the bent figure.

I thought in the stone silence. I had told Ool I was from the south. Thuran knew otherwise.

"From afar," I said.

Nothing stirred for a few seconds.

"He says he is from the southlands," said Ool, standing beside Thuran.

It now seemed as if the whole world of Ur was contained in this stable, and I felt a surge of mental power searching the twilight. Not Vorta, though.

"No," the old crone mumbled. "I see within Thuran's thoughts that this man is from the stars, another world. Gargan, he calls it. Yet his own mind is shut to me."

I blanched. So the old hag had mental powers of her own! The Dream Lord culture was not unique!

"He must be a spy! A Zurk spy!" shouted some of the men.

"Be *still*, curse you!" threatened Afagal, and all was so at once.

"You say you are from Gargan, beyond the sky. You come from the heart of our enemy's camp, cast out by them?" Her question brought a murmur of deep shock to the gaping audience, and I realized that Afagal must have guessed about me.

"Yes," I said simply. Thuran scowled and I wondered why he was so annoyed. Ool had a stern look on his face, too. But Afagal was trembling, still holding the stage, and now her voice rose.

"You see! A stranger from the sky who protects a pale horse. A man whose mind is closed to those who would try and read it!" She moaned, and another loud gasp broke from the lips startled onlookers. I was wary of the old witch, for I knew only too well the implications of her words.

Thuran now looked on blankly. He knew what must follow, but why did he not stand by me? For some reason I felt that if he had not feared me, he would have turned against me.

"We shall see," went on Afagal, whispering hoarsely. "Take off thy smock, stranger."

I demurred and stood back. Behind me I felt sudden movement—I had forgotten Holjeen, the midwife—and with one quick jerk, he ripped the thin cloth off my back, and it parted off my shoulders leaving me naked from the waist up. Naked that is, but for Chalremor's medallion. The winged horse gleamed in the twilight. Afagal almost fell to the straw, so much did she shake.

"Blessed Powers! This must be the one. This must be the Chosen One!" she proclaimed excitedly. And with cries of bewilderment everyone began falling on their knees in supplication. Ool knelt and so too did Thuran. My eyes met Thuran's for a moment.

"Do you still doubt that I am from Chalremor?" I asked him softly. I could have probed his mind, but it was a talent I disliked.

"No. My life is yours," he said quietly, and briefly lowered his eyes.

"As is mine, my Lord. Forgive me for disrobing you," said Holjeen with unfeigned humility. He came and knelt at my feet, and I felt amazed at the transformation. But these were primitive, superstitious people. I gripped the midwife's shoulder gently.

"Rise, Holjeen. All I ask of you is that you spare the foal," I told him.

"Yes, Lord. If I had known that it was more than a pale horse...but that of the legends...I shall guard its life until you require it," he replied, full of remorse for what he had almost done, and I thought for a brief second of the horse I had seen in the Finger of Dusk back on Zurjah.

Now it seemed to me that Daras Vorta would look upon the face of the Pale Rider that I had seen—Death. These people around me were silent in their worship. They saw me as a God incarnate, the promised hope of their dreams. But the role no longer awed me, and I felt a heady wine of power filling my head. I was young and hotheaded. Why should I not believe that the Gods had chosen me to lead these people that I had adopted for my own? Ah, but if Taria could have stood beside me in this, I would have felt invincible.

"Arise! All of you! Our differences here were but the work of the Gods. Now you know me, and you know why I have come. So prepare yourselves! The end is coming to Karkesh and its foul master, this I swear to you in the name of your beloved prophet, Chalremor!" I lifted the medallion and kissed it, holding it for them to see.

"We shall take the cursed God Shaitan and pull out his horns!" I avowed, and they got up, cheering and laughing joyfully, while others came to see what was happening. Amidst the jubilation and the commotion, Thuran came to my side.

"Word of your coming and the birth of the Pale Horse will spread. We must leave with all haste," he said softly as he bowed.

Chosen One I might be, but I still relied on Thuran in such a situation.

"You are fully recovered, I take it?" I asked him.

"Yes, sire. Afagal has strange but potent powers. She can see into the future, so they say, but I would not care to linger and hear her prophesies. Ool has prepared us a boat, for we are to cross the Poison River."

"Very well. If it pleases you, we shall go at once. You are still my guiding light," I told him warmly, and my words seemed to soften his stiffness a little. He nodded and helped me through the noisy crowd. I felt a shadow near me and turned to see the old hag looking up.

"So you have come to us, Pale Rider," she breathed from the darkness of her rags. "Woe unto all who cross you. You will reward them all with Death."

I would have grabbed her and spoken more with her, but she melted away and Thuran urged me on.

"Make way! Make way! The Chosen One must go to the Lion. The Gods must plan. Make way!" he cried.

We left the stables and I heard cries of, "The harbinger! The harbinger!"

As we struggled through the swelling throng of exultant villagers, Thuran told me something of his plans.

"Forgive my questioning of your purpose in the stable, Galad, but I thought this incident untimely. I had wished your identity to remain a secret until we reached the Warlord. The people will expect you to ride upon Karkesh tomorrow, such is the heat of their fanaticism. You will constantly be mobbed and cheered unless we can stem the news."

"I am sorry to have appeared rash, Thuran. At first I sought only

205

too protect the horse, but it seems a greater significance was attached to the incident," I said and he nodded.

"It is not my place to question the Gods," he said solemnly.

The incident had aroused a mixture of strange emotions within me. It had been a remarkable coincidence. How much of the legend did Thuran believe, and how far did he accept my role? He knew just how vulnerable and mortal I was. My thoughts were pushed aside as Ool came abreast of us.

"All is ready for your journey to Mooten," he told us. "I have dispatched more pigeons to tell the Warlord you are here."

Thuran whirled on him, his eyes betraying his alarm.

"You have not told him that I come with the Pale One?" he said tersely.

Ool looked startled. "No, sire. I thought it a risk, no matter how small, to send such a message. The Zurks..."

"You did right. Do not announce any further news. We do not want the whole country in an uproar."

"My Lord?" said Ool, obviously dumbfounded. He turned to me, but I was nonplussed. Why should the Warlord not be told of the coming of the Chosen One?

"You must trust me," said Thuran to Ool.

"The time for the war is not yet ripe," I added. "The preparations must be thorough before we move. I know you are anxious to ride against the Zurks. You will in time."

"Very well," complied the huge warrior.

We came then to the main stockade of Vendl, and at Ool's signal, two fresh horses were led to us in the fading light. The crowds gathered to cheer ecstatically as Thuran and I mounted.

"Here," said Ool, handing us each a thick, green cloak which had been brought from across the compound. "The night on the marshes will be bitter." We thanked him and wrapped them around us.

"Fare thee well, Ool We shall meet again, be sure of it," I told him, and he bowed.

"Your servant, Lord," he said softly. "I knew when I first saw you fight that you were something more than a man."

I waved to the milling Barbarians, and they cheered.

"Vengeance shall be ours!" I shouted. New power surged in my veins. I thought of all those who had died and suffered under Daras Vorta's evil yoke. Now I would sweep him and his minions back to the Hell that had spawned them. I would carry the throne of a world back to Taria. Soon there would be massed armies behind me. Chalremor's prediction that my destiny had reached out for me had come to fruition.

So Thuran and I rode out into the misty gloom of evening, the cheers of the villagers receding behind us in the vapors.

CHAPTER V
The Sacred City

Thuran and I rode for most of the night, our way winding through marshes and swamps, and it was a miracle to me that the warrior found his way through safely. Some time before dawn we came to some hutments and here were met by a party of warriors who were to ferry us over the Poison River. It was like a lake of seething, boiling pitch, its oily waters flowing sluggishly and thickly for hundreds of miles into the wasted area known simply as the Sea of Death, where none ever went. Mists cloaked us as we ferried over that foul-smelling river of effluvium, and dawn had broken when we reached the marshes and reed banks of its farther shore.

We left our guides and rode through the waving stems, hung with webs and shrouded in wispy mist, until we came to another Barbarian village. This was Mooten, its presence hidden from aerial eyes by the tall reeds. I saw little of its extent, but Thuran told me there were several hundred houses here and a strong garrison of soldiery. We changed horses and had a brief meal before riding on into the day. Now for the first time I began to see parts of Ur that were not so blighted or disheartening.

Ahead of us stretched the ragged peaks of the Forlorn Mountains. We rode swiftly over the plains, where grass grew sparsely and genetic mutations were less frequently apparent. The air was cooler and fresher, and I began to glory in the fever of the ride. Thuran was silent and ever watchful. The Zurk air boats had never been seen this side of the Poison River, he told me, but one could never be sure when they would venture across. In my enjoyment of the journey, I had almost put thoughts of the Zurks and Karkesh from my mind, until we came to a river and paused to water the horses. The river— the Silver River as I was told—was fresh and the water safe to drink.

It came down from the valley of the Sacred City.

As I knelt to drink, I felt something in the air around me. I knew at once what it was: the mind sweep of Daras Vorta. I had sensed it before—once on Gargan when I had first fled Vorta's agents and since then when the Warden had tried to sense me. I threw a mental cloak over myself and Thuran and, after a time, felt the probe of Vorta fading away. He must be scouring the whole of the surrounding terrain for a hint of my presence.

I said nothing of this to Thuran and presently we mounted and rode on. Soon we came to the mountains, and to my surprise Thuran led me to the base of a sheer cliff of granite. A tall waterfall gushed and cascaded down from the perilous heights, and I turned to my guide with a frown.

"This is one of the most beautiful places I have ever seen on any of the worlds," I told him. "But is it not a dead end?"

He gave a rare grin and rode on slowly to the very foot of the roaring falls. Beyond the last shoulder of granite, beside the deep, foaming pool, was a crevice. Thuran led his steed into it, and I followed. A subsidiary stream had etched a way through into the solid wall of the mountain, and we splashed our way through into the darkness. After what seemed an eternal climb, I saw light ahead, with Thuran outlined against it. We came to the exit quite suddenly and found ourselves standing on a small ridge, high up in the mountains. I looked in wonder on the valley below.

On our left, about three hundred feet below us, the Silver River entered a narrow gorge where it cut its way through the mountains to emerge as the waterfall we had seen beyond. The river wound its way from high up the valley, twisting and curling, often lost among the thickly wooded slopes. Our precarious ledge had been chiseled out of the sheer red cliffs, and it led along the mountains in front of us. It was no more than six feet wide, and the cliff face dropped, sheer, down from it. Above towered more unscaleable rock walls, dotted here and there with sparse, brown bushes, and across the valley the mountains rose high and jagged in the clouds.

"The Sacred City lies beyond the bend," said Thuran, leading the way along the dizzy ledge. I now kept my eyes firmly in front, for the sheer drop frightened me—though not the horses. Heights have always held an unprecedented fear for me. We traveled along the ledge slowly, rounding two bends in the cliff face, and at long last I saw before me the beautiful Sacred City.

In the center of the valley a huge block of rock—probably volcanic—soared up a thousand feet top the sky. Its uppermost pinnacle reached a height greater than that on which we stood. From the valley floor, hundreds of feet of vertical cliff rose up from its base, then its sides steepened for a further five hundred feet and were thickly wooded, giving a peculiar impression that the block had been man-made in sections. High above the wooded slopes the mountain became sheer cliff again, one of the sides sloping inwards from above. It was on the top of this latter cliff that I could see the distant temples and buildings of the City. On the extreme top, a huge golden disc blazed with reflected sunlight.

"Well, Galad," came Thuran's soft voice, "we are home."

"So this is the Sacred City," I marveled, gazing enraptured at the gleaming spires high up beyond. "The place must be impregnable. How do we enter?"

"We must descend to the river," he replied.

We rode further along the ledge which came to a final ridge. This was steeply sloped and forested, and we were able to leave the mountain side and enter the cool shade of the trees, going on down through a thick carpet of rustling leaves. Right down to the river we made our way, coming out in the shadow of the titanic block of rock. Thuran's horse seemed to know the way, and it gently forded the pebbled river to the base of the rock. We rode slowly along this until we suddenly came upon a tall cave. From within came strange echoing sounds, and I heard the babble of many voices. But Thuran urged his mount forward, and we went in unchallenged.

Once my eyes grew accustomed to the light, I saw that we were in a vast cavern, hundreds of feet high and across. Scores of caves were cut into the cavern sides at all levels, each level connected to a neighbor by roughly hewn steps. The lower caves were mostly used for stables, armories and blacksmiths, while above them were stores, and on the higher level were shops and dwelling places. Horses cantered to and fro, and hundreds of people were crossing and criss-crossing the whole cavern; many called out or waved at our approach. Thuran spoke with a number of them, and there were shouts of joy at seeing him safely returned, as they had thought him lost.

I looked above me at the curling ceiling of rock, now noticing that the huge walls of the cavern were covered with incredible paintings and murals of vast expanse and great detail, depicting mounted warriors of steel locked in combat with outrageous beasts and other vivid scenes of battle. It seemed as if I gazed upon the art of another age, for there were many things in the paintings that I did not understand. We came to the far side of the busy cavern and entered one of the many tunnels that led off it. I drew in my breath in surprise.

The walls were lit, not by primitive firebrands, but by glowglobes, or something akin to them. I had not thought Barbarian society so advanced. Presently I was further numbed as two doors slid aside to reveal an elevation chamber. Thuran may have sensed my surprise, but he made no comment. How had the so-called primitives availed themselves of this sort of technology?

The ride upward was smooth and silent—a thousand-foot shaft to the city above. The doors opened, and we stepped out into another chamber which opened onto daylight. I could not contain a gasp as I looked up at the exit. Etched in naked rock, guarding the way out, was a winged horse, bearing the skull-faced rider of my nightmares. Again Thuran paid me no heed, and we passed out into the sunlit citadel. The superb buildings were constructed out of solid gold blocks, with curving gables and picturesque gargoyles. Each had its own garden of wondrous flowers and small trees, and the streets were paved with gold, having thin central flower beds running down their entire lengths. There was an abundance of magnificent, bejeweled fountains, and this surprised me at the time—though I later learned that there was a reservoir up near the top of the mountain. The city was not big, the bulk of its people (as I also came to learn) living below, inside the mountain.

As I passed down the miniature boulevards, I understood the City to be an incredible feat of engineering, built into the mountain as it was, easily comparable to anything achieved by Zurjahn standards. On my left, beyond the rooftops, the opposite side of the valley loomed up into misty heights, and on my right, terrace upon terrace climbed up the mountain above the shining citadel to its peak. Thuran led me through those glimmering streets, and the people that passed (dressed mostly in robes of splendid white and gold) nodded and smiled, so that I felt a growing security here. They seemed like holy people to me, such was the air of reverence surrounding this place. Along the rooftops, row upon row of doves and pigeons cooed noisily to each other, and I thought how ironic it was that the inhabitants of this paradise were called Barbarians.

We walked to a long, low residence that sat squarely up against the cliff wall, overlooking the dizzy drop below. In its small, lawned gardens, a young maiden of about twelve years was playing with a black and white puppy. Thuran leaned on the silver gate and smiled lovingly at the scene, but so intense was the child's concentration on the yapping pup, that she had not seen him. The warrior's sudden mellowing moved me, for he seemed such a brooding, solemn man, more used to the ways of the sword than of this sanctuary.

"Ho, there, Melida!" he called, and at once her eyes flashed up at him. Her long black hair swirled about her in shining curls as she shot up and came skipping across, her cheeks flushed.

"Thuran!" she cried as he opened the gate, and flung herself breathlessly into his open arms. "You have come back!" she said excitedly, tugging at his thick beard joyfully.

"Surely you did not think I had deserted my little Melida, eh?" he laughed. The puppy scampered madly across the lawn and leapt about our feet. I bent down and lifted him up, fondling him as he licked my face.

"Hey. Your little friend here is jealous." I smiled to the girl, stroking the puppy's warm coat.

"Do you like him?" she asked in her delightful, cultured voice. "His name is Totus. I named him myself."

"I think he is charming, and I think you have named him well," I told her.

"There you are, little one," rejoined Thuran. "Galad approves. He set the smiling girl down and she curtseyed to me.

"I am very pleased to meet you, Galad," she said with dignity, and I bowed graciously.

"I am pleased to meet you, my lady," I replied, and this seemed to please her very much.

"Thuran!" came a voice from the house. A tall man in a flowing white robe stood in its doorway. "I cannot believe the testimony of my own eyes! Have you returned from the dead?"

Thuran chuckled at the man's disbelief.

"Nay, Prosocles, noble friend. I am very much alive, as you can see. How are you?"

The two men strode forward and grasped each other's hands warmly. Prosocles was in his fifties, and he had gray hair and patrician features, carrying himself with no less dignity and bearing than a Zurjahn nobleman. There were no lines of worry about his brow, and he seemed suffused with vivacity.

"I am well," he said. "And the sight of you adds to my happiness. This is indeed a wonderful moment. We have mourned you every day since that fateful expedition to Pyron."

"Then mourn no more, dear friend, for I am well. I would like you to meet my most gallant friend. This is Galad Sarian. Galad, this is Prosocles, one of the Sacred City's noblest inhabitants."

I bowed and shook the man's firm, outstretched hand. "I am deeply honored, sire," I said.

"You are more than welcome in my home, Galad. I see you have already met my younger daughter, Melida." He smiled, putting a hand on her shoulder affectionately.

"Yes, sir. And this delightful bundle." I laughed softly, scratching Totus, whose tongue darted for my face again.

"Oh, yes. Totus is quite a handful. Melida, dear, take him from our guest."

I handed the puppy to Melida, and she pressed him to her sweet young face.

"Thank you, Galad."

"You must come in. Both Eome and Vellarna will be delighted to see you. Come." Prosocles ushered us politely inside, and we went into a long room, with a low, wide window which overlooked the magnificent valley so far below.

"Do you like the view?" our host asked me.

"I have never seen its equal," I told him truthfully.

"Be seated, please. I will fetch my wife and elder daughter. Melida, go to the kitchens and ask the servants for some of our best wine. Thank you, child."

"Yes, father," she cried, scampering off dutifully, Totus hard on her heels. Prosocles excused himself and left the room, while Thuran and I sat back and relaxed. It was a rewarding sensation to feel silk cushions beneath me after so long.

"Well, Galad, how do you find our citadel?" said Thuran, incongruous among such finery.

"I am amazed. I never imagined such a fortress could exist. Your people have equaled the cities of Zurjah."

"Aye," he said, nodding thoughtfully. "And speaking of that, I think it would be best for now if you allow Prosocles and any other you might meet in the City to believe you are from the southlands. There is good reason for—" he began, but cut himself off when Prosocles entered the room once more.

"Thuran. Galad. Allow me to present to you both my dear wife, Eome, and our eldest child, Vellarna."

He led firstly his wife to us, and Thuran bowed, kissing her proffered hand gently; then I did the same. She was tall for a woman, and had gray, curled hair, and was dressed in a modest, flowing gown of pink satin. Her eyebrows slanted regally, and her voice was deep and precise. She would not have been out of place among the elite of Zurjahn society.

"Blessings on both of you, gallant sirs," she said as we bowed. Then she turned to her daughter, lifting her hand. "Come, Vellarna."

The girl was perhaps nineteen, and at once I was taken with her great beauty. She had long, jet black hair, like her younger sister, and deep blue eyes. She curtseyed daintily in her light green dress, and Thuran kissed her fingers. Yes, she was very beautiful, I thought, as I fancied that she flushed as our eyes met. I could not repress a thought of Taria, for here was a maiden that I could look upon with more than a passing interest.

"Please sit down," said our lady host after I had kissed her daughter's trembling fingers, and Thuran and I did so.

"We are immensely overjoyed to see you alive, Thuran. We had lost all hope," said Eome, shaking her head.

"Aye, Thuran," said Prosocles. "Tell us how you escaped the Zurks, for the Gods must have had a hand in it."

All attention turned to the General. I glanced from time to time at Vellarna, but she watched Thuran closely. My own thoughts were sad now, lingering on the girl I had left, so far from my reach. At that moment, Totus bounded in, followed by Melida, who carried a silver tray on which stood a tall wine flagon and goblets inlaid with precious stones. Totus settled himself at Prosocles's feet, and our host scratched his ears playfully.

"Good girl, Melida," he said. "Set the tray down on the table." He waited till she had done so, then poured us all a drink. When we were refreshed and had again sat back, Thuran began.

Melida sat next to her sister, and I heard her whisper. "He called me 'my lady'," she said, and Vellarna smiled, motioning her to be silent.

Thuran told the fascinated family of his engagement at Pyron, his subsequent capture, and of our fight in the arena and our eventual escape. He succeeded in greatly embarrassing me by describing graphically my part in the drama, and Eome was deeply moved, while Vellarna lowered her eyes from mine every time I looked her way. Melida, totally absorbed, had come to sit between Thuran and I.

"So we have a venerable fighter in you, Galad," said Prosocles. "That is good. The City needs such men."

"Thuran has exaggerated grossly, my lord." I smiled, and the General chuckled.

"Not at all, not at all. He has made a habit of saving my life!" he told them. They were all thrilled by the tale, especially Melida, though all fell silent when Thuran spoke sadly of Gastar's passing. After a long discussion, Thuran and I were allowed to bathe in a heated pool, and I treated myself to the luxury of a proper shave. Afterward we sat down with the family to a superb meal of roast boar.

"Will you stay the night?" Eome asked of Thuran at the table.

"I am honored to be asked, my lady, but I must hasten to the Temple of Light," he replied. "I must speak with Annulian. He has had word of my coming from Vendl, and the watchers in the valley would have seen me pass through. The Warlord will want a full report immediately."

"Of course. And what of the noble Galad?" Eome said, turning to me, but Thuran answered before I could.

"I would appreciate it, my lady, if you would shelter my friend for a while. He is from a distant place and flees Zurk persecution. I will inform Annulian of his coming, and should the Lion want an audience, I will return for Galad."

"Why, of course. It is our pleasure," replied Eome, looking to her husband, who nodded agreeably.

"For as long as Galad wishes," he said.

"You can tell me all about the arena again!" said Melida, squeezing my arm, her eyes sparkling.

"Now, Melida, our guest is tired. Let him rest," said Eome.

We returned to the large room and Prosocles left Thuran and I alone. The General gazed out over the valley.

"Well, Thuran," I said, "we have come through some trials together."

"Aye," he nodded, clapping me on the shoulder. It was plain that any suspicions he may have had about me were banished. "However, now I must leave you for a while. You are in good hands here. The Lion will be impatient, so I'll away. You will mention nothing of your own purpose?"

"No. As you wish. I would not incite the people to premature action. And what of the Lion? You will tell him from whom I come?"

"I...must do so, it seems. The news will be a shock to him...but," he said falteringly, and his discomfort was clear. Why should the Warlord feel thus?

"A shock?"

"Of sorts. We are a superstitious race, Galad. I dare not say more. Trust me. All I can say is that Annulian is the king, the Lion, the Annihilator. He is well versed in the legends. He will accept you..."

"But he will be jealous of my power over his subjects, is that your meaning?" I asked with a grim smile.

"Perhaps. I best not tarry. Remember, the time will come for action."

"Very well," I nodded. Prosocles entered and saved any further embarrassment. Thuran then took his leave and left me with a conflict of emotions inside me. My mission, Taria, Vorta, the beautiful City—all jumbled inside my head.

CHAPTER VI
Enter the Warlord

I lived with Prosocles and his family for three months, during which time Thuran came often and told me of the Warlord's plans and of how he was gathering together the last scattered remnants of the Barbarian tribes. I was becoming restless, for I had still not been taken before the Lion, though Thuran still insisted it was for good reasons and that I must be patient. Meanwhile, Prosocles taught me much about the Barbarian way of life. He said that after the war, what few people there were left alive lived in widely separated tribes, mostly in remote mountain regions. It took many years for them to unite into a nation of any size, and now the work was almost done. There were still, however, many thousands of square miles of the planet about which little or nothing was known. The Sacred City was the result of many years' work, and in it were the remnants of technology and the priceless leftovers from before the war. Most valuable of these was the Book of Prophecy, which was kept somewhere in the vaults of the Temple of Light, and about which my host would say very little.

Prosocles himself was a banker. Here in the citadel there were such places as banks, libraries, shrines, and private houses, while down in the caverns were the armories and stables, as I had seen. The Barbarian nobility lived in the citadel—bankers, generals, priests and such like. The others lived in the caves, the captains and higher ranks in the uppermost and the ordinary fighting men and refugees in the lower. These caves were not squalid places, but well-furnished and comfortable. Most Barbarians were soldiers, now that the Warlord was preparing for war on a grand scale. Their pay was low, as it was for everyone, but it was a necessary state of affairs until Zurk rule could be broken in the west. This was the prime function of all Barbarians: smash Zurk rule. There was much training and practice (in which I participated frequently), and when a legion was considered fit, it was sent to one of the camouflaged villages to relieve those already there, and sometimes given a chance to fight against Guard patrols or new fronts. The Barbarian forces were always fully prepared to be on the move in strength. Thuran's attack on Pyron had been the first major offensive on a Zurk outpost, and was a complete disaster. The Zurk weaponry had been superior. The Warlord, said Prosocles, would not allow it to happen again.

During my long, restless stay, I amused myself with Melida and Totus, who would both play energetically for hours, and I spent much time also with the lovely Vellarna, who came to be less shy with me. She listened avidly to my tales of far-off lands, although I withheld from her the true nature of my home. My medallion still hung from my neck, but was always carefully hidden. Thuran had told the family I was from a distant place in the south, where I had led an open revolt against the Zurk Empire, and no one questioned the fact.

Vellarna told me of her secluded life here in the citadel, and surprised me one day by saying that she was to marry the Warlord and be queen. She had been taken to the temple one day by the handmaidens of the mysterious Priests of the Inner Sanctum. There she met Annulian, who told her that she had been chosen to marry him, being the maiden of noblest blood in all the lands of the Barbarians. I gathered from her words that she feared him, but was prepared to do her duty, and that from her tone, Annulian had avowed his love for her. But she was loath to dwell on the matter. As she unburdened the problems of her heart to me, I naturally told her of Taria and of my love for the girl I might never see again. Afterward we would both fall silent, for Vellarna was always saddened by my words.

So the days passed. I accompanied my host about the golden city, and we traversed the walls which guarded the endless drop below. High up above, the sun glinted on the huge, blazing disc, and the pigeons flew to and fro from the distant mountains. One morning I was sitting in the garden beside the house, looking out from the heights at the sliver of silver which was the river below, when I heard a movement behind me. It was Thuran, whom I had not seen for some time.

"Greetings, my lord. I am sorry to have been away for so long," he said, and we shook hands.

"I was beginning to think that you had deserted me," I laughed, and he sat next to me on the wall under the shade of a leafy apple tree.

"Nay, lad. I have been busy. Events are at last drawing to a head. The Warlord has been away these last two months, for he has to administer to the very limits of the known world. However, at last it is time for you to meet him."

"How very condescending of him. I have been patient as you requested, Thuran, but his attitude irks me. He appears to have taken the news of my coming with little enthusiasm," I said shortly.

"Aye, aye. Yet you will come to understand him in time. And now you must come with me. Are you ready?"

"One moment. I will get my sword," I told him and went inside and strapped it on. A warrior never went anywhere without his sword.

We bade the family good day and left together, walking up the glittering street. Thuran was evidently nervous, and he said little. I sensed this, but did not press him for facts—neither did I try and read the troubled thoughts in his mind. Instead I walked quietly with him to the foot of the trellised gardens. A gate of twisted iron stood before us, guarded by two tall men in long, white cloaks, emblazoned with a lion's head. They wore simple, undecorated masks, held short, barbed javelins, and had curved daggers thrust into their belts of chained gold links. I felt the unmistakable probe of a mind search—not unlike that of the old hag, Afagal—but closed my mind to it easily. After a pause the men opened the gate for us, and we began the climb up the steep stair of engraved gold which wound its way high up towards the mountain peak.

"These are Annulian's Priests of the Inner Sanctum. There are fifty men in all, and they are the most loyal and trusted men in our ranks. All are said to be touched by the Gods at birth, and the limits of their powers are not known," Thuran told me softly as we passed two more Priests. There were pairs of them standing on either side of the twisting stairs at periodic intervals.

The sweet scent of honeysuckle came to my nostrils, and in the gardens, roses bloomed, as did large rhododendron bushes and other gorgeous flowers of all colors. We came at length to the topmost steps, halting in the entrance of a small chamber. Two more of the Priests stood beside the way in, and each of them held an ugly iron mace.

"Greetings, Thuran," said one, saluting. "Enter the gates of the shrine. The Lion awaits you."

We went through the dingy chamber and came to a hall lit by a row of glowglobes. Flames licked up at the vents in the roof from three huge saucers where incense burned. Thuran led me through the smooth-walled chamber to yet another stairway, and we climbed in silence for some way. More Priests lined the top of the stairway, and a panel of steel hummed open. We passed into daylight. A semi-circular court opened out from the mountainside, uncovered and ringed by a wall of granite a few feet high. Many of the Priests stood silently around the perimeter, facing inwards. Thuran led me across the superbly mosaiced floor, and beyond the low wall I saw the snow-topped peaks of the mountains across the valley. An unusual, pointed design was the centerpiece of the floor, and we stopped on this.

"Turn around, and keep your feet within the design," whispered

Thuran.

This puzzled me, but I obeyed in silence, thinking it part of the ritual of the sanctuary. This time I had no need to read Thuran's mind. His fear pulsed there like a heartbeat, and I felt a twinge of surprise, for he feared not for himself, but for me. I looked up to see the enormous blazing disc, becoming vaguely aware that a figure was seated with its back to it, some twelve feet off the ground on a dais. The reflected glare of the sun was so harsh that the figure could only be seen in silhouette, and I had to tear my eyes away from the blaze. This must be what Vellarna had meant when she had told me that 'no man may look upon the face of the king and live,' by right of Priestly law.

"I see you have brought Galad Sarian to me, as I bade you, Thuran," said a powerful voice from the dark figure. I stood before the Lion at last.

"I have, Annulian," Thuran said, bowing. A faint breeze ruffled our hair, and I heard the rustling of treetops lower down the slopes.

"I thank you, noble General. You may leave us. Be good enough to wait in the Fire Chamber until I return your charge to you." The voice was neither that of youth nor age, but of a man probably in his thirties, rich, deep and imperious. It was a voice accustomed to being obeyed, brooking no insubordination.

"Very good, sir," said Thuran with another bow, then left me alone with the unseen Warlord and his silent retinue. The Priests were not hostile, but their minds exuded an aura of defensive protectiveness.

"I bid you greetings, Galad Sarian," the Warlord addressed me, and I bowed. "I have heard that a stranger from the heart of my enemy's camp has come among us, wearing the medallion of the Prophet that only he can wear. You are this man? You are from Chalremor?"

"I am," I said, carefully extracting my medallion and showing it to the figure. The Priests around me sighed and it was like a passing breath of wind. I replaced the medallion inside my tunic.

"That is good. I have it reliably that you are indeed the one whom my master promised me would come. Chalremor sent word from the Dream Lord halls that you were coming. I gather your journey has been fraught with difficulty since you left your Zurjahn home. It is with relief that I now look down upon you," he said slowly, and something about his tone suggested that his last words were meant to be read two ways.

"The journey was harrowing. But the Gods are said to look after their own," I replied, unable to see what reaction the words would have. I heard a soft laugh.

"Yes. But I have faith in the Wise One. He controls powers which we little understand. The Gods guide him wisely. Yet, in spite of the foul machinations of Daras Vorta, you are here, even as the Book says. Now we can finish the work that Chalremor began."

"The destruction of Karkesh," I said grimly.

"More than that, Galad Sarian, much more than that. By his wicked devices, Daras Vorta has brought the very Devil incarnate within an inch of our world, as it was foreseen of old he would come down and try to rule it again."

"The Devil?" I said, slightly bemused, for the exact term was new to me. I had heard of devils, but this was something more.

"Aye, the Devil—Shaitan. Chalremor speaks of the circle that knits...the coming of the cosmic confrontation. And it is true that soon the Last Battle, the Armageddon, shall be fought. Light against darkness, Good against unspeakable Evil. Earth must be rid of the evil powers for the rest of her days!"

"You speak to me with new words, my lord," I said. "Earth...it is not familiar to me."

For a long moment there was silence from above, and then the suggestion of further soft laughter.

"Earth. The name of the true motherworld. The world that your Dream Lords have spurned in favor of tempestuous Zurjah. *This* world is Earth," he said. There was power in his voice, and a devoted fanaticism that I sensed verged on religious mania. He was born to command, that much was very clear.

I could understand now the fear in Thuran's mind, for was I not born likewise to command? Was I to contest the leadership with Annulian?

"It is a good name," I said, masking my thoughts.

"Not one that is often spoken—not while we bow to Zurk rule. But that will soon pass. For the time, tell me of yourself, Galad Sarian. What has Chalremor taught you? How much has he left for me to teach you?" he asked. I relaxed somewhat in the warm breeze and recalled in detail all that had befallen me in the Finger of Dusk, where I had first met Chalremor, and of my life since. As was always the case when I lived those first moments, something of the aura of the old sorcerer hung like a nimbus about me, and the Priests appeared to sense it. A prolonged silence followed my conclusion.

"So you know little but your general purpose and few of the details. That is as well. All shall be revealed to you in due course," said the Lion, dissolving the spell. He seemed almost pleased at my apparent ignorance, and it angered me.

"In due course!" I said indignantly. "Why am I not furnished with the details now? Chalremor told me, his apparent Chosen One, that the people of Ur—of Earth—would flock to me, and those that have seen the medallion have done so with unrestrained reverence. But still you hold from me the secret of my destiny. Why?"

"All is under the eyes and control of the Gods."

"So I may take it that I have your own support? I am to be accepted then? Or perhaps there are those who feel I am but a Dream Lord spy, or Vorta's creature?" I taunted him, and the Priests ill concealed their alarm.

"Of course not!" burst out Annulian, a little too quickly for my absolute comfort. "I understand your impetuosity. You may justly have wondered why Thuran did not make more of your coming. But he was right. Should everyone know that you are here, they would want an immediate crusade, and that would be disastrous. You see, everything is almost ready for war. I have spent my life organizing this. Once the people have been totally rallied, then can the Chosen One be presented to them. They will know that once the Four Horsemen ride, nothing shall stand in their way, not even the blackness in Karkesh!" His words were, after all, thoughtful and sensible, but I still suspected an undertone.

"Just what are these Four Horsemen? I have heard of them and have dreamt of them often. Chalremor proclaimed me to be one. What is their true significance? Am I to be kept in ignorance of this as well?" I said testily, agitated by the control in his level voice.

"The Four Horsemen are the prophecy given to us by the Gods. They are in the Book of Prophecy that had survived all wars. Once they ride, the Last Battle against evil shall be fought on Earth."

I tried then to pry into his mind, but instantly felt a shield drop across my probe. Was he possessed of Dream Lord powers, too? But, no, I realized, it was the combined screen of the Priests. I withdrew my probe.

"And am I to lead them?" I asked in a more restrained tone.

"You are indeed to be one of the Four. The Pale Rider. You have been proclaimed the Chosen One—by the Gods as much as Chalremor. Surely you must know your true heritage? Passed down through the endless years. Now that this Earth, a mere speck in the great cosmos of Creation, is to be the scene of the final struggle between the powers of Light and Darkness, you, Galad Sarian, are to be the instrument of the Gods, even as Daras Vorta is the instrument of the Devil. You, and you alone, must hold high our standard, and lead us to the eternal destruction of the legions of Shaitan! Ask me not what you are here for!" he said, his voice rising to a shout.

Although I grasped the meaning behind his words, I felt something beneath it all—zeal, jealousy, I knew not. There followed a terrible silence, and I wondered if such events could really be on the scale he had suggested. The Priests stood motionlessly, their masks making them inscrutable.

"So you see, Galad," Annulian said more softly, "we must not be rash but must wait until our time comes. The Gods have waited eons for this. Let Chalremor be our guide. He alone is conversant with the Powers of Light. He alone has shown you the path. He alone has shown me what I must do. In time, he will summon you to the Pool of Thought. There he will speak to you across the star void. Ask me nothing further of this. You must trust in me. Chalremor will furnish us all with the last details in our cause."

I would have questioned him on this enigmatic Pool of Thought, but decided it would be best to obey him for now. I preferred to be master of my own destiny, rather than the Warlord's puppet—but I had been Chalremor's puppet since the night we had met on Zurjah.

"I see things more clearly for your words, Annulian," I told him, trying to sound convincing. "I apologize for my rashness. You must know that my one waking thought is to bring down Daras Vorta and all his foul conjurations."

"As you say. Fear not for our trust. I understand only too well your misgivings. But all goes well for us. Worry not about plans and campaigns. You have only to lead. All Earth will rally to the Four, come the day."

"Then I am in your hands," I replied, but it was like cat and mouse, and I wondered who was the cat and who the mouse.

"And I am in the hands of Chalremor, who does only the bidding of the Gods. We draw our comfort and our strength from that knowledge."

I nodded silently at the words. The Priests chanted a brief prayer.

"And while we wait for Chalremor's last delivery, the first blow shall be struck," said Annulian.

"How so?"

"I have been fortunate in my travels, for recently I had imparted to me one of the ancient secrets of this planet. My scientists are working on its formula, trying to perfect it. It is a very old weapon and had become very much outdated by the sophisticated standards of the war. Should we perfect it, it will be a great boon to us. Dream Lord decree states that only the supposed homeworld of Zurjah is permitted weapons of any standing. But Vorta has used arms other than mere sword and spear against us. Now he shall taste his own medicine."

"You will test the weapon against him?"

"Yes. You have heard of Pyron, where Thuran was captured?"

"Of course."

"It is an outpost of some two thousand Imperial Guards and Karkesh's most recent encampment. It lies far to the northeast of the Black City, north of the forest of Budian. I intend to destroy its entire company of vermin with but a handful of men and this new weapon. I'll teach the Warden to steal our herds," he said with more than a little conviction.

"Is that possible?"

"We shall see. With this weapon I can move a handful of men in darkness and be done before our presence is known. Vorta has his thought detectors probing constantly, but I will take Priests with me. And Pyron will fall. Then shall we begin the war in earnest. You, Galad, shall hear all you need to know, and we shall drink to the razing of Karkesh and the fall of Shaitan and all his legions of devils. There will be nothing to stop our reclamation of our world. When we have done, the Zurks will never set foot here again!"

However, his words did not comfort or inspire me as they should have. Somehow I felt that the strife would only begin in Karkesh.

CHAPTER VII
The Pool of Thought

Another month dragged by after my meeting with Annulian, and I began to wander moodily about the citadel. At last Thuran appeared and took me once more up into the Inner Sanctum. His face was grave in the cold, blustery twilight, and I sensed that he too was tired of inactivity in the Sacred City. He had wanted to accompany Annulian on the attack on Pyron, but had not been chosen. I asked him if the Warlord had returned, but he had no news.

The Priests met us in the Fire Chamber, where incense burned to their Gods of Light.

"If the Warlord is still away, to whom are we to present ourselves?" I asked Thuran, but a solemn Priest stepped from the shadows.

"Galad Sarian," he said softly, his masked head inclining to me, "be so good as to accompany me into the heart of the mountain to the Pool of Thought."

I knew at once what this meant. Somehow Chalremor would speak with me. Thuran motioned for me to follow the Priest. I left him and went down the dark passages of the shrine, the Priest holding aloft a glowrod to show the way. We reached a cavern in the innermost part of the rock, and I saw that its walls were lined with chanting Priests, their heads bowed in supplication. Before me was a wall of crystal or glass, its surface shimmering in the eerie glow. The Priest that had led me here joined the ranks of his fellows and took up the chant. The floor of the cavern was broken and dusty like any simple cave, but my attention focused on the shimmering wall.

A haze seemed to blur and distort its shape, and for a moment I thought I was looking into a deep pool of glowing liquid. The liquid shifted until it had molded from its many hues the outline of a face. I opened my mind to the face, for it suggested warmth and friendship. It formed more clearly—Chalremor! Calling from across the ether.

No sound came from that glowing wall, but a voice spoke in my head.

"Galad. Are you receptive to me?"

"Chalremor! But how can this be? What manner of device is this?"

224

"An old secret. Thought transmitters are not unknown in your father's house. But let us not waste words, my boy. This is the only time I can speak with you, for the Dream Lords will quickly trace our communication and stop further contact. You are safe among the Barbarians?" The features of the face had become clear in the shifting light. I looked to the chanting Priests, but they had heads still bowed and saw nothing.

"Yes, but what news from outside?" I thought, my words filled with urgency.

"I have grave news from Zurjah, though you must be told. Your father, Dotas Sarian, is dead."

"Dead! But...how...so soon?" I gasped.

"I regret to bring you such sorrowful tidings, but it is true. Since you disappeared on Gargan, he has grown worse, and now he is no more. His enemies—your enemies—even now prepare to move for power on Zurjah. The Dream Lords are considering the application of Ravas Tarak for your seat."

"My father...dead," I thought-spoke. This had come as an enormous blow. "But...surely Ravas Tarak was discredited after the revolt on Gargan..."

"Not so. The whole affair was smoothed over by Vorta's agents. Most of the Garganians who rebelled against the so-called oppression of the Empire were killed, and those that escaped swore that Wortan Heynar had used the rebellion to gain control of the planet for his own ends, independent of Zurjahn rule. Dream Lord ships landed and cleared the debris and settled the last riots. Now Zurjahn rule is stronger than ever on Gargan and the natives are left to their own ways. Ravas Tarak and Daras Vorta have not been implicated in any way. The Dream Lords believe you to have died in the rebellion. They appealed to the Garganians to give you up if they were holding you to ransom, but of course they could not. The Dream Lords sent agents to mind sweep the entire world, and when no reply was forthcoming, they presumed you dead. Now they have to consider Ravas Tarak's promotion to the triumvirate, as he is next in line to you."

"Then we must hasten our war on Karkesh," I said.

"Yes, the day draws closer. But be warned, Galad. Daras Vorta's suspicions are aroused. Up to now he has been content to rule from Karkesh, concentrating his energies and resources on worming his way into Dream Lord power. Now that you have escaped him, he realizes he can no longer ignore the Barbarian hordes that roam free in the wastes. He does not expect a full-scale war, but he knows that you are there to unite them and lead them against him. And so you must beware his powers. Your will bested his on Gargan, but he was a world away. Now you face him in his own den, and the Imperial Guards are not without weaponry. Nothing too advanced, luckily, as the Dream Lords still manage to retain strict control over what leaves Zurjah, but they have certain armaments that the Barbarians cannot match in any number. I have my spies in Karkesh, and there are those in the Black City who even now sabotage for me."

I asked for no details of this, for there was no telling what eavesdroppers might be listening, even to our mind speech.

"The Warlord has gone out to test a new weapon," I told Chalremor. The face in the pool of thought remained impassive.

"Thunderpowder, yes, I know of it. An ancient but deadly thing. It will balance the powers at play when you ride on Karkesh. But the Warlord will show the way in battle. He is a brilliant man, though dangerous. I would rather not have to say this, but beware of his jealousy. He hates the Zurks more than any man alive. They killed his father horribly after a battle at Orezza, and he has never forgotten. When the Zurks are subdued, he will want his planet free of them forever. You must be the one to show the people that the men of Zurjah and Gargan and all the worlds, belong on Earth, the true motherworld. That is your prime purpose, Galad. Let the Annihilator be the one to lead the Barbarians to success, but after that, you must take command. The leaders of all nations will look to you after the Apocalypse."

I started to ask about the war, but the Pool of Thought began to ripple like a lake in a wind and Chalremor's face clouded.

"I dare not speak to you longer. Let the Warlord furnish you with the details of the Riders when he returns. It will be soon...soon..." And the voice was gone as if it had never been more than a thought. The wall shimmered and after a moment became blank rock like all other walls. I shook my head to clear it and felt an arm on mine. I spun round, but it was only one of the Priests.

"My Lord, the Lion has returned from Pyron. Will you wait in private chambers for him to come?"

I nodded and he took me to a small room off yet another

passageway, then left me to my thoughts. I felt numbed at the news of my father's passing. I had known he was dying, but even so it came as a bitter blow. Now I was alone against Vorta, with Ravas Tarak anxious to win my place among the Dream Lords.

As I sat in the dim chamber, I heard soft footsteps, and then the gentle sobs of some unseen maiden. Quickly I got up and went to the passageway without. I saw none other than Vellarna running down the narrow corridor, face in her hands. Stepping out I gently barred her way. She jerked to a halt and looked up, fear in her red-rimmed eyes, and then shock as she saw it was me.

"Galad!"

"Hush. What are you doing in the Inner Sanctum? And why the tears, Vellarna?" She started to cry anew, and I put my arms around her shaking shoulders.

"It would not be well to be seen here," I told her. "Come within."

I took her to the seat and sat her down, my arm about her shoulders for comfort. She dried her eyes on her pretty gown and shook her head, her hair billowing about her and filling the air with perfume.

"But what is it, girl?"

"Annulian. He has returned from Pyron."

"Well, that should not distress you. Unless...by the stars...is everything well with him?"

Her eyes widened at my concern.

"Oh, he is alive, fear not. The engagement was a success. Pyron is no more."

"But that is good news!" I cried, my spirits rising.

"Yes, I suppose so," she said softly, pressing her head to my chest. I stroked her black hair and murmured words of encouragement to her.

"Then what is wrong?"

"It is Annulian," she said again. "I was summoned by his grim Priests this night. How I hate them, with their blank masks and mysterious silence! Annulian was pacing his room like a...a...caged beast. I heard first of the victory, and when I did not respond joyfully, he threw a tantrum. He is mad!"

"Soft, Vellarna. Be careful what you say in this place. The walls are more than stone," I chided, but I had thrown a mind shield over her as soon as I had seen her.

"Yes, blasphemy. The Warlord is mad. And I am to be wed to him! He says the war will begin soon, and after, when Karkesh burns, I will become his wife. I would rather burn with Karkesh!" She began to cry again and I was moved by her feelings.

"I did not think you hated him so," I said, as her arms tightened around me.

"No? How could I love a man whose face I have never seen? A man whose sole purpose is to kill? A man whose mind is ever on his throne, his dominion of Earth? Tonight, as he announces the wedding plans, he shouts with rage and indignation that the Priests are against him. The Priests! The most loyal and trusted men in the City. Now they foresee his doom, he cries. They prophesy that a king will fall in Karkesh, and he says they have lost faith in him."

Her words puzzled me. Why should Annulian believe such a prophecy? Yet he was superstitious, like all his subjects. I gripped Vellarna's shoulders.

"He is overwrought," I said. "Soon we must ride to war. Not just another battle or skirmish in the plains, but war. Once it is done, Annulian will be able to relax, for the strain on his shoulders is greater than that on any other man's. Then he will have time to devote to you."

"You don't understand, Galad. I do not want his attention! I...I *hate* him. He is like his father, Brossitan—mad! I would rather be touched with a sword than by him."

I caressed her face softly and she suddenly gripped my hand and pressed it tightly to her. Our eyes met, and I felt a strange emotion stirring. But this was foolish...Taria...

Vellarna kissed my hand and was about to speak when another spoke first behind us. I turned and was up in a flash. A huge man stood there in the door, taller even than Thuran, and Vellarna shrank back with a cry. The man wore splendid trappings of silver armor over a rich red tunic. On the chest plate of his armor an embossed, roaring lion stood out from a sheet of beaten gold, and on his arms were studded bracelets and rings of pearl. I could not see his face, for he wore a golden helm, cast in the shape of a lion's head, and only his eyes of piercing green—like those of a cat—showed through it. The helmet was the most wonderful piece of artistry I had ever seen, beautifully etched and engraved.

"This is no place for the daughter of Prosocles to be hiding away," said the firm voice I had first heard up above by the disc of light. Annulian's cold stare never left my face, and I sensed the deep anger in it.

"Return to your home until I send for you again," he said, and Vellarna wasted no time in leaving.

"Your intended bride is distressed at the proximity of war," I said, hoping the Warlord had not misinterpreted my comforting of the girl. But he said no more on the matter.

"My Priests inform me that Chalremor called for you from his Zurjahn prison. I would have been there to see him, but I was not told," he said in equally as cold a tone as before.

I refused to be intimidated. "I thought you were at Pyron, otherwise I would have insisted that you be at the mind-speak."

"What did the Wise One say?"

"My father is dead and Vorta moves for power on Zurjah as well as here. We must not delay any longer. You are to instruct me and the war is to begin."

He thought for a while, then his cold mood seemed to change. I almost detected a smile.

"Pyron is no more. With kegs of thunderpowder I have scattered it and its troops to the winds. We burrowed like rats beneath the stockade and left our deadly wares under the center of the settlement. Then we sent a trail of fire into the tunnel, and the Gods did the rest. By the Powers of Light, there was all Hell released before us! Walls of flame, blasts of thunder from below! The Zurks must have thought the very legions of the underworld had come to claim them. Not one lived, my archers saw to that. As they reeled from the smoking ruin that had been Pyron, we shot them down. Two thousand, and not one lived to crawl back to Vorta. Pyron is ashes!" And he laughed, throwing back his head and slapping his thighs. He had forgotten Vellarna in his retelling of the victory.

"Then we can use it on Karkesh," I said.

"Yes! With the thunderpowder we fear no one, not even the horned one himself!"

"So we prepare."

"At once. Come, Galad, to the Inner Sanctum. I have already spoken to Thuran. He awaits us there."

I followed the huge figure through torch-lit passages deep down into the bowels of the cave system. We came at length to another chamber and entered. In the half-light where tapers burned, Thuran stood wrapped up in his own thoughts. It was a small room and had a low dais at its end. On this two candles burned, dripping hot wax into engraved bowls below. Between them on the marble table that was draped in black rested a huge grimoire, its covers torn and dusty, its pages loose and soiled with age. In the poor light I could make out the statuesque faces of the ever-present Priests, who lined the walls. Annulian pointed to the book.

"This is the fabled Book of Prophecy, which is said to be almost as old as man himself. Herein is foretold the coming of evil to the world and of how it shall be finally vanquished, allowing the Powers of Light and Goodness mastery for all time."

The Warlord spoke with deep reverence, and the Priests began a soft litany. One of them stepped forward to the dais. Annulian nodded to him, and he tugged on a concealed cord. The red velvet curtains on the wall parted to reveal a glittering inscription of gold.

"Behold, the very words of the Legend, as taken from the crumbling pages of the Book," said Annulian.

The Priest read it out to us. "From the Book of Prophecy:
...I heard, as it were the noise of thunder...And I saw, and behold a white horse...
and he that sat on him had a bow;
and a crown was given unto him;
And there went out another horse that was red:
and power was given to him that sat thereon to take peace from the earth, and that they should kill one another;
and there was given unto him a great sword..
And I beheld, and lo a black horse;
and he that sat on him had a pair of balances in his hand...
And I looked, and behol, a pale horse;
and his name that sat on him was Death, and Hell followed with him.
And power was given unto them...to kill with sword and with hunger, and with death, and with the beasts of the earth..."

I shuddered at the Priest's sepulchral rendering of the awful words of doom, seeing at last the true meaning of the role of the Pale Rider.

Annulian spoke again. "These words from the Book of Prophecy were written untold centuries ago by the servants of the Gods. Now has the time come for them to be fulfilled. Chalremor, the Wise One, has seen and learned their meaning, his mind governed by the Powers of Light. Four Horsemen have been chosen. One shall ride a white horse and carry a bow, and wear a crown. Chalremor has spoken in a dream to the Priests of this Inner Sanctum and has told me who this is to be." He paused in his address, and I reflected that he wore the crown of kingship.

"Thuran shall ride the white horse," he said suddenly, pointing at the startled General, who trembled at the news. Annulian had taken on the appearance of some awful demigod in his stern wrath. Why should he give his crown to Thuran? Unless, as Vellarna had said, he feared for his own life.

"I, lord?" muttered Thuran, as puzzled as I, his face bathed in perspiration.

"Yes! You shall carry the bow that I shall give you, that has rested in our secret vaults since time immemorial. You shall wear also my crown that I shall give you."

"But sire! You are the king!" protested Thuran, horrified, and I began to seriously question the Warlord's motives.

"I know. But time dictates our needs from hereon, Thuran. The crown is yours for two reasons. Firstly, you ride the white horse of plague, to which all our enemies must bow. The crown is a symbol of the power of pestilence. Secondly, the armies need a leader, and I must ride far to the east to rouse the Nomad hordes, who are ready to join us. Therefore you will ride the white horse at the head of my armies. Question it not, for every move serves the Divine purpose. I will be there at the Lost Plain, where all the armies of Earth shall join together, and there shall they see the Four Horsemen. I shall be upon the red horse of war, and I shall carry the sword of the Gods, which also rests in our vaults. Beside me when I come will be Chungsar, Emperor of the Eastern Nomads, and he will ride the black horse of plague to the Lost Plain."

I sensed the Warlord's nervousness, perhaps through fear of a reprimand from the Priests, but the silence of the grave followed his address. I kept my eyes on the dripping candle wax, for I knew my part in this only too well. In my mind I saw again the awful vision in the Finger of Dusk. Thuran shuddered beside me.

"Galad, the staff of Chalremor, Chosen of the Gods, shall lead us all astride the Pale Horse of Death," Annulian said grimly, and all his earlier resentment of my leadership was there in his voice. Thuran swallowed hard.

"You are sure this is the way the Gods will it?" I asked, for Annulian was fearful of something. Though the Priests still hid his thoughts from me, I sensed that he was ill at ease.

"It has been written thus," he said.

"Is it wise to assemble all our forces on the Lost Plain? Vorta will know of it at once. Is this not rash?" I asked dubiously. Annulian's eyes flared up, fired by fanatical madness.

"Rash! How can you call it rash! We obey the Gods in this, none other! They have planned this for centuries, and you call it rash! No, Galad Sarian. I say it is not rashness that impels us. We must act according to the Divine Plan. You know only too well why you are on Earth and your role in the Legend. Has not Chalremor shown you? Can you deny the truth of his words? Have the Gods not watched over you? You speak of the armies...we have the powers now to divert Vorta's watchful mind. Shields! The Priests, the shamans of the wilderness—yourself. Your combined minds will blanket our actions until we are at the doors of the Black City!"

He seemed to me then more of a man possessed than ever. Yet what he said was so, and I thought of Gastar and Tegara Sahdi and my Garganian friend, Pthorthe, and my father—all dead by the workings of Vorta.

"Yes," I said simply.

"So be it!"

And so we retired to his war rooms where for hours we planned and discussed strategies by which to wage war on Karkesh and her satellites.

"I ask only one favor," I told Annulian.

"And that is?"

"The privilege of plunging my blade into Vorta's black heart. You may have his head to do with what you will," I added brutally.

"Very well," said Annulian. "Then we are at war. Let us sleep on it."

And so Thuran and I left the inner warmth of the Temple of Light and came out into a foul night. Storm clouds obscured the moon, and huge drops of rain splashed down on to the wet streets. We went our ways, Thuran with a deep frown on his handsome features, while I came again to the house of Prosocles. As always, my room was open, and I went in, stripped off my wet clothes and lay down wearily on my bed. Outside the storm raged, and a shudder ran through me, so I pulled the furs over me. There was a vivid flash of lightning then, and a shadow fell across me. I was surprised to see Vellarna standing before me.

"Galad," she whispered, drawing near.

"Vellarna. What is it? The hour is late. Dawn will break soon." I sat up in the darkness.

"I would talk to you," she said. I could not see her face clearly.

"It is late."

"Soon it will be too late," she returned, and her words disturbed me. I tried to search her expression in the dark, but could not. She moved closer to me, her thin robes rustling as she moved.

"What do you mean?" I said softly.

"Soon the war will begin and you will leave," she said, and in another flash of light from outside I saw her face, but her eyes averted mine. She was very beautiful in the glow.

"But I shall return."

"Shall you return to me, though?"

"Of course. I must come again to the Sacred City when the victory is ours."

"There, you see. War and victory—you think of nothing else. You return not for me at all." Her voice caught in a sob.

"Annulian will return to you—" I began.

"Oh, Galad, are you blind?" she said suddenly, and I felt my cheeks flush. It was unusual for a girl to fluster me so. "If not, then surely you must know of my feelings for you! How I have felt since first you came here, and since first my eyes looked upon you" she said passionately.

"Vellarna, you must not speak this way. I admire you very much. Nay, do not interrupt. I have thought much about you, and there will always be a place in my heart for you, but there is another—"

"But Taria is so far away! You may never see her again!"

"You must not say that!" I snapped, hurt by the truth of her words.

"Forgive me," she said humbly, lowering her head. "I have watched you, walked with you, thinking that one day you might favor me as you did her."

"I am not angry, Vellarna. But I have told you often of my love for Taria. Only the thought that one day I might be reunited with her has kept me alive for so long."

Tears welled in her eyes and shone in the storm light. There was a long pause.

"And if you are, will you bring her here one day?"

"If the Gods will it."

"Then...then, I would be honored if," she broke off with another sob, and I drew her to a sitting position and put my arm around her to comfort her.

"You must not weep for me, Vellarna," I told her, and I felt her warm body tremble as she silently cried.

"But I love you!" she said, and filled me with utter helplessness.

"It would be wrong for us, though. Remember you are betrothed. Annulian is, for all his faults, a fine man. You may come to love him in time," I tried to solace her, but she sobbed the more.

"Never! He is a madman, cursed with dreams and haunted by those awful Priests who frighten him with their soothsaying. Lately they have changed him for the worse, and their last prophesy has made a bad-tempered devil of him. I can stand him no longer."

"The prophecy..." I mused, thinking of how Annulian had been afraid in the temple earlier.

"I forget the words," she said, burrowing deeper against my chest, her slim arms about my neck.

"Come, come, dry your eyes. Here." I lifted a corner of a silken sheet to her eyes. She brought herself under control at last, and her sobs subsided.

"Tell me of this prophecy, Vellarna. It is important that I know."

"The Priests told Annulian that a king would fall before Shaitan's last dawn. I know not what it means, unless Annulian is to die in battle. If that is so, I will be free of him." She watched my face intently, but my eyes were on the storm outside.

"Yes, I see now why he will make Thuran ride the white horse and wear his crown! He fears for his life," I said, realizing why the Warlord had been so devious. Vellarna's face was pressed to my chest, and after a moment of silence she sat upright. I had forgotten my medallion, and she had seen it.

"What is this? Galad! The medallion..." she murmured.

"It is nothing...uh, nothing. It was given by a friend in..." I began, but she straightened up with a shock.

"The winged horse! There is only one. You could not have got this from a friend. It is the medallion of the prophet, Chalremor."

"Nonsense," I bluffed, but she knew the truth.

"Oh, Galad, I understand now why you have come. The secrecy...the meetings with Annulian...why did you not confide in me? Why did you not tell me? You are..."

"Yes, but it was best that no one knew until the war began."

She tossed her hair back, and her beautiful black tresses filled my nostrils with a heady aroma of perfume. My resistance to her was very low. Only my conscience held me back.

"Even though you are the Chosen One, you still have my heart. I shall marry the king, as my duty commands, but know this—he shall never have my love, and his reign shall be a barren one. No man shall have my love, save you!"

"You must not—"

"No, do not speak," she said, putting her fingers to my lips. "There is no man or god who will tell me who to love. I have chosen you, even as they have."

So saying, she leaned toward me and kissed me fervently with soft, trembling lips, and her arms went once more about me. I responded ardently, unable to hold back my own emotions. Then she broke away and stood up. In silence she undid the cords that held her thin robes, and they fell to the floor, revealing her young and beautifully molded figure in all its splendid nakedness. I watched in fascination as her up-tilted breasts rose and fell.

"What are you doing?" I said stupidly, my mouth dry.

"Soon you will be gone, and I shall never see you again. Take with you this gift, for it has been long since you were comforted, Galad. Nay, do not demur. You cannot go on your quest without love."

With that she pulled away my cover and came beside me on the bed. There was no longer any way for me to resist her, for my passion had been roused. As she made gentle, understanding love to me, I felt a great release of tension and fears. I sank with her into a reckless pool of ecstasy, but when she had gone, my thoughts flew to Taria, whom I had betrayed, and more than ever did I crave to have her beside me.

CHAPTER VIII
The Unleashing of the Armies

One cold, windy night, when the silvered moon drenched the valley and cliffs of naked rock beside the Silver River in its bright light, I rode silently and unnoticed out of the sleeping Sacred City and into a blustery darkness. I was riding out at last on my final mission of destruction, my head full of tactics and plans which had been worked on in depth this last month. I was bound first tonight for the treetop village of Vendl. As my steed trotted along the moonlit ledge, high above the waving treetops, I reflected on the recent events that had led me to this solitary journey. Annulian, the Lion, mighty Warlord of Earth, had at last cast the die in deciding the fate of Karkesh. He had summoned Thuran and I for the last time to the Inner Sanctum, and there in the vaults he had shown us an encased collection of magnificent, priceless weapons. To my noble companion he bestowed a tall, thick bow, encrusted with sparkling jewels, and a crown of beaten gold. Thuran was reluctant to take the crown, and I nearly spoke up against him doing so, facing Annulian with the words of the prophecy that Vellarna had told me of, but for some reason I held my tongue, and Thuran did as he was bidden. To me Annulian had given a suit of mail and a skull-shaped mask, the features of which would have put fear in the hearts of the bravest. He also gave me a weapon which I recognized at once as a star lance. He was unaware of its powers, but said that I would know its purpose. Indeed I did—it could be used either to spit flame or as a heated rod—and I took it with a grim smile of satisfaction. These items now lay wrapped in a cloak across my mount's back.

Since that last meeting, the Warlord had gone to the east, where Chungsar was making ready his army, and together they were making for the Lost Plain at this very moment. I rode across a haunted, empty landscape, and I felt like a gaunt god coming through the realm of dreams to the portentous dawn. If the Gods were at war, they were moving through the phantasmal skies tonight. A chill wind blew across the dusty palisade in choking gusts as I rode into the deserted Vendl. Leaves eddied past in spirals in the gloom. At first I saw nobody and no sign of life whatever. It was as though no one had ever lived here. Then a muffled neigh broke the melancholy silence. A dim figure was crossing the paddock toward

236

me, leading a horse that showed ghastly pale in the moonlight. It was the horse I had saved on the day of its birth, now grown to a great size for a yearling stallion, tossing its mane in the spectral light.

I tethered my horse to the rail inside the open paddock and walked over to the ghostly pair. The shadowy figure dropped the reins in the damp grass, and the proud stallion trotted across to me. As I came up to him, I confidently stroked his firm muzzle to show him I was not afraid, and he rubbed his nose against my face. We were old friends, for I could tell instinctively that he knew me. It was uncanny. I mounted him while he stood motionless, allowing me my will without question, even though none could yet have broken him in. I soothed his mind, and it was as though he knew the reason for our partnership. I stroked his thick mane, patting the broad shoulders.

"Have you the accouterments?" I said to the unmoving figure.

"They are in the stable, lord," he said, keeping back. His superstition filled him with dread.

"Very well," I said, dismounting. "Take him and saddle him up. Prepare him for me. We have a long ride yet."

I gave the reins into his unsteady fingers, and he led the splendid animal away. I watched for a moment, then crossed to the horse on which I had come. From their wrappings I took my armaments: the star lance in its scabbard of gold, the silver mail coat, and the skull helmet, with its black, sightless, staring eyes. I donned my armor and strapped on the scabbard, listening to the leaves rustling in the sighing treetops. I buckled on lastly the thin, metal leggings that the Lion had given me.

Now, with the frightful helm under my arm, I walked across the silent paddock to the stables. Black clouds were piling up high in the distant mountains, while overhead, smaller ones streaked raggedly across the bright moon. A storm was brewing in the brooding heavens. I felt as though my surroundings were lifeless, as though I walked some desolate, astral plane. Perhaps I was indeed Death personified. Only the dust stirred. Inside the creaking stable, I found my steed prepared, but of the man, there was no sign. I was alone again. A superb saddle elaborately worked with runes and ancient letters graced the horse's back, and beneath this was a black saddle cloth, on each side of which was emblazoned a grinning skull.

237

The horse also wore a coat of thin silver mail to protect it in battle; I knew this metal to be a particularly hard alloy, despite its thinness. Winking jewels were embedded all along the leather work of the horse's harness. He stood peacefully chomping hay. I put my boot into one silver stirrup and mounted him. All was ready. Outside, the wind moaned like some demented soul in torment, anxious for me to be on my way.

So out of empty Vendl we rode, two creatures forged into one mighty machine, a powerful engine of destruction. On into the chilling vapors of night we traveled, riding hard in the spectral darkness for hours. Through swamps and reed banks, over mossy hummocks, past crumbling menhirs of ancient civilizations, across weed-strewn clearings which might once have been roads—on and on we rode. At last we saw the distant foothills of the mountains and rode now the more furiously. My steed never tired, reveling luxuriously in the gallop, and I felt an exhilaration such as I had never before known. The howling wind tore at us as we charged across the grassy plain; above us the threatening cloud banks rushed ominously across the striated sky, blotting out the moonlight. Spasmodic drops of rain brushed my face, but the storm held off. I wondered for how long. The air was close and oppressive despite the wind, and sweat soaked my inner linen.

We reached the foothills where I found a spring in the rocks, there watering my grateful mount. I had brought some food, so I ate what I had and gave the horse some fruit. Then I cantered him along the edge of the hills until we came to the ruins of an ancient city. Falling walls and heaps of tumbled rubble thrust up from the dusty, cracked streets, and I led my horse up a dry gully to where a flaking tower leaned drunkenly against the skyline. This was the place I sought. I tethered my horse and climbed the steps of the old tower. From its broken ramparts I could see for miles in either direction. Then, satisfied with my night's work, I drew my cloak over me and slept.

Distant sounds awoke me. I looked up at a low ceiling of overcast clouds. They were swollen with rain, which must surely fall soon. The sounds below me attracted my attention, and I looked down on the Lost Plain in wonder. Thousand upon thousand of mounted Barbarian warriors were filling it from my right, as far back as the eye could see. Their mingled multitude of voices drifted up to me on the calm air, and I heard the clank and jingle of metal very clearly.

Ahead of this sea of men rode a lone figure, who had come almost abreast of the point where I watched, far down on the Plain below. Even at this distance I recognized him, sitting stiffly astride his white charger. It was Thuran, whom the human tide behind would believe to be the Warlord.

Never before in the history of the Zurjahn Empire had such an army marched. There were bowmen by the hundred thousand, lancers, swordsmen, ax men, mace bearers, and all manner of other soldiers, virtually all mounted. Hundreds of white flags, edged with gold braid, fluttered in the warm air, all emblazoned with roaring lions. I knew the number of the Warlord's forces, but to see them before me was a sight of incredible awe and magnificence. Among the seething masses were great carts pulled by many horses, containing all kinds of supplies necessary for a period in the field: food, medical and extra arms. A peal of distant thunder away to my left made me glance across at the endless plain there.

I gasped. Yet another immense army was approaching. It was surprisingly close, and as I peered down from my lofty perch, I saw for the first time the giant figure that led this body of men, sitting on a black horse. This must be Chungsar and his eastern nomads—men who were said to roam the eastern deserts in separate tribes, now banded together in a common cause by the efforts of Annulian. But what a titanic array! It stretched back along the edge of the foothills to the hazy limits of the Lost Plain, its size incalculable.

Slowly but surely, the two enormous armies came to face each other below me. Their combined roars and cheers set the mountains behind me echoing. Chungsar and Thuran saluted each other, then met and rode together in the direction of the gully below me, stopping about half a mile from me on a grassy ridge, overlooking the howling armies.

Annulian had planned well. The Priests would be in the ruins behind and around me, prepared to shield from prying Zurk eyes and minds the gathering of the armies. In the ranks of the nomads, which now began to mingle in places with Thuran's army, I could see strange war engines, catapults and rams. Strange devices adorned the flags of the eastern horde, and the men wore long robes hung with metal. Their shields were small, and their helmets of black metal, inlaid with letters of some language unknown to me.

Now the imposing figures of Thuran and Chungsar turned and

239

faced the gathering armies. I studied the latter closely. He wore a tight-fitting undersuit of black silk and over it an incredible leather coat, from which protruded dozens of long, metal spikes. His brightly painted helmet was cast in the shape of a dragon's head, and this also had many projecting, though smaller spikes. On his steed's sides hung two long saddle cloths, almost reaching the ground, and each of these was embroidered with the scales mentioned in the Book of Prophecy. Swinging at the Emperor's thickly studded belt was a huge mace, wrought from solid gold, and he carried a long, three-pronged fork of black iron. Chungsar was the most terrifying warrior I had ever seen. His black leather boots were laced to the knee with thin chains of gold, and his horse was well-protected with thin sheets of silver armor.

Thuran sat beside him on the proud white steed, wearing the familiar lion-helm of the Warlord. This was now adorned with Annulian's priceless crown, and across Thuran's shoulder was the huge bow, strung with twisted steel rope, given to him by Annulian. A velvet quiver, full of iron shafts hung across the General's back, over his thick, shining armor, and on either side of the white horse's flanks dangled rows more of quivers, full with gleaming arrows. He also carried a heavy broadsword at his side, and being the same build as Annulian, passed for him without difficulty.

Above me I heard rumblings in the scudding clouds. It would be dark soon, despite the daylight hours, for the thunderstorm would certainly break. Flickers of lightning were crackling faintly behind me in the mountains. I heard also a whinnying horse, and at first I thought it to be mine. I turned to see a scarlet rider descending from the rocks beyond the gully, unseen by the masses below, and mounted on a red horse. Annulian! He wore a tight suit of red leather, reinforced with metal armor, and had on a hideous mask, with protruding fangs of silver. Scarlet plumes sprouted from its crest, and his chest was ringed with bands of etched steel, as were his arms and legs. Three javelin hafts of ivory jutted up into the air on each side of his saddle, and at his side was belted the enormous sword, which needed both hands to be wielded. He trotted his lightly armored horse up to the other two, standing between them.

A deafening roar went up as the clustered armies saw him atop the grassy slope, and it swelled as it was taken up by those in the distance. A crash of thunder answered them, high above me, as though the Gods joined them. Soon the storm would be on us. Now was the time for me to act. I went down from the tower, donning my grim helmet, and mounted my pale horse. I undid his tether, then picked our way carefully down the gully, still out of sight of the waiting hordes. The hillock rose before me, and steadily I cantered the horse up it. The three riders came into view against the black sky. A forked tongue of brilliant lightning split the heavens in a crescendo as I topped the ridge in full view of everyone, and I heard screams and cries of alarm mingled with uncertain cheers rising above the booming of the thunder. Those in the front ranks drew back.

Now did the storm choose to break loose in all its terrible fury. Sheets of driving rain swept across the Lost Plain, and dancing flames of fire zigzagged across the fuming skies. It seemed as though the Gods spoke for us, filling us with power and might for the task. The appalling Four Horsemen were ready to ride. We made a fearsome sight, standing before our armies, oblivious to the howling madness of the enraged elements. The Powers of Darkness whined about us but we were not moved. As one we held high our weapons, and the rain-lashed army saluted us from the deluged Plain.

All was in order for war. Annulian had called together all his chiefs and generals in the Temple of Light and given them all strict orders. Our plan of attack had been worked out precisely: we must be swift and effective, destroying the environs of the Black City and as much of Karkesh itself as we could, and bringing to earth the Space Receiver Station at its heart so that Zurjah could not send reinforcements. Thuran was was to lead one quarter of the army to the northwest, with Bastagal, Salanar, Mordruicus, and Gavantaz as his Generals. Chungsar and Annulian were to take half the army southeast to a place called Olan's Forest, where they would divide with Annulian's force in the north and the Emperor's in the south. I was to take the remaining quarter of the army to the fringes of the Cursed Forest, with Ool, Prosocles, Hoymanian, and Fatho as my Generals. At the appointed hour, our forces would attack the Zurk satellite towns of Arbore in the north, Orezza in the east of Karkesh, and Ultima in the south simultaneously, reducing them all in one three-pronged swoop before Karkesh could retaliate. Thuran and Chungsar would then meet west of Karkesh and destroy Loyul, then advance upon the Black City, while Annulian and I would march upon it from the east and the ruins of Orezza. We were counting on speed and surprise, having put our faith in the Priests and shamans to blanket our activities.

Three nights later, the war began at midnight. I rode to a hill overlooking Orezza and waited for the signals to attack. The town was nothing more than a glorified barracks, housing several thousand Zurk troops, who patrolled the borders of the Karkesh kingdom. Its destruction was swift and brutal. Firstly a small band of Barbarians rode from the cover of the swamp and attacked the gates and walls with fire arrows and thunderpowder kegs. A host of aroused Zurk cavalry came recklessly out in pursuit, and with that I gave the signal for my men to ride down in force from the hillsides. From north and south of the town we rode, crushing the Zurk infantry and killing them to a man. We circled the town and blasted its thin walls and rained down more fire arrows. Tamed ibathenes, controlled by the mysterious shamans of the forests, trampled their way into Orezza, and after an hour our forces scorched through the streets like a prairie fire and put every living thing to the sword or torch.

The fighting was savage, the Zurks battling hopelessly to stem the flood of invaders. I watched with little compassion for them as barbarians took a cruel revenge for all the years of oppression, burning the houses, destroying everything. We turned night into day with the foray, and the streets were paved with blood and the mangled corpses of the slain. I trotted slowly about the transformed town after the battle, Death looking upon death. The charred streets were piled with corpses, mostly Zurk, and houses were gutted or leaning at absurd angles. The gutters were stained with dried and clotting blood, and the side streets and alleyways were choked. This was my cause, my calling. To kill, and to counteract everything the Dream Lord creed had taught me. But it had to be done, no matter how ugly a deed, for there could be no peace on Earth until Vorta's hold was smashed.

Now that Orezza was no more, the army marched east to Karkesh. It camped in the valley, and in the early hours the army of Annulian rejoined us from Olan's Forest. Now we could sleep and await news of Chungsar and Thuran. The hour to strike for the Black City was only days away. I entered my tent and collapsed with fatigue, my head still ringing with the shouts and clash of battle.

It was broad daylight when I awoke. I left the tent and sought that of Annulian. We were up in the hills that overlooked the valley leading eventually to Karkesh. Down below me the army was encamped.

"The first blow and a complete success," said the Warlord when I confronted him in his tent. His eyes watched me closely from inside the garish mask.

"Were there any prisoners?" I asked, but I already knew the answer.

"Prisoners? Don't ber a fool, my lord. We show no mercy to the Zurks. We put them all to the sword. Word has come from Thuran. He has razed Arbore, driving all manner of wild beasts into it from the jungles, and slaying its inhabitants to a man. Ultima has fallen, too. Chungsar's fanatical nomads swarmed its walls and gutted the place in minutes. Not a Zurk lives outside Karkesh's walls after last night's carnage. It now remains for the combined forces of Chungsar and Thuran to wipe Loyul from the map and for us to annihilate any reinforcements that Vorta might send. The smoke from Orezza boils upward in a beacon of filth a mile high."

I said nothing for a moment, regarding him grimly. It was I who wore the helm of Death, but the coldness of the man before me suggested it should be him who was named the Reaper. His determination to slay the Zurks to a man bordered on the obsessive. Yet it was true that Zurk oppression had been equally as ruthless and unfeeling. The wheel was turning.

"So Vorta will send troops out to meet us on the plains before Karkesh?" I said.

"Yes. He will send the cream of his army to face us. I have had word sent to him via my spies that a Barbarian force is even now poring over the spoils of Orezza. Vorta will howl and send his best to wipe us out easily—or so he thinks. Once we have smashed his picked troops, Karkesh will be our goal."

Again he was to be proved right, for shortly after midday, I saw a cloud of dust up the valley. A host of Zurk cavalry spurred down the valley. But Annulian had planned his moves carefully. All morning his troops had been lacing the valley with thunderpowder. Now the main body of men were concealed behind the banks of a shallow river and beyond it, out of sight of the oncoming army. The tents had been struck and everything moved, ready for battle. From the hills, the Warlord and I watched.

When the Zurks came within a certain distance of the river, they were allowed glimpses of Barbarian warriors on horseback. Beyond was the black plume of burning Orezza. The Zurk generals must have cursed at the sight of it, their lust for revenge prompted by the thought of the Barbarians even now looting beyond. So they spurred their men onward with all haste, straight into the waiting trap. A chain of explosions churned the valley floor into a melee of dust and confusion, as keg after concealed keg of thunderpowder burst among the bewildered Zurk forces. Annulian's men behind the river banks yipped and shrieked with glee as hundreds of assailants were blown apart.

Confusion took over among the Zurks. They scattered in all directions as the ground blasted apart and tons of earth and rock flew skywards, heaping up the dead and smashing their ranks indiscriminately. It was difficult to see in the blanketing clouds of dust, and now the Barbarian forces chose their moment to attack. Out from their cover they spurred, their battle horses tearing into the bemused ranks of the Zurks. Annulian laughed as wave after wave of our men galloped to the bloody fray. Thousands of warriors hurled themselves at the confounded Zurks, and the ring of steel and the screams of the dead and dying reached our ears.

The dust cleared a little, allowing us to see the battle. That proud column of Zurks had been chased and harried into groups and surrounded by vengeful Barbarians. A rain of arrows wiped out most of the survivors. Swords clashed, blood flowed like spilled wine, and horses screeched among the carpets of dead. I looked on in amazement, never having witnessed such scenes of death and horror before. Through it all, the Warlord was silent. His eyes were cold and merciless.

For an hour the warriors hounded the cream of the Zurk forces, and after that it became a case of clearing up the dead and wounded. Gradually the dust settled and vultures swooped daringly down from the blue skies to feast on the lifeless multitude. Thousands of corpses were strewn about, man and horse alike, and not one Zurk lived or had escaped to warn Vorta of what was coming to Karkesh. Annulian climbed on to his red horse and spurred it down into the valley of death. I watched as our forces regrouped beyond the river bed and made ready for another march.

Later that day, a lone rider came hurrying up the hillside and leaped off his steed at the feet of Annulian. He garbled some message before the Warlord dismissed him and then galloped off down to the tents that had been unfurled below. Annulian came to me, his eyes dancing with an unfamiliar warmth.

"Good news. Thuran and Chungsar have been triumphant in the west. Loyul is no more, crushed between the twin armies in one sweeping assault. The Devil in Hell will be overworked this day with so many Zurk souls to contend with. Now can we ready ourselves for the final offensive. Only Karkesh stands against us."

"Remember your pledge," I said quietly.

"Which was?"

"Vorta is mine."

"So be it. But I will be there. The days of the Zurks on earth are numbered. We attack in two days. Let Daras Vorta conjure up all the fiends of the underworld—they will not avail him against my killers."

I did not feel such confidence. Although we had smashed the satellites, the real conflict had yet to begin.

CHAPTER IX
Shadows Over Karkesh

Karkesh, the Black City, rose in an ugly sprawl before me, cloaked in an aura of evil and corruption. I sat astride the pale horse, in full battle dress, refreshed after a two day rest. To my right and left stretched line after line of Barbarian warriors, glinting in the harsh sunlight. The jingling of spurs and the clang of arms blended to stir the still morning air. Annulian rode forward far to my right, while Prosocles and Ool were over on my left as we converged as one on the high, grim walls. Somewhere beyond this grim city of death, another army would be marching, led by Thuran and Chungsar. The crude road that led from Orezza wound its way before us, up to the huge eastern gate of the city, and from its twin towers and lofty ramparts the ant-like Guards looked down upon us in consternation. I turned to watch Annulian. When our forces were a mile from the walls, he lifted his sword. I did the same, and the whole vast army halted. Annulian was to attack the gate by which Thuran and I had earlier escaped the city.

The air was strangely silent. Vorta had sent out a number of air rafts to see what kind of host opposed him, and I had scorched them out of the sky with my star lance. Vorta could have had but few of the aerial machines, or he would have had them attack us constantly. Faintly I could hear the excited cries of the Zurks as they stared at our mammoth ranks. I looked about me with an air of calmness. The men waited expectantly. Far away clouds drifted aimlessly across the blue vault. Someone coughed.

"Bring the thunderpowder!" I yelled. As the murmurs rippled across the tide of warriors, the ranks around me parted. Scores of kegs were brought forward and laid in front of the army. Annulian had given a similar order to mine, further down the line.

"Carriers! Load up." At my order, a chain of horsemen stepped forward, and the warriors lifted one keg each, holding them across their legs in readiness. I sheathed my sword, bent down, and heaved a keg up by the rim. The men waited tensely.

"Archers! To the fore!" I called back, and a company of mounted archers split from the main body, riding out before us and forming a spearhead. Dust eddied about in thin flurries as the horses fidgeted. I looked back.

"Prepare your arrows and cover us," I said. A thousand voices cried in jubilant readiness, and I lifted my arm to show Annulian that all was ready here. He waved back. Before I committed my men to the charge, I sent my mind flitting along those battlements to try and gauge the nature of the defense, but there were no dreadful weapons of war lined against us.

"All right!" I shouted. The men hung poised for the charge like ravenous wolves, their faces grim under their daubs of paint. I gave them one last glance, their faces showing how eager they were to be at the walls. Satisfied that the moment was ripe, I cried out the order to attack. Led by the spearhead, we rode hard to the gates that loomed above us. The intention was to break open the doors with all haste and be in the city before Vorta could mass his defenses. So far he had not taken the Barbarian successes seriously, and I wondered if he knew that it was I who stood against him.

As soon as our front runners were within range, the Guards on the battlements began unleashing a steady hail of their own arrows at us, and our leading bowmen fired up into the blue ranks high above, covering our advance. We galloped furiously, churning the black earth to dust as we drummed forward. Arrows fell in thick clouds, bouncing off my helm and breast, while next to me a horse fell squealing, discharging rider and his precious load in a flying somersault. We were losing men fast, especially up front, but we drew ever nearer the gates. My eyes smarted in the swirling dirt, and I coughed in the dense clouds of dust that we disturbed.

Some of the Guards began throwing down rocks on to the advancing archers, many of whom fell prone or injured. Riderless horses charged madly off along the rim of the walls. I swung my star lance and sent a sheet of flame scorching up at the walls, burning down a score of Zurks. Still the storm of missiles fell upon us, but eventually we made the gates. Above me the Guards were falling and tumbling to the ground, pierced by our whistling arrows, though our own casualties were far heavier. There was no other way for us to get the gate open, and we had to open them. The star lance would have done it, but in the time needed I would certainly have been shot down. We rushed in madly, depositing as many kegs at the foot of the gates as we could, then whirled away to safety. I came under the cold shadows of those foreboding walls and cast my keg at the thick doors, wheeling away quickly as a huge rock hit the ground nearby, bouncing dangerously close to me before smashing into a valiant warrior and bowling both him and his horse over, crushing them.

We had built up quite a substantial pile of thunderpowder I saw as I looked back over my shoulder. Annulian's forces were moving in further along, but I could not see the gates they attacked for the curve of the city walls. Most of our brave front men and their steeds were down, twitching in death. Many of the valiant keg-bearers were struck by fatal arrows as they tried to spurt away, and catapulted headlong into the dust. I turned again to see how we had fared, raking another line of heads up on the battlements with the star lance flames. The path to the huge doors was littered with our dead, and the Zurks were jeering, thinking they had thwarted us. Annulian had also retreated, his work apparently done, and I saw arrows pinging off his armor as he rode back to the ranks.

The Warlord would burst open the gates by using fire archers, but I had the star lance. I waited as the last of my warriors galloped back to the safety of the ranks, though pitiful few had survived that deadly hail of arrows and rock. The Zurks could not understand what our motives were, but they continued to fire impotently long after the last of us was out of range. Choosing my moment, I spurred forward again, my star lance steady in my hand. I released a stream of crackling heat at the foot of the gates, and the thunderpowder went off with a devastating detonation, like the sound of a hundred thunderclaps. A shower of broken rock and dust rained down on me and the waiting army, and I fought to control my prancing steed. As the black clouds parted I saw that we had achieved our aim. We waited amidst noisy cheers while the last of the dust cleared. The gates were broken and twisted on their hinges, and huge chunks of charred wood poked out from the great smoking hole we had made. I opened my eyes as I saw the left tower; huge cracks like rivers were spreading up its height, then with a sinister rumble it split into pieces, crashing down upon the battlements, crushing scores of Guards, and sending them dropping off the walls mingled with chunks of debris. Parts of the wall itself split open, and chunks of loosened masonry fell onto the plain. The result was more than we had dared hope. Roars of triumph burst from every throat, almost drowning another explosion on our right—Annulian had also succeeded and blasted open his gate. Now the men were eager to charge forward, but still I restrained them.

"Bring the ibathenes!" I roared above the din. Behind me the ranks parted once more, and up the road came three of the reptilian beasts, three times taller than a man, tails flicking, teeth bared, dripping with foam as the riders goaded them on. The shamans that sat astride the bronze collars of these beasts had something of the Dream Lords powers of telepathy, and could force the ibathenes to respond to basic commands. With so many men around, it was hard to control them, but the shamans bent their wills. There were Priests among our numbers too, and they concentrated on goading the ibathenes forward with their own peculiar mental powers. I added what will power I could to their efforts, and at once felt the groping presence of my sworn enemy. Vorta had found me with my mind screen partially down.

"So it is you, Sarian! I had guessed as much. Your mental powers are growing. To shield the minds of so vast an army from me—it is no small achievement. I applaud it. But now you and your stinking army of Barbarian filth are doomed. You have only the vaguest glimmerings of what the power of the mind is really like. You are a flea among titans! You will see, my boy, you will see. I will raise up such opposition that your minions will fly back to the wastes. Until we meet, Sarian!"

The Zurks were now vainly trying to prevent the approach of the lumbering ibathenes. Nothing could penetrate the thick armor of their hides, and the beasts moved sluggishly and ponderously to the leaning gateway. With mad roars, goaded by its tormentors, the first beast entered the gaping orifice, bellowing its hatred and anger as it entered the city. Not only would it release a tide of terror among the people within, it would also ensure that the Guards did not try to barricade the gateway. Painfully slowly the other two ibathenes were led up to the gates and passed within, while the helpless Guards above could do nothing but watch.

I led our army closer to the gates, still out of range of enemy fire. I looked across at Annulian. He had sent another three ibathenes into the city. He raised his glittering weapon and then charged. Behind him his forces rallied, riding like the wind for the city. We must now enter Karkesh systematically, for we would be reduced rapidly if we all charged together. I yelled instructions and led the first column forward. We encountered that deadly hail which took its fearful toll, but the archers above could not hope to stem our flooding numbers. Forward I thundered, my steed kicking up huge clods of earth, regardless of the flying arrows. My fellows fell about me on all sides, and the ground trembled at our coming. With a jubilant war cry, I leapt through the gates on my pale charger, splitting open the nearest Zurk head with one swing of my drawn sword. I used my star lance to singe them and my sword to slash them aside as they came at me.

But we were inside the walls! Now we could pit ourselves man to man. We followed in the destructive wake of the rampant ibathenes, which had gone on into the suburbs, and now we set everything to the torch, discharging more kegs of thunderpowder on every side. I cut and burned my bloody way to a flight of stairs leading to the ramparts, where Zurk archers lined the way upward, firing incessantly into our milling warriors. Thousands of us were pouring through the broken gates now, releasing a withering shower of arrows at the Zurk forces, which broke before the deluge of assailants in the streets. Ool had spurred his men deeper into the city, cutting down the opposition like wheat stalks with his crimson, double-edged ax.

"To the ramparts!" I yelled, and forced my steed up the first steps, kicking aside two Guards as I did so. Below me the houses burst into flame and blazed as I fought the men on the stairs. Realizing that their arrows were useless against my resisting mail, they drew swords. Men followed in my rear, hacking and thrusting with gusto. My steed reared, sending Guards to their screaming deaths on the cobbles below as I urged him on. Then something heavy hit me from above and I fell clumsily to the lower steps. My men swarmed over me protectively and on into the bitter fray. The Guards above were stoning us in a desperate bid to keep us from the ramparts. Once there, no one would stop the flood of warriors through the gates.

Caught up in the whirlwind of my own warriors, I was hustled up the stairs, and as many of us as could grabbed fallen shields and held them over our head for protection. My horse had found his way down to the foot of the stairs again, and he would be safe there for a time. Meanwhile we pressed the fighting Guards higher and higher up the stairs, while still our men poured into the city. Everywhere below us was aflame, and from all directions came the sound of exploding thunderpowder. Vivid scarlet and yellow tongues reached up into the blue skies, enveloping the buildings in black fumes. The Zurks fought like dogs for their lives, and I soon found myself leading the assault on the ramparts again.

My star lance was a silver blur as I sent Guard after Guard tumbling off the stone stairs into oblivion, soaking the stones below in pools of gore. I was kicked and buffeted, but I no longer cared. When I am involved thus in battle, I am gripped by a madness and the strength of ten and cannot hold me back. Up and down flashed and crackled my deadly weapon, burning through flesh, bone, and steel alike, and step by step I forged upward. Beside me fought a tall mammoth of a man, drenched in Zurk blood. He swung his ax with all the strength his huge bulk could muster and was almost hacking the opposition in twain, booting any that fell over the edge.

Together we led the irrepressibly ascent, until a javelin from above buried itself in his thick neck. Without a sound he toppled outward in an arc, falling into the inferno below. I attacked all the harder, and two men replaced the fallen giant. Time loses all proportion when one is fighting for one's life, and so I know not for how long we battled up on to the walls. Missiles flew thick and fast like buzzing flies and men grunted and cursed each other, spitting insults at every thrust. Eventually we forced our enemies back, until hundreds of Barbarians followed us, leaping joyfully on to the ramparts. With frenzied charges they began sweeping the Zurks over the sides in merciless abandon. I paused from my slaying and momentarily left the battle front. I leaned over the side of the wall and searched out my horse. He stood patiently in the ruins below.

My eyes caught sight of movement in the billows of smoke above the streets, and I cursed as I saw a fleet of air rafts bearing down upon us, their sides bristling with Zurk armament. I fired on them with the star lance, nodding with satisfaction as the first one burst into flames and crashed down into the city. I swept the stream of fire to and fro in an attempt to bring down more of the air rafts, but a new wave of them appeared. I expected to be cut down where I stood, but with some confusion saw the new wave set upon the first. My expression changed to one of glee as the air rafts entangled and fought above the bedlam on the ramparts. Some of the air rafts appeared to have been commandeered by our own troops!

My men were fighting furiously along the ramparts, dealing out bloody death to the Zurks, who would soon be cleared from here altogether. Above me the Zurk air rafts were falling like leaves, each party of attackers involved in close quarter thrusting. With another burst from the star lance I was able to reduce the odds in favor of the second wave, and soon only a handful of the rafts were airborne. The leading raft floated above me, and a familiar face grinned down at me. It was Brusiphylon, Vorta's chief of staff.

"We meet again!" I called above the din of battle, and he waved a bloody sword.

"Your helm masks your face but not your voice, Galad Sarian," he called back. "You will not have to contend with any more air rafts. The rest have been sabotaged from within. And so have most of the war weapons Vorta has hidden here."

"By the stars! Then you are with us?"

"Of course. Vorta will howl when he realizes!" laughed the General, and I echoed him grimly. The deception had indeed been remarkable.

Brusiphylon leaned over the side to watch the fighting, then suddenly straightened up, his features twisted in a mask of agony.

251

His eyes bulged and blood ran from his mouth where his teeth had bitten into his gums. I tried to see who had delivered the death blow, but there was no one there. Brusiphylon let out one piercing scream of agony, then tumbled out of the air raft to the blazing ruins below. I turned to my men once more.

"Fight on along the walls. Clear them of all Zurks," I told them, then ran down the slippery stairs to see if the General had died. Still our armies flooded into the city, waving jubilantly at me as they galloped headlong past. I mounted up and tried to find a way into the fire, but it was hopeless. Brusiphylon was dead. A cloud seemed to pass over the sun as I thought about his passing, then a sinister presence flickered inside my mind.

"So," came the thoughts of Vorta, unmistakably him, "you found an ally within my camp. I was a fool to trust him. But you see what happens to those who betray me, Sarian. To die in agony...you will know what it is like, when you come to me."

As quickly as the thought-voice came it had gone. I shuddered. Then a fresh wave of warriors burst through the gates. Recognizing me at once, they rallied to me and we thundered up the now deserted, war-torn streets in search of more plunder.

CHAPTER X
Horror in the Pits

Charging down the streets of Karkesh, with the abandon of a madman, I led a pack of a thousand warriors across the city. The Barbarian army was everywhere, burning and sacking. Now that the gates were down, the Zurks had not had the time to organize a solid defense, but fought in disjointed pockets all over the city. Whether Vorta was too preoccupied with his evil practices within the citadel to mass a defensive blockade, I could not say. I concentrated on a swift invasion of the inner city. We burned as we went, my men casting flaming brands into doorways, pausing only to watch the flames catch at the timber and straw. I used my star lance to sweep aside the parties of horsemen that rode for us, leaving a path of charred, stinking flesh. Now I was seeing in ghastly detail the realization of my nightmares. Buildings toppled into ashes, roads were pitted and littered, whilst roaring fire devoured everything. I was indeed Death himself, surging down upon my victims with an insatiable lust, carving a bloody way through the Zurk troops. Behind me came the pillaging hellions, spreading crimson death in waves as they tore on in my wake.

Covered in filth and sweat I rode on, while at my back my screaming band sent more shafts of fire up into the open windows, trampling down all those who withstood us as brutally as I. Karkesh would be doomed unless Vorta could perform some frightful miracle. The tenacity and velocity of our siege had caught the Zurk forces completely off guard, and now there was no way they could stem the invasion. But Vorta's silence and seeming refusal to unleash his own awful powers puzzled me.

Ahead of us in an empty square stood a deserted Guard Centre, its troops having raced to the walls or the palace, where the fighting would be thickest. My marauders and I charged under the archway and into the inner compound. Several men rushed bravely at us, then halted as they saw how many there were. We cut them down without a second glance. We wheeled around in the cobbled yard, throwing spears through the windows and cursing any occupants. One of my men rode up as I reigned in, preparing to lead them out in search of more victims.

"Your pardon, Lord, but there is some kind of gateway yonder," he said, pointing. "Could it lead to the pits?"

"Gods of Light, yes!" I nodded. "Your head is not befogged with battle as is mine. Let us see. We may be able to descend and free our fellows. Ahoy! Gather around you men. We seek a way to the pits. If we can free our fellows, our forces will multiply."

A cheer of approval went up as I blasted the gates with the star lance. A sheet of flame flicked at the wood, and after some time the gates fell in ashes and a tunnel gaped at us. We clattered into it and made our way down its sharply twisting decline, meeting no one until we came to the first level. Here we were seen at once by a disheveled gathering of bewildered Guards, who ran like scalded cats through the passages, yelling in disbelief. We rode on down, the first mounted men to descend into this festering filth. Once we were seen by the prisoners, they began cheering and yelling with delight.

"It cannot be true!"

"My eyes are mocking me."

"See! The Pale Rider! Death has come for his own!"

"It is an illusion," I heard them yell. Some came and pressed themselves up against the bars that confined them, others cowered back in terror, their eyes white in the shadows. Blood coated me and my skull mask must have terrified them.

"Hear me, prisoners of Karkesh! I am no illusion. This is real blood on my armor—Zurk blood! Your torment is at an end," I roared, and the cheer that went up echoed around the damp walls.

"Let us cast off your chains that you may join our fellows, slitting Zurk throats and bellies above! Know you this, that the hand of doom is upon this Black City. Armageddon is come to Karkesh!"

Our mounted party soon ran the scuttling Guards to earth. The Zurks fought miserably and desperately, but we cut them down within minutes, yanking keys from their mutilated corpses. The clamor set up by the exultant prisoners was deafening as we began unlocking the cages everywhere.

"To the lower levels!" I shouted to my mounted warriors, leaving the prisoners to release all the others. We searched successfully for the passages that led below, meeting and spitting the odd Guards that ran in terror from our flying hooves. Most of the jailers were quickly killed and relieved of their keys, and all the remaining Guards appeared to have gone into the city to join their fellows in battle. We liberated thousands in that triumphant raid on the prison levels, and some of the freed men surged up into the streets like demons, bent on terrible vengeance and full of new-found zest, while others followed us down into the pits.

As I rode past the last cells of the second level, I caught a glimpse of a familiar bent figure, shambling off into the further depths below. It was none other than my former jailer, Yarkeron, and I spurted after him with a shout. Behind me followed the mixture of mounted warriors and liberated prisoners. I rounded a curve in the evil-smelling walls that led down into those well-remembered depths, and did not notice the dwarf skulking in a dark nook. As I came abreast, wondering where the little man had gone, he darted out and plunged a long iron javelin hard up into the soft belly of my proud steed. Deeper and deeper sank the fatal shaft, and with a terrible cry, the great pale horse reared high in the mildewed tunnel, a stream of its lifeblood issuing from the wound and gushing to the floor. With a strangled whinny the horse fell backward, sending me crashing heavily to the slope.

The men were shocked into silence as they drew up, their faces masked with horror at the struggling stallion's plight. I scrambled to my feet and ran to the horse in disbelief. He lay motionless now on the dimly lit ramp, the hateful shaft embedded in his vitals, drinking deep of his precious blood. I cradled his head hopelessly, and his eyes looked beseechingly into mine. Then with a last spasm of movement, he coughed out blood and died. A murmur of sorrow broke from the lips of my men, and behind me I heard a shufling sound. I turned to see the dwarf hobbling down the tunnel for safety.

"Yarkeron!" I shouted venomously, until the walls rang with his name. He stopped and turned. Slowly I picked up the star lance and advanced. He made off again.

"Come and fight, you abomination!" I yelled, breaking into a run. Anger washed over me in ever increasing tremors. All my loathing of this sick, debased city flooded back to me as I ran, concentrating on this one fleeing figure. The Barbarian laws were just—there should be no mercy for our enemies. Yarkeron could not outrun me, and had to face me once more. He drew back against the wall in fear, seeing the ghoulish skull-mask I wore leering at him.

"Are you ready to die?!" I snarled at him. The approaching men watched in silence. Yarkeron babbled inanely. I slipped the lance into its sheath and whipped out my sword, raising it as I strode forward. Yarkeron lifted his gnarled arms, and for a moment I felt pity. But then I thought of the horse, and so I split the jailer into two chunks of flesh, kicking that flea-ridden carcass aside. The incident held no joy for me: I felt nauseated, and had no wish to linger over my victory.

"On to the pits," I said to the men. They rode wide-eyed over what was left of Yarkeron and in scorn we descended to the last unholy level. The Priests of the Inner Sanctum had prophesied that a king would fall in Karkesh, and so one had. My steed had been a monarch among horses. But that would not have been their meaning. I pondered the enigma as I went down. As we came to the pits, we were set upon by several more jailers, but madness goaded me to a superhuman endeavor and I slashed about wildly with the fury of a whirlwind. I had killed everyone that beset me before my followers struck a blow. We achieved the same level of success down here as we had above, liberating everyone and putting all our enemies to the sword.

I was bitter about my irreplaceable loss, but made the Guards pay dearly. At length we had set free everyone on all levels and stood reeking of blood and sweat in the midst of our slain foes. We had set free the prisoners under the very nose of the Warden. Yet still he had not taken the offensive. Why? Some of the prisoners motioned me to yet another tunnel, and I found to my surprise that it led down still deeper into the fetid earth. One of the prisoners waved severed chains at the black hole.

"Here lies the way to the Sacred Altar, which goes down to Hell itself! Below lies the secret chamber of the Goat worshipers," he cried.

Burning torches were snatched from wall sockets as my warriors dismounted. I sheathed my sword and pulled out the star lance, flicking the haft button on. The weapon glowed blue as I went down into the tunnel, heedless of what might be down there. The men came after, thirsting for the scouring of the Goat. After a brief, clammy descent down narrow, crumbling stairs into oppressive air, I came to a macabre chamber, with a low, charred ceiling. A steel door barred the way, and from beyond it came a foul, necromantic dirge, as though the foulest slime in Hell had been given speech to mouth obscenities to some bestial deity. Vorta must be there, gearing his mind powers to the production of some new foulness with which to blast the invaders with madness. I waved my men back and set the star lance flame to the door. It melted slowly, and the din beyond increased.

At last, with the energy of the star lance fading, the door was molten and dripping. As it cooled, I passed into the chamber beyond. I expected to be set upon by the grotesque horrors of Vorta's worst excesses, but the chamber was disturbingly empty, despite the continuing dirge and atmosphere of many *presences*. The bizarre walls I could see in the glow of the star lance to be painted with terrible scenes of torture, and the rank floor was scattered with human bones and skulls. They *floated* in a sticky pool of blood. In the misty distance was a stained altar, shaped in a curve with long goat horns at either side. Black candles and flickering bowls of incense lit the foul scene, and behind the demonic slab was a bleak miasma formed in the likeness of a horned devil, with twin eyes of red fire that blazed with a semblance of life.

"Vorta's chamber of horrors," whispered an awed man beside me, clutching firm his stolen Zurk sword, and not trusting to speak too loud in this forsaken place.

The room had gone chillingly cold, and the voices rose in volume as though the place was crowded with the spirits of some forlorn domain—Shaitan's domain. A gust of intense evil seemed to seep out of the very walls and ruffle us. Images leapt through the air—images of demons and hobgoblins performing foul and licentious deeds. The wicked eyes of the blurred shape fixed upon my mask with a malevolent gaze. Crude and inhuman pictures whirled before me. Vorta was here! He had begun his attack.

My warriors began to scream from inside the chamber and without, and I knew that Vorta was using his own ability to read their minds to show them the things they feared most, coupled with obscene acts performed on their loved ones. Blood fountained out from the walls and men howled as serpents of green slime wrapped about them. They saw each other as men from whom the skin peeled in festering chunks, gazed on bare bones, skeletons. A thick mist of black fumes swam around me, and I felt drawn outward into a void as though I stood in the realm of infinite nothingness beyond the extremes of the universe. I held high the star lance, its blue glow warding off the hellish things that flitted around it, fangs slavering.

The pitch darkness became total. Silence. Absolute.

Then a point of light. It whirled closer and closer, and in a split second of time I saw an image of Daras Vorta, beckoning to something shapeless and unknown from the remotest regions of consciousness. So that was why he had not come to the speedy defense of his city. He had been immersed in some ungodly ritual to bring into material being the very essence of the Goat-God, Shaitan.

I bent all my powers of will against him, and Vorta wavered. The darkness enveloped me, and the chorus of awful sounds came back. Vorta's power was split in two—trying to go through with his demonic pact and trying to destroy me and my warriors. Thus divided, he was vulnerable.

"Damn you, Sarian! Damn you!" his thought seared me, but for the moment he was beaten.

With startling abruptness, the inhuman choir ceased and the mists cleared from the chamber. Silence of a different kind descended. My men had stopped screaming, those that had not been killed or maimed by the bewildered others. I searched the chamber; the devil-miasma had gone. The blood had gone from the floor, but not the bones.

"What is happening?" cried a warrior behind me.

"Vorta is here. We must find him. He has ceased his attack only for as long as it takes him to summon Shaitan."

The men drew well back at the name. I took no notice and began frantically searching the chamber. Behind the altar was a weird tapestry, covered with the intricate designs of some hellish order. I hacked at it angrily with my blade, sundering it in two. There beyond was another stairway, leading upward. I heard the echoing of footsteps. So Vorta had been here! And now he fled.

"Come!" I shouted to the men. "I hear the fleeing footsteps of the Warden. He has seen the face of Death and will face me no longer."

Now they were with me again. The armed warriors came first, kicking aside the rattling skulls as they crossed the chamber, then the host of prisoners, armed with whatever they could lay hands on. I led the assault force, now in better spirits, up the cobwebbed stairs. Up and up they led, until I thought there would be no end to the narrow spiral. Spiders and rats fled my coming, and behind me the chattering warriors came on, grunting words of enthusiasm to each other now that the accursed chamber was below them.

I could now draw my own comfort from the thought that somewhere ahead was the man I most wanted to see in all Karkesh, or in all the nine worlds. I stopped quite suddenly, for there before me was the head of the eternal staircase, and beyond it a dark passageway. Motioning the men to silence, I moved on, and they kept close behind, swords ready, poised eagerly for action. Many passages led at intervals off this one, and I was undecided which to investigate. The floor here was polished and free of dust, implying recent use. After a brief pause for thought, I decided to continue along the passageway, which appeared to be a main one. It ended in a thick metal door.

My star lance would be useless until it could be recharged in sunlight, so I told the men to break the door down. As many of us as could put our shoulders to it. For long moments we could not budge it, but we heaved and butted frantically at it until finally we felt it giving. The runners squealed in protest, then with one last tortured scraping they ripped from the wall, and the door crashed into the chamber beyond. I held both sword and star lance at the ready and sprang forward, murder in my heart.

However, the chamber was empty. It was round and about sixty feet across. In its center was a familiar object—the hideously garish goat's head throne of Daras Vorta. We were inside the stepped dais of his mighty throne room! Outside these walls must be the vast upper part of the palace dome itself. Men had followed me into this circular room and were now preparing to wreck it, subject to my approval. I told them exactly where we were and that if we could get into the chamber above, we could storm the palace from the inside. They cheered exultantly once again, and then they did proceed to rip up the furniture and fittings. The word had passed back to the anxiously waiting ranks, and back down the stairway, and I wondered how strong a force we were.

Before I could form a definitive plan, someone's sword struck accidentally against a hidden lever on the weird goat-throne, and above us the ceiling opened to reveal a square of light, about six feet across. Simultaneously the throne hummed and began to rise toward it on four metal rods. So this, I mused, was how Vorta operated his royal throne.

"Reverse the process at once," I said urgently. "If there are any Guards upstairs, they will be alarmed if they see an empty throne rising from the dais."

The warrior who had triggered the action stopped it, and the process reversed itself. We then entered on a long discussion on how it would be best to continue the attack. All the passageways were searched, but of Vorta there was no sign. Time passed as we plotted. I had called for a massing of all the men, and word came that there was a vast army of prisoners and warriors behind us, ready to burst out upon the unsuspecting Guards of the palace at a word from me. We would attack from within and reduce the citadel to ashes before Vorta could hurl his last and deadliest assault at us.

CHAPTER XI
The Battle for the Palace

Slowly and carefully my faithful Barbarians dismantled the grotesque goat's head throne of Daras Vorta. When it was done, the word was passed back that all who followed me should prepare.

I nodded to the warrior who stood beside the operating mechanism, and he pressed it. We waited with bated breath as the ceiling opened with a dull whirring. The rods lifted, now throneless, up into the space, then stopped with a click. The ceiling was only about twelve feet above us and it was an easy matter for us to climb up and through the hole, using each other's shoulders. I went through first and stepped lightly to the top of the dais.

Our luck held, for the vast chamber where first I had met Vorta was empty. I descended the steps cautiously, and one by one companions followed, gasping at the beauty of the gold and silver floor. I made straight for the gigantic windows to see how the siege was going. A wall of flame could be seen in the east of the city where Annulian and I had smashed our way in. Crossing the hall, I looked out again, and to the west I saw scores of fires. Chungsar's catapults would be raining fused kegs of thunderpowder into the city, while the combined forces of his army and Thuran's must be even now outside the walls.

Far down below I could see the walls of the palace lined with busy Guards, all firing and casting spears into the streets below. The rest of the prisoners and the advance guards of the Barbarians must be trying to storm the palace. We had to aid them from within, for should we take it, Karkesh's last vestige of hope would be gone. There were stairs next to the lifts leading down to the next level— where the Space Receiver Platform joined the palace dome—and with a cry to my gathered men, I led our swarming force down the broad steps.

"Horns of Shaitan, what is this!" yelped a startled Guard below as he saw the ragged band coming down the golden stairway upon him. Others joined him, drawing their swords in horror.

"Aid, comrades! The Barbarians are in the palace!"

"Attack!" I bellowed, my voice ringing back from the high-vaulted walls.

The thronging horde behind me followed, all screaming hoarse war cries as loud as their lungs would allow. I leapt out from the stairs and crashed amidst the waiting Guards. Three fell senseless beneath me, and I split two more skulls with my sword before anyone was quick enough to retaliate. Hundreds more were coming up the foot of the widening staircase, drawn by the noise of our cries. Now could we avenge our dead in earnest. My star lance was short on power, so I sheathed it in favor of the sword.

There on the shining stairs, the two contingents flung themselves together, steel swinging and flashing. I began thrusting and jabbing at the blue tunics around me, finding my mark and drawing scarlet rivulets among the foe. Hundreds more Barbarians came tearing down the stairs and flung themselves outward among the uncomprehending Zurks. They fought with swords, chains, iron bars, crude clubs, and anything they could lay their hands on, facing cold steel absolutely without fear. Some valiant warriors fought with their bare hands, goaded on by the pent-up hatred of years of incarceration. They drew on reserves of energy that it seemed impossible for them to have stored, but they were sadly cut down in the end.

However our hurricane attack drove the soldiers back step by step. The huge hall was full with straining fighters. Sparks crackled in the atmosphere, and the noise rose to unbearable dimensions. Some of the Guards drew back in consternation from my ugly mask, having perhaps heard of the legend of the Four Horsemen, and they paid for their hesitation with their lives. I was in no mood to show any mercy, whether they were Zurjahn-born or not, for they were all tainted by Vorta's foulness. My sword splintered enemy shields into shards of steel, ripping open their bodies as it would have paper, and I marveled at its edge. My demonic advance into the heart of the enemy was temporarily stopped when a brawny Zurk clubbed me heavily with the butt of his javelin, and I staggered back under the massive blow, feeling blood trickle into an eye beneath my helmet. Before I could retaliate, two warriors chopped him to pieces and he tumbled down, dragging three thrashing companions with him. They were all trampled to death in seconds as the advance went on.

So intense was the struggle that a perfect stream of blood soaked the stairway, and none but the strongest hearts could go on in this. Never could a more frightful encounter have been staged before. To say that the blood on the stairs ran freely would be no exaggeration. My men were like desperate, fierce animals, loose from their cages, dealing death with terrifying abruptness and delight to the slowly retreating Zurks. Our masses pressed from behind, clamoring to join the fray, so that keeping our balance on the corpse-choked stairs became hazardous.

The Zurks were forced to fall back under that weight, for nothing could halt our descent. Some of the warriors further back began tossing Zurk corpses into the midst of the enemy, causing further confusion. We were winning the hall inch by inch. I was using my fist as much as my sword for we were so tightly compressed, and I thought of the fields at Orezza, where I had at least been mounted. A thick arm wrapped itself around my neck, and before I could kick out, I stumbled over a torn body, falling with my antagonist among the scuffling, bloodied feet.

I was seized by a terrible panic, for I knew what that forest of stamping legs would do to me if I did not rise quickly. Movement at this level was badly restricted, but somehow we turned and twisted as we grappled. Those choking fingers were at my thrtoat, and I felt the world going black. But my luck held, for someone trod clumsily on my attacker and he momentarily released me. I acted as best I could, and somehow rammed my sword up under his chin, soaking myself in his steaming blood. He thrashed about for a second, then I wrenched free and tried to rise. I was still held down by the compact bodies above, but eventually forced my head up again, having hacked savagely at a few Zurk legs to make room. Almost at once I was battered across the head by a mailed fist, and I felt myself weakening. Someone near me was splitting Zurk skulls, complete with helmets, with a three foot length of chain, and he cleared a space as he swung, the sound of crushed skulls sickening to hear.

Suddenly the whole front line of Guards collapsed like broken twigs, and the weight of the men behind pushed us forward. We trampled over the screeching Guards, struggling for footing, and I felt further nauseated by the crunching of bones beneath me. The slayer with the chain was doing the work of ten with that rattling weapon of his, for none of the Zurks could get under that flaying guard. They retreated faster and faster under the hammering blows of our new assault. They decided that it was impossible to compete with this force of suicidal madmen.

Slowly they broke and fled downstairs to the next level—which was ground level—while others were forced to swarm out on to the Space Receiver Platform. I called a halt to our warriors, who would have given pursuit at once. It took many minutes to bring the excitable mass to a halt. I took stock of our situation, my breath coming in ragged gasps. We now held this level and the one above.

"We must hold these stairs at all costs!" I shouted to the near-exhausted men, and found that my voice carried surprisingly well. Everyone, it seemed, listened to the Pale Rider. Faces grinned down at me from the stairs, and I saw that we were still a powerful force.

"To ensure that we hold them, all the armed warriors who came with me from outside the city, stand firm here," I told them, pointing with a bloodied sword to the top stair of the next level. I saw that at least a hundred of my original raiders were dead.

"The liberated prisoners come with me. Arm yourselves with Zurk shields as well as swords, and pick up any bows that you find. And javelins. Take them also. We shall advance on the Space Platform outside and deal with the Zurks who fled there."

This brought no sighs or groans of displeasure, but yet another enthusiastic roar. By the stars, I murmured to myself, but these were heroic men. They gathered up their arms in a moment and were ready.

"For the freedom of all the Children of Light," I shouted, and as one they returned the cry. My one eye had closed up, but I was forced to go on by powers within me over which I no longer seemed to have control. I could not rest until we had taken the palace. We burst out into the sunlight and onto the blistering landing pad. A large force of remaining Guards was getting organized in opposition to our ragged ranks, reinforced by members of the observation towers around the Platform.

"Spread out!"

By now my eye was badly swollen, and worse still, it had begun to run. I shook my head. To the men who faced us across that high Platform, way above the city, I must have seemed like a conjured evil, caked as I was in blood and offal. I lifted my sword.

"Show them no mercy!" I cried, realizing as I did so that I spoke the words of Annulian which I had once condemned. Yet we charged like bulls and I grinned as arrows flew from our ranks at the wavering Zurk soldiery. Not all of our men were befuddled with blood-lust. The Guards marched resolutely forward, shields foremost, Some of them fell at once, pierced by the whispering shafts. Then the two forces clashed head on with a rending of steel, cascading blows upon each other. I knocked the first shield of a bewildered opponent straight out of his hands and into the face of his neighbor, mashing his nose to pulp. He thrust at me, but his sword bounced harmlessly off my buckled armor, without which I would have died hours before. I dispatched him with one blow, smashing my free fist into the face of another.

Beside me I glimpsed the warrior with the chain. He was an amazing fighter, fit to be a king. He swung that chain over his head and with it bent shields in two, cleaving heads like pears. We were losing men, but were successfully pushing the Zurks ever backward. Soon they had spread out wide to avoid going over the edge. Flights of arrows, thicker now, swished overhead at the Guards, whose ranks were so close together as to make the return of fire impossible, as at Orezza.

Someone hacked at my leg, and I felt red hot needles shooting through my kneecap. I fell sprawling on to the metal floor, smelling that odd metallic diffusion intermingled with sweat and death. Above me the prisoners closed in, driving the Guards back. Pinfully I arose, my leg sending more shafts of agony up into my thigh. I must rest soon or my part in all this would soon be over. The men behind me still pressed forward, so I limped on, not bravely but out of sheer necessity. Again I clashed weapons with the Zurks, snapping swords in twain and cutting into booted legs at the knee. I took many rough blows, but my mind was past registering any more pain as I hacked on. I could only go on swinging and striking, arms like lead, for if I stopped now I would never rise again.

Once more the impact of our drive forced the Guards further and further backwards, until at last they stood on the very edge of the Platform, where there was no wall to save them from going over. One Guard lunged at me with a staff and I grabbed it, ripping him open from navel to chin as he came on, and tearing his weapon from his hands. I pressed forward with it, holding it before me like some miniature ram, slashing frantically with my sword at those who tried to turn the staff, and carving a path through the remaining Guards. Some fell with gurgling cries to the cold stones so far below, and others tripped and fell up here, stumbling helplessly into their fellows.

I stood near the dreadful brink, swinging my staff as if possessed by all the demons from Vorta's Hells, splitting faces and skulls, sending Guard after shrieking Guard to his doom. The chain slayer had reached the last lines too, and with one almighty swing he knocked six men over the edge. Shower after shower of arrows, javelins and even shields fell thickly into the Zurk rearguard. One by one they fell, twisting and tumbling in a mixed tangle of kicking legs, to fall flat and smashed on the flagstones way below.

I sent one last Zurk to his death, then sagged down on one knee among the clustered corpses. My left leg felt shattered, though I knew it could not be broken. We had triumphed though; we held the Space Receiver Station, and the Palace was almost ours. My right eye had closed completely, and I peered through the other, looking at the blackened buildings that jutted up out of the smoke. The fires were coming ever nearer. I nodded to the chain slayer, who came over.

"Are you well, lord?" he asked.

"Aye, man. Not done yet. Are they all slain?"

"Every last dog. Shall we rest awhile, before we finish our work in this black place? The city cannot withstand the invasion much longer. See, the fires of our advance," he said, and again I nodded. He saw that I was lost in thought and so went off to tend the wounded. I needed to sleep, but could not yet. Vorta was still somewhere in the palace. I would find him before too long. And there would be none to help him. My only prayer now was that no help would come to Karkesh from off world.

I watched the excited Guards on the ramparts of the palace wall below me, firing down into the seething ranks of the prisoners outside. Whether those prisoners were harassed in the streets by other Zurk troops was hard to say, but I saw them hurling missiles of all kinds at the high palace walls. Our forces must surely take those walls, I mused, as I knelt on the edge of the Space Receiver Platform. The Barbarian hordes who followed the other three Riders were closing in gradually around the palace, and soon those of us inside would find ourselves under extreme pressure, for the Zurks would make this their last stand. The chain slayer, Janharah as he was named, came over to me and rested one massive hand on my shoulder.

"There is fighting again within, lord," he said, nodding in the direction of the palace dome. "Zurks from the ground level are trying to retake the palace, and our men are hard pressed."

"I see. Come, then. Enough of rest for now. Let us trample them back. We *must* hold the palace," I said as fiercely as I could, and got painfully to my feet. I felt a little better for my rest, but was still weary.

"Are you strong enough, lord?" asked the blood-bespattered giant.

"We shall see," I returned after a pause, then led him and those around us who were fit enough back into the hall of the palace. The gallant armed warriors were driving back a fresh attack of Guards on the stairway to the ground level, and for a while it looked as if they did so with apparent ease. They were casting anything solid into the Zurk ranks: spears, stones, statues from the walls, and even ripped-up flagstones and furniture. I stood on the balcony overlooking the heaving conflict.

"Death to the Zurks!" I cried, holding high my bright blade. They roared the louder and began thrusting forward with renewed vitality. The halls and other stairs were lined with the dead, and everything was broken and torn to shreds. The beautiful but demonic paintings on the walls were holed and splattered, and windows and mirrors had been smashed. Priceless carpets were ripped and cut, as were the gorgeous tapestries that had graced some of the walls. The prisoners had taken a terrible revenge on their captors. As I wiped my sword clean, preparing to attack once more, I wondered anew where Vorta would be.

I put the thought momentarily from my mind. We must take the palace first at all costs, and my men would need me to lead them, for the presence of the Pale Rider spurred them on and put naked fear in the hearts of our enemies. With another battle cry, I leapt over the bizarre balcony rails and crashed feet first among a group of panting Guards, knocking them like dolls to the ground. Almost at once Janharah was beside me, a whirlwind of tremendous power. We began our slaughtering afresh, forcing the Guards back down the steps, oblivious now to the death about us.

The noise was ghastly. People were using anything as weapons: clubs from chair legs, broken lumps of masonry, snapped swords and splinters of wood. Some kicked, others tore with fingers and punched, while yet others swung about them with buckled shields. One man near me was wielding a long shard of mirror-glass, his hand badly cut from the effort of holding the pointed fragment, but he put it to frightful use, before a length of Zurk steel eventually pierced his own heart. Once more the Zurk ranks had to retreat. They cut down many of our wild warriors, but could not achieve any measure of progress on the stairs.

I fought myself into a trance, my movements growing slower as the bones of the men about me cracked and shattered like the glass of the windows. We were outside at last, and up above us the walls loomed, Zurks upon them firing into our unprotected ranks, cutting down scores. One star lance up there would have finished us all, but Brusiphylon's saboteurs had done their work well. However, Zurk attentions were divided, for outside, the prisoners were battering incessantly at the steel doors, which even now were bulging ominously. The courtyard was a writhing mass of bodies as the relentless struggle went on. The ornate flower gardens that had adorned the entrance way to the palace doors had been churned to mud underfoot. Our men were still fighting gamely, but were gradually being reduced, and I could see now that we would not succeed without help.

For nearly an hour more we fought on desperately, and it became our turn to retreat. We found ourselves backing on to the stairs again, only a thousand or so of us remaining. The Imperial Guards were bedraggled and grimy, but they found new heart and my sword did not cleave open as many heads as it had earlier. Inch by inch we backed up the stairs, Janharah and I the last to give way, and at that moment, when all seemed lost, the doors in the palace wall burst asunder, falling in on and crushing scores of Guards. A flood of prisoners poured into the compound over the fallen gates, and now was the tide indeed turned. The Guards before us turned to see what had caused such a commotion, and with wild yells of delight, we again leapt at them.

Finding last reserves of strength, the few who were left on the stairs began a new offensive, and soon the Guards were hard pressed. The ensuing struggle was both terrible and rapid. The masses that had burst in from the streets were poorly armed, but sacrificed themselves unsparingly in an effort to wipe out as many palace Guards as they could. Once we had slaughtered all that remained in the grounds, splitting them down into small groups and steadily bludgeoning and butchering them, we took to the walls, where the last defenses sought to withstand us. There we carved another bloody trail along the battlements. The Guards were broken at last. They fled in all directions. Most of them were cut ruthlessly down, and some managed to get into the streets where they melted into the city. It was still something of a puzzle to me why no one came from the city to the palace's defense. Maybe the fighting out on the fronts was too demanding for anyone there to have been spared.

I was almost done. My right eye ached abominably, and I could hardly stand. My armor was clinging to me in battered segments, and my helm was cracked and almost broken in two. The sun's rays glowed fainter over the jagged skyline, mingling with orange tendrils of spreading fire. It was late evening when we cast the last bodies of the Zurks over the side of the walls and out into the reddened streets. Those that remained of the warriors, many of whom had died so valiantly, had at last conquered the palace. Now we must hold it, for the rest of the receding Karkesh soldiery would certainly try to shelter within its bounds.

"Barricade the gates!" I shouted from aloft, and my men began piling everything available into the gateway. We cleared the battlements of corpses, dropping them into the rapidly filling gap, and I had guards posted all around the walls to keep me informed of any forthcoming Zurk attacks. Should they come to the palace seeking a citadel, they would be disappointed. A few Zurks did appear in the streets, but we shot them down or sent them scuttling back into the shadows. It was nightfall when I took Janharah up on to the Space Receiver Platform. I prayed that no Zurjahn solar ships would arrive from out of the night sky.

"Our armies draw tighter about the palace," he commented, pointing around us at ever-nearing explosions and fires. I took off my helm, laying it gently on the metal floor. My companion gasped.

"What is wrong?" I asked.

"My lord, your eye. It badly needs attention!" he replied.

"I will bathe it shortly," I told him. He gave me the impression that he would rather do so himself, but something held him back—my assumed godliness I supposed.

"Meanwhile we must secure our grip here," I went on. "The other Riders will be pleased to see us holding the palace when they arrive. Our holding the walls can guarantee us the victory. My only hope now is that Zurjah will have no time to send reinforcements before we have conquered the city. If so, we would be finished."

"Then let us destroy this Platform," replied Janharah, looking about him as he spoke at the hillocks of dead that covered the landing area. The observation towers leaned at acute angles over the city, and one was in ruins down on the streets below.

"No. It must be destroyed only as a last resort, if our armies out in the city are somehow repelled. If we win, as the Gods will surely grant, we will need this Platform. The riders will have business elsewhere."

"I do not understand you," said Janharah, frowning. He seemed suspicious, as Thuran had been when I first met him.

"Do not question me!" I snapped, for my nerves were so taut that I thought they might snap. It was the best way to act, for the Barbarians respected my authority.

Janharah lifted his shoulders stiffly, his massive, almost primitive bulk framed by the consuming fires in the city behind him. "You pardon, lord. I did not mean to do so," he said, and I nodded, waving the incident aside.

"I am tired. The men are tired, too. We must all rest. Tomorrow there is certain to be a terrific onslaught, and many of us will die. We must be ready."

Janharah nodded, resigned to the fact, and together we went into the palace. He went below, and I bade him goodnight. I wandered up those blood-drenched stairs where so many had died, threading my way through the mangled mass of corpses. Among the motionless sea of dead was strewn the debris of battle. Some of the stairs had crumbled, and two of the thick pillars of marble had been displaced, leaning now against the walls, paused ready to fall as if frozen. Other pillars were cracked from foot to top.

As I climbed, kicking aside swords and helmets, shields and breastplates, I felt a numbing weariness creeping over me, as though my body had just realized what it had been through this day. Glittering chandeliers were shattered and spread wide over the frightful scene, and light twinkled star-like from the tiny glass splinters. This was to be the Last battle— Karkesh was falling and Chalremor's promised cosmic circle was knitting. But for how long after the war would man be peaceful? Would the race of Barbarians tame the lusts and fires of battle that burned like molten lava within their veins? My strength was fading. My own will to go on had dulled.

After an exhausting climb, I sank down in Vorta's huge throne room. Where was that vile being? Spitted in his own den, perhaps. Or was he marshaling his evil minions in one last gesture of defiance, somewhere down in the bowels of this grim citadel? I dared not send my mind out to try and pinpoint his, for I was too weak. Let tomorrow tell. Now I settled myself in a corner, the sole occupant of this silent hall, and soon I felt into an uncomfortable sleep.

It was still night when I awoke. I had no idea for how long I had slept on these cold floors. Nothing stirred within the hall. Outside I saw the leaping blaze of the city, much nearer now on all sides. I got up agonizingly slowly, discovering that my leg had stiffened and was too damaged to walk on. I crawled across the chilled floor to where a spear lay with its point snapped off. I suppose that it had been cast scornfully aside by one of my men when first we had passed through. I hauled myself up by it, using it as a crude crutch.

My inner self insisted that I must find Vorta, whether he was alive or dead. Perhaps I would be successful if I searched the chambers beneath the throne dais, where my men had looked earlier. Something deep in my subconscious urged me on. I hobbled over to the steps, the echo of my tapping crutch thudding around the cavernous hall. With great difficulty I climbed the dais, went down into its interior, and began searching every tunnel that led off from the chamber beneath. I found no sign of Vorta or any of his men.

These were his private apartments, though, that much was obvious. They were provided with all the comforts that a man could desire, and more. I utilized the extravagant bathing facilities and scrubbed myself. My eye was swollen severely and puffed out in a blackening lump. I took pains to bathe it carefully, treating it with some of the salves that were kept here. My leg pulsed with pain. Somehow I left the bathing chamber and fell across a velvet bed of golden silks, dropping at once into a fitful sleep.

My dreams were of Vorta, his face laughing at me in a thousand forms, his finger pointing, his lips curled in a sneer. I saw also Taria, her sweet face clouded with worry, and for a moment I thought I was back on Zurjah. Lastly I dreamed of Chalremor, whose swelling visage dissolved into dust, and out of the dust rode the Four charging Horsemen, my skull-helm in the fore.

CHAPTER XII
The Passing of the Storm

I awoke shivering. A slow, encroaching pain insinuated itself into my every muscle. Events began to flood my memory. Outside the palace, the war would still be waging, and I must go. With one heave, I pulled myself off the bed, then began dressing myself in my battle-scarred armor. My eye was now bandaged, and I donned anew my buckled helm, the symbol of doom. Today would the fate of Karkesh, and perhaps the fate of mankind, be decided.

I came out into the glaring sunlight and blinked. The warriors that manned the palace walls were refreshed, cheerful and confidant as the sounds of war drew nearer in the city. It was good to see morale so high; it took some of the horror out of it all. Janharah greeted me with some concern, and I told him that I was well enough. My leg felt better, though it still ached. We waited patiently on the smoke-hung ramparts and after some time heard two tremendous explosions from very close. Columns of flame and masonry shot up into the sky, and I knew that Annulian and the others were closing in. What few remaining birds there were in the palace dome took off now in a flurry of feathers.

Below us the streets began filling with fleeing Zurks; almost at once we began firing. Our men had accumulated a vast store of missiles, which they had drawn up into heaps all around the battlements: arrows by the thousand, spears, javelins, hammers, axes, broken furniture, and anything that could be thrown down on the ranks below. If we ran out, then we intended to pull the very walls apart, and fling chunks of stone at the enemy.

Between distant houses I caught a glimpse of one of Chungsar's war engines—a tall, wooden catapult. It was casting fused barrels of thunderpowder across the buildings as I watched, blasting great heaps of rubble skyward. The Barbarians were closing in for the kill. Karkesh was paying for its sins. In the shadow of the palace walls, the Zurks were caught in two minds—whether to try and force an entry into the palace and risk death from our deadly missiles, or to reform and stand firm with their fellows against the oncoming hordes.

We had no way of telling how many Zurks had died out in the city, or how many of our own men had perished in the siege. It seemed logical to expect that huge forces of both sides were still locked in furious combat. Looking up the broad streets that fanned out from the palace like the spokes of a wheel from the hub, I saw that the Zurk front line was only a mile away.

I walked around the walls, checking to see that all our preparations were complete. The men nodded respectfully, keyed up for the attack that would soon come. I murmured a few words of encouragement as I passed. Above me the mist was evaporating in the morning sun, and the heat grew as the tension began to mount. Below us the Zurks had sensibly retreated, forming a vast ring around the frowning walls of black stone.

The booms of echoing explosions came more and more often to our ears. From up here I could easily see the terrible conflict that was raging in those distant streets. The roads to the east were suddenly full of retreating Guards, and I soon saw why. One of the ibathenes that we had unleashed into the city had been cornered by the Barbarians and forced to attack the Zurk barricades, with the result that it had broken through to lumber down the street, wildly destructive in its rampant rage.

The main Barbarian forces had frightened the other beasts as well, and now the huge, cumbersome reptiles were taunted by firebrands which they hated. All six beasts were shepherded towards the central palace and the helpless Zurks ran before them. Discovering their new plight, the Zurks had no alternative but try an assault on the palace. As they ran across the streets at us, we jettisoned our piles of weapons, killing hundreds of the enemy with our first hail of arrows. Then our spears tore into them, gathering momentum from the long drop, and the rocks that we flung down crushed groups of six and seven as the seething masses came on. It would have been more difficult to spear fish in a garden pool. We were so few, compared to that multitude, yet were able to slaughter thousands, until the very level of the street was raised as the corpses piled higher. But despite our constant bombardment, the milling thousands began pushing aside the vast pile of dead and the debris which choked the palace gateway.

The ibathenes were creating bedlam out in the streets, whipping their tails about furiously, but the staggering barrier of carnage was slowly shifting from the gates. As I ran for the nearest steps, in preparation for the coming onslaught, I cast one last glimpse at the

Barbarian advance, fully thinking that when it got here, its members would find us all dead. In one broad street they had broken through, and I saw to my joy that they were led by Thuran and Chungsar, who were both charging down the street, carving a crimson path of destruction as they came, just as the Riders had in my dreams. Our archers had quickly organized themselves, and we opened up with a remorseless fire on the Zurks as they swept in through the palace gateway, laying level a thousand with one shower. Desperation drove our enemies on over their own dead and dying.

"We must hold the palace, or they will summon help from other worlds!" I shouted across to the men on the walls, and I led some of those from this parapet down to meet the swirling Guards below. So choked was the courtyard with the slain that the Zurks made very slow progress to the palace doors, and the warriors who filed quickly down from a dozen stairways on the walls were able to head them off in good time. We leapt upon them with a resounding clash of steel. My star lance I had discarded, for it had taken so many blows in its scabbard that it no longer functioned. I had to rely on my sword for survival. The ringing of weapons and the groans of the injured were all that I could hear now as I drove forward, intent on cutting off the enemy advance to the palace doors. If I were to die here, I would see that it was to some purpose.

Somehow our war-mad men formed a line before the palace and we stemmed the charging Zurk horde. Beyond it, outside the walls, thousands more were gathering, for the Barbarian advance had evidently broken through on all sides. I cannot say how many of us withstood that titanic thrust, but we could not hope to hold on for long. All around me the battle raged with a new fire, bodies falling like flies, trampled to pulp beneath the weight of the surging army.

Inevitably we were driven back. My sword flicked to and fro, fending off as many as five blades at a time. Janharah was creating havoc nearby, his chain red for its whole length. Sheer weight of numbers forced us back up the stairs. The Zurk forces had to press us even harder, for thousands swelled to bursting point behind them. They crushed scores of their own men to death against the walls. Another thundering explosion came tempestuously out of the sounds of battle, almost on top of us, and I saw one of the gate towers shake and crumble, slowly toppling into the crowd beneath in a cloud of dust.

Annulian's forbidden weapon had almost won us a city, and I wondered how the Dream Lords would take the news. There would be no surrender here—Annulian had made that much clear to the Zurks, though I would intervene wherever I could to sue for eventual peace. I found myself defending out of sheer reflex action now, cutting men down to right and left, only to have them replaced at once. The sword which I had wielded so long and so proudly was chipped and notched, but I determined to use it until it snapped. Javelins were thrust at me, but could not penetrate my indestructible armor. I sliced three of the shafts into pieces with one sweep.

Both my own men and the Zurks must have gawked at my determination to hold my ground for as long as I could, but I had good reason. There were so many Zurks crushing and trampling each other in the screaming chaos, that it was important to block their main line of retreat, so that we could keep the suffocating pressure on them. It cost us dearly and time was fast running out. My men would not turn and flee while I stood my ground. Into the blood-red hall above the stairway I had to back with my remaining men. We were pitifully few now, but we would die at great expense to the enemy while we drew breath.

We hacked and chopped all the more ferociously atop the stairs, but could never hope to stem the torrent of humanity. Further back they edged us, as we thrust and parried to right and left. We were steadily forced out on to the Space Receiver Platform, where only the day before we had cut down the Guards and hurled them to the flagstones beyond. Now we must surely suffer the same fate. Seeing my men dying around me on all sides, I felt that it would be unavoidable, but Karkesh would fall soon after us. That was a surety. Annulian would be the victor.

Angered by the thought that I was soon to die, I set upon the enemy with fresh reserves of strength, carving open their faces, cleaving their skulls and spilling out entrails. The stink of the sweating combatants mingled with the rotting stench of the previous day's slaughter, and as the intensity of the burning sun grew, the smell became intolerable. Flies swarmed over us, sticking to wounds and faces. Down in the streets I saw hope. Our main forces were snarling into the Zurks with such energy that hundreds of the foe were being torn to shreds. I could see the spiky form of Chungsar on his black charger, digging his three-pronged fork into the heart of the enemy.

The Zurks had manned the palace walls again, now that they had slaughtered its usurpers to a man, and they poured a frantic hail of arrows into our ranks below. Our struggle up here became more equal, for the better part of the Zurk troops were occupied in withstanding the siege below. Whole sections of the palace wall were reduced to smoldering ruins by the catapults, and as they fell, depositing hundreds of shrieking Guards on to their fellows beneath, hordes of bloodthirsty Barbarian warriors rushed in for the kill.

I looked down with my one eye, now watery with effort, and saw that it would soon be over. Our forces could not be contained. Defense of the congested palace. Down in its courtyard the armies of both forces were thronging, clawing and tearing at each other like wild beasts. The entire city was on fire, and the wind blew reeking gusts, hot with the stink of charred flesh, across to us as we renewed our attack above.

"Hold firm! Aid is on its way! The day will be ours!" I shouted again, and my diminishing warriors shouted their fierce war cries in reply, alarming the Guards, who thought us mad. My joy at this new hope below was cut short, for near me I saw brave Janharah staggering, a jevelin run through his throat, protruding fully four feet from the back of his neck. Even so, despite this terrible handicap, he held two Zurk heads in a death lock, one between each thick arm, and he choked them both to death as the blood ran out of him and over them. I had to turn my head to engage the enemy once more, so did not see him fall. I again fought myself into a stupor, oblivious now to everything but the obstinate will to survive. I clung to my life with avaricious tenacity, so that some of my assailants were forced to draw back in bewilderment.

Time has no meaning when one struggles in the clutches of the enemy, cutting and thrusting with flagging arms, evading death with every turn of the blade. I cannot say for how long I and my last few gallant men fought on the Platform, high above the smoking city. I had been isolated by a band of Guards, and had to jump up on to one of the careening observation towers that hung out over the drop. None followed me out on to the swaying construction, and for a moment I fended off their blades more easily. The heat from below grew more unbearable. My opponents were as exhausted as I, and fought with fading drive.

A growing commotion somewhere at the rear of the Guards drew my attention, and I looked that way to see a fresh wave of Barbarians coming out on to the Platform. They had broken into the palace at last, and were led by none other than my ally of old, Thuran. He still rode his magnificent white horse, and his armor was soaked in blood, dripping gore. I gazed in amazement as he hacked at the enemy with his huge broadsword, and the Zurks backed off in terror as he rode relentlessly on to the Space Platform. Behind him came the most ferocious fighters the world had ever bred, who had been bathed in blood, so were they stained. The fighting in the city must have been incredible.

Again I shouted loud the battle cry, leaping off the dizzy tower and caving in an unwary Guard's head as I landed. I swung about me madly, sending two more ripped men tumbling out into space. My last few slashing warriors were defending themselves in scattered bunches, and between us we dealt out death with murderous fury and with no compromise. Thuran had seen us and was making his way across. I was then smashed hard on the helmet by someone's ax, and though I had taken several such blows, this time I was almost knocked senseless. I slipped over and fell among Zurk corpses, hanging on to the very brink of the Platform. One lick now would send me over. My eyes focused dimly on the heaving armies still in the palace grounds below, and there I made out yet another familiar figure. It was Annulian, thrashing out with his two-handed sword, his red steed gone from beneath him.

I felt a new surge of energy and shook the lethargy from me, but as I turned to rise I saw two leering Guards preparing to send me over the edge. They advanced grimly, spears at the ready. Before they could achieve their aim, their heads miraculously burst like squashed grapes and the two decapitated corpses fell beside me among the dead. Thuran it was who had so dispatched them. He came toward me, his dripping blade held at his side.

"Thuran." I coughed, my voice scarcely more than a whisper. He knelt beside me, holding my arm tightly to save me from falling to my doom.

"You are hurt," he said with grave concern, as I wrenched off my helm. The Space Platform was an inconceivable jumble of carnage. It was impossible to conjecture how many lay dead up here.

"No matter about me, Thuran. I am alive, though that is a miracle.

Had you come any later, you would have found my own corpse added to those that surround you now."

"The Gods are with their own," he said simply. "I was shocked to find you in possession of the palace. Had it not been for your occupation, the battle could have raged for days— weeks. And the result might not have favored us." He began an inspection of my eye. "This will have to be treated at once, or you will lose your sight in this eye." He shouted to his men for a physician.

"The men with me fought like Gods, Thuran. Like Gods drunk on celestial wine. How many of them live?" I asked, peering about me at the mounds of slain.

"Only yourself, Galad. Every other man up here is dead, save a handful of Zurks. We were too late to save the others," he said sadly.

I hung my head dismally. All dead! Not one of that mighty band of warriors had lived, save myself. We had won, but at what a cost. I felt that I must surely break down right here in front of the victorious Barbarians. To have fought so hard and so long only to die at the finish. I shook my head and groaned at the news.

"The word from the city is good," said Thuran. "We have won. Everywhere is carpeted with Zurk corpses. The walls, the streets, the drains, the gutters—all run red with the blood of our enemies."

"And what of our army?"

Thuran fell silent. I knew how many thousands must have died. And now, to Vorta. I must find him. He could still raise up some frightful creation from the depths of barbarian superstition and yet confound us all.

"What news of Vorta?" I asked Thuran.

"Vorta? We have not seen the Warden. But he will be found. Our warriors will scour the palace stone by stone before it is razed."

I tried to rise, but could not. Thuran pushed me back.

"You must rest," he insisted.

"I must find Vorta. He is preparing for an attack that could undo all our carnage and yet reverse the victory."

"He cannot. He has left it too late. I am surprised that he did not confront us before."

"Vorta was busily working on some new rites of depravity when the siege began. All his attention was needed for his work, for if it succeeded it would bring into being a terrible power—power enough to crush us all at a single blow. That is why he ignored us.

He knows we burn this city, but he cares not, because he believes he will still defeat us," I told Thuran steadily. I could not hope to explain to him the potential of Vorta's mind and its inconceivable powers.

"Then we shall find him in his den of iniquity and end all his vain schemes," said Thuran bluntly. "Every hole in Karkesh will be investigated. Our warriors will bring us his head."

I sank back with a sigh. I prayed for my own strength of mind now, for if Vorta did attack, my own powers would be infinitesimal beside his own.

CHAPTER XIII
The Death of a Warrior

Physically and mentally I felt completely drained. A physician inspected my eye gently, bathed it and renewed the bandage. Everywhere now, down in the palace and streets, the Barbarian hordes were reducing what was left of the Zurks without mercy. I watched in fascinated horror as Karkesh burned from wall to wall. Its buildings crashed down in ruins. Occasionally I heard the sounds of sporadic explosions. We had taken a terrible toll.

Up here on the corpse-laden landing area there were a few warriors moving about in the littered debris, searching for possible survivors. Thuran supervised the collecting of weapons, and after a while I saw Annulian emerge from the palace, striding across the ground toward me. He was badly cut across one arm, where his mangled armor hung loose, and his breast plate and leggings were bent and twisted. He still wore his bestial helm, though its plumes had been cut away.

"Galad!" he exclaimed, seeing me, and I wondered if he was pleased or disappointed that I had survived.

"You are alive. Was it you, then, that we have to thank for holding the palace?" He removed his dangling arm bands and flung them casually aside. I told him briefly of what I had been through since entering Karkesh, and of how I was the lone survivor of my original outfit. He seemed in exceptionally high spirits, despite the grim news and his bleeding injuries. It seemed that our earlier conflict of purposes could be forgotten.

"You did more than I dreamed any man could," he said, grasping my arm in his vice-like grip. "Now it is virtually done, as the Gods foresaw. We are the victors! Look about you! Is it not a wonderful sight? Karkesh burning up in the very Hell-flames it sought to harness. But where is the head of Daras Vorta that you promised me? Have you slain the tyrant?" he demanded, his eyes glittering with fanaticism through the helmet.

"Neither he nor his body have yet come to light," I confessed softly, wiping a fresh trickle of blood from my forehead. Annulian straightened.

"What! Not yet found? You have searched the palace from the depths to the highest tower?"

"Even now Thuran's warriors are at that task. I have spent my time fighting here. There has been little time for diversions."

"Vorta will be found!" Annulian growled. "Until then let there be no more victory talk. I shall see to the hunt at once."

I nodded as he turned and went back to the palace, the epitome of war in his scarlet armor. I was far too weary to reply or do anything. Instead I sank down. Beside me, in a pool of dark blood, lay the sword that had wrought so much slaughter. How many had died on its edge? It lay chipped and dull, its jewels lost. With one last sigh I lay down, unmindful of the dead, and was soon oblivious to the holocaust around me. Dreams haunted my fitful sleep. Shapes swam in a thick mist—the horned mist from the chambers below, Vorta's face, lined with consternation as he struggled to bring into being his dark god, Shaitan. There were screams, whether from the dreams or the battle below I could not distinguish.

Rough hands revived me long afterwards. It was still daylight, and my eyes smarted under the glaring sun. Annulian stood over me. I looked around and saw that the Platform was edged with our most important warriors. Thuran stood nearby, impassively gazing out at the furnace, and I saw also Prosocles and Ool, who was leaning wearily on his great ax. Bastagal was among those in the rear, together with other chiefs I had met and a number of nomad chieftains. Everyone murmured as I got to my feet. In my hand I held my skull-helm.

"The foe are vanquished," announced Annulian, still wearing his own grisly helm.

"Are there many Zurks left alive?" I asked.

"A few Guards are left in the city, hiding and running from our hunters. And there are women and children out there, though not many."

"Then no more need to be killed. The victory is ours, so we will not make animals of ourselves. Bring all the prisoners to the palace," I told him, putting as much authority into my voice as I could, making sure my warriors heard my every word. Most of them nodded in agreement with what I said. Annulian did not countermand my order, but I sensed his displeasure.

"Are we to confine them in the pits?" he said.

"We are not. Have them sent to the throne chamber."

"Very well, Chosen One," he said, so that no one else could hear, his tone bitter.

"And Vorta?" I asked.

His self-assurance and pride welled up anew, and his eyes narrowed. "I have done what you failed to do. We found him, hidden in some innermost vault, communing with all the blasphemies and horrors of the legend. He was calling upon Shaitan, but his satanic master heeded him not, or so it seemed. We braved his festering minions, and a score of my stoutest warriors hacked him into a thousand pieces. Then we fired his ungodly temple and came away while it fell, burying him and all his works."

My eyes widened at the news. Vorta was dead then? Cautiously I lowered my mind shield and sent my mind out. There was no response. I searched Karkesh for a flicker that would prove Annulian wrong. But there was none. I opened my mind wide, wider, as wide as I ever had. If Vorta lived he would never find me more vulnerable than now, but I had to be sure. There was nothing. Only a void. Annulian had not lied. The lord of nightmares was no more.

"And now," said Annulian with authority of his own, "let us remember our people." The fire in the city was not as fierce now and seemed to be receding. Even so, parts of the palace were yet alight.

"Let the Four Horsemen stand before their people, so that all will know that the will of the Gods has been done, and that the legend and the prophecy have been fulfilled."

I nodded wearily at his words, and stepped with him to the very brink. Thuran and Chungsar came and joined us.

"It is done," said Annulian. "We have broken Zurk power on Earth." Below us the survivors stared up in awe, then cheered and laughed, the sound of their mingled joy coming up to us like music.

"The Gods were kind to us," breathed Chungsar.

"Now all that remains for us to do is to destroy the palace and this Space Platform that they may never return!" cried Annulian, waving to the Barbarians.

"Not yet," I replied gently, turning to face him. His masked face turned around sharply to meet my level gaze. The others watched us closely.

"What do you say?" Annulian snarled, his hatred for me laid bare, a raw nerve.

"We must not destroy this landing area yet. We have conquered the Zurks here, but there is work to be done yet on Zurjah."

"Work! What work? The only work we shall ever do is with the sword!"

Everyone's attention was riveted on us. Below us the people still cheered, unaware of what transpired above them.

"That is foolish talk," I snapped. "We have ended Vorta's evil rule, that I grant you. The Zurks no longer hold sway on earth. But we must communicate with their rulers, the Dream Lords, so that they sanction your rule and so that Earth can take its rightful place in the Empire," I went on slowly.

Annulian was incensed. "The people of Earth no longer belong to anyone's Empire. Let the Zurks come again and we shall lead the Riders of Death against them and bring them down as we have this day!" he cried, hoping to gain the support of the warriors. But they were quiet, unsure of where their loyalties stood. They loved their king, but me they feared.

"Do not be a fool," I hissed, and Annulian was so embittered by the remark that I thought he would attack me. "When the Imperial Guards return to Earth and see what we have done here, they will want an explanation. I shall give it to them. Why do you think Chalremor sent me here as his right arm? Because I was born on Zurjah—born the son of a Dream Lord and heir to his position. And they will listen to me when I tell them of Daras Vorta and foul Karkesh and all the horrors that were perpetrated on the people of Earth. But if you offer them violence and your swords, they will think that Vorta was just, and they will wipe you all off the face of the planet! You know nothing of the weapons they would use. Look about you! See how Karkesh crumbles into ashes. If you try to make war on the Empire, so will it turn the Sacred City to dust, and every home you have. The Dream Lords are not warmongers and fools. They are not like Daras Vorta. And they will listen to *me*. There will be peace. We will become joined in peace. This was the Armageddon spoken of in the Book of Prophecy, and all that the Gods have willed has come to pass. The Last battle has been fought here. Would you disobey the Gods?" I asked of Annulian. My voice had risen higher and the assembled warriors were murmuring among themselves. My words had impressed them.

"This is the Last Battle," said Annulian with a nod, "but it has only just begun."

"No!" I thundered. "All war must end here. If we do aught to anger the Dream Lords they will send another Vorta, and build another Karkesh. Look down into the streets. See how pitifully few our numbers are now. We have routed the enemy, yes, but how many have we lost? How can we hope to fight on with so few?"

"We shall grow stronger than ever before, now that the Zurks do not blight our world," Annulian persisted.

"Earth will flourish as never before if the Dream Lords help us to rebuild it," I told the gathered warriors, and they gave our words silent thought.

"Tear down the palace and this Platform and they will not be back until we have mustered another mighty army!" Annulian shouted to the warriors.

I shook my head. "Do that and this day shall be repeated over and over, throughout history, until the Earth is consumed by the flames of a war worse than even that in which she nearly perished so long ago," I promised. They knew then that I was right. They had had enough of death, and whern I, Death, the Pale Rider, said that no more would I kill, they knew that it was time for peace. Only Annulian stood against me, and it seemed to me that his jealousy had driven all reason from him.

"You heard his admission! He is himself a Zurk. Do you trust a Zurk spy? With your own ears you have heard him claim accession to the Zurk throne! He will sell us to them," he said, punching out every word venomously.

"The Prophecy said that he would come from the camp of our enemies," said Prosocles, stepping forward.

"He has shown himself to be as much a hater of Zurk ways as

you and I," said Thuran.

"He is a spy, I tell you! Would you disobey the Lion? Warlord, Annihilator, king?"

"And I have said that you must not disobey Chalremor, the Wise One, mouthpiece of the Powers of Light. I say that henceforth shall Earth live in peace and harmony with Zurjah, as is the will of the Gods, and from now on we shall enter the Empire as a sub-race no longer, but as brother men to the Zurjahns. The Zurks ended here. The rest are not like them, so call them Zurjahns."

My words had a profound effect on the warriors, who were naturally dubious about any Zurjahns, but who had firm faith in the Prophecy. And after the dreadful carnage during the siege, no one could have stomach for more.

"*Brother* men!" Annulian cried incredulously. My own anger was burning within me, and I was resolute that Annulian should not undermine my wishes. I had not fought here just to whet his own manic ambitions.

"If you defy Chalremor, and if you wish to question the one who taught us, if you, *you*, who instructed me in his teachings, are against him, then wait until he comes again. Then will you see how he punishes disobedience," I retorted. Annulian was furious, but the warriors buzzed with excitement.

"My lord," cried Prosocles. "What does this mean? Will Chalremor come again to Earth?"

"When he learns that we are victorious, he will do so almost certainly. But if he learns that his wishes have been defied, despite my warnings, he will be angry. If we live in peace with the Zurjahns, they will no longer chastise him, seeing at last the truth in his words. It was Vorta who poisoned the Dream Lords' minds against him. Now he will be freed and can return."

This carried more weight with them than anything else I had said, and some of them shed tears at the news that the beloved Prophet of old would come again.

Yet Annulian, gazing into the jaws of defeat, would not submit. "I for one would rather die than enter any alliance with Zurjah. I defy any man who imposes such a law upon the free peoples of Earth!" He spat into the dust.

"Then you defy me!" I countered, all patience with him gone. The warriors drew back, for my anger frightened them. They sensed a brewing storm.

"You will have to kill me, Annulian, if you intend to force your will upon the people of Earth. Would you forsake Chalremor?" I asked again.

"I have never forsaken him! It is you who betray him, twisting his words to your own purpose. Nothing will make me subject my people to Zurk rule! Chalremor would not wish it either."

"You will not be subjecting them."

"Yet you would call the Zurks brothers. Brothers! We have just slain thousands! Will your Dream Lords turn a blind eye upon the mountains of their dead?"

"There has been enough death. Would you add mine to the tally?" I said coldly, and a ripple of anxiety ran through the warriors. I felt motivated by something outside my own will. But the Warlord had to be challenged.

"Does the Chosen One challenge me?" he said softly.

"If you persist in your insubordination, then I have no choice," I said simply, without fear. The warriors were horrified, but none dared interfere.

"Insubordination, you say. I, Annulian, who have led my people since my father's death, whom they love and call Warlord. I, the Annihilator, who have schemed the destruction of Vorta and all the impossible odds that he heaped against us. I, who have cut down a thousand men, and smashed Karkesh to rubble. I, who have slain the tyrant in his very den. You call me insubordinate. I ask my people—" and here he turned to the warriors in supplication—"have I not been a fit leader? Am *I* not fit to be your Chosen One? Have the Gods not smiled upon me?"

There were frowns and many shaken heads among them as he said this, and he saw with a terrible understanding that they were refusing his blasphemous offer.

"Who speaks now of betrayal?" I asked.

"Very well," he said quietly. "If this is the only way I can reconcile you to my will, then I shall slay you. We shall see who the Gods protect."

There was a thoughtful pause. I felt myself shudder, though not with cold or fear. What madness had prompted me to fight this man, this Annihilator? It was plain to all that Annulian was wrong, but must we fight to decide the future of this planet? It was too late to go back on our words, for his broadsword was in his hands. I found my helmet on the floor and slowly put it on. Thuran made to stop us—he knew how unfit I was—but something cut him short and he receded.

"So be it," I murmured, lifting my sword once more. A wide circle had formed around us as the warriors watched in petrified silence. No one spoke against this fight, for they knew it was the only way.

Annulian's sword came down sharply, and I barely managed to dodge to one side, betraying my injured leg. His sword was far longer than my blade, which seemed puny by the side of it. I tried to rush in close to him, but he dropped back quickly, swinging his blade for another blow. One strike with that and I would be finished. I somehow deflected the blow as it split the air, and the sword crashed on to the deck, carving a slice of metal out of it. I wondered what material the deadly blade was forged from. He moved quickly and surefootedly, holding me easily at bay. Slowly I backed away, my face beaded with sweat, my eye bandage damp inside my helm. Annulian brought the huge sword swishing down at me again, and I ducked sideways as it clanged to the metal floor. I could not get close enough to thrust at him, for despite his size and his own battle-fatigue, he was very agile.

Gradually I was forced back to the doors of the palace, and the warriors parted to give us room. I stood with my back against one of the marble pillars, already gasping for breath. Only the knowledge that if I did not move I would be split in twain gave me the ability to keep eluding him. That terrible sword came whistling at me again, and again I swerved away at the last moment. As his blade smashed into the solid, black marble, it shattered near the hilt end, leaving the Warlord with only a short sword. I heard him curse as I leapt in, anxious to finish this quickly lest exhaustion be my undoing.

We fought furiously, and I sought in vain for a vital opening. Annulian's broken blade was everywhere, desperately thwarting my blurred movements, and now it was my turn to force him back. Smoke still drifted across the Platform as we battled perilously close to its edge, and some of the people below saw our struggle and pointed up, wondering what could be amiss. Seeing Annulian slip for a moment and leave an opening, I rushed him, but just when I thought I had at last penetrated his defenses, he anticipated my move and grasped my sword arm. He tried to get at me with his blade, but I grabbed his wrist, and together we swayed on the brink of eternity, the warriors gasping behind us.

"Must you steal everything from me?" Annulian said hoarsely as we grappled.

"Your way is wrong," I grunted. I had to heave with all my waning strength to push him back, and I came near to going over. We broke and circled each other warily.

"Perhaps. But it is not my kingdom you want, is it?" he hissed. The warriors could not hear his words, nor mine. I felt a pang of conscience as I realized what he meant.

"You are a fool to sacrifice your kingdom for a woman who does not love you," I replied, for it could only be his jealous love for Vellarna that had driven him mad with anger. If I had not interfered, he would probably have accepted peace with Zurjah. He hated me, and had to kill me for what I had done.

"Vellarna loves you. I know you are lovers," he said, his voice rasping with effort.

I felt an overwhelming flush of pity for him, for I had indeed wronged him. I dodged a lunging thrust and backed off. We fought for peace, not for a woman, I told myself. He came on again, intent on ripping open my throat, but I slipped aside and caught him about his own.

"You are wrong, Annulian. We are not lovers. My bride to be is on Zurjah," I whispered. The warriors heard only muffled words, and read them as taunts.

"You lie in your teeth, Zurk! You have shamed us all with your act. The Priests have spoken to me of your meetings."

I blanched at his words. The Priests! I had forgotten them. But I had no time to look for them now.

"I..."

"My kingdom means nothing to me without my queen," Annulian said gruffly, and there was a growing despair in his voice. We split apart again, and our swords met with a flurry of sparks. His actions came slower, and his breath came in great sobs.

"I am sorry for what has happened," I said lamely. He was right in this. "I would willingly bestow her love upon you if I could," I said slowly, word by word.

We were circling again. He thrust at me, but I avoided the blow. Our breathing was becoming labored now, as we both gulped in mouthfuls of the smoky air. I could not last for much longer.

"You took her and used her to appease your own carnal appetite, like any other Zurk. You would scorn Earth's fairest daughter, even now," he said, tears in his eyes.

"No, no," I said, remembering the hot embraces of Prosocles's beautiful daughter, who had first vowed her love to me that stormy night and many times since. I loved her, but my love was pale before that of my love for Taria, as the moon pales before the sun. Annulian would never understand that.

"Long have I hated you for this," he said, his voice almost inaudible. "And now my hate has led me to disobey Chalremor and cast the fate of Earth on one play of the sword. Am I cursed by the Gods?"

He fell silent after these words, his sword arm hanging limp. It would have been the work of a second to run him through, but I could not find it in me to strike. It was I who should die.

Suddenly he became a mad whirl of frenzied activity, raining blows at me in frantic succession, as though possessed by devils. I staggered back under such ferocity, instinctively protecting myself. Then I took a terrific butt on the chin as I slipped in a pool of blood. I sprawled backwards over a rank corpse, blood dribbling from a torn gum inside my helm. My elbows came to rest on the extreme edge of the Platform, and my head and shoulders jutted out into space. Annulian stood above me, sword lifted for the kill. This was to be death, then.

"The Priests never lie. They foresaw the death of a king in Karkesh, and so I gave my crown to Thuran. But it was you they meant," he said, his boot upon my sword hilt. I looked up helplessly, and some of the warriors came closer, eyes wide in disbelief as they saw that the Pale Horseman was to die.

"No!" cried Thuran, and Annulian paused.

I wrenched my sword free. Something was wrong with the Warlord. I was at his mercy. Why did he pause so long? Then with a yell he fell upon me in a mock attack, holding his shattered blade high above him, exposing himself recklessly. He wanted to die! Yet I could not do it. My head throbbed, and I fought to control my sword arm. It had taken on a life of its own, though, and I could do nothing to prevent myself from striking. I watched in horror as with one swift upward thrust, I sunk my sword beneath Annulian's armor and into his heart. He screamed at the mortal wound, and his blade clattered down beside my head.

"Annulian!" I cried.

"Peace, Galad," he gasped, and I smelt his rasping breath on my cheeks. He coughed out great gouts of blood, staring from agonized eyes. "Your way is right. Priests...not to...be...defied. The Gods...not to be...scorned. A king has fallen. Priests right. Look after...Earth...my queen and people..."

I yanked out my cruel sword in a useless attempt to undo what I had done, and felt a warm glow as his blood soaked me. Then, with one last groan, he heaved himself off me, plummeting over the brink and into the crowd far below. The warriors rushed forward, gazing down on his remains. Yet he could have killed me and gone on to become master of Earth, at least for a while. Now I knew what had stayed him. It was the Priests. It had been them who had entered my mind and willed me to kill him. I had been open to them, now that Vorta was dead. They knew Annulian's way was wrong and that I must live.

I could hardly move. It was Thuran who got me to my feet. Sure enough there were Priests among the warriors, masked as ever. I sealed my mind off from them. Instead I turned to the people below.

"Warriors of Earth! Karkesh is no more!" I roared, still gasping for breath. I paused, standing on the edge and lifting my arms, as if in supplication. They heard my distant voice ringing out and looked up. My words bounced off the opposite buildings, where the fires had ceased. The people began to cheer.

"You have seen the Four Horsemen. Now there are but Three, for the Red Horseman of War is dead. There shall be no more war! Annulian the Warlord is no more! You have a new king. Here he stands. Salute him! Salute Thuran!" I cried, lifting up Thuran's arm. The crowd cheered the louder.

"And never again shall the Pale Rider cross your world," I added, flinging aside my skull-helm. "Salute your new king, who shall rule over you with peace!"

Thuran shook his head in bewilderment, and on his helm the crown of Annulian sparkled.

"No, Galad. This cannot—"

288

"Be silent! The Priests foresaw Annulian's determination to rule by the sword. They could not permit it. They told him he would die, have you forgotten that?"

Both the people below and the warriors above set up a roar so loud that we could no longer hear our own words. I turned to glance at Prosocles, and he nodded, his face radiant with joy. And beyond him, the Priests were leaving, content that their own purpose had been achieved.

CHAPTER XIV
Envoy from Zurjah

At first Thuran was utterly confused by my pronouncing him king. Thousands of jubilant voices roared up at us from the crowded streets, testament to the popularity of the decision, while the evening sun shone on the swords we held skywards. Some of the warriors on the Platform were nonplussed as well as the General.

"Have you lost your senses?" he said to me under his breath.

"Not at all. Annulian lies broken below, does he not?" I replied, still waving.

"Yes, but..."

"You wear his armor, his helm, his crown. You have his horse."

"What are you suggesting?"

"Annulian is the last of his line. There are no other claimants for the kingship. The people love you. You are a just man. And Annulian bedecked you in his own trappings. When the people hear of that, they will know that he has as good as pronounced you his successor."

"But the Priests will not accept this..."

"They have ordained it, believe me, Thuran. Had it not been for their intervention, the Warlord would have been the victor in our conflict, not I. Do you remember his words the night he showed us the inscription from the Book of Prophecy? When he told you that you must ride the white horse in his stead?"

"Yes, clearly. I protested, not understanding his motives, though he said it was the will of the Gods."

"Aye, and so it was, though he knew not how much of that was true. You see, his Priests had told him that a king would fall at

Karkesh, and Annulian, always in dread of their powers, schemed a way by which he could temporarily be rid of his crown, thus hoping another—you—would be the one to fall. When he saw that you had survived, he turned on me, thinking, hoping, that I was the one the Priests had meant. In the end he realized he was wrong, and when he could have killed me, he stayed his hand."

"Why did the Priests turn against him?" Thuran asked, unable to see why the nation's champion would be so rejected in his hour of triumph.

"Because he was a warrior, and would have been so until his death. He would never have permitted peace with Zurjah. Perhaps it was a hard decision for the Gods to make, but there was no other way. The people worshiped Annulian, no less than they worship the Chosen One and Chalremor—nay, listen—but they fear the Pale Rider of Death. Oh, they respect me, yes, and see me as their savior, which I have been, but I was never meant to be the one who rules after Karkesh is no more. Even now my task is almost at an end. You are the most able man they have, Thuran. You are one of them and you know the dangers of prolonging the war. Unless peace is enforced now, your world, our world, will be brutally reprimanded. We will have gained nothing."

Thuran gave my words long and deep thought. "Perhaps I am the one to wear Annulian's crown. Yet there will still be problems of accession. What of the queen to be? What of Vellarna?" he asked, and his words caught me off my guard. I masked my feelings with an effort. As far as I knew, my affair with Vellarna had been secret. And whatever transpired hereafter, she could never be the one to sit beside me.

"You must be the judge of that, Thuran. You are unwed. She is from the noblest house in the Sacred City. The people would hail any ties you made."

"She may not take the news of Annulian's death well."

"You must make the decisions. You are king," I said with finality. I had spoken from a conviction that his union with Vellarna would be more than favorable.

"I must give the matter much thought," he murmured.

"Then you are king. Accept your new role."

"As you will it."

"I told Annulian repeatedly that it is imperative that Earth live in harmony with the rest of the Empire. It is senseless prolonging this bloodletting. Soon there will be an investigation here, for I am certain that some of Vorta's men escaped to Zurjah—there are no ships here. I shall speak for Earth, and my voice will carry weight with the Dream Lords. I am still my father's heir. I shall do everything to secure an alliance, and you need have no fears. My right will not be denied me, nor you yours. The common path is peace, and it is all the Dream Lords would want," I told him with conviction, and he nodded.

"Then they shall have it. Our time of strife is ended, praise to the Powers of Light. Come, let us gather together all the chiefs and leading warriors and explain to them all you have told me," he replied, breathing a great sigh of relief. He waved a last time to the people below and their joy was like thunder.

And so the Barbarian and nomad chieftains and Generals went into a long conference with Thuran and I, and I told them why the Gods had decreed Annulian's death, and that they had chosen Thuran to be king in the Sacred City. Eventually they were in agreement, and gladly received Thuran in his new role. Annulian's claiming to be the Chosen One had disturbed a good many of the faithful warriors, and they saw the wisdom of my own peaceful policies. Some even spoke up and said that the Gods had guided my sword into him, when it was for him to take the victory. It was a popular belief, and I let them have their way in that. I had no qualms about Thuran's accession to the crown, for the Priests had virtually chosen him themselves.

Outside the palace, the excitable army began the completing of the destruction of the city, and any survivors that were found were not killed, but brought to the palace. My command that no one else was to be slain was obeyed religiously, and it pleased me to see that the Barbarians still treated me with reverence. I would need that when the time for the new union was at hand. The Zurks were given a free choice in the matter of their futures, for gone was any malice that I once bore toward the people of Karkesh. They were allowed to go west if they chose, or await Zurjahn investigation, and perhaps return to the Empire's principal world. All who promised to give a full account of their service to Daras Vorta and his evil ways were promised asylum, and many there were who threw their fate on that promise. Slowly the Barbarian armies were given the order to depart, taking with them the wounded and any dead that they wished to bury with ceremony. Karkesh fell into ruins, and only a handful of us remained on the Platform and in the palace.

The Zurjahns came, just as I had expected. Three days after the last of the Barbarian armies had gone, the sky darkened, and we saw the shadows of the Zurjahn war fleet slowly descending. It was well that the Barbarians had not wanted to fight on. The ships, some hundred or so, hung motionless in the sky above the smoldering city. The directly above the Space Receiver Station, now cleared of the dead, I saw the huge shape of the flagship of the Zurjahn Air Navy. A smaller craft detached itself from the hold and floated down, touching gently the deck of the landing area. All my remaining followers were hushed in awe, and the last of the defeated Zurks stood with bated breath, depending on my promise to obtain pardons.

As the doors of the by no means small craft opened and the ramp unfolded, I walked alone on to the deck, dressed now in the simplest of clothes. I still wore the rusting sword at my side, and my medallion around my neck, though it was with some pain that I crossed the deck, for my injured leg throbbed and forced me to limp. I had bandaged my right eye again, for it had closed altogether, affording me an occasional knife-stab of pain. I could not have made a very impressive sight. But I walked as proudly as I could to meet whatever delegate Zurjah had sent. High above me the fleet hummed, its ships like expectant vultures.

My heart sank as the Zurjahn forces emerged. Twin columns of hoverbubbles bobbed down the ramp, each Imperial Guard armed with both star lances and light rods—deadly weapons both. There must have been at least a thousand men, and I surmised that they were all crack fighting troops, fresh from the training grounds in the Red Mountains of Gargan. They spread out in rigid formation at the foot of the ramp, their weapons ready for discharging at the slightest hostile move. Zurjah had lost none of her old caution. I came to a stop, my hand resting on my sword hilt, returning the unblinking stare of the rigid Guards. If they chose to fight, at least the Barbarians would be well away in the Forlorn Mountains, although this force would be equipped with air boats and surface gliders, so that the combined efforts of the Priests to shield the presence of the Sacred City would be to no avail.

My fingers played with the edge of the medallion, and I prayed to whatever Gods had watched over me while I had fought. My attention was caught by the appearance of a tall, well-built figure at the top of the ramp. He did not sit astride a hoverbubble, but stepped slowly down the ramp into the sunlight. My heart leapt into my mouth. Zurjah had sent none other than my greatest friend, Gundar Sabian.

I wanted to rush across to him and embrace him on the spot, but dared not. One sudden move and the Guards would fry me alive. Gundar walked slowly toward me, and his face betrayed nothing of his emotions. He stopped only feet away and scrutinized my face as though he had forgotten it.

"By the stars!" he gasped, almost inaudibly, his eyes widening in disbelief.

"Thank the Gods it is you," I said, my own voice a whisper.

He frowned. "You realize they have sent me to put down this revolt, and to slay every living Barbarian on this world?" he said at last, as if his mind were a thousand miles away.

"We are Barbarians no longer, old friend. The people of Earth have been maligned too long, but justice has been done. The devil who ruled here is no more. Now the men of this world are ready to begin a new life in brotherhood with the men from...the homeworld," I told him, my voice rising. Only the wind high up on the dome behind us broke the silence. Thuran was looking at me from across the Platform as if he had been turned to stone. I unstrapped my sword.

"Once, Gundar, you gave a boy a star lance, when he was banished from Zurjah. I no longer have it. Weapons of such power are almost unknown on Earth. So I give you my sword." I handed it to him with both arms outstretched and here I prayed that the men in the palace would not misinterpret my gesture. It was the ultimate test of their faith in me. Gundar's arms hung by his sides, as though he were an automaton. Behind him the blue plumes of the Guards fluttered in the breeze. Gundar's eyes flickered and at last the spell seemed to have been broken.

"Galad!" he blurted out, then pulled me to his huge breast and hugged me with the strength of ten.

"By all that is wonderful in creation, I cannot contain my joy longer, no matter what you are responsible for here! Keep the sword, keep it. I know you would never use it on me."

"The Gods forbid it!" I laughed, and we slapped each other's backs like the old comrades we were, all the barriers of ceremony and time falling aside in that warm moment.

"But tell me, how is it that you are here, of all places? You were said to have been murdered on Gargan by Wortan Heynar, the rebel. I have never reconciled myself to your death. By heaven, but you have grown! You are a man."

The world and its problems had receded.

"I have survived a hundred deaths, and only the Gods know how. But I have served the one purpose for which I was bred, Gundar, and you must hear every detail," I told him, with a slight frown. He smiled and looked around him.

"In good time, lad. You have involved yourself in something of vast importance, that I can see. But you say you fought *with* the Barbarians, or did I mistake you?"

"You heard right. But you will know why. The yoke that Daras Vorta placed on this world had to be cast off, and it has been. The prodigal children can return. The Barbarians here are few now, for they died in their thousands to win their rights, and I must tell you that I am their spokesman."

"I see," he breathed uncertainly.

"This world, Ur as you call it, is the true homeworld, Gundar. I will prove it to you. You will learn to accept Earth, and so will the Dream Lords now that Daras Vorta is dead."

"The Dream Lords will be delighted at your return. We must away to them with all speed. And you must have a physician. That eye looks bad," he said, scowling at it.

"There will be time enough. There will be time to speak of me later. First you must meet the king and his retainers. And remember, these are not savages, they are as human as you and I. They are my people."

"Very well, Galad, I will respect your wishes in this. I am prepared to listen to reason. But the Dream Lords have strict legislation concerning Ur."

"Earth. Yes, I know about that. But believe me, old friend, they will change all that after I have spoken to them."

"You will have a chance sooner than you thought. I am only military Commander of the Fleet. Allow me to summon my superior.

He is on the flagship."

"Superior? Are the Dream Lords here, then?" I asked with renewed hope.

"Not exactly. But your cousin, and until your appearance just now, the new heir, Ravas Tarak, is in command."

I drew back with a curse as he said it, and his features clouded with suspicion.

"Ravas! By the Powers, I had forgotten the swine. So it was he who fled to Zurjah and told of the war. Listen, Gundar, you must trust me in this. If ever our friendship meant anything to you, then let it motivate you now."

Gundar looked perplexed.

"I will explain. But for the time, do not contact Ravas. As I live and breathe, he is the Empire's most deadly enemy."

"If you can prove this..."

"I will, Gundar, my friend, I swear it. For now, bear with me. If Ravas knows I am alive, he will have me executed at once. Come with me and speak to the king. You are not bound to speak to Ravas for a while?"

"He will not set foot here until I have cleared the way. He awaits my word."

"Good. Come, then. You are mystified, I know. But you will see."

He had not changed after all these years, and he knew I was no fool. I took him and a handful of his principal soldiers into the palace hall after he had given his troops orders to await him.

"Gentlemen," I addressed the warriors. "This is Gundar Sabian, Master at Arms in Chief to the Zurjahn Empire. He is one whom I hold in great esteem and is close to my heart are are you all. He was sent here to investigate the fall of Karkesh. He is a fair and just man, and will listen to the telling of the wrongs that have been done to you, as you shall see."

They all bowed courteously, and one by one shook hands with the splendid Zurjahn and his men. I was very proud of them, and could see that Gundar was impressed, if a little dubious, his men likewise.

"I am honored," he said to Thuran when I introduced them. Thuran was nonplussed, for he secretly feared treachery—a natural instinct—despite my earlier insistence that all would be well. Gundar spoke pleasantly to them all, including the somber

Chungsar, who cut a powerful figure. He had removed his helmet and armor and could be seen to be a man of Gundar's age, eyes twinkling, and he had a long, drooping mustache which came to his waist. Both he and Gundar eyed each other with evident respect.

There then began by me a recital of all the important incidents that had befallen me since first I had met Chalremor. Gundar listened avidly, and slowly he began to realize the truth about Earth. He had always thought of the Barbarians as primitive savages, and while he could see the military potential inherent in these warriors, he appreciated their reasons better. Prosocles spoke to him about the sacred City and he realized then, I think, just how prejudiced his own views had been. The tension slackened and soon the company, including Gundar's captains, was exchanging views and discussing freely all that had happened here. Gundar paled when I told him exactly what Vorta had planned—trying to oust me from my place and substituting Ravas Tarak—and then overthrowing the Empire. At the end he declared openly his apologies for the biased opinions he had held of Earth, saying that he would do whatever was in his power to put matters right. I was moved by his words because I knew what it meant to him to admit that he—and indeed the Dream Lords—had been wrong. I felt able to relax at last. My efforts had drained my strength, and I had to find a place to rest.

A meal was prepared for everyone, and Gundar talked on with Thuran, Prosocles and Chungsar about Earth and the progress of rebuilding. A new attitude of mutual trust had already started to build up and Gundar promised to hold off his army. He came to where I was resting and left the warriors and soldiers to discuss the aspects of the new alliance among themselves.

"So Daras Vorta is dead!" he said, kneeling beside me. I was exhausted.

"Aye, thank the stars. And there are plenty of his former retainers here to testify that all I have said about him is truth. He ruled through terror."

"Peace, Galad. Your noble friends impress me. I hope the Dream Lords see reason, though I think they will. Vorta blinded them."

"Promise me you will thwart any attempts they make to retake the world in their name," I said feverishly, clutching at his arm.

He patted me in a fatherly way. "There will be no more bloodshed while I command."

"Then is my heart at rest. Or almost so..."

"You should rest. I will have physicians tend you. Surgeons can correct your wounds. What else must you know before I have you sedated?" he said with a grin.

"There is one whom you have yet to mention. It has been long, but..."

Gundar's face clouded for a moment, but he hid his feelings with another grin.

"I think you should rest before we discuss..."

"Not yet, Gundar. I must know."

"Then I must impart bad news. I would that it were otherwise, but I will tell you. Your father is dead, Galad."

His eyes looked away, and I felt a pang of guilt. Of course, he had no way of knowing that it was not news to me, and that it was Taria I had been thinking of.

"I have heard, old friend," I said softly. "These things have a way of reaching us here. I heard that he died."

"I am sorry," he said simply, and I nodded.

"I only wish I could have been with him. But tell me, what of Taria, daughter of Bordin Sulian, the noble. How does she fare?" I asked anxiously. For a second I thought Gundar had frowned again, but he was quick to mask his thoughts.

"Taria? Why, yes, the fair maid you wooed so secretively. I remember her. She is well," he said evenly.

"Has she worried overmuch?"

"She has been unhappy, of course, for all Zurjah thought you dead and mourned your passing."

"Then she will be overjoyed at my return. I have dreamed of returning to her for so long. There are so many places here on Earth that I want her to see. And if I am to be a Dream Lord, I would do well to take a wife."

Gundar lowered his eyes uncomfortably. His whole manner suggested that something was amiss. "You still love her," he said quietly.

"Why, yes. Is that so amazing! You must have guessed how it was with us, despite the taunting about my flirtations with other maids?" I asked with a grin, but his reticence disturbed me. He spoke again.

"I knew it then, of course. But that was long ago."

"I fail to understand you, Gundar. What is amiss? What has

297

happened? You told me she is well. Is that so?"

"Yes, but you may not cause her joy, Galad. I fear your return may cause her bitter distress."

"Distress!" I gasped. "But why? What does this mean? She loves me, I know it. Do not toy with me, Gundar. Speak your mind. You told me I had become a man. Then speak to me plainly." I gripped his arm and he winced.

"You have been away so long. Even I, who never gave up hope, thought you dead."

"Yes, yes. I understand that she would have grieved, but I live. Taria and I avowed our love. We were to be wed! And now that I am to return," I protested, but as I said these words, I was struck by a sudden icy fear. "Unless—"

"She had her duty to consider. She is married," he said, his voice now very low.

I felt as though I had been struck. My mind whirled.

"Married!" I repeated, the word barely audible. "That cannot be so. Tell me you jest!"

"May I be cursed for being the one to bring you such unseemly tidings, Galad. I knew not the way of your heart. Yet it has been so for a year now. If she was a reluctant bride, I cannot say, but her sense of duty and family pressure would have been enough to make her take the step."

I was terribly shaken but managed to steady myself. All the pain and discomfort I had suffered in the campaign and over the last few days were nothing to this.

"Married," I muttered, still hardly able to believe it. I had risen and now paced restlessly about the hall, and my warriors watched, wondering what was wrong. I was hardly conscious of them.

"Tell me," I said, whirling upon Gundar, my voice shaking. "Does she love him, Gundar?"

He grimaced at my hoarse words. Time stood still for a moment. He could not bring himself to face me.

"Your silence speaks for you. She does not love him," I said, seeking to convince myself that it was so. Then at length, Gundar turned and spoke, damning my hopes forever.

"She is with child."

CHAPTER XV
Across the Skies of Earth

I passed a restless night. Gundar had returned to his scout ship, from where he had relayed orders to his most trusted men on board the flagship that Ravas Tarak was to be confined to his quarters until further notice. Gundar proposed to accompany me to the Sacred City before making a full report to the Dream Lords, but I had declined his offer to let me sleep aboard the flagship. I preferred to remain with Thuran and the others. The last of Vorta's Guards had been sent aboard to await trial on Zurjah.

The next morning Thuran came to me.

"This Gundar Sabian seems to be all that you say he is, Galad," he said calmly. I nodded and roused myself.

"I thank the Gods that it was him the Zurjahns sent us. I have no closer friend on Zurjah. You may rest easy about Earth's future now. Gundar will see to it that there are no more hostilities. When he withdrew his troops last night, it was for the last time. The next time those men set foot here, it will be as unarmed civilians," I promised, and Thuran knew now there were no deceptions involved.

"It is well that the Zurks—uh, Zurjahns, I should say—listened to reason. With the weapons they brought, we would indeed have been an easy prey."

"Well then. No more talk of war."

We were interrupted by footsteps. Gundar was awake and now came to see us once more. He had three of his officers with him, though none were armed. Neither was Gundar, and again the Barbarians were reassured. They bowed to him and he to them.

"Greetings Galad, Thuran," he said, and we nodded. My face was still grim with the news he had brought me.

"Soon," said Thuran, "you will see the Sacred City. It will convince you that we are not all sword-bearing savages on this world." Thuran grinned as he said it, and Gundar smiled, removing any last vestiges of tension between the two giants.

"It will be an honor, Thuran," said Gundar.

"You will receive strange looks, for until yesterday your people were our deadliest enemies. I have sent pigeons to tell them we come with friends."

"Pigeons?" said Gundar, puzzled.

299

"Yes," I said. "Messenger birds. You'll learn all about them."

"As with so many things," Gundar chuckled.

"Let us waste no more time," I said, a trifle stiffly, and made ready to leave.

"Will you go by horseback?" asked Thuran. Gundar could easily have declined and offered to take us to the City more speedily in air boats, but he was as tactful as I would have hoped.

"Horseback? Why, yes. It has been too long since I felt a steed beneath me. And perhaps your people would be a little disconcerted to see Zurjahn ships coming upon them."

Thuran nodded affably. I was looking up through the windows of the palace dome to where the navy hung suspended over the city.

"My lord?" asked Thuran.

I turned to Gundar. "Before I join you, there is one person I must see."

Gundar frowned. "Can it not wait until we are back from the City, sire?"

"No," I said simply. I looked meaningfully at Gundar. The day before I had warned him not to speak of Ravas Tarak in front of the warriors and he had not done so. If they knew he was up there they would want his immediate execution. Gundar and I stared at each other in silence for a moment.

"Very well," he said. "We will wait for you."

"There is no need. You go with Thuran and the others, and I will be with you shortly." He could see that I was resolved in this.

"I'll have an air boat pick you up at once," he nodded, before excusing himself and going back to the scout ship.

"You will forgive me for this interruption," I said to Thuran. "But I must speak to the Dream Lords. They believe me to be dead. I will put matters right and prepare them for Gundar's report." I did not relish lying, but I wanted to keep the presence of Ravas a secret.

"We will see that the noble General is treated with all due cordiality," said Prosocles.

"Of course," I nodded, gripping his arm. "And soon we can rebuild in earnest."

Gundar returned with another Guard. "My man will take you aboard the flagship. An air boat is standing ready."

"Thank you, Gundar." I walked with him outside and saw a single air boat beside the scout ship.

"Be careful," he warned me, out of earshot of the others. "I know what Ravas means to you. Do not be rash. Not now that this new union looms so very close."

"No. Ravas will live to pay for his crimes. And I have faith in you."

"Then go to Ravas. Keep your sword. I have told the men who it is that will step aboard."

"Fare thee well, then," I said, and went with the one Guard to his air boat. I climbed aboard, and he settled at the controls. We lifted gracefully into the warm air, and I waved down to Gundar and the warriors. High above us the flagship blotted out the sun. We curved up to meet it. Karkesh was a blur far below us when a commotion broke out under the belly of the flagship. I could see flashes and could hear shouts, but the shadows under the hull blotted out the details. The pilot Guard accelerated, and we swooped faster up to the huge ship.

Suddenly another air raft came hurtling at us from the ship, a solitary figure at the controls. I squinted to see what was going on. Behind the newcomer there were flames billowing from one of the belly doors from the mother ship. My pilot took evasive action as the small air boat flew over us. And now I could see who the crazed driver was.

Ravas Tarak!

Somehow he had freed himself from his confinement, and was making his last bid for freedom. As he passed, he snarled, for he had recognized me. I looked on in horror as he levelled a star lance at our air boat and raked it with a sheet of flame. I dived down into the bottom of the boat and felt the searing heat pass above me. But the pilot was not so fortunate. He screamed as the fire caught him and seconds later he was a ball of flame, his blazing body tumbling over the prow of the boat to drop into the void below.

The air boat spiraled down, and I scrambled to my knees. Ravas had passed me and turned to look back. I had to risk getting to the controls and revealing myself, or the boat would nosedive to its doom. I managed to reach the controls in a crouch and fought to steer the boat on a level plane. It took long moments to right, but eventually the craft was flying smoothly. Ravas did not come back to finish me. He was more intent on saving his own worthless hide. Instead he had turned southeast of Karkesh and was headed out high over the Southern Waste for the Sea of Death. I wasted no time in deliberating what I should do.

With a twist of the controls I sent my craft after his. I could see the already receding dot against the blue haze of the sky, but to be sure I did not lose him I switched on the monitor and tracked the green dot on the screen. For a long time the two crafts sped high across the scarred face of the devastated world, and from up here I could see how badly the ancient wars had damaged the planet. If the rest of it was like this, it would take a titanic effort to restore it.

My mind flew to the fleeing air boat ahead. I could clearly see the gleaming waters of the Sea of Death far below, and I noticed on the monitor that Ravas was losing height. Whether by accident or design I could not say. I looked back over my shoulder to see if we were followed, but there were only the ships of the navy and no other air boats—but there would be.

My own craft dipped toward the sea in pursuit of Ravas. Now we both came within feet of the surface, and I saw with some degree of disgust why the waters were named as they were. For it was more like a vast expanse of oil or bubbling black mire. Weird fingers of petrified wood twisted up from the silent sea and nothing stirred.

For hours we sped over that awful glutinous expanse, the smell rising to sicken me. The distance between us never changed. Both craft sped on at maximum speed. Then at last came a break in the dreadful monotony of filth below us. On the horizon a small island rose from the sea like a ridged hummock of mud flat. Nothing grew on its broken surface, and greasy waves lapped viscously at its bare shores. Ravas chose this isolated mount to stage his confrontation. His craft nestled down between two of the muddy ridges out of sight.

I took my own craft in fast, determined to keep out of firing range, or I would be shot from the sky. The air boat veered to one side then came in at a different angle from Ravas. I let it skid to a halt on the mire beyond another ridge. As the boat settled, I left the controls and made for the side. The craft lurched and I fell back with a curse. The island was as unstable as the sea itself.

When I was sure it was moored, I made to climb over the side. My only hope lay in surprising Ravas. Yet it was too late for that now. A dry laugh made me look up.

Ravas stood on top of the ridge, his star lance pointing at me. His lank black locks hung loosely down, a waft of his tart perfume drifted down to me. His lips curled in a sneer of triumph.

"So, cousin, we meet for the last time," he said, again laughing.

"You knew I would come for you," I said grimly.

"How you escaped Vorta's clutches I shall never know. I only know he was furious. Yet still you thwarted him, Galad."

"I did. And Vorta is dead."

"It hardly seems credible. A pack of Barbarian animals led by an upstart Dream Lord cur, yet they plundered Karkesh. To no avail. You may have destroyed my master, but you will never take me."

"Where will you hide?" I taunted him. "You can kill me easily enough, but not all the men of Earth. And now that the Zurjahns will return here in peace, you will be hunted like the animal you are. Even now the ships will be searching."

"With you dead, I will be Dream Lord. There will be no peace while I sit on your throne."

"You are beaten, Ravas," I said with a shake of my head. "Gundar is against you, and Thuran and Prosocles. There are men here and on Gargan who will testify against you and Vorta. And on Zurjah there is Chalremor. He will be pardoned and given a new hearing."

Ravas laughed and this time the sound made me shudder.

"Chalremor!" he scoffed. "Chalremor is dead!"

"Dead..." I echoed, the word not registering fully.

"Yes, dead! I went up into his den myself."

"You—"

"He was no more of a man than you and I—less so. A length of steel through his belly, and he was no more immortal than a worm. I flung him from the ramparts of his tower and let the moat take him."

I choked down my horror, my fists clenching on the rail of the air boat.

"And as for that pretty tart you thin so much of—" he began, but it was too much for me. I snatched out my sword and leapt from the boat. Ravas leveled his star lance at my chest. I would be dead before I even reached the ridge.

"Still a tender spot," he jeered. "But it means nothing now."

Sweat broke out on my brow. Ravas would fire at any moment. There was no way out of this. I had blundered into it—a victim of my own temper, my own seething hate.

"This time, Sarian, there is no escape. I bid you adieu."

As he raised the star lance for the kill, a last desperate ploy came to me. Once, on Gargan, an Imperial Guard had made as if to torture me with a star lance. He had touched it to Chalremor's medallion, and it had been the Guard who had died. I tore the medallion from my neck and flung it at Ravas as he fired. A stream of heat reached out for me and the medallion tumbled into it.

There was a blinding flash, and I was knocked off my feet and sent rolling over and over in the stinking mud. Sparks showered down and my one eye felt as if it had been seared by lightning. Smoke and ozone clouded everything, and I shook myself. I was alive. I scrambled away from the air boat. Ravas would finish me once the screen of smoke had cleared.

I still held my sword, and within moments I had taken cover behind an adjoining ridge. I waited while the smoke cleared, my breath coming in great sobs. Now I could hear another sound. It was Ravas. I could see him, kneeling on the ridge, etched against the backdrop of sky. His star lance was beside him, and both hands covered his face. I had to act quickly before he recovered.

With a last heave of strength I got to my feet and ran across the mud. I struggled up the slope, sword gripped tightly, praying that he would not look up and see me. I was still yards away when he dropped his hands and stared straight at me. I froze, knowing that this time he would end it. His eyes widened as though looking through me.

"*Blind!* I'm *blind!*" he shrieked suddenly.

He made no move, tears streaming from his sightless eyes, and I went up the last of the slope slowly. I had no need to hurry now. His ears seemed to pick up some new sound.

"Galad? Galad! Is it you? No...I hear...hooves. But not here, not possible...not hooves! Am I mad...hooves?"

I stood before him and raised my sword. There could be no mercy.

"I see! I see! *The Pale Horseman!*" he screamed, his eyes boring into mine. But he made no move to stop me. I brought the sword down and it sliced into his skull. Over and over I struck, even when his body became lifeless, my own tears running freely. At last I shook and turned away, vomiting. My final enemy was no more. Victory was mine.

And yet I had won nothing. Nothing at all.

EPILOGUE

The sea ripples now on the mud and rocks around me. Only the sound of those whispering waves, lapping near my feet, disturbs the tranquility of the timeless days.

No one has come.

I sit here restfully, my sword by my side, and dream of days past. I see castles and cities, warriors and wars, and sometimes the face of a beautiful girl.

Ah, Taria. So fair, so lovely. Perhaps I was never worthy of one so fine. But that is no matter; my purpose is served. I have answered the call of the Gods.

Perhaps there are none.

My blade is clean. I have polished it to its former shine as a good warrior should. Or as a good servant of the Gods should.

Perhaps there are none.

There is now but one life left for the weapon to claim. The Pale Rider will be seen no more.

The day has been long; it will soon be evening.

Very soon.

Book III:
Retribution

THE DREAM LORDS

Man has reached out and conquered the planets of his tiny system, crossing the black voids of empty night and setting down on alien worlds—hostile worlds that he has tamed only by perpetual strife and hard labor and, not least of all, cunning. He has found new and ingenious ways of working miracles, making the worlds that were once inhospitable and barren now bearable and even pleasant. The Dream Lords, with their mastery of illusion and sending of visions, have made this new acceptance of these outlandish worlds tolerable to even the most nostalgic of homeworlders, so that the truths and legends surrounding the history of our race have become blurred.

And it is they, the Dream Lord masters who rule with iron laws from Zurjah, who have also sought to travel the realms of inner space, searching for powers hitherto unknown to mortals. Mortals? With their newfound abilities, they have set at a remote distance the gaping jaws of death and have prolonged their lives and the lives of their chosen disciples. They perform wonders with these powers of the mind, and yet they have inadvertently unleashed upon their minions darker powers, reaching into the deepest lairs of nightmare and dredging up from those nethermost vaults of the mind abysmal terrors possessed of unbridled dangers.

There is a goodness within man and a capacity for love, creation and peace, but the Gods have balanced this with the darker emotions, so that there is also a capacity for destruction and war and self-annihilation. The cosmic circle of power will turn, inevitable as the oblivion which claims all, so that each era of peace and civilization will resolve into one of chaos and barbarism, no matter how grandiose man's achievements. And the greater the civilization, the greater the chaos surrounding its collapse. If there are Gods at all, it must amuse them to watch our petty retrogressions.

And so man has made the solar system his own, straddling the nine planets ostentatiously, yet the cosmic circle closes in while Man bows before the yoke of the nightmare powers, so that there may at last be an end to his insignificant fumblings. All these things have I learned since leaving the Dream Lord courts—I, who have been banished by my own; I, who have brought down the evil masters of a world; I, who have ridden at the head of the Four Horsemen and brought Death incarnate upon the servants of the Devil.

309

I, Galad Sarian, who should be dead.

CHAPTER I The Sea of Death

There is a sea on Earth, a black, miasmal expanse of viscous effluvium and polluted oil-mire, into which the poison-laden rivers and sluggish waterways discharge their deadly loads of waste, fruits of their courses over the ravaged, desecrated lands, so that for untold hundreds of miles there is nothing but a vast excreta of contaminated filth, where no creature, normal or mutated, stirs. Not unkindly, it is called the Sea of Death. From out of its foul surface there emerge but few solid shapes. There are, it is true, occasional black, metallic hulks, rusty and eaten away by the acid slime, relics of millennia gone by when the sea was clean and navigable, but for the most part all that can be seen is the infrequent hump of an islet, thrust up like some growth on the cankerous hide of a leviathan.

It was upon such a shifting islet that I slew Ravas Tarak, the foul apostle of Daras Vorta, whose own life had ended at the fall of the Black City, Karkesh, where the servants of darkness and madness had sought to raise Shaitan himself. It had been a terrible conflict, that apocalyptic war, and many thousands had fallen. Yet Vorta's insane ambitions to put Tarak in my seat of power and to thus tilt the scales in the ruling of the solar system had fallen with the burning ruins of his odious city.

There should have followed a time of rejoicing, of merrymaking and feasting and of reunion. My old friend from Zurjah, planet of my birth, Gundar Sabian, had arrived with the war fleet of the Zurjahn overlords, but swift talks had followed—the war was at an end. Gundar listened sympathetically to me and my faithful generals and to Thuran, now the king of the Barbarians. The elderly envoy from the Dream Lords had it within his power to salve my bruised and war-torn body with a few mere words—how fared Taria, the girl I had been forced to leave on Zurjah? Yet I heard from Gundar only his muttered, apologetic revelations as he stole from me my last vestige of hope and will to live.

Taria, from whom I had been ruthlessly torn by my father and his fellow Dream Lords, and who had shone for me throughout my years of trial on Gargan and Ur like a brilliant star, had given me up for dead (as had most of my old friends) and had taken a husband. Gundar had hesitated in revealing this news to me, but I had insisted on the truth. Even now Taria was with child, and I could only hope for a shadow role in the remote corridors of her heart. I had brought destruction and death to the agents of Shaitan, and had emancipated a world of slaves; I was revered by my new-found people like a deity, but all this had suddenly become nothing to me.

Without Taria, my life was empty. I had endured years of trial, bloodshed and death, and both my mind and body were exhausted, calling out for succor. My mind shrank back inside myself, and I cursed all men and their infernal struggles. Thus it was that I stood brooding upon the lonely islet far out in the lost wastes of the Sea of Death. I took my sword and polished it clean of Ravas Tarak's blood. And I set the haft to the ground, the point beneath my heart. I would cast myself upon it and this withdraw from this mire of seething emotions that was my life.

As I knelt in the black mud, on the verge of impaling myself, my eyes saw movement at the edge of the islet. I looked up, startled, and there, garbed in filthy, ordure-encrusted rags, hunched an old man, his lined visage screwed up like a dried fruit, his eyes strained to see ahead of him as though vainly searching for something. My first thought was that this haunting figure must be Death, come to escort me to the after-realms. It was an ironic thought, for I, too, had been Death, riding before the Horsemen, destroying all who came near. I voiced my sullen thoughts.

"Are you Death, old man, come to claim me at last?"

The stooping shape peered even more closely, taking a number of clumsy steps forward.

"Not Death, not I, though I may enter his domain soon enough. Who are you to talk of Death—you who are but a youth?" he answered, coming up the slope to me. I quickly lifted my sword and reversed it, so that he could not see what I had been about. Digging its point into the ground, I rested my arms upon it.

"My affairs are my own," I retorted, growing impatient at this unwarranted intrusion. He stood near me, his head on a level with mine, his rheumy eyes still screwed up so that I could hardly see them. He was leaning precariously upon a gnarled stick, his bent legs shaky as though the island rocked gently upon a cleaner sea.

"So they are," he said with a nod. "You must forgive an old man

311

for being curious. I have my own life to lead. And I value it, short a time as there may be left to me. It is why I took it upon myself to seek out the cause of so many strange auguries."

I looked long and hard at this wizened figure, no bigger than a child, and the stirrings of an unnatural fear made my bare neck cold. Well did I remember Chalremor, the wise old man of Zurjah, whose own divinations and prophesies had mapped out my turbulent life well before time and with an uncanny accuracy. Once I had laughed at superstition, but experience had tempered my derision with respect. I knew that Chalremor was dead—yet he had wielded strange powers. Surely this could not be an illusion of his making.

"Are you, then, a prophet?" I asked the oldster.

He cackled, the phlegm rattling in his withered breast. "Nay! But here in the Sea of Death all is tranquil, or so it seems most days. Not so this day. Ships that travel in the sky, burning lights that even my fading sight made sun-like and you, young man, alone upon this bank of mire, a thousand miles from the haunts of the last men. These are ominous portents and ones which called for the attention of the lord of these wastes."

He was looking about him, head bobbing like that of a doll.

"Who would be fool enough to claim ownership of this pestilential morass?" I sneered.

"Why, I!" he said proudly, and the senile gesture brought a half-smile to my stern features. "No one has disputed my claim."

"No. Nor do I, old man. And no one who comes after me will, be assured. You may live out your life and go in peace. Go—I will not remain here long."

"By what means will you leave? I have carefully scrutinized the isle. I see nothing to take you from my domains. And how came you here?"

My brief amusement at his tottering figure was seeping away with my patience. Why did he not go?

"I came by the airship you saw in the sky. It is no longer here, having sunk in the mire. The...explosion you heard and the blinding light...it was the ship crashing."

This was a lie, for the light had burst across the island when Ravas Tarak had aimed his star lance at me and fired—the stream of fire had hit my horse medallion, knocking Tarak senseless and disintegrating the golden talisman that had been my protector for many years.

"But there were two such flying things," croaked the old man, still looking about the bare islet as if expecting to see a band of outlaws leap up from nowhere. I was thankful that I had cast the corpse of Ravas Tarak into the sea, together with the airships.

"Both are gone. I am all that remains. And I will soon be gone—be assured."

He nodded, but he I could see his discomfort remained.

"It is strange for visitors to arrive here. What possible purpose could they have?" he mumbled, as though to some other attendant listener. It was plain that I would not rid myself of him easily. "And how did you come to be here, old man?" I asked him testily, getting to my feet. He hopped back like a ragged bird.

"I have lived here for years, choosing the seclusion and the silence to the old life on the mainland. It may be deadly and foul smelling here, but I prefer it to the violent ways of men ashore. You seem to have time only for killing and destroying one another—the ancients left their curse upon you when they burned up the world. Now the last of you scrabble in the pitiful remains like slavering dogs after offal. Only when you are all dead will there be any peace. I can see from your trappings that you are no different. There is blood upon you, and your sword is worn. Your eye is closed—the kiss of steel will rob you of more than your eye, you will see! You are all cursed! You come here and you laugh at me and my spoiled lands! You spit on my silent realm. But there is peace here such as you will never have!"

I nodded sadly. Looking at the Sea of Death I wondered at what Man had forfeited to attain his peace.

"Yes," I said to the old man. "There is peace in death."

"Pah! Death...what is so wrong with life? I have been alive for more years than you would believe. Do I seek the surcease of death? Not I! I would gladly exchange the brief flicker of life left to me for a new life. I would had I your youth—then I would show you how to use it wisely! Warring and destroying? Pah! I would find better ways of spending my days. I would enjoy life and be happy."

Gradually his words were beginning to take on a more meaningful edge, though he could not realize that. Surely he could not have guessed that I had been about to destroy myself when he arrived. Yet his words lashed me now as though in punishment for the very act. I had reviled the gods for denying me peace after I had served them well—and I had even laughed and shouted to the sky that there were no gods—but now I sensed a chilling purpose in my meeting with this old buffoon.

"I have fought and killed," I confessed to him, "but it was for good reasons."

"Excuses! Pah! There is no justification for this!" he spat vehemently, pointing to the dismal sea around us.

"No. I make no excuses for this. I, too, would see an end to man's perpetual warring. I told you I fought for a cause—it was a war to end all wars. There were forces of evil at work that had to be brought down. Now that they have been destroyed, Man can think about rebuilding this world and living in harmony with his neighbors."

"For how long? You are young and full of hopes. I am old—I have seen such hopes before. Always the pattern is the same. These evil forces you speak of—it is *Man* that is evil!"

"Then he must learn to be wise." His grim logic annoyed me.

He shook his head morbidly. "Too late for that, with his world dying around him."

"Earth will thrive again. There is a new peace coming. The Dream Lords will change the laws," I persisted, but there was a hollow ring of doubt about my words. The old man shuffled about uncomfortably. "I have heard of these Dream Lords," he said. "Cruel rulers from beyond the skies."

"They have the power to set this world aright."

"So you say! And even if it were so, they would use the men of earth like slaves to do the work, then reap the harvest and cast us out. Barbarians they call us."

"No longer, old man. The fall of Karkesh has changed that."

"For a time, maybe. I have seen too much blood. I will stay here while the mad dogs of the mainland tear the world apart between them as they would a chicken carcass! I want none of their promised peace."

His words horrified me. How many of the world's scattered hermits had no faith in the legend of the Horsemen? Had it all been a clever scheme of Chalremor's and Annulian's to cast down the Empire? I had been taught that all men of Earth believed in the rebirth and the coming of a new era of enlightenment. Now I was ready to take my life, knowing that the Dream Lords would be instrumental in the coming of the new age of peace. For a moment I was nonplussed, but then my melancholy overcame me again. Why should I longer care about the wars and the strivings—I had fought blindly and I had gained nothing for myself. The old man was right, men were born to fight and would always fight.

"Will there be more of your kind coming?" he asked, gazing up anxiously at the clouds.

I shook my head. "No. There may be a few men in ships, seeking me, but they will not come with intent to disturb you. They will quickly leave."

"And you—how will you leave? You have no ship."

"That is my affair."

He regarded me for long moments, his thoughts hidden behind his lined expression. I could have seen into his mind with my own, but I hated using my mental powers unless I had to. The old man coughed and spat noisily.

"I have a ship. I can set you on the path to the mainland if you wish it. That way you will soon be gone from my lands."

"No!" I turned away from his unsettling gaze.

"But you cannot survive here for long!" he protested.

"That is of no concern to you."

"Quite so," he said, sniffing and again looking skyward. "I came here to be sure that my existence was not in any danger. I am satisfied. Your life is your own, to do with as you will. Go back to your fellows and kill yourselves. I care nothing for you, or your rough companions of the sky."

"Then leave me!"

He seemed taken aback and eyed me curiously. I had to go through with my plan. There was no way I could go back and face the Dream Lords and Taria now. I had had more than enough. Let the gods mock me in my moment of shame—I would thwart them yet.

The old man was moving around, his stick poking idly at the mud.

"As you wish. I shall leave. Though you will have to suffer me for a while longer."

"Why so?"

"You see, there is no wind. Without wind I cannot leave the isle."

"What, then, of your ship? Does the wind carry it like a leaf, or does it have the wings of a bird?" I was mocking him.

His face clouded in anger. "My ship is safe and worthy enough! Unlike yours, it has no need to take to the skies of its own volition. It travels upon the surface."

"How can a ship travel upon this excrement?"

He stamped his foot like an impetuous child. "You young men give no credit to your elders!" he cried, waving his twisted stick at me. "We are more than cabbages! Impossible to take a ship over the Sea of Death—how often I have heard that said! Pah!"

I could scarcely refrain from smiling at his tantrum.

"I apologize," I said, mollifying him somewhat. He sniffed and pointed to the edge of the islet.

"My ship has sails. The word may be a new one to you. Men knew of sails before they ever took to the skies. You will see. The sails are like sheets—they catch the wind and the wind carries the ship over the surface of the sea. The sea is slippery and my hull is sleek, worn thus by many journeys so that it can slide fast. I made this ship years ago when I was agile enough for such labor. As soon as the wind rises, I will leave you to your gloomy despondency."

I looked around indifferently but saw no such craft as he described. It sounded intriguing, but I had no real wish to see or examine it. I wanted only to be left alone. There was a long silence, punctuated by the wheezing of the old man, who still insisted on staring at me as though I were a museum curiosity. I could bear this no longer.

"What is your name, old man?" I said finally. He jerked upright, as though he had been dozing off, then made an effort to straighten himself with a show of dignity.

"Scarge."

"I see."

"And yours?"

"Galad."

"What land are you from? The plains, the mountains, the jungles?"

"I was not born on this world," I told him, and for the first time I saw his eyes as they widened. He seemed deeply intrigued and shuffled closer, peering more intently than before at my face.

"Is that so? Yet you look like a man of earth, for all your scars. Where, then?"

"Never mind. I have not the heart nor the patience to spill out my story. We would be here too long."

"Are you hunted? It is no secret that the men of Earth hate the alien men of your race. Is that it, my boy?" He almost whispered the words, as though in conspiracy. "Is that why you are here at the edge of the world?

"No. Those that seek me are friends," I said, but I could see the disbelief in his eyes.

"Then if you have nothing to fear from them, I will tell them that you are well, should they happen on me."

"No!"

He drew back. "They cannot be friends if you fear them."

"I no longer yearn for their company."

"And if I meet them? What am I to tell them?"

"Tell them that I am dead."

"Pah! You are a fool! I know nothing of what you flee, but only a coward would take his own life to escape his dues."

I scowled at him, my hands gripping my sword hilt tightly.

"Yes, Galad. I can see into your heart easily enough. I had guessed what you were about when I first came upon you. My eyes are old, but my wits are not so worn as to play me false all the time. You mope like a dog that hides in the shadows after a master's curse—you flee either justice or some unpleasantness, and you seek to find relief in death! I am not so old that my senses have completely deserted me. I know the pangs and rigors of defeat, too, shut away here."

"You chose this life."

"Aye! Over death—for I would have been spitted elsewhere for a false seer. So I shouldered my grief and came here—to live!"

"You made your decision. I will make mine."

"Pah! You are like an old crone!"

My hand shot out and grabbed his filthy rags and drew his face close to mine, ignoring the stench of his breath. I had fought my way across a world and into the heart of a city, careless of a thousand deaths, and this bundle of filthy bones called me a coward.

"Aye! Kill me, too! Another death to your credit! Death is all you are fit for now. There is no one else, so you will kill me and then turn on yourself. Man deserves no better!"

I shuddered as I looked hard at him, but in the end I cast him from me, disgusted with myself and my weakness. Scarge swore and struggled to his feet, ignoring the muck that coated him. I buried my face in my hands, fighting to control the waves of grief that threatened to flood over me. I stood motionless for long minutes, then something light touched my shoulder. I looked up hazily and saw Scarge's twisted visage.

"I spoke harshly," he said. "But I would rather not see a young man uselessly cast away his life."

I said nothing, for I had lost the will to do anything, even that.

"Come with me, Galad. Your offworld status means nothing to me. I have provisions, a fire, some wine. There must be many things happening in the world of which I am unaware. Come, sail with me to my humble home."

He was the only person on the planet whom I had met who had no reverence or awe for my name. To him it meant nothing. I was not a god or a savior, or a bringer of peace—I was merely a troubled youth, a sorrowful man full of self-pity and misery. I must have seemed very foolish to Scarge, whose own life must have been far more troubled than mine. He picked up my sword and motioned me to my feet.

"If you have truly forsworn war," he said with a grimace, "then I will place this with my trophies. The Sea has given up many relics to me."

We went around the islet and there, half hidden by a mud-flow, was his craft, its lone mast pointing skywards, the sails already beginning to stir at the first suggestions of a breeze. I looked back at the hillock where Ravas Tarak had died. Something of me had died there, too, and I knew that it could never be recalled from its dark well of rest.

CHAPTER II
On the Brink of Madness

Scarge's island was larger and firmer than the one on which I had ended Ravas Tarak's life, and I was surprised to see a strain of mutated grass growing here, evidently cultivated by the old man. There was hope for this most forlorn of regions, then. From somewhere among the fallen hulks and twisted debris of the Sea of

Death, Scarge had managed to scavenge pieces of metal and rotting wood, and had somehow constructed a weird, leaning shanty which served him as a long, low-roofed home. Beside this was a makeshift larder, in which he had stored pilfered barrels of corn and other foodstuffs that I realized must have come from the mainland. Amazed by his food stocks and supplies of water—a rusty canister was propped against the shanty, filled with a liberal supply of rain water—I asked him where he had obtained them and, after a show of petulance, he finally revealed that he got them from small settlements on the mainland to the west. He apparently traded with the folks there, bartering and exchanging things from the filth of the Sea of Death. And, I was later to learn when he was in a more garrulous mood, he occasionally performed small rituals of what he called magic, and healing—he disliked people, retaining his misanthropic status as best he could, but he had to give in to the demands of survival.

I was in no mood to mock or praise his life-long efforts, already beginning to wish that he had not stumbled across me, if chance meeting it had been. He made a fire as evening came and gave me stale bread and coarse wine, of which he seemed to have an inordinately large supply. Slowly, as the sun sank and the wine dulled my melancholia and loosened my tongue, Scarge dragged from me a summary of recent events—the tyranny of Vorta, the rise of Annulian and then the coming of the Horsemen. I withheld from the avid scavenger my own true role in the whole affair, simply telling him that I had been one of the many thousands involved in the fall of Karkesh.

Thankfully he did not press me for further details of my own circumstances, which was well, for my temper grew short as the wine-bag emptied. Each moment that I remained alive brought a renewed sense of shame and degradation to me, and I began to wallow anew in my self pity. I began to drink more freely, something from which I had all but abstained in the past. This new-found well of alcoholic despair was my source of indulgence for days afterwards, so that the waxing and the waning of the moon blurred with the movement of the sun. At first Scarge left me outside, where I did nothing but drink and stare vacantly out at the dreary sea. My sinking down into almost constant drunkenness drew oaths from my rescuer, while I cursed him cruelly, withdrawing at last into the shanty, where I found myself in a corner and called for more wine. In the dark shadows of the ramshackle house, day and night blended into one long, drunken cycle of depraved despair. My brain began to spin and sink down in a vortex of jumbled, besotted dizziness, turning inexorably into a sponge for the fuddled images that coursed about me.

Scarge tried to revive me and cut me off from the potent wine, but I grew cunning and cruel. I thrust him away and stole whatever I could find to drink while he was away, threatening to destroy his home if he did not furnish me with more wine. He rued his finding of me and at length left me to my degraded ways. My ravings and wine-sodden murmurings of devils and horses and foul beings intrigued him at first, as he must have tried to piece together the puzzle of the Apocalypse, but I became monotonous, and he ignored me. Rather than trouble himself by trying to forcibly eject me, he left me there in the darkness, and the world began to ebb away from me as though it had never existed, or as though it had been a dream. Taria's face floated to the top of my sea of despair, only to be driven away by my clutching fingers, sinking deep below the waters of intoxication. Even Daras Vorta did not come from out of my terrible visions to laugh at me.

How long this continued I have no way of saying, save that it must have been weeks, and perhaps months. My body began to lose its vitality, I ate less, and my eye ached as though its sight was lost forever. Had there not been a new turn of events, it may well have been that I would have succumbed to the wine and one day would not have awakened from its strong, alluring caresses. But I was not to be left to die the death of the gutters.

Distant voices seeped down into my brain, like water sinking into the ground. My drunken hallucinations were often accompanied by skirling sounds. I grunted and rolled over in the filth of the hut. Scarge had long since stopped sleeping within, preferring the seclusion of his ship. I opened my bleary eyes. Sunlight filtered through tiny crevices in the cracked and tumbledown walls. I reached out instinctively for the wine bag, but it was empty and no nectar dribbled to my parched lips. My mouth had dried up like a river bed in the desert sun, and my head set up a rhythmic throbbing like the echoes of a mighty heart.

I could hear the voices more plainly. Not a dream then. But who would be speaking? Scarge often muttered to himself, but he was not alone. He spent most of his time away in his peculiar sailing ship, but now he was outside, arguing and haggling with someone. I drew back further into the darkness. I now heard clearly the other voices outside. They were sharp and abrasive with words of command, uttered in imperious tones. I slumped back and regarded the sagging roof through bleary eyes. No one must see me.

"He is here," said a voice outside the doorway. It had become very clear, and I recoiled as the cloth hanging was thrust aside by Scarge's withered arm. I peered up to see him shuffling through it, hands clasped about his gnarled stick as though it were a priceless relic. A taller figure stood behind him, having to bend over to get within the hut.

"This is a sty for pigs! There is no one in there, you old oaf!" rumbled the voice as the head began to withdraw. I tried to growl something derisive, but my vocal chords failed to respond.

"You are wrong," cackled the oldster, his teeth like black crags within his mouth. "Look more closely. You will find the one you seek in the darkness. Take him! He is lower than the pigs you describe! I have no use for his drunken carcass, and even the sea rats shun this hovel."

Reluctantly the man again pushed his head within, wrinkling his nose, then came into the hut, bent near double. He came closer, probing with his foot. When he reached me and felt my balled up body, he gasped.

"There is a man here, but it cannot be the one I seek..."

"It is he—ask his name," insisted Scarge, delighting in his moment of revenge. I tried to turn away, but a shaft of sunlight slanted across my bearded face.

"Galad? By the powers, is it you there? This is some jest of the gods."

What little sanity remaining to me blanched at the sound of the burly man's voice, for it could be none other than Gundar Sabian himself. I tried to shrink even further into the lice-infested blankets, but could not.

"No," I managed to blurt. "Go from here. I am not he."

"He lies!" snarled Scarge. But Gundar's hands pulled me into a larger pool of light and his face stared intently down into mine, horror dawning upon it as he recognized me, despite the filth and beard.

"Galad...it is unbelievable."

"Get away, Gundar. Let me die in peace."

Gundar looked even more horrified. He turned with a curse on his lips and roared at Scarge.

"Old man, go outside and have a tub brought from one of the ships. My men will do as you ask. Fetch the tub and have it filled with water. Don't stare at me as though I had given birth, man! Hurry!"

Gundar gripped me and I muttered something as I tried to break free of his iron-like fingers, but he hauled me up from my sanctuary as though I were made of straw. He yanked me to my feet, ignoring my crude protestations, and pushed me towards the door. I fought him limply and was thrust out into blinding daylight. I was dazzled and fell to my knees, whimpering like a child that has been whipped for disobedience.

"Get to your feet," said Gundar in my ear, but I shrugged him off.

"Who in the Empire is *that?*" said a sardonic voice, its pitch a little too high. I could not see the speaker, but the maliciousness of his tone cut through to even my besotted mind.

"You will see," said Gundar, controlling his evident distaste with difficulty. I had shamed him. He had no sympathy and rightly felt only nausea at what I had become. "Good, set it down here," he said to unseen figures.

A heavy tub full of clear, cold water was set down on the mud before me. Gundar wasted no time in swinging me haplessly to my feet There was nothing I could do to resist—my head was thrust beneath the water. It was ice cold and like a searing fire at the same time. I came up gasping for air and was instantly ducked again. Three times more this happened. I lurched and gripped the wet sides of the tub to support myself, my hair plastered to my face. I fought down the urge to retch—I had shamed myself enough.

"All my men are treated thus when they forget themselves and their duties," said Gundar, his voice controlled.

"Why… have you...come here?" I gasped, wiping water and dirt from my face.

"You are not the man you were, Galad Sarian."

"You cannot talk to me—"

"You are a disgrace," he hissed, and I had the feeling that

someone of importance was here, otherwise I would surely not have received such treatment. I was not wrong in my surmise, for someone came forward and began examining me as if I were some lowly beast dredged up from the bottom of the Sea of Death. His was the cold voice, and he wore elegant clothes and had the unmistakable haughty mien of the Dream Lord hierarchy.

"You are Galad Sarian!" said Gundar firmly. I looked up at him, but there was little mercy in his cold features—I deserved none. I could see with but one eye, the other having been closed by the fighting at Karkesh, but I tried to find some shred of dignity as I rose unsteadily to my feet.

"So," said the haughty men beside us, "this is the man on whom the Barbarians pin their hopes for a free world." His voice was thick with loathing, and I feared not for myself, but for the people I had deserted.

Gundar turned to him with the merest of bows, and I guessed that his deference rankled with him. "Yes, this is Galad, son of Dotas Sarian, the Dream Lord."

"Really, Gundar, it is quite appalling to think that this is the Sarian heir. Come, reconsider, man, surely you are mistaken?"

I balled my fists, the scathing voice doing more to sober me than all the duckings I had had. I managed to take an unsteady step forward.

"And you—who are you in your finery?" I challenged thickly.

Gundar put a restraining arm on my shoulder and easily pulled me back.

"This is Mygol Feyd, ambassador to the Dream Lord Triumvirate, and their Investigator. He is here to listen to the people of Ur on behalf of the Dream Lords, so that any decisions that will be made regarding the planet's future will be fair ones. Already he is familiar with Thuran, Chungsar, and many others," said Gundar, his eyes deliberately avoiding my own.

The Ambassador scowled. "I had hoped to be able to talk to the so-called Messiah of these people, but under the circumstances..."

"Forgive my impertinence, Ambassador, but I will make the necessary arrangements. Evidently the strain of recent months has taken a heavy toll upon Galad. If you will retire to your craft, I will see that he is made presentable," said Gundar stiffly.

Feyd gave me another cursory glance before nodding sourly.

"Very well, Gundar. Though it may take a week to sober him. I am entertaining strong doubts as to whether this journey into the wilderness was necessary. I will await you, but time is getting along." He moved away among the Imperial Guards that ringed us like statues.

Gundar watched Feyd leave, then impatiently waved the Guards back to their craft.

"Now," he said, a little less coldly, turning tome and shaking me roughly but with something of his old camaraderie. "What is the meaning of this performance? What got into your foolish head, Galad? You have always found a way of flouting authority—first as a youth on Zurjah, and now, when you are needed most, you flee from Karkesh."

I shrugged away embarrassment. "My part was over..."

"Over? But it has only just begun!"

"No. Karkesh has fallen. You came from the Dream Lords with an army fit to chain a world, but you saw that the rebellion was over—you saw the truth of things on Earth, or Ur as you call it. I slew the real enemy. Ravas Tarak, last of that vermin, is dead. It is done."

You cannot believe matters are as simple as that, you young whelp! I cannot hope to satisfy the Dream Lords that Ur is ready for peace and a new way of life without your help. The generals and the orators of this world must have unity and a spokesman, and I am not that spokesman, much as they have come to trust me. The task was always and still is yours!"

"No more, Gundar. I have had my fill of all this strife, can you not see that?"

He shook me angrily this time, his eyes filling with heated vexation.

"Why have you given up? It is contrary to everything that I know about you. You championed a hopeless cause and won. The people have told me about the marvels you performed, Galad. Why have you turned away from them when they need you most?" he persisted.

"Cease!" I cried, tearing free, but he gripped me anew.

"You have no right to desert them! Not now! It is unfortunate that your life has never been your own—the gods use whom they will. You must see your ordained fate through to the end."

I shook my head dully.

"I understand only too well why you are like this. But it is a fool who allows his heart to rule his head."

I cursed under my breath.

"Does it sting you? To think that a hero of thousands could sink to his knees because of one woman..."

I made to strike at him for that; Gundar, my greatest friend and ally, but he rode the soft blow and cuffed me mightily, so that I fell sprawling in the cloying mud.

"Come to your senses! You may crawl away and drown your petty sorrows in a sea of wine when this is finished," he said angrily. "But first you will perform your duty like the man I once knew! You will go to Zurjah if I have to drag you!"

We stared long and hard at one another, the atmosphere between us charged with pent-up violence.

"I will not return to Zurjah for you, nor for all the treasure and power in the entire Empire!" I snarled, wiping blood from a split lip. Gundar stood menacingly above me, his fists balled like huge hocks of meat, his body like a Titan's thrust up against the swirling sky.

"Not even to thwart the machinations of Daras Vorta?"

I glowered at him. "There is no one left who will speak for him, unless you cull the devils in hell. Even the last of his men in Karkesh promised to speak against him for their freedom."

"Vorta will speak for himself."

I failed to understand what he meant by this. Vorta was dead—Annulian had taken a score of warriors to his chambers and cut him to pieces. Could Vorta's voice speak to us from his grave? Could he have learned to bridge yet another gulf to blasphemy with his necrophiliac powers?

"Vorta's rule is over."

"The cause of all your agony," mused Gundar. "And the cause of all our ills. He will speak for himself at the reckoning."

"What are you saying?"

"He is alive, Galad, *alive*."

I felt the word like a physical blow. "*No*!"

"Yes. Alive. Even now he is on Zurjah, speaking with an ever-glib tongue about the savage ferocity of the Barbarians and of their terrible uprising. Of how the false prophet, Galad Sarian, abused him and his efforts to maintain peace..."

"This is a trick! You lie!"

"I swear not."

I kept shaking my head. "But...how? Vorta died."

"You saw him die?"

"There was no need. Annulian took a score of armed men into the very pits of the city even as Vorta was attempting to summon Shaitan. They carved the tyrant to pieces! Annulian hated him even more than I!"

"Yet you did not see this?"

"I..." But I had to shake my head. The import of Gundar's words had begun to dawn on me. Vorta alive! It could only mean disaster.

"Vorta had Dream Lord powers of his own, perverted though they were. You tasted them. He tricked Annulian and his blood-crazed men. None knows better than you the strength of Vorta's mental powers."

Yes, I knew them well enough. I remembered a terror-filled night on distant Gargan when I had thought my beloved Taria to be dying under the sacrificial knife of Vorta's goat priests. I must not think of her now.

"The altars at Karkesh, the temples, they fell to rubble and were scourged with fire," I protested.

Gundar shook his head. "Vorta must have fled and shut down his mind to fool you. He hid like a rat among the destruction. I cannot say how the deception was carried out. He lives. I swear it. As soon as he knew that you were missing, possibly dead, he managed to find a way back to Zurjah. And there he has been decrying everything that you and the men of Ur have fought for."

"You are sure he is alive? You have seen him?" I said wildly, gripping his arm.

"He is alive. I have not been back to Zurjah since first you saw me here. I have had so much to do, listening to your people, visiting the Sacred City. I cannot fight on all fronts. *You* are the one who has to answer Vorta's challenges. The Dream Lords have sent Mygol Feyd as their ambassador to learn what he can of the war here. He is a hard man, steeped in pomp and arrogance, but he is reputed to be just. However, for all his lack of bias, nothing can be achieved without you, Galad, can you not see that? I am beginning to realize you have suffered much anguish— mental as much as physical, but it is time now to put others first. You cannot allow Vorta the victory after such a lengthy campaign."

I nodded slowly, my eyes dropping. As always, the old warrior spoke wisely.

"I am so tired, Gundar, my friend. The war has sapped me of my senses. And Taria..."

"You must learn to shoulder the pain. There will be far more difficult tasks ahead. Prosocles and many of your allies from the war are still scouring the country for you. And Vorta's confidence grows. The Dream Lords are stretched on a cruel rack of dilemmas. They have my preliminary reports, but against the fiery invective of the Warden, my reports are insipid things. So go to Zurjah, Galad! Shrug off this abysmal shroud of gloom. Think about all those who have died."

How could I resist his wishes? "So be it. Take me to Karkesh," I said, my voice hardening.

"Karkesh has reaped the curse of the Four Horsemen. Death, plague, the war and famine have done their worst. Few ships travel there now. But Feyd awaits us."

And so I was taken aboard Gundar's airship. Scarge cursed me as I left him, but I wished him well for all that. I was bathed and rested, then at last I came before Mygol Feyd. Gundar spoke favorably about me, his bitterness having melted now that he could see something of my old spirit returning.

"The youth has suffered terribly," he told Feyd. "His eye needs skillful surgery if his sight is to be fully restored, and his leg must be attended to. It seems that the telling war has all but robbed him of his mind—you have heard how he spearheaded the assaults."

"I have heard a good many things," Feyd said sharply. "However, there is more I would hear from the lips of the Heir himself."

Gundar blanched. It was clear that his respect for this officious ambassador was limited. Feyd represented all the things I hated about Zurjahn pomp and elitism. He eyed me coldly and leaned back in the cushioned furnishings.

"Tell me, Galad, for what reason did you flee the cause you had fought for so tenaciously?" he threw at me. My heart was filling with anger and hate—Vorta being alive had fanned the heat of my blazing wrath. I looked without fear at Feyd, returning his arrogance.

"I pursued Ravas Tarak, the loathsome being that was my cousin. When I had cut him to pieces, I found my way back to be barred by the endless filth of the Sea of Death. I was weary and half dead. I succumbed to the feeling of depression, as my spirits had been drained. More than once Vorta sought to drive me over the brink to madness."

"I see," he replied, idly chewing at an emerald ring. "So we waste time looking for Ravas Tarak. It would appear that all those who stood beside Daras Vorta in this suggested plot to overthrow the Dream Lords have likewise been disposed of."

"Suggested!" I fumed. "You speak as if you are unaware of what has been transpiring on this world!"

I felt Gundar's hand on my arm as he tried to subdue my anger. "Soft," he said.

"This is no time to bandy soft words!" I persisted. "Daras Vorta set himself up as the slave of Shaitan, sworn to bring our Empire to ruins, so that the monstrous powers of darkness could sweep over us and feed upon our souls for all time!"

"So it has been said, but of course, this has yet to be proved conclusively," said Feyd, his voice a rebuke. I had met his kind before and my temper snapped in the face of this refusal to listen to reason. I strode forward before Gundar and his Guards could hold me. I gripped the robe front of Mygol Feyd and tore him out of his comfort to his feet, my face inches from his.

"Listen to me! I left Zurjah to the cries of doubters and mockers like you! My own father told me to forget my fears. But I came to Earth and found a monster eating at the heart of our Empire. Now Vorta's Black City is a shell. Countless thousands have died to rid the world of the foulest tyrant in history. Now you come, echoing the same pathetic and faint-hearted doubts that still ring in my ears from years gone by! Vorta was a fiend. Know this, then—when I return to Zurjah, it will be to cut out his black heart and hang it from the highest tower!"

The red-faced ambassador spluttered as my grip tightened, his eyes filling with terror. Gundar, remonstrating frantically with me, at last pried me loose and Guards rushed in, none certain how to cope with the situation for, despite my past exile, I was still a Dream Lord.

"You young imbecile!" gasped Feyd, rubbing his throat with soft fingers. "You cannot wrench the law from your superiors..."

"My father was Dotas Sarian, the Dream Lord. Would you

question my birthright?"

He scowled, then chose his words carefully. "That is not my intention. I am not here to question the validity of your claim to ascendancy. I am an Investigator. Since there was no way of knowing if you were even alive..."

"Well, you can see that for yourself. You have wasted enough time. There is no need to continue squabbling here. Let us make all speed for Zurjah, and put an end to this procession of lies and deceit that has plagued us for so long."

Gundar still had to restrain me, for the strain of months past and my returning anger spun up giddily and threatened to smother my reasoning.

"That sits very well with me!" snapped Feyd. "My orders are to escort you back to Zurjah. Until you have validated your claims pertaining to Vorta's alleged heresies, you are to consider yourself under my command," he said pompously, regaining some of his crusty composure.

"Galad Sarian is no man's prisoner," I growled, but Gundar diplomatically led me away, much to Feyd's relief. Outside, Gundar favored me once more with an annoyed gaze, which swept over me like a hot blast from the desert.

"It would be foolish to make an enemy of that one, Galad. I know he speaks with too much caution. But think on this—he is the eyes and ears of Vidor Karset, the Dream Lord. And you need the support of the Triumvirate if you are to bring Vorta to retribution. The time of the sword is finished. Use tactful words."

I nodded sullenly, biting back a reply. Vidor Karset—I remembered him well. He had been the one most opposed to me when I had stated my cause first on Zurjah, years ago. And my doings on Earth would have done nothing to foster his change of heart about me.

CHAPTER III
An Empire in Crisis

Mygol Feyd had evidently been a little more than incensed by my outburst in his ship, and he gave strict orders that I was to be confined rather than be given the opportunity to rejoin Prosocles,

Thuran, and my other companions waiting at the Space Station in Karkesh. This served only to inflame my temper at first, but, as there was nothing I could do, I lapsed into a morose mood as before. I was told that apart from the Space Station at Karkesh, the city was mostly out of bounds now, as there were all kinds of vermin infesting the place, and plague had broken out and spread like wildfire. Eventually I was escorted aboard the flagship that was to take me back to Zurjah, and although I was not kept shut away as a prisoner in the way that Feyd had insinuated I might be, I had little freedom of the vessel.

I did not allow this to irk me, for I had come to feel scant comfort in the company of my fellow men—least of all in that of friends in whose eyes I must have seemed a disappointment. Gundar was the only one to whom I could talk for more than brief periods. He sensed and had come to understand my gloom and sought often to wrench me away from the numbing melancholy that held me like an ague. I softened a little, for he had filled my father's place in earlier years, when the latter had too frequently been enveloped in his Dream Lord duties to attend my troubles.

Much of what had happened to me since leaving Zurjah was mere myth to Gundar, and slowly he drew from me the telling of the fall of the Black City. At last, after an endless voyage across the dark vaults of space, we neared Zurjah, and my apprehensions grew, together with my unbridled hatred for Vorta. Gundar entered my apartments and, seeing me staring out at the endless darkness, drew me from my bout of reverie.

"Before you go to the Dream Lords, Galad," he told me, "there are things that you should know. Since the days of your banishment to Gargan, there have been many changes and upheavals—the structure of Dream Lord society is weak."

"I have known upheavals and the bringing down of false prophets myself," I replied coldly.

"Indeed. I do not doubt the causes for which you have fought. But there have been difficult times on Zurjah since the death of your father. As you well know, the Dream Lord Triumvirate cannot function fully reduced as it has been to only two primes. It has been of paramount importance to secure an Heir to fill the shoes of Dotas Sarian. You are his Heir, but you have long been believed to be dead."

I nodded. "And so Vorta sought to put his puppet on my father's seat of power—Ravas Tarak, my heinous cousin. And for his grasping ambitions he died."

"Yes, but your cousin was smooth-tongued and not without certain mental powers of his own—he at least concealed his true ambitions. You cut down the tree, but the roots prevail. Vorta is also smooth-tongued. He still seeks his place of power."

"Vorta is not of the true Dream Lord blood line. He knows full well that he is not eligible for a place on the Triumvirate."

"Yet he will seek that place in the light of the confusion."

"Vorta will never be elevated to the Triumvirate while I am alive!" I said through my teeth, my eyes averting Gundar's steady gaze.

"Even so, he will seek the position. And I realize that you place his death before all else. Yet there are other things to think on."

"Gundar," I said, my voice less excited. "Daras Vorta is the vessel of powers from the farthest and most terrible nightmare realms. Through him, they will find the gate into reality, and our entire system will be swallowed up in boiling chaos. Nothing is more vital than the death of this odious monster, so that the gate will be sealed."

"That may well be so—I do not dispute it. But you will find Zurjah much changed. The Dream Lords cannot control its ferocious atmosphere and hostile environment unless the full power of the Triumvirate is in operation constantly. Without an Heir to make the third link in that power, the world's survival has become jeopardized. You are still the Heir, so you must think seriously about your duties as such."

I laughed, my scorn like bile. "Am I to leap into my father's shoes so easily, then? Are all my so-called misdeeds and blasphemies to be swept aside and forgotten as though nothing more than boyhood fantasies?"

"Certainly not," he said mildly. "Not by the Dream Lords, who saw your outbursts as deliberate heresy. But they *must* have an Heir elevated."

I reflected in silence for a moment, picturing the dilemma of my perplexed masters. "So the prime reason for my recall is a bid to save their own putrid souls...Earth still means nothing to them. It never has. And now they seek to use it as a screen so that the people of our decadent Empire will be shielded from their own crisis."

"You must convince them that they are wrong about Earth. It can be done. Galad my boy, don't be ruled by fire! You have been wronged and so has Ur and her slaves. And the people of the Empire are not all worthy of contempt. You can rectify the sins of the past."

"By bowing to the ones who spurned me and cast me out like blighted wheat?"

"Listen to me," he persisted. "The Dream Lords have spent many months priming the entire stock of the highest strains of subordinate Dream Lord nobility. They have done this because it may well fall upon these lesser strains of Dream Lord power to take over the ultimate power of the present depleted Triumvirate. Laomidian and Vidor Karset cannot control the Zurjahn image structure for long without a third prime. If you had died, as was thought, and no other man from the blood line had been available, the Triumvirate would have been forced to hand over their powers to the nobles. It would be like giving them into the hands of children."

Again I nodded at his words. "That would inevitably mean disaster—centuries of ultimate power and knowledge prematurely put into the hands of the unprepared and untrained. It would mean the breakup of the Empire."

"Precisely," said Gundar.

"Which is why I am accorded such attention. Without me, they will fail."

"There is the other possibility, which you seem to insist is not a possibility at all. I assure you that it is."

I scowled.

"Vorta has powers, evil as they may be, that rival those of the Dream Lords. He presses for a place on the Triumvirate, swearing devotion and fealty to the survival of the Empire."

"And I have sworn by all the powers of light and dark that I will have my vengeance. While I am alive, Vorta will never attain his desires."

"No one would deny you your rights," snapped Gundar, his patience with me evidently fraying. "But you must make Zurjah and the thousands who live upon her your prime consideration."

"Must I? Why should I show any compassion to a world that treats its own kind like animals—worse than animals! Dwellers in a morass of filth, unfit to do anything but serve as slaves and sacrifices to their dominion! Why should Zurjah have a place in my heart? I *hated* the place, even as a child...I always knew that it was hostile—alien! Men were never meant to tread upon that accursed planet with its storms and hellish, toxic blasts. Those who fled from the wars on Earth in shame had the audacity to call it the Motherworld. Shame—that is the foundation on which the Dream Lord Triumvirate was built and the reason for its secretion on Zurjah."

"You were born on Zurjah, whatever her sins. You must have some loyalty."

"My loyalties are with *Earth*! The so-called Barbarians that have died by the thousands like flies under the cruel yoke of Zurjahn tyranny are my people. Zurjah's own kind! Damn Zurjah and its lies, its deceits, its false visions, its blind, unquestioning faith and its bigoted rulers!"

I was trembling as I spoke. I thought by Gundar's expression of horror that he would strike me as he had on Scarge's island, but he lowered his head and shook it slowly, an expression of deep sorrow replacing the one of awe.

"I was not wrong when I said you had changed. You have done so more than I could ever have realized."

"Yes! I am full of bitterness and hate! Why? Who put it there? Who made me what I am? The gods? No. It was the slave masters, that is who. These unmoving, unfeeling creatures who control the nine worlds. They made me what I am."

Gundar sighed. "Galad, you must know that I have little love for Zurjah. I love the outdoors, the chase, the freedom to roam over natural terrain, just as you do. I have come to understand the old lie behind the legends about men coming from beyond the stars to settle on Zurjah. Earth is the true Motherworld. You have shown me that. I accept it. The Empire sought to hide its shame at the near destruction of Earth by covering its past and alienating its people. But you have made Earth's people men again, and they are free. Would you now reverse roles? Would you make slaves of the Zurjahns? Would you show them the lack of mercy they showed you? Would you show your own faults to be equal to and even worse than theirs?"

His words stung me, for there was truth in them, but in my heart there was little room for mercy.

"I have no power over the Dream Lords!" I protested. "They act in all things by their own will."

"You do not understand how ill Zurjah fares. Its common people believe her to be the Homerworld. Their beliefs are sustained by the dreams and images that the Dream Lords constantly transmit. Remove this blanket of images and the people will soon see the truth. Chalremor showed you the true guise of Zurjah, and it was that which set you on your course in life. If the Dream Lords fall, the common people will riot and rebel, those that do not lose their grip on sanity altogether, and there will be many such. Zurjah will eventually return to what is was before men came, and no one will survive her terrible vengeance."

"You are right," I said, though without a shred of compassion. "Zurjah will expel Man as she has sought to do since first we thrust our usurping ships into her storms, millennia ago. It will be a fitting end to our sojourn."

Gundar weighed my words unhappily. "So you would see the Dream Lords toppled?"

We looked at one another, friends who had become strangers.

"Gundar, you are no lover of their ways. You know they are unjust."

"They are. But justice must always be tempered with mercy! Have your bloodthirsty campaigns taught you nothing? Do you think that life has been so terrible and so cruel to you that you must destroy life itself? You claim to have lost everything...your friends, your causes, your lover..."

His words bit into me like the passing of steel along raw nerves.

"Well, then. Life is hard. Yet you have the power to change everything. You alone can resolve the chaos that threatens to suck the last of us into its looming vortex of oblivion."

"Man has summoned his own doom to him as though seeking its cold embrace, its final, sterile peace."

"No! The races of Earth, Zurjah, and all the worlds have been as pieces in a game! And it will be Vorta and his likes who will triumph if you persist in your spurning of the common people. Change the laws of the Empire, but do not destroy it. That is Vorta's goal—to let in the nightmare gods you spoke of, to give everything to darkness. By condemning Zurjah, you serve those gods, not your own."

"That will never happen."

"You have told me that death sickens you. You have told me how your grim role as the Pale Rider has surrounded you with death—friends and foes alike. Then, if you truly desire to relinquish the role, forego your rejection of Zurjah, otherwise you will have the heads of thousands more to add to your Reaper's tally."

For a long time I contemplated his words. Gundar's age had bequeathed him patient wisdom. The bitter seeds that had been planted in me when my own father banished me had born terrible fruit. Now I had indeed become the epitome of the Pale Rider—Death, riding as remorselessly as the Horsemen of my childhood nightmares. Was I fated to play out the grim role until I myself fell to the shears of the greater Reaper? Was I reluctant to quit my destructive part in the affairs of the gods?

Tiredness began to weigh me down. "I am sick of war."

"I know that, Galad. You have suffered worse trials than it is given most of us to bear. Yet all strife must have an end.""I pray so," I sighed.

"On earth it was necessary for you to take up the sword and wrench power from Vorta violently and in bloody war. Now, on Zurjah, you need not have recourse to the same physical insurrection. Will you not be patient with the Dream Lords?" he said anxiously.

"If you say that I must, then so be it. But I will not accede to any wishes that I know to be contrary to the well-being of Earth. She is free. It must be understood that I fight for the ending of all Dream Lord powers on Earth."

"Zurjah must endeavor to put her own house in order. I do not think your desires will be questioned severely. And with such men as Prosocles to testify to the rebirth there, your case will be a strong one."

"Earth's severance from the Empire is my fondest wish, save one, and that is to see Vorta brought to just retribution."

"I hear that Vorta has been named Snake by some—on Gargan, where you thwarted his attempt to supplant the Zurjahn officials with his own, for example. It is a worthy name for one with such a smooth, double tongue. You must be wary. Vorta has already been the ear of Vidor Karset."

Again I recalled the man who had been open in his scorn of me when I had first spoken of the Barbarians as fellow men. He had resented me and shown me least compassion among the Triumvirate.

335

"Then is Vidor Karset sympathetic to Vorta?" I snapped.

"To my knowledge, no. But I am uncertain. However, I do sense Vidor's animosity towards yourself. Laomidian, though, is a just man. He will have no bias either way, and had you but to convince him of the justice of your cause on Earth, the task would be easy. But Vidor resents you—even I, in my capacity as Master at Arms, am not greatly in his favors, and that, I suspect, is born out of my friendship with you when you were growing up on Zurjah."

"I knew that Vidor resented me in those days, although I never understood why—I never tapped the roots of his aggression. Do you think that our mutual dislike will weigh in Vorta's favor?"

"It is possible. Vorta is truly a snake. I have read transcripts of his speeches before the nobles. His defense of his actions on Earth as Warden of the planet were full of confidence and self-justification. He swore that he was forced to maintain a grip of iron on the Barbarians and that he turned Karkesh into a hell hole merely as an example to chastise the rest of the free Barbarians. They were always ready to strike out against the Empire, he claimed, and he used your rebellion as the crowning example of the age-old curse, the men of Ur were born only to destroy. You used some ancient weapon in the war, too..."

"Thunderpowder? Yes, but it was very primitive."

"Vorta has made much of that, claiming it to be an example of the development of free Barbarians and saying that it could lead to the rediscovery of more terrible powers, such as those that ravaged the planet in the devastating wars of ages gone by. Nothing frightens the Dream Lords more than those old powers and their grim secrets."

"So Vidor Karset will be contemptuous of me."

"It may be that he will be your real opponent."

"Yet you say that he and Laomidian will seek to win me to their ranks?"

"Their tenuous hold on Zurjahn ecology puts them in an ironic position."

"I will have a private audience with Vidor. If I am to settle differences, the future of an Empire must not hang on a rootless dislike. How deep do you think his contempt of me goes?"

Gundar looked uncomfortable. He had given me some bad news before now and on such occasions had always been slightly embarrassed, reluctant to speak words that might distress me. Now he seemed to be equally as uncomfortable as he had on those previous foreboding occasions.

"Come, Gundar, you cannot disguise your thoughts from me. I have no need to dip inside your mind—I read something in your face. Speak! What is it about Vidor that I must know?"

"Very well. You would have discovered it for yourself soon enough. I would not see you hurt, but you must be properly armed for your coming ordeals. I would not have your reason unseated at an inopportune moment. I know too well your temper—if it is to explode, let it be before me, and not before those who would use it against you."

"Then speak," I said, smiling gently at his concern.

"Vidor has reason to despise you. I suspect that it was the reason he had no love for you when you were a youth on Zurjah."

"Surely he was not jealous of me? Although he, too, was young, he was a Dream Lord—a prime. I was not even a promising student, even though my father's Heir and next in the line of succession."

"It was not your attainments that fostered his jealousy."

"What else, then? I had nothing...unless..."

"Vidor it was that chose and married Taria."

I gasped, my mind turbulent with images.

"Oh, it was never her wish, Galad, be assured. I know that more than you can. No one knew of your affair with her better than I, and I am still not without her confidence in certain matters. But, consider this, Galad—Taria is of the highest breeding, an essential factor to Dream Lord evolution. Bordin Sulian, her father, is one of Zurjah's most favored and esteemed nobles, being none too far down the scale after the primes. And Vidor had to have an Heir. An Heir that would be of the best stock and of the purest blood lines. His bride was a logical choice—Taria. Even Vidor, whatever his personal feelings towards her—had little say in the matter. Thus, the two were wed—the ceremony was brief, for you know Zurjahn laws..."

"A mockery, a convenience to maintain the blood lines and to enhance the species," I said tonelessly.

"Even so. Now Taria bears his child, though there is nothing between them. Taria has made certain of that. Since the news first came that she would be having an Heir, she has shut herself off and refused to have dealings with any man."

"She does not love him."

"I am sure not. Vidor knows of your affair with Taria before you were banished. So, I say again, he has reason to despise you."

New shafts of emotional pain sank deep into my already tortured mind at these revelations. So she had not deserted me of her own accord, even though she must have thought me dead. Law had forced her to mate with this imperious Dream Lord—another cursed law and ritual that was forced upon the servants of this corrupt system.

Gundar may have expected me to receive his words with another vehement outburst, but I did not flare up and release the anger inside me in the torrent of invective that should have come. I just nodded dully.

"So," I said, after some reflection, "I must tread warily."

"You begin to see the delicacy of affairs on Zurjah."

I nodded. Looking back down the twisted tunnel of the past, I could visualize Chalremor in his prison turret, telling me that I was the one to do the work of gods. I had never wanted the full mantle of power that he had cast upon me, but there had never been a way to throw it off. Always must I go through with what had been ordained, and it seemed that I could never hope to master my fate.

"Soon," said Gundar, relieved that my antagonism had at least temporarily abated, "we will be landing. How well are you?"

I shrugged.

"Let me inspect that eye more closely." He did so, nodding with satisfaction. "Can you see?"

"Not clearly. But the surgeons performed miracles. My vision improves daily. I will miss little with it when I stand before the nobles, I promise you."

"Excellent. And your leg?"

"It no longer troubles me, though I fear I will never be as nimble in combat. There are some things that not even the most advanced of surgeons cannot repair."

Gundar flashed me a skeptical look, but contented himself with a nod.

"There should be no further need for combat."

"We shall see," I returned, matching his skepticism.

CHAPTER IV
The Great Assembly

Zurjah greeted me with all the reluctance and coldness that she accorded any offworlder. As I left the buildings of the Space Center with Gundar and the escort, I had ample time to reflect on the huge world that Man had barely tamed and learned to call Homeworld. We rode out on horseback—once there would have been hovertrucks to take us to our destination, but there was a power failure and the hardy ponies that had readily adapted to the sub-dome terrain bore us steadfastly. The buildings of Zurjah, the principal metropolis in which the Dream Lord stronghold was housed, appeared to be beautifully designed, interlocking smoothly like a sequence of chamfered pieces in an elegantly dovetailed sculpture. The blocks and towers soared majestically, the streets were broad and clean, and the stonework was white and unharmed by the acid advances of erosion. So did the common people see the city that they lived in. Yet I was able to see the truth behind the fantastic image-weaving of the Dream Lords, for to my eyes the streets were compacted and choked with grime. Walls had developed cracks and the huge stone blocks resembled scattered monoliths heaved up and rough-hewn from some vast, drab quarry. There was no majesty in what I saw, for the city had been lumped together by desperate builders in an attempt to combat the fierce atmosphere of a world determined to oust the usurpers on all fronts.

When I had left Zurjah, the city, when viewed without the obscuring veil of Dream Lord beauty, had been as stark and rugged as an ice-scarred mountain range, but now it had become much worse, like some desolate outer bastion of the northern crags. The Dream Lord images clung to the stones like cobwebs that were slowly being reduced to dust by the inexorable breezes of time. As their potency was weathered away, the erosion of the old city poked through like the bones of a starving horse, grim harbingers of a more final decay.

Overhead the sky was piling itself up in layers for another of the perpetual storms that constantly war and boil like seething oceans of volcanic fire, bursting asunder and raining torrents down upon the restless surface, sending long fingers and spears of lightning crackling for hundreds of miles across the atmosphere. A

339

combination of technical powers and subtle image-weaving had reduced these apparent storms over the city, so that the common people had learned to believe the planet was bowing to man's achievements. Today, though, I could see the heaped clouds racing headlong into black banks like savage wolf-packs, ready to detonate apart as thunder rolled across the heavens in booms and crashes, like the beating of drums played by wild gods. Dream Lord power had developed holes as ragged as those in the skies above. The discs and vehicles that could defy gravity and other laws of science were absent from the winding road, and our small party bent under the cascading rain that came down in blinding sheets. I preferred the feel of a horse beneath me, having been too long in the steel cocoons that webbed the nine worlds. As we rode upwards through the streets to the foot of the castle's towering hill, I glimpsed the commoners rushing indoors, wary of the impending hurricane. The rain increased, coming down in huge blobs that felt like angry, demonic fists. We hugged our clothes tightly about us, fighting to keep the horses moving. I felt the cold more acutely than ever before, my bones chilled agonizingly by all of Zurjah's freezing caresses. The skies lit up with colored fire and shooting stars of light as the first rolls of thunder pealed in from the horizon and made the skies cacophonous overhead.

Increasingly slowly we fought our way up the hill to the castle gates. I looked up through the torrential rain at the crumbling edifice—for crumbling it was, and in this deluge it looked as if it would melt away. There was no longer any pretense about its mighty ramparts. Now it looked like an old, old man who no longer tries to deceive his friends with his age. The wrinkles and the pits showed through the image-weaving, and I could see the great building would eventually tumble and be one with the crags from which it was hewn. I searched for the Finger of Scorn, the lone tower that had thrust up defiantly at the roaring sky and that had confined Chalremor before Ravas Tarak had slain him.

My breath caught in the deluge, for the tower had gone. Whether it had succumbed to the storms that washed over it like a restless tide, or whether the Dream Lords had had it taken down, I could only guess. Perhaps it fell when Chalremor died, symbol of his passing wisdom. And with this passing and the knowledge that the old image must indeed have been erased, there went from me much of my spirit and determination. I was alone against all those ideals and people that I despised. And Zurjah, her winds sucking the last breath of warmth from my freezing marrow, mocked and chided me with her incessant fury. See how I have humbled them all, she seemed to say, like some shrieking virago. I bent my head and passed through the castle gates into a brief respite from the maelstrom without.

Thankfully I had not long to wait before Dream Lord procedures got under way. I slept, then woke to be bathed and frugally fed. My apartments were quiet and I was not pestered by curious officials. The Dream Lords did not contact me, and I made no attempt to contact them—Gundar explained that everything was to be done in front of the gathered nobles, who were likely to have a big hand in the planet's future, now that the Empire's fate hung in the balance. So came the first great convening of the nobles to hear the testimonies of the men from Ur, the name that they still gave to Earth. Gundar was ever by my side, a huge protective angel, his face cold and serene as marble, his back stiff with pride. He had no fear of letting it be seen where his loyalties were couched.

Up into the castle we went, this time riding the discs that still carried men everywhere within. There were scores of Imperial Guards here now, and I wondered if the Dream Lords expected me to openly rebel against them here as I had when I was banished. Certainly the castle atmosphere, once relatively calm and untroubled, a balm to weary nerves, was charged with anxiety. Men fingered their star lances nervously, and as we passed them they snapped stiffly to attention, with far more alertness than the dreaming figures from the past with which I was familiar. The castle, once the haven of peace and the charisma of the laws of peace, had become a hive of suspicion and intrigue.

Then came the moment when we stood outside the great halls of justice, where the nobles had already gathered. I was not yet to have my private interview with the Dream Lords – protocol must be observed, and I cursed it. This time the whole of Zurjah's nobility was to hear the facts, as it should have years before, when I first spoke out. As I passed into the titanic hall, my first thought was for Daras Vorta—where would he be? My injured eye was almost miraculously healed, but I could not pick out the vile Warden in the seething humanity around me.

The hall was vast, its domed ceiling lost high up in a tangle of crossing vaults and aesthetically carved beams that curved and twisted like the finest artwork of a mighty cathedral. Pillars sprang up from the ovoid central area of the floor to support the great canopy of masonry overhead, their sides etched and carved with beautiful archaic symbols and designs, inlaid with filigreed gold and set with gems beyond price. Here there was no need for imagery or mental connivance, for the artisans and artists who had created this place were the most skilled men in the Empire, and rivals for the finest that humanity has ever known.

Tiered seats spread out from the center of this area and reached up and back in concentric rings to the far walls of the hall among the towering pillars, and in the central arena resided the marshals and officials who would hear the case for the Barbarians of Earth and conduct the proceedings. Still I looked in vain for Vorta, for above me on all sides a sea of faces leered down as one, blended into a buzzing, babbling beast, sensing scandal and the thrill of the hunt. There were hundreds of nobles here, from the lowest of the novitiates to the highest of the blood line, their voices all mingling impersonally, regardless of creed or status. At the lowered edge of the tiered seats was a long ring of armed Imperial Guards, each with a star lance, the weapon that could shoot fire and wipe out a hundred men in an eye blink. There were days when they would have been allowed nothing more than a spear, symbol of their rank.

Banners and pennons hung limply in the air beyond the far reaches of the uppermost tiers, depicting the presence of every royal member of Zurjahn nobility. From the central dais of the arena rose carved seats and tables. Gundar led me to a set of steps and motioned me up to a seat. As I stood by it, silence dropped over the multitude as though its components had been plunged into a vacuum and the noise went out like a snuffed candle. Gundar stood arrogantly by me, his eyes open and unblinking, ignoring what he saw. There were already a number of officials here with us, but presently Mygol Feyd arrived with a contingent of weasel-faced scribes who rustled around him like a brood of finicky hens. He gave me a curt nod and sat himself in one of the raised chairs.

Below me were other rows of seats, and now these were taken up by more officials, many by men whom I recognized. There were important Zurjahn functionaries here, and also the men who would testify for me—I could see Prosocles, the banker from Earth's sacred City, whose drawn face tried to pull itself into the semblance of a smile for me. Thuran had not come, for his place in this time of crisis was on earth, reorganizing, but there were many of his finest warriors here, who had fought beside me at Karkesh.

At last the presiding Marshal arrived with his entourage, and he sat at the seat at the apex of the arena, his lean body wrapped in purple and white robes, his face stern but as unemotional as the stone carvings around us. This was Galatian, long-serving voice of the Dream-Lords, who would conduct proceedings in their absence. They were not truly absent, for they would be somewhere above in their sacred place, seeing, feeling, and absorbing every emotion and detail that went on down here, assessing every word.

"We are convened to hear the testament of Galad Sarain, son and heir of the late Dotas Sarian, Dream Lord of the Empire. While it is to be understood that no charges against him have yet been made, you are to bear in mind all that has been said and also to weigh the words of Galad Sarian with care and judgment. Charges may be made against the Heir later, but first we must hear from him and of events that have befallen him during the long years that he has been away from the Homeworld. Please stand forth, Galad Sarian, and address the nobles." Galatian so began the day's speeches, turning his regal features to me and nodding.

I walked to a rostrum and returned his gaze.

"Before I speak, I would make a solitary inquiry," I said, as impassively as I could.

"Ask it," he said in a neutral voice.

"My words are for all leading dignitaries of the Empire—every living soul with status is concerned. I do not believe I see Daras Vorta, the former warden of Earth, among the assembly. Surely he should be here."

In the silence that cloaked the entire hall from paving stones to vaults, my voice pierced the farthest wall and remotest corner, amplified by the superb acoustics. A faint breeze of surprise at my audacity drifted among the members of the great gathering. Galatian's head inclined towards a trio of black-browed men opposite me, who fidgeted in their seats as though a cold wind had come in from outside to molest them.

"Daras Vorta is not compelled by law to be present. He has

chosen to abstain from today's proceedings. These men will speak for him."

I gave them a withering look of scorn that was not lost on the nobles. So Vorta was taking every precaution—he would be listening in, rather than attending in person. And these puppets would speak the words he fed them like jerking dolls.

"Very well." I nodded, forcing myself to refrain from making scathing comments that would only have eroded my standing with Galatian and the other officials.

"I am sure that the Dream Lords are most anxious to hear a full account of your movements from the day you left Zurjah to this," said the Marshal pointedly.

"Of course," I said, bowing. "Yet first you must allow me to summarize briefly the reasons for my leaving Zurjah."

At this a distinct murmur went up and Galatian looked angrily at the ranks around him. They subsided and he turned his scowl to me.

"The reasons are well known," he began, but I cut him short. When I had gone to Gargan, the Dream Lords had put it out that I was going to that planet's Centre of Learning, and undoubtedly they had suppressed the fact that I had been banished.

"If I am to give my testament, I must place before you the facts in their entirety. It is my right."

My voice was calm and controlled, though icy with will. I saw the Marshal stiffen and so, too, did Mygol Feyd. Galatian was forced to nod his approval.

"To begin with, I was banished from Zurjah. My father, Dotas Sarian, sanctioned the Dream Lord proposal. Why? Because I upheld certain beliefs that were considered obnoxious to the Dream Lords and to all of you gathered here. Namely, that the men of Earth—which you in your ignorance call Ur—whom you call Barbarians, are of the same stock as Zurjahns and all other men in the Empire of the nine worlds. I was sent away to Gargan where I was to be schooled in all the ways and teachings necessary to raise me to my full stature as Dream Lord Heir, and I was meant to have my heretic thoughts purged from me by three years of hard life on Gargan. I was to have certain facts branded into my memory—that the Barbarians are the scum of the Empire, fit only to be spat upon or used as beasts to do the foulest work needed to keep our just and compassionate civilization flourishing.

344

"For a long time I worked hard at my duties under the tutorship of Ardat Vellor, my master on Gargan. And my tenets about Ur and the Barbarians began to metamorphose into the beliefs I was required to hold. My potential work as a future Dream Lord inspired me and imprinted its importance upon me, and I became a dedicated scholar."

And so I went on to reveal how all this had changed when the machinations of Daras Vorta had begun on Gargan. I told of his plans to kill me and ultimately place Ravas Tarak on the Dream Lord Triumvirate. I gave full details of my escape through the sewers and of the awful confrontation in the Ancient Forest, and of how I had thwarted Vorta's plans and destroyed his leading henchman on Gargan, Wortan Heynar, only to be snatched by Ravas Tarak and smuggled off to Ur in a prison ship.

"You are saying," interrupted Galatian, "that Wortan Heynar, the Zurjahn primate in Melkor, Gargan's principal city, was a traitor to the Dream Lords and that he actively encouraged a revolt by the native Garganians?"

"Precisely. There are countless witnesses." My words hushed the nobles, whose whispers had risen to rumbled of surprise.

"This whole discourse is preposterous!" stormed one of Vorta's three spokesmen. "Sarian claims to have fought with Daras Vorta upon Gargan, and yet the Warden has never been there in all his years in office on Ur! We have countless witnesses who will testify to the effect that throughout Galad Sarian's sojourn on Gargan, Daras Vorta was on Ur!"

"I have explained the powers of Vorta's mind and how he was able to project it across the gulf between worlds. Do you deny that this is physically possible for a man of Dream Lord potential? Do you need a demonstration?"

They could not deny it, for by doing so they would be openly admitting Vorta's unsuitability to be a candidate for the vacant Dream Lord seat. Before they could think of a way to undermine my words, I went on to describe the mental conflict in more detail, and there followed a good deal of arguing and heckling from the trio of Vorta's spokesmen.

"I will call my own witnesses," I ended. "Pthorthe, the Garganian elder, cannot speak for me, as he was murdered. But there are others—men of Empire and natives of Gargan."

345

"Very well," said Galatian. "Each person that you specify will be brought here and given the chance to verify your story. A comprehensive list will be complied later and action taken. Meanwhile, describe the events that occurred after you left Gargan. Afterwards, all your testament will be correlated and every attempt will be made to verify it, using as many witnesses as are necessary."

"I left Gargan in a stinking prison ship—and not as the result of a Garganian plot to kill me and overthrow Zurjahn rule as you have been falsely led to believe."

For two hours I related the events of my life on Earth. I spoke coldly and clinically, patiently revealing each and every intricacy of the evil spun by the tyrant Vorta. I spoke of the endless cruelties of his oppression and the needless tortures that he performed to satiate his Goat Brethren and its black gods, Shaitan in particular. I omitted nothing and managed to keep my temper under control, stating facts rather than making generalizations, so that a clear picture emerged. At the end of it all the torrent of questions began—even the nobles were allowed to ask of me what they would, and they did so thoroughly. All the old taboos had come loose now that I had unlocked the old mystery surrounding Earth and her culture. The debate went on endlessly. Vorta's minions sought to whip up the emotions of the gathering, appealing to the snobbery and the bias of the nobles, using as their most effective defense of Vorta the bellicose nature of the Barbarians, while I tirelessly sought to show how the aggression was the lap-dog of the Warden and merely the touchstone for the Barbarian revolt.

Eventually Galatian called for silence, and it was a long time in coming.

"There are many witnesses whom we must hear," he said. "It will take many days to hear them all. So before they are placed before us, we shall hear from an unbiased source. Namely Mygol Feyd, whom the Dream Lords recently sent to Ur as their Investigator into the uprising."

Feyd got up with characteristic pomp and began smoothing his spotless robes like some elegant bird preening itself before a gathering of females.

"The uprising was something larger and more disturbing than that. I found Karkesh in ruins, its buildings gutted and its army practically wiped out to a man," he said, and I disliked his approach at once. "The war on Ur had been brief but horrifically devastating. Apparently the whirlwind offensive of Galad Sarian and Annulian had succeeded in uniting the various tribes and as one they tore Karkesh apart, stone by stone. My initial response was quite naturally one of disbelief that anyone could generate such violence. The sights and smells of the aftermath were far too terrible to elucidate upon here. Suffice it to say that the carnage was total and had spared pitifully few.

"Gundar Sabian, who had been sent before me to put down the insurrection when first we heard of it, met me as I landed and explained that there had been no need for him to unleash his own men in measures of vengeance or retribution. Apparently the situation was as Galad has described it—the Barbarians were under his supreme command. He had given his word to Gundar Sabian that the war was over and he also handed over his sword as a gesture of submission."

I boiled at his words, for there had been no surrender, neither given nor asked. Feyd was concerned that I should lose face, no doubt still smarting from my affront to him on Earth.

"Galad Sarian had indeed said that he wanted only peace and a reformation of the laws concerning the Barbarians, and he felt that Gundar Sabian would sympathize. The latter was thankfully tactful enough temporarily to suspend his orders—orders that would have meant the annihilation of the people of Ur. When I arrived, these people met me cordially enough. I was treated with respect, and although I visited a war-torn landscape and saw some highly primitive standards of living, I could not help but feel compassion."

Feyd was not a fool. He dared not allow any personal dislike of the men of Earth to poke through his mask of indifference. Even so, I felt a flood of relief at his words. He was not about to condemn the war. It was not easy for me to measure his sympathies, or I saw a potential enemy in every man connected with Zurjahn power—it was the result of my exhausting war against blind authority. Now I hoped I could see in Mygol Feyd certain humaneness, despite his overbearing nature and his supreme haughtiness. He did not seem about to deliver crippling blows to my cause.

"I was taken to a remarkable haven in the mountains, to a place known as the Sacred City. If this magnificent place could be seen, it would be favorable testimony to the true level of Barbarian culture.

I try to speak to you with an unbiased tongue, but it must be stated clearly that only an advanced people could have built that city. I also met many Barbarian chieftains and leaders—scholars and philosophers blessed with creditable intellects. Others were rough, violent men, from awful terrain where softness and temperance would do little to harness the environment. I will not over-embellish—let them speak for themselves as many have come from Ur to do so.

"So...yes, I saw that the war had been as terrible and uncompromising as any of its predecessors. However, the case for the Barbarians bears investigation. They must not be dismissed without a thorough weighing up. It was not something that a single Investigator could do. I strongly suggest that deeper investigations be started."

I was amazed. This was the first time that I had seen a ray of light and hope for the Barbarian cause from within Zurjahn circles. Vorta must surely come to his just deserts at last. But Feyd had other things to say and I could see the wiliness of the fox in his words.

"Although I neither condone the war in any form, nor do I bless its purpose, the Barbarians had some cause for rebellion—they are evidently far more advanced than we have given them credit for. And they were under a stringent doctrine of reprisals—their turbulent past gave us cause to keep them in check. Yet their method of outcry was grim—and Daras Vorta, however rigorous and harsh a taskmaster, was savagely repaid for the execution of his apparent duties as Warden. I submit that we must here establish the justification for the war, with regard to Zurjahn law concerning Ur, and that the scope of this investigation is far beyond the involvement of individuals. It is vital that personal factors are not pushed to the foreground and that the people of Ur are given a fair hearing."

Feyd sat down to applause, and I barely registered the urge to leap to my feet in anger. Vorta must not be allowed to get away with his crimes so easily. I turned to Gundar.

"I will have many witnesses speak of Vorta and his foul citadel, and of how he used the people like cattle for slaughter to appease his own vile appetite. Let the nobles view those facts with indifference!"

Gundar broke his stern gaze and put an arm gently upon mine.

"Feyd will do anything to avoid disruption among the Dream

Lord hierarchy. You must be thankful for the ground you have undoubtedly won through his speech, however safely he played. He has conceded that the people of earth have a case...and remember, he speaks for the Dream Lords. True, it has not been established that Vorta has been nothing more than over-zealous in his Wardenship, but if you remain calm as you have done today, you will slide away his resistance and show him in his true light. I have faith in you."

"You are a rod for my back," I told him as Galatian again called the buzzing nobles to order.

I had begun to think that the breakthrough was truly coming, but still the undercurrents of a new fear rippled around me. Could Vorta somehow avoid his punishment? He must know that the odds were against him—too many would vouch for the Barbarians and tell of how they had been dreadfully persecuted. Yet Vorta could cling to his justification for performing duties handed to him by the Dream Lords. I must ensure that he did not evade justice.

Galatian stood up. "No one here has the power to pass laws. The Dream Lords do that, and we respect their wisdom. We are concerned with facts. Cold facts. Provided we have been given details of events as they have transpired, the facts will emerge. For today we have heard enough. Tomorrow the first of Galad Sarian's witnesses will come forward to correlate his testament."

And so the gathering was disbanded, and not without relief. I dwelt on Gundar's words—and his earlier revelation that the Dream Lords were primarily seeking a solution to Zurjah's dilemma and not Earth's. I would cling to my own faith, though, even if it meant rejecting the planet of my birth.

CHAPTER V
At the Tower of Treachery

That night I was allowed to sleep again in the cold room where I had spent the nights of my Zurjahn youth. Gundar was patient with me now that I had thought twice about launching into a verbal assault on the Dream Lords and Vorta. He saw to it that I was left alone and not disturbed, for I was in no mood to talk to anyone after the ordeal of the day. I threw myself down upon the bed, but could not sleep. Here I was too close to the source of my troubles. The

Dream Lords, their minds locked away as they spread their dreams over the city; Vorta, too devious to show himself to any man now that I had arrived; and somewhere within the castle would be Taria, wife of a man she cared nothing for. I was determined to see or speak to her, though I dare not try to touch her with my mind—the castle was like a living organism, its many minds closed, but still sensitive to mental activity of any kind.

I thought hard about my course of action. I decided that I would do all I could to ensure the safe future of the men of Earth and then I would return there, and be grateful of its warmth—I could never become a Dream Lord, I realized that only too well. Nothing could induce me to remain longer than necessary on this storm-torn world. And I would find Vorta, I swore.

As I tossed and turned restlessly on the bed, even as I had in the nightmares of my childhood, with the hurricane elements battering like demons at the windows of my room, I sensed something new in the atmosphere, some vaguely mysterious emotion that had come back like the ghost of another memory to stimulate my nerves. I sensed it as surely as a man would sense the oncoming mist over mountains in the early morning—as I had seen and felt the cool, white wisps coming on Earth when high in the Sacred City. For long moments I tried to decide what the cause of such uneasiness could be.

At last I realized, and marveled at my own stupidity at such a poor memory. For it spoke of Vorta! When he had tricked Annulian and his men (and me with them) into believing him dead, he had dropped his mind shield that all men with Dream Lord powers can erect automatically, and had thus erased the pulse of his being, so I had accepted his fake death as truth. But now, here in this crawling darkness, it had been the revival of his dark mind that so disturbed me. It was a minute and subtle flow of energy, but I knew it as surely as I knew his bloated visage. Now I allowed my own mind to flow as furtively as a vole, seeking the source of that psychic emanation, for there I would find Vorta himself. Yet his barriers remained firm.

Why had he suddenly found it necessary to shield himself this way? He could easily have protected his mind from Dream Lord interrogations without needing this strong shield against attack from prying minds. Vorta was somewhere within the castle, and ensuring himself extreme secrecy. Why? My suspicions arose like the nape hairs of my neck, for it could only mean that he was plotting and scheming some menace with his usual vile motives. What thoughts were coursing through that devil-ridden mind?

I could not hope to learn by trying to pierce his shield with my own powers—it would mean violent conflict and the arousal of the entire castle. I could, however, seek him out physically. Perhaps I would even gain the opportunity of killing him, one which I would embrace gladly. I would not respect the laws of the castle if that chance arose, for I would kill Vorta without rancor and take the consequences indifferently. Vorta alive was the only reason I had returned to Zurjah.

I left my room. Outside stood a quartet of sleepy Imperial Guards. They raised their brows, but if they had been given orders to restrict me to the room, I used a mild mental sedative to nudge them over the edge into, if not sleep, deep drowsiness in which I was merely a shadow to be ignored. I could have summoned a disc and sped down the corridors, but I chose to walk. My feet echoed down the flagstones and my contorted shadow passed by the lurid murals that graced the curved walls. Occasional Guards watched me, but again I numbed them, obscuring my identity, that they relaxed, instantly forgetting me as I passed by.

As I moved on, my mind slowly homing in to the vague suggestions that would eventually pinpoint Vorta's proximity, I came near to a cross corridor which led to the apartments of Mygol Feyd and his staff. Footsteps that were not my own echoes bounced at me from that direction. Someone unseen approached. I drew back into the shadows, for here I would certainly attract attention. The man passed me—it was Feyd himself, his eyes darting to and fro like those of a conniving conspirator or secret assassin bent on some serious misdeed.

I thought to challenge him, but demurred and watched silently as he made off quietly down another corridor. When he turned a bend out of sight, I drifted silently after him. I could not determine where he was making for. He certainly did not seem the type to go on a late tryst with a castle wench of his choosing, which was common enough practice among the nobles. Then the truth of his nocturnal venture dawned upon me. He had come to a corridor that few people ever trod, for I recognized it. It led to the remains of the Finger of Scorn, the shunned tower, where the old sorcerer, Chalremor,

Prophet of the Barbarians, had been housed. I could never forget this passage, for it had been along its chilling route that I had first crept to that portentous meeting which was to thrust me away from Zurjah, and into a cosmic conflict beyond my dreaming. Some of that bygone magic still clung to the stones, and I imagined that I saw my own ghost going on befor me to meet the sorcerer.

With a swift glance behind him that almost unmasked me, to see that there were no marauding Imperial Guards in these neglected quarters of the castle, Feyd climbed an old stairway to a thick-beamed door that shut it off abruptly. I was momentarily nonplussed, for the door had not been there in the past. Feyd turned its iron ring slowly and carefully, and the door creaked open, spreading a cloud of dust. The motes danced in the dim light as Feyd went through the black opening. I saw nothing but heard the wind moaning as the elements stirred, as though preparing for another onslaught upon the castle battlements—the door led not to some secret chamber but to the outside. It closed gently and the ring twisted.

Cautiously I stole over to the stairs and the door. I prayed that Feyd had not locked it from without. After allowing a little time to elapse, and satisfying myself that Feyd would have moved on, I tried the ring. The door opened. Beyond it I glimpsed a broken stairway, where once the stairs had curled up inside the Finger of Scorn. Instead of that forbidding tower, the ruined ramparts of the castle now straggled away up to a lone and flat tower, roofless under the storm-tossed sky that seethed like a cauldron of boiling foam.

Straining to see through the wind-whipped darkness, I saw Feyd scuttling through the rubble that spanned the distance to the derelict tower like a narrow stone bridge, the sides dropping sheer for thousands of feet on either side. Feyd hugged his robes to him as the fingers of the clawing, roaring wind tried to drag him over the precipice and dash him to pulp against the black bastions below. On the tower opposite were flaming firebrands, guttering furiously in the gale, though the howling wind tried in vain to extinguish them. I pondered this primitive scene. I could see by the wavering light there were armed Guards up there, and most intriguing of all I could sense the source of Vorta's mental shield. He was there, in the loneliest, remotest and most abandoned segment of the castle.

I sought in vain for a clearer view, then set off in pursuit of Feyd, bending low and keeping to the mounds of rubble and heaped stone that littered the narrow bridge. I stumbled and fell close to the edge, and rain began spattering down, sharp as needles. It seemed to whisper against the old stone, insinuating that I should roll further, over the brink. Light flickered and crackled around the horizon and clouds painted the night blacker with their deep mantle of tarry gloom. Shaitan's sub-world hells could be no grimmer than this bleakest of planets.

Approaching the edge of the flat-topped, crumbling tower, I saw a string of steel-shod Guards, all bearing star lances, thrust outwards and primed for attack. Feyd had passed through their cordon of death, but there was no way I could do so. Vorta was far too cautious. If I was to surprise him and an audience with Feyd, I would have to find an alternative means of getting up there. The tower was solid, its old floors within having fallen and blocked off any internal passages. I strained my eyes in the dark. The stonework of the tower was broken like a moldering loaf, and many of its blocks had come adrift and plunged below, leaving an erratic, pitted structure of jumbled masonry. There might be a chance of climbing around it.

So I was forced to leave the dubious safety of the bridge and seek footholds in the decaying tower's rubble. Slowly I edged away from the bridge and moved around the tower like a beetle climbing a tree trunk, my fingers digging for a grip in the flaming mortar. One slip would have sent me plummeting to my doom in that bottomless fastness. As if sensing this, the wind and driving rain buffeted me anew, howling dementedly, laughing at my efforts. It seemed that Vorta had set the very elements to guard him in his forbidden seclusion, but my hatred for him urged me on to superhuman efforts, as it had in the past, so that gradually I worked my laborious way around the tower blocks. Clouds piled past, like the waves of a solar ocean, so huge that they seemed to have the power to mould the planet's crust into new vistas, eroding away Man's efforts here scornfully. I pressed my face to the icy stone, shutting out the frightful images of destruction above me.

Once away from the bridge where there was no chance of being detected by the Guards, I moved slowly upwards, until after an eternity I was but a few feet from the edge of the tower. My hands were dead with the cold and I could have fallen easily, but I heard the voices of Daras Vorta and Mygol Feyd, drawing upon the remaining dregs of my will to push up to the last inches of the lip. I dared not try and scramble over, for Vorta would have dispatched me easily before I could have landed a blow. Instead I clung there tenaciously, like a drowning man fighting to retain his grip on a log that means safety. My mind was completely shielded from any probes that Vorta might have set.

Presently I sensed movement only inches from where I straddled the gaping drop.

"If you come here to me expecting my congratulations for the weak and lusterless efforts you expended today, you are to be disappointed Feyd! There are no excuses," growled the voice of the one man that I had learned to despise with a pathological loathing.

"But, my lord Vorta, this whole enterprise can only be achieved gradually, discreetly, and with infinite pains," came Feyd's protesting voice. So—the reason for Feyd's dislike of me became clear, personalities aside, for he was another who had been tainted by the Goat's evil shadow! Vorta's voice rolled out above the thunderous heavens.

"Do not imagine that I did not see and hear everything that transpired in the halls of justice today! The nobles waver—I can sense their thoughts. When I returned to Zurjah after the disastrous events on Karkesh, I had them eating from my hands! They were made to believe that everything I did there was justified. You were to underline that belief! Instead, the Sarian brat has made them think again! And now he is to produce a host of witnesses to further bring the verdict in doubt. You are supposed to be closest of all men to Vidor Karset! Can you still promise me his backing while this accursed Sarian child flaunts Karkesh in our faces?"

"I felt that today's proceedings began to bend our way..."

"How so?"

"The nobles will see that the major concern is for the future of Ur and Zurjahn legislation there—not for your so-called atrocities. I have done all in my power to suggest that you are being maligned by the Sarian upstart. I have had it put out that you acted as you did on Ur because it was absolutely necessary. The Barbarians cull no favors among the nobles—their past sufferings will easily be forgotten. But the persecution on Ur must end. It is vital that we now give way to their demands for freedom. We must allow the Dream Lords to accept them back into the Empire as an equal race. Bow to this and your supposed guilt will not weigh heavier than feathers about you!"

"Your whining, conniving method of handling my affairs is far from pleasing to me," Vorta snapped, but Feyd had the nerve to hold his ground. I had not heard a man under Vorta's black banner that could stand up to him before now—Vorta could scare any man with his warped powers.

"Sarian," said Feyd, "is no more than a powerful pawn. Yes, he is a man who commands respect when he speaks—especially to the nobles. He will speak defiantly for the Barbarians. Let him! Let him champion them. Let them justify their war. Let them be forgiven for the past—and the Dream Lords can wipe aside the stigma upon their own records. While this tide of goodwill and vindication flows like wine at a libation to the Goat, it will be an easy task to depict you as nothing more than a man who ruled firmly, if extremely, but always under Dream Lord instructions. The worst that can be said is that you over-reached yourself..."

"I should have your tongue torn out for taunting me with..."

"Hear me out, Lord Vorta, I entreat you. No one appreciates the immensity of your powers more than I. You are never a man to make idle threats, I appreciate. But you will have your opportunity to take revenge on those that have hindered you. Subtlety is our best weapon now. If you allow the Dream Lords to believe that you acted harshly on Ur merely in the interests of the Empire, so that the rabble could be controlled, I am certain that I can induce the sympathies of Vidor Karset. It is no secret that he has no love for the Sarian cur. And I have played his prejudices like a fish, that I promise you."

I felt sickened by Feyd's odious attempt to curry Vorta's favor.

"Perhaps you are not such a fool, Feyd," said Vorta. "I admire cunning in a man. Cunning and ambition. You have both. Serve me well in this and you will win for yourself undreamed of powers. I will play the subtle game and even lose a little face if it moves me nearer my goal. But Galad Sarian must be discredited! No pains must be spared to drag his pain through the mire! Allow him to appear as the savior of the Barbarian pigs, yes, but his hour of glory must be short! You must paint him as a bloody warrior, reveling in his war. Say that it was just if you have to, but bring forth men who will swear that he wallowed in his killing like a primitive beast!"

Feyd allowed himself a sharp, barking laugh. "It will be done as you say, Lord Vorta. Tomorrow, though, Sarian's witnesses will begin to give their testimonies. Many of them will speak ill of you."

"I cannot prevent that. I dare not warp their minds here! The Dream Lords would counter at once. And I cannot fight them all. If only I could call upon Shaitan to aid me -"

"That will not be necessary yet. You need have no fear of these witnesses," purred Feyd. The elements seemed to have temporarily abated as though they, too, strained to know what these two monstrous minds plotted.

"They cannot all be easily discredited," said Vorta.

"Those from Gargan will be. You will easily be vindicated of all connection with the events surrounding the incompetent Heynar. You were not there, so it cannot be proved that you incited the Garganians to rebel—besides, they themselves believe that it was their own gods that led them."

"Very well, you may dispose of that line of attack easily. What of Ur? There are many of my own foul underlings who have promised to speak against me in order to obtain pardon for their part in the running of Karkesh. I would have sent word to them to speak for me, even now, but they are very carefully watched—any movements I make to win them back will be seen as an admission of guilt."

"Set aside your doubts. They know you are alive. It is enough! Many would have spurned you dead and saved their miserable hides, but when it became known that you were alive, their yellow hearts turned to water and their mouths clammed up with the bile of terror. *I* have had word sent to them all that the horns of Shaitan await all those you testify against you."

Vorta laughed at this.

"As I said today," Feyd went on, pressing his verbal advantage, "I admired the advanced stages of Barbarian civilization. I will go on to say that, in spite of it, there are many bad elements among them— men who are bred to war through hardship. Men with *supposedly* good hearts, but men who have harbored nothing less than undying hatred for Karkesh and the Empire it represented."

"Go on," said Vorta, though I sensed his skepticism.

"When men like this come forward to testify, the nobles will see that their words are twisted and bitterly biased. They will make you out to be some evil demon from the darkest of their hells. Exaggerating the facts, they will paint an uncompromising picture. Then I will place matters in their true perspective, making ludicrous the excesses of the Barbarian speakers. You will emerge at last as a stern and determined Warden, but one who believed firmly in his decisions and in the ultimate power of the Dream Lords. And in the face of Barbarian savagery, what choice did you have?"

Again Vorta laughed, and I shuddered. "You will counteract all of them?"

"It can be done. You may not emerge as a popular figure, but you must remember, your position in a precarious one at best."

"And you, dear Feyd, must remember that your own position is far more so. Should you fail me, you will be the first to perish and go down to the eternal embrace of Shaitan!"

"We will not fail."

"Only one man has the ability to upset our meticulous plans. Sarian! By the darkest powers in the cosmos, but I would have had him slaughtered a thousand times when I had him before me if I had but known what he would bring about by his infernal interference! Set him at my feet, I pray, Shaitan—he will feed your soul for all time!"

For the first time in many long months, a slender grin of genuine amusement touched my lips at Vorta's ironic plea. He had only to lean out over the parapet and he would discover the realization of his wish. But I thought of the mocking gods and my humor died— how could I tell that Shaitan had not answered Vorta? Feyd's next words tore away my hopes like the searing winds.

"You spoke of discrediting Sarian," he said.

"We must!"

"It can be done."

"If you can devise a means whereby it can be done with total satisfaction, then you rise in my estimation," growled Vorta.

"Vidor Karset is the potential touchstone of Sarian's downfall. The Dream Lord dislikes Sarian for a number of reasons. Paramount among them is that while the youth was here on Zurjah, prior to his banishment, he broke a number of sacred vows and committed sins of the flesh. You know well the affair he had with Sulian's daughter, Taria. It was Vidor Karset's misfortune to marry the Lady, who was partner to Sarian's sin. While the Dream Lord has little to do with his wife now that she has performed her obligatory functions and bears his son and Heir, the knowledge that Karset was not the first..."

Vorta roared with cruel mirth, and only by a supreme effort of will did I restrain my quivering muscles and keep myself from thrusting myself over the parapet and at his throat.

"Do go on, dear Feyd." I could envisage the smirk on the vile Warden's face.

"The triumvirate wavers—Zurjah is not a healthy world while they are weak. They must have a third prime. I will see to it that Sarian is so discredited that the position can never be his. I have heard from a young handmaiden of the secluded Lady Taria that she is wont to visit the gardens in the castle where it is said she and Sarian used to conduct their carnal affairs. Tomorrow morning, in fact, she will walk those gardens. It is most unlikely that anyone of any import will be in the vicinity with the present debates in progress. I will see to it that Sarian is caught in some kind of compromise with the woman. It would be too much to expect them to indulge in any of their bygone sins of the flesh together, but Vidor will see enough to alienate him from Sarian forever."

"How will you get Sarian to the gardens? He is suspicious of every breeze."

"I have the confidence of Taria's handmaiden. She will teach me a way to lure Sarian to the gardens. Have faith in me."

"Excellent!" Vorta laughed.

I felt a new wave of hot anger—I would make this traitorous Feyd pay for every foul-mouthed insult. He would burn with pain before I avenged myself on his wickedness.

"Afterwards, Sarian's every word will be treated with a degree of distrust and skepticism. His motives will be in constant question. And, of course, his aspirations to the position of Heir will clearly have to be forfeited."

"Yes! It is time that I took it for myself. With Vidor's backing and the danger of the Empire's collapse, it will have to be given to me! Ravas Tarak would be a prime now but for Sarian, curse the man! But the Empire can no longer afford to reject me, in its hour of supreme peril."

"No. And once you are elevated to the Triumvirate, Lord Vorta, you could begin the eventual revocation of any new laws that are passed concerning the Barbarians. You can enslave them anew, and more—enslave the nine worlds."

"Indeed! I shall grind the entire Empire under my heels. With the pool of enslaved minds that would be mine to control, I could chain even Shaitan to my will!"

I shuddered again at the words. Vorta was insane. I had always known his megalomania had unbalanced him, but now it was plain to see the extent of his madness. His mind, weakened by the conflicts of the past and sapped by his terrible attempts to unleash incalculable horrors on mankind had drifted well inside the borders of madness. Like myself, he had lost much of his mental strength at the Apocalypse, and I realized that never before would he have let a lesser man like Feyd do so much of his reasoning and planning for him. Feyd was deadly, although Vorta was still the deadliest foe a man could face.

"See to all these things, Feyd," he intoned above me.

"With all speed, Lord of Darkness."

And the voices were gone as though they had been no more than intrusions inside my head.

CHAPTER VI
Death in a High Place

There is no sunrise on gloom-wrapped Zurjah to herald the coming of day. Instead, the clouds that roll overhead like a remorseless sea of ghosts allow insipid light to filter through their screen, so that day ushers in slothfully, scarcely noticed.

As the gray light outside my window gradually brightened early the morning after my visit to the ruins of the Finger of Scorn, I sat quietly in my room, going carefully over the details of the plan of action I had devised. To remain passive while Vorta's agents were so busily engaged in the attempted overthrow of the Triumvirate was no longer feasible. I had to act, regardless of consequences. Now that it was confirmed that Mygol Feyd himself was servant to Vorta's will, I could hardly hope to fight my case verbally. I had not been born to wield words and barter thrusts of scholarly wisdom—I fought with fire, and I no longer had the patience to do otherwise.

I waited in my room in silence, thinking of earth. There the chorus of birds and insects that heralded the dawn made it a joy to be awake as the golden sun washed the heavens with its glory, whereas here it was cold and sullen, infusing its bitterness into my mood. It were better for the people of this place to burrow underground, where they might at least find a degree of warmth.

After some time there came the knock on my door that I had been anticipating. It was very early in the day still—no castle official would have disturbed me at this hour. Therefore I concluded that it must be an agent of Feyd's: if so, I was more than ready for them. I called sharply for them to enter.

I had not been mistaken, but my luck held, for it was Feyd himself who quietly joined me, glancing a shade apprehensively behind him. He did not want to be seen. He closed the door.

"Ah, Galad," he said with a false air of pleasantry. "You must pardon my intrusion at this unseemly hour. However, the business of the hour is of a pressing nature."

I stood motionless, nodding with apparent unconcern.

"As you know, I mediate freely between the nobles, and, of course, the Dream Lords also, in these troubled times."

"Come to the point."

"Yes. Well, apparently Vidor Karset has expressed a wish to see you privately in order to clarify a number of points raised by the Barbarian issue. You must understand that although the Dream Lords are following closely the events described in the halls of justice, there are certain things that you could explain to Vidor better in private. And there are other important factors governed by your return to Zurjah which would be better discussed privately. I need say nothing more, I take it?"

I made a pretense of eyeing him skeptically.

"It will be some hours before today's hearings are convened," he went on. "Therefore, it will be in order for you to come to Vidor in private."

"This is against all normal codes of practice," I said, my eyes studying his face intently. I knew he was lying, but I wanted to squeeze as much discomfort from his traitorous hide as I could.

"Quite so," he blustered. "Yet there are mitigating circumstances. You are, after all, the son of Dotas Sarian. I have...raised doubts about that in unhappier occasions on Earth...but here, well, despite your past, you are the Heir. And I believe that you were accorded a private interview with the Dream Lords once before."

"Before they banished me, yes."

Feyd scowled at my evident annoyance. But he dared not be too whining with me—it would be out of character and would likely arouse my suspicion. He acted his part well.

"The choice is yours," he said, masking his anger. "You are not bound to it. Do you wish to take advantage of Vidor's offer?"

"He wants me to go to his private chambers?"

Feyd glanced away, out of the window, concealing his deception with the practiced skill of an orator. "That would be a little too direct. A certain amount of subtlety is called for in these matters."

"Then explain what is expected of me."

"Of course. It seems that Vidor has only consented to this private interview on the intervention of his wife, the Lady Taria. She, who it seems knew you quite well before you left Zurjah – both as companion and fellow student—has asked Vidor to be patient with you. He is a reasonable man and, naturally enough, has acquiesced to her suggestions."

"I see," I said quietly, holding down the fury that seethed inside me at these lies that slipped so easily from this serpent's tongue.

"In fact, the Lady Taria herself will speak to you and conduct you to Vidor. So have I been instructed to tell you."

I frowned with open suspicion—if I fell into this trap too easily, Feyd would likely become suspicious.

"The Lady Taria?" I echoed. "Why can you not take me directly to the Dream Lord?"

Feyd made a passable showing of looking embarrassed. "I gather you have not seen your former companion for many years. No doubt she would like an opportunity to pass on her good wishes personally. It is not unlike a woman's behavior. And the gentler sex are curious, are they not?"

I thought of his words of the night before and of Vorta's sickening laugh, but again I fought back my anger. "And where am I to meet her?"

"I have been asked to convey to you the details. The Lady Taria walks in the gardens before the day's early meal. If it pleases you, I am to conduct you to her."

"And then I am to speak privately to Vidor?"

"Quite so," said Feyd, with a bow.

I made a show of pondering the offer to me, then slowly nodded. "Very well. Allow me to robe myself. I feel a distinct chill in the vapors of this world."

Feyd bowed again, his expression impassive, and I left him alone.

When I returned again, some moments later, he was staring out of the window at the wakening city. I had slipped a voluminous white robe over my shoulders.

Feyd turned. "Ah, ready, then."

I nodded.

Feyd made for the door, hiding his evident satisfaction. No doubt he thought he would soon have me bound in his web of intrigue. Before he had gone more than a few steps, a low moan came to us from the room beyond. Feyd's mild grin faded and his brows contracted. He looked at me, but my face gave nothing away.

"What was that sound?"

"It seems to have come from in there," I said blandly, pointing.

"Something is amiss..."

"Perhaps you should investigate?"

He scowled. "You'll forgive me if I..."

"Yes. Go and look."

Extremely puzzled and now very much on edge, he went through the doorway and into the room beyond. There, propped up against the wall, was an Imperial Guard. He had been assigned to stand solitary watch over my doorway in the last hours of the night, and earlier in the morning I had asked him in on some mild pretext. It had been an easy matter to drug him heavily and deposit him here.

Feyd gasped. "What is the meaning of this?" he cried, turning to face me. Beads of perspiration had already begun to form on his creased brow. I remained cool, the ghost of a smile on my face. As Feyd made to brush past, I lifted aside the parting of my white robe and revealed the weapon I had taken from the Guard—a star lance. I rammed its end hard into Feyd's stomach, and he doubled over in agony, retching, his fingers groping spasmodically at the air as he staggered and fell to the floor. His eyes streamed with tears, for I had not dealt him a soft blow. He managed to open them and stared up at the wavering end of the star lance. I had not activated it, but put the cold steel beneath his chin and lifted his head so that our eyes met, and I saw naked terror in his face.

"One twist of the haft, Feyd, and you would be incinerated. Do not doubt my threat. Should you die, you would be among the least of those that I have destroyed," I told him with slow deliberation.

He tried to speak, but could not, dragging air into his lungs.

"Now, I have heard enough of your evil subterfuge. You will hear what I intend. Listen attentively, for my patience has been worn very thin by your lies. You are to take me to the private quarters of Vidor Karset immediately. There you will see to it that we both gain an audience with the Dream Lord."

"Impossible," he protested, eyes yet filled with pain and fear.

"I think not. You are a mediator, as your own words have condemned you. So you will use your obsequious powers. Deviate one step from my instructions, and I will destroy you. Remember who I am, and what I have done in the past. One more death will mean nothing to the conscience I lost years since."

"I cannot understand your reasons…." he blurted, and I pushed the star lance harder under his chin.

"Daras Vorta. He has sucked you into his schemes. Nothing that fiend does escapes me, Feyd. I shall hound him to the bowels of hell."

Feyd gasped, a new wave of terror breaking over him. "He'll kill me!"

"I have thrown a mind shield over both of us. Oh, yes, I inherited my father's gifts, be assured. Vorta will not know where we are. No doubt he will be focusing his attention on the gardens of the Middle Terrace!"

Feyd shook his head, but he knew protest was useless.

"We have wasted enough time here. Get up! Take me to Vidor. And remember my promise. To die by the star lance is not a pleasant death."

I slipped the weapon from beneath his chin and concealed it under my robe. Feyd arose uncomfortably and I nodded for him to lead on. We went out into the corridors where a hoverdisc stood waiting. There were two of Feyd's Imperial Guards here, but he waved them from the disc and we climbed aboard. His face was coated with sweat, but his rank and mine were far too high to be questioned. Presently we were skimming up and along the corridors that would take us to Vidor Karset. Feyd made a last sibilant attempt to reason with me.

"You cannot hope to achieve anything by confronting Vidor, least of all with that weapon," he whispered as we went past Guards and early risen officials. I pushed the star lance through the fabric of our clothes and pressed it against his back. He flinched in terror.

"Be silent."

At last we reached the hallowed corridors of the private apartments. There were many Guards, but the whole complex was threaded with sensors and scientific devices designed to forestall and unwanted intrusions. Feyd, however, was well known here, having done much mediating between the Dream Lords and their subjects. In spite of his terror, he managed to control himself sufficiently to speak calmly to the Guards.

"An urgent and necessarily secret audience with the Dream Lord, Vidor Karset," he said, managing an aloof expression.

"This is not recorded, sire," returned the Officer of the Watch. "Are you expected?"

"Of course! But the meeting is to be held in absolute secrecy— as little recording and forewarning as possible surrounds it. This is Galad Sarian, Heir to the Triumvirate."

The Officer scrutinized me and bowed—I had known him when I had been a youth.

"Very well, my lords. Pass within." The Imperial Guards stood aside, and we heard the robotic voice of the alarm system negating its circuits to allow us passage.

When we reached the inner rooms, the lights were dimmed. There was little in the way of furnishings and the walls reflected light from their crystal surfaces. At the far end of the low room stood the shadowed figure of Vidor, idly scanning some papers and charts, evidently immersed in his work. He appeared not to have seen us— he must have been relying entirely upon the scientific gadgetry that surrounded his inner chambers to protect him. For a Dream Lord this was extremely unusual. As Feyd and I stepped out of the semi-dark, Vidor looked up, wearing a puzzled expression, one of doubt and concern. He was a middle-aged man, his hair flecked with gray at the temples, his face bearing early lines, etched there by the demands of his position. His eyes, rimmed with dark shadows, were still sharp, his nose long and thin, his mouth a soft line that could have been a gash in his clean-shaven face.

My star lance grated up against Feyd's spine and I marveled that it had not been detected.

"I am accustomed to unscheduled visits from you, Feyd, but I fail to see what either of you hope to gain by bringing Sarian before me. Who bade you enter this place?" snapped the Dream Lord as he walked towards us.

"It is unwise for a Dream Lord to leave such gaps in the curtain of his security," I returned coldly.

"You are not the man to teach me my duty, Galad Sarian!" he fumed.

"Let us not waste energy in useless bickering. There are pressing things that you should know about. Things which may not come to light in the hearings."

He looked at me without a shred of feeling. "Is that so? Explain yourself. And I hope you are more convincing than you were when you came to your betters before."

I ignored the barbed insult and pushed Feyd lightly. "This time your own chosen Investigator will talk for me."

Feyd fell to his knees, his fears shaking him like a dog shakes a rodent.

Vidor frowned at him. "What in the Empire is wrong with you, man? Has he riveted your tongue to your mouth? Speak, damn you!"

"Tell him what you know," I snarled at Feyd, nudging the quaking figure hard with my knee.

"I...I..." he babbled, his mind in a torment, a heaving sea of confusion and terror.

"What have you done to him?" Vidor snapped at me angrily. "Why is he quivering with terror? Have you used your mental powers on him, you young fool?"

"If I had, you would have detected it with your own. Or is your power drained by your night's servicing of the city? Keeping its illusions alive, barely." I said coldly. Vidor's expression told me I had more than glanced along the truth.

He let his eyes drop to Feyd. "Then if you have not bent his will with mental intervention, why is he so craven?"

Feyd was now trembling uncontrollably, as though forced naked into Zurjah's howling atmosphere.

"I...cannot speak. He will...kill me..." he gibbered. It was horrifying to see a man of his position so cowered by fear. Yet Vidor needed to see this.

"Feyd! What are you saying? Sarian will not kill you, or anyone! You are under my protection. And you, Sarian. I ask you again the reason for this unwarranted intrusion. If you have in any way brutalized Feyd in order to gain my attention—"

"There is a conspiracy," I said calmly. "And Feyd has been a party to it. Feyd, tell the Dream Lord what you know!" I stood mercilessly over the Investigator, my eyes burning into his.

"Enough of this! Let him up!" said Vidor, coming forward. "Up, Feyd! Face us like a man. We are not gods!"

Our wills were bubbling and crossing, though none of us sought to forcibly extract information from each other. And as the unspoken writhing of mental attitudes intensified, I felt something else—the sluggish awareness of another mind. Vorta's mind, turning like some bloated leviathan in a deep-sea cavern, focusing not on distant events, but on the very happenings in this room. At once I shielded my own mind from his probing, casting my defensive web also over Feyd, for if Vorta knew that he was about to be denounced, he would try to intervene. I must act quickly.

"Tell Vidor why you came to me and about your secret meeting last night," I shouted at Feyd as the blackness thickened at the rim of my mind. "Tell him!"

Feyd moaned, hands clapped over his ears.

Vidor seemed nonplussed, though bitterly annoyed. He could sense the tension, but his own mind was exhausted by the work of the night.

Inexorably I felt Vorta's mind seeping in like a lapping tide. He was fully aware now, and he knew that I was protecting Feyd from him. He began exerting more of his own hellish power from whatever corner of the castle he was hidden in.

"This is pointless!" snapped the Dream Lord. "Let Feyd be. There is no need to persecute him. Let him alone, I say!"

He sensed the growing atmosphere of evil power that so charged the room with fear, but his befuddled mind could not read the implications clearly.

"It is not I that abuses power, you fool!" I shouted. "Don't you understand what is happening?"

Yet I could say no more. I was forced to give my attention to Vorta's terrible bolts of energy. The warden knew the danger he was in and was determined to kill Feyd. The man writhed now upon the floor, moaning and thrashing about as though flayed by fire. Vidor sensed the play of violent mind powers, but he seemed to think I was responsible, attempting to force my will upon Feyd, trying to force him to admit things that he did not want to. Vorta increased his efforts to kill Feyd by driving him out of his mind, and now Vidor's hand was forced into protecting himself, from me, as he thought. If he had been in full control of his sagging powers, he would have blasted Vorta's will aside.

Yet instead of that he projected at me and the defensive shield I had erected. For a moment our wills locked and wrestled like huge saurians in a primordial sea. Then Feyd shrieked. Blood suddenly gushed from his nose, his mouth and ears. Vorta had found a way through the weakened defenses. Vidor's assault on me had inadvertently let Vorta in. And now the evil one withdrew and was gone with the speed of thought, gone beyond recall.

Feyd was dead at my feet, his face a twisted mask of agony.

"You murderer!" Vidor gasped, his face ashen. He looked at me as though preparing to repel a fresh onslaught.

"You've been tricked," I told him. "I was trying to protect Feyd! If you hadn't projected at my defenses, he would have been safe. And you would have had his confession, and heard the truth."

Vidor's scowl darkened. "What nonsense are you talking? Protect him! You have killed him!"

"It was not I that killed him. Did you not feel the other mind— the relentless press of darkness? Daras Vorta..."

Vidor seemed lost in confusion. "Vorta! You are obsessed with the man. I felt only your mind, and a confused melee of thoughts that could only have been Feyd's terror."

"You are certain of that?" I said, lowering my voice. He stared at me, then at the grotesquely twisted corpse. "Vorta would not be fool enough to thrust his mind into this inner sanctum," he retorted, but without total conviction. I had to cling to that.

I swore and shook my head. "I wanted Feyd to denounce Vorta. He was in league with him, working away at your innermost defenses with guile and clever words. You trusted Feyd?"

"He has been a close confidante for a long time. He has an unblemished record. How can you expect me to believe he was against me? What could he gain by setting himself against the Dream Lords?"

"He served a man he thought could rule you all—Daras Vorta. Everything Vorta touches, every person that he contacts, becomes contaminated by his perverted schemes. He knew that I would try to make Feyd confess this to you, and so took drastic measures, risking everything in order to silence him. Subject Vorta's mind to a thorough scrutiny—let your psychometers probe its depths. You will learn who killed Feyd soon enough!"

Vidor looked tired. He turned scornfully from the body. "You are as wild in your accusations as you were years ago. Your words border on the hysterical."

"You waste time—vital time. Bring Vorta before you and cut out this canker that threatens to destroy us all."

"When will you learn that you cannot force yourself and your views on the worlds? There is a series of hearings going on now that will give you, and your adopted people of Ur, a chance to speak. Nothing can be gained by continued violence and usurping of the law!"

My hands were clenched tightly around the star lance haft, but I fought back my anger. "How many deaths will it take for you to see that you must fight back, or be engulfed by this evil that festers throughout the Empire, like a disease?"

"You threaten me with more deaths?"

"Not by my hand. By Vorta's. His is the only death that I crave."

"I can see that! You put personal vengeance before all else..."

"This is *not* a personal vengeance! A mad dog does not discriminate when it attacks its victims."

"Enough! We must rule with peace! For millennia we have sought to stabilize the worlds, trying to wipe away violence and barbarity. You have evidently been corrupted yourself by your years on Ur among the Barbarians. They may yet learn to respect peace. But you have not, evidently!"

"There can be no peace for any of us while Vorta and his like force their inhuman ways upon the Empire."

"That is for the hearings to decide. If Vorta is found guilty of all the things that you would charge him with, he will be dealt with. He will answer to the Triumvirate. But not before!"

I stood facing him in my fury for long moments, but his resolve was set. He would not bend to me. I wrenched away my gaze.

"I am prepared to suspend judgment on Feyd's death," he said. "I will have this incident investigated further, but I am not at all impressed with the way in which you have behaved. Whether Feyd died by your doing, I cannot be certain—I am loath to give you no opportunity to clear yourself, although the affair here seemed straightforward enough."

"My conscience is clear."

"Perhaps. But you are to return to your quarters until further notice. You will be placed under strict guard and kept there. You are not to leave your rooms until I summon you. As for today's hearings—it will not be necessary for you to be present. Any dealings that are to take place with Daras Vorta will be attended to by myself. Any efforts you make to contact him in any way will be severely dealt with. Your intentions may be well-founded...but you will learn to respect the law. Laomidian and I have to concentrate not only on the hearings, but also on the running of the planet. We have little time to spare for senseless diversions, so do not cause further disturbances. You will have an opportunity to state your case later. Is that clear?"

I stared at him, my dark mood obvious, but said nothing. He moved away and I heard Guards approaching, though I had not seen him summon them. They saluted Vidor, standing on either side of me.

"See that Lord Sarian is returned to his quarters." He gave them explicit orders concerning me. Was there no grain of comprehension in this decaying Empire? Had Vorta so bemused them all that they would go to their doom in ignorance and blissful incomprehension? As I left Vidor, I clung to but one consolation—the Guards were wary of me and my office and they neglected to search me, so that I retained the star lance.

CHAPTER VII
The Mind of Daras Vorta

Wearily I returned to my quarters, slumping down, staring blankly at the bare walls. There seemed to be an inevitability about everything that was happening here on Zurjah, as though Vorta's evil had permeated the air and blighted everyone and everything here. Reason no longer seemed to prevail, and it appeared that a huge abyss had opened up, ready to drag sanity down to the deepest oblivion.

I sat motionless for timeless hours, my mind running over the faces and events that had made up my turbulent past. I wrapped the star lance in the folds of the discarded robes. If the eventual verdict that the Dream Lords went in favor of a pardon for Vorta, I would seek him out myself and destroy him, regardless of what might happen to me. I no longer cared for Zurjah and her people. They were remote and self-supporting, caring only for their own powers and their guided evolution. The commoners of the Empire were treated like sheep—lesser beings who were expendable once they had ceased to do their chores and duties. For them I grieved, but they had the choice of futures. There was no call for them to remain here if the Empire foundered.

No one was allowed to visit me during the day, so that by the time night wrapped the world in its Stygian gloom, I had sunk into a deep reverie, my mind closed to the outside world, dwelling in the remotest recesses of memory and inner visions within me. I lay as one catatonic, oblivious to all but inner space.

As I lay there my dreams swooped and eddied around inside me like windblown, directionless fantasies: a whirling, image-wracked storm of fragmentary pictures, some meaningless, some connected to the bloody deeds I had witnessed on Earth. From time to time the Four Horsemen thundered through the echoing corridors and canyons of my mind, and I experienced again the terrible dreams of my youth. I understood them now, for I had seen Karkesh in blazing ruins and had watched the pain-filled faces of the dying. I relived the horrors of Karkesh as the armies of the Barbarians had ridden in, cutting down all in their path, and I saw friends die, their lives gushing out of them horrifically. And I saw my own proud, unforgettable charger—the pale, mutated horse that I had spared at birth—ruthlessly destroyed by the skulking dwarf in the pits of the citadel.

Deep into the Zurjahn night I dreamed, and then at last I found myself in the blessed surroundings of perpetual darkness and silence that heralded inner peace and true sleep. How this contrasted to the terrors of darkness in the external world—the darkness that had chilled me since birth.

It was a peace that was not to last.

Somewhere in the nameless vaults of nothingness into which my resting mind had sunk, a light began to grow. I focused upon this intrusion so that the nimbus cast its pale glow upon the shape of a reclining man, lying as one dead on a billowing shroud that slid away from him, sleek as velvet. His face was serene, his body straight and still—as completely relaxed as I was. It was Vidor Karset, deep in the dream sleep of the Dream Lords. That vague nimbus that surrounded him was the watch-light that his slumbering mind had set to control any interference with his rest. It should have burned with dazzling radiance, but it glowed feeby, the events of the day having sadly taxed even the Dream Lords' immense powers.

As my own dreaming mind watched, there came into the shapeless void surrounding the nimbus a series of distorted circles of deeper blackness, more solid in their tangibility than the void. Slowly those intruders moved inward, bubbling towards the sleeping Dream Lord like effervescing air rising from a polluted mire. Vidor's nimbus flared in an instant, and the garish light illuminated for a short time the contorted, gruesome faces of the watchers, who hovered like gremlins of the air. From thick folds of cloak and robe of night the hands thrust out like tongues, and in the poor glow I saw the burnished glint of knives.

I tossed and turned in my sleep like one thrown about on a heaving sea, but still my nightmare held me in its trance. There was no severing of its thread. I saw the Dream Lord wake, his staring eyes seeing the flash of knives that rose as one to take his blood. At once he rallied and fought to blast aside the minds that came to dispatch him, but something huge and obscene loomed out of the night and hovered like a vast pall of death over the figures.

Vorta had sent his odious mind into the vision, and now it brazenly wrestled with that of the Dream Lord. I groaned and fought in my sleep as Vorta and Vidor Karset began a titanic struggle, wrapping themselves like waves in a whirling maelstrom of light and darkness.

The diversion was enough for the bobbing shadow-shapes with the knives. The cruel steel came down repeatedly, tearing silently through the Dream Lord's defenses as easily as ripping fabric. Blood stained the white linen that covered the Dream Lord. The velvet shroud became a bloody, torn cerement, as the man writhed and convulsed in agony. His white nimbus began to darken until, like the sky streaked with crimson dawn, it stained deep red, so that my whole vision was seen through mists of bloody light.

Vorta's grotesque hulk coiled within itself like a huge serpent and vanished as though it had never been. Only the murderers remained, their knives still flashing, dripping blood. Then they too, satisfied that their sickening task had been accomplished, flitted beyond the range of the vision like black ghosts returning to the grave.

Vidor was all that remained, his blood fountaining from his throat and chest as though it would turn to a sea and wash him out into the ultimate darkness from which there is no return. I awoke with a cry of horror and tumbled among my sheets. I shook my head and stared numbly into the pitch-black night around me. Surely it had been no more than a ghastly dream. The thought repeated itself—a dream. Vorta, despite his driving mania for power, would never dare attack a Dream Lord here in the very heart of their Empire. Even though he must have known Vidor was weak, he would not risk everything on a mad gamble and invade the holiest of places.

Yet I felt that what I had seen in my dream had been a fragment of the truth—precognition perhaps. Then my door burst open and a glowtorch was rudely thrust in. I stumbled from my sheets and skins as two burly Imperial Guards stared aghast at me, as though it was I who bled from a hundred wounds.

"My Lord?"

"Sire?" they cried.

I looked up in stupefaction. It must have been my scream that had brought them to me. I struggled to my feet: my face must have been white.

"Is all well, sire?"

"With me, aye. But others may be in danger. You must take me to Vidor Karset at once." I hurriedly put my clothes on.

"But, sire! Both Dream Lords are deep in sleep at this hour. To disturb them, while they dream could risk disaster..."

"We have strict orders not to..."

"Listen to me! Vidor is in deadly danger, precisely because he sleeps."

They exchanged looks of deep fear. "How do you know this?"

"I have Dream Lord powers of my own. I sensed Vidor's dreaming mind. Time is precious! His very life may be forfeit if we delay. Bring as many men as you need. Have no fear of me. Guard me as you see fit, but take me to Vidor at once!"

They hesitated as I snatched up the white robe with the star lance wrapped inside it.

"Should we take you to him, he cannot have an audience with you at this hour."

"We..."

"He may be under attack!"

"Attack? From whom? Who would dare?"

At that moment an alarm came to my rescue for the castle suddenly vibrated with life, like a hornet's nest that had been brutally overturned, the blood of anxiety coursing through its corridors. More alarms began wailing and there came shouts and the humming of discs as they skimmed by the door outside.

"What is happening?" cried one of the Guards, rushing out into the corridor. His companion stood before me, his manner changed, his face a pool of suspicion.

"What do you know of this? You know more than you have said—what is amiss?"

"There is no time for delay," I shouted, shoving aside his weapon and pushing through the doorway. A hoverdisc was coming up fast, manned by two other Guards. Quickly I hailed them and leapt aboard before I could be stopped.

"Hey! What do you think you are about, fellow?" began the man nearest to me, trying to adjust his star lance in the confusion.

"I am Galad Sarian, son of Dotas. I must get to the Dream Lords. They are in grave danger and desperately need my assistance!"

"How do you know of this—no word has come to us concerning the source of the alarms," growled the other. We had sped on out of earshot of the Guards outside my room, which was well, for they had seemed determined to shackle me rather than let me rush away into the castle.

"My own power has communicated to me the danger. Vidor may be fighting off an assassination attempt!"

The disc sped away up the corridors, from which dozens more discs came whirling, all converging on the private apartments of the Dream Lords.

"We are glad of your concern, my Lord. But I fear you must disembark at once. When we know what transpires..."

I wanted no further time wasted in senseless arguments. Instead I waited until we swerved around a bend and then heaved with my shoulder at the cramped Guards. Both of them were thrown off balance and went tumbling over the lip of ther disc to crash down hard on to the stone floor. There were altercations in other craft, but I shifted balance and took control of the disc, pulling it up short of

Vidor's doors. A gathering of Imperial Guards was lined up there, motionless as robots, three deep and pointing their star lances at my chest.

Jumping from the hoverdisc, I leaped before the motionless ranks.

"Let me through!" I cried, but they continued to ignore me. "You know who I am! Let me through. I must see Vidor. It is imperative that I speak to him."

I realized, though, that they would not let me through. Whatever had set the alarms shrieking had banded them together like metal and no one was to pass. Behind them the doors opened inwards and a lone figure emerged, his face haggard and lined with disbelief. It was Gundar Sabian.

"Gundar! What is happening? I must know!"

He parted the ranks of the Guards, motioning them to lower their weapons and he stood before me, his face clouded with horror.

"Why are you here?" he said softly, seemingly concerned for my safety.

"I have had terrible dreams. Vidor..."

"Vidor Karset has been assassinated," he said, his voice almost a whisper so that I barely caught the words.

I sucked in my breath. "So it was no dream. Not a projection."

"What do you mean? Quickly, explain yourself."

"I saw what happened."

"You?"

"My mind locked on to Vidor's thoughts as the knives went home."

Gundar nodded bemusedly. "I see." He appeared to be totally dazed.

"Let me go to him."

He came suddenly awake. "No. It is not something anyone should see, Galad. Gods, but there has been nothing like this on Zurjah..."

"Take me to him!" I commanded, and he knew that I was not to be denied. With Vidor dead, the Triumvirate would be in ruins, and my own powers were more vital than ever if total collapse were to be prevented. Gundar nodded and led me through the Guards and into the bloody chamber of death. I approached with trepidation the divan on which the Dream Lord lay. Vidor was stretched out just as he had been in the dream, his mutilated body a hideous criss-cross of wounds and slashes where the steel had ripped into him. The floor about the soaked drapes was sticky with blood.

"He would not listen to me," I said with a groan.

"What?" murmured Gundar, almost afraid to speak in the semi-light, as though his voice would awaken further tragedy.

"I spoke to him early this morning. And I warned him that Vorta would strike."

"This is Vorta's work?"

"Yes."

"You are certain?"

I scowled at him, annoyed. "Do you doubt my word?"

"Not at all. But we have found the men responsible for the murder. See, there, among the shadows, their bodies line the wall. Vidor did not die asleep—he at least managed to blast asunder their minds, even as they cut away his life."

I went to the wall and stood over the mangled bodies. Gundar was right. The seven cloaked men who had somehow stolen in here to commit their foul murder were all dead, their faces wrecked masks of horror. Blood seeped from their every body orifice—they had died as had Mygol Feyd, their brains turned to pulp by the mind projections of a man of Dream Lord powers. Yet it could not have been Vidor who had slain them.

"These men," I said, bending over and examining therm. "Were they dead when you arrived?"

"Indeed. In dreadful disarray about the chamber, their wasting blood mixed with Vidor's."

"So you had no opportunity of speaking to them, of questioning them?"

"No. All were as I have described them."

"I see. Vidor did not kill them. They are agents of Daras Vorta. He employed them in this foul work and then he destroyed them himself, to silence them."

"How do you know this?"

I gripped the revolting face of one and studied it.

"Two of them at least fought at Karkesh. They were among those who promised to testify against Vorta in order to save their necks. But when they learned that Vorta was alive, their fears must have changed their plans. So they were ready to serve him anew. Why were they not chained up below?"

"None of the witnesses from Karkesh have been imprisoned. You know that. There has been no need for renewed hostilities. In the interests of peace..."

"Peace!" I thundered. "You speak of a myth!"

"The Dream Lords sought to avoid tensions within the castle. Everyone had their freedom, with certain restrictions."

"So this...this filth, disguised as Imperial Guards, were able to penetrate even these hallowed halls? Were those morons outside not on guard! And the electronics? What happened to them?"

Gundar looked utterly bemused. "I cannot understand it. Somehow Vorta must have outwitted them all..."

"So you accept that it was Vorta?"

"Your word in this is sufficient for me. And I can imagine no other who could have set such deeds in train."

A shadow fell across both of us and I leapt up, the star lance in my hand leveled at the man who stood before me like a wraith. His face was old, but dignified, framed by pure white, thinning hair. Lines were etched so deeply into his face that they might have been burned there, so the skin looked cracked and dry as a desert, and his eyes were set in deep hollows, black and melancholy as though watching for oncoming death at any moment. He was tall, but stiff with age or weariness, and seemed to draw breath with difficulty, leaning upon a carved cane for support.

"Laomidian," said Gundar, surprised, for the last of the Dream Lords rarely ventured out from his chambers in his normal form. For years he had been nothing more than a disembodied mind, floating in the light of knowledge that was his sacrosanct shrine.

He looked with infinite sadness at the corpse of Vidor, then at the star lance that threatened him as though it were no more than a dead branch. I lowered it as if I had been struck. Old and tired he was, but there was still power in that wrinkled shell of a man.

"Who is responsible for this outrage?" he asked crisply, his emotions so under control that he seemed completely unruffled by the horrific events in this chamber.

I was aghast. Was it possible that he had not felt the vibrations of Vidor's death? He, a Dream Lord?

"Your face speaks of shock, Galad Sarian. Why do you menace me with that weapon? I read in your mind that you bear me no malice."

"And I do not," I said. "Though I cannot credit that my mind is the only one you read. Did you not see as clearly as I what happened here, even though it was from the depths of your dreams?"

He sighed and rubbed at his wasted features so that I thought they might come away. "I am tired, my son. Years of Dream Lord sleep crowd in on me, demanding their price for the energies I have used. Slowly my powers are draining away. When we were three, we harmonized and our power was unblemished. Now I am content to use the nights to rest and renew my strength for the ordeals of the day. True, I had a brief nightmare, but this...horror...evaded my senses."

I looked at him incredulously, seeing for the first time the true dissolution of Dream Lord power.

"This is the work of Daras Vorta," I said bitterly.

"You can prove this?"

"I saw it all. The powers you have lost are still at their height within me."

"Yes, your father's powers. The blood line is strongest in you."

"Even so. I *saw* Vorta act. He must have killed his henchmen after they had slaughtered Vidor. Thus he destroyed the evidence. But he reckons without me."

Laomidian shook his head in disgust, and I knew then that there was no doubt in his mind that I was telling the truth. "But why has Vorta done this?"

"He knew that his time was running short. The evidence of his crimes has built up like a mountain, condemning him out of hand. All his efforts to discredit me and the people I have fought for have slowly been beaten back. Mygol Feyd died this very morning so that Vorta's secrets could be kept—and Vorta must have seen then that I would secure Vidor's belief and support in the end."

"Yes. Vidor spoke to me of the incident. He seemed to think there was an element of truth in the story you told him, although his initial thoughts were that it was you who had killed Feyd."

I nodded, picturing their discussion clearly.

"If Vidor confided in you and suggested that I might not be guilty, Vorta, his mind trying to pick up every whisper here, would have known at once. He would have seen the last rays of hope fading. And, insane as he is, he decided to act out this perfidious tragedy and destroy Vidor before he voiced his feelings to the nobles. And you would have been the next to die, everything blamed upon me and my rebellious followers."

Laomidian shook his head in despair. He looked like an aged man who is fast losing his grip on the will to live.

"With Vidor dead," he said, his voice reduced to a thin rasp, "the Triumvirate will collapse. We had hoped to find some salvation with you, Galad, but..."

"Yes, I am aware of that. But it is too late! I tried to warn you. Now you must do what you can to accelerate the learning powers of the nobles. Zurjah's future lies with them. You are not fit enough to continue as you have been, that is plain for all to see. I will not serve here. I wish only to return to Earth, my home, once my business here is finished."

Laomidian nodded sadly. He had neither the heart nor the strength to argue with me or command me further. The Triumvirate had indeed come to its pitiful fall. It was a strange ending to come to—no crashing down of powers and falling of illustrious heroes and armies, but instead the exhausted whimper of defeat that sighed out, the death rattle of an old man, almost too feeble to lift an arm in protest. I could have snatched command of an Empire that spanned nine worlds, and few would have stood against me, but I spurned it and all that it offered.

"For now we must bring Daras Vorta to justice," I said with grim determination. I would not rule the Empire, but I would command. I would be the one to lead, the one to extract vengeance. No one would stand in the way of my will, and it would be here on Zurjah as it had been when I had forced the belligerent warlord, Annulian, to bend to my will on Earth. Power surged through me, though its waters were an icy torrent.

"Gundar," said Laomidian softly. "Bring Daras Vorta to us."

The faithful warrior bowed.

"Bring him directly here. There is no way he can leave the castle," added the Dream Lord.

"Do not be certain of that," I said. "He has wormed his way out from under death's foot before now."

"I will give the order for every door to be sealed again," said Laomidian. "I will use what strength I have left to project defensive walls around us all."

"I cannot stand here patiently," I said. "I will seek Vorta out for myself."

Laomidian rested his thin arm on mine. "Do not take the law into your own hands as you have done in the past. For once, bear with us, Galad. Vorta must be brought to trial before all of us, so that the nobles and the common people can be shown the truth. The future of the Empire rests in the understanding of that truth."

I looked into eyes that spoke of more weariness than any others I had seen. And for the first time I saw defeat—defeat for a man who had spent his life covering a web of lies, and who had at last come to terms with the need for a revelation of all the lies.

"Very well," I breathed. But I was not deceiving myself. I understood that somehow, the Dream Lord knew it, too. Then I turned with Gundar and we went from the chamber of death.

Down through the castle we plummeted on our spinning discs. When we came to Vorta's chambers, we were not surprised to find them empty. There were dead Imperial Guards in the nearby corridors, so there could be no doubt that Vorta knew we were coming for the kill. He had gambled recklessly and brought this pursuit on himself—his reason must have completely failed him.

Gundar leaned over the corpse of one man, cradling the head, and I realized the man was not dead, although soon to pass into oblivion.

"This poor fellow is alive," said Gundar thickly, his fingers coated with the blood that gushed from a deep wound in the man's side.

"I knelt down."

"Where is Vorta?" I said softly.

The man's face twisted in a silent scream of agony, blood frothing at his gasping mouth.

"Galad, be patient," said Gundar, but I was adamant.

"Speak! Where is he?"

"...the...gardens..." moaned the man, his eyes glazing over and closing as he lost more blood.

I leapt up with an oath. The gardens! Of course. It was where Taria would be. I should have known at once that Vorta's madness was not without purpose. He last hope would be to snatch the girl and barter her safety with his life.

Before Gundar could move, I had rushed to another disc and set it spinning away. Through the castle I shot, making for the Middle Terrace, leaping off at the unguarded gate to the gardens. This was always unguarded, for it was a place of sanctuary, and during the course of the present debates, few were likely to go there.

I burst through into warmth and light, standing in the humid, silent air of the beautiful gardens. Verdure and foliage gleamed in the clouds of steam, and light played down from the scintillating orbs high overhead in the glass ceiling like radiance from the sun underwater.

"Vorta!" I roared in sheer anger, but the dense vegetation absorbed the shout, and only silence answered me. I thought that I could hear a laugh of scorn, but it could have been my own mind playing tricks from within me. The gardens had not changed since I had last been here, years before, when Taria and I had hidden our affair in their secluded walks. I rushed down the narrow paths, walls of leaves above me, and I flicked on the star lance, holding it glowing before me. Should I find Vorta, there would be no trial, just a stab of light and a fiery death. I made my way to the secret place where Taria and I had held our private trysts, away from the prejudices of the world we had known. Tiny birds fluttered out from hidden branches and flashed brilliantly as they darted away, and insects chirped as though chafing at the speed of my passing.

Before I had reached the hallowed place, a sound reached me and I stopped dead, my ears afire, straining to catch the source. It was a piercing scream—the unmistakable sound of a woman in terror. It must be Taria, Taria whom I had thought of and longed for since first I had been forced away from this unfeeling planet. Smashing my way through the trailing creepers and growths, I prayed that she would still be alive when I reached her.

CHAPTER VIII
Abduction and Flight

Through the undergrowth I plunged, charring the leaves and the branches that clustered around me as though deliberately barring my way. I burst out into a clearing and saw before me the one sight that I feared to behold most—on the little wooden bridge that crossed the meandering brook was Daras Vorta, his face a malign mask of glee, his ungainly arms wrapped around the neck and waist of the struggling form of Taria. Her long, golden hair tumbled over her face as she wrestled with the leering Vorta, and her hands clutched vainly at air, trying to rip into his skin.

"Vorta!" I shouted again, aiming the star lance in the direction of the grappling pair. Vorta's saucer-like eyes turned on me and hate faced me as though a tangible force. He spun Taria before him so that she shielded the huge bulk of his bloated body.

"Fire if you will, Sarian, but she will be the first to die," he said maliciously, an ugly laugh bitten off as the girl fought to tear free. I stood motionless, half in anger and hate, half in choked emotion as I looked at Taria. For a brief moment her eyes lifted and gazed into mine, and I saw deep pools of pain. All that had passed since we had parted seemed to melt away, releasing emotions within me like a released floodgate. But I snapped out of the flickering moment as Taria began twisting and trying to free herself.

As I stood impotently watching for the first opening, my lance held rigid, I felt something slide along the back of my shoulders and reach stickily for my exposed neck. I spun about, ready to face whatever minion of Vorta's he'd summoned, but there was only the undergrowth. I realized what was happening at once. Vorta was exerting his will over mine and projecting a series of visions in the form of a plant attack. He had immediately seized upon my emotional weakness when I saw Taria helpless in his evil grasp, and was quick to take advantage.

I countered his assault with energy from my own tired mind, but quickly found myself surrounded on all sides by the twisting and searching plants. Vines slipped down from above and tried to curl about me. I was gripped by something smooth and flung to earth, but I was up on my feet fast. Roots burst out from the ground like serpents, stretching out white tendrils and seeking holds on my feet. I cut and sliced into the growths with the star lance and the smell of their burning was almost overpowering.

I fought desperately, now only half able to see Vorta and his beautiful captive. He snatched her feet from under her, lifted her and dragged her into the screen of bushes beyond the bridge. I was temporarily helpless to follow, for if I relaxed my concentration for a moment on the weaving foliage of Vorta's mental projections, I would succumb to their attack and be crushed. I tore into the leathery leaves that converged on me like the walls of a gigantic vegetable, singeing and burning through layer after layer of greenery. My star lance hissed with the spilling of thick sap and green juices, and my feet stung from the droplets of hot ichor that ran from the scarred leaves and roots.

Round my feet these roots still burst up from the churning earth as though the ground had awakened to horrifying life. I kicked frantically and blundered toward the clearing, my arm suddenly gripped by a long stalk. I almost dropped the star lance, but kept on beating at the plant that held me with my free fist, finally pulping the thing and tearing free. Fire had started to lick convulsively at the shrubs, and it crackled around me as it took a hold, so that soon I was in danger of being surrounded by walls of flame. Coughing as the thick smoke swirled, I felt the gradual cessation of the weird assault—Vorta was fleeing and his projections weakening.

Slowly the grotesque movements about me wavered and then began to ebb as though night were drawing the plants into slumber. I shook my head to clear it of the drug-like visions. With a last wild swing and chop of the star lance, I staggered on to the bridge. Vorta had cheated me once more. He had stalled me long enough to disappear, and now that the brief attack was over, he had spread a black mental blanket over himself and Taria, so that it was impossible for me to seek him out with my mind.

I felt groggy, but I rushed on through the bushes beyond the bridge, thinking that I would not be attacked further—Vorta's deception had served its purpose. As I ran I tried to fathom where Vorta would be headed. He could not hope to survive long in the castle and would have to find a way out, for the entire contingent of Imperial Guards would be hot on his scent.

Through the narrow passageways and paths of greenery I weaved, coming eventually to the far gate of the gardens. I went out and looked up and down the steel corridors, but no one was in sight. If Vorta had somehow managed to commandeer a disc, he would increase the gap between us, for I could find none. There were no guards here; they must all be above, searching in more promising places.

Blindly I ran on, ignoring the pains that had returned to stab through the leg I had wounded at Karkesh. If only Vorta would seek to forestall me further, I could find his whereabouts in an instant. Yet only a dark silence met my attempts to probe his dark mind. At length I came up into the castle and found myself surrounded by frustrated Guards.

Gundar came to me, his face lined with concern. "My Lord," he began, but I cut him short with an angry gaze.

"Where are they? Have you seen them?"

"The castle is being searched, inch by inch. Every last corner..."

I nodded, looking out over the balcony at the castle gates. Rain was sheeting down outside, and flickers of lightning jarred into garish luminosity the silhouettes of the grim, doomed city. As I watched, my face a terrible vision of hatred, there came an altercation from below.

I leaned suspiciously on the balustrade and looked down. Several Imperial Guards were strewn around the compound near the gates as though buffeted there by a giant hand.

"What is wrong?" roared Gundar to the men below.

One of the technicians came running from the gates.

"The gate control, sire! Jammed. We are trying to locate the fault, but most of the locking units are burnt out. It must have been the storm."

I wasted no time listening to more. Instead, I launched myself down the steps like a wolfhound and pulled up short by the pale-faced technician, wrenching his tunic so that it tore in my hands.

"Has anyone left the castle recently?"

He looked dumbfounded, wincing as my fingers dug into his shoulder. "I do not think so, sire."

"Think? Damn you...what is wrong with these men?" I demanded, nodding at the bemused Guards who had started to get up and dust themselves down.

"The gate, sire. When the fault occurred, there was a field distortion for a moment or so. Most of us blacked out...the shock waves..."

"You fools!" I snarled, pushing him away so that he almost crashed into a rising Guard. This was Vorta's doing—he had tricked them easily.

"What is it, Galad?" asked Gundar, putting himself between me and his men so that I could not vent my unreasonable temper on them further.

"The confusion is Vorta's work, for certain. He has found a way out. Every second is vital if we are to stop him. Fetch me a horse! Come, you there! Fetch me a horse at once."

The man I had addressed saw the look in my face and turned at once to comply.

"Where are you..." began Gundar and I swung round upon him.

"Vorta has fled the castle. He will try for a ship offworld, I'm sure of it. You! Technician! You told me no one has left the castle."

The man paled. "Well, there was a grain floater, but there were only the usual two grainers on board. I didn't think you..."

"Too late for that now! You see, Gundar—Vorta has made his escape. But he will not get far."

Gundar nodded and began bawling out instructions to his men.

"I'll rally as many as I can," he said as a horse was brought into the courtyard for me. I grasped its reins and with one flowing movement leapt up on to its sturdy back.

"Follow as swiftly as you can. I will attempt to head Vorta off, though there is so little time left to prevent him leaving Zurjah."

Gundar made to reply, but I yanked the horse's head away and urged him into a gallop. Through the gates we clattered, then out into the driving rain. Zurjah had unleashed another storm upon her luckless people with the full passion and zeal of her fury. Rivulets of rain cascaded down the sloping roadway, forming deep runnels and rivers, while rain danced back up off the metal surfaces. Thunder boomed constantly overhead and the clouds pressed down like a thick weight of ocean swells, ready to pummel and obliterate the ragged terrain below.

I could hardly see as I fought to keep the terrified steed from veering off the road into the deep storm drains. My clothes were soaked, my hair plastered to my face, my fingers numb with the bitter cold as the elements raged. Down into the outhouses of the city I rode, where nothing stirred outside as the full fury of the storm burst and the wind raged like a company of demons.

Through the streets I raced at breakneck speed, but there was nothing and no one in these concrete canyons to stay me. I pulled up at the gates of the space complex and bawled at the Guards. After a heated argument, they gave in to my demands, no doubt urged to do so by the appalling weather than anything else, and I rode on to the heart of the complex and the docking areas. Ships rose up out of the roaring darkness, rocking at their thick chain moorings as Zurjah tried to pry them loose and shatter them.

Coming to the courtyards I flung myself from the horse,

splashing through rivers of gushing rainwater. I reached the doors of the reception area and a number of Guards rushed up to me from the scant shelter of the buildings, their faces protected by the waterproof coverings of leather that showed only their mouths and eyes.

"What is your business here? This is a restricted area," shouted the first, barely able to better the howling of the wind.

"Has Daras Vorta passed through here?" I shouted back, trying to see into the buildings behind him.

"Daras Vorta?" he echoed, his expression blurred by the mask.

I growled something and made to push past, but the men locked together against me, their eyes hard as steel.

"I'm sorry, sire, but this area is restricted."

"I know that! But my mission is one of prime urgency. Have you seen the Lady Taria?"

There was a frustrating silence, but then one of the men pushed forward.

"I have, sire. Not long since. She went through here to the docking area with one other. Both had passes."

My eyes lit up—it would be Vorta, probably disguised in some way. My clothes were soaked now as the deluge continued unabated. I sought to find a way through these men, for I had to reach Vorta before he got aboard his own private ship. He had free passes to this area, still being a leading Zurjahn figure and could soon be through the decontamination protocol. In fact, he had personal retainers who could attend to it and ensure that Taria was kept by his side.

"*Sarian*!"

The voice suddenly boomed inside my head and I jerked up like a doll at the sudden pressure. Instantly I protected myself from any projected attack. Vorta's voice still filtered through into my mind, though, and his words were like an invisible lash.

"You think you have beaten me, you interfering fool! But it is you who have lost everything, not I. Even now I am leaving this hell world for the last time—and as insurance against my security I am taking the lovely Lady Taria, whose pretty neck you value so much. I shall break it before I allow you to take me! That I promise you above all things, Sarian. You have thought to cheat me in my desires—you shall never have yours.

"This planet is also doomed—I have ensured that. With that fool Vidor Karset dead, the Dream Lord machine is shattered beyond

385

repair. Let the nobles try to emulate their masters—they will fail in the teeth of their destructive environment. Already the forces of a world are gathering like warriors of iron to bring down the citadels here. I want nothing further from this place. I bequeath you Zurjah's doom!

"And Earth will fare no better! You think you have destroyed my powers there, but again you are wrong! Already a place has been prepared for me, a place that no man ever dreamed of, far from your Barbarian climes. Soon I will conclude my preparations and I will release my ultimate army against the last of the cities that dared oppose me and Shaitan's will. All Earth shall toil under my rule. Come to me if you dare. Seek to bring down Shaitan's powers. And feel the wrath of his limitless minions!"

I made to respond, but the projected voice winked out like a projected light, leaving only the deep and familiar void of silence. I stood, numbed more by the words than the deplorable, cold rain.

From behind me came the clattering and splashing of hooves, echoing over the rain-swept yard, and I came out of my reverie to look up at the huge figure of Gundar, who had led a score of armed Guards into the compound.

"Is he here?" he shouted, dropping from his steed and coming to me, his eyes screwed up against the lashing rain.

"He has been. Now he is on his ship," I replied, just loudly enough for him to hear.

"Let us through!" he snapped at the other Guards, and when they seemed in doubt, he placed his hand on the first chest and heaved the man back as though he was no more than a door. Seeing that he was the supreme commander of the army, the men at last parted and Gundar and I burst into the buildings.

Maddeningly, Vorta's head start turned out to have been enough. When I finally reached the docking area, I could see that his ship had already ascended into the thickening strata of atmosphere that swathed the planet. I cursed, deliberating whether to risk an immediate pursuit. Vorta could kill Taria at will—though he had goaded me into following.

I had to take the gamble that he would keep his hostage alive as long as he could.

"How soon can a ship be prepared to follow?" I asked one of the bewildered officials. He blustered for a moment and I reviled him for an idiot. Gundar tried to calm things.

"How soon!" I shouted and once again Gundar put a restraining arm on me.

"Well...I...I'm not sure..."

Another official flustered. "The matter will have to be cleared at the highest levels. Unorthodox flights..."

Gundar gave him a withering look. "Galad Sarian is the Heir of the Dream Lord, Dotas Sarian. He is now elevated to the Triumvirate in the light of Vidor Karset's death! I trust you respect this level of authority?" he said tersely.

The effect was instantaneous. The man stiffened.

"Prepare a ship at once!" I said and the distraught officials bustled away as though scalded, leaving Gundar and I alone, staring up through the glass wall of the dockside area at the heavens.

"You want to pursue him with all speed, without making full preparations?" Gundar asked me. "There can be few places that can shelter him now." His men had tactfully withdraw to the edges of the area in which we stood, standing motionlessly, star lances drawn.

"I remain skeptical," I said. "Vorta could secrete himself anywhere on Earth. So little is known of its desecrated lands. I must get to him as soon as possible."

"We can have a thousand picked troops at your disposal within the hour," suggested Gundar.

"Then prepare them. If a ship is ready before then, you will have to follow. I will leave full directions for you at the Karkesh landing area."

Gundar was about to comment when another of the officials came panting up, apparently at long last fully aware of the urgency of matters.

"There is only one ship due out from here in the next two days. It is not a fast craft, as was Daras Vorta's, but if you do not wish to utilize it, sire, it will mean a wait of several hours while a ship is fueled and prepared for you." He mumbled further apologies.

"And what is this ship which is due to leave?"

"A sea harvester, bound for Aquarn."

I made my mind up at once. "Then commandeer it and prepare it for take off as soon as possible. Tell the captain that we are bound for Earth. And I will brook no further arguments! Is that clear? Good—get the ship ready to move as soon as you can."

Something in my expression froze any further remarks in the man's throat. He gulped and went off to carry out my orders.

Gundar was frowning out at the rain. I spoke quietly.

"I must pursue Vorta with all speed. There is no telling what horrors he intends to perpetrate once he gets back to Earth. He will not be content with hiding for long. For certain he will seek to raise a new satanic army and lead it against my people."

"I see that, Galad. But you cannot go alone. You must allow me time to gather a following of the best picked men."

"There are men on Earth who will ride with me. This is their war as much as Zurjah's—more so."

He nodded and remained thoughtful for some time. "And what of Zurjah?" he finally asked.

I sighed heavily, scanning the flickering horizons and the drab, flaking buildings. "The dream here is ending, Gundar. Men were not meant to live on this planet."

"All is not yet lost! You could help Laomidian restore the old powers. The nobles could be given the higher knowledge, and the Empire could still be made to flourish."

I shook my head." To what end? To enslave the minds of all lesser men? To use them as slaves to keep them while the masters dream away the centuries? It is wrong to subjugate minds, even if it is for some vaster purpose such as this evolution into greater life that the Dream Lords have always sought. Minds at least should be free. When I was a prisoner in Karkesh, Gundar, my body chained along with thousands of other men, it was our spirit, our free thoughts, that kept us alive. Our will to overcome the evils that held us. If a man must be locked inside his mind, his thoughts at least should be free. Take away the freedom of mind and you destroy the man utterly."

"And you believe this is what the Dream Lords did?"

"Look out at this world. Tell me, is this a fitting homeworld? Is it a natural habitat for man?"

Gundar scowled.

"Yet," I went on, "the Dream Lords decreed that the past be obscured and that this place should be called the homeworld henceforth. And they set up dreams and visions to fortify their corrupt decision, so that in time the people became brainwashed. Earth is our homeworld, no matter how scarred, how torn. And the people there, Barbarians or not, are from the selfsame root race.

"You ask me to stay here and save this planet from its death throes. I say again, my loyalties are with Earth. I must go back there. If the gods do weave a fate for each man, then mine is to be on Earth, my life woven inextricably with her future. Even if Daras Vorta were dead, I could not remain here."

"Yet, Galad, you can return to Earth—even live out your life there. For now, though, do what you can to help the people here. They, too, have been deceived."

"Zurjah's fall is coming, Gundar, as sure as night follows day. No power in the system can save it. It is you, not I, who must help here."

"I?"

"Yes. Laomidian is dying. He will try and pass on his waning powers. Man's future lies on Earth, whatever worlds he dwells on now. The salvation of the people of Zurjah will not be found on this collapsing titan—an exodus offworld is the only hope. And there is no need for it to be me who spearheads the migration."

Gundar looked sorrowful, but he understood the truth of my words.

"Do you have faith in the gods, Gundar?" I asked.

"Why...yes, I think perhaps..."

"There have been times when I have cursed them and doubted them. No one can be sure they exist. But if they do, then I believe that all that has happened to me—the conflict with Vorta and the war on Earth—has come about so that Man could be restored to his true world. It is as though the gods are satisfied that he had paid for his past and that he is ready to go back and begin anew."

"So Zurjah is to be given up without a fight?"

"Who would oppose the gods?"

Gundar made no answer.

"As for me...I told you my fate is wound up with Earth's. And my personal need is to defy Vorta to the death. So I go to meet my destiny."

As I finished speaking, another official arrived.

"I have made the necessary arrangements, sire. The ship will be ready to leave shortly."

"Excellent," I told him, and he bowed with evident relief. I turned to face Gundar.

"I will meet you on Earth," he said.

"Perhaps. I will waste no more time here. But you—you must

attend first to Laomidian. Help him and the people steady themselves. If we are to meet again, old friend, let it be in happier times."

"So you are adamant—you will not return to Zurjah?"

"I cannot."

I turned away and the official escorted me to the doors. I did not want to prolong my parting from Gundar, and he left it as it was.

Once on board the Aquanx ship, I gave the confused captain orders to track the craft of Daras Vorta and to pursue it with all speed. Then I went to my quarters, shutting myself away from the crew. I had no wish to watch the world slipping away below as we took off. I had taken my last view of Zurjah, and I knew in my heart that I would never see that world again, although I felt no shred of remorse.

CHAPTER IX
The Desolated Lands

The voyage across space seemed interminable.

For hours I gazed into the screen where the motionless green light that was Vorta's ship hovered, mocking me with its never changing distance, though I knew that my own ship was slowly losing vital ground. I hid my exasperation with difficulty from the others on board, eventually deciding to avoid further torture by going below. In the drawn-out days that followed, I was frequently to be seen pacing the control deck, only to return to my quarters in frustration I had half expected Vorta to taunt me with a string of threats and foul suggestions of what he would do to Taria, but he had thrown a shield over his ship and his mind remained a closed door to me. I doubted that he would kill Taria—he knew that I would follow him now, whatever the cost. I had sloughed off my gentler emotions, thriving upon the hate and the need to destroy as though it would be the only source of energy capable of sustaining me.

When our craft finally lowered itself into Earth's atmosphere and hung high over Karkesh and the desert surrounding it, I wasted no time in procuring a surface flier. The ship itself was too big to land, and the station was in a state of disrepair that made any landing treacherous.

I spun down to the surface area in Karkesh, thankful that I had given orders after the siege not to have it brought down. Vorta's ship was a blue shadow in the sky high above me, although my scanning system had already shown that he had landed a light flier here himself. Despite the long chase across millions of miles of space, he would still be only a matter of a day ahead of me.

The warm air of Earth hit me like a furnace glow, but I breathed it in gratefully, glad to be home. As my flier touched down on the pitted surface of the landing area, I spared a brief thought for the merciless hand-to-hand battle that had raged up here when we had driven hundreds of Vorta's Imperial Guards to their deaths over the brink. Now Karkesh had become a huge mausoleum for the dead and dying—a plague city infested with vermin, its outlands in the grip of famine, its survivors gone away like dust dispersed by an ill wind. Few remained, manning the landing area in isolation from the charnel scenes below.

I ran across to the broken buildings, looking around for any sign of another flier, but there was none to be seen. Figures detached themselves from the remains of the gutted palace where Vorta had once held sway and rushed towards me, star lances in the hands of the uniformed Guards, and swords in the hands of the Barbarian representatives. They halted before me, fiddling uneasily with their unkempt uniforms, patting at thick dust and wiping away the grease stains from their mouths and beards. I cared nothing for that: these men had been through terrible times and their faces were etched with signs of stress that could never be removed. When they saw that it was me who stood before them, they looked horrified, and their weapons waved aimlessly in the heat.

"My Lord, Galad," began one of the Imperial Guards, bowing and trying to tighten his unbuckled harness.

"I have no time to spare for explanations. Quickly—tell me— have you seen anything of Daras Vorta? His ship hangs above us," I snapped, my own star lance sheathed in my belt. At mention of Vorta, the men all exchanged looks of bewilderment.

"But surely he is dead, sire? Killed during the war," said one of the Barbarians.

I scanned all of their faces, but recognized none of them. Most of the important leaders and chieftains were either on Zurjah or back in the Sacred City. Another figure emerged from nearby buildings and I saw by his uniform that he was a Sergeant of the Guard.

"What is this?" he said. "Karkesh is a plague area—no one is to land here until decontamination processes have been completed."

I glowered at him and he realized who I was.

"Vorta," I said. "Where is he?"

"I assumed, sire, that he had fled to Zurjah and that he was standing trial there," he said, his face reddening.

I pointed with my star lance at the dark ship overhead.

"That ship is Vorta's," I told him grimly. "Vorta has left it in a flier. Our scanners traced him. He must surely have come here. If you think to hide him—"

"I assure you, sire, that he has not been here," said the man, his unease growing. "Our receiving equipment is destroyed—those ships that come up there usually unload fliers bound for the Sacred City and King Thuran. All of the legislation takes place there now. Karkesh is unfit to live in..."

I swore softly to myself. Wherever Vorta was, he was gaining more time, widening the distance between us. I looked searchingly at the men—how strange it was to see Barbarians and Zurjahns side by side. No doubt they had even been drinking together before my arrival. Yet it was a good sign.

"I did see something a trifle...irregular, sire," offered one of the Earthmen nervously. They would always look upon me with awe and many with fear. It was not easy for them to forget the Pale Horseman, who had been a god incarnate, indestructible and murderous, leaving a ragged trail of death and agony wherever he had ridden.

"And?" I prompted.

"Yesterday—a small craft left the mother ship there and headed south. Sometimes ships go out to inspect the lands and see how Earth fares."

"But never south," ventured another.

"South? Be more specific. Where, exactly? Show me."

The man led me to the broken lip of the landing area and pointed to one section of the still smoldering city.

"Since men have come to us from the sky, sire, ships travel everywhere." He spoke confidentially so that the others could not hear. "In the south are the most ill-favored regions—you will know the tales told about the jungles there."

I nodded silently, remembering something of Barbarian folklore.

"I saw a ship head that way, sire—a solitary craft. I took it to be a Zurjahn patrol."

"Who is in charge of this area?" I said, cutting him short and indicating the station.

He frowned and puzzled it over. Then the sergeant came to us, his face grave.

"There has been a certain amount of re-organizing in the ranks, sire, since the King and the various officials of state returned to the Sacred City. I have a mandatory command here while Ool of Vendl is away. He should return before evening."

I would have grumbled at the further seeping away of precious time but I still felt taken at the idea of Zurjahns and Barbarians linked together as these were. I knew Ool well—the big, blustering chieftain of the jungles, and it seemed a miracle that he could command the respect of men from the haughty Empire. So the dream of union had become something of a reality here on Earth while I had been away, even if it had not on Zurjah. It would be vital in the years to come, for Zurjah's people would have to return to survive—and the role of prodigals would be reversed with bitter irony.

"I have no time to lose," I told the men. "When Ool arrives, tell him that I am in pursuit of Daras Vorta. Yes—the Goat still lives, despite our war and all our attempts to destroy him. Tell Ool that Gundar Sabian and a company of men are due to arrive soon. They are to await me here. *Here*. Is that clear? I will return soon enough. Whatever dark hole Vorta is fleeing to, there will be others waiting for him, servants I am certain. I will seek out his haven and draw upon you all then."

Mention of Vorta, the goat of myth and legend on more than one Empire world, made them all shudder, but they were a quick-witted company for all that, and they had soon moved off to gather their fellows together. I returned to my flier, and without a glance at the two ships above, headed out over the ruins of Karkesh to the south. My mind probed the surrounding wastes, but Vorta had blanketed himself off thoroughly. I flicked the switch on my regulating panel—it would automatically pick up and relay the course of any other flyng craft within a radius of fifty miles, but it remained dead.

As I sped south, the charred landscape beneath me that had stretched bleakly on all sides like the burnt-out shell of a lunar surface gave way gradually to deep-gullied and ash-faced ravines, where nothing grew. If Vorta had come this way, he was plunging deeper into unknown territory—lands that were clothed in legend and fear, lands where the most adventurous of Earth's wanderers never set foot. Here there were the realms of fantasy, where all manner of horrors were said to stalk, and there were said to be jungles of indescribable mutations, the worst products of the ancient wars. Superstition took a powerful part in the building of the legends that made these southlands so awesome, but below me I saw the arid desolation and ruination that enhanced the fables and brought them to grim reality.

For hundreds of miles my craft flew on, the only sign of life the barest traces of seared plants. I began to wonder if these polluted lands might be fatal to life as were the Wastes around Karkesh. But I went on—Vorta must be here somewhere.

Eventually my craft looped up over a ridge and, as I leveled the flier out and swept down into another of the interminable valleys, the panel before me winked into faint life Vorta's craft was registering! As I flew on I could see that it must be stationary—I had found his haven. The valley had a peculiar uniqueness of its own. It stretched away like a gigantic bowl for hundreds of miles, and within its basin I could see the rich green verdure of an endless jungle. As I overflew the first straggling growths, I knew that it was a mutant zone, for the plants and trees (if words could describe them thus) were bent and twisted in the most hideous ways, an insult to all things natural, their metabolism strangely altered by the holocaust of the ancient wars, as though lunatic deities had scorched them and gnarled them, using evil powers from beyond Man's knowledge.

Evil. The word permeated my mind as though the jungle below me breathed the very images familiar to it, wafting it up to me as a last warning to avoid landing. It became difficult to scan the horizons over the silent, unmoving mass, for the air became humid and clinging, as though it, too, were blessed—or cursed—with sentience of its own. I concentrated on the panel before me, noting with grim satisfaction that the blob of light in its center was growing larger—Vorta's craft could not be far away. I cradled my star lance as though drawing strength from the touch of its metal.

From out of the thick jungle below there rose up lone buttes and crags, their spires and bastions runneled and scarred, their faces etched, scoured and sheer, their tumbled chimneys black and lifeless, surrounded in morbid, birdless silence. In fact, there was not a shred or trace of life to be seen anywhere in that impassive wilderness, although the greenery below me seemed somehow to retain a repugnant awareness of its own, as though a single, vast organism sensed me as it sensed the play of light and heat along its verdant corridors. And it would know me as an outsider.

My disturbing thoughts were interrupted as the sun sparkled on something lying near a flat rock outcrop below. I caught my breath. With a careless twist of the controls, I took the craft in swiftly, skimming the treetops, and then I could see the craft I had pursued for so many hundreds of miles! It could only be Vorta's. I flew above and around it, but I saw no sign of either Vorta or Taria, so unless the craft had been forced down for some reason, this very jungle must have been Vorta's destination. It would be the perfect sanctuary for one who knew its forbidding labyrinths, and a chilling opponent for an outsider.

I prepared to land my craft, for the chase must go on. As I came slowly down to the flattened rock area, a sudden beam of fiery light stabbed out of the pressing jungle and slammed into the underbelly of the flier like a huge fist. I stumbled forward as the craft shuddered, my head banging against the control panel. I rolled back groggily, fighting to stave off nausea and unconsciousness as the craft went into a fatal spin. Its nose crashed into the naked rock and then the dish jerked upright, tossing me away from it as a huge wave would have done. I tumbled down among the rocks, the skin scraping from my knees, elbows and hands. As I made to get to my feet, there came a detonation behind me and I was picked up and hurled forward again. My back felt as though it had been scalded with boiling water, and I plummeted over the edge of the rock outcrop and into a tangle of matted plants. They broke and snapped under my weight, and I sank down through them into a deep fissure, barely hanging onto consciousness as the dark abyss swallowed me.

I should have been wary of a trap on landing, but there was no time or strength for recriminations now. In my haste to get at Vorta I had assumed that he would be anxious to flee as quickly as he could on landing. Now he was still free and my craft was destroyed.

Crashing hard into the ground, I groaned and tried to clear my head in the darkness. I fell motionless, my bones feeling as though they had been pulped. Above me I heard vague, distant sounds. Something moved within the bushes there. Light crackled and I realized that Vorta was using his star lance in an effort to ensure that I was dead. Another beam of fire stabbed out, and the bushes above me burned and plants were seared. Vorta was determined to finish me, but fortunately my fall had been a long one. Desperately I hugged the rock wall of the fissure into which I had tumbled, and at last the flame from the star lance died, but not before it had singed the very floor of the fissure. Everything went very silent except for the faint crackle of burning undergrowth above. It was some time before I could assume that Vorta had gone. After that I sank down in the cold moss and slipped beneath the dark surface of oblivion.

When I came to, it was to the trickling touch of water. My face was pressed into some dank growths on the ground and I rolled over and peered through the darkness. I could make out a slit of light not far from me and through it saw the golden wash of evening. I gently flexed my arms and legs to see if I had broken any bones, and finding myself luckily uninjured got to my feet, though still groggy from the fall. My hand reached out and touched something cold among the vegetation, and I bent to feel the star lance. My luck held: I retrieved the weapon, without which my plight would truly be hopeless.

Wriggling between sharp-edged rocks, I emerged into a noisy jungle, where the crawling insects and gibbering twilight creatures were already filling the sinister surroundings with their deafening cacophony. The trees here were low and thickly clustered together, their leaves long and thick, moving in the breeze like tresses of hair or voluminous skirts. Ignoring the dirge from the insect world, I sought a path through the matted verdure. I had been in mutated forests before, but this one, a thousand miles from the edge of civilization, seemed altogether more foreboding, potentially more hostile than any of those. Its growths seemed to have been made of wax and then melted and dried into parodies of vegetation, twisted, gnarled and contorted thickly like strands of crumpled material.

I had gone but a few feet when the ground itself began to tremble gently like the flanks of a horse twitching to remove an irritable fly. I realized that the turf formed a large expanse of islands that must be floating on a morass that threaded the entire floor of the jungle. If I could climb back to the rock from which I had fallen, I might be able to see a pathway through, but on looking back I could see that the task was impossible. Rock walls rose sheer and overhanging behind me.

There was nothing to do but go on. Cautiously I tested every step as I progressed around the perimeter of the floating turf continent, and as I approached the first clump of rustling trees, I heard sounds further out in the gathering night. Splashing sounds, as though something huge stalked blindly through the marsh. I moved to the dubious shelter of the trees, the leaves of which hung down into the sticky mire beneath and seemed to take nutriment from that oozing surface. I made certain that the leathery surface did not brush my skin.

After listening for a while, I moved on, finding an area of solid ground that threaded the clumps of dwarfish trees. I became aware of the fact that I was not alone in the watching jungle, for my mind detected jumbled, incoherent thoughts around me, as though the trees were alive and would suddenly reach out with their weird branches to claim me. I twisted the star lance haft and the weapon glowed. One touch with it would sear any predator to ashes. The lance cast an eerie glow about me, and at once I saw something shuffle back from the arc of light.

Other spectral shapes were gathering, and I remembered the terrible mutant men of the north, where Thuran and I had almost died under the prolonged insanity of their attack. Something about these glimpsed shadows unnerved me, though, for I could sense thoughts and more—the sharing of thought. There could be any number of creatures tracking me, but they appeared to think *as a unit*. Before I could evaluate this discovery, there came a rush from behind me that I had anticipated. I spun about, the star lance spitting a stream of liquid fire as I indented the button at the base of the haft. In the brilliant glow I saw two human shapes fried alive before I switched off. The stench of burning flesh was overpowering, and I looked to see who or what I had killed. They had been men, and not the horrific caricatures that the northern mutants were. Their skins were sickly pale, their skin dried and wrinkled, but they were not malformed as I had expected. The bone structure was vaguely anthropoidal, and the jaws prognathous and heavy, giving a brutish appearance to the beings, but something about them suggested an intelligence of sorts. Before I had time to think further, a whole host

397

of them rushed forward from all sides and I swung the star lance about, cutting down a good many as they sought to overwhelm me.

With night coming on quickly I could not afford to drain the power of the lance, for it relied on solar energy to sustain its charge. I had to be content with the secondary power of the rod, which sizzled and burned as it touched the naked flesh of the antagonists. They fought without spoken words, but their minds were a terrified jumble of outcries, as though they feared me for some incarnate devil from the heart of their mythology. They grunted occasionally and some shrieked as the star lance bit cruelly into their pale flesh. I swung with frantic abandon, knowing that one instant of respite from my defense would see me brought crashing down, never to rise.

Just as it seemed that the hulking shapes around me were about to claw and tear through my ring of fire and rip out my vitals with their ugly talons, something else moved nearby in the jungle. The splashing I had heard earlier had returned, its volue increasing as though the trees themselves were moving. For a second I wavered, my attention riveted on the edge of the clearing where I fought. I must have felt a pang of uncertainty and fear for somehow the assailants picked up my thoughts and as one they stopped to listen and watch the jungle. My worst fears were confirmed, for something unspeakable was disgorged from the depths. Through the groves of huddled trees a long, ringed worm came slithering, its segments gleaming with slime and mud as it propelled itself across the surface of the marsh. It had thin, transparent fins that were crossed with pink veins, and its white body writhed and pulsed like an obscene organ, churned up from the floor of this hideous marsh.

At once the beings scattered as the huge worm-thing lifted its blunt, featureless head and bore down upon us, clearly scenting its prey. The maw opened like a tunnel into another world, and I could see plainly the rows of sucker-like pads inside, contracting and glistening with saliva. As the monstrosity came closer, the throbbing veins stood out inside its wriggling body as it undulated and rippled like a vast serpent.

I had little time to react, so quickly did this horror from the primeval depths of the jungle move. I lifted the star lance and poured a steady stream of fire into that hungry orifice that readied to scoop up any living things in its path. For tense moments it seemed that the worm would ignore the fire and come on regardless, but it began to writhe and squirm as though impaled on a gigantic hook. Filthy water and thick muck slapped at the tree bases as the thing wallowed in agony and thrashed about, its mouth a scalded, burning ruin. The veins inside the translucent skin pulsed madly as though they would burst and pump forth the ichor within.

I gagged on the stink of charred flesh, and the worm began to curl and roll up tightly into a humped, quivering ball, the tail slopping wetly against the shaking tree bolls. Even with the amount of blazing energy that I had poured into it, the creature took an age to reach its final spasms of death. It turned over again and again, half submerged in the morass before coming to a standstill. I watched for signs of further life, but there were none. The men from the swamps were returning. I looked to them, ready to defend myself again, but they obviously watched me with a new respect. Even so, they were surly and their minds spoke to me of mistrust.

"Attack me again and I will destroy you all as I did that monster," I said to their minds, but it was a forlorn statement, for I doubted they could relent. They were uncouth, clothed in filthy, ragged hides, their hair greased and lank, their skin coated with muck and grime from the jungle. Compared to these bestial looking men, the so-called Barbarians of the north were like Zurjahn noblemen.

Mercifully it did seem that I was not to be set upon at once. One of the men, bent over, his knuckles scraping the ground like those of an ape, shuffled up to me in an act of bravery and lifted his ugly face to mine. His fingers scratched at his thick beard as though searching there for lice.

"Who are you...Death Watch?" came the crude whisper from his mind. So these creatures were telepaths! Despite their appearance, they were not so backward, and I wondered what quirk of nature had set them apart from other men. Was this another far-reaching effect of the ancient wars?

"I know nothing of the Death Watch. I am from far away. I come you your jungles seeking an enemy and mean you no harm."

It brought a unified mental sigh of relief from the whole company and they began to speak. I did not expect them to use any branch tongue of the Earth languages that I knew, and although these men had strange accents and thick-tongued ways with words, I was able to pick up mental images enough to be able to understand them. They babbled at me and bombarded me with questions, and I drew back, alarmed at the degeneration in them. But men they were, and not mutants, and it was impossible not to pity their plight. I had told them I was not Death Watch, which seemed to ease their tension considerably. Apparently the Death Watch were held in abhorrence and were dealt with ruthlessly.

When it became plain to these swamp dwellers that I could not speak their tongue, but could talk to their minds, the spokesman at my feet took over the questioning on a mental level. I ignored the bobbing fears that still swirled around his main stream of thoughts and began to try and sooth his nervousness.

"You are not from the evil places?" he growled, like a wary animal protecting its cubs from potential danger.

"Evil places? No. I am from the northlands. There are cities there."

"Cities?" The word echoed around the massed minds.

"There are no cities!" came one sharp thought, and I saw the sullen figure who had aimed it at me like a knife. "We know there are none! You must be from the evil places!"

The man beside me snarled at him and he recoiled. "I am Karl. I lead here! I will talk to this one."

"I am Galad Sarian," I told them.

"You speak of an enemy—who is the one you seek?" asked Karl.

"I have followed him across many lands. He has hidden himself somewhere in your jungles. He is an evil one."

They muttered suspiciously among themselves, and I knew that I had sparked off some chord of recognition in their minds.

"If he is evil, he will be with the Death Watch in the evil places. Have you come to destroy them with your bough of fire?"

I looked at the star lance, then nodded. It seemed to please them greatly.

"You must tell me more of these evil places."

They flinched uniformly and I caught cross-thoughts and black images of some unhealthy terrain as they collectively tried to thrust aside their fears of these evil places. Karl nudged closer to me and I could not suppress a smile at his scowling features.

"First you must come to the village. Gast must be told of your coming."

CHAPTER X
The Moon into Blood

I was escorted by the still suspicious men of the swamps through a series of twisting groves and floating islets of turf that grew thick with shadows. Although I found it increasingly difficult to pick out details in this morass-ridden landscape, it became apparent to me that the men had a peculiar kind of night vision of their own, perhaps another birthright from the mutated lands. The hunched figure of Karl was ever near me, as though he had singled himself out to be my personal guide, and he moved like a medium in a spirit world, guiding me to some sacred haven. We reached a place where there was a thicker entanglement of trees, trailing their fronds like skirts around them, and the leaders of our groups swept them aside and passed through fearlessly. Soon we were beyond the rustling leaves, and I made out bobbing lights, high above the dense forest floor. At first I felt a pang of hope, for I thought it might be air rafts come from Karkesh with Gundar Sabian, in spite of my orders, but closer scrutiny showed me that a peculiar type of plant grew in the area around here. It had long, translucent stems which were topped by small, bulbous sacs that were filled with some luminous resin, glowing exotically against the wall of night behind.

The sight that they illuminated in their glowing amber and violets fascinated me further, for among the weed-strewn marshes I could see clumps of gnarled trees, from the trunks of which had been hewn openings and hollows. It was among this ideally camouflaged village that the swamp dwellers his themselves from the perils of the strange jungle in which they lived. I could not see the hidden eyes that watched from a hundred holes and from behind carefully drawn fronds, but my mind sensed the alert vigilance and the curious pondering that emanated from them as a palpable force.

The inhabitants still evidenced fear—the natural fear of an animal for anything alien to its domain—and I knew that those fears would usually prompt them to kill anything suspicious and that I was therefore fortunate to still be alive. We waited at the edge of the marsh, which at this point looked impassable, but shortly a number of earth and root turf islets were propelled towards us from the trees in the mire, and we clambered on to them, my feet unsure on the rolling earth boat. We then ferried over to the tree village.

"I will take you to Gast," said Karl, and I sensed that he was incapable of reaching any major decisions of his own. Evidently Gast's power was supreme among them. They all nodded and I could feel the slackening of tension—Gast would take control of the situation and there was security in that. When my feet again touched relatively solid ground, I was taken through the stunted trees and whispering leaves to a central point where a huge mound rose like a humped-up hillock. Its surface was covered in thick, tall grass which rustled in protest as we began to climb and push through it, like the sensitive hair on the flanks of something dormant. I wondered at the unnatural location of the hill and felt the stirring of my nape hairs. On the crest of the hillock the grass thinned to almost nothing and I saw a single huge plant. At first I thought it to be some enormous vegetable, vaguely rounded, with a series of tendrils and roots sprouting outwards and down into the soil like the internal wires of some infernal machine, but as we approached I saw that the plant moved, not as though swaying and rustling with the light breezes that were at play, but as though shaking itself tremulously like an animal rousing itself from sleep.

At once the men with me bowed low and after a moment began directing torrents of garbled thought images *at the plant*. In a moment my strangest evaluations were confirmed, for this was the being that they knew as Gast! I watched in unfurling horror as the thing shuddered and tiny balls of crystal-like flowers rustled up on the crown, hanging delicately on minute threads and seemingly sensing every vibration in the atmosphere. And I felt the first stirrings and probings within my mind—it reminded me of the cruel scientists of the Empire that Vorta had once employed to rape my mind with their psychometers. But this probing was gentle, sympathetic. I still closed my mind at once and felt the immediate reflex action of the plant.

Carefully I projected questions of my own and presently felt the first of the gentle probes returning.

"Now that you are aware of my existence, you are anxious to screen your thoughts from me," came the mind-voice of the plant. It was like the rasp of a dry breeze alongside my ear.

"You are sentient," I replied, amazed. I had seen many weirdly mutated creatures to the lands and jungles of the north, but this was something unheard of, even in the remotest parts of Barbarian legend.

"That is strange to you?"

It had picked up my unguarded thoughts at once and, even more surprisingly, I realized this thing had strong emotions and that my indiscretion had bruised them.

"Indeed it is. How is it that a plant can communicate this way?"

"Well, the explanation is both simple and yet complex, Galad Sarian."

At the use of my name I must have evidenced shock, internally and externally, for the men around me seemed agitated, as though they were the nerve ends of this peculiar life form. I had no clear idea of how much thought they could pick up and translate into images, and although my mind would be blank to them, they would see something of its workings in the mirror of the plant's mind.

"How is it that you know my name?" I marveled.

"I have been reading much of what has passed in your tumbled mind since you crashed here in the jungle. Oh, yes, I am aware of everything that transpires in these green wastes. Your mind was vulnerable after your accident, and it was I that sent the men to find you and bring you here."

"You?"

"I will explain. However, first you must know more about me, or else you may well fear and doubtless alienate me. You ask how it is that a plant can speak with a mind. I answer with a paradox—I am not a plant. Outwardly, yes, I have all the accepted characteristics of a plant. Although there are facets of my visual biology that would horrify and even disgust you—aspects which I have learned to shield—I am more human than I would appear. I can tell you little of my biological development—my memory cells cannot recall events and cycles from millennia ago. Yes, I have existed for many years, more than a thousand human lifetimes. But if I have known childhood, puberty, adolescence, and old age as do normal men, I have forgotten them all. You can see that I am no ordinary man. My condition must be attributed to the results of the war that was waged so long ago, for I am an ultimate product of that disastrous conflict— not only I, but all this wild and insane jungle around us. My mind is one with most of it, even the ground on which I stand. I sense the movement of nutrients from below; other minds feed me, and upon me."

"Mutations..."

"Even so. I may well be a unique form, but there are many unique life forms here. The war released diabolical powers, and life forged heedless and unchecked along often monstrous paths. There was an unholy *fusion*. Gradually the jungle became as one single organism, so although it is made up of millions of components, each shares harmonious symbiosis with the others. Thus I am able to project my mind anywhere and attune it to developments elsewhere. There is much hostility and conflict.

"In me you have a plant-like branch of human biology, with the chemical make-up of a vegetable, together with the vastly developed mind of a man. The sub-branches of humanity in this jungle are generally retarded, despite mental powers that their ancestors lacked. Therefore, despite my physical shortcomings, I have the power of leadership. I slipped quietly and unobserved into your thoughts at a time when you were half-conscious, and I learned, with some degree of surprise, that your own mind far surpasses even my developments. Had I sensed evil, I would have shut myself off and left you to the mercy of the jungle, the combined mind of which would soon destroy you. But my probings detected other things.

"It was easy to read your name and details of your home, though there is much that baffles me. You are not from these lands, but come from the far north, way beyond the limits of this tropical region. And I sense greater distances beyond my comprehension. Will you open your mind to me on this? You need not fear hostility from me—you must be aware by now that you could destroy me with ease."

"I am a Dream Lord," I told him, but it meant nothing to him. His mind had ranged far and wide in this jungle terrain, but its boundaries represented the limits of his own scope. I allowed him to see the unfolding of my trust, for he was correct in his assumptions that his mind was vastly inferior to my own. In fact, it had taken many years for me to appreciate the true strength of my mental capacity. In my struggles with Vorta, necessity had matured it to be able to counteract annihilation.

"You must tell me about that," murmured Gast. "I am anxious to know how true men fare and to learn how it is that their minds have so developed."

"You shall hear. But first you must tell me about this jungle. My time here is limited. My mission draws me urgently."

"You are no enemy of mine, I am certain. I know that you have come here seeking a source of evil, and it may well be the source of evil that has been threatening our existence for some years now."

"You know of Daras Vorta?" I asked incredulously.

"The name is not familiar to me, but the images I read in your mind that you associate with the name tell me we speak of a connected source."

"Then tell me what you know of him," I urged.

"There are many things that I must explain. Firstly, you are only partially aware that the jungle here is more alive than it seems—oh, yes, you have sensed vibrations new to you, but know that the jungle is full of sentient creatures. It is basically a primitive sentience and the peak of it is seen in these sorrowful specimens around us. They cannot hear our present thoughts, do not fear. For millennia the jungle has been a mass of conflicting entities—each plant, tree, and creature all alienated from its neighbor and basically hostile. This began after the mutation set in. Normal Biological development became grotesquely warped. Humanity and botany and other biological branches grew intermingled in bizarre new cultures. Eventually, the plants became the new dominant species, and in order to remain so they had to find an alternative method of locomotion—after all, the fastest hunter makes the greatest number of kills. So mental powers were developed and refined—hence plants exercise new control over their physical abilities, and more important, over the movements of other, more mobile beings. There are many plants in the jungle that can dominate human forms and will them to obey—a grim method of nutrition. Survival, of course, makes harsh demands.

"So the jungle advanced its mental potential, but remained internally hostile to its parts. I may have gone on this way, but some years ago there came into the jungle a new power—a power from outside which proved capable of shielding its own considerable mental strength from myself and all other sentients. At first, the intentions of this black power could only be guessed at, but soon it became horribly apparent. It sought to unite the various individual powers of the jungle and subjugate them to its own will, so that the jungle would become one vast extension of that will like a second body, subservient and helpless before this superior power.

"When you crashed here, I thought *you* might be that power."

I shook my head, fascinated by what he was telling me.

"I know now that I was wrong," Gast went on. "But the power is an erratic one. For some reason it has only exerted itself at certain times. For long periods, months sometimes, it became as though it had withdrawn completely. Yet it persistently returned."

"And it returned today, not long before myself?"

The plant shuddered. "Even so. It seems clear now that this Daras Vorta you speak of is the source of the power. He comes to the jungle from time to time, experiments, then returns to his own lands."

"I understand. I have fought him for a long time. His evil has by no means been confined to your jungle. Elsewhere he has been crushed, so that now, ruthlessly hunted down, he has taken his last desperate refuge here. He will not leave now."

"The picture clarifies itself. When this Vorta first came here, he sought out the most advanced life forms. Sensing the evil at work, I managed to shield my own powers, which are feeble beside his. I also managed to gather about me the faithful swamp dwellers who built their village around me. We represent one of the few bastions against this nightmare power that seeks to control the entire jungle."

"And where is Vorta now?"

"He found a source of servants, far from this remote outpost. You were questioned and challenged with being from the Death Watch?"

"Yes."

"Nothing and no one is more despised and reviled in this jungle as much as the Death Watch."

"What are they?"

"Once they were true men, back in the mists of antiquity. Their nation, Trucia, was powerful, with distant boundaries, armies, a rich culture, science. Much of its history remains fabled. The war obliterated everything, and these people altered terribly. Now they are still a race of men, although it is a questionable term in which to couch such blasphemies. However...who am I to speak of blasphemies? So, let me tell you of the Death Watch.

"They dwell in the mires and filthy lakes of the inner valleys of the jungle. Underground, in holes and in caves of night, you will find them—eyeless and putrid, never seen by daylight—skulking monstrosities that moved and writhed mindlessly like worms with brains the size of peas until the black power of the man you call Vorta found them out and began to make use of them. They were easily controlled, offering no resistance, and he uses them now to spread and multiply in the evil places as we have named the worst parts of the jungle. They obey Vorta and worship him as the living embodiment of all that is foul and diseased in the world, too witless and debased to think for themselves. Like a plague of vermin, they permeate the vilest places and reproduce like flies, readying for whatever unholy task Vorta has set for them."

Gast's revelations were profoundly disturbing. They had come as an unpleasant surprise rather than as a shock. It was so typical of Vorta. He had lost the last of his human consorts and chattels, and now, as his last hope, he had fallen back on the sub-human.

"Where is Vorta to be found?" I asked again, and the urgency of my demand was not lost on the plant-man.

"You emanate hate as the sun emits heat," he said.

"Not without cause, I promise you."

"You would be foolish to oppose him alone, Galad Sarian. He has taken the more advanced of the Death Watch and welded them into a strong bodyguard. To stand face to face with your enemy would give you an equal chance, but he is no longer alone. Why not go back to your own world in the north, where men are men and not monsters?"

"I cannot! Not only does Vorta have possession of the one person I hold most dear, but also, if he were left to rule your jungle, he would soon seek to overthrow the lands from which I come. He would not be satisfied with the seclusion of this place for long."

A mental sigh came from the plant, which rustled and shimmered in the pale light from the bulb plants overhead.

"You are right. I only seek to avoid the death and pain that these conflicts bring. Yet you must bring an army! Alone, you will be destroyed, even before you found him."

"I could command ten thousand men, it is true, Gast. Though it seems to me that in all this vast green sanctuary, Vorta has a million bolt-holes. If he knew that an army sought him, he could go to ground and might never be found. As it is now, he may well think me dead after his ambush. My one hope of discovering him is by stealth. Tell me where I am to find the Death Watch."

"Perhaps you are right, but your bravery is rooted in foolishness. The Death Watch will be found in the south, near the heart of the jungle world. The way there is long and will be fraught with peril."

"I have effectively shielded my mind from Vorta before. He need not know that I am coming."

"If I could move," sighed the exasperated Gast.

"Can you aid me in other ways? How far can you exert your will?"

"I can reach the very edges of the jungle, but alas, I could hardly control anything under the power of this Vorta. I could even control a horde of the Death Watch, but not if Vorta already had them under his direct will."

"There will be no need. All I ask is that you ensure that the jungle is not hostile to me. You said that it would kill me. So protect me from it. Let it aid me. Make my journey south to Vorta's retreat unimpeded—disguised."

"Yes!" he agreed, seeing that he could be useful after all, and I sensed at once a rising of his dull spirits. "I can make your passage easier. And I can create your diversions. Vorta will think the jungle is in a state of upheaval, and your passage will be nothing more than another facet of it. The jungle often vibrates to some all-embracing tremor like a hibernating animal turning in its sleep."

"Excellent, Gast. You see, I need not be alone in my offensive."

"You will still have to stand against the Death Watch. I cannot protect you from them. You carry that dreadful weapon that spurts fire and heat as though sucked from the sun itself, but there will be many of them. They swarm like an army of rats ready for conquest."

I could not ignore his warnings, of course. My drive south had brought Vorta within my reach again, but Gast was right—there were no limits to what I could do, even alone. I looked around at the swamp men, who had remained silent through my mental conversation with Gast.

"How many of these men are there?"

Gast seemed alarmed by the implications of my question.

"Surely you do not expect them to help you oppose the Death watch? They are simple, peaceable people."

"They were ready to kill me when they found me."

"Fear moved them then. *I* did not want you dead."

"No, but they must protect themselves. They go in terror of the Death Watch."

"Precisely. They have taken great pains to avoid discovery."

"Hiding here in the darkness in shame is not the answer. In time, if the Death Watch are allowed to multiply, they will infest the entire jungle and then all your men will be absorbed into their ranks, corrupted and enslaved!"

"I know, I know," said Gast sadly.

"I sympathize with the situation, Gast. You have no wish to see them embroiled in a war that will see many of them dead before its ending. Their choices are poor."

"I am...selfish. I have no one else. Without them..."

"Gast, Vorta must be destroyed! If I can reach him and bring to an end his foul existence, the Death Watch will be like a beast without a head. Without Vorta's power to motivate them, they will be easy prey for your own men. And the entire jungle will be yours, my friend. The swamp men will begin the steady rise back to the light and to a proper evolution. People from the north will come to their aid. Do you not see, you have to risk everything or eventually you will have it all torn away from you. The choice will no longer be yours."

"I know, I know. I am selfish, selfish. Yet the loneliness before you came...you have no idea."

"I am sorry," I told him gently.

"You are right. I cannot remain detached. I cannot expect others to do my work for me. You need men to accompany you and guide you. You must overcome their terrors. Let me speak to them first."

"Good. They will find a purpose in this. However we fare, it will make them men again. They will feel pride coursing through them. They cannot relish their confinement in this dismal region. Vorta's evil is the worst kind and must be opposed. And for him the light is fading. He has evaded me for too long."

"There has been little light or hope in this unfortunate place for centuries. We have already plumbed the depths of our own misery. I will exhort them to follow you."

With that he began to project his thoughts at the swamp dwellers. They listened attentively, like children hearing a worshiped parent. All remained silent until suddenly, with no prior warning, the baleful eye of the full moon glowered out from behind a cloud bank. At once all was confusion. I was amazed—the men fell to earth as though by doing so they could burrow away from the bright lunar glare.

"Gast! What is wrong?" I asked, puzzled.

"Superstition! I have taught them to hide from the moonlight.

Darkness is our protector from the evil abroad. They think that the moon is the eye of the evil ones."

I watched the pitiful swamp dwellers cowering from the moon like helpless children. I had to rally them, to give them a new belief in themselves if they were to aid me in my renewed battle.

I stood in the clear, my hands raised to the moon as though in some prehistoric, ceremonial ritual.

"Listen to me, men of the swamps!" I cried, opening their minds to my words. At once their eyes swung to me, their terrified attention riveted.

"You see the eye of the evil ones!"

"We see! We see!"

"The time has come to fear it no longer! Watch!"

With that I made a rare use of my mental powers. I disliked having to project false visions and hallucinations, but I had to free these men from their superstitious chains. Into each mind I sent a picture, and that picture was of the moon turning to blood. They looked up from their hiding places and saw the great orb in the night sky glazing and filling with crimson, as though its veins had burst and its sight was stabbed out in flowing agony.

"See—the power of the evil ones wanes. I bring death to the Death Watch. Rise up! Stand with me!"

They may have feared me more than their enemies, but they obeyed and soon were able to find the courage to jeer at the bloody moon.

Gast was amazed, but pleased.

"You will follow me?" I shouted, and the men waited to hear the mental words of Gast.

"Obey him," he said, and they clustered around me like faithful dogs.

"You have your men," Gast told me privately, and I nodded. As I saw the first of the clouds, racing up to obscure the vision I had made, a sound came to me from beyond the hill—a sound I had not heard for a long time, and it made my blood run cold.

"Tell me, Gast," I said to the plant-man, "are there horses to be found in this jungle?"

"Not for many miles. In the south, the Death Watch dwell near the herds, but they are small."

I shuddered again, for the sound that I had heard had been the steady drumming of passing hoof beats.

CHAPTER XI
Jungle of Terrors

Gast spent a considerable time explaining to the men of the swamps my purpose in coming to the jungle. With some reluctance he told them that their time had come, and that if they were ever to rid their lands of the growing horror of the Death Watch, they must act with me now. Their trepidation and fear spread quickly like waves across a lake, and I sensed the other minds within the village, all seething and bubbling with the turmoil I had brought.

However, their faith in Gast and his apparent leadership was not to be briskly denied. After many deliberations that went on deep into the night, their spokesmen, of which there were many, agreed to support me. Karl was loudest in his shouts for the downfall of the Death Watch, and he kept close to my side, his loyalty clear to everyone. Eventually I was taken to a tree hole of my own, and there I was left undisturbed to sleep until the first glimmerings of dawn light.

It was the raucous chorus of insect and bird life that awoke me, just as the sun was spreading its early fires in the east. I slipped from the tree and joined the swamp men who were already gathering in the clearing, and their eyes locked at once on to the star lance, which had become the symbol of their deliverance. I sensed their awe and disturbed peace of mind, but soothed it with subtle vibrations. Karl, who had slept beneath my tree, shambled forward, his face reflecting my own concern, but I smiled and he returned the smile with a crooked grin of his own.

"You heard the words of Gast last night. It has been agreed. It is time to go forth from here and seek out our enemies before they come to worry us out and kill us. The reign of fear must end now!"

They murmured restlessly, their numbers swelling as they came to see who it was that stood up and spoke so openly against the Death Watch. There were men there who had only heard half the talks of the previous night, and they were yet filled with fear and skepticism.

"How can we fight?" cried one old man, leaning on his

411

immediate colleague for support.

"Arm yourselves. All of you. Take what weapons you can. I have this," I cried, holding aloft the vaunted star lance. "With it I will burn a way to the core of the evil places and there I will cut out the heart of our enemy."

The images of Vorta's death that my words conjured up were sufficient to start them all thinking. I had not imposed my will upon them mentally—something I had never been wont to do, with the exception of Vorta, with whom I had engaged in mental struggles several times. These swamp dwellers must choose for themselves; if they still refused to accompany me, I would go on alone. Gast, lingering on the edge of awareness and hearing these present discussions, kept out of the arguments. He had said his piece the night before.

"It has been agreed!" shouted Karl. "No more debate! I will go with you, Galad Sarian." He beat his chest, and that seemed to act and a trigger, for presently they all began shouting their support anew. In the end their fervor had reached an important apex and their morale and confidence surged from their minds in waves.

"Then let us make our plans carefully before we leave."

And so it was that that evening, having designed a string of tactics that we could employ when we reached the so-called evil places, we set out with Gast's blessing. He would exert his own peculiar influence on the jungle terrain while we journeyed south. Through the straggling trees and across the shaking turf islands we went, my guides running on ahead and searching out the most secretive passages south. Gast had promised to stay alert for signs of plant hostility, and for a while none of the weird growths attacked us. I shuddered at some of the unspeakable things I saw, many of which would have taxed the sanity of simple men, but forced myself to pass on. I knew that our progress was watched, sensed by all living things around us, and at times there was eerie movement and at others none at all, which lent an even more sinister aspect to the grim verdure, as though lurking predators were always ready to spring and devour us. I stretched my mental powers and tried to shield the men as best I could from any probes that Vorta might send out.

Deep into the night I called a halt at the edge of an expanse of marsh that we would take time to skirt, and told the men to find niches among the trees and then camp. Certain trees would have been unsuitable, some being hostile to all other life forms, but Karl told me those here were safe enough. The jungle had fallen silent around us and nothing stirred; it might have been hewn from stone. If there were eyes or minds studying us, I was not aware of them. Even so, I imagined that I felt the distant ripples of Vorta's mocking laughter as he had defied me on Zurjah when he had snatched Taria and made good his escape. I dared not allow myself to dwell too long on her predicament, for that way lay the path to inevitable madness. She must be alive, and I must retain my belief in that fact if I were to succeed.

Restlessly I twisted in the flattened grasses beneath a tree boll, hunched up, exhausted and covered with dirt and grime. Around me the men were falling asleep, leaving a deep mental void behind them as they succumbed. These surroundings, though semi-hostile, were natural to them. I found sleep impossible to woo, dozing fretfully until eventually I foundered off the shores of wakefulness and managed a broken rest. Unintelligible images peppered my half-sleep, driving back relaxation. I tried to utilize Dream Lord control, but the conflicting shards of consciousness persisted. Something sinister tried to thrust itself into the mixed and feverish dreams that flashed witlessly through my turbulent mind, and I awoke with a jerk and banged my head against the rough bark of the tree. Only a few of the men were awake, but even those on watch seemed oblivious to the subtle disturbances in the night air. Karl shot a glance at me, and seeing my evident discomfort, gripped the rough club he had fashioned and scowled into the darkness. I could see very little through night's drapes, but I knew that something stirred, and it was hostile.

I got up quietly and went to the edge of the brackish swamp. I looked down and saw that its surface trembled very slightly as though ruffled by a breeze. Yet there was no breeze, and not a sound. The world seemed to be dead, a cold rock, devoid of life or thought, like the asteroids beyond Gargan. However, I knew the illusion of calmness was false and evil. Out there in the scum-lined marsh, something was gathering itself. Karl stood close by and he sensed something amiss as a hound scents its prey.

All that I could make out in the gloom was an island of turf that seemed motionless. Scanning the edges of the swamp, I could see nothing but thick-leaved trees, bowing down to the foul waters as though nodding in sleep. I was tempted to wake all of the men, I was so certain that menace was abroad. It was as though I sensed the incredible nightmares of a madman—the incoherent images tugging away at the recesses of my consciousness. Was the bulky turf island out in the dark moving? I concentrated on it, watching and probing. Then I knew that I was right: some discreet current eddied around this swamp. And that island was moving slowly towards the shore, like a vast bulk slithering silently across ice, the darkness concealing the movement so that nothing appeared to change. Gast had been right; the jungle was more alive than I would have guessed, for in that island of matted turf I sensed thought, and it was hostile.

My realization amplified the reality of whatever blasphemy drew near, for suddenly the island burst upwards as though pushed rudely from beneath by a gargantuan hand. Filth and slime splashed back into the lake of mud as the first lashing growths that could have been either thick roots or tentacles reached out for me. I leaped back in sheer horror as I saw the vile mouth of some unspeakable vegetable monster opening and closing like the red petals of a flower. Whatever the thing was, it writhed forward, rearing high out of the marsh, a contorted colossus.

All the men were shaking themselves awake, crying out both aloud and mentally as they fled into the dubious refuge of the jungle, as if Hell had unleashed a pack of its worst demons. I drew back as waves of muck slopped at the shore, leveling my star lance at the writhing mountain of leaf-wrapped terror that had erupted from the floor of the swamp like some volcanic ejection. Foul air heaved over me like released gases born in pits of excrement. The creature came shoreward, its hideous probes licking out like clammy tongues, rich and thick with mucus. I directed a stream of searing fire into the sucker-filled mouth, and the flames spat and hissed as if cast into a cauldron of fat. The writhing and twisting and thrashing about set the whole swamp to rocking with a tide-like motion, so that the turf islands were tossed and washed by repulsive waves of mire, and the trees at the edge were set to shaking as though by a sudden storm wind.

Despite the havoc and blistering destruction that I had wrought with the star lance, the huge monstrosity still propelled itself forward and reached out for me. Thick, rubbery tentacles wrapped remorselessly round me, coating me in foul-smelling ichor and fetid scum from the marsh. I was dragged towards that revolting mouth, my weapon lunging, thrusting and chopping madly as I summoned up the last vital reserves of my energy. I slashed sideways and burned into the tentacles, searing and charring them so that many crumpled and fell away, but rootlets and saplings swung from above me and renewed the terrible grip. The entire island was alive, each growth a part of the whole, each plant, root and flower commanded by the central will that served as a mutated brain. My feet crunched into the very lip of the awful maw and somehow I wedged myself there, hacking madly at the suckers that protruded like sticky tongues in abundance.

For a moment I had reached a temporary impasse, for the working mouth could not open enough to devour me whole, and I had now wedged myself deeper as I had cut into its sides. With the burning rod of the lance smoking and smoldering, haft-deep in the flesh, I directed a mental bolt at the source of the twisted intelligence behind this vilest of beings and at once felt the whole mass shudder. I fought on, sickened and nauseated by the stink and the overpowering odor of the thing I battled. On the shore the men must have rallied, for they had begun hurling flaming brands at the denizen of the swamp, and many of the tentacles that clung to me unlatched themselves and seemed to waft shoreward in search of other victims.

I burned huge holes in the leathery framework of vegetation and was soon able to break free of the rancid tentacles. With a lunge I toppled out of the dreadful maw as though spewed up and sank beneath the putrid surface of the swamp. Blindly I groped for the shore, feeling roots and broken rocks dragging at me, while the monster still tried to hug me down into the abyssmal depths. I managed to find firm ground with my feet and broke surface, whirling about to hack through a cluster of reed-like roots that waved before me. I gagged as I clambered ashore.

Mercifully the creature seemed to have been effectively stalled, for a number of fires had broken out among its thick leaves and roots. In order to douse them it had to sink lower in the mire, and then my men rushed to me, dragging me away from the last of the cloying mud and taking me quickly into the jungle away from the marsh, where the awesome creature would not follow. My body was covered in blood and filth, bleeding from a hundred ragged wounds caused by the tentacles and suckers of that sickening mouth. But I would live! I repeated that to myself and drew strength from it. If it had been Vorta who had goaded the lumbering horror into attacking me, he had been thwarted again.

Slowly I was nearing him, cutting away at his powers, eking away his resources, hemming him in. I relished the thought of the kill and allowed myself to slip into oblivion.

It was dawn when I woke, and at once my men were gathered around me, faces grave. Karl thrust his curious companions aside and stood over me watchfully. I had been bathed and my wounds were taken care of. There were many of them and there would be a danger of infection, for the marsh must be a well of disease, but they had smeared all manner of pungent herbs over me, so that I looked as white as a ghost. I forced a painful smile and got up, albeit groggily.

"The herbs will protect you from the spirits that burn," said Karl. I nodded, looking at my coated body. Then I laughed and a chorus of relieved cheers greeted me. The men were far more buoyed after that, although I sensed that some of them were thinking hard about a speedy return to their village.

"You see," I told them. "I survived the attack. It was our enemy, seeking to unleash upon us the creatures of the jungle. But we are their equal! Come, let us go on and spurn all his attacks as we did last night! The swamp creature has gone back to the bowels of the earth to lick its wounds, probably to die!"

It was true, for when we returned to the edge of the marsh, there was no sign of the living turf island that had so nearly ended me. A thick pall of smoke hung in the air, and nothing lingered but the stench of charred plant flesh.

"We are not afraid!" shouted Karl, stamping his foot on the muddy bank, then turned to eye his men to see if any of them would back down from going on. Some wavered under his scowl, but there were no objections voiced.

"Lead on," I called to the guides and they did so, now with rueful grins.

"We have still to meet up with the Death Watch," grumbled one of them, though, but Karl silenced him with a glare of annoyance. Soon after that we had cut into our fruit provisions and had begun the journey south anew.

The jungle valleys got steeper and narrower, and I could see the scarred faces of the buttes jutting up out of the tree-lined ridges. We were entering a system of steep sided ravines and clefts in the jagged rock outcrops. High up in the sunlight I made out the dark forms of winged creatures, but they never came close or low enough for me to distinguish their features clearly, yet I knew they were nothing like the birds I had known in the past and were better left unseen.

Our passage through the jungle became gloomier as though we were going down into a tunnel bored inside some gigantic plant, its sides green and pulsing with rhythmic life. Marsh had given way to rock and small boulder outcroppings. The vegetation underfoot was tangled but sparser, so that our passage, although slow, became less fraught with danger. Or so it seemed. I had felt since the night before that Vorta and the jungle would surely attack again. No matter how I shielded my mind and the minds of the faithful followers, word would get back to Vorta, perhaps through the silent but vigilant plant life that infested this scarred land, a blight upon it.

I was soon to be proven correct in my assumptions. One of the scouts came back from ahead and began speaking of a stream where we could drink. I had always been wary of water sources on Earth, but it seemed that here in the jungle, as remote and as diseased a place as it was, there were streams from which water could be taken and drunk in relative safety. It had to be boiled, but it was not poisonous. Gast had told me something about it, suggesting that the plants were slowly cleansing the water sources in a natural re-cycling action. Perhaps the war-blasted land was slowly returning to its former state.

We emerged from the tunnel-like vegetation and I felt a sense of relief. Gast claimed to be able to exert an influence on the jungle, but that vegetable stomach could have closed in upon us and digested us all too easily for comfort. Before us was a fresh, clear stream in which there grew a number of normal plants. Karl pronounced the water fit to drink. As I bent gratefully to scoop up the water in a skin, a beautiful butterfly flew past my head. I stared at it in amazement, for it was larger than any of the tiny creatures of its kind that I had seen before, and its brilliant, multi-hued body flashed in the light. The delicate creature landed silently on the naked arm of one of the men, who had not noticed it. I watched it, seeing the huge, splendid wings closing. As the man turned to speak, he saw the wings folding up like the gorgeous leaves of an exotic bloom. Instead of evidencing pleasure, he let out a startled shriek and smashed a hand down at it, shaking bloody remains from his fingers and scrambling back in horror from the broken body.

I saw why, for on his arm there was a clear trickle of blood. His jumbled thoughts confirmed what I had quickly concluded, for the butterfly had been *feeding*. The next moment the clearing was suddenly filled with a cloud of the fluttering shapes as hundreds of the huge butterflies came from out of nowhere and began trying to settle on the alarmed men. I felt the sting of the bloodsucking horrors and swiftly began trying to crush as many as I could with my bare hands.

Fighting off these grim, vampiric shapes was impossible, for it was like attempting to forestall the passing of a cloud of down. Everywhere the air seemed blanketed with a mist of the beautiful shapes, and wherever they landed on flesh they left a trickle of blood with their tiny probosces. I tried using bursts of fire from the star lance to sear some of them, but they sensed its heat and moved bodily away from it. The glowing rod did appear to attract them, though, and soon I found myself fighting off a fresh cloud vast enough to threatened to darken the sunlight.

Running and stumbling blindly down the ravine alongside the stream, I came at last to a deep pool, fed by a number of little rivulets, and at once plunged in. I swam away from the shore and surfaced, for a moment having thwarted the deadly butterflies. Men came bursting through the underbrush, following my example, and soon the pool had filled with struggling swamp men. We dived and dived again, remaining under water for as long as our lungs would allow, until finally the butterflies departed back up the ravine. As we climbed wearily out of the icy waters, we knew that we had lost several of our number. None of us dared to return to see if the butterflies were feeding off their luckless victims. Karl emerged from the water shivering, his hair masking his face like streaming cloth. We nodded grimly at one another.

I urged the remainder of our company on so that we could quickly leave the vicinity of these winged devils, and soon we had stumbled down to reach the valley bottom and were able to look up at the towering, sheer walls of a cliff face opposite. Vegetation here was sparse and stunted. We wound our way round the base of the foreboding outcrop and kept every sense alert for signs of further attack. The jungle had fallen silent as though each of its atoms strained to hear and watch us moving, ready to betray us to their brooding master.

We found a dry gully that led round the sheer walls like a knifed pathway on to the south. Pausing to take fresh supplies, we recovered something of our shattered wits and I endeavored to raise the spirits of my men. But a resigned gloom had slipped over them like a dark mantle, and I found Karl to be the only bright company. He was able to converse with me and told me something of his life in the jungle. We went on, but before long I raised an arm and signaled for absolute silence. My acute ears had picked up a sound down one of the tributary gullys that led from the valley which we now followed. Drumming, or something akin to it. But, no—I remembered the thunder of hooves that I had first been haunted by in Chalremor's tower on Zurjah and knew this for a similar sound.

"Are there horses here in the jungle?" I whispered to Karl, waving at the terrain. His eyes flickered from tree to tree and along the ridges on either side of us. He did not understand what I meant by horses, so I showed him a mental image. He nodded, but he was too frightened by the sound of hooves to comment.

And then I saw it, galloping from the gully, a thoroughbred with tossing mane and sleek black hide. Its eyes seemed to look momentarily into mine as it thundered nearer, and I knew that this was no engine of my destruction, for there was no horse that I could not reach out to and tame. The proud stallion stopped, a cloud of dust rising up around it, and it bucked wildly, raising its hooves, neighing and voicing its unbridled freedom. It stood defiantly watching us, as though challenging us all to pass it. I had rarely seen such a fierce, magnificent beast. With this I could spur into the heart of Vorta's citadel and ride him down to dust!

Slowly I walked towards the steed, still thinking of the sapient Chalremor, whom many had scorned with the name sorcerer, and the thought of his words that horses would mark my passage in life spurred me. I lifted my fingers and felt at my neck for the golden medallion with the winged horse emblem, but then remembered that it had been destroyed in my duel with Ravas Tarak on the Sea of Death. I would miss its shielding magic, but here was a horse of flesh and blood that would serve me amply.

The horse made no move, standing stiff as beaten bronze, eyes ablaze. I came within feet of it, my men holding back in barely concealed terror. I looked at those eyes as I reached out to touch the flowing mane. And slowly, as though I woke from a drugged sleep, understanding dawned. I recoiled! Something deep within those twin orbs of feral fire blazed with an alien light—a sinister, deceit-filled light that reflected the hateful visage of Daras Vorta himself. I knew at once that this was an illusion and that I had let slip my guard at seeing so familiar and desirable an object as a horse. Vorta had lost none of his cunning.

I backed away, my star lance ready for any attack, and the horse dissolved to become a sickly plant with leaves of tacky gum, coated and smeared with slime, ready to trap and snatch anything that as much as touched it, as I would have done a second later. I felt a chilling laugh echo in some distant corridor of my brain as Vorta must have seen my brush with death. As I returned to the horrified men, I turned contemptuously from the quivering plant of doom and pointed on down the valley.

"We must keep moving," I told them all.

Karl came to me, worry burned into his features. "What was it?"

"Gast cannot hope to protect us from all evil forces in the jungle. Evil ones were at work, but their danger is past." Yet I guessed that Vorta knew of my coming and that he would be ever-vigilant from now on, whatever distant Gast did to help us.

"Karl, do you know anything of the horses?"

He reflected on the image I had cast earlier, then spoke. "They are wild and untamed beasts. We have nothing to do with them. They would trample us if we went near. They live further south. Some of the Death Watch may herd them."

I nodded and waved him on. If there were true horses here, I would attempt to find one to suit my needs. My affinity for the creatures would win them over, I felt certain. I ran a finger through the last of the white herb stains that the water had not cleansed away. My shielded mind was already thinking ahead to the time when I must at last confront Vorta in his lair.

CHAPTER XII
Return of the Pale Rider

Through the steep-sided ravines we threaded like ants, until the sun began to sink, bathing the tops of the mesas around us in distant, rusted gold. What vegetation there was between the rearing rock walls rustled in the stealing dark. I sensed the agitation of the men who followed me, and knew that soon we would be in the territories of the Death Watch. I had had much time to contemplate and evaluate my situation, and now that the end of the chase drew nearer, my mind was calmer and less impulsive. At first I had sped from Zurjah in violent, heated pursuit of Vorta, my whole being quivering with hatred, driven on blindly like an automaton, but now that so much time had gone by without my being able to quench the volcano of hate within me, I had cooled down a little and had come to rationalize more carefully. I saw now that I had plummeted myself into a very dubious revenge, being in such a precarious situation as I was. Despite my yet smoldering loathing of Vorta and my determination to bring him to justice, I found myself weighing the odds against me and they were far from favorable. Chalremor had long since warned me of my temper and impetuousness—now I must ride the consequences. However, I was neither morbid nor downhearted. I felt the glowing determination that had been with me from the start, although I had to be ever-watchful and awake to the numerous pitfalls with which Vorta would sew these lands. But it would be Vorta whose nerve would be put to the test now. Our roles were reversing; I had become the calm, patient Nemesis, while he had become the one to act impulsively and out of desperation.

We filed up between two rock outcrops and beyond them saw a small, crater-like valley, ringed by a jagged edge of rock and filled with a weaving sea of dark vegetation. On the far side of this valley there rose up in the distance another mesa, much larger than any of the others we had seen, its top eroded flat like a gigantic table. Karl pointed at the huge geological formation, then quickly dropped his hand as though it might be singed.

"The evil places," he said, face wrought with fear. I felt the mental abhorrence among the men as their eyes caught sight of the eerie mesa. Somewhere there I would find Vorta, hidden away in his final place of refuge.

"We'll camp down in the valley," I told the men, and they shuddered as though a cold wind were blowing from down among the strange blossoms. The men's resolution was quickly fading. When we had set out from their village, Gast and I had been able to instill into them a sense of purpose and a will to defeat the evil that constantly beset them and penned them to their dismal part of the jungle, but now that strength was waning like water seeping away underground. Perhaps action of some kind would restore their faith.

The trees in the valley were equally as weird as the hybrids we had passed on our journey. These were huge, thick-bolled and tall as cliff faces, their foliage so tangled and interlocked that the green canopy overhead seemed to be one huge blossom, while the trunks had the appearance of massive roots, burrowing into the thick, black loam. It was cold and dark, but we found a clearing and set up a number of sentries. Night was falling and we settled back to snatch what restless sleep we could take in these grim surroundings.

For my part, I was still unable to sleep properly. I twisted uncomfortably among the curled hides and skins that served to keep me warm and between the waking moments of troubled half-sleep I seemed to hear again the distant thudding of hooves. I shook myself awake and glowered out at the enormous trees that obscured the sky, remembering some of the dreams that had haunted my childhood and my youth, and of how the Horsemen had ridden through them like reapers in the cornfield of life. If Vorta sought to plague me with his trickery, I would not be fooled.

Yet the sounds that had wakened me came from the earth, as though muffled, and I bent down and put my ear to the ground. It was no illusion this time. The sound of hooves was unmistakable; there were horses somewhere close at hand! Gast and Karl had both said they existed in these parts. I rose quietly and threaded my way through the sleeping figures around me. Some stirred and moved over in their sleep, but no one hailed me or questioned my passage.

As I reached the edge of the clearing and the last of the tall trees rose majestically into the darkness, I heard the rustle and snap of old roots and undergrowth. I spun round to see Karl facing me, beaming with an expression that was half guilt, half amusement. I nodded and smiled in silence, then passed through the last of the sentries I had set up as a cordon. We went stealthily through the gloom and I sensed Karl's growing fear. Among the tangled roots and heaps of forest debris we went, and Karl saw terror in each dark hole and concealed opening.

"The Death Watch lair in such places," he whispered, pointing to the base of a tree, which was a matted complex of fibers and roots. Many of the holes between the gnarled growths could have been tunnels, widened by the passage of animals or other denizens of this wild region.

"Then we will go silently," I replied. "There are horses near, and I need one."

Karl nodded dumbly, and with only the star lance glow to guide us, we wound through the trees, coming to a slope which led up to a rock outcrop. The forest floor beyond slipped gently away, devoid of trees, giving way to grass banks that brooded silently, and down among the thickets and clumps of low, stunted bush in the distance, I made out restless shapes.

"There!" I whispered, and Karl tilted his nose upwards, sniffing and nodding uncertainly. He showed no deep fear of the horses, but it was evident that they meant little more to him than the other creatures of the jungle.

"What do you want with them?" he grunted.

"We must capture as many as we can."

"*Capture* them?" he echoed, aghast. He bent over in the darkness, his eyes squinting to see the shapes below.

"Yes. You have told me there will be many of the Death Watch in the evil places. If so, we will need anything that will strengthen our assault. These horses will help us to outwit our enemies."

The prospect of taking horses and trying to teach the swamp men some rudiments of riding was a daunting one, but I had to clutch at any straw that could bolster my attack on Vorta. How I would bring my ragged followers to terms with this new element I would fathom once I had caught the horses I needed. There seemed to be a large herd of them. I only hoped they were not too wild and were less hostile than their environment.

"Keep close to me," I told Karl as I doubled up and slipped over the rocks and down the slope beyond. Karl, shadowing me, kept glancing back over his shoulder, almost bumping into me a dozen times as we carefully approached the horses. Heads rose among the herd as the beasts sensed our movement in the grasses, but for the moment they were still. I began to think that our chances of capturing a few of the horses were excellent until Karl jerked up stiffly behind me, his hand gesturing wildly at the lip of the slope from which we had descended. There, near the rocks over which we had clambered, was a fissure, and from it now emerged a crouching shape, its eyes gleaming in the light of my star lance.

"Death Watch!" cried Karl, shuffling back against me as a number of them came into view. I raised the lance like a torch and tried to scan them, but the shadows obscured the overall picture, warping my impression of them. They were as large as a man, with long, simian arms and their flesh seemed totally devoid of hair, pale and bare, hanging in folds as though decaying and sloughing away. I sensed the rank odor of their repugnant bodies and heard the primitive grunts and snarls that they emitted like wild beasts. From up on the ridge, a number of them blended with the outline of trees, their contorted arms and bow legs giving them a sinister silhouette.

Their apparent leader snarled, baring slavering fangs and spitting saliva, and he lunged down the slope like a bull ape, his ugly fellows at his heels like a wolf pack hungry for the kill. Karl shuddered and put me between him and the oncoming horrors, and I swung the star lance, ready to cut as many of them down as I could. Six of the brutes came leaping at me, more beast than man. I could see them closely now; they had pale, mottled skin, blotched and sickly as though scorched by acid or fire, and a curved bone comb that swept back over their thick necks and on to their broad backs. Their eyes were terrible, like round, milky orbs, staring widely and seemingly blindly, used to darkness and subterranean lairs, and smarting at the proximity of the glowing star lance. Creatures of night, they hunted by what little power of the mind they had, their raking talons and gleaming fangs drawing closer.

I stepped forward to meet the furious onslaught of the first and swept the star lance into the blotched flesh, burning and cleaving a passage to the foul creature's vitals. It screamed out with a horrifying yelp of bestial rage and agony before crumpling into the grass. Two of its revolting fellows fell with it as I brought the deadly lance slashing into their thick skulls, sizzling the brains that gushed forth as I smote madly. Karl cried out in terror as the last of them tried to hurl themselves upon me, but I was far too fast for their clumsy movements, and the star lance's fire burned them, filling the air with the sickly stench of roasted flesh and charred bone. Karl kicked at the twitching corpses, then banged his crude club into them, assuring himself that they would do us no more harm.

Beyond the rim of the surrounding forest I could see more shapes rising up from their nocturnal burrows as though the ground were disgorging a legion of dead from their graves.

"There are too many!" I called in frustration to Karl as he finished his grisly work with the fallen. I whirled and grabbed his arm. "Quickly! We will be ripped to pieces if we don't act now! Make for the horses! Come, do as I say!"

Fearfully he ran alongside me, while up on the rim of the valley bowl the ghastly Death Watch began shambling forward like aroused anthropoids, their white eyes glaring as though they could see as well as any man. Snarls and roars came from above, and the horses began whinnying nervously. I thought of using the flame from the lance, but there would be no way to recharge it at night, and I was loath to lose its power unless in an extreme emergency.

Karl and I got close to the horses, who were frightened by our hurried advanced, and at once they began to scatter. The shape of the valley bowl and the cluster of thick scrub at its far end meant that they could not avoid us completely, and several even rushed headlong at us, lips drawn back over frothing mouths in a rictus of terror. I dropped to my knees, dragging Karl down with me, and I held aloft the lance, praying that it would divert the stampeding hooves that came too near. As I had suspected, the horses were unfamiliar with fire, and new terror reflected in their eyes as they bolted away from the light source, passing on either side of us.

I struggled up and ran deeper into the sparse vegetation beyond the horses. The Death Watch were still pursuing us, coming over the lip of the valley in increasing numbers, but most of them lay directly in the path of the wild horses, who were galloping up into the jungle above. There seemed to be a multitude of the horrors from beneath the earth, and I knew that Karl and I would have to find a way past them and back to our companions if we were to avoid them and a grim death, carved apart by their talons. Karl's mind seethed with terror, but I drew one fact from it to the surface: there had rarely been so many of the Death Watch seen together at one time. It could only mean that Vorta had a hand in this, calling up the multitude.

As the horses continued uphill into the first waves of the Death Watch, they neighed fiercely and rode down the stumbling creatures, who seemed to be ignoring them. The horses kicked them aside with flaying hooves and bit at any who came too close. The noise was terrible as the wild charge cut down scores of the lumbering, clumsy brutes from underground. There were still a good many horses in the valley, and I saw in them a possible way of besting the milling Death Watch who were still bent on pursuing us. I began setting fire to the underbrush, working my way to the end of the valley with the intention of rounding up all the remaining horses and driving them out into the jungle. They were rearing and neighing frantically, unsure of themselves and of all the frightful shrieks and howls.

Karl's mind emanated a constant stream of terror-filled images, and I could see from his desperate whirling about that he was little better adapted to this situation than the animals around him. In that wild moment I felt a wave of compassion for the man, who had been dragged into this perilous pass by my own selfish needs. I tried to soothe his mind, but everything was happening at breakneck speed. Gradually I sent fire to clutch at the extreme edges of the valley, and the last of the horses made ready to race away up the slopes. I sheathed my star lance as the oncoming Death Watch were battered aside by the impact of the horseflesh.

There was one last act to perform if the escape was to be effected. I watched the horse that I had singled out earlier, a young stallion with a dark, smooth coat who seemed totally bewildered by the fire and the panic among his fellows. He left his own dash to freedom until the last possible moment, and as he crashed by, I sprinted for him, grabbed at his thick mane and swung myself up on to his rippling back. I expected a difficult ride and indeed, it was like being astride a whirlwind as the magnificent horse attempted to fling me from its heaving shoulders. It had boundless energy, but I was determined to harness it. I had mastered some defiant horses before, and now called upon all the remembered knowledge of happier days as I strove to win the spirit of the black stallion. All the time I spoke to the prancing, bucking beast, my hands tangled in its thick mane, my legs locked about its lathered trunk. It leapt every way and tried every trick to throw me, but soon my calmness and its own fear of the fire got the better of it.

Slowly I brought its tempestuous nature under control and it ceased its wild bucking and kicking and began to realize that I would not be dislodged. Still speaking reassuringly to it, I wheeled the horse and trotted it toward the petrified Karl. He cringed as though Shaitan himself had come for him, but he had to straighten up and run towards me anyway as the first of the Death Watch had broken through the fleeing horses and were bearing down upon us again. Everything happened at lightning speed, and I acted from sheer instinct.

"Karl! Don't be afraid!" I shouted to him, but he began to run blindly away. I spurred the stallion forward, bent across its shoulder and my arm swooped down for the fleeing man. I grabbed him and heard a yelp of terror that might have come from a whipped cur, but presently I somehow swung the struggling figure up with me, my balance almost failing me. The stallion gave a tremendous surge and leapt forward so that we were almost both thrown to the ground, but I clung tenaciously to its mane and managed to regain control.

By now the Death Watch were upon us, those that had not been trampled to bloody ruin. Karl gripped the horse and shivered uncontrollably. I urged it forward, and its hooves came up and smashed into two skulls, drenching others of the Death Watch in brains and gore as the black stallion crashed through their disorganized ranks as though they were made of straw. Still they seemed to know no fear. I kicked out at them, their clawed hands ripping for us as we passed, as though they were being goaded by something far more powerful than their own puny wills. Vorta must be driving and pushing them with his demented mental powers. I smiled grimly in the sweat of battle, for the Death Watch assault had the stink of desperation in it.

Up the valley sides we raced, sweat coating the three of us as I drew and swung the star lance down at the last lines of the groping Death Watch. We left a bloody trail behind us, and many of the Death Watch lumbered on into the fires like senile old men, devoid of senses. Through the silent trees we plunged, the stallion's great heart pumping like a generator. Karl gave a low moan, his head buried in the mane of tangled black hair, but I patted him like a child. The worst of it was over, for the Death Watch were not giving further pursuit. We left them to lick their wounds and crawl back into their dark lairs.

At length we paused in our breakneck flight as we came to my men's camp. My heart sank as I saw it, for other Death Watch had been here, and the many had not fared any too well. There were still a few pockets of resistance giving fight, but all around the clearing lay the dead and the dying, and many of the mangled bodies of the slain were being dragged away to subterranean labyrinths by the Death Watch who had barely noticed my arrival. The worst of the fighting was over, but I wasted no time in attacking the Death Watch still here.

I raced at the nearest party of them. Some fled back to the root tunnels that were their dirty homes, while others flung themselves at me in deranged fury. Round and round the clearing I goaded my charger, hacking and kicking at the uncouth shapes, while the last of my followers fought tigerishly for their lives. Screams blended with the roar of the half-men, while out in the jungle there were the snarls of other creatures, maddened by the stench of blood and battle.

At last it was over and the remaining Death Watch slunk off into their filthy passageways of earth. I swung down from off the stallion and made a quick inspection of all those still alive, but there were pitifully few of them left. I called the last of them to me and they responded wearily, coming out of the thick gloom, their faces pale and drawn.

Karl, surprisingly, was holding gently on to the stallion, and he led it over to me slowly, running his leathery hand over its nozzle in a new-found and wondering affection.

"The Death Watch will return before dawn," muttered one of the wounded men, wiping blood from the talon marks across his chest.

I nodded. It was pointless my using these men to aid my own cause further. They would all die if I continued to urge them on.

"You must go back to your villages. The jungle here is full of the Death Watch. You will march to your deaths if you go on with me. I see that now. You cannot hope to survive the wrath of Daras Vorta. It is for me to stand against him. I release you from your service. Go back."

There were no arguments, no cries of determination to stay with me, and I had expected none. It seemed that I had fulfilled my old role of Pale Horseman and brought death to these people as surely as though I had wielded the tool of their destruction myself.

"I will ride on alone," I ended.

Only Karl disputed my decision. He thrust himself forward defiantly.

"Galad, we cannot desert you now. You told us that we must fight for our freedom! Fear rattles us like a high wind, but we must no longer cower away in the dark like the Death Watch below us. You have shown us that they can be beaten! We must fight!"

For Karl it had been an unusually long and impassioned speech, and I gripped his shoulder in silent thanks, though I could see that the others were beaten men.

"Fight to defend your homes," I told the apprehensive men around me. "I will not force you to come to the evil places. Those that wish to follow me may. The rest of you, go back to Gast without dishonor. You are as sand grains before a tide. Nothing can be gained now by your dying."

Karl looked at the despondent band and read defeat in their silent faces.

"I will come with you!" he avowed fiercely, expecting others to second him, but none did. Their eyes remained downcast.

"Let them go back to their homes," I said without bitterness. "I have my horse and a star lance. Vorta has tried many times before now to destroy me. I am still alive. Only when he is dead shall I rest. This conflict is between the two of us."

Slowly the men began picking up weapons that had fallen in the skirmish and the last of their scant provisions. They huddled together in silence, and then, like smoke blowing idly away, began to move back the way we had come, melting into the shadows, their combined minds a mixture of relief and sorrow.

Karl brought the stallion forward, his thick jaw jutting proudly as he met my gaze. I grinned and slapped the stallion's flanks.

"So you will take me the remaining distance, Karl?"

"My heart bulges with terror, but I have not come this far to shrink away. If the evil ones are not stopped now, they never will be."

"Do not think harshly of your people. Vorta calls upon abominable powers to serve his foul ends. There is no limit to the degradation he can heap upon this world. If you have doubts about going on—"

"None," he said emphatically. I felt a pang of guilt, for there had been others like him who had followed me, and many of them ended in the cold embrace of death.

"Very well," I sighed.

"Shall we seek out Daras Vorta now, or do you wish to sleep for a while? I will watch over you."

"No need. We will go on, before the Death Watch's thirst for blood rouses them anew. But first, can you find me the mixture of herbs with which you smeared me after my fight with the thing in the swamp?"

I detected his puzzlement, but then he nodded, looking about him at the vegetation.

"With ease."

"Then do so. Prepare as much of the white paste as you can. It will not be for me, though I have cuts a-plenty to wipe clean. It is for the stallion."

Karl looked totally baffled.

"I have my reasons. I wish to change him from a night-black horse into a pale one."

"But a black horse...it will not be easily seen in this darkness."

"The Death Watch see with their minds. I wish to be seen. I wish our enemies to see the pale horse of Death riding for them. Prepare the mixture and I will explain. When it is done and the horse is transformed, we will be ready for the last stage of our journey."

"I will be ready long before the dawn! I long to ride down the evil that haunts the jungle!"

"Even if it means our death?"

He scowled, but his face cracked in a new smile. "Yes! It will be a small sacrifice to make."

With that he darted off, leaving me with the horse. I watched Karl seeking out and plucking herbs, keeping an eye on the jungle to see that he was not set upon. The trees were like solemn sentinels, breathing and listening, conveying my every move back to the monster at the heart of these godless lands.

CHAPTER XIII
Lair of the Death Watch

Karl clung to me as I raced the now pale stallion through the trees that crowded in like ebony walls, the brush crackling and parting beneath the flying hooves. Within the pitch darkness of the dismal forest we heard the regathering of the Death Watch as they shambled forth from their filthy hiding places deep within the earth.

We burst out of the tree bolls and rode on past the valley in which I had begun the stampede with fire. The brief brushfire had burned itself out and there was nothing left but scorched undergrowth and only the stiff, blackened stumps remained as we rode among the ashes. Wisps of smoke clung to us and we reached the end of the valley.

Beyond it we came to a defile and I guided the stallion through it cautiously, expecting an attack from the surrounding crags at any moment, but none came. At last I could look out from the rugged hills. There before us was an eroded plateau that rose from the surrounding lands like an outcrop seared and gouged by the hands of a giant. It was the huge mesa we had seen from afar. Darkness threaded among its time-eaten corridors of stone, and gloom hung its haunted buttresses as though daylight never dared seep within its morbid domain. The naked rock seemed to be alive, crouched and quiescent, anxious to embrace us in its mantle of cold shadows.

"The evil places are fast within that plateau," said Karl's nervous voice in my ear. I stroked the mane of the stallion as it sniffed at the air uncertainly, smelling the polution that permeated it. Gently I nudged him on down the ravine. His coat was smeared with white, herbal juices, giving him an eerie presence.

"The way within is defined by a single pass," Karl went on, pointing at a black crevice that looked from here like a monstrous sword stroke cut deep into the bare rock of the plateau walls, a ragged, forbidding gash.

"Is there no other way in?" I asked him. This pass would be narrow and easily defended and our chances of using surprise within it were minimal.

"Not unless our charger can grow wings. Only the vultures enter the evil places by routes other than the pass yonder."

I looked around but could see no other way up the sheer walls.

"Very well. Be ready to fight if we are set upon. There is still time before dawn breaks, though there will be precious little light in that place of nightmare."

We left the defile we were in and crossed a sooty waste that led to the very base of the huge plateau. I looked up at its foreboding ramparts, their brows knitted like the scowl of an enormous demon. Like a huge castle of titans that had never been taken, it jutted up defiantly, mocking our minute figures. A faint gust of wind whipped up the dirt and dust about the stallion's feet, and I thought that I caught the snickering tones of laughter whispering back at me from the rock walls. Vorta would be waiting for me now, no longer determined to keep me at bay; there was no need, for the odds would be heaped up in his favor. I knew that this last assault was a libation to death itself, but there was nothing left for me in the life I could still go back to by fleeing.

"Why do you not enter the pass?" grunted Karl, for I was allowing the stallion to circle, watching the towering cliffs.

"Karl, you have served me faithfully, but it would be foolhardy for you to come with me now. Beyond the pass, death lies in wait for me. Nothing else. You need not cast aside your own life for me. Take the horse and ride back..."

Yet somehow I knew that his fate was wound up with my own, and that he would be with me to the end. I shuddered at the thought, for I saw small hope for me, and none for him.

"Perhaps I would return, Galad, for I feel the fingers of terror wrapped about my innards when I look into the black tunnel there, but it is too late for me to go back. See!"

He motioned over his shoulder and I gasped. Behind us, filling the defiles and canyons of the escarpment from which we had emerged, there now came veritable legions of the Death Watch, scurrying forward like an army of ghouls seeking their food. Up on the nearest crags there were other half seen shapes watching us, and from a pile of shattered boulders nearby a lone member of the Death Watch stumbled into view. Its huge eyes, white and empty as the stone around us, fixed myopically upon me as though looking into my soul.

"Sarian!"

The deep sound hissed from between its drooling, misshapen lips as it staggered out into the open like a dead man imbued with life. I watched the hideous face, transfixed by the sound of my name so awkwardly spoken. My horse shied, but I kept it still.

"Sarian! You know me! You have pursued me for too long," came the awful voice, guttural and hoarse as though the creature's larynx was unused to human speech. And I knew why instantly, for the voice, disguised and distorted as it was by the low, growling tone, was that of Vorta himself. From his distant lair he was using this brute as a vessel for his own message of hate.

432

"Show yourself!" I cried angrily, my voice ringing back of the weather-chiselled rocks.

"Not yet," growled the odious voice as the creature shuffled closer. "You have almost stumbled upon my citadel. But I welcome your coming. Yes, I welcome it! As a spider welcomes the arrival of a fly before digesting it! A place has been prepared for you, Sarian—beside the slender form of your precious lover!"

"Taria!"

"Indeed. She lives yet. So, be swift, Sarian. My patience runs away like sand. You have thwarted my desires for too long. Once, in my slave city of Karkesh, you set your curs yapping at my gates and tore down my armies before I could complete the rituals I had begun in summoning Shaitan to aid me. This time it is far too late to save yourself or your pitiful world. Come to me and see the raising of the most powerful deity of them all, and see the beginning of his eternal rule! Come swiftly, little Sarian. Bring your dwarfish fellow with you. We are all eager for your souls. Come, try your powers against me and watch how I suck them up and spit them back into your face!"

I screamed a curse and pointed the star lance at the contorted face of his messenger, releasing a stream of fire which showered him and set him to blazing like a torch. But as he fell to his molten death, the canyons rang to the laughter of Daras Vorta, as though thunder rolled overhead from some netherworld of madness. I wasted no more time in reflection and urged the stallion into a gallop. The black walls of the pass enveloped us and we rode hard through the scree, leaving the Death Watch legions well behind. I knew, though, they would be following, closing off our retreat.

Karl was trembling in terror at my back, but my anger and bitterness had bubbled and welled up anew, filling me with all the old recklessness and blind determination to destroy Vorta. Madly I kicked the frightened stallion through the often tortuous winding of the pass, holding high the star lance for a semblance of guidance in this remotest of places. A fall among the broken rocks and tumbled boulders of ages may well have finished us both, but I had not come this far for such a death.

A draught of bitterly cold air washed over us as we at long last burst out from the confines of the pass and there before us was the final goal. It was the incredible ruins of a long forgotten city, so old and neglected that its scattered ruins were fallen and decayed almost to their foundations. Piles of stone blocks had crumbled, while sporadic heaps of what had once been pylons thrust lopsidedly up at the slate skies. Millennia of dust and sand had drifted over the whole city like the coverlet made by a shroud, time's mildewed web, and nothing stirred. Even the breeze and the desert wind had long since shunned the place as though it was from here that the blasphemous wars of so long ago had been precipitated. It was like looking through a time haze at some other world, a world long dead and rotted into atoms that now blew like dust through space.

"Here lies the heart of the old empire of Trucia," Karl told me, mesmerized by the silent remains.

"Yes, forgotten for countless centuries. How many other places must there be like this?" I said, speaking aloud my dark thoughts.

"Nothing has lived there for years," said Karl, but his words slipped over me. Instead of further speculating, I urged the horse forward once more and the last of the scree passed beneath the stallion's hooves.

"There is life of a kind here now," I said. Then we were riding down what had once been a boulevard, our eyes watching the sprawling ruins on either side, which stretched as far back as could be seen. The sky above was streaked with violet and the horizon was ringed with a band of white as the sun prepared to slide up over the rim of the world. Not a skirl of wind, not a trickle of falling dust moved as we went down that history-laden street. Something in the atmosphere of the devastation around me told me that Vorta was close. I could not probe his mind nor sense his thoughts, but I felt him listening to every footfall, as though the hoof beats of the stallion echoed down the tomb-like alleys of stone and rang back loudly to him in his lair. We rode on for a long time, passing row after row of collapsed temples, pylons, warehouses, and eventually we reached the inner heart of the city. Here stood a sprawling hill, and up on its crest stood a peculiar edifice that had barely lasted the acid erosion of time.

"Such a strange edifice," muttered Karl, looking straight at the anachronistic building that had somehow defied time for millennia, its garishly sculpted spires jutting up unbroken at the dawn. When it had been built, eons since, it had been carved and designed in the most intricate and fantastic of ways, but erosion had enhanced the

434

architectural whims of the sculptors and had added bizarre and macabre effects of its own, so that now the warped stonework took on a sinister, even maniacal aspect.

"A cathedral built to gods that have long since been forgotten," I replied to Karl, surprised to see it in such apparently unimpaired condition. Its gargoyles and crenels were black and etched with age, but were unbroken as though the hands of those same eon-old gods had stayed the collapse of the solitary building.

"You have heard of this place?" asked Karl, appalled.

"No, but I was taught years ago about the old religions, or shared such poor knowledge of them that survives. This is a cathedral, although I have seen modern equivalents that would shame it."

"How is it that this place yet stands, while all the city has returned to sand?"

"I cannot answer that."

"And are the evil ones worshiped here?"

I frowned at the dismal building, etched against the pre-dawn sky. "History changes. Once a place like this would have been a harbor against evil. But no more. It seems as though its very stones have altered to lend it an air of wickedness. Daras Vorta is in there. His black powers will have tainted any goodness that clung to the foundations, believe me."

We approached the hill with caution, and I drew the star lance, ready to burn my way through any doors that might be sealed to me. As we went through the pale grasses, we saw many stones and boulders half concealed therein, etched with runes or carved with unusual shapes or script. I wondered about them, for the hill seemed to be sewn with them. Something about them was familiar, but the memory was so deep-rooted that I could not bring it to the surface.

We came upon a stone cross, its base lost in roots and tangled grasses, and the realization came to me that these were old graves. Karl and I were passing over a hill of the ancient dead, though their bones would long since have decomposed and become one with the earth. I said nothing to him, for fear flooded his veins.

From behind the stone cross a grinning figure appeared, its face a rictus of glee. The stallion reared up in terror, and before I could check its wild plunge forward, it surged on up the hill. It had been one of the Death Watch that had surprised us and I knew there would be more about us. As we dashed on, the ground gave way beneath the stallion's front legs and I was flung headlong into the damp grass. I was up, shrugging away the pain of a bruised arm as the horse regained its balance. Both Karl and the horse appeared unhurt, and I turned to see the grim figure coming towards us, a scarecrow shape in the early light. It was unlike any of the others of its kind, for it was robed and had a purpose about it that chilled me.

I yelled for Karl to get back and made for the figure, but as I stepped forward, the earth folded up beneath my feet like thin film of dried mud and I felt myself sucked down into the black earth of a pit. As I tumbled into that gloomy womb, the last sound that I heard was the mingled laughter of the shambler above and the groan of horror from Karl. Dirt and earth fell with me and I felt myself buffeted briefly against solid walls, until I thumped down to the base of the hole, the wind punched out of my body.

Showers of loosened earth cascaded down, and I dragged myself aside, avoiding the black deluge. At first, coughing and staggering, I thought I had fallen into some rotting mausoleum, but as my eyes became accustomed to the dim light here, I surmised that I was in a sepulchral maze that connected numerous subterranean galleries, though for what purpose I could scarcely guess. Only the thinnest shaft of light penetrated the ruptured earth ceiling above, and I could see from the heap of fallen earth and stone that there would be no way to climb back. I peered around for the star lance, but it had either fallen from my hand up on the surface, or was buried beneath the earth fall. I would have to go on and face Vorta without it.

I wiped filth from my face and pushed on through the root-laced walls, until at length I came to a broad passageway. Its uneven surface had not been walked for many years, perhaps centuries, but it seemed to lead on towards the foundations of the cathedral. Cobwebs hung the stone pillars that reinforced the roof of this grim place, stretching like white curtains across my path. I ripped them aside, heedless of the scuttling shapes that gathered around the fringes of decay. My feet kicked at layers of dust that were as deep as sand upon a beach.

Presently I was nonplussed to see a light far ahead—a light that wavered and shivered like a night creature flitting aimlessly in a wind. By its guttering glare I could see that the ceiling had become higher and that a forest of stone columns supported it. I was in an intricate series of catacombs, nearing the cathedral cellars. I came up to the light, which was a single cresset thrust into an iron holder in one of the columns, and I wondered at its purpose and who had placed it here.

Nonetheless I took it and looked around me at the fantastic runes carved into the stonework of the columns. They must have been older than the first Zurjahns, perhaps even older than the wars that had sent men away from this world to the neighboring planets. I could understand little of the messages in the rune work, but the paintings depicted men in strange and unfamiliar clothing and showed machines unlike any known to men of my time.

I wandered on through the seemingly endless rows of pillars, and around me now could see stone slabs and what could only be the sarcophagi of the long dead. Kings and nobles of this once thriving city, perhaps, but all rendered to nothing by time. Brushing dust from one, I saw the ancient writing, and the carved image of a face, serene in sleep, but then I paused in my discoveries, for my ears had acutely picked up the first sounds I had heard since falling into the earth. Out there in the pressing darkness I sensed movement. It was as though the pillars of stone were breathing and coming to life, for shadows moved within the shadows of the catacombs, and eddies of dust stirred as feet began an almost imperceptible movement. I held high the firebrand, scattering darkness like a bat cloud, but the movement had been too far out in the void to be discerned.

A weird humming had begun, emanating from all directions in a long, drawn-out throb, so that I felt myself encircled by a complete, living organism just as I had been in the jungle, as though the earth moved like a huge beast, closing its walls in upon me like some grotesque plant. I fought down the urge to scream or flee uselessly and set my back to the old slabs of flaking rock behind me. As I listened, calming my fears, the droning hum became a chant, the blended sound of hundreds of deep voices, and the shadows beyond the pillars seemed to pulse, as though an army had gathered there. I found myself fighting against the belief that Vorta had called up the massed dead of the hill and set them upon me. A reeking stench of decomposition permeated the air, and the darkness throbbed to the hellish wail of the chant.

This was no illusion, this amassing of shrouded figures. I would not believe that Vorta's odious powers could extent to calling up the dead, even as an image in my mind, but the chanting grew louder as though the uniform voice of a monstrous pit-dweller from gulfs beyond wildest imagination. Soon faces appeared among the tombs. These were the inner acolytes of Vorta's degenerate faith—Death Watch who had barely raised themselves from the lowest levels of existence. They swayed as they moved in upon me, their bodies wrapped in cerement-like robes, their huge, sightless eyes laced with red veins and gleaming in the flickering glow of the torch.

I snapped out of their hypnotic clutches and looked to see if they had left me any avenue of escape. There was one path through the pillars where they did not seem to be in evidence, and without pausing to think, I ran for it. I could not hope to fight so many of them off, not without the star lance. As I heard my footsteps ringing back at me and the swelling of the chant from behind, I realized that I had not chosen this path myself, but it had been the Death Watch who had guided me to it. I stopped and swung about, my face dripping sweat on to the dusty stones of the floor. On either side the Death Watch closed in, forming a living aisle, while from behind me they also pressed, walking unhurriedly toward me, hands out as though in supplication. Their purpose was clear. They did not mean to kill me, not yet, but were leading me to a chosen place.

"Vorta!" I yelled at the low ceiling of black earth. "Show yourself! All the armies of Hell will not keep you from me now! Where are you cringing away? Let me set eyes on you for one solitary moment and I will settle all our differences! Vorta!"

My voice rang out in the catacombs, raised above the woeful, powerful din of the incessant chanting. At last I had the answer that I thought would never come. A low whisper drifted out of the charnel air, wrapping itself around the uncouth company like fog, its sound the rattle of a man speaking from beyond the grave.

"Be content, Sarian. I have not cheated you. Everything reaches the final stage of preparation. You have no need to come secretly to me. Rise up from the bowels of my citadel and come into the halls of worship. You will not be prevented."

I turned, looking for the source of the voice, but saw nothing and knew that Vorta would not be here. The Death Watch still moved purposefully towards me and I backed off down the aisle that they had formed. I saw the end of the pillared walk that they lined, and there was a flight of eroded and narrow stairs that must lead up into the cathedral itself. Without hesitation I ran for them, ignoring the swaying Death Watch, and as a last gesture of contempt I turned and flung the torch into the faces of the last of them, though it was a futile gesture.

As I quickly mounted the time-worn stairs, I forced down all the thoughts of the insanity of my cause. Alone as I was against Vorta's hordes, my chances were infinitely small. But I drove myself up the stairs, filled with hate, seeing before me the awful countenance of the Pale Rider, Death. Many were those who had died by my hand and by my workings, and now only a handful more need die to fulfill the needs of whatever gods watched over me. Those that had died must not be allowed to have done so in vain, and I must drive myself to the end, bitter as it might be.

Sounds and light above me alerted me and I went more slowly, not wishing to lose my head now. I could look up and see the end of the stairway and high, high up above its opening the crossing vaults and beams of the inner cathedral. I reached the top of the stairway and frowned at what I saw. Here was the last array of evil that I had ranged my powers against, and my heart pumped at what it beheld.

I was within the very heart of the cathedral, standing now in an aisle that led straight to a huge altar. Over the altar had been thrown a black cloth that fell to the incongruously carpeted floor on all sides, and behind this grim object was a golden seat, carved into the shapes of strange figures from a bygone, despicable mythology. On either side of this burned two huge candles, black as night, the smoke filtering up into the giddy heights of the cathedral dome. Looking around at the assembly, I felt the closing in of icy tendrils on my heart, for the hideous multitude outnumbered any preconceived estimations I had made.

The place was filled with the Death Watch, all decked out in funereal garb, and they lined the aisle where I stood in silent throngs, awaiting their signal. Yet they seemed to ignore me, watching the altar and the drapes by the empty throne. Chalices stood at the foot of the altar, and beside them were ornamental knives, smeared with a dark substance that could only be blood. I could smell the overpowering stench of incense, and somewhere in the smoke-obscured walls of the cathedral there burned tapers and braziers that clouded them in thick palls of gray. Looking up at the higher galleries of the immense building, I stifled a groan at the sub-human shapes that watched me from up there. Their shapes were hidden by

439

the filtering smoke, but I glimpsed the flash of red eyes and saw the leathery sweep of wings not meant to beat in earthly skies. What manner of hellish beings Vorta had set up around his shrine, I could not say, and I was thankful for the masking smoke. It was as though I had walked into a gruesome antechamber of Hell itself.

Dazed by the horrors around me, I walked forward, for there could be no retreat from this vile den. I stepped slowly towards the altar, as though going willingly to my own sacrifice, and as I did so, the thick drapes rustled, then flicked aside. Vorta's obese bulk came into view. He mounted the steps to the throne and flopped down like a landed sea-beast, his hideous eyes falling upon me, his thick lips twisted with evil humor. Every tortured memory that I had of him flew aside at the renewed sight of him now, bloated and swollen with gross living and unspeakable hedonism, the epitome of all that is vile and monstrous in Man.

"At last we meet," he breathed simply, his voice a gasp from the vaults of doom. Behind him towered a huge cross of solid gold, encrusted with gems of unsurpassed beauty and value. The symbol of the ancient religions thrust up over him like a pillar of faith—but the ancient religions had been religions of Light, not the evil of Shaitan. Something about that cross was wrong. Even though I was mesmerized by its glittering stones, I realized what it was.

It had been inverted.

CHAPTER XIV
Hell's Cathedral

The sight of the face that I loathed and despised above all others tempted me to rush the last remaining yards between us and grasp that obese neck in my bare hands, but somehow reason prevailed. If I were to destroy Daras Vorta, the conflict would have to be on a mental level. I stood before him and stared long and unflinchingly at him, but there was no tremor of fear in his corrupt features, only the sheer arrogance and certainty of his own victory.

"Galad Sarian," he said, his voice deep and sonorous, rolling across the cathedral as he savored the name he detested. His huge bulk was wrapped around with thick robes of black velvet, symbolic of the nightmare powers he served. His bloated fingers stroked his face, rich rubies gleaming in the candle light. I saw movement near his feet, and there were tiny beings there, watching me with sharp fascination, creatures of the jungle that obeyed his will like dogs.

"Yes. You have set many pitfalls for me, yet I hound you still, Vorta. You have sought to thrust countless deaths upon me, but I have laughed in the face of them all."

However my words rang emptily among the assembled multitude of the Death Watch and other beings. They began to murmur softly and deeply, beginning some forbidden incantation to the night walkers that they worshiped. The air coiled upon itself as their words reverberated.

"You are a fool, Sarian," snorted Vorta, his face a bestial mask of sadistic amusement. "I could have had you killed at any time. Look around you now! How many of my servants do you see? How many more are there out in the jungles that surround this plateau? You stand alone. How can you hope to pit yourself against me?"

"For all your minions, I have reached your altar of shame."

"Only by my will! The gulf that separates us yet may as well stretch from here to Zurjah, and you know that. You are harmless. You are less to me than the feasting worms in the graveyard around the cathedral. You think you have come here to see the last of my powers pushed back, but you are wrong. It is only the beginning! I will launch new powers that will spread from here like an irreversible plague. One day even Karkesh will be rebuilt. Zurjah will die, her peoples with her. Already I have delivered the death blow there, ending Dream Lord control. That of her people who come whining to Earth for shelter will find new masters. Ruling them all will be the divine Goat, Shaitan!"

At mention of the name, the Death Watch began to raise their chant so that the massive walls of the cathedral echoed and rang to the mournful sound, vibrating jarringly against my very soul.

"And you," snarled Vorta, flecks of spittle coating his thick, reddened lips, "will be the greatest of the sacrifices. Your soul will be the last link in the chain that draws Shaitan from his distant realms to unleash him on this plane of existence. For this I have spared you, puny mortal. You think I could not have destroyed you numerous times? You are a fool!"

His expression had twisted itself into a feral glare, and I read nothing but sheer insanity in his eyes. I controlled myself with difficulty, trying to shut out the terrible swell of the chanting.

"What of the girl, Vorta? What filthy scheme have you devised for her demise? Or have you already flung aside her frail form? If not, release her. Spare her, for you have me to work your worst upon," I said bitterly, hopelessly, my anger seeking an outlet.

"Ah," he aid, laughing evilly. His voice dropped to a derisive purr. "The Lady Taria. So your foolish heart still beats a little stronger at the thought of her? Well, she lives. I would not have her harmed until you were here. Any fate that I mete out to her will be conducted before your eyes, I promise you. Rest assured, her time is near. She is to be the most potent ingredient in my awakening of Shaitan. Even more important than your self."

I tried to see into his meaning, but in my confusion I could see nothing clearly. "What do you mean?"

"I am well versed in my arts. Millennia of rituals have taught me much about dealing with Shaitan. There is nothing more powerful in the exercise of summoning the dark gods than human blood. And there is no blood richer in significance and omnipotence than the blood of an unborn child, pure and untainted by life beyond the womb that bears it!"

"No!" I gasped, stepping forward, my eyes aflame with horror at his unthinkable words. But his will reached out and our minds locked so that I could not move. Sweat broke out on my brow. The conflict would soon begin.

"Yes, Sarian. Taria and her unborn infant await my pleasure in the steeple behind us. So you see, you will all play your part in the calling of Shaitan. And you begin to see why I allowed you to come to me. Once in Karkesh you interrupted my ceremonial offerings and forced me to flee as the city burned around me. Now you are as a leaf upon an ocean—the ocean of my will!"

"I will never bend to you!"

He laughed, a dry, mirthless sound that grated along my nerves as if on unpolished steel.

"Then fight. Test yourself!" he taunted me. "See if you can hold me back. He rose to his heavy feet and glared at me across that altar of ultimate sacrifice.

I jolted at the release of powers that he could summon from the depths of his will, but forced my own hate and anger to funnel my own will into a concentrated defense in order to oppose him. The duel that I had feared but longed for had begun in deadly earnest. Gradually the surroundings dimmed as though dark mist was encroaching and blotting out the gathered figures, the candles, the pillars of fluted stone—everything. Sounds of chanting swelled and then began to dampen as though being muffled by colossal paws, and all my senses slipped away. I found myself standing in a total void, with neither light nor sound to guide me. Somewhere opposite, as though from huge distances, I sensed the uncoiling serpents that were Vorta's mental exudations.

Balls of night darker than any interstellar void began crowding in around me, jostling like primordial scavengers from the bottom-most depths of the human psyche, anxious to envelop me and drain me of all sanity with their weaving, rolling touch of Hell. I rallied, causing a sphere of dim light to cling to me like a nimbus of pale fire. Gradually its intensity grew, and the dark shapes swept slowly back into the void, ever hovering, seeking a way past my radiance. Chalremor had aided me once in my struggle against a psychic attack from Vorta, but this time I would be completely alone. I mastered my will, driving all thoughts from me but the desire to force back the spheres. I began to gain the advantage.

Slowly, like the anemic dawn of Zurjah, wan and feeble, a gray haze swam up on the edge of my vision, revealing not the cathedral interior and its ululating acolytes, but a dismal plain of viscous filth. The stench was overwhelming, but I shut it out forcibly. I watched its surface writhing and heaving like molten mud, and then something rose up like a gargantuan hand and reached for me, dripping rivulets of foul putrescence. I countered with mental energy that seared the groping horror, and as it drew back into the endless sea of filth, more such amorphous shapes rose up and clawed at me.

I shuddered with effort but would not allow one shred of my sanity to desert me. In each succeeding attack I saw the will of Vorta, and I in turn fed on my endless well of hate. It was this that upheld my dogged defense. At last the horizons clouded and the mud receded from view. Instead I stood upon a lonely, bare islet. The sea around me was pure and deep blue, as it must have been centuries before men had all but destroyed Earth. Clouds sped away overhead, leaving an azure vault. Clean, unpolluted sand stretched beneath me, soft to the touch.

Yet I was wary. Vorta would never be beaten so easily. The

expected assault was not long in coming. The clouds were heaping like a sea in heavy swell and thunder rolled across the heavens. Racing clouds of darkness flew overhead, whipped on by whirlwinds, and the sea began readying for a tidal assault. From out of those clouds came a sudden downpour of rain, which quickly turned to a thick, treacle-like substance that I recognized only too well as blood. The crimson shower beat me to my knees in the sand, which now began to heave and pulse with all manner of vile creatures—crabs, scorpions, spiders, vermin.

I could not help but howl my anguish, hurling bolts of mental energy back at Vorta in retaliation. Then heavy seas rose up and crushed down upon me and the island as the tide broke in a flooding deluge. No water this, but waves of pollution and filth and unholy excrement. I felt it thrusting into my mouth, my ears, up my nose. Yet I fought on and clung to my powers of reason. Vorta was battering away remorselessly at my resistance, but I would never give in. Still I dragged air into my lungs, closing my senses off to the tidal effluvium that had drowned out everything.

Abruptly the grim assault ended. I found myself in darkness, now able to breathe relatively clean air. Laughter rang out around me, sharp and confident, as though giants watched ants uselessly trying to avoid their stomping feet. I was on my knees, my head spinning wildly as though I had taken too much wine. All I could see were the few paving slabs on which I knelt, for beyond them was the eternal night void again. Painfully I forced my eyes to look up. It seemed that I looked across from one mountain pinnacle to another, higher pinnacle. There opposite me was Daras Vorta, his revolting body blown up to three times its normal size by the egomania directing his mental projections. Writhing around his arms and limbs were snakes and serpents, caressing him sensually in obscene abandon.

"We have hardly begun, Sarian, and already you reel like a drunken sot," he snarled, his voice mocking inside my vain. I knew then that I was lost. He had toyed with me and I had barely survived. I would go on until he ripped away my sanity, but I could not hope to match the overpowering strength he held.

I detected inhuman sounds coming from behind me in the dark. Somewhere in the unseen, fathomless realms of darkness, a host of unknowable horrors were crawling or drifting towards me. Vorta's face writhed in ecstasy. He sensed my defeat. I got sluggishly to my feet and drew mental spheres of gold to me, sending them out at whatever that invisible host of terror was. Suddenly tendrils of liquid mucus slithered from the darkness and tried to flick out and wrap themselves around me, drawing me into a sickening, stifling embrace that would surely plunge my soul down into eternity.

Fire cracked and sizzled as I fended them off, but they were like a swarm of flies, numerous and determined. My will was being sucked from me, a twig dragged away in a strong current. It screamed soundlessly to the gods, to anything that could assist it. As I drew upon my innermost reserves to combat that gruesome menace, some new force exerted itself and entered the conflict.

I could not see what it was. For a moment I was numbed as a bright trail of fire spat like a molten tongue at the crawling nightmares. One by one the slime-hung tentacles drew away or burst. I renewed my defenses, and the hugely inflated bulk of Vorta that presided over this insane contest began to shrivel to its normal size. Fizzing balls of fire still aimed at the mucus tendrils and I added my own. As the last of the things slid away, I faced Vorta across the chasm of night, the redoubled halo of fire around me. For a moment he looked appalled, and it came like a flash to me what had happened.

It must be Taria! Somehow she had sensed the grim contest of wills, which must be setting up all manner of psychic vibrations throughout the cathedral, and she had drawn upon her own small Dream Lord powers and projected her will blindly into the battle. It had not damaged Vorta, but it had upset the balance of his attack, giving me a vital boost and a respite. Vorta may have guessed what had happened, but he merely sneered.

Monstrous shapes coiled up from the space behind him, and I looked upon the amorphous horrors that crawled and swam in the unsightly havens of Shaitan. An army of ghoulish and macabre nightmares reared up and filed away back into infinity behind Vorta, ready to be summoned one by one and unleashed into first my mental world and then the Earthly realms. So this was the ultimate blasphemy that he sought to control and use to master the world. He was insane, his mind a cesspool of all that was foulest in man, if man he still was.

Some of the bulging horrors slithered or flapped across the vault on grotesque wings and made to devour me with mouths that yawned, but I sent shafts of light at the shapeless heads. Taria's thin will was still with me, although our combined energy seemed to be slowly crumbling as the horrid legions crowded forward, anxious to envelop us. Gibbering imps and shrieking gargoyles leaped into perspective, pouring across the abyss, a black swarm. Just as it seemed that a cavernous mouth would scoop me up and suck me down into a revolting digestive tract, a new beacon of fire speared into its fetid depths. With a sickening shower of protoplasm, the thing burst asunder, and I knew that we had again foiled the assault. But how? I could barely stave off the psychic waves, and Taria operated from afar, her own tired mind capable of only minor beams of energy. I could not see how the new spearhead of energy had dissipated the thing that had gaped for me. I was all but drained, and Taria must have drawn upon her own last fiery resolve.

Whatever it had been, it had temporarily balked Vorta. He looked across at me, or us, for I could not help but think that Taria stood beside me, even though not cloaked in her natural contours. I made an attempt to sear Vorta with my energy, but he simply laughed. Behind him the host of slithering entities had for a while drifted back to the edge of their unplumbed realms.

For the first time since entering the psychic arena with Vorta, I began to hear external sounds. Yet there could be no salvation in them, for it could only be the chanting of the Death Watch amassed in the cathedral. I could not see them, but their awful cacophony swelled and hammered upon the eardrums, seeking to reach something huge and dreadful. Vorta raised his arms and closed his eyes and began a new, terrifying incantation that blended with the grim harmony.

And then I saw the thing I feared most, and my body felt bathed in a column of icy water as though all heat and light had been torn away from the very galaxy and an onset of withering frost had closed in from some external gulf outside the universe. For there, raised up behind Vorta like some titanic shadow, was the dark entity, its shapeless head set on both sides with the unmistakable outline of horns. The Goat god, the dreadful Shaitan, the absolute deification of evil—Vorta was seeking to bring it through the psychic levels and into absolute reality. I knew that I stood upon the threshold of the Devil incarnate, and that the doom of a universe drew in upon me as irrepressibly as time.

My will combined with the last efforts of Taria were nothing like enough to stem this. Everything I tried was of no avail, like wind howling at an immovable rock. The putrid emanations from the huge horned shadow swelled and began to take on solid form. Vorta's eyes opened for a moment, reflecting an expression of absolute glee and triumph. I prayed fervently and called upon every source that I knew or had known. I fell to my knees, calling upon the gods that I had forsaken, and upon the forces that had ridden as the Four Horsemen against the might of Karkesh. As a last resort I sought to recreate the images of the Riders and the potent image of the Pale Horseman.

Silence clamped down and reigned for a long time as the figure of Shaitan coalesced into substance, bulging and billowing. Then...a sound.

Hoof beats thrummed in the darkness around me, and Vorta turned his wild eyes to my face. He remained imperturbable as the shudder-some monstrosity behind and above him welled huger and grew its own eyes of green, baleful light. I forced the last dregs of will into solidifying my horse images, but Vorta let out a maniacal howl of laughter.

I tottered, the veins standing out on my brow, then I crashed to my face. I could not halt Shaitan's coming. I was defeated.

The darkness flew away as though torn aside by a hurricane, and the legion of the Death Watch was there surrounding me. I lay in the aisle of the evil cathedral, the shouts and chants of adulation ringing in my ears. And towering over all was the cloud that was Shaitan, readying to take my soul and become one with the realm around it. Its power grew by the second, no longer governed by Vorta's will, but by its own black designs.

As that horrendous darkness dropped for me, solidifying and cementing itself into concrete form, I heard a crashing somewhere in the background. I managed to turn my throbbing head and look back down the aisle to the end of the cathedral. The tall wooden doors there had burst apart as though smashed asunder by the mailed fist of a giant. Standing amidst the confusion and scattering bodies, cloaked in spiraling dust motes, stood the stallion that Karl and I had daubed white! It lifted its hooves, kicked out wildly and galloped forward, down upon me. I renewed my efforts to create a Horseman image, for somehow it had been that last effort that had brought the garish charger here.

I had to roll quickly aside as the flaying hooves beat swiftly past, and I looked up in amazement to see the tiny figure of Karl, holding himself upright on the horse's back, his eyes blazing with fanatical light. He had lost his own reason and was goaded on by my blind resolution and command. He aimed the horse straight for the towering shadow of nightmare above the altar. In his hands he clutched a skull that he must have pillaged from one of the graves— the skull-faced Rider of my projection must have imprinted itself on to his brain. At his waist was the star lance I had dropped.

Vorta's expression had become one of horror and disbelief, contorted by his madness and frustration. He screamed out in terror as the horse rose up before him like the curse of the gods. Karl, motivated by I knew not what forces, hurled the skull at the centre of Shaitan's shadow. I sprang to my feet and, with Vorta's wall of mental energy shattered, summoned up powerful images of blazing light, driving back the walls of darkness that stifled the air in this vile cathedral. Shaitan's shadow writhed as though caught in a vortex of ferocious cross winds. Hundreds of the Death Watch fell to their knees as a searing pall of heat burst over the altar. Winged shapes flapped down from balconies and pandemonium broke out among the unleashed creatures, their minds free from Vorta's binding will.

I shielded my eyes as Vorta pulled himself together and concentrated his flagging powers on the stallion and on the shouting form of Karl. I knew that my poor ally was doomed, as I had known from the first he would meet a cruel fate. Vorta hurled a mental bolt and the horse and rider crashed to the ground, the stallion falling on top of the luckless swamp dweller and crushing him like an insect. The shadow of Shaitan was fast flowing away to nothingness like mist dissipating before sunrise, and I ran forward. Karl barely moved, his hand just touching off the star lance. A stream of fire licked out at Vorta, but he had evaded it and it slammed into the golden cross. Karl was still as I reached him, and the stallion was dying, blood seeping from its nose and mouth.

I was up and racing for the altar, where Vorta was standing on unsteady legs, his black world as shaken as he was. Bedlam reigned around us as the Death Watch became hysterical, fighting with each other and the things that flapped and crawled from the darker niches.

Vorta, whimpering, grabbed a sacrificial knife and held it up, ready to thrust it into me if I got near him. I stood looking into the eyes of a raving madman. Foam dribbled from his pale lips and in his eyes I saw not my own face, but the reflection that would have been there if I had been garbed in the skull and war-gear of the Pale Horseman.

"Look upon Death, Vorta! Look upon your Death!" I shouted.

Behind him the great cross of solid gold moved, and I watched it in fascination. The heat from the star lance had turned its base into a molten mass, and its weight made it top heavy. Slowly it began to topple forward. Vorta sensed the movement and turned. But he was too late. The old religions of the past eons reached out over the gulfs of time for him. The heavy cross fell and smashed into him, crushing his spine up against the stone slab of the altar top. Bones snapped like dry wood and his head smacked on to the stone as the cross rammed itself into his hideous face, burning into the flesh as though its metal were cast in solid fire, stifling the shrieks of agony, in steaming, sizzling heat. I heard Vorta's thick neck snap, and the head lolled over the front of the altar, the eyes almost bursting from their sockets as they looked upon some awful vision, the source of which was mercifully shrouded from me.

Vorta's oily blood washed out over the altar in a dark tide, as though his sacrifice cleansed the evil done here. Every bone in his obscene body had been pulped by the colossal weight of the cross, and I had little doubt that Shaitan had ripped out his soul as he departed and had fled with it back to whatever realms of filth he had emerged from.

I drew in great sobs of air, looking around almost disinterestedly at the utter chaos. Without Vorta's controlling mind, the host of the Death Watch had become lost, and devoid of reason they were as brainless as vegetables, wandering aimlessly. They tumbled into one another, clawing and biting ineffectively. Many fell and never rose again. They would offer me no resistance if I kept away from them. I prayed that the Death Watch out in the jungles had likewise been reduced to a level of idiocy. Gast would then have little difficulty in subduing them.

I looked again to Karl, but the unfortunate swamp man was dead. He had somehow found his way in, his mind locked on to my own last desperate pleas for help, and at a time when he was most needed. I shook my head, for I had known his fate would claim him here.

449

Now I could spare no time for thought. I snatched up the star lance, although its power was nearly drained. I had to find Taria. Vorta had said she was in the steeple. I yanked aside the drapes behind the golden throne and found a stairway. I hoped that this would take me to her.

I sent out a mental call to her, and I thought that there was a distant reply, but it seemed tired and drained, as though it was ebbing away rapidly. With a fervent prayer I raced headlong up the old stairway that led higher into the apex of the steeple, crashing into the walls as I negotiated the spirals. Surely the gods, who had aided me after all in my bid to destroy Vorta, could not reward me with Taria's death.

But Man cannot command the gods, nor his fate, and both can be the cruelest of all.

CHAPTER XV
The Shores of Oblivion

Although I had raced across the void between worlds and had pursued Vorta across the blighted face of Earth for hundreds of miles, my race up that staircase of the steeple seemed longer than all the days of the chase that had gone before. When I finally came to the head of the spiral, I found two of the Death Watch blocking the way, but both seemed bemused as though befuddled with drink, I snarled and smashed them ruthlessly aside, and one went crashing down the stairs and the other cracked his head against the stone wall and collapsed senseless or dead. I did not pause to see which.

The door to the solitary room resisted me for a moment, but I brought my heel down and the woodwork splintered as the door banged inwards and wrenched away from squealing hinges. I found myself standing within a room that was dark, lit by flickering candles, as if a resting place for a bier. Incense hung on the air and something else that might have been the scent of blood.

"Taria!" I called to the shadows that hovered over the furnishings like dark drapes. Despite the gloom the place seemed well kept; no doubt these were Vorta's private apartments. I prayed that he had not tricked me and that Taria was still alive. I went into the room and a slight sound turned my head. A large bed with embroidered curtains

450

occupied one side of the room, and I dimly made out a shape stirring among its linen. I snatched a candle from a table and walked cautiously towards the bed, holding it over the coverlets. There were sheets strewn around the floor and evidence of a struggle.

My heart almost thudded to a stop as I looked down at the bed and into the drawn features of Taria. Her eyes were lined with gray and her cheeks were hollowed. Her damp hair clung to her head like straw and her lids fluttered on the edge of consciousness. She tried to say something but could not. A pale smile lit her face for a second, then her eyes closed.

"Vorta is dead," I told her, setting down the candle by the bedside and leaning over her. I looked around at the room and saw a pitcher on a nearby stand, and some linen draped by it.

"We must get away from this place," I told her softly. "Are you well enough to move?"

But it was an unnecessary question, for I could see she could hardly move at all. Her thin arm came out from the coverlets and groped for mine. I held it, and her icy fingers tightened. I could scarce believe that we were facing each other once more, after a gap of years. She was haggard and lined with weariness, but beneath that beat the heart that had lived for me long ago and I knew that my own love for her had not been diminished by the minutest fraction in all that time.

"I had thought you long dead," she managed to murmur, tears gleaming in her eyes.

I nodded, my throat constricting, and lowered my own eyes. As I did so I saw that there was blood along her bare arm.

"You are hurt!" I cried. "What has that madman done?"

"Soft, Galad," she whispered, clutching me and pulling me closer. I scowled at the room, remembering the faint scent of blood I'd caught when I entered. There were dark stains on the scattered sheets.

"Not Vorta," she murmured.

"Who, then? How badly are you hurt?" I said fearfully.

I leaned close to her, and her fingers came up and brushed my lips for silence.

"When you fought Vorta, locked in that struggle of wills by the altar, I sensed it all. I have small mental powers of my own, pitiful by your standards, but what I do have, I sent to aid you."

"Yes! I had guessed that somehow you had..."

"But it was not enough. Vorta was too strong for us."

"You held him back long enough for me to recover," I said, stroking her hair.

"Perhaps. You recall the unspeakable thing that gaped to take you..."

"Yes," I said with a shudder. "But we destroyed that, too."

"You and I—and one other," she said so quietly that I had to put my ear to her lips to catch the words.

"I don't understand..."

"The bolt of light that destroyed the thing was from a third source. One that could concentrate itself into one brief burst of energy."

I stared into her pain-filled eyes.

"The child, Galad. Vidor's unborn child," she said, her face ashen in the flickering light.

I drew back in surprise. "But how?"

"A child is so much a part of its mother. I felt its disturbance within me. Perhaps it had inherited something of it's father's Dream Lord powers and sensed the threat to me . It was the child that added to our strength against Vorta, even if only for a moment."

I shook my head in amazement, words failing me.

"The price for the help it gave us was heavy," she sighed, and I looked with renewed horror at the bloodstains.

She nodded calmly as she saw my agonized expression. "I lost the child," she said simply, hiding what she must have felt.

I cried out in anguish, and she pulled my head down to her shoulders. Shuddering, I fought to keep back the tears. How cruel could the gods or fates be? Surely they could not treat mortals so? Another life had been wasted in their scheming. How high was the tally in the struggle against Vorta and his foul masters? Surely this must be the last. Surely the gods would not rob me of Taria, too.

After I had been pressed to her for a long time, she sighed, then stroked gently at my scarred eye, studying it as I sat up.

"I grow cold, Galad," she whispered, as though reading my gloomy thoughts. I cradled her head.

"I have sought you for too long. I cannot let you slip away from me now," I told her, trying to force a smile. She pressed her face against my hands.

"I must rest."

"Sleep, then. I will bathe you and find food. There is none to come and harm you now. Vorta's servants and his foul army have broken up. Without him they are mindless. We are alone here."

She nodded, and reluctantly I left her side to look for water and food. I found a small chalice and filled it with cold water from the pitcher. With the water I bathed Taria's broken lips.

"The gods work strange courses," she whispered.

"Do not speak."

"I thought you dead, many years since. I longed for you, always. But I had no choice but to marry Vidor and to bear his child..."

"There is no blame attached to that. It was your duty, and you had the future of our people to think of."

"Maybe so, Galad. But you see, the gods reward the faithful. They have taken Vidor and his child away from me...and given me you. Perhaps it was their design from the beginning..."

"Do not dwell on that now," I said, continuing to bathe her.

"We are united, after everything, even if for brief moments," she went on, ignoring me, her eyes closed. I feared she was dying and gripped her tightly.

"You must not speak so. There will be a new life, far from here, and other children..."

"I think not," she whispered, almost inaudibly.

"*Taria!*"

"There are some places...where even you, my lord...cannot follow me..."

"I would follow your soul to the very afterlife itself and drag it back..." I avowed, but her breathing was weakening, her body colder still, and motionless.

I was desperate. I refused to believe that I had come upon her only to find her dying. I sent my mind spinning into hers, trying to establish a last link, to give her a final burst of strength, to entreat her soul to stay.

And it was as though I had plunged myself into another deep vortex of total darkness. Gradually I saw vague shapes below me and what seemed like a gray, austere landscape of blasted rocks and ashy deposits sprang up, more dismal and miserable than even the worst of Earth's withered terrain. I began to run along the undulating land as though in a dream, my feet dragging as if held by strong currents of water. Somewhere ahead of me a glimmer of light bobbed away among the upthrust rocks—Taria's soul, fleeing towards the darkness from which there would be no return.

I forced myself on, trying to call out to her, but there were no sounds in this awful vacuum. On and on I struggled, getting no nearer to the wavering light. Up she climbed and then was lost to view beyond a ridge of teeth-like crags. I forced myself headlong in pursuit, knowing that if I lost the light altogether, Taria would be lost to me forever. Eventually I came to the crest of that last ridge.

The sight beyond froze my insides to ice more readily than any of the earthly horrors I had looked upon. For the rocks slid away to nothing, and all that was left was a sloping, misty flatness that went downwards to an ocean of shifting nothingness. I could see nothing beyond the hem of the ocean and I knew that this must surely be the realm of total oblivion.

Taria's ghostly figure moved steadily down the slope towards the distant emptiness. I felt overwhelmingly beaten, for I could never hope to catch her and turn her back. The sense of hopeless loss fluttered like a trapped bird inside my vitals, and claws strong enough to tear away my sanity more easily than all of Vorta's worst workings ripped at me.

As I watched the receding light in cloudy despair, something emerged from the region of emptiness and stood upon the shore like some fatal sentinel, waving the souls into its dismal lair. My heart pumped madly against my ribs, for it was familiar.

Vorta!

He stood, arms outstretched to receive Taria's oncoming figure, his bloated face bathed in unholy glee and final triumph. I tried to scream, but nothing came, and I tried to roar out Vorta's name, but it was impossible. Taria stepped irretrievably near to that monster.

I shouted inside my own mind. For an instant nothing happened, but then Vorta looked up from the place where he stood on the awful shores. His face saw mine, but his grin remained fixed like a dead man's. I felt the ultimate waves of despair about to crash over me, but then Vorta's face changed to an expression of stark terror. Behind me, something vast had moved. I dared not glance back, my head held rigidly so that I stared at the distant Vorta. Light seemed to be flooding from behind me and down on to the shores below.

Now Taria stopped, turned and looked back, and I raised my arms and tried to shout to her. As I did so, my shadow fell across the entire width of the slope, and its tip fell across the face of Vorta. He screamed without a sound, as though washed with fire, for the shadow had fallen in the shape of a cross. Behind Vorta the emptiness seemed to waver and writhe. Tendrils of the stuff drifted outwards like hands and began to wrap like confining mist about him.

He was engulfed and jerked inexorably back, his face a hideous mask of agony. I yet held my arms out in supplication to Taria.. She spared one glance at Vorta as he disappeared for eternity. Then, very slowly, she began to walk back up the slope towards me.

I waited in agony as she turned from time to time to look back wistfully at the emptiness of Death below, but at last she reached me. I flung my arms around her.

It was like bursting up to the surface of a deep pool. I sucked in air and opened my eyes, looking down into the face of Taria, who lay cold on the bed beneath me. The room in the steeple had not changed. I put my fingers to her mouth and felt escaping breath.

Presently her eyes opened.

She smiled faintly and looked around her as if waking from a long sleep. "I thought..."

"You are alive," I told her.

She seemed perplexed, but then sighed and snuggled against me, slipping this time into an untroubled sleep. I knew now that she would live on—the gods had given me the sign. After a while, I went to the pitcher and threw water in my face, slumping down on the bed beside Taria in utter exhaustion. My quest had reached its end.

*

We remained in the steeple for many days and Taria began to regain something of her strength. There was food and water to last us for many months, though we wanted to get back to our own lands when we could. In time, Taria was able to travel, and I saw with returning happiness that her strength grew daily. She was far from her old self, but there were signs that one day she might be.

When we left the devastation of the cathedral behind us, there was not a sign of life to be seen anywhere in the city or indeed beyond it. The Death Watch and other horrors had melted away as though they had been figments of our minds in distress. Our progress was unhindered, and we even had the fortune to come across horses

455

at the fringes of the jungle. I managed to catch one, so that we approached the forest with more confidence.

On the last of the bare ridges that flanked the evil places, we sat on the back of the docile mare that I had caught, and looked down at the whispering greenery of the jungle. Its former sentience and hostility seemed to have abated, though I still carried the star lance in case we were set upon by predators.

"I think we are going to have a storm," said Taria, her head close to my ear, her arms wrapped tightly about my waist. I looked up at the overcast sky where heavy clouds were piling together ominously.

"You are right, but we should make the jungle before it breaks."

I stroked the mare to calm her, for she also scented rain in the taut atmosphere. High up over the jungle I could see shifting shapes in the clouds, and I fell silent for a while, watching them. As I looked, I began to see a distant pattern emerging.

"It has gone strangely dark and silent," said Taria softly. It was so, for the heavens had become dismal, the sunlight dimming. I pointed to a cloud formation that surged across the horizon, tearing along at a frantic pace like a gigantic wave flecked with boiling surf.

"Look!"

"What are they?" said Taria.

The horse reared as though it knew what we had seen rolling towards us, for the cloud formation was unmistakable—three plunging, rearing steeds, their manes streaming out behind them, and upon their backs the titanic shapes that represented warriors. Closer and closer they came, covering the sky, thunder booming around them like the hooves of immortal titans. Taria screamed as we saw the distinct god-like horsemen tower right above us.

Instinctively we ducked and the first heavy drops of rain fell, to be followed by a heavy shower. Overhead thunder echoed explosively and my horse reared, throwing me to the ground. I had a brief glimpse of the three terrifying horsemen, then buried my head in the soft earth.

The storm burst in all its fury around us and I felt Taria pulling at me. Stubbornly I got to my feet, my face averted from what I had seen. For an age I let her hold me tightly, not daring to look up at whatever monstrous visions the gods were unleashing. At last, Taria wiped my face with the hem of her sleeve.

"It will soon be over," she said soothingly. "See, the clouds are already rolling away."

I looked up to see sunlight breaking through the shifting layers of gray. Then I turned to look back the way we had come, and I gasped. The three formations that had seemed to be horsemen bearing down upon me were boiling away like disappearing riders, but now I could plainly see a fourth horse among the clouds, and upon its back a barely seen figure.

"Why...there are *four* of them," murmured Taria, studying the receding figures in wonder.

"Yes," I said, understanding. "The burden is lifted from me. The Pale Horseman has gone back to his own."

Taria frowned in puzzlement at my odd words, but I smiled, for I felt as though a colossal weight had been removed from my back and my soul. I laughed and threw my arms around her, and we both knew instinctively that something nightmarishly evil had gone from our lives, and from then on our fates would be our own.

EPILOGUE
A Brief History of the Zurjahn Empire After the Rebellion

Extracts from **The Annals of Enlightenment**, official archives of the Empire.

...The revolution that took place on and burgeoned out from Earth became known as the Great Rebellion and over the next century of Man's existence it had repercussions that reverberated in even the remotest corners of the Empire of the nine worlds, and indeed led to its inevitable collapse.

The Dream Lord hierarchy on Zurjah was in total disarray after the Great Rebellion, and with the assassination of Vidor Karset of the Triumvirate, and the permanent withdrawal of Galad Sarian, heir to his father, Dotas, Laomidian was the sole member of the Triumvirate left on Zurjah. Without the combined powers of the full Triumvirate, it was impossible to maintain the control of the planet's wild energies and keep the mental shields intact. There was no one among the nobles capable of being elevated to Dream Lord status as this relied almost wholly on blood lines. The consequences were inevitable—Man was forced to begin the exodus from Zurjah and return to the planet of his birth.

Thus the vast Empire began its dissolution, for without Zurjah's central control, the other worlds similarly began the gradual process of sending their populations of Man back to the Homeworld. Gargan, or Mars, was the only planet to escape this fate, as it had become self-sufficient enough to be able to continue to support human life in conjunction with its indigenous species. Laomidian oversaw the exodus from Zurjah, with Gundar Sabian appointed Supreme Commander of the Imperial Guards on Earth. Prosocles, from the Sacred City, was made Primate of Earth and the three made a new core of power that was designed to serve all peoples on all worlds.

Galad Sarian spent a brief period with the new authority, refusing to become a formal part of it, and a few years after the new settlers came to Earth, he and his wife, Taria, left the centers of population and began a new, hermetic life in a remote, relatively unexplored part of the planet, where they shared minimum contact with their former friends, allies, and warriors. Laomidian, who suffered from ill health brought on principally by exhaustion, retired to Mars, where he took no further part in the new rule on Earth, and died within the first decade of settlement. The many tribes of Earth set aside their weapons and concentrated on rebuilding the shattered world, much of which remained uninhabitable. As new waves of settlers came from the other worlds, there was an uneasy truce for several years, but the Zurjahns brought invaluable technology with them and gradually the integration programme accelerated, with new, healthy centers of population growing up.

Gundar Sabian, Prosocles, and King Thuran, all lived long, productive lives, and their efforts to reunite the people were the foundation stones of the new peace. When the last of them died, fifty years after the Great Rebellion, Karkesh was being partially restored around the old Space Platform, vital for contact with Mars, although the former Black City remained a place of shadows and ruins, a reminder of the bleak past. An Administrative center was established in the city, under the stewardship of Galatian, former Marshal on Zurjah, and he formed part of a larger planetary Council that continued to oversee the development of the free peoples.

Dream Lord powers were no longer concentrated in an omniscient Triumvirate, their blood lines weakened and dispersed unevenly. These old mental powers, once so crucial to sustaining the Empire and controlling its disparate peoples, were eventually outlawed by the presiding Council, considered blasphemous, aberrations. The danger that they would corrupt any who attempted to develop and apply them overrode their potential practical uses. Thus the remnants of Zurjahn rule passed mainly into the realms of myth and legend, although the new rulers were ever watchful, determined to flush out any last pockets of dark powers once wielded by the evil cults of the former Warden of Earth, Daras Vorta. The Council trained a new breed of warriors on Mars, the witchfinders, men and women whose purpose was to seek out potential enemies of the state on either planet, who might be tempted to walk the paths of the nightmare gods of the past.